MARION
ALIVE

BOOKS BY
VICKI BAUM

Marion Alive
The Ship and the Shore
Shanghai '37
Tale of Bali
Sing, Sister, Sing
Men Never Know
Falling Star
Helene
Secret Sentence
And Life Goes On
Grand Hotel
Martin's Summer

VICKI BAUM

MARION ALIVE

THE BOOK LEAGUE OF AMERICA
NEW YORK
1942

PRINTED AT THE *Country Life Press,* GARDEN CITY, N. Y., U. S. A.

MARION
ALIVE

"*The great thing is to last and get your work done and see and hear and learn and understand; and write when there is something that you know; and not before; and not too damned much after.*"

—Ernest Hemingway

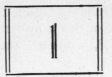

1

ARLY THAT MORNING Christopher came strolling into Marion's room; his hair was wet with morning mist, and he chewed a grass blade as usual. His heavy shoes were wet too, and tiny beads of dew clung to the rough homespun of his coat.

"Where's Michael?" he asked.

"He went over to the doctor," Marion said.

"Anything the matter with him?" Christopher asked.

"No," she said happily. "It's more like a last check-up. We've won our battle."

"Yes, you have, Marion," he said, "and that's more than many people can say of themselves just now." He hung one long, lean leg over the railing of the gallery and took out his pipe. She could see that he was deeply occupied by something.

"Don't break my geraniums," she said. Marion liked the heavy clusters of red that cascaded down the outside of most Swiss houses, but Christopher saw colors only when he didn't think. Like most men, thinking made him deaf, mute, and color-blind. He was thinking now. Marion knew it by the unseeing expression of his eyes behind his glasses. She had got so used to watching eyes during the last two years, when she was afraid her son Michael would lose his eyesight, that it had become second nature with her.

"Another date the poor schoolboys of tomorrow will have to remember," he said. "June 14, 1940. The collapse of France. Paris has surrendered. Not that it matters."

"It was to be expected, wasn't it?" she said, just to say something.

"Oh, definitely," he said, hoisting in his leg and beginning to pace up and down the narrow space of the gallery.

Marion had thrown out the radio weeks ago because it upset Michael too much and yet gave only half of everything. Since then Christopher usually furnished her with a brief digest of the news, and, sometimes, with a dry comment. She leaned over the railing and looked down into the valley. The mist had settled into compact, round little clouds which the sun slowly punctured, plucking them into shreds of white cotton. Behind it there was the glitter of the lake and the slow swaying of treetops. The air was brisk and full of the good smells of pine and of freshly cut kindling wood and of the green, frothy brook beyond the little garden. But as Marion leaned over the railing she could see the sandbags they had built around the ground floor, and they spoiled the morning for her. The children from the mill farther down the brook came marching up the trail, each one wearing a little gas mask. They were an odd-looking procession. The oldest girl carried the baby, and the baby too wore a tiny little gas mask, which made it look like some sort of a larva. They sang a muffled song into their contraptions and marched stoutly, but once in a while they had to stop and slap their knees because things seemed so funny to them. All the children in the village had lots of fun with their masks, and they had invented all sorts of new little games. The baby from the mill especially seemed to adore her little apparatus and cried every time it was taken away from her.

"Do you think Switzerland will be in it soon?" Marion asked Christopher.

"Who can tell? Probably," he answered with the same absorbed expression. "Look here, Marion, why don't you pack up and take Michael and go back to the States while it's still possible?" he added after some more thinking.

"It won't be long now," Marion said. "Dr. Konrad thinks he

can let Michael go safely in about two months. It wouldn't make sense to break off the treatments now, would it? There is too much at stake."

Christopher gave no answer. He had been near them ever since they had come to Staufen in spring 1939, when Marion Sprague had brought her son to have him treated by Dr. Konrad. The doctor was a badly battered German refugee who had chosen to live and work in this out-of-the-way Swiss hamlet, and when Christopher had met them first, Michael had been an almost hopeless case of tuberculosis of the eyes. Christopher had soon become their friend. He had watched their valiant struggle and learned to love them both, mother and son, a cheerful duo pretending that getting blind was nothing to be unhappy about. There was no need for Marion to explain to Christopher why they were not scrambling for a boat to the United States, now that Michael was almost cured.

He took out his pipe and gave her a little grin. "Following another one of your hunches, eh?" he said. "The instinct of the field mouse, or how to get into trouble against better judgment. Marion, darling, will you never learn?"

Marion had told him about the field mice that always left her grandfather's farm before a flood or some other catastrophe befell it. But if the field mice stayed on, her grandfather knew that there was no danger. It was one of her grandfather's best stories and had greatly impressed her as a child, it seemed.

"I couldn't jeopardize Michael's recovery, could I?" she said.

"Jeopardize! What a nice big word for someone who hasn't been brought up in the English language," Christopher said, obviously amused. "And besides, we don't like to run away, neither from death nor the devil, do we? And that's the length and breadth of it."

"Are you so sure that running away would help?" Marion asked hotly. "What about the people who ran away from Holland and Belgium and Paris and God knows where and got bombed on the roads? If we go off on the next boat, are you so sure it won't be sunk? And if we get back to the States, who tells you that we won't be in a plane crash or an automobile accident? Why, there are even people who die from a simple pneumonia or an infected tooth. No one thought of running away the last time we had a war; why should I run now? I feel just as safe and much quieter behind the Seven Brothers than I would anywhere else. And so do you."

He looked to the mountain range across the lake: the Grauhorn, the Brothers, the Arlistock. They were his best friends. He knew every fold of them, every glen and slope, every glacier and ridge. They still wore their old-fashioned flannel nightcaps of clouds around their white heads, but their flanks were clearly etched into the scintillating morning air. Marion could follow Christopher's eyes as they wandered across the lake and up the narrow zigzag trail that led to the Kees and the Grauhorn glacier. At this distance you could discern the herringbone stitch of that trail only if you had climbed it many times and knew every bend and loop of it. She believed that she could follow Christopher's thoughts as well as his eyes, but she was wrong as so often before. He talked so little about himself that news of a personal nature usually came as a shock to his friends.

"I'm leaving Staufen today," he said. "I'm going back to England."

Marion hoped that she didn't gasp. She felt her scalp contract and grow cold from the nape of the neck upwards; it was an odd sensation. Mercy, my hair stands on end, she thought.

"You? Leaving? Why?" she asked, stiff-lipped and foolish. It had never occurred to her that Christopher could go away and leave them behind. Sometimes she had pictured how they would go away, leaving him behind, buried in this valley, laboring over his eternal, never-finished Rise and Fall of the Byzantine Empire. To think out this parting in every detail and consequence had sometimes kept her awake at night. So now she was to stay behind and he was going away. She licked her lips to get them warm, but even the tip of her tongue had grown cold with apprehension. The Seven Brothers rocked before her eyes as if a bomb had blasted them that very moment.

"What time are you leaving?" she asked.

"Around one o'clock," Christopher said.

"There's no bus," she said, knocked out by the shock. The next railway station was more than two hours off. All the motorcars and even the bus had been commandeered for military use when Switzerland had mobilized, and people did their errands on bicycles.

"If I start out at one o'clock I'll be at the Arli Hütte around sunset," he said. "I'll stay there overnight, and tomorrow early I'd like to climb up to the Grauhorn summit once more before going over the pass to Arlingen. I've figured it all out. If I start out around one o'clock today I could easily be in Geneva the day after tomorrow in time to catch the plane."

"What plane?" Marion asked feebly.

"Plane to Lisbon. It seems a bit roundabout, but that will be the best way to get home," he said.

She looked at him. He sat astride the railing again, with his legs between her geraniums, and she said foolishly, "You've had a haircut, haven't you?"

He brushed over his sandy new crop and laughed. "Yes, I finally broke down and trusted my tresses into the hands of old Hammelin," he said. "He did a smart job, don't you think so? He was rather timid about it. He says it's hard to be the village barber *and* blacksmith and to keep the fine touch if you don't shoe horses in between."

"Why do you want to go home, Chris?" Marion asked.

"I have to," he said, still with the same amused air, while his eyes had grown deadly serious. "I simply have to. I know it sounds idiotic, but things seem to go so badly at home that I simply have to be there for the final mess."

"But you don't believe in war and the British Empire and all that," Marion said helplessly. The lofty structure of their long evening talks toppled over and came down with a crash.

"Oh no," he said. "Who would? I was quite a big boy when my father came home shortly before the end of the last war. What a wreck of a man he was for the rest of his life! No wonder I was brought up on pacifism, pure and undiluted. We all were, weren't we? Studying history doesn't make you believe in war either. Makes you believe in cycles, though, and according to it our time is up. The trouble is you can't win a war if you are sober and disillusioned as we all are, and I wonder if Mr. Churchill's brave little fanfares on his tin toy trumpet will make one bit of difference. But I've cheated myself when I thought that I could stay here and finish my awfully important book while England is going down. I can't. There you have it; I simply can't. I know the idiocy of it, and I loathe to think of the filth and mess and stink I let myself into, but I can't keep out of it. Look here, am I talking too much?"

"Michael will be pretty desperate if you go," Marion said.

"Oh no, he understands. We've talked it all over, and he agrees with me. He would do the same if he were in my shoes," he said. "Of course, we all are a bit dizzy. We thought of ourselves as the postwar generation. Suddenly we have to find out that we have been prewar all over again. It's a filthy little trick and slightly confusing. But Michael knows his way more or less."

"He was on the verge of becoming a Nazi before we came to Staufen," she said. "I don't know if you realize how much your influence has changed him. If you hadn't become his friend——"

"Oh, naturally," Chris said lightly. "Hitler's antics are quite fascinating, and Michael is still very young. But he is a fine boy, and I don't think it would attract him much to sympathize with a successful conqueror. A saturated hero stops being a hero, and success has ruined every one of them from Jenghiz Khan to Napoleon. When the moon is fullest it begins to wane, the Chinese say, and they ought to know."

"Damn the Chinese!" Marion said. "Damn your being abstract and detached about everything! You are making a lie of your whole past life, and you expect me to applaud you for it. Well I won't. I'm not going to tie flowers to anyone's bayonet."

Christopher came from the gallery into the room; suddenly he was so close that Marion could feel the warmth of his body and smell the smoky smell of his coat.

"Look here, Marion," he said. "Will you come with me as far as Geneva?"

"Well——" she said, catching her breath.

"It's only two nights and days. You could take the train from Geneva and be back the day after tomorrow."

"I don't know if Dr. Konrad would like Michael to go away just now——" Marion began, but Christopher put his hand on her arm and stopped her. He turned her toward him so that she had to look into his face. She could see herself in his eyeglasses, very tiny and with a cramp of a smile around her mouth.

"Forget Michael for a moment," he said. "This is about you and me. I don't want him to come along. I want to be alone with you for once."

Careful now, dangerous ground, Marion thought in a panic. "I don't know if I am in shape for a strenuous mountain trip. I'm like an old car—I begin boiling on steep grades," she ventured.

"You're in perfect shape, and you've been to the Arli Hütte twice without even puffing," he said, very strict now. "Of course, you won't have to go to the summit with me if you don't want to. You could wait for me at the Hütte. It won't take me more than five hours to get to the summit and back. We would go across the pass tomorrow afternoon or even take the funicular and stay the night in Arlingen. There is the loveliest old inn, you'll like it. The train for Geneva leaves at six-twenty in the morning, but as you don't mind getting up early——"

"It sounds like a very crazy enterprise," she said feebly. Steady, Marion, steady now, she told herself. You've behaved very well so far, don't slip now, don't let yourself be carried away by some emotional nonsense, now, at the last moment. And why not? Why not snatch two nights of happiness out of the cataclysm? It's done all over the world when men go to war and women stay behind . . .

"I hoped you would see me off," she heard Chris say in his even, unemotional voice. "I thought you would stand there on the airfield and wave good-by and I would look down and see you getting smaller and smaller. Maybe it's childish and ridiculous and anything you want. But somehow it would give my going away some sense."

"It's a funny idea, Chris. Why should I of all people——" She tried, but he stopped her short.

"Good Lord, Marion, don't let's pretend now," he said. "You know that I love you. It's odd, but love seems to be the only thing strong enough to blot out the whole confounded rest of it all."

Marion's mouth went dry. She knew that he was right, but she could not admit it. There was a difference of fifteen years between them, an unobtrusive but deep abyss and no bridge across.

"I saw three men off during the last war," she said more brittle than she intended. "Not one of them came back. I don't like repetitions."

Ever since this war had started, Marion had been surrounded by ghosts. Everything had happened to her before. Ghosts of speeches, of words, of things said and things felt and things suffered before. All of them so familiar, so worn out; she could look through them as through the ghosts in the funny papers. Chris was young; to him everything happened for the first time. I'm old, Marion thought. I've been through it before, I know the beginning of it, the climax and the end.

"Now you're being plain silly," she said. "Silly and conventional. Like every soldier, you want to go to bed with some woman before going into the war, that's all; and as I am about the only woman in Staufen you really know . . . But, heavens, Chris, I have three grown-up sons, I could be your mother, so don't be absurd. In fact, I'll be a grandmother before fall——"

Christopher smiled down at her. "Come on, Marion, darling," he said gently. "You don't have to put it on so thick. Better bring out your hobnail boots and get yourself ready to go with me. It will be lovely up there tonight. So quiet, and the sky so close, and the stars so ripe and big you can pluck as many as you want."

Marion pulled herself together. There is something like dignity and self-respect, and she held onto hers as best as she could. She made herself stiff as a stick inside as she said: "Whatever gave you the idea I could carry on with my son's best friend? It would be a nice spectacle, and Michael would love it, wouldn't he? Do you know how much older I am than you?" (She had figured it out time after time and chewed on it and sucked so much bitterness from it that it had poisoned all her pleasures.) "Do you realize that I was a grown-up girl when you were born? Aren't you a bit conceited, you with your stars? Why, I might have changed your diapers and powdered your little behind when you were a baby. I might have sat you on your potty and spanked you when you wet your first pair of pants. Love—my eye!"

He took his hands out of his pockets where he had anchored them; he put his pipe away, and at last he took off his glasses. She had never seen him without them, and his face seemed suddenly undressed, nude, a new face, much too intimate, almost obscene. It was funny and very dear to watch him make all these circumstantial preparations before he took her into his arms and kissed her. His lean, hard mountaineer's body trembled against hers as if he were afraid of his own doings. She mustered all her will power and turned to stone. She didn't struggle and she didn't respond. She behaved. It was the crowning achievement of many months of self-denial and self-control and not losing her head and not giving herself away and not forgetting that she was forty-four and fifteen years older than Christopher. When he let go of her she felt her whole body ache with the strain of not having responded. He pushed her away and stared at her; his eyes had gone dark, and Marion could see that he was hurt and furious.

"Sorry," he said. He restored himself, becoming his own, unemotional English self again. Pipe in mouth, eyeglasses, hands in pockets.

"It's true then. You really do not care for me," he said. "A foolish misconception on my part. You must forgive me. Maybe you are right and I have lived in this valley for too long a time. I hope you'll forget what I've said. I wouldn't have done it if it weren't for my going away."

After that they sat down and talked like two marionettes on their little stage. Marion could almost feel the string that jerked her into silly, flighty little gestures that were not her own. Someone spoke their lines for them, wooden words without sense or meaning. When Christopher became polite and treated her like a lady, she understood how deeply he was hurt. They sat there, each one of them broiling in his own little hell, talking about the weather. The rain corner beyond the Arlistock was clear and there would surely be no thunderstorm for some days, and the view from the summit would be good and old Hammelin, who was something like a prophet besides being the

barber and blacksmith of Staufen, foresaw at least four sunny
days. Suddenly Marion discovered a life belt floating toward her
through an ocean of distress, and she grabbed it and said:
"Maybe the Lisbon plane will be sold out for weeks."

Christopher shook his head. "I've got my reservation," he said.
"I telephoned the air line several times. Fortunately someone
turned back his ticket and I got it."

Fortunately, indeed.

Well, I think I must go now, Marion. I won't detain you,
Christopher. Good-by and take good care of yourself. Bon
voyage, or what does one say if a man goes back to his country
when the odds are one to one hundred . . . "If it's too lonesome
for you to fly off without anyone seeing you off, I wouldn't
mind making the little trip with you, really," Marion said at the
last moment. He stopped at the door and looked at her.

"But you wouldn't want to pluck the stars from the sky with
me tonight," he said with a tortured little smile.

"I wouldn't want you to draw any nonsensical conclusions if I
come and see you off," she said.

"I'm no charity case," he said. "I love you. I want you. If that's
a nonsensical conclusion to you, I don't want you to come along.
It would be hell, don't you see? I would feel as if I had black-
mailed you into something. No, thanks, Marion. Forget this
whole silly little incident."

"Chris," she said desperately, "don't you understand? I'm no
cradle-snatcher, that's all."

"You Americans have such lovely words for everything," he
said. "Well, I must run along now. Good-by. I think there is
still mail going from and to England—for a little while yet anyway. I'll keep in contact with Michael."

"I could row you across the lake at least," Marion said. Her
throat felt as if she had swallowed dozens of knives.

"No, thanks, really," he said. "I'd rather not have you around
for my exodus. It would be nice, though, if you could send
Michael over to the hotel."

"Certainly. The moment he comes back from the doctor."

"Well—good-by, then, Marion."

"Good-by, Christopher. Everything may still turn out all right in the end—with England, I mean."

"Certainly. It's only that the old girl never had the measles when she was young. They say it's much more dangerous after you've come of age."

Will somebody tell me why I fell in love with you? Marion thought desperately. Because of silly little things; the way you smoke your pipe, the way you smile with closed lips, the way you hang your legs over the backs of chairs, the way you wrinkle your forehead, the sound of your voice, the shape of your ears, the subtle, precious something that formed the corners of your mouth—call it breeding, resignation, countenance, pluck to face things unpainted and without make-up. Don't go away, Christopher, don't fight for things in which you don't believe, don't let them kill you, don't die, please. Steady, Marion, steady now. The main thing is to keep your equilibrium, that's what Grandfather used to say, isn't it?

Christopher's hand was cold as he shook hers, which was cold too. She knew that his lips would have been cold had she kissed them.

"By-by, Chris. Try and don't be too much of a hero."

"Certainly not. And you be sensible and go back to the States. It wouldn't make much sense to have Michael hit by some infernal bomb just when he is well again."

"I'll think it over, Christopher."

"Do, please. And thanks for everything."

One moment his hand was still in hers, a heavy, cold weight, and the next moment there was only emptiness. Marion did not know where he had kept his grass blade all the time, but when he left he had it between his lips again, chewing frantically. That's how she would always remember him: wet with dew and chewing a grass blade that he had picked up on his morning stroll.

Remember all the fuss and posing and chichi and flag waving we had in the first war? she thought. We've become awfully silent since. We're shying away from big words and display of emotions. Seems this time only prime ministers are capable of

uttering those resounding hollow tirades that everyone blared
out in 1914. Better dead than slaves. Save freedom and civilization. Our brave soldiers, glorious battlefields, your country
needs you, God is with us. Poor prime ministers, whistling in
the dark! They are like old operatic tenors, singing the same old
arias, but the audience won't listen.

I believe the Bible calls them The Last Things: Love. Faith.
Sacrifice. Death. They are still there, but we don't talk about
them.

When I was young the big words dropped from us, sweet and
profuse, like the soft, too ripe pears dropped from the tree in
my grandfather's back yard. Plop, plop, plop. Today it would
make us cringe to listen to all the blab we flounced into one another's face.

Well. Good-by, Christopher. Good luck to you.

Ever since I was a little girl of four I've been in love—and
with you it was the last time. Exit love. Exit life.

On her way downstairs Marion passed a small mirror in a dark
wooden frame, and what she saw in passing made her stop and
turn back and sternly scrutinize her reflection in the shadowy
depth of the greenish glass. A pale, drenched, drawn mask with
big dark holes for eyes stared sternly back at her. Don't be ridiculous, Marion told herself. No reason for looking like Me-
dusa just because a boy you like is going to England. She gave
her image an encouraging little grin. Excuse me, this is where I
came in, she thought. Another world war with the same heartbreak.

Who are you, with that silly grin and those frightened eyes?
she asked herself. Where do you go from here—and how, in the
name of heaven, did you get here and become what you are,
Marion, my girl?

WHAT I REMEMBER most vividly just now are the laundry days
when I was a child. The turmoil on Monday nights when the
maid took out the dirty linen and my mother counted it on the

kitchen floor before it went into the tub to be soaked. So many men's shirts, so many women's shirts, so many camisoles; night-shirts with ruffles, petticoats and more petticoats, and my father's funny under-drawers, and then my own prim little underthings. There were two crochet patterns rampant in our family, a wider lace to embellish the underwear of the grown-ups and a narrow, skimpy little edge of lace for the children. But the petticoats I wore in school had no lace at all, for even that clumsy bit of crochet was thought pretty frivolous and not quite befitting for a nice little girl.

My mother had seven sisters, and six of them had daughters, and every female member of this widespread family was eternally seen dragging around a roll of that damned lace, crocheting every spare minute. There were few things in my life I hated more than that lace. My own roll was very dirty, almost black, and when I unpinned it to see how much of the stuff I had crocheted, it was only a few inches long and very disappointing. That was be-cause I took to dreaming most of the time, and then I slipped up on my pattern and my mother had me unravel the whole thing and do it all over again. She was merciless in that respect, al-though almost too gentle and yielding in many others. But she had a few firm principles, and not to have that traditional pat-tern spoiled was one of them. In a way that crochet pat-tern was something like the tartan of a Scottish clan. Even to-day, if I should meet somewhere in deepest Africa some pitch-black Zulu with a scrap of that lace around his loins, I would be sure that he must be some sort of relative of mine.

Laundry day was every second Tuesday, and the wash was collected for that day in the big drawer at the bottom of an odd piece of furniture called a table-bed. It was a chestlike con-traption, very big and solid. The top was scrubbed with sand till it was clean and white; during the day this top served as a kitchen table where the manifold doughs of the Austrian cuisine were slapped and kneaded and beaten and pulled and rolled. Therefore that top had always the faint sweet scent of fine flour about it, and a thin film of flour clung to its well-worn face like powder to the face of a busy woman. Come night and the top would be taken off, revealing the maid's pillows and eider-downs inside, for that was where she slept. I envied our maids bitterly for this bed, it was so deep and cozy, and to sleep in it must have been like having a little house all to oneself.

Only once did I have the good luck to sleep in that bed; that was the night some comet was running wild and the end of the world was forecast as probable even if not as certain. My parents had gone to a party, and Vefi, the maid, took me into her bed because I was afraid and she too. I still remember how warm and safe I felt under the heavy eider-downs; I fell asleep, and when I woke up in the morning the world was still there, unscathed. Since then the feeling that the world has come to an end has become so permanent we hardly notice it. We pull some ideological eider-down over our heads and try to sleep through the night, and maybe the world will still be there when we open our eyes again.

It seems, though, that Vefi must have been afraid of sleeping alone in a general way, for I remember very distinctly one morning when there was a terrific rumpus because August had been caught with her in that table-bed. August was my first love. A tall, handsome fellow, dressed in the swanky uniform of the Imperial Guards, high, shiny boots, wide flowing cape, and an especially dashing horsetail waving from his helmet. August had a most attractive mustache with which he used to tickle me when I sat on his lap and purred. He was allowed to visit in our kitchen after dinner because that was safer than letting Vefi go to the park with him. I thought it wonderful to have a tall, strong guardsman of our own to watch over all of us and even to take the trouble of sleeping in our kitchen. But my parents were outraged, and August was forbidden to ever show up again. Vefi cried, and my mother cried, and August stood there in his underthings, very little of a hero, looking as if he would have liked to cry too. I was interested to see that he wore the same sort of long under-drawers as my father, only they looked different on him.

On Tuesday mornings I would always wake up at six to sneak into the kitchen when Kathi, the washerwoman, arrived. I loved Kathi and I loved laundry day and therefore the Tuesdays were so many holidays to me. True, I would have to go to school at eight, but for the time being I was propped up on a high kitchen stool and secretly had breakfast with Kathi and Vefi. We ate from the top of the table-bed, which was primly closed again. We had rolls with poppy seed, and they were still warm, for the baker had just dropped them at our door. We drank coffee from thick, muglike cups with very red roses on them, and I held mine in both hands and had both elbows on the table-bed like Kathi and Vefi, and I tried to make just as much noise gulping down my coffee as they did. It smelled of the burning wood that crackled in the stove, with that fine, fleeting smell that is a little bitter and a little sweet, like most good things in life. Breakfast finished, Kathi would get up and go to the tin tub in the corner where the drinking water was kept, until the time when we became swanky people with a faucet right in our kitchen. She would take the pewter pitcher from its nail and ladle it full of water and take a good, long drink. "Ah," she would say, wiping her mouth with the freckled back of her hand. "If there is anything better than water I still have to learn about it." As it went down her throat I could taste its goodness and tang and freshness, and I got very thirsty myself. I would hop down from my stool and dance with impatience until Kathi had drunk all she could hold, and then it was my turn with the pitcher.

I think Kathi was the happiest woman I ever knew in my life. I've learned a lot from her, and off and on I've tried to imitate her trick of being happy. But where I succeeded only for hours at a time, she could keep it up perpetually. There was hardly anything from which Kathi couldn't wring a few drops of joy. I don't know how old she may have been, because to a little child most people seem very old. She was broad-hipped and red-headed and rather ugly, and her face was sprinkled with freckles. When she arrived on Tuesday morning she smelled of starched linen, a good, fresh smell that was kept in the folds of her white apron. "Now let's get to work," she would say, taking off that apron and tying an old, faded blue one around her ample waist. During the day she changed her smells several times, and there was sweat and dampness and soap and the smell of hard work in her repertory, interspersed with the smell of coffee, beer, bread, and goulash. "Bread," she would say and roll her eyes in delight. "Never bite into a piece of bread without thanking your Lord, for He made it." It sounded merry and gay and not at all like the sour sort of religion a thin-lipped Herr Kathechet would pound into us at school. "Beer," she would say. "Is there anything as good as beer in paradise? If not, thank you, I better go to hell." The moment she began to work she opened wide her mouth and sang, not loud but softly and beautifully. "Kde Domov Muj," she sang, for Kathi was Bohemian. She laughed and winked at me until I took heart and came out with my own little voice, joining hers in some clear, pleasing harmonies, as people do in Austria.

Kathi was crazy about her profession. "Tell me anything better a person can do than be a washerwoman," she would say to the world at large while examining a particularly dirty piece of linen. "When I come, everything is dirty. When I go, everything is clean. What would you do without me?" Yes, what indeed? In whatever condition she found the dirty laundry, she was delighted with it. "Not very dirty this time," she would say. "Jezizmaria, that's no work at all, that's fun."

"Pretty dirty today," she would say some other Tuesday. "That's when it's really a pleasure to wash it. You see at least what you've done."

One Tuesday Kathi didn't show up. Instead, my mother received a postcard which said: "Have been very lucky, run over by carriage of Count Hoyot. Am in General Hospital, very fine hospital, like it very much. Doctor cut off left leg, but Count will pay money to me. Am very happy. Excuse I cannot come today. Will be back next month."

The first Tuesday of the following month she hobbled into our kitchen, lifted her skirt, and proudly exhibited her new wooden leg, "the finest leg in the whole of Vienna, and the count bought it for me." It was not one of those super-de-luxe artificial limbs they learned to manufacture during the World War; just a solid wooden stump. But Kathi was infinitely proud of it.

"Best thing a washerwoman can have is wooden leg," she cried happily. "Washerwoman must stand in wet places all her life, no? Now I won't get wet feet any more. Come, Milucka, let's sing."

All I see when I think of Vienna are plumes of Persian lilac in every shade from white to deep purple. And chestnut trees. There were chestnut trees everywhere, clumps of them in the public parks, avenues of them, groups of chestnut trees in all the dreamy old gardens behind the baroque houses of the nobility and a sea of chestnut trees in the Prater. Everything was very big and tall and wonderful in Vienna when I was a child. Later on it began to shrink and to choke me, so that I had to go away from that dying town. And when I went there for a visit many years later, I was just another American tourist, Mrs. John W. Sprague, who shocked the hotel porter by understanding when he swore in German; and the streets looked dark and narrow, and everything was cramped and crowded, and the elegant big house where we had lived had become small and shabby.

But when I was a child there was no Social Significance to the fact that the maid slept in the kitchen and the laundry was washed there too and the food was prepared on top of a bed, because everyone I knew lived like that. I suppose that expression didn't even exist then, or, if it did, it lived a hidden printer's-ink existence, somewhere in the pages of Karl Marx's Das Kapital and unknown to wider circles.

But it actually was a very elegant house, in so far as it was old and stood in the heart of Vienna and that was where the right people lived. It had four wide sweeping staircases that were not quite marble but almost. We had kerosene lamps until I was six, but then that old house began to reform, and with much hammering and knocking and yelling workmen and empty beer bottles everywhere we got the faucet in the kitchen and gas light in the rooms, and in the end even an elevator was installed in the wide, generous almost-marble staircase. But we never used it, for it was said to be very dangerous, and to this day I haven't overcome my deep distrust of elevators.

The house stood in the swanky, quiet quarter near the Opera and next to the Academy of Arts. From our front windows we looked down on a tree-shaded little square, called the Schil-

lerplatz, where the Italian models sat on benches and ate salami
and cheese and the art students walked around in their flowing
capes and big slouch hats. One of those ill-shaved young men
with burning eyes and large flat cases with sketches under their
arms was a young genius whose application was refused on the
grounds of lack of talent. Boy by the name of Adolf Hitler.
What would have happened if the professors who had to judge
his Roman landscapes had been more lenient? Maybe the frustrated and suppressed ambitions and visions would not have
started to rankle and to burn and at last turn into evil for the
world, but would have found release in oil and paint. Maybe
we would have one more mediocre but successful painter today
instead of a genius of destruction. . . .

In the center of the square Schiller was perched up on a high
pedestal, surrounded by a crowd of symbolic figures. A lot
of black marble had gone into that monument and its groups,
some dressed and some in the nude. Yet even the nude ones
were decent in that a drapery or garland of black marble con-
veniently hid their private parts. The front of the academy
building too was covered with figures—reproductions of famous
Greek sculptures, I found out as I grew up—and all the men
had fig leaves in front, which I thought part of their bodies.
It took me a long time, even at maturity, to get rid of the
notion that certain portions of man were created in the shape
of fig leaves. But what I loved best in that green square was a
crab-apple tree. Every spring I was afraid it would forget to
bloom, and every spring the miracle happened again and I was
overcome with a strange sense of excited happiness. Yes, and of
safety too. It was good of God not to forget my little crab-
apple tree.

We were good, bourgeois middle class, and the way we
lived, housed, ate, dressed, and behaved was as typical and unchangeable as the nest and feathers of a certain bird will be.
Up to my time you were born and raised in a certain class,
and that's where you belonged for the rest of your life. Our
parents started us out the same way, and look what's become
of us! It makes me laugh to see what happened to my own
generation, how we got kicked around, how all security and

continuity went out of our lives, how we were catapulted far and wide. Living, to us, has become something like an extended visit in the fun house at a second-rate amusement park. It's not up to us what we are doing or where we are going. We are juggled and rattled along, dropped through trap doors, pushed ahead, pummeled and rolled and kneaded, we're hit over the head, swung in dizzy circles, the ground gives beneath our feet, the floor revolves, the ceiling drops down on us, and sometimes we have trouble knowing what's the top and what's the bottom of this crazy world. The best we can do is to get a few good laughs and take it all in fun because we know that at last we must reach the door with the sign: Exit.

I don't really like that phrase, "my generation." It sounds so stiff and pompous. But what would you call all these people between forty and fifty, that whole hard-boiled, hard-bitten, up-rooted lot of us, scattered over the face of the earth? The main part of our lives has been sandwiched between two wars, and what we believed yesterday is not true today. We've changed professions and places and ideas so often that we've lost all contact with our own past, let alone our future. Christopher said the other day that this holds true only for Central Europe; he claims that in England and in France people are still clinging pretty solidly to the background into which they were born. I wonder for how long yet. I rather believe that we, who began wandering quite some while ago, were the vanguard of the biggest migration since that last big shifting of the human race—I must ask Christopher how many centuries ago.

If I ever see him again, that is.

Two years ago I asked Martin, my first-born, what he would rather have, liberty or security. "Security, of course," he said. It gave me quite a jolt. We, when we were young, had all the security we could stand, and we threw it to the winds and didn't care a hoot for it. What we wanted was liberty, and we got it—with several wars and revolutions thrown in for better measure.

I remember my parents' home as a never-ending succession of card games and little family gatherings and gossip around the table in the dining-living room, with the strong, aromatic coffee

of Vienna and cakes, pies, and pastry piled high on china plat-
ters with the old rose pattern. I didn't like our guests, for the men
yanked my pigtails and made silly jokes about me and smelled
of tobacco, and the day after their card game I had to dig their
chewed-up cigar stubs from the soil of the potted palm where
they had squashed them. Mother's parties were still worse, because her friends discussed me and my health and my pinafore
and the way I should wear my hair and, worst of all, they
kissed me. Their kisses felt as if snails were crawling over my
face, and I went straight to my room and washed it without
being told to. When Mama's friends or sisters had something
important to discuss, I was ordered to "go and look at the
album." I did so, while perking my ears and trying to understand why they were whispering and giggling. Most of the time
their talk seemed dull or silly to me, and after a short while I
got usually interested in the album and forgot about the silly
grownups. In one side of the album a little music box was
cunningly concealed. It had a little roll with bristles on it, which
slowly revolved and played always the same short, sweet tinkling tune. The other side was inhabited by the photos of all
my relatives, from my great-grandparents down to my youngest
uncle, who was a handsome officer and became my second love
after I was through with August.

I fell in love with Uncle Theodor when he came back from
some military outpost in Bosnia. He was sun-tanned and slim
in his blue tunic, and he brought an eagle along, which he tried
to settle down on my grandmother's kitchen balcony. It was
a sad and cross-looking animal—the eagle, I mean—and it confused me no end to find out that eagles had only one head, not
two like the ones I had seen on all stamps, flags, and official
emblems of Austria. The eagle refused all my advances and
died soon after, and Uncle Theodor was very sad. He resembled
a romantic and unhappy young man by the name of Ratcliff I
had found in Heine's poems, illustrated edition, four beautiful
gilt-edged volumes bound in red morocco leather, which were
given to me whenever I was ill. I was forbidden to read the
poems, except a very silly one about a mouse, but was to look
at the illustrations only. As soon as I could read I read them all,

and nothing would keep me as quiet and well-behaved as reading Heine's poems. I thought them absurd and ugly, and I still do. But the strict taboo made me believe that something utterly wicked must be concealed behind their words, and they gave me a lot of food for thought.

After Uncle Theodor came back from Bosnia he stayed for a short term with my grandparents, and this made my week ends with them ten times as exciting. Sometimes he would tell stories about the little garrison where he had been for three years, and sometimes he would show me picture postcards with minarets and mosques and veiled women, and altogether Bosnia sounded like a far-off, unreal, wild country and gave me a vague idea that Austria was spreading out all over the globe.

What a puny, provincial thing patriotism is! All we learned in school in the way of history or geography was that Austria was the most beautiful, the most important, the most perfect, the mightiest country in the world. We were the finest people, we had the best government, our emperor was the best, and the rest of the world was depicted to us as an insignificant appendix to our own glorious country and nation. Let's go on teaching children such things in every country of the world and let men believe what they were taught in school and we'll have wars until the end of time. As for the tottering Austria of my childhood, ruled by a likewise tottering monarch, it never occurred to anyone I knew that things might not be quite so wonderful with us as we thought.

Like every child I had two sets of grandparents, and they were as different as grandparents could be. In fact they abhorred each other and were rarely on speaking terms. Sometimes I can feel my grandparents having a fight and a scuffle inside of me, and the outcome of it is usually that I get into a jam. Only I don't call it a jam, but a soup, as my grandfather did. "Child," he would say, "now you have cooked your soup, now you have got to eat it." It's a sound principle, and it's the one thing I can say for myself: I have eaten most of the soups I have cooked for myself, and they didn't always taste very sweet.

I used to call my mother's parents my Fine grandparents and my father's my Common grandparents. My Fine grandparents lived in a big apartment. They had a living room and a library, both filled with fat, big, overstuffed furniture, plush-covered and solid. They had paintings on their walls and books in their cases, and they ate pastry with every meal, which in Vienna was a symbol of high-class living. At home we had pastry every second day, and my Common grandparents, who lived in a tiny flat and in the wrong part of the town, had it only on Sundays. My Fine grandparents' family branched out into the low nobility, and my grandmother had been a baroness before she had married my grandfather. But my Common grandparents were what was known as Little People; they had a little stationery shop, and my grandmother sold copybooks across the counter. But in my Fine grandparents' living room, which was called a salon, there stood that marvelous, sumptuous, splendid grand piano which became such a deciding factor in my upbringing. If my grandfather hadn't been the son of an old and wealthy family he would have become a musician, and probably a great musician at that. But his family was against it; it wasn't done, and maybe he had not enough grit to fight it out with them. He was the second of the six sons of the Dobsbergs, and he was put into The Firm as were all the others.

The Firm, Dobsberg & Sons, was a big and mysterious power on a high, invisible throne, ruling the lives of all of us. The name Dobsberg, in Austria, meant wood, timber; it meant the possession of entire provinces of forests, and Dobsberg wood went into the building of most houses, ships, railroads, and furniture of the country. It appears my grandfather didn't do so well in The Firm; I suppose all the suppressed music rummaged in his veins and made him restless and of little use in business. After he had put through some very damaging deals and done the firm a lot of harm, his brothers indicated that he would do better not to overwork himself and to live as a gentleman of leisure. He was a handsome, tall man in checkered trousers and with a high, shining silk hat, and, as he had nothing to do, he divided his time between playing the piano and visiting his eight daughters. At such occasions, however, he seemed slightly bored and also a bit vague about the names, age, and number of his various grandchildren. Yet he never forgot my name, and I think he liked me a bit better than the others because I was a single child, and also because we had a little secret between us that had to do with music.

Each Saturday night Vefi delivered me at the door of my grandparents' apartment. "Now be a good girl and don't over-eat," she said, foreseeing the worst, for the dinners at my grand-parents were rich; the word "diet" was still unknown, and I always returned on Sunday evening with stomach trouble. There was a smell of hot butter and roast meat and yeast cake even in the entrance hall, and I could hear Grandfather playing the piano in the salon. My grandmother, who was a very worldly lady, was in the bedroom, changing into a black silk dress for dinner, and I knew that she would not want to see me during that important process. I tiptoed through the green plush library and into the blue plush salon where Grandfather was having a fight with the grand piano. That, at least, was how it always struck me when he played: as if he were a lion and the grand piano another lion and that the two of them were fighting a battle of life and death. Grandfather snorted and grunted and groaned as he leaped over the keys and hammered out his savage passages and trills; his body bounced up and down, and I watched fascinatedly how his bottom was lifted from the piano stool and then banged down again in some fierce rhythm. The stool responded with a rhythmical squeak, and I wouldn't have been surprised if fire had emerged from Grandfather's nostrils. But it all ended with some thunder in the basses and a heavenly melody in the right hand, and then Grandfather leaned back, dried his brow, and discovered me.

"Oh, it's you, midget," he would say. "Did you listen? Did you like it? That's good. That was Beethoven, the greatest of them all; the Appassionata, and don't you forget it."

Grandfather wanted me to like Beethoven, and he was very pleased that I could recognize his sonatas without fail. Less successful he was in teaching me to hate a thing called Wagner. Wagner was what I liked best because it pulled some string inside of me, it touched some nerve, it gave me a little cramp which I called to myself The Nice Bellyache.

"This is Wagner!" Grandfather would yell at me while play-

ing something from Tannhäuser or Lohengrin. "I want you to
know that it's awful, it's horrible, it's unethical, it's devil's music.
You can't understand it yet, but I want you to remember it.
Listen! Destructive! Indecent! Ugly! Phooey! What a swine he
is, Wagner!"

In spite of that, I liked it better than any other music. Everything seemed tame and dull compared with Wagner. If this was
the work of the devil, I might like the devil too, even if I didn't
dare say so. I felt utterly wicked. I put Wagner into the same
pigeonhole with Heine's poems and my mute passion for Uncle
Theodor and felt important, having my own, dark secret.

When Grandfather had got himself tired out he would take
me on his lap in front of the piano and have me play things
by ear. That is, I had no trouble in picking out with two fingers
some of the melodies I had heard, and this delighted him out
of all proportion. Sometimes he would screw up the squeaky,
much-used piano stool and perch me on it so that I could reach
the keyboard. He would pull up a chair for himself, and we
would play à quatre-mains. It was wonderful fun, because all
I had to do was to hold onto my little two-finger melody while
he worked up the most complicated variations and paraphrases,
and such mighty noise rose from the piano that the windows
began to rattle. When we were through with it and looked
around, my grandmother was standing in the door and laughing
at us. "Aren't you two ever hungry?" she called, throwing
her head back with laughter. She was small and quick and very
gay. She walked young and talked young and was always up
to some mischief. But she was a very, very old lady of at least
forty-five when I was seven, and she had even begun to wear
the indication of a bonnet on her head, as a gesture toward age
and dignity. But it was the most flippant bit of a bonnet, and
to me my Fine grandmother always seemed a child like myself,
but hiding her face behind the mask of an old lady, just for the
fun of it.

Eating at the Fine grandparents' had something very festive
about it. We had plates with hand-painted flowers on them, and
when you turned them around there was on the bottom the beehive, which was the mark of the real good old Vienna porcelain.

I had my own little ruby-red wineglass, with a huntsman and a stag engraved on it. My fork and knife were such heavy silver that I had trouble handling them, and I had to be most careful of my table manners. More than once my grandmother clamped a book under each of my arms, and I had to clutch them tightly while eating, which gave me a very arrogant, high-shouldered air indeed. Grandfather carved the meat for Grandmother and myself, but Grandmother ladled out the soup, which came in a steaming, big tureen. The chairs in the dining room were big and, of course, covered with plush, and they were much too low for me. Grandfather always brought a batch of music along and perched me up on Mendelssohn's Lieder ohne Worte combined with Bach's Well-Tempered Clavichord. The joke was that my grandmother too was just a bit too short for those chairs. She shrewdly slipped a little cushion onto hers and then she sat there, high and proud, presiding over the table.

As soon as the coffee was served—thick, aromatic, black coffee in a big-bellied silver pot—my grandfather began to examine me. It was all about music. How many sharps had E major? How many E minor? What's the difference between major and minor? Tell me a piece in D minor that I played tonight. Listen, midget, how would you like to play the piano as well as I do? Wouldn't it be fun? Eh? What? Of course you would have to practise a few hours a day . . .

I didn't understand then that Grandfather pursued his own little dream with all his urging and questioning and talking about music. I poked my finger at the belly of the coffee pot and was sorry for myself. I could see myself in the rounded silver; I looked funny and distorted, with an enormous nose and a tiny forehead. I felt short of breath, filled with food as I was, and I had no ambition whatsoever. "I'd rather wait till my hands grow a bit more," I ventured timidly. Grandfather took my hands and flexed my fingers in his thoughtfully. "They will grow and stretch as soon as you start training them," he said. "You don't want the child to get big hands like Ida," my grandmother said. Ida was my mother's second cousin; she lived in Berlin and came once a year for a visit. She was a Prussian, and she seemed very strident and ugly to all of us. Austrians didn't like the Prussians then, and never will, in spite of Hitler. Grandmother looked down at her own hands, which were very small indeed, and Grandfather lifted these little hands from the table and kissed them, one after the other. Then he put them back with great care, as if they could break any time. She played a bit with his gray hair and said: "Well, Herr Dobsberg, how about a little bit of medicine?" The medicine came in a brandy bottle, and my grandfather took it after every meal.

I was with my grandfather when he died, and the funny part is, he didn't die of an illness but of a pastry, which, after all, isn't a bad death for an old Austrian. That pastry bore the untranslatable and absurd name of Marrillenknoedel. It was a national dish, sweet and rich and heavy; it consisted of dumplings that were filled with apricots, rolled in buttered bread crumbs and served with more melted butter, which made them swim in a hot, golden puddle. I wonder if the seasons in Vienna are still heralded in by those Knoedel, which are filled with cherries in June, with apricots during July and August, with plums in fall, and with preserves in winter. Every family staged great and festive competitions and tournaments in Marrillenknoedel-eating. My grandfather once ate forty-five, the proud and amazing achievement of a champion Marrillenknoedel-eater.

It was a Saturday night, and Uncle Theodor was staying with the grandparents for a short visit. He didn't look like Ratcliff any longer and he had quit the army. He had entered The Firm like any other son of the Dobsberg clan, and he had just returned from America, where the firm had sent him on some vague business trip.

"Let's see who can eat more Marrillenknoedel," Grandfather said, and we went to it as if it were a serious athletic tournament. For a while Uncle Theodor was in the lead, with Grandfather a close second. Grandmother was third all along, and I had not even a chance, although I ate so much and so quickly I felt like bursting. In the last stretch my grandfather overtook Uncle Theodor, winning the race by three and one-half dumplings. He had eaten twenty-eight and one-half altogether, but not for the world would he have been able to down that other half Marrillenknoedel. We were all breathing heavily, and I noticed that Grandfather opened a few buttons of his waistcoat behind his napkin. It was not like my swanky grandfather to let himself go like that, and Grandmother noticed it too, for she said quickly, "How about a little bit of medicine now, Herr Dobsberg?"

Grandfather took two glasses, but after a while he put down his unfinished cigar and said, "I think I want to go for a little stroll. I ate too much. Like to come along, midget?"

We went slowly down the street, Grandfather stopping several times to take a deep breath. "It's very warm, isn't it?" he said. It was warm. The evening shone with a queer light, mauve, between gray and purple, with a reflection on the faces of all the people, and I have never forgotten it. In the shade of every house door maids were standing with their lovers. There was a scent of lime and jasmine, so heavy you could hold it in your hands. The janitors of all the houses had brought out their chairs; they sat in front of the house doors, their big hands resting flatly upon their broad laps. Dogs were taken out for a late walk; they sniffed happily at every street lamp, and the lamplighter went around in his white linen coat and lit the gaslights. We walked as far as the corner, where Grandfather bought himself an evening paper and some cigars, and then we walked slowly back again.

"Wait a moment," my grandfather said and, to my surprise, he went into the little hack drivers' joint, farther down the street. I waited outside, for this was definitely no place for a little girl. Neither was it a place for my elegant grandfather. The smell of stale beer and fried onions streamed thickly from the door into the street, and I could hear the hack drivers laugh and haggle and shout inside, where they were drinking and playing at cards. The cabs were lined up along the sidewalk, and each tired horse had a feedbag tied to its mouth. They hung their heads and crunched and munched and seemed very contented. After a while Grandfather came back with a siphon bottle in his hand and we went on. We didn't walk up the stairs but rang the bell for the janitor to let us up in the newfangled elevator. As usual I was terribly scared of it. What if anything goes wrong and we fall down the shaft? I thought. Grandfather shook his head as I grabbed his hand. "The damn thing makes me sick," he said. "Me too," I said, slightly relieved. "The main thing is to keep your equilibrium," Grandfather said; I was impressed by the big, unfamiliar word, and I have never forgotten it. Steady, Marion, steady, I would say to myself ever so often in the years to come. Steady my girl. The main thing is to keep your equilibrium.

I'm saying it now to myself, now, this very minute.

As we left the elevator on the third floor, Grandfather's equilibrium was not too good. Just then Uncle Theodor came from the flat, whistling and rather dashing with his straw hat and choke collar. "Going out?" Grandfather asked him. "A little rendezvous," Uncle Theodor answered nonchalantly, and I felt my love return with a pang. Grandfather gave a little snort of amusement. "See that the husband doesn't catch you," he said, and, as so often, I looked down long avenues of the incomprehensible secrets that grown-ups shared and children couldn't understand. Uncle Theodor entered the elevator whistling, and Grandfather let go of my hand and went straight to the kitchen. As he arrived there with his siphon bottle and asked for a glass, he stirred up quite a flurry of excitement, for he rarely ever dived into these regions of the apartment. He patted the big old cook on the back. "You didn't cook enough Marrillenknoedel," he told her. "I wanted to eat thirty, but there were only twenty-eight left for me." The cook grinned and cackled, and Grandmother came into the kitchen and shooed us out. "What are you doing here, for the love of the Lord?" she asked, and I heard him answer, "I've got myself some soda water. I'm feeling funny."

He went into the library and sat down in his big chair to read the evening paper. There was an old-fashioned kerosene lamp standing at the side of his head, with a round white glass shade shaped like a globe. I liked that lamp because on its foot it had a picture of the pyramids and two camels. I crouched down next to Grandfather and studied that picture. After reading for a while Grandfather dropped his paper and leaned his head back. The light of the lamp glistened on his face, which was covered with a fine film of moisture. "Warm," he said. "Come on, midget, tell me something; a bedtime story."

This was a good joke, because usually he told me bedtime stories when I stayed there on Saturday nights, and they were all about Paganini and Liszt and a funny friend of his by the name of Dinckelmann. But I was willing to oblige, and also I had something important to tell.

"I've been to the opera," I said proudly. "Papa and Mama took me along, not to a matinee but to a real performance in the evening. It was past ten o'clock when we got home."

"I declare!" Grandfather said. "What opera did you hear?"

"There was no opera, there were three ballets," I reported. One of them, called Die Puppenfee, had driven me into a frenzy of enchantment, and I was still full of it. As I went on telling Grandfather about it, he closed his eyes. "Do you remember some of the music?" he asked me after a while, and I said, "Of course."

He told me to play some for him, and I went into the next room, left the door open so that a faint gleam of light fell onto the piano, climbed onto the piano stool, and set my two fingers to work. "Like it, Grandpapa?" I asked eagerly, and I heard him answer in a sleepy way, "Yes. It's pretty. Go on." I played on and on, because all of a sudden I seemed to remember a lot of music; once in a while I could not find the right key, but most of the time I was very pleased with the melodies that I could find with my two fingers. "Like it, Grandpapa, like it?" I would ask. "Yes, it's pretty, I like it," he would answer every time. Then, after a while, he didn't answer and I got bored. I hopped from my stool and went into the library. He still smiled at me, with his head leaning against the back of his chair and the light of the lamp on it. He didn't say anything and he didn't move, and I tiptoed out of the room so as not to disturb him.

My grandmother was in her bedroom; she sat in front of her mirror and soaked her hands in a little bowl with warm milk, which was said to do miracles for your skin. The chambermaid stood behind her and was brushing Grandmother's thick switch, which hung at the side of the mirror. Grandmother took off her braids every evening, and the maid held them in her big hands and brushed them, with an absorbed expression on her freckled face. At the side of the milk bowl was the household book, and Grandmother was counting up the figures, shaking her head and muttering, for she wasn't good at additions and subtractions or at handling money.

"Well, child?" she said.

"Grandpapa sleeps like a rabbit," I said. "With his eyes open."

Grandmother went on muttering and counting. "You ought to go to bed yourself, it's much too late for a little girl," she said. When we went back to the library to say good night to Grandfather he was still smiling, and he was dead.

Putzi was the nickname of my Common grandfather, my Little grandfather. To him I came with all my troubles, and I never needed to tell him lies as to the other grownups. Friday was my day with the Common grandparents and, in a way, I liked them even better than the Fine ones. They lived in the wrong part of the town, and their flat was so small that beds were concealed in every one of the three crooked little rooms. After dinner those beds blossomed out from the most surprising places, from pieces of furniture that looked like cabinets or easy chairs or even like splendid Venetian mirrors. Indeed, the wall beds of the average furnished room in the American rooming house had no surprise for me. They certainly could not live up the ingenuity of beds in disguise in my Common grandparents' home.

Boiled beef with horse-radish, and stewed prunes for dessert, served on chipped-off stoneware plates. A slatternly maid whose heels peeped through the holes in her stockings like round, dirty faces. The pear tree in the back yard, and the old retired pushcart, which in succession became my throne, my sailboat, the stage for my dramatic renderings, and the place where an unpleasant boy with buck teeth tried to steal the first kiss from me. And the old, green bench in the yard that had a story of its own. It seems that this bench and a coat of lambskin were the only things left after my grandparents' farm had burned down. There was also a wonderful penholder with a tiny peephole in it where you could see the Eiffel Tower. It made you want to go away and travel far and see the wonders of this world. There were the windows from which one could watch the slow freight boats coming down the Donau Canal, with half-nude children on them and always a broad woman who would wave and shout to someone and an excited dog running from one end of a boat to the other and barking at other boats. And there was the door that gave onto the yard, a door made of bits of colored glass— green, red, blue—and when you looked through it the world changed into something out of a fairy tale.

Every evening my grandmother, a tall, strict woman, brought a little tin box from the store; I can still hear the sound of coins dropping on the tin as she counted the intake of the day. The store itself was a dark, musty-smelling paradise, filled to the ceiling with stationery and copybooks and erasers and penholders and colored pencils and all the things children cherish. It gave me quite some distinction among my school friends to have such easy access to the dream things of my grandparents' little store. By some elaborate plan children could get small premiums thrown in after a purchase of at least twenty pennies. This was a means of trying to beat the competition at Weiner's, across the street. Weiner's, that was the big, powerful enemy of my Little grandfather. Weiner's had two windows and more money to back them up, and they were shrewder and they undersold and they gave things away just to spite us, and they were Jews. Sometimes my grandmother would bring out her old opera glasses and look through them across the street, to find out what bait Weiner's had conjured up this time. My Little grandfather was too proud to walk across the street and have a look at Weiner's display, but he sent me over as a spy. I would mingle with the other children and promenade nonchalantly up and down in front of those two windows until I knew exactly what we were up against.

"Mutzi, today we've got to work like Turks," Putzi would say to me as he pulled down the blinds in our own little display window, and then we would go berserk with paper streamers and confetti, with a village and zoo made of cardboard, with Easter bunnies in spring and children in the manger around Christmastime, and with a sign throughout the year which screamed: "Positively highest price paid for used schoolbooks."

I suppose my Little grandfather was far from being impressive or perfect in any respect. He was funny, ugly, red-headed and cross-eyed, and he even limped a bit. He claimed that his eyes had taken to squinting while as a boy he had worked in a drafty workshop, and for his limp he had also a rather flattering reason. It had something to do with that fire on the farm wherein only that lambskin coat and the green bench had survived and in which Grandfather claimed to have saved the three children while risking his own life. But I think he was born imperfect, cross-eyed and limping; he had never saved anything or anybody and, on top of it, he might well have forgotten to pay the installments on the fire insurance. But I think I was so fond of him *because* of all his faults and shortcomings—for that is how fondness is constituted. He was wise and kind and mellow, he never talked down to me, and he never seemed a day older than myself.

It was Putzi who took me to church and made me pray, yet it was also he who afterward gave such a funny imitation of the priest and his Catholic Latin that I rolled with laughter. Each Sunday we went to a different church or cathedral, and all of them were beautiful, filled with crowds of gay, fat baroque angels and saints who looked like cupids and pagan deities. And there was incense and fine singing and slanting sun rays that streamed through the windows and stained the marble floors, and flowers on every altar and the golden tinkle of the acolyte's bell when we all knelt with our eyes cast down. But I peeped up and got a glimpse of the holy monstrance, and it was all rich and exciting and fantastic like a theatrical performance. For such was religion in Vienna that it might well compete with the stage and the imperial opera house, and that is how the Church kept her power over the fun-loving, lively Austrians.

There were other days when Putzi took me down to the market at the bank of the Donau Canal where the broad, flat boats arrived from Hungary, loaded with melons and apples and sun-tanned peaches, with corn in green husks and chains of red pepper, with cages of cackling chickens and fat ambling geese, with fish and fowl and with all the abundance of a rich country. Putzi was able to rattle off some Hungarian jokes, for his parents had come from Hungary, and these jokes met with great laughter and success and helped him to beat down the price. He taught me how to market and to choose and to bargain. How to break the feet of the chickens and the breastbone of the geese to see if they were young and how to squeeze the bellies of the fat carps we bought for fasts, to be sure that they had roe inside or spawn. Once, when we went there to buy everything for the Christmas holidays, Grandfather had me pick the goose and the carp. And when we came home the goose had two large livers inside and the carp turned out a freak, with roe *and* spawn in its innards. And Putzi laughed himself sick about the trick he had played on me and about my baffled face.

Putzi took me to the menagerie in Schoenbrunn, where one of the guards was his personal friend, so that I was allowed to enter the cage of the orangoutang, Peter, and play with him. And the seals came every time Putzi whistled, and somehow they resembled each other, the seals and Putzi, only the seals had no red beards. And Putzi showed me the giraffes and kangaroos and taught me their names, and he showed me big, funny birds, pelicans and flamingos and pepper birds. Later I remembered them in one of the tougher spots of my life and carved them out of wood, and they helped me through and even made me famous in a small way. . . .

And Putzi took me out for long hikes in the Vienna woods. Every spring we went out to find the first violet, just before the meadows became a purple, scented carpet of them, and every fall we picked the last bramble and boughs with red and yellow leaves to take home, and in winter when there were no flowers we blew our breath against the frozen windowpanes and made ice flowers grow. Putzi took me to every parade and procession in Vienna, and there were many. He showed me the Emperor in his carriage with the golden wheels, and he showed me Johann Strauss, who was an old man then, with dyed black hair and a violin. And he took me to the Prater and let me ride on the merry-go-round, and he held my head when I got sick from it. And he took me to the circus and to the opera and to the marionettes, and he even took me to the wax figures where, in a separate little room, you could hear—for the first time—something that was called a phonograph and see something called living photos. The phonograph, with much scratching and squeaking and groaning, produced a torturous scene at the dentist's, and the living photos showed a spasmatic and convulsed crowd chasing after a man who fell over an apple cart. Putzi was very thoughtful afterward. He shook his head and said, "I hope Weiner doesn't see that stuff or he will put it into his window."

Putzi showed me Vienna, he showed me Austria, he showed me a good, rich part of the world. He had no money and many debts; he could not buy things for me, but he had friends everywhere and he had done little favors to everybody, and he knew all the fun you could get free of charge. When we went out together on a spree we were royally entertained and the whole town was our theater. Compared with my remembrance of my grandfathers, my parents seem a shadowy and blurred and thin-blooded lot. There was so much more strength and vigor in the two old men who formed the roots of my existence.

There is another one of the new words we had to learn: The subconscious. I discovered it in an article in the papers when I was eight years old and I liked the sound of it. I startled my uncle Theodor by asking him very seriously: "What do *you* think about the subconscious, Uncle?" Poor fellow, he had never heard of it and just then he was entangled in a very strenuous love affair with my grandmother's housekeeper, the one he married later on. "You're a precocious little brat, aren't you?" he said, pinched my cheek and forgot the very next second that I existed. It made me rather proud to think that I had a subconscious of my own; I pictured it like a purple-colored velvet bag that hung inside of my chest, near the heart; sometimes it throbbed and sometimes it felt sort of swollen and sometimes again it was heavy with emptiness. From it I could pull dreams and crying spells and the odd, sudden flashes of understanding things far beyond my scope, which are so frequent in ten-year-olds.

I wouldn't have been a very good object to demonstrate Freudian theories, because there were no fixations whatever in my relations to my parents. I liked my mother in a tolerant and slightly condescending way, for she seemed helpless and very childish at times. I didn't trust her to be able to manage anything, because my father bossed her around the house and treated her as if she were a child. And what, in the name of heaven, should I think of a woman who bawled at the slightest provocation while I wasn't allowed to bawl at all; who couldn't cross a street or ride on a street car without getting into a flutter and doing everything wrong? As for my father, I was absolutely indifferent toward him. I didn't like him particularly, neither did I dislike him.

My father had a set of very strict yet wholly haphazard rules, opinions, and disconnected principles and made us live accordingly. To wit: Red wine was good and necessary for your health but only bums drank white wine. Fresh fruit was very dangerous, especially for children, and cucumber salad was the common cause of cholera epidemics. (There were still cholera epidemics during my childhood.) People who drank cold water were apt to catch pneumonia. People who bet on the races were scoundrels and would die on straw. (That I would die on straw was the ultimate verdict my father spoke over me whenever he was angry with me.) But people who played in the state lottery and bought every sweepstake they could lay hands on were good providers and fine characters. People who read books went crazy and ended up in the state insane asylum. Girls with curly hair had bad tempers. Women had no sense at all, the poor darlings, with the exception of one's own mother—that is, Father's mother.

I don't know whether he liked me or not. Sometimes he seemed bewildered at having sired a creature as different from himself as I was. He kissed me twice every year, on Christmas Eve and on his birthday, after I had recited some silly poem. He seriously worried about my figure, especially about my legs, which were thin when nice plump calves were the fashion. It seemed to embarrass him that I was thin and long-boned and boyish-looking at a time when girls had to have a lot of meat.

When my father was angry at me he shouted that I was crazy like all the Dobsbergs, as if he had had nothing at all to do with my pedigree. Sometimes I pleased myself by pulling out of my purple velvet bag a vague notion that, maybe, this intolerant stranger wasn't my real father and that I was a foundling. I have never seen a child who didn't have that notion at one time or another.

When I was eight, sometime after my Fine grandfather's death, my mother took me to a concert of Sarasate: it was the most wonderful thing I had ever seen or heard, and I decided that I would study to play the violin and tour around the world and be very rich and famous and please my grandfather in heaven. Then Putzi took me to the circus and I saw the lion-tamer. She wore a red hussar uniform and had a whip in one hand and a gun in the other and she put her head into the lion's mouth. It struck me to the core of my heart. This was exactly what I had always wanted to do: put my head into a lion's mouth.

I told Putzi about it on the day when we had filled wine from a barrel into bottles. We did it once a year, and this day was one grade better than a real holiday. A few weeks before, I had gone out with Putzi as he was making the rounds of the wine merchants and choosing just the sort of wine he wanted. Then that barrel arrived and two men with leather aprons trundled it down into the cellar where we were busy cleaning last year's wine bottles. The cellar was a wonderful world in itself, grimy and dark and filled with wine fumes which gave me a flighty feeling in my head. The spiders had diligently woven filmy little curtains from one bottle to the next, and I was sorry I had to tear them to pieces, they were so fine and neat. Several times I tried to fold up a few of them and take them home and keep them for my dolls; but the moment I touched them they were just a dusty bit of fuzz. I used to scoop up whatever seemed pretty to me and experienced some great disappointments when I brought home such beautiful but evasive objects as icicles, dewdrops on leaves and the beautiful water from a puddle in which a rainbow had reflected its colors. Man belongs to the collecting group of animals, together with squirrels, badgers and chipmunks. Let's collect furniture, money, filthy bits and ends of everything and worry how to keep and defend them. Let's live like a dung-beetle, roll all the dirt we are able to collect into a neat little ball, hide it in the ground and then sit on it and fight for it with our lives—and there will be trouble to the end of this world.

Putzi was humming and whistling, and I felt very important with galoshes on my feet because the cellar floor was damp and my sleeves rolled up like a real workman's. Putzi filled water into last year's bottles, and I put shot into them, and together we rattled them until the greenish film inside disappeared. Then came the great moment when the bung was hammered into the bunghole and a hose led from the barrel into one bottle after another. It began to smell of wine. We knelt in front of the barrel, and I was allowed to hold the bottles. Every time before Putzi stuck the hose into the neck of the next bottle and the next one and the next one, he put it into his mouth to siphon the wine down, for that was the correct way of filling wine into bottles. There was a silent law of honor that forbade drinking wine while filling it in, but the little pulls on the hose kept Putzi quite happy. Wine would drip down his chin and he would wipe it off and laugh at me. I was slightly intoxicated from the smell and the gurgling sound of the wine flowing into the bottles; it spilled over my fingers, and once in a while I would lick them to get my mouth filled with the tart, bubbling taste. There were puddles of wine on the floor; my knees were wet with it, and the skin of my hands and arms was washed with wine. Ordinarily I didn't care for wine because it was supposed to be Good For You and I hated everything that was administered to me like a medicine. But the day we filled the wine into bottles I loved it because it was so much fun. Grandfather too loved wine, not in a gross manner but with the delight of a connoisseur. He smacked his tongue after every suck at the hose and wiped his beard, in which golden little drops lingered on. "Not bad," he would say, "not bad at all. Almost as good as in 1898, only a bit lighter." He had lovely words to describe the taste of wine. Some year it had velvet and some year fullness or fire or sparkle. When all bottles were filled, Putzi drove in the corks with a little apparatus and a good final slam on every bottle, and I laid them in neat rows upon the wine racks, pretending they were children who had to be put to sleep. My legs were stiff from kneeling and my head felt funny.

"Mutzi," Grandfather said, "what the two of us need now is some fresh air and some bread and salt."

And so we left the cellar. When we reached daylight again we blinked and we swallowed huge chunks of air and Putzi drummed upon his chest. It was late in the afternoon, for we had worked all day long; the vesper bell was sounding from some near-by chapel, and the shiny leaves of the pear tree in the yard looked tired. We sat down on the green bench, feeling very good, and for a while we listened drowsily to the pleasant muffled sound of ripe pears dropping into the little patch of grass there. Putzi rubbed salt onto the pieces of bread he had taken out of his pocket, and we chewed contentedly. I was still a bit dizzy, and suddenly I was overcome by a rush of courage and noble emotions.

"Putzi," I said, "I want to become a lion-tamer."

He looked at me from the side, chewed on for a while, and grinned.

"Well, that's not the worst idea," he said peaceably. "I knew a lion-tamer once, when I was a soldier, in Pressburg. She had beautiful blonde hair sewn to her hat. When she took off the hat the hair came off with it and underneath there was only her bare skull with nasty scars on it. A lion had torn off her scalp, just in fun, you see. He didn't mean any harm, just feeling playful, I guess. The hair she had sewn to her hat was her own all right. Like your doll with the real hair, sort of, what's her name?"

Well, this wasn't exactly what I had wanted to hear. I thought it over awhile, licking the taste of wine from my arm.

"Last week you wanted to become a fiddler," Putzi reminded me. "It's time you make up your mind and then stick to it. You promised to make a lot of money and buy me a rocker chair. I was looking forward to it. You can't let me down now."

That was true. "Maybe I could make a lot of money taming lions," I suggested, but Putzi shook his head.

"Look here," he said, "you're not a little baby any longer, are you?" (I wasn't nine yet.) "Now I'm talking sense to you. Your mother wants you to study music, you know that. Herr Dobsberg wanted you to study music too, and he looks down from heaven and wonders if you'll do it, bless his soul. Nothing could make your mother happier, and you want to make her happy—or don't you?" Of course I did want to make my mother happy. Yet in some sensitive but inarticulate part of my heart I felt being pushed and shoved and coaxed toward becoming a musician, whether I liked it or not. It had been like that ever since I could remember. Herr Dobsberg, as Putzi insisted on calling my dead grandfather, had wished for it and had handed his wish down to my mother. My mother herself would have liked to become a musician, but she had been too weak and soft for it. Parents are that way. They want their children to achieve what they themselves were unable to do: it's a very subtle bloom of egotism, but it's egotism all the same.

"Of course no one is going to tell you what you ought to become," Putzi said shrewdly. "It's entirely up to you. If you want to become a lion-tamer, no one is going to put any obstacle in your way. If you want me to, I'll take you to the circus Renz one of these days: I know one of the stablemasters, and it's a cinch to introduce you to him. That's very easy."

That took some of the wind out of my sails. If Putzi had refused to let me become a lion-tamer, a lion-tamer I would be, for if anything was strictly denied to me I had to go and get it. I suppose I'm still like that, and I've bumped my head quite badly in the pursuit of things that were marked: "Keep Off."

"Lion-taming is much more dangerous than playing the fiddle," I said. Big pink bubbles of courage rose inside of me. Putzi looked at me and said nothing. He chewed his last piece of bread with salt, then he stretched his arms with a little groan and got up from the green bench. He limped to the little patch of grass under the pear tree and carefully selected one of the dropped, overripe pears from the ground. He came back, smiled down at me, and dropped the pear into my lap.

"Yes, Mutzi," he said. "Lion-taming might be a bit more dangerous. But playing the fiddle is more difficult. Oh, it's much more difficult. Compared with playing the fiddle, lion-taming is child's play."

And that decided it.

"Well," I said grandly, "if that's a fact, I guess I'd rather play the fiddle."

WHENEVER anything important has happened in my life I have had a headache or a sore throat or a huge fever blister on my upper lip. I had all three of them the day my mother took me to the Uncles to have it out with them. The Uncles, Grandfather's five brothers, sat high up on the family throne, an autocratic bunch of old men who ruled the lives of all of us. They spent their time in an expensive office with super-de-luxe leather chairs and an oil portrait of the founder, Leopold Dobsberg, and photos of themselves, each one stiffly standing next to a pitifully small round jigsaw table.

The Uncles regulated the existence of the whole clan; they decided what the sons should study, how big a dowry should be appropriated to the various daughters, nieces, and grandnieces respectively: less for the pretty ones and more if they were ugly or had other shortcomings; how much allowance had to be ladled out to the widows in the family; how many more sons-in-law could possibly be unloaded onto The Firm; which black sheep had to be sent on a mission to South America and left there to his fate; and whose debts should be paid just one more time.

How small and neat a woman my mother was as I marched at her side down the Ring toward the Uncles' office. She had such small hands and feet that I was proud of them, whereas my own hands and feet seemed to sprawl and grow and took up an embarrassing amount of space. My mother always wore tiny, much-cleaned white kid gloves that emanated a fine odor of benzine. In her left hand she gathered up her skirt in a most ladylike way that I could never hope to attain, and in her right she carried a little bag with petit-point embroidery.

She wore a black hat with tightly curled little ostrich feathers and a veil into which she blew from time to time, to stretch it a bit, for it was pulled too closely around her face and twisted into a little knot under her chin. She made very small steps while I strode along in big, flat-heeled shoes, miserably conscious of my black-ribbed cotton stockings, which had a tendency to rumple around my long thin legs sticking out from under a pleated, short little-girl's skirt.

"You should have been a boy," my mother sighed once more as she examined my entire appearance, so utterly void of graciousness or refinement. I thought so myself. In fact, there was, deeply hidden inside of me, the vague and ridiculous hope that I might yet turn into a boy someday. In those days to be a boy was so much better than to be just a girl.

"Now don't be afraid, Marion," my mother said in a small, helpless voice when we reached the house where the Uncles resided. "Why should I?" I replied arrogantly, but my knees felt funny.

"I've knuckled under all my life, but this time I'm going to fight it out," my mother said nervously. I felt terribly sorry for her. She seemed so utterly unfit to go into battle for anything or anybody.

"You don't understand it yet, but I want you to be independent someday; that's why I want you to study music," my mother said. I didn't answer, but I understood it quite well. The word "independent" had a ring that made me feel hot and cold. Even today, if I were asked what I treasure highest in life, it would be that fleeting, intangible thing, better than love or happiness or wealth: independence.

"Now don't forget to make a nice curtsy to the Uncles and don't shuffle your feet and don't fiddle with your gloves and speak only when asked," my mother said before she pushed the button next to the discreet brass plate with the name DOBSBERG & SONS on it. Anton, the office boy, opened the door and bowed politely. He was an old man too, and he wore dignified white side whiskers like the Emperor. "The gentlemen are expecting you," he told my mother, and then he turned to me and examined me severely. "My, how you are growing," he said. "Soon I'll have to call you Fräulein, hey? How old are you, Fräulein Marion?"

"I'll soon be eleven," I said, blushing. Anton led us through the long, dark entrance hall where the gaslight burned all day long, opened double doors, and led us through several rooms where bookkeepers and cashiers and clerks were busy, some sitting at desks, some standing and scribbling into ledgers that were placed on high writing stands. But there were also—first dawn of times to come—two crude typewriters, handled by two sexless, efficient-looking creatures, with spectacles, no bosoms, and high, stiff, white collars. My father hated them and could never be reconciled to the disgrace of having women in the office.

It was funny to see Father in the office. He looked up from his desk and nodded, just as the other men did, but otherwise he treated Mother and me as if he didn't know us. I suppose it wouldn't have been dignified for him to show too much familiarity. Besides, there had been quite some quarrels at home about this matter of my studying music and my father was strictly against it. That same morning he had left the breakfast table in a huff, his eggs untouched, his napkin flung to the floor and behind his insulted-looking back the door had banged close with a sound of finality. Here he was now, looking like a moody stranger, with eyeglasses which he never wore at home and a black alpaca armlet pulled over his right arm. His white cuffs with the big golden cufflinks stood on his desk, next to the inkstand.

"Good day," I said, intimidated. "Good day," he muttered, bending over his books and ledgers again as if he hardly remembered knowing us.

My father was one of the sons-in-law who were favored with a job in The Firm. He worked in the main office as a bookkeeper, and only the faintest reflection of the Uncles' pomp and splendor reached our humble household. I suppose the Uncles had so many nieces and grandnieces to take care of that they were compelled ever so often to throw a good job into the bargain to get them all married. Getting all female members of a family married must have been a harassing test in that period. Whenever I was told to "look at the album," my mother's sisters, cousins, and friends unfailingly went into a heated discussion of some betrothal, engagement, or marriage, of planning ways and means to push ahead some girl's chances of getting a husband, and a flurry of figures was always connected with all this difficult mating business.

Before I was six years old I had decided that I wouldn't marry, ever. I wouldn't have a husband who had to be paid for taking me and who would command me around the house and expect me to wait on him, hand and foot. To me all husbands were made after the image of my father and I didn't want to be married to a man like my father, oh no, thank you. So far this was my own one-girl-rebellion. But there must have been millions of little girls who decided just the same around the beginning of this century. If someone would have told me that I was part of the movement for the emancipation of women I wouldn't have known what they were talking about. We never know exactly where we stand and what we are until many years after. Christopher said the other day that we are all only tiny particles of the Great Decline that's under way just now—with the Barbarians destroying an old culture—our culture;—and then they would set up a new culture and after a few centuries that culture would be old again and a new crowd of Barbarians would come and destroy that one and so forth ad infinitum. If he meant it as a consolation it didn't serve its purpose, because I don't feel like declining, and all the examples of the Romans and the Persians and the Khmers don't mean a thing to me. What means something to me is that all the things I believed in and the goals toward which I strove seem just now to have been utterly and ludicrously wrong. Maybe man is meant to be a killer, like the lion and the python. Maybe it's human to fight, to conquer, to kill and to show no mercy. If so, all our virtues have been failings, and to be kind, tolerant, peaceful and free are the marks of degeneration. Maybe I am what my stepson Johnny in his more inspired speeches calls A Stinking Liberal. Poor me, poor tiny particle of this and that, pulled here and there by every current, blown hither and thither by every wind that stirred my times. . . . Maybe if, back in nineteen-hundred-and-six, I and a few other millions of little girls hadn't rebelled against family and marriage, hadn't dimly wished for independence but had decided to be obedient wives, give birth to many children and raise our sons to be good soldiers, we wouldn't be in the thicket of the Great Decline today. But what's the use of philosophizing now? We were as we were and we had to go after the things we wanted.

Anton opened another impressive double door, my mother gave my pigtails a little tug, and we entered the sanctuary. The Uncles were there, all five of them, which meant that this was to be a serious conference. Up to then I had seen them only on great occasions, at my grandfather's funeral, for instance, at Aunt Caroline's wedding, and when I brought them flowers at the fiftieth anniversary of The Firm.

"Good day, Uncle," my mother said to each of them and gave them her white-kid-gloved hand, as if she were a little girl herself.

"Good day, Uncle," I piped and made my curtsy.

"Good day, good day, Betty. Hello, little Marion. It's a rare pleasure to see you two young ladies here," said Uncle Leopold, who was the oldest one. They were all charming, worldly gentlemen, and they patted me in turns and pinched my cheeks and said what a big girl I was and how did I like it in school. They even had a box of candy prepared for me, and Uncle Julius, a dapper little man with an iron-gray beard, asked me to do him the favor and try some. It was all very urbane and friendly and absolutely wrong, for I was no baby and we knew what we wanted, my mother and I, and it wasn't candy. I fastened my eyes to a big painting on which the Uncles were to be seen, sitting around the same green-baize table where they sat now and looking very important with little decorations in their lapels. Only in the painting my grandfather was with them, and that gave me some sort of confidence.

"Well, and what brings you here, bright and early?" Uncle Heinrich said, looking at his watch as if to indicate that they were busy men and had not much time for nonsense. My mother came forward on her chair; she was so small that her feet didn't reach the floor if she didn't sit on the edge. "It's about

Marion, Uncle," she said. "I understand you don't want her
to study music."

"But no, that's a misunderstanding, child," Uncle Leopold
said good-naturedly. "Let her play the violin, by all means.
Why should all little girls play the piano? Let her play the
violin for a change. She'll stop playing as soon as she gets
married and has babies, just like you did, hey, what?"

"That's just it, Uncle," my mother said. "The child has too
much talent and too much ambition to dilly-dally around like
that. Fräulein Gans, who has given her lessons up to now, may
be good enough for the foundation, but now it's high time that
Marion began to study seriously and with a real teacher."

"Far be it from us to interfere with that," said Uncle Leopold.
"If little Marion doesn't mind practising an hour a day, let
her go ahead. I understand Fräulein Gans is a very good violin
teacher. She gives lessons to some of the young ladies in the
convent of the Savatian Sisters, and everybody has only
praise for her. But if you prefer another teacher for your little
girl, no one will hinder you."

My mother swallowed hard. "I wouldn't bother you if it
were that simple," she said, closing her eyes as if she were
running through a blazing fire. "But if Marion is to study we
need money. We can't afford it on my husband's salary. I talked
to Professor Szimanszki—he is the best master in Vienna, maybe
the best in the world. He thinks he could finish her within four
years, but he is very expensive. And she would need a good
violin soon—up to now she played on a three-quarter fiddle,
but Szimanszki wouldn't take her on if she hadn't a real good
violin."

There was a little silence. Uncle Leopold pulled on his cigar.
Uncle Johann made doodles on a blotter. Uncle Heinrich examined his nails. Uncle Julius pushed the candy box toward me.
"Have a candy, Betty. Have a candy, Marion," he said, embarrassed. Uncle Robert, who had been silent so far, made a
faint effort at easing the tension. "I know Szimanszki," he said
good-naturedly. "He plays the second fiddle in the Philharmonic
quartet. You know, we have chamber music in our house every
Wednesday."

"Phsh! The second fiddle!" Uncle Leopold said contemptuously.

Uncle Leopold threw his cigar stub onto the ash tray. "It sounds like complete nonsense to me, forgive me, Betty," he said irritably. "Why make an issue of it? Why spend good money on a hobby like playing the violin? What do you think would be the outcome of it all?"

"I want to become a virtuoso like Sarasate and play in concerts and travel everywhere and earn a lot of money and later I want to buy my mother a villa in the country," I said, forgetting that I was to talk only when asked. Uncle Heinrich laughed and patted my head. But Uncle Johann put a big period behind his doodles and angrily pushed the blotter away.

"What we don't want in the family is a girl who would play in public," he said. "It would be a scandal. After all, we are somebody in Vienna, even if I say so myself. What light would it throw on us if one of our nieces went out with the fiddle and played for Krethi and Plethi. Play for money—a young girl! Imagine!"

My mother looked as if she would like to cry, but this time she didn't. I wasn't too sure I wouldn't begin to bawl myself, for there was a lump in my throat as big and hard as a fist.

"The child has made up her mind to learn something and have a profession and be independent later on," my mother said. "And I agree with her entirely."

"What does a little child like her know? Whoever put that bee under her bonnet?" Uncle Leopold shouted, forgetting his suave manners.

"My father did. Your brother," Mother said, pointing with her chin to the painting on the wall. There was another little silence.

"I am sorry if that sounds rude, Betty," Uncle Heinrich said after a pause. "But we all know that your dear father was not a very practical man; a good, kindhearted, charming fellow and a true gentleman, yes, but not very able to manage his own life—let alone the lives of his children and grandchildren. You shouldn't take his little whim too seriously."

"It wasn't a whim," my mother said, and now she did cry after all. "It was his serious wish that Marion should learn an instrument and not just as a hobby, and you know it."

"It seems a crazy idea," Uncle Johann muttered, and the others nodded their heads in agreement. Mother's eyes were dry again, as if she had swallowed her own tears back from where they came, and she straightened up and grew a little. "Look here," she said, trying to sound sensible and not at all crazy. "If Marion happened to be a boy you would certainly let her—him—study something and you wouldn't refuse her—him—some funds for a good education, now would you?"

Uncle Leopold slammed his hand down on the green-baize table. "But Marion is a girl," he said.

"Uncle Leopold, Uncle Johann, listen," my mother said urgently. "There is still my dowry, we didn't touch it, why can't I use it for my girl now?"

"Your dowry belongs to your husband," Uncle Heinrich said curtly. "He is a thrifty and levelheaded man, and I am sure he wouldn't spend his good money on a crazy adventure like this. You should be grateful for having a husband who saves for his and your old age and won't throw your security to the winds."

My mother hung her head because she knew that this was true. Even I knew it, because scraps of my parents' nightly discussions about this had penetrated from their bedroom into my chamber.

"If I am right," Mother said stubbornly, "you have been kind enough to provide a little trust fund for Marion. Wouldn't you consider to advance us some of that money now and let her study the violin?"

The Uncles looked at one another and then at me and then at my mother. Uncle Leopold took the water carafe that stood in the center of the green baize and poured himself a glass of water, which he drank in hasty gulps, as if to calm himself down.

"Betty," he said afterward, "you know that we try our best to provide for the future of all the girls in the family. The trust fund is solidly invested in five-per-cent bonds so as to provide an appropriate dowry for Marion as soon as she reaches her twentieth year. It looks as if she will become a nice-looking young lady and there won't be much trouble in finding her a good husband, but all the same, that trust fund will come in very handy when you begin looking around for a good son-in-law. It would be absolutely irresponsible—irr-responsible—to spoil Marion's chances for a good marriage by touching that money for such a flimsy pretext as learning to play the fiddle. That's my last word. No more about it."

"How do you know what's good for her? What do you know about her chances? Bonds and five per cent and a good husband whom you'll pick for her, that's your idea of making her happy. Well, it's not my idea, not by a long ways. If you had let me study something I might be happier than I am—much happier, maybe. All right, it wasn't done when I was a girl. But this isn't eighteen-eighty, this is the twentieth century, and this is my child, and I want her to have a better chance in life than to be sold off like cattle on the market, and I won't go from here before I have your consent to let her study with Professor Szimanszki."

The water carafe rattled. The Uncles looked as if an earthquake were the cause of it. But it was only my mother's little kid-gloved hand fumbling excitedly on the green baize. It was the streak of Dobsberg craziness coming out in her all of a sudden, and she reminded me of my grandfather when he had a fight with the piano.

". . . And why don't you want the girl to learn something and be able to do something and take care of herself? Why not?" my mother cried, trembling with excitement. "Why is it a scandal to play in public and why is nothing a scandal that's kept hushed up and covered? When my sister Caroline ran away from her husband on her wedding night you sent her back to him, didn't you? He was a sick man, a dirty, rotten, sick man, she told you so, didn't she? But she had to stick it out, she had to live with him and to pretend, just so there was no scandal in our blessed family. Look what you have made of her, look at the poor wretched thing today! And Maria! She tried to commit suicide and you know why! And Corinne who had the pluck to get a divorce! You treat her like an outcast, you keep her like a prisoner, you are ashamed of her instead of taking her side. And Jenny, who didn't get a husband in spite of your wonderful dowry at five per cent solid, just sitting in her room and shriveling up and drying out and going crazy with no one to talk to and nothing to do. And Fanny— and Georgine—and Ida . . ."

A few years later, when I discovered the plays by Ibsen, it was an exciting experience, but it was nothing new to me. I had known it all along that the foundations were rotten and that we lived in a swamp of lies and false pretenses. That's why we young people grabbed Ibsen so eagerly and devoured every word of his. Here was one man who knew how to express the things we had carried around with us in a mute and inarticulate way. Funny, two years ago I saw a play by Ibsen again, Ghosts, and I could have cried; it was so old, so dusty, so covered with cobwebs. But when I was fifteen, it was new and shining, almost blinding like a sudden flash of lightning by night, which lifted every dim, dark detail into a sharp merciless brightness. I still do not know whether it was something good or bad, this breaking down of the respect for the family. It seemed the only right thing to do at that time. Yes, but the Chinese have survived more than four thousand years by hanging on to the rule of the family, and they are going on to survive, Christopher says, while Europe and America are not so very successful—or are we just now? Well—I don't know, Christopher, my darling. I suppose I have to get still a lot older to know the right or wrong of it. Getting older is like slowly going up in an airplane. The horizon is getting wider and wider, we overlook more ground the higher we rise; but at the same time everything becomes smaller and less important in our panorama. Rivers are a trickle, deserts a little sand and the enchanted forests of our youth are only dim little patches on the surface of our past.

We left the Uncles' office with flying banners. My mother's cheeks glowed like an overheated stove, and she pressed my hand in hers reassuringly. We marched past my father, who bent low over his ledgers and pretended not to notice our exit.

By the mysterious way in which office gossip travels he knew even then that we had won our battle. "Good-by, and don't be late for dinner," my mother called to him, a challenge in the very sound of her voice.

"See that you don't get run over by an automobile," he answered sourly. Anton opened the doors for us and led us out through the dark corridor with the sizzling gaslight. "Congratulations, Fräulein Marion," he said. "I hope you'll give me a free pass for your first concert."

I DON'T REMEMBER exactly when I stopped wanting to be a good girl and began wanting to be bad. I think it was after the night when Aunt Caroline told me that there was no God in heaven.

Aunt Caroline was my mother's youngest sister, a helpless creature whose hair had turned gray when Mother's was still a rich chestnut brown. Everyone knew that she had a sick husband, because he had been wheeled around in a chair for several years before he disappeared in what the family called an "institution." There was an air of whispered secrecy around his disease, and I hardly knew him, because even before he was left to oblivion he had been kept in a back room of their little flat. Since Aunt Caroline had thus returned to the single state, she was boarded in turn by every one of her seven sisters, staying a month at each place. "She's not a visitor but a visitation," my father used to say of her. She would arrive in her shuffling way, with two traveling bags and a number of grouches, deposit herself in any corner that was allotted to her, take off her corset, and be ready to stay for a few weeks.

"Caroline, you've got to wear your corset. You can't let yourself go like this, it's bad for the figure," her sisters would try to persuade her, but Aunt Caroline shook her untidy head. "I'm having my backache today," she would say. "It feels as if every vertebra would break the moment I put on the corset."

"Don't go around in bedroom slippers all day long, dear," my mother would plead with her. "It'll make your feet big." Aunt Caroline would lift her shoulders and drop them in a gesture of utter resignation, as if to say: Who cares how big my feet are? She had headache days and backache days and gall-bladder days and days when she just felt bad in a general way. To have Aunt Caroline around was enough to make you healthy for the rest of your life. A chaise longue had been pushed from my parents' bedroom into my little cubicle, and that is where Aunt Caroline slept. She liked me very much, but I didn't like her at all.

At that time I was still a good little girl and said my prayers every evening after going to bed. That is, I didn't kneel down and blare them out like a baby; but after the light was turned off and I had crept under my meager blanket and pulled my knees up to my chin, I would whisper my "Our Father Who art in heaven" and let the Ave Maria trail after, for it was a nice, cozy feeling to converse with the Madonna whose picture hung over my bed, and she wore a blue coat and had watched over me ever since I could remember.

And then, on a cold, white, translucent night, with snow settling in every corner of the window frames, Aunt Caroline told me that there was no God in heaven and no Madonna and no Immaculate Conception. She made fun of my praying, and she laughed at me, and when I climbed out of my bed to see if perchance she could be delirious, I discovered that she was crying, all tied up in a knot on her chaise longue.

"I'm not crying," she sobbed, "I'm laughing. I've been laughing for years. It's all too damnably funny, the whole bluff. It made me laugh when I heard you pray like a good little girl. Listen, Marion: It's no use praying. It doesn't get you anywhere. There is no one to listen to you. It's no use believing anything people tell you. They don't tell you the truth anyway. It's no use being good. It only gets you into a mess. God Almighty, you don't know what a mess a good little girl like you might get herself into. Don't believe a word your parents tell you. All they tell you is silly lies."

When I heard these amazing and utterly unbelievable words, I felt my whole world shaking at its roots. Yet somehow they sounded like an echo of something that had been brewing for quite some time in the back of my mind. I was scared. Weakly I tried to remonstrate. "You mustn't say such things, Aunt Caroline," I whispered. "It's wicked."

"Wicked, indeed! You don't know how wicked people can be, but I do. There is no God, there is no heaven. There is no one to pray to and no one to watch you and no one to help you. It's all a huge, ridiculous fraud, and only fools believe in it."

This was terrible. I felt my knees shake as I waited for a bolt of fire to strike us or for the ground to open up and swallow us right there in my little room. But nothing happened. It was very quiet; I could hear Aunt Caroline sniffle; I heard the tick-tick of my alarm clock and the thump-thump of my own heart.

"If there were a God He would surely have created a better world than this here. Don't believe the lies they are telling you, Marion, it's all wrong," Aunt Caroline said. "Babies aren't brought by the stork, and there is no guardian angel to watch every step of yours, and our dead don't fly into heaven, and there is no old man with a white beard, sitting somewhere high up, to punish you when you do wrong and to give you a reward if you only say your little prayer every night. It's not as simple as all that, oh no. Look at me, just look at me. I've prayed too, I've done no wrong—and I've been punished all the same. Jesus God, how I have been punished!"

Yes, I think it was that night that I began wanting to be bad. On the outside it made no great difference, but within a few months my entire attitude toward people and things and experiences changed imperceptibly. First it was too daring and frightening not to believe in God, and I went to Putzi for support. It was on a day in February when he had come down with the flu and was in bed with a poultice around his chest and rather defenseless.

"Putzi," I said, after beating around the bush for some time, "Putzi, do you know, there are some people who say that there is no God in heaven."

Putzi scrutinized me for a while. "Is that so?" he said dryly.

"Well, is there or isn't there?" I pressed him. "And don't tell me a fib. I'm not a baby and I know there is no Santa Claus. I want to know whether all this talk about God is just the same sort of a swindle."

"It's time to give me my medicine," Putzi said instead of an answer. I counted twenty drops of quinine in a spoon and fed it to him. He shivered because it was bitter, and then he leaned back on his pillows and closed his little squint eyes.

"Look here, Mutzi," he said after he had thought it over. "I'll answer you as well as I know how to. I'll tell you the truth as I understand it. But, mind you, all I can tell you is my own truth. The real truth is too big or too precious or too high for us to grasp it. Maybe Jesus Christ knew it. Maybe someday someone will come and know it again. All I know about God is this: you might not believe that He is there when things go their daily humdrum way. But when you are really happy, you'll feel Him and you'll say, 'Thank God for this.' And when you're really unhappy, you'll cry out, 'Help me, God, please help me.' Remember the Bible? What Jesus said when things were too hard even for him to bear: 'Eli, Eli, lamma sabacthani?' Well, that's it, Mutzi, that's it."

I was disappointed with this answer because what I had hoped for was a straight yes or no. And I began being bad by losing my trust in Putzi. For a while it felt a bit lonesome and chilly, with no heaven above and having to live without a God or a dead grandfather up there to protect me. But on the other hand I was rewarded with the arrogance and self-reliance of the sworn atheist, which soon took possession of me. I had a few minor tussles with God, that's true. I dared Him to strike me with a thunderbolt if He existed. It was February, and no thunderbolt came, and that was that.

After I had cleared this matter of religion I turned to less important problems. That babies weren't brought by the stork I had suspected even before my night talk with Aunt Caroline. Kathi, the washerwoman, told me the facts of life just as tactfully as any progressive school might do it for the enlightened children of today.

"You're getting fat again, Kathi," I remarked one day. "You've

eaten too much. Someday you're going to bust." Throughout
the years I had watched the phenomenon of Kathi swelling on
and shrinking back to normal size, and it seemed as natural to
me as the moon tides.

Kathi went on rumpling a dirty shirt while she looked up from
the washboard and smiled at me, amused and thoughtful. "Don't
you know what it means, Milucka?" she asked me.

"What means what?" I said.

"How old are you?"

"Almost eleven," I said impatiently. I had been almost eleven
for an endless time, it seemed to me. "Why?"

"It's another baby coming," she said, and now she stopped
washing; she rinsed the soapsuds from her wrinkled hands and
dried them on her blue apron.

"What baby? Who? Where?" I said, flabbergasted.

"I thought you knew," Kathi said. "It's time you learned
about it anyway. It's growing inside of me, another little one.
Want to feel it? Been jumping around all day long, the little
fellow." She took my hand into her soaked, wrinkled fingers
and pressed it to her body. "Listen," she said with a smile as if
hearing something far away.

I felt it, and it was wonderful. It was alive, like a little kitten
in a bag.

"When are you going to take it out from there?" I asked her.

"He'll come out all by hisself soon as he is good and ready,"
she said.

"Won't it hurt?" I asked, with the first faint stir of a woman's
inherited knowledge.

"It sure will, Milucka, it'll hurt plenty. But them are the good
pains, good, strong, blessed pains. You don't need being scared
of them. Now run along, and don't tell your mama; she might
not like it."

By that time I had given up telling my mother about any of
the things that occupied my mind. It never occurred to me that
she might be able to understand them. I was building a little
shell around myself into which I could retire with my own
secret, bad, wicked, adolescent life. I was a little woman, and
what Kathi had revealed to me neither scared nor surprised

me particularly. I broke the little clay pig that had served as my penny bank, went to a bookshop and bought myself, one by one, a series of enlightening little booklets called You and the World. I devoured them greedily, squatting on the stairway that led down into our cellar. It was dark there, but a little lantern stood ready, and in its dim light I filled myself to the rim with Darwin and Evolution and a muddle of the planetary system, the sex life of the birds and the social order of the beehive. There· is still that hollow, moldy dank smell of the cellar in my nostrils whenever I am confronted with serious knowledge. It was, I believe, the only time in my life when I really wanted to *know*.

It's funny to watch how women acquire what little they ever really know of abstract things. Most of us know only as much as we learn from our men; the rest somehow doesn't stick; it rolls off like water from a duck's tail. If a girl knows a lot about astronomy, you can bet that she is interested in the young assistant of the planetarium with whom she has been dancing a few times. As for me, I learned more from my sons than from my father; I learned some from my husbands and a bit from my lovers, and a few of the most important things I learned from strangers and passers-by.

WHAT AN EXCITING, complex little world that old Vienna Conservatory was. Its very wall dripped with traditions, with a hundred and more years of music, handed down from Haydn to Mozart to Beethoven, on to Schubert, to Brahms, Bruckner, Mahler, and down to the old men who were our teachers. They were a gay, wayward bunch of high priests, our professors. Strict about such serious things as counterpoint, the form of a sonata, the phrasing of a cantilena; yet easygoing about conventions and what in other quarters was called morals. Teachers and pupils were eternally tangled up in crushes, flirtations, and real love affairs. The walls of the toilets, where track was kept of the latest romantic developments, looked much like any of today's gossip columns. I still can see the thin scribbling on the cream-colored walls, the hearts pierced by arrows and marked with lovelorn initials, the crude sobs and screams of love carved into the doors and on the benches that stood along the dark corridors of the old building. I still can hear the confessions and the gossip that were babbled out at all hours between the two cells of the girls' toilet. I don't know what is so inducing about Johnnies to make girls shout out their secrets as soon as they are comfortably placed on a churchseat, but this is one custom that hasn't changed since I was a child.

The old building was so filled with music that it sometimes seemed as if the roof must blow off. There was music behind every one of the green-baize doors; it drifted through the walls, it dropped through the ceilings, it rose up from the basement, where Chorus Class Two was practising. There was the deep, oceanlike roar of the sixteen-foot pipes of the big organ vibrating through the entire building. There was fiddling and blowing and singing in all five stories, there was the tinkle of twenty pianos and the squeak of forty wind instruments. Basses rumbled and piccolo flutes pierced the air with their shrill pinpricks. A famous string quartet rehearsed in the smaller auditorium, and the school orchestra, thundering and sweating over Beethoven's Eroica, worked in the larger hall. The chorus classes—One, Two, and Three—sang at the tops of their lungs, and somewhere a future prima donna held a strident high C above all the noise and hubbub. The air trembled with ambitions and jealousies and disappointments and five-minute triumphs. In one corner of the corridor an old attendant copied music and sold bread and butter to hungry pupils. Soft, warm butter, which he kept among his scores and which he spread very, very thinly on very thin slices of bread; his knife too was worn thin by the use of many years, and every time he had finished one slice he licked the last bit of butter from this long, thin knife with the serious dexterity of a sword-swallower at a fair. In another corner five girls tried to prevent a sixth girl from going off and jumping into the Danube. She had just been notified that she wouldn't be permitted to play Mendelssohn's D minor Variations in the next school concert. Somewhere a young boy stood in front of a closed window and looked intently and with an expression of utter desolation into the dark nothingness of the air-shaft outside. Maybe an unhappy love, maybe hurt ambition, maybe such poverty that it had become impossible for him to go on studying music. While somewhere down the corridor someone shouted with delirious joy: a cellist who had found a job in an orchestra, a young composer who had won a prize. Young, thin, vivacious bodies, young, eager faces, everybody high-strung, near suicide today, in heaven tomorrow. It seems to me that in the old Vienna Conservatory the temperature was always a few degrees above normal. I don't know whether they overheated the old box or whether we pupils were so full of vibrations and invisible rays that we gave off heat like so many living stoves.

In each corridor there was enthroned a chaperone to watch out that the girls didn't speak with the boys—some little old woman, wearing old mittens and knitting new ones, a creature as bleached and dried out by the years as a piece of driftwood. "Ladies! Ladies! No conversation with the gentlemen, please," she would call out at regular intervals, rapping her little table with her stiff knuckles. No one paid any attention to her. The ladies were a brash-looking lot, and they did awful things to their faces. Some went so far as to use rouge on their cheeks, some others obviously painted their eyebrows, for heavy brows were supposed to be beautiful. Cosmetics were still in the state of innocence and consisted mainly of a harsh, white rice powder, while mascara and lipstick existed only in stage make-up. But the conservatorists achieved their fresh and indecent appearance by a little push they gave to their hair and by the way they wiggled their hips, in spite of stiff-boned corsets. The gentlemen wore their hair long, and they had a feverish, wolfish, and hungry look about them; they had long, fine, nervous, very unmanicured hands, and they were extremely amorous. The constant occupation with music seemed to keep us all overexcitable, thin-skinned, with a seismographic sensitivity for every emotion. Young girls, at that time, were treated like dynamite, as if they might explode in a big blast the moment a young man came near them. In the corridor of the conservatory girls were never allowed to sit on the same bench with boys; the chaperones took care of that. But the air between the benches fairly crackled with sparks of suppressed sex.

As for me, I had completed my being a bad girl by getting myself engaged to Pepi Jerabeck, who was several years older than I, who knew many Bad Words, who was the leader of a gang of rowdies, and who was the son of our janitor. Each house in Vienna had a janitor who ruled with an iron scepter over the tenants, locked the house door every evening at ten, watched over the proprieties, extracted tribute from maids and masters alike, and knew every shred of gossip in the house. I also associated in school with a ratty girl who made a sport of pulling other girls into corners and whispering dirty little secrets into their blushing ears. "All right, so you know where the babies come from," she whispered to me. "But do you know *how they get there?*"

When she told me, I refused point-blank to believe her.

"My parents couldn't do such a thing," I said, as millions of children had said before me.

"Oh no?" she said, with more scorn than I could endure. I felt like hitting her in the face but thought better of it.

"Well then, the Emperor couldn't have done it," I said, and that was final.

"Or work or die!" Professor Szimanszki yelled at me in every lesson. It was the motto of his life: Or work or die. He was a genius, or so, at least, we pupils thought. He was a Pole, and although he had lived in Vienna for more than forty years, he had never managed to learn the language. He made up funny words for himself and used them like a whip. "Don't she woodle!" he would yell when I played sloppily. "This is not music, this is swine stable! Don't she swallow her left hand, goddamn for, verflixter woodlepoosh!"

He was possessed by a wild and merciless impatience. He paced up and down like a caged tiger while I played, he tore his thin, white hair, he wrung his hands, he pulled faces and looked like an old baboon gone mad, he beat the time with his fists on my shoulders, and he threatened to kill me, to kill me with his own hands, if I ever played a sour note again. But whenever I touched the strings with my bow, sour notes would drop from the fiddle, like the toads which dropped from the mouth of Pechmarie in Grimm's fairy tale whenever she spoke. "She issa criminelle," Szimanszki would growl. "She rape a magnifique cantilene. Poor Kreutzer, he rolls in his tomb." He always spoke in the third person singular to me, which was his way of expressing disgust and contempt. The études by Kreutzer were my Mount Everest. Breathless and vanquished, I gave up after each lesson, only to start a new expedition up its steep slopes again. On rare occasions Szimanszki grew gentle and sentimental. "Potshato," he would softly breathe, "Potshato, sweet, soft, make she the fiddle sing, sing, sing, God damn her, sing! spiewniey! or I'll break her neck." And there were tears in his wise, heavy monkey eyes.

And then there was that little matter with the Mozart Concerto in A Major. I had started to study that concerto during my third year in the conservatory, and it soon became the central point of my life at that time. It's a beautiful piece of music, the sort of music that sounds simple and easy, but to attain this simplicity and beauty is one of the hardest tasks for a violinist; especially if that violinist is a girl of thirteen, a confused, feverish little creature in the throes of beginning puberty, of mental and physical growing pains, overworked and underweight, with trust in no one, not in the grownups, not in God, not in herself.

Every morning I shook myself awake, I threw myself out of bed, and then I stood reeling in the cold, dark little room. The floor was chilly under my bare feet. I groped around for a match. I lit the gas flame, and it came to life with a soft hiss; good, friendly circle of light. There was the familiar muddle of my room. In the morning it always looked as if it had been away on a long, secret journey during the night and had barely managed to return in haste, to be there when I opened my eyes. Yet my dress and my meager underthings were lying on the chair just as I had flung them off last night. The Mozart concerto, open on page seven on my music stand, made faces at me; the violin slept in its soft little nightshirt of green silk in her case, which I had been too tired to close before I went to bed. I dropped my own nightgown and hesitated in front of the stand, the sponge with the ice-cold water poised in my hand. I closed my eyes and tried to memorize one of the passages that gave eternal trouble, but my brain was still encased in hazy dreams. I opened my eyes again and looked down my body, which was thin, white, and childish. Every morning I hoped that a miracle might have happened during the night, that I would wake up and have full breasts like a grown-up girl. I went over to the little mirror to inspect myself in successive portions; now the face and neck came into view, now that disappointing flat little front of mine, now the back with the bones sticking out, then I traveled down the legs, which were too thin too, and then I shivered, left the mirror, and hurried to the washstand in the corner, dimly ashamed of myself.

While I brushed my hair I memorized once more the eight bars on page seven that refused to stick to my memory. While I gulped down my too hot coffee I worried about the double stoppings in the last movement. Maybe if I write down those eight bars from memory I'll fix them in my mind, I thought. I tried it with slightly shaking fingers, nervous because it was high time to prepare for my piano lesson. The notes were leaning forward like little men walking against a heavy storm. Holy Madonna, it was almost seven and I hadn't yet done my homework for the history-of-music class. Let's see the oeuvres of Haydn: 125 symphonies, 77 string quartets, 35 concertos for the piano. Masses. Divertimenti. Cassatas. Damn Papa Haydn's fertility. How many solo arias? How many operas—and all of them forgotten? Why do we have to learn all that junk?

When I think back to those days I see myself always in a hurry, always worried lest I should be too late, always short of time. The schedule of my days was overcrowded and hard to keep up. It began with the piano lesson from eight to nine. I played my étude from Czerny's school of velocity, and old Fräulein Steger nodded mild satisfaction. I galloped from the conservatory to my near-by school and arrived breathlessly and shaky, just as the bell shrilled through the dull, gray building. There was the smell of ink and chalk and of many children.

The tramp-tramp of shoes on the stairs and the yelling in the classrooms, cut off as though with a knife the moment the teacher entered. While the teacher droned on, the poised, dear theme of the second movement was gradually overtaken and conquered by a different breed of music. Wagner, Tristan, the duet of the second act. Oh sink hernieder Nacht der Liebe. . . . I knew it by heart; it was enclosed deep within myself; I was a shrine of music; I closed my eyes and floated away on a great, blue barge with red sails, over an ocean of longing, urgent harmonies. . . .

"Sommer! Would you consent to join our little discussion? Would it be asking too much if I requested you kindly to tell us the Roman emperors? The subsidiaries of the Danube? The exact date of the battle of Aspern? Sorry to have to disturb you, Sommer, but it is my unpleasant duty to pump a store of knowledge, however scant, into your thick, inattentive skull. Once again. The battle of Aspern . . ."

Twelve o'clock and I would gallop back to the conservatory. I hastily swallowed down two pieces of bread and butter, purchased from the old attendant in his corner of the corridor. No time for lunch. The classes for music theory. The classes for music history. The classes for chorus singing and training of the ear. Three o'clock and I was on my way back to school. Five o'clock and I raced once more to the conservatory. This was the most important, the only important, part of the day: the violin lesson. By that time all faces looked pale to me, probably because I myself was pale with excitement, fright, and fatigue.

"What's the matter with you, lassie?" Shani Kern would mumble to me in a corner. "What are you scared of? No one's going to kill you. Cold hands? Come on, I'll rub them warm for you."

Shani was my only friend in the conservatory. He was the boy who accompanied us on the piano, and he seemed to like me better than the rest. He had a face like a Scotty of doubtful pedigree, and somewhere in all that black hairiness were two very blue eyes, hidden under bushy brows, surprising like blue plover eggs in an untidy nest. He had the finest touch, singing fingers, and he had a secret only I knew. He was composing a cantata, something called Paumanok, a title which sounded most outlandish. Once he brought me a frayed little book containing the poems of Walt Whitman and let me read it.

> Out of the cradle endlessly rocking,
> Out of the mocking-bird's throat, the musical shuttle,
> Out of the Ninth-month midnight,
> Over the sterile sands and the fields beyond, where the
>   child leaving his bed wandered alone, bareheaded,
>   barefoot . . .

The words were new and different from anything I knew, and they echoed in my mind for quite some time. This, I think, was my first, very faint acquaintance with anything American, and I was rather baffled by it. I gathered soon, that Paumanok was to Shani what the Mozart Concerto in A Major was to me: the navel and center of his world, his shining hope, the wall against which he bumped his head every day and every hour.

I believed in Shani, and in his sprouting cantata Paumanok. In return Shani believed in me, if only in a restricted form. "You've got it in you. Even if you played the cadenza like a pig yesterday, don't give up. You've got the thing that can't be learned. You're a lazy, stinking little rabbit, but you've got talent. You've got a great big pile of talent. Now go and show them how that second movement should be played. No excuses, no alibis. Go!"

I went into the classroom; I played and I played very badly. I woodled the first movement and got stuck in the second. My memory slipped in the same eight bars I had muffed every time so far. Through a haze I saw Shani creep behind his piano and disappear from my view. I saw Silber, my enemy and competitor, grin condescendingly as if to say: Didn't I tell you she would never learn it! Worst of all, Szimanszki stopped yelling at me. He became very quiet and polite all of a sudden and, without using a single one of his self-made words, he said: "Thank you, Sommer. I don't care to hear the rest of it today. However, I advise you to go and learn cooking; maybe you will do better in the kitchen than on a concert platform. Silber, will you release her and play us the second movement as it should be played?"

Beaten, crushed, in ruins, I dragged what was left of me from the room. I slunk toward the girls' toilet to cry in solitude. But, as usual, both cells were occupied and a chatting line of girls waited in the room outside. I withdrew and reached the corridor once more, choked and blinded by tears of fury. I dropped down onto the last bench, the one in the darkest corner, hoping that no one could see me there crying. I could hear, or at least I imagined that I could hear, Silber playing the concerto in the classroom. Slickly and glibly he went through the second movement, without hesitating he took the hurdle of those crucial eight bars, he went into the variations of the last part, raced brilliantly through the cadenza and the double stoppings and finished with a flourish.

A few minutes later I heard the familiar sounds that accompanied the closing of our violin lessons. The door of the classroom opened, some of the pupils sauntered out; in there, chairs were put in place and violin cases shut. The shuffling of Szimanszki's feet in galoshes. "Good night, Herr Professor." "Bon soir, mes enfants!" I hid my face in my arms so no one should see me. I was a beaten army all by myself; I was Napoleon at Waterloo and Wagner after his Tannhäuser had flopped in Paris. Someone plunked down at my side. It was Silber. I should have known. I should have recognized the smell of his parents' delicatessen store that clung to his clothes forever. Smoked brisket, dill pickles, and fresh horse-radish. Instead of repulsing me, these odors suddenly made me so hungry that I felt my stomach cramp and roll to the side like a heaving boat. "Go away," I said faintly.

"Bawling, eh?" Silber said with great satisfaction. "Ain'tcha crazy to sit here and bawl? Whatcha care how ya play? You're a girl, ain'tcha?" He pulled his long fingers until they cracked, as was his obnoxious habit. "Comes a nice man and marries you, it's good-by fiddle anyway, so whatcha care? Your folks have plenty of money, haven't they, so whatcha worry about the Mozart? It's too difficult fa' ya anyway. You don't need playing in concerts, do you? Of course, with me that's something different."

I stopped crying at once, growing cold and dry with fury and hatred and disgust, while Silber kept on rubbing salt into my wounds. I sat up and stared straight into his eyes.

"We'll see who is going to play that concerto in the end," I said, choking with my own words.

"We sure will," Silber said, and at that moment I swore to myself that I would play it even if I had to give up eating and sleeping altogether. I felt so sorry for myself that I would have started crying again, had not Shani popped up and come to my rescue.

"Leave the lass alone," he said sharply, and his eyes crept out from their nest of black hair. "She's tired, can't you see? And if you want a piece of my mind you can have it. You'll be a good second fiddler in a nice second-rate orchestra when this lass here will be touring the world. Now leave her alone or you'll be sorry for it."

"I don't mean no harm," Silber muttered, took his case and left us without another word.

"Thanks," I said, sniffling all my tremendous grief back into my soul. "I'm glad he was so mean to me. Now I'm *determined* that I'll play in the concert."

Shani kept on looking at me with a mixture of pity and amusement. "Determined you are, are you?" he said finally. "All right, if you are determined you might want to go back in class right now and have me coach you a bit. It's that second movement you have to work on. The cadenza doesn't worry me a bit. It'll come all by itself. Come on, let's work!"

Dear Shani, he was like a good, long, straight road that takes one to one's goal in the end. "Determination is a good thing," he said as we entered the empty classroom. "Did I ever tell you what determination did for me? I played the piano in a brothel for three years to make my living, but I was determined to get out, and out I got." He slammed the lid of the piano open and fished some harmonies from the keyboard. "Or maybe you don't even know what a brothel is," he added with an angry little snort at himself.

"I certainly do," I said with dignity. I believed it to be a place where illegitimate babies were kept, foundlings and bastards and such, and I wondered why Shani had to play the piano for them. I unpacked my violin, and without another word we began to work.

In April it was decided that I was the one who would play the Mozart Concerto in A Major in the school concert, if I kept on working like that. In early May I went on a secret outing with my boy friend Pepi Jerabeck, the one who knew bad words. We went to the Prater to see the two Renner boys who claimed to have constructed a dirigible balloon and were going to fly with it as high as one hundred meters and in any direction they chose. We went there on the sly and against the definite protest of our parents, because janitor and tenants agreed that children had nothing to do at such hazardous undertakings.

The balloon was a shapeless thing with a gondola fastened to it. It heaved a bit, like an asthmatic bellows; the two Renners pulled ropes and gave commands and perspired profusely; the balloon flapped once or twice, then the air went out of it and it folded up and was no more than a bundle of old, patched-up canvas. Pepi uttered many of his worst words, because he had spent all our money getting to the Prater, what with omnibus fare and candy and soda pops. Afterward we were caught in a rainstorm and I was soaking wet when I returned home. First I got the sniffles and then I got a cold and then I got a cough and a fever and what our doctor called first a bronchitis and then a congestion and finally a pneumonia. I came very, very close to that dark door through which we all have to go sooner or later, but I didn't pass through it, because something called me back. I wanted to live and I wanted to play the Concerto in A Major, which meandered in and out through my fever dreams and delirious mumblings.

The school concert took place on June 18—I never forgot that date—and Silber played in it. He played quite nicely and had a moderate success. I sat in the audience, still a bit wobbly, and applauded as was expected from me.

"I tell you something, my lass," Shani said to me afterward. "That Silber boy is as important as a hole in a doughnut."

That's the story of the Mozart Concerto in A Major. I never went through any disappointment as painful and burning and deep as that one. Or maybe that early grief made everything that came later appear less important and easier to bear.

Michael once told me that scars make the tissue much stronger and less sensitive to pain than it was before the injury. Maybe each scar our heart receives makes it stouter and abler to endure the pains of life. And that's what people call growing up.

AT THE TIME I grew up the world was full of taboos and superstitions, especially for a blind mouse like me, a groping, blundering, precocious girl of thirteen. We all were cursed with an abundance of soul. It hampered us at every step, like those wooden blocks sheep have dangling between their forelegs so that they can't run away. We had no sex, no glands, no hormones, no complexes, and no obsessions. But we had soul and a lot of it. Men, we were given to understand, had no soul; they had a lower nature and were carnal. It made them rather attractive, I thought. I had heard rumors according to which men lost their senses and turned into beasts, into snorting, grunting, atrocious animals the moment they got power over a girl. I also knew that there were girls who had done IT. In fact we had one of them in our class; Jarmila Swoboda was her name, a Bohemian girl with broad hips and a broad smile. She had more teeth than a shark, she played the fiddle with sweep and gusto but very sloppily, and she was No Virgin. I remember that I never dared sitting down on a chair where Jarmila had sat before, as if being No Virgin were a contagious disease like the measles, only much worse and very catching. Yet, by some strange fascination, I circled around her all the time, hoping darkly that some of her forbidden knowledge would transpire or emanate from her. I hoped that I could learn something about the great mysteries of life by staring at Jarmila, by throwing a timid word into the conversation, and by sniffing her odor, which was mixed of perspiration and Milles Fleurs. I also waited for her to become pregnant, to have a baby, to kill it, and, in turn, be hanged for it, like Gretchen in Faust—for such was the fate of girls who were

No Virgins. But Jarmila soon left the conservatory and joined a girls' band that played in some beer garden in the Prater. There she could be seen and heard by everybody, fiddling, smiling, attractively dressed in a starched white dress with a wide blue ribbon across her chest, and apparently entirely unscathed.

By that time I had grasped that people got married for the sole purpose of doing just the absurd thing that was so horrible when committed by unmarried people. I tried to fathom this out and put carefully veiled questions before my mother. My mother quailed and squirmed and the tip of her little nose got very red with embarrassment. Women, my mother said, were born to suffer and to sacrifice themselves. A good married woman had to submit and to surrender herself to the awful doings which the low and carnal nature of men demanded. There was not the faintest indication that any nice woman could derive the least bit of pleasure or satisfaction from those terrible unions that seemed to be necessary for the perpetuation of the race. It sounded like a pretty hopeless and yet incomplete information, and I turned to my old reliable oracle, Kathi the washerwoman.

Kathi laughed at first and then grew serious. "You're too young, Milucka, for this," she cried. "Wait a few years and when the right man comes along you'll find out whether you like it or not. This is one of them things nobody should talk about, see?"

"You're a married woman," I said, obstinately sailing my course. "Tell me just one thing: Is it terrible to let a man do those things with you or does it happen while you are asleep?" I had heard Pepi Jerabeck talking about people sleeping together, with an innuendo that this was IT.

"Jezizmaria, listen to that child," Kathi said, bending lower and rumbling violently on her washboard. "I don't know how it is with rich people. Maybe they are asleep. For poor people it is the nicest thing they have in life. Now run along and don't ask silly questions. If your mama catches you . . . ."

I don't know how it is with men, but girls know a lot about love long before they get acquainted with the real article. They dream about it, worry about it, are afraid of it and feverishly ready for it, whether they know it themselves or not, whether they are brought up in a progressive, experimental, coeducational school or behind the walls of a convent. My source for anything that had to do with love and related subjects was Wagner's Tristan. I never missed a performance if I could help it. I was one of the entranced group of young people that always crowded the uppermost gallery of the opera house when Gustav Mahler conducted Tristan. I bit my lips, I clenched my fists, I pressed my nails hard into my palms with excitement, I got lost in an ecstasy of music and sex and sensuality and longing. If surrendering to a man was anything like that second act of Tristan—let it come then. I was willing and ready to do it and to bear all the sinister consequences.

But just when everything sank into the strangely changed twilight of puberty, a new influence entered my life and helped me clear up things and pull through without damage: My friendship with Clara.

Remember the dull beginning of it? Remember the sour smell of the little dairy shop where we first met? Buttermilk was prescribed to me, because buttermilk was one of the things that Are Good For You; that is, if taken in with great precautions and after manifold preparations. You had to be sure not to drink water an hour before or after. You couldn't eat fruit the same day you had buttermilk, not even stewed prunes, which, on other days, were Good For You all by themselves. No wonder I hated buttermilk.

For several days I had watched a girl, a bit older and taller than myself, sitting there and eating the best thing there was on earth: whipped cream. She ate it nonchalantly, almost reluctantly, not heaping her spoon full of it, but only dainty little blobs into which she licked little ornaments with the capricious tip of her tongue. This girl was something so wonderful that I couldn't take my eyes off her. She wore her hair short, only down to her shoulders. It was soft and of a silvery blond and made her look like the page boy in my old, much-thumbed, illustrated copy of Ivanhoe. She wore something I had often dreamed of but never possessed, a leghorn hat with a bunch of moss roses on one side, and she didn't wear it on her head but hanging down her back on its black velvet ribbon, as if it meant nothing to her to have such a hat. She wore a white Sunday dress with a pink sash, although it was only Wednesday, and she had little pink socks and patent-leather shoes with a bow in front and the least bit of a heel in back. I was still in the black-cotton-stockings-and-laced-boots stage. She looked wonderful and not quite real, and she didn't seem to mind my staring at her.

That Wednesday all three tables in the shop were occupied, and I took a heart and sat down at hers. She seemed to look at me while I kept my eyes everywhere but on her; I could feel her glance like little ants crawling all over me; it was a pricking but not unpleasant sensation.

"You like whipped cream?" she asked all of a sudden, and when I nodded she shoved her bowl to my side. "I don't," she said. "Tastes like making soap bubbles."

"Why do you eat it every day?" I asked her, dumfounded.

"It's supposed to be good for you," she said. She looked down at her firm, sun-tanned legs and flexed them a bit. I was confused beyond speaking. Whipped cream, in my world, was something almost sinful and very, very bad for you.

"Eat it, eat it," she said. "It gives you a good figure."

Girls at that time didn't know they had bodies; they had figures consisting of curved hips, bosom, and calves. My own dangling, thin structure was nothing to brag about; but I saw with a hot pang of envy and jealousy that the girl carried the round fullness of young breasts under her white dress.

"You like making soap bubbles?" I asked her in the way of making conversation. My mouth was full of whipped cream, soft, gushing sweetness, which tasted so luxurious that I was almost sorry to gulp it down.

"I did when I was a child," she said. Without ceremony she grabbed for my glass of buttermilk and took a sniff at it. "What's yours? Oh, buttermilk. Phooey. It's the shits."

That gave me a short, sharp shock, but a second later I began to grin with delight. This was even better than Pepi Jerabeck who knew bad words.

"Really," the girl said, "reminds me of the things babies do into their diapers. Well, never mind."

"I like babies," I said timidly. There were always new babies in our family, what with Mama's seven sisters zealously perpetuating the clan. I had hoped for a little baby sister myself for quite some time, but had given up after finding out what my mother would have to do to get it.

"So do I," the girl said. "I've got a little nephew, only seven months old. The sweetest thing you've ever seen in your life."

This too was something different and exciting: having a nephew instead of being a niece. "What's his name?" I asked.

"Salvator Benvenuto Amadeos," the girl said. It sounded like a joke.

"Big names for a little baby," I said. "He sounds like an archduke."

"No, he got them from his father," she said. "He's Count Hoyot's baby."

"Oh," I said respectfully. "Are you a countess?"

"Countess, my foot! My sister has had an affair with him for five years," the astounding girl said calmly.

The ceiling didn't drop down on us and I didn't die of a stroke right then and there, although I blushed so hard it felt as if my throbbing cheeks would burst with the pulsing heat inside.

"Is he the same whose carriage ran over our washerwoman?" I asked, groping for my evaporating countenance.

"Quite possible," the girl said. "He is a wild bird, but I like him. He always gives me presents. Look, he gave me this."

She stretched out her wrist and showed me a little bracelet with many charms dangling from it. "What's your name?" she asked me after I had admiringly inspected the little trinket.

"Marion. Marion Sommer," I said.

She pointed with her chin at my violin case, which I had deposited on a chair. "Working hard?" she asked. No child had ever asked me that question.

"Pretty hard," I said proudly. "Five, six hours practising on my violin, and two hours on the piano, and then all my theory and harmony and music history and all that——"

The girl wrinkled her nose. "I'm working hard too," she said. "You see, I'm in the ballet, what they call an *élève*. They break all your bones there, they work you so hard. Eight hours' practice and being on duty almost every evening. Ever been to the opera?"

"A million times," I said. "Ever since I was a baby. I'm crazy about the opera."

"Well, then you must have seen me," she said, a bit like a queen about to disclose her incognita. "I'm Clara Balbi."

Indeed I had seen Clara Balbi, and one had to be an opera fan as I was to remember her. She was the so-called stage child. She played the Duke of Brabant in Lohengrin and William Tell's boy in the Rossini opera. Her name was the last one on the program, but it was her name, you could see it in print, and she was part of that world which so far embraced most of the fascination, enchantment, and intoxication I knew.

"I'll finish the conservatory this year. I might even play in the graduation concert, and next fall I'll go on tour with my violin," I said, not to be outdone, although the memory of the Mozart Concerto in A Major hurt me as though I had undergone an operation and a few stitches hadn't been taken out.

"I'll have to be fifteen before they take me into the last quadrille," Clara said speculatively. "You know, there are too many old battle horses in the ballet; they would rather poison us young ones than give up their place. But Nicki has pull, and he promised to get me advanced soon—Count Hoyot, I mean. My sister is one of the solo dancers and she is only twenty-one. My mother was a ballet girl too, see, and she brought us up the right way. Say, d'you like ballet?"

I struggled between being polite and being sincere. I didn't want to hurt Clara Balbi's feelings or jeopardize this new and wonderful acquaintance. On the other hand, what sort of a friendship was it going to be if I had to lie to her like to a grownup?

"I did like it when I was a little child," I finally said. "Now I don't. It's stiff and old-fashioned. It bores me. It's always the same. It's like the little music box in the album that plays the same piece every time you turn it on."

"What album?" Clara asked, and I told her. Up to that moment she had treated me not unfriendly but slightly condescendingly. All of a sudden she seemed to warm up and change her attitude.

"It's funny you should say that," she said thoughtfully and very serious. "It's something that bothers me all the time. I'd like to dance something different. But you should have heard the row when I showed our gouvernante a dance I had worked out all by myself."

"What sort of a dance?" I asked.

"You wouldn't understand," Clara said. "Ever heard of Isadora Duncan?"

"The one with the bare feet? I've read in the papers about her," I said. "She must be crazy. She doesn't even wear a corset."

Clara's mouth became a stubborn straight line. How often since have I seen that straight line in her smooth, soft face! "I'll show them," she said, "crazy or not. You don't know what you are talking about. Ever been in love?"

This was familiar ground. "Often," I said. "I'll tell you a secret. Right now I'm engaged to a boy who's almost three years older than I am. He is tough. He is the leader of a gang. His father wants to send him to a reform school, but he won't go. He'd rather cut his throat with a razor, he says. He is no sissy."

Clara listened with growing amusement. "You're still a baby," she said. "You don't know a thing. But I sort of like you. Want to come along and see my little nephew?"

I knew that I was not supposed to go and look at a baby who was a child of love and a fruit of sin. That's just why I did it. I wanted to do everything that was forbidden, and I had a craving hunger for the wrong experiences. The baby, Salvator Benvenuto Amadeos, by the way, was as lovely a tiny creature as could be dreamed of, and his mother, Corinna Balbi, looked, talked, and dressed very much like one of my mother's third cousins who had married into the low nobility. Mama Balbi, on the other hand, who had also been a ballet girl, was a garrulous woman with a carrot-colored flock of hair, and her impetuous caresses and outcries frightened me at first. Later on I got to know her as one of the kindest and most tolerant and helpful creatures I've ever met, and the flat of the Balbis became my secret refuge when I felt like molding and rotting away in the decorous and saturated correctness of my own family.

My acquaintance with the Balbis was my own deep secret, and it took an awful amount of lying to cover up my visits there. But it was wonderful to have a double life and to learn so much about sin even before I was fifteen. I quickly acquired an amazing amount of worldly and skeptical wisdom from Mama Balbi, and I learned to joke with Nicki and his friends on equal terms. They were all gay blades without much distinction but with a lot of charm. And from Clara I learned many useful and important things: To smoke a cigarette without getting sick. To drink champagne without getting tipsy. To soak raspberry candy drops in water and rub my cheeks with them to make them glow. To stuff rolled-up stockings into the places where my nonexistent bust would have belonged. She also relieved my mother of the task of explaining to me about the strange things that happened to my body just then. Mama had made a few feeble efforts at talking to me about the curse of womanhood but had been gagged by her own words and given up every time, leaving me mystified and slightly worried but not in the least enlightened. Clara took care of that and many other neglected points in my education. And on a veiled, moonlit night Clara went with me to the Schillerplatz and, on the lawn under the chestnut trees, she took off her shoes and danced for me the dance she had worked out all by herself. It was a great revelation to me and tied in with all the other new things that had begun to grow up around us: Music by Richard Strauss. Sculptures by Rodin. Crazy paintings in the galleries on the Ring; odd designs on houses, furniture, and on the fabric of the very dresses we wore. Queer ideas in the books I brought home and a strange fever in us that I shared with her and that had gripped all of us who were young. Ibsen. Nietzsche. Oscar Wilde. Tolstoy. An odd assortment of food for thought, and we suffered a lot of mental indigestion. We were rebels against anything that was handed down to us, in art, life, and ethics. We were Isolde, Salome, and the prostitute Natasha, in short little-girl's skirts. But when, in the excitement of the graduation concert, my enemy Silber tried to grab me and kiss me, I slapped his face, and then I washed my hands and cried with outraged feelings.

And for more than a week I was afraid that something had happened to my precious virginity.

I HAD A SORE THROAT and a headache and two fever blisters and, on top of it, I "had my days" when I played in a real concert for the first time. I had left the conservatory behind, I had embarked on a career, and for the first time I played as a full-fledged person in the auditorium of the old building that had become so much of a home for me during my four years of studies. I played the concerto of Mendelssohn with the accompaniment of the orchestra; I had cold hands, and my knees felt numb and inconsistent like cotton, and all the time I played I was afraid my memory would give out or my right arm would get stiff and tired as it usually did during the last movement. I hoped urgently for the miracle that sometimes happened when I played the violin at home and no one was listening. Then something like a glowing emptiness, a misty yellow cloud, would close around me and I would forget everything about technique and fingering and bowing; something would lift me up and carry me away, and I would play as light and lost and enraptured as Clara had danced on the lawn for me that night. But nothing of the kind happened when I came in front of an audience. I stayed wide awake and alert; I watched myself playing, cool and detached. No, I didn't make any slips, but produced my little tricks as I had been taught; and all the time I felt like the little trained monkey of an organ grinder. What amplified this feeling was the fact that they had put me into a very short, pink dress that definitely marked me as a child prodigy; my hair, which I had worn up since my thirteenth birthday, had been taken down again and I had been put through an endless ordeal with the curling iron. My breasts, pride and joy of my youth, which had at last begun sprouting, bless them, had been flattened down in a tight little camisole. And to top it all, I was advertised as the twelve-year-old wonder child, Marion Sommer, although I had celebrated my fourteenth birthday quite some while ago.

I felt old as a rock; as old as only children can feel. I was choking full of skepticism and Thus Spake Zarathustra and Dorian Gray, and Clara had told me two days before what Demi-Vierges were and that one could do IT and yet not have a baby if one didn't want to—and there I was standing in front of an audience that seemed to consist of uncles, aunts, and grand-uncles only. Wherever I looked I saw the same expression on every face; a lenient and sugary smile that seemed to scream at me: How cute!

The only exception was Szimanszki in the second box. He obviously was highly displeased and made faces at me all the time. He had an enervating habit of grimacing and pulling his mouth as if to whistle when he was dissatisfied with one of his pupils. And there he was grimacing and pulling his mouth all the time, like a fish on dry ground.

The cadenza, the end, the applause. It fell down like a patter of rain, and the heads of the audience looked like a bed of flowers under a gust of wind. I made my bows as I had learned them, first to the audience, then to the orchestra. I shook hands with the concertmaster. I saw the conductor Kant applauding, politely and somewhat bored. The orchestra, too, applauded. I left the platform, and the applause kept on falling, with the patter of rain and the rustle of dry leaves. I was pushed out again and I bowed and I left the platform, and the audience cheered, and I was pushed in again and suddenly there was Shani Kern at my side, whispering. "The encore!" The sudden silence of the audience as I lifted my violin to my chin almost frightened me. My hands weren't cold any longer, they were damp, moist with sweat and fear and excitement. The strings had given a bit, and it was too late to tune them. The Perpetuum Mobile, which I played as an encore, should have come off with an easy, insolent virtuosity, but now I had to be careful, and I played it the fraction of a fraction too slow. I heard Shani at the piano trying to hurry me, but I wouldn't be hurried. I was afraid my fingers might slip on the moist strings, and I was glad when the piece came to an end. There was more applause, and I bowed and left the platform

with Shani in my wake. As soon as the doors closed behind us
the applause out there died down.

"How was it?" I asked Shani, who tried to avoid my eyes.
"Lousy," he said and left me standing there. Well, that was that.
I had known it all along. I would have liked to creep into a mouse
hole or drown myself in the Danube. I slouched off toward the
artists' room and put my fiddle into the case.

Badly as I had played, I seemed to be a success. People streamed
into the room to tell me so. There was Mother, with tears in her
eyes and too much chalk-white rice powder on her nose,
squeezed into her eight-year-old black evening dress, which was
outmoded and stiff as a board. She wanted to kiss me but didn't
dare; she laughed high and loud; her lower lip quivered and
she had gone to pieces. My father, ill at ease, with white kid
gloves and black pearl studs in his stiff dress shirt and his
mustache smelling like something out of the Song of Songs.
Putzi, slightly stewed and quite indecorous, giving me a good
slap on my fanny. My two grandmothers, looking daggers at
each other, though sweet as licorice. And behind them the whole
God-forsaken clan, the Dobsbergs and the Sommers, aunts and
uncles, cousins and relatives, with all their offspring. The whole
blessed family, all with the same expression of pained satisfaction and deep embarrassment. A whole big flock of ducks who
had hatched a scraggy little swanlet and didn't quite know what
to make of it.

Finally an old attendant cleared them all out and I took a deep
breath. In the sudden silence after their exodus I heard faintly the
beginning of Richard Strauss's Don Juan played by the orchestra. I loved this music, which was called crazy and obscene, just
as my grandfather had called Wagner. Suddenly I had a hazy,
inarticulate, yet overwhelming feeling that I was I. I'm through
with them, I thought, through with all of them; and I meant the
whole family, even Putzi, even my mother. In a sudden panic I
gripped my violin case to get away before they could come back.
But there was no escape. The door opened once more and
Szimanszki entered, ushered in by Shani and preceded by a baldheaded, friendly little man, the impressario, Herr Krappl.

I expected an eruption, a hurricane, something in the nature of an elementary catastrophe. But no, Szimanszki, for once, kept himself in check. He was all sweetness, a put-on, badly overacted sweetness, and he spoke French, a thing he did only when he was very mad.

"Charmante, ma petite," he shouted at me. "Excellente, ma petite gosse. . . . Elle est charmante, cette petite là, n'est-ce-pas? Elle sera une grande vedette, ne croyez-vous pas, mon cher?"

Good old volcano, he kept all his self-made cusswords down, but I could hear the subterranean rumble. He put on an act for Herr Krappl's benefit, he kissed my wet forehead and yanked my tresses and treated me altogether like an idiot. Shani watched the strange spectacle in silent irony; his blue eyes crept out from under his bushy brows like two curious little animals, and his enormous mustache trembled with hidden laughter. Herr Krappl bowed and kissed my hand. He kissed my hand as if I were a grown-up lady. The decorations on the lapel of his tail-coat gave a fine little clanking. "Yes, I think we'll make something out of her," he said, keeping my hand in his and kneading it absent-mindedly, as if it were some sort of dough. "We'll make something of her. She went over big with the audience. We'll have to give her a lot of liquor to keep her small and stop her from growing," he said. He was a jumpy, good-natured little man and he was only joking. Although I knew it I got sore at his little joke and took my hand away and rubbed it in the folds of my skirt.

At last I was left alone in the room, red in the face and suddenly very tired and sad, with a feeling as if I would cry if I didn't watch out. There was a huge plaquette of Wagner set into the wall. He looked down at me reproachfully over his superhumanly big nose. I had received a lot of flowers, huge arrangements, each flower a little corpse stabbed through the heart with a stiff wire. The room had begun to smell like Grandfather's funeral. I went to the big mirror in the corner and looked at myself. I had never seen myself in a full-size mirror, and I examined the girl in the glass inch by inch. I wondered whether I would ever be as pretty as Clara. I doubted it, though I wasn't displeased with myself. I pulled my short skirt down to make myself look taller and more grown up, and I began pulling up my hair from the nape of my neck and piling it up on top. I was so engrossed in experimenting with my looks that I hadn't noticed that Don Juan out there had come to an end and that the following applause had subsided. It gave me a start when the door opened and Kant, the conductor, came in.

"Aha!" he said as he discovered me. Kant was a very famous man and, to my mind, a very old one, over thirty at least. He had a silky little black beard, he was pale and had a haunted look, very much like the Flying Dutchman. He was said to be so demonic that ladies frequently swooned at his concerts. I was scared of him, and no wonder.

"Aha!" he said, brushing me away from the mirror. "Here we have little Marion! You played very nicely and you had a whale of a success. Congratulations!"

"I played awful and I know it," I said. I had enough of being patronized. He looked at me with a slow smile that kept itself somewhere in his little black beard, and he said, "Well, that's better. Do you know what's the matter with your playing?"

"No, I don't," I said, and I felt that I might start to bawl any moment now, as if I really were only twelve. "Maybe I would have done better to become a lion-tamer after all," I said, furious with myself.

"Oh no. Oh no, Marion. You're too pretty to be thrown to the lions," he said. "You are pretty enough to make a success even if you play still worse than tonight. Do you want me to tell you what is the matter with you? You played as neat and dry as a good little music box. Ever heard one?"

"Yes. I know. It's awful. I'm sorry," I said. I thought of the album at home. I was afraid of Kant. Now he stood in front of the mirror. He was as pale as a ghost, his face shone with sweat, and I could see in the mirror that his stiff white shirt was heaving because he was still breathless with the exhaustion of conducting Don Juan. He turned around and came toward me.

"It's all here," he said, knocking against my temples, "and nothing there." I shrank back a bit as he touched the place where my heart was supposed to be. It pounded anxiously inside of my flat little camisole.

"Tell me, Marion," Kant said, "you are not as young as Krappl wants to make the audience believe. You can tell me the truth."

"Naturally not," I said, relieved and angry at once. "I think it's ridiculous to stick me into a dress like this and to make all that fuss as if I were a child prodigy."

"How old are you then? Wait, let me guess. Sixteen?"

I nodded, flattered and happy.

"You know what the Bible says? 'Though I speak with the tongues of men and angels and have not love I am become as sounding brass or a tinkling cymbal.' That's what's the matter with you. You don't have love. Not yet. Someone ought to awaken you."

This sounded familiar. The general belief in the conservatory had run to the conviction that girls had to be awakened before they were able to give a good performance. Some of the teachers were constantly busy awakening one or another of the budding talents.

Kant came closer, took my head between his hands and tilted it back. Then he leaned over me and very carefully, very deliberately, he pressed his experienced lips upon mine. There was the smell of cigarettes and Parma violet brilliantine and beard and man. It felt terrible. It felt like being sucked in by some undercurrent and it felt as if a cannibal were about to swallow me, eat me up, skin and bones. I was disgusted and I was scared out of my wits. Yet, at the same time, I was proud that such a thing should happen to me. Clara will be surprised when I tell her, I thought in the midst of it all. This was not like being grabbed by a nobody like Silber, and certainly I couldn't slap Kant in the face.

I struggled free, and he strolled away from me, laughing softly. "Mind if I smoke?" he said, taking out his cigarette case as if nothing had happened. "Care for a cigarette, Marion?"

"Thanks," I said huskily. I grabbed my flowers, my violin case, my evening cape, my shawl and scrambled toward the door. I dropped some of the flowers, and Kant picked them up. He reached for the violin case to help me with it.

"Thanks," I said furiously. "I carry my violin myself."

Thanks, I carry my violin myself. It sounded like something symbolical to me, like a leitmotiv or something. . . .

"Good night, little Marion," he said. "I hope we'll play together again."

At the foot of the stairway I found Vefi waiting for me as usual, with August loitering in the shadow behind her.

"What do you want?" I said. "Why are you waiting for me? I don't need you, I can find my way home alone. Leave me alone. I have to think."

"But Marion, that's impossible! It's past eleven, you can't go alone! And your mama—she had a headache and went on home, and she told me to wait here for you and to see that you don't catch cold. Holy Maria, Marion, what has come over you? Now be a good little girl and——"

"I'll take a cab," I said. "You go to hell."

I think that this was the end of my childhood. Soon afterward I got my first long dress and I made some money, and one day I had all the plush peeled off the furniture in my room, which I had inherited from my grandfather. I took down the heavy dark curtains and, to the distress of my parents, I had it all done over in cretonne, Nile-green and with a design that looked like water lilies gone insane and growing on rainworms instead of stems, and I paid for it myself.

And with this revolutionary enterprise I began the second period of my life.

2

ALL HER LIFE Marion had harbored a strict faith in the healing powers of a stiff walk. She removed her blanched reflection from the mirror, scribbled a little note for her son: "Out for a walk" and left the small house at a brisk pace. She took the trail that meandered past the mill and then turned uphill into the slender shade of the fir trees. She was careful to avoid the village and the hotel where Christopher lived, and soon the old remedy worked its simple miracle.

What Christopher loved in her—if Marion had but known it—was her unlimited ability to enjoy life and treat it as fun; her curiosity, which was always hungry for new experiences, good or bad ones alike; her eagerness to squeeze the best out of every disappointment, sadness, or misfortune. "My mother has the constitution of one of the amazing earthworms they have been using lately to fertilize barren land," Michael had said of her once. "You can feed her a few acres of dry dirt, and after she's through with it, it'll be a blooming field."

And so, being very sad and unhappy, Marion also had a lot of fun as she marched up that trail to get over her sudden farewell from Christopher Lankersham.

The feel of the trail under her boots. The speed and rhythm of her own steps. The gurgling and babbling of the young brook alongside the trail. The sudden miracle of yellow sun splashed over a slab of gray granite, lifting two million sparks from the old stony face. A bird flying ahead, teasing her with always the same three notes: Scherzo of Beethoven's Ninth Symphony. The scent of mint and moist fern and herb and moss. Rosin dripping from the trunks of the firs and the small stars of feathery mountain pinks dancing across the trail and hiding in the grass. By and by she began humming a melody of her own making. Walk, walk, walk, Christopher is gone, he is gone, he is gone. Christopher s'en va-t'en guerre, s'en va-t'en guerre. Look, two dragon-flies linked together, a whirring little ornament of ecstasy. Then a song by Schubert, born by the rhythm of her steps and the chit-chat of the stream beside her. Ich hoert' ein Baechlein rauschen. Soon she felt warm again and things began to smile at her and to give her sly little winks.

When Marion was upset or unhappy or frightened she didn't cry, she didn't flutter, she didn't throw plates. But she got cold down to the marrow of her bones. She had been very cold when she had left the house. But when she came home an hour later she was warm and flushed, and tiny beads clung to her forehead and to the delicate wings of her nose, which was one of the attractive features in her face although she didn't know it.

As she took the last turn of the trail toward the house, she saw that Michael was sitting on the bench outside their garden fence, examining with deep attention something he held in his hand. He still could be as seriously absorbed in any silly little object as a baby playing with his wooden blocks. The trouble with his eyes had left him with that intent and childish expression. "Hello, gorgeous," he said when he looked up and saw her. He liked to make fun of the snappy flatness of the American vernacular. Sometimes he would talk for days like a Middle Western high-school kid, or like a certain gas-station boy in Great Neck or like the Puerto Rican who had worked in the garden of Elmridge, or like the colored cook Ethel in New York, or in a highbrow circumstantial German like his professor of biology in Heidelberg. He put on accents and languages like costumes and trailed them around and played with them because his father had been an actor.

"Hello, stupid," Marion said, willing to cooperate.

He looked up and saw her. These few words contained Marion's whole life. Guilt and punishment. The brief joy and the lasting heartbreak. Fear and courage, weakness and strength, failure and victory, a bit of everything. He looked up and saw her.

"Look, I have something for you," he said, getting up. Now she discovered what it was that he had been examining with such utter absorption: a tiny bunch of wild strawberries as they grew along the mountain trails. A few were red, but most of them were still green, and there were even a few pale pink blossoms among them. The summer came late to the high altitude of Staufen.

"Strawberries," Marion said, delighted, for to her there were few joys as round and complete as plucking wild strawberries. They are little samples of that rarest of all things: perfection. Their color, their shape, their glow, their scent, their taste. In each red little globe there is the shade of the woods and the heat of sunny slopes, the humming of bees, the flicker of butterflies, the jeweled flitting of lizards, the rustling of hedges, the lively feel of sun-warmed stone and grass, the whole, hot summer bliss.

"The first ones. I found them down near the mill," he said proudly. They both were still so proud of his eyes that they were apt to brag a bit about them. No reason to be bashful about such an amazing achievement as being able to find red strawberries hidden in the grass and fern of the mill stream's green bank.

"You are a hog, Mike, to pluck them all," Marion said. "You know how I would have liked to find a few myself."

"Hog yourself," he said. "I left some for you. We'll go down together and I'll show them to you."

He watched his mother eating the berries. They were hard and sour and not quite ripe, but Marion gave a good show of delight for his benefit. As he stood there leaning against the fence it struck her what a good-looking boy he was. Like all mothers she sometimes wondered how she had managed to bring forth so much manliness, that whole large male structure of strong bones and flexible muscles and hard skull and firm legs.

They say he has my eyes, the Dobsberg eyes, she thought, and he is tall as my grandfather was. The hands are his father's, and the quick change of expressions on his face and the high forehead and the long eyelashes. Yet there is so much that is Michael himself, neither me nor his father. I don't remember how his father looked, but I know that he was not a bit hand-some. That is, my brain knows how he looked, but I cannot conjure his picture out of nothing and hang it before my closed eyes as I can do with Christopher's picture at any time.

Marion had a little secret all her own. Ever since she had been a child she had stored things away and saved them up to remember them in her dying hour. Whenever something seemed very, very lovely or very, very funny, so that it made her cry or laugh or gasp, she always made up her mind and said to herself: Of this I'll think in my dying hour. Christopher's face was one of those things.

"Mike," she said when they sat on the bench together, "there is a bit of bad news I've got to tell you."

"I know," he said quietly. "They had to shoot Nero."

"Oh," she said, startled. "Did they have to do it?"

"It wasn't much fun for him to live any more, was it?" Michael said bravely. "Not since they have all that noise and commotion in the village, soldiers marching and bugles calling at all hours, day and night, and rifle practice and all that. I tell you something, Mony, and I have it from old Hammelin who knows dogs. Nero had been insane for many weeks. Something cracked in his brain when they mobilized, see? He couldn't understand what it was all about, so he went mad and howled day and night and bit anyone who got near him. It's a shame, for he was a good dog. I liked him an awful lot. You liked him too, didn't you?

"There you can see what happens to anti-militarists," he added, and it was only half a joke.

"In the last war we had to kill our dogs too, but it was because we had no food for them," Marion said. She wondered how to find a transition from Nero's execution to Christopher's going to England.

"How come you're always on the losing side, Mony?" Michael asked her, amused as he always was when she mentioned the way the Germans had been starved in that first World War. "Last time you were all for Germany. This time you're all for the Allies. It can't be very pleasant."

"It's part of my personality," she said. "I've never won a sweepstake or a bingo game or at the races for that matter. It wouldn't be natural and would embarrass me no end."

Even then they could hear the noises from the village that had made life unendurable for old Nero, the St. Bernard dog: Crackling of shots from the rifle range, followed by a slow, faint echo from the mountain-wall across the lake. An insistent, repeated, distant bugle call that seemed to excite all the village roosters and made them crow with great belligerence.

"They asked me if I wanted a rifle too," Michael said thoughtfully. "Every man, child, and granddad has been given a rifle. Did you see them? It's that long, double-barreled, old-fashioned Swiss model."

"Would you like to have one too?" Marion asked him. He shrugged. "What do they think they are going to do with their rifles?" she asked.

"Shoot at parachutists. Defend the threshold of their homes. It's pathetic, isn't it? One of Hitler's dive bombers would snuff out the whole of Staufen within a few minutes," Michael said. He sounded like a resigned, wise old man.

"For the time being Switzerland is still at peace. And there are still the mountains," Marion said, looking across the lake.

"You and your mountains!" Michael said with a lenient smile. "But Chris says Switzerland is lucky, having no oil wells or gold mines or ore; just hotels and tourists and people with a spot of T.B. Who'd want them anyway?" He made a little hollow of his hand and bedded his eyes into it. It was a gesture that had become a habit with him during the last two years; as if he would retire for a few minutes into the blackness that had threatened to become his permanent abode. When he came out of his little shelter he looked bright and cheerful.

"Spank me," he said, "I almost forgot. I've got mail for you. From Martin."

Marion took the letter with the Clipper stamps of the United States and smiled down on it. She had been waiting for some news from her older son for quite some time. Letters have faces like people, she thought, reading the address. You don't have to open them, you know by looking at the envelope who wrote them and what's in them. Martin's letters always came in swanky but businesslike envelopes with the names of trains or hotels on them: Statler Hotel, Cleveland, Washington Hotel, Terre Haute, The Challenger, Fred Harvey's, Bowling Green, Iowa. She could trace his route across the Middle West, where he was trying to get contracts for the Sprague Water Drill and selling pneumatic tools.

"What does he write?" Michael asked without much enthusiasm.

"He seems to be doing all right. Judy has gone to Chicago to spend the summer with her parents. Her mother wants her to stay there until she has the baby—that'll be around the end of September," Marion reported. "I think that's quite sensible. He writes that they are toying with the idea of building a little house on the FHA plan. He thinks they could do it for around fifty-two fifty a month—that's not more than they are paying for rent now—and it would be their own. He seems to dangle that in front of me as a little bait. Maybe he thinks it would make me scurry for Chicago to have a hand in the designing. A little grandchild and the prospect of planning a home, it sounds fascinating, doesn't it? He seems to be worried about us being over here, even if he doesn't say so. Good old Martin! Can't you see him sweat in the waiting room of the maternity ward when Judy throws her litter? If I were a better mother I would really be there to cool his brow," she said, trying to sound funny. She was homesick for her older boy, and she had been homesick for him for quite some time. Martin was as good as a solid, heavy flatiron. Everything became flattened out and even and without any wrinkles as soon as he took it into his reliable, practical hands. Sometimes, and without much success, Marion tried to look at life his way. How ridiculous the emotional confusion of this last year would appear, seen through Martin's sober, sensible eyes, she thought with a deep sigh of self-reproach.

"Does he say anything about America getting into the war?" Michael asked impatiently.

"No, nothing about the war. They don't seem to be quite aware of what's going on over here or what really is at stake. He writes that business is fair even if the stock market is more than sluggish," Marion reported. She turned the letter upside down to look for more. Martin had a funny little habit of scribbling in pencil one or two lines around the margin, and these lines usually contained all the nice things which he was ashamed to peck out on his orderly typewriter. "Here he says that it's high time for us to come home and that I should slap your silly puss for not writing him more often. And a shipload of love," she finished with a sigh.

"So the stock market is sluggish, eh?" Michael said. "Good little Babbitt! Good little Regular Guy! Isn't it nice for you to have at least one son who is no problem child?"

"It's restful anyway," she answered. "Two problem children out of three is sufficient. But I suppose Martin thinks that I am a problem mother. He couldn't present me to the local chapter of the D.A.R. without great embarrassment all around. I didn't even do for the P.-T.A. in Great Neck."

Michael didn't listen to her. He was thinking of something else. Marion could see it on his face. They had stopped shooting in the village and had gone home for their lunch and the time reeled off and she hadn't told him about Christopher yet.

"The children from the mill are having a funeral for Nero this afternoon," he said at last. "I promised to help them dig the grave and make the funeral speech." He leaned his head back and looked up into the sun with wide-open eyes without flinching. During the last two months Dr. Konrad had trained him to do that for thirty seconds at a time, and Michael loved to prove to himself again and again the strength of his eyes.

"Would you like to go back to the States before things get worse here?" he asked. It was a sudden attack and startled his mother.

"Would you?" she asked back.

"I don't want you to remain here on account of me, if that is what you mean," he said. "Somehow I would feel much easier if you would take the first boat possible and be out of the way. But I couldn't go with you, and you know it."

Yes, Marion knew it. "Couldn't you?" she asked without conviction. He shook his head, still staring into the sun. His face was much darker than his hair, tanned by mountain air and snow and violet rays.

"No, it would make me feel miserable to be over there and read in the papers about Europe. I can imagine their headlines and the boom in extras," he said, trying not to sound too serious. "Remember what Pixie always said about my compositions in school? Too Continental. That's me. Hard as you've tried, you haven't made an American of me. Europe is where I was born, and Europe is where I belong. I don't know what it is. Take an apple. It tastes different, it looks different, it's something different altogether when it grows here. It's not perfect and big and luxurious like Mr. Burbank's glorious creations over there. It's small and hard and maybe sour and maybe full of wormholes. But it tastes better—to me at least. Take this," he said, bending down and scooping up a handful of soil from the ground. It was dark and moist, and a little rainworm, pink and slick, was squirming in it. Not much of a sight, but Michael looked at it with an odd sort of rapture.

"See it? Smell it?" he said. "It's a different soil, old soil or something. It's European soil."

"And what about Renate?"

"Well, what about her?"

"Wouldn't you like to see her again soon?"

Michael smiled leniently at his mother. "What are you trying to do? Matchmaking or procuring?" he said. "Of course I would like to see Renate. And you know why? You know why I like her so much? Because she is Europe too even if she lives in U.S.A. now. That's why."

He went back to looking at the sun. "In a way it's better for me not to see Renate too soon," he said. "Don't forget, she's only seventeen. Let's put her on ice until this war is over and I'll have got my M.D. degree and there is peace or something. This is not the sort of world for a blooming romance, is it?"

Renate was Clara's young stepdaughter, and Marion had

helped them to get away during the Anschluss of Austria. Silently she wondered if Renate, after two years in a New York high school, would still be as European as Michael seemed to remember her.

"Dr. Konrad thinks that I could go to Lausanne in the fall and pick up my studies, provided Switzerland doesn't get into the war," he said. "Anyway, I couldn't go away now. I would feel like running away when my mother is sick. Sort of," he added, because it embarrassed him to use such big words and he knew that it was the best way of making Marion angry.

"Don't dramatize yourself, little punk," she said promptly. "If we wait here long enough Martin and Johnnie will eventually come over too, dressed in nice, new khaki suits, and meet us with a few neat, well-equipped American divisions." She felt herself that it was a poor joke and made no impression on Michael.

"I'd like to be in on the fight," he said thoughtfully. "The trouble is, I wouldn't know for whom to fight or for what. I wouldn't know who is right. It seems to me that all parties concerned are wrong. I wish I had never gone to the States; I would be a Nazi today and I'd have no qualms about anything. It must be wonderful to have someone do all your thinking for you and to be so sure that you are right. I wish you hadn't sent me back to Germany. It was an overdose of my own medicine and made me good and sick of Hitlerism. That's why you did it, wasn't it? What a mean old thing you are, Mony! I wish I hadn't met Christopher either. I didn't like the English before I met him; that made things much simpler. The more you know and look around, the wobblier you get in your opinions. If England has many people like Christopher she'll pull through, don't you think so? Maybe I could become an ambulance driver or something, somewhere. It makes me feel like a cripple to hang around here and just wait to see what's going to happen. I've been a cripple for too long anyhow. Would it be all right with you if I became an ambulance driver? I believe you have to have a little money when you apply for it——"

"We'll talk about that later," Marion said, reaching out for some hook to hang her news on. "As for Christopher, I have to give you a message from him. He is leaving, Milky," she said, carefully treading her way. "He is going on a mountain trip— I don't know how long he plans to be gone. He wants to start out at one o'clock today and he would like you to come over to his house before he goes."

She felt like running through fire, but she got the whole story out in one big lump, and she congratulated herself for the sly bit of half-truth she had managed to sneak into it to cushion the blow for Michael. He rubbed the moist soil between the palms of his hands and it trickled softly to the ground.

"Yes, I know," he said quietly. "I passed by the hotel on my way home and he told me. I'm glad he is going back to England. You don't like your best friend to be a piker."

Marion gasped. There she was; just a woman, locked out from the world of men. They have their own way of handling things, she thought.

"I don't know what makes a man a piker," she said angrily. "A convinced pacifist dropping bombs on any old place is just as much of a piker as a soldier deserting from the army. It's the old question, and no one has answered it yet: who has more courage, he who fights or he who refuses to fight? Come on, Milky, can we talk nothing but war? What good did it do me to throw out the radio if we go on like this? I'll give you a bite to eat and then you can go over and help Christopher pack. He may want you to row him across the lake; I suppose he'll start from the Seewinkel."

"I'm not hungry," Michael said, and that was his only indication that Christopher's going had hit him hard. "I'd rather go over right away. His books and things are packed, though: he had them stored away for more than a week. He didn't want to worry you."

Male conspiracy again. "All right, Milky, go then," Marion said. She felt a bit as if all her bones were broken, as if an express train had gone over her and left her on the tracks, alive but unable to move. "Give Chris my love and my good wishes and all that. See that he gets off without forgetting to take along his own feet or his eyeglasses or something."

"Aren't you coming?"

"No. No, I don't think so. You know I can't see people off. It makes me wobbly. I curdle or turn into jelly. It's a very unpleasant sensation. No, I won't come along."

Michael scrutinized his mother with the absorbed expression he usually reserved for flowers or butterflies or the strange habits of bugs. "As you please, Mony," he said, rubbed his hands on the seat of his trousers, and shuffled off. Before turning the corner of the garden fence he stopped and came back once more.

"You shouldn't try so hard, my girl," he said.

"Try what?"

"I don't know what. Fighting it off, I guess. Keeping yourself aloof or whatever the hell it is you think you are doing."

Marion felt foolish, helpless, confused. "I don't know what you are talking about," she said waveringly.

He smiled down at her with the fatherly expression that six-foot sons have for their mothers. "You are not being stingy, are you?" he asked. "You are not making some old-fashioned fuss about something very simple and natural? This is a hell of a time for refusing a chap his little happiness, if you ask me. It's still not too late to change your mind. In fact, I've said good-by to Chris and promised him to send you over, complete with hobnail boots, ice ax, and toothbrush."

It stunned her for a moment. Is this the way to talk to your mother? she wanted to say. But somehow their relation was not like that. Marion began to grin.

It's funny how children always believe they have discovered continents of which their parents knew nothing at all. If I had been stingy as you call it, you wouldn't have been born, my little Michael, she thought. It made her laugh, sore as she was inside.

"What's so funny about it?" he asked.

"Nothing. Someday I'm going to tell you," she answered, still shaken by a laughter that at any moment might crack and turn into sobs. "But I'm not stingy and I don't make a fuss. I simply don't feel like seeing anybody off. Go now."

He hesitated for another moment, still with the same half-angry, half-suspicious expression on his sun-tanned, handsome face, and then he turned without another word and left.

It was ten minutes past eleven, and while Marion still stood there and pretended to look at the dill in the vegetable garden, the bell in the church spire down there chimed the quarter. She went into the house.

I WAS SURPRISED when I found out that what they called their Mauve Decade in the United States was our European Fin de Siècle. But I remember that we, in Europe, had our own mauve decade some ten years later, just when I began to be grown up; plenty mauve and sad and exaggerated, like a too beautiful, too flashy sunset. To be grown up was in itself somewhat of a mauve and sad and beautiful condition. It was a dizzy feeling, like being suspended on a thin thread somewhere high up, expecting to tumble down any moment into something unknown, inevitable, very dangerous and very wonderful.

It all began with an indecent dream that I have not forgotten in all these years, although it was made of a vague, fluffy substance, floating in the midst of nowhere. It seemed I walked on mossy ground in a landscape that I recognized after a while as the one in Botticelli's "Primavera." Under those dream trees I felt lighter and happier than I had ever felt before. A man stepped out from the dark background and came toward me. He looked so beautiful that it frightened me. It turned out that I had good reason to be frightened, because my dream man, without a word, lifted me up as if to carry me off, put me down gently on the ground and proceeded to rape me on the soft, green carpet of moss. The alarm clock jerked me rudely out of this dream just as he was melting into me, and I found myself staring at the unfamiliar wallpaper of a small provincial hotel; for I was on my first concert tour and we had played the night before in a middle-sized town in Moravia. I was shocked and at the same time inordinately proud of having been capable of dreaming such an extraordinary thing.

By and by I had managed to be almost sixteen; along with the rest of my generation I had passed through a period of deep absorption with Russian literature; Dostoevski, Tolstoy, Chekhov. I had left behind me Anna Karenina's adultery and the sacred prostitute Sonia, throwing myself into the arms of French decadence. Baudelaire, Verlaine, Rimbaud, Huysmans, Maeterlinck. And now I had even been raped in my dreams by a beautiful stranger. . . .

I met Charles Dupont in March, at the Spring Festival of the New Art, and to say that it was love at first sight would be wrong. I had been in love with him even before I knew him, ever since I had seen some of his paintings. When he kissed my hand—not the back, as gentlemen used to do in Vienna; he turned it around and pressed his lips into the hollow of my palm—I thought: Fate. Or some such big, inflated, nonsensical word. . . .

The New Art people were a loosely knit society for the propagation of anything new and revolutionary in art. Their club was like a bulb wherein were sleeping most of the things that since have developed into the present, into this fateful, pregnant 1940. It was a new design for life, a new beauty—sparse, hard, tough, and true—to replace the fat, overstuffed, much too obvious "BEAUTY" of a God-forsaken bourgeois period. It was a first, sketchy conception of this our new, twentieth century, and everything we have today was in it—maybe even this war.

I had stumbled into the New Art Festival through Clara and Shani, and also through the conductor Kant, the one who had given me that first, cannibalistic kiss. Clara had pestered Shani for a long time to write some dance music for her. Not a sweet waltz, not a coquettish polka, not even the barbaric new thing that had come from America, the one-step. After many sessions there evolved something called "Pierrot Mélancolique." Melancholy Pierrots were very much the fashion among us. We girls went around in straight black reform dresses with big white ruffled collars on which our faces were served as on a frilly china platter; and with more ruffles around our wrists, to make our hands look exquisite and precious and limp with fatigue— for that was how men liked us to appear to them.

Remember the excitement and the fuss and the heartbreak before we got "Pierrot Mélancolique" set? The New Art was still a walled citadel, a secret conspiracy, something evasive and esoteric. The strings we pulled, the letters we wrote, the auditions we got, and the refusals we took on the chin! So far we were three little nobodies. Clara danced in the last quadrille of the petrified opera ballet. Shani was an unknown, unsightly, ill-mannered fellow playing the accompaniment in third-rate concerts. I myself, being something like a midwife to our melancholy Pierrot, had a thin scrapbook with a few provincial write-ups to my credit and that was all. But after Shani had played his music for Kant; and after Clara had danced Pierrot for a small jury of the New Artists; and after we had promised to get the necessary chamber orchestra together, free of charge; after Count Nicki Hoyot, the gay blade, had advanced some money for the purchase of costumes; after Mama Balbi had cut and sewed miles of organdy the color of autumn crocus; after we had slaved and sweated and rehearsed and studied; after we had quarreled and hated one another and made up again and given up in despair and cried on one another's shoulders; after we had driven ourselves almost insane, there it was at last: "Pierrot Mélancolique." The first revolutionary, the first modern piece of dance.

I suppose it was all quite funny, as most beginnings are, but we took ourselves most seriously. We were torchbearers and banner carriers and fighters for a great cause. Youth wants to believe in something and to fight for something or it will rot at the roots. We fought for a new style in life and in art. Of the other half of the world who fought for a new social order we had not heard in our ivory tower. That came only later, when I met Walter.

The event took place in the Secession. There were modern paintings on the walls, and modern sculptures flanked the entrance. A little stage had been improvised, two gray pylons and a gray backdrop, all completely new and arty. Clara danced as nobody had ever seen anybody dance before, and Shani's music was thin and linear, all bones and no flesh, a slap in the faces of Wagner and Richard Strauss. Shani played the piano and I the first violin in the six-man orchestra, and Kant conducted without a baton and very pale and excited. I wore my black dress with the white ruffles, and I felt myself being something very wonderful, a black water lily, for instance, or a singing reflection of moonlight on a dark pond. I felt as wonderful as you feel only when you are not yet seventeen.

When it was all over and the people applauded we were all a little delirious and I felt as if I had a fever, with shivers down my spine and a dull roaring in my temples. It was Kant who introduced Charles Dupont to me. I saw them swimming toward me against the current of the crowd that surged out of the room, and I remember bracing myself as for the impact of a huge wave.

"Marion, this is Charles Dupont," Kant said. "He wants to do you in oil. Don't let him persuade you. His portraits are libelous."

Charles took my hand, turned it around, and kissed my palm. He did not bend over it as he did so, but kept on looking into my face. "Your right side is very young and childish," he said, "but the left side of your face is very old, very, very old and very, very wise. As if you knew everything."

"Don't listen to his arias, Marion," Kant said. "And if you do, don't make me responsible for introducing him to you. Don't say I didn't warn you. Charles is a seducer of virgins and a debaucher of the worst sort."

"Blow it," Charles said. "Evaporate. Transport your obnoxious presence somewhere else. In other words, disappear."

Kant disappeared whistling, with an innuendo, something from Don Juan.

"Is it true?" I asked.

"Is what true?"

"What he said about you?"

"Nonsense," Charles said. "I am the typical paterfamilias. I am happily married and have three children—one set of twins and a girl. Or don't you believe me?"

"No," I said, helplessly. "Why are you making fun of me?"

"Forgive me. I don't know what I am saying," he said, not taking his eyes from me. His glance was so direct that it felt as if he had touched me or kissed me. I tried to break the spell.

"You don't look like your picture," I said.

"What picture?"

"Your self-portrait."

"Oh, so you know that one? No, not one of my self-portraits is good. But on the other hand, whatever I paint turns out to be a self-portrait. Landscapes. Flowers. A tree. A woman. They all look myself. Not on the surface. More—more as if you put a candle inside of a shell. The light will shine through, the inner light. Or, if you want, the darkness within. You understand what I'm trying to say? Yes? I knew you would understand me. We don't have to make conversation, not we, you and I. Words are such poor—how did we call it in school?—poor conductors."

I stood dazzled as these fireworks went off around my head. He looks like an actor, I thought. What made him look like an actor was the fact that he had skipped ahead of the fashion that prescribed a little brushlike mustache. He had his face shaven clean. It was the first time that I saw a man's lips uncovered. They were red and firm and expressive, and the unwonted sight gave me a thrill.

"You look like an actor," I said, as the silence descended once more upon us. We were left alone on the gray velvet stage. From the next room, where a champagne cup was served, the voices and laughter came to us with the sound of a distant water-fall.

"You remember that we have met before?" he said.

"No—where?" I asked just as he wanted me to ask.

"In Egypt. Two thousand years ago. You were a slave girl of Princess Hatchupset and I was one of the palace guards. That time we both got executed because the princess was a very amorous woman and a very jealous one. And later—in Venice—don't you remember? You were the youngest daughter of the Doge and I was a poor good-for-nothing, a painter, as I am now. But you eloped with me all the same. In fact, you have eloped with me in every century at least once. Now it's our turn again. I knew that I would find you someday—I've waited for you. Last time I saw you was during the French Revolution."

Yes, it sounds funny now, but it was wonderful when I heard it for the first time, and I swallowed every word of it. Charles had a whole store of lines like that, and I fell for every one of them. The past is always comical and only what happens to us just now looks like very serious business. To look at us as if it were from a distance of ten years is the best remedy against taking ourselves too seriously. How funny it will be to remember this day, won't it, Marion? It was the day France had collapsed and I had a middle-aged crush on some young Englishman, I forgot his name, he was long and thin and very shortsighted. What became of him? Oh, nothing outstanding. They planted him into some office in London and after the Allies had put a stop to all that Hitler-nonsense and England had gone through her quiet and most respectable revolution, he became a teacher at one of the People's Universities and got married and had two children. Yes, I saw him a few years later in London but he didn't recognize me. He was very shortsighted. I forgot his name, my memory is letting me down lately, it's old age, you know. . . .

Yes, Marion, that's what you hope it will be like. But in all probability it will be quite different and there will be very little reason to make jokes about today—even ten years from now.

In the midst of my conversation with Charles, Shani popped up with two glasses in his hands. He seemed to run a temperature too, or maybe he was a bit drunk. "Drink, lassie, drink," he shouted at me. "This is a great night, this is the night for all Pierrots who believe in vertical music. Let's get drunk because nous sommes arrivés!" Obviously the success had gone to his head. He forced a glass into my hand. The fine sharp green scent of Waldmeister rose from it, the herb that is picked in the Vienna woods in spring to give the cup fragrance. "To our future," he said elatedly. "Yours and mine, my lass."

Only then did he notice Charles Dupont. "Say, and who are you?" he asked rudely; I could see that he played at being drunker than he was to cover up his bad manners. "Oh, I see," he said. "One of the New Artists. Goddamned New Art is written all over your physiognomy. D'you mind if I tell you that I don't like your face?"

"My name is Charles Dupont; I'm an old friend of Marion," Charles said smoothly. "And I agree absolutely with you about my face. Do you mind if I tell you that I like yours very much? And your music too."

It did not take more to start a veritable sunrise in Shani's eyes; he took Charles's hand and pumped it vigorously. "Excuse me," he said, "I seem to be drunk. I don't know if you remember how it felt when you sold your first painting. How d'you like Walt Whitman? Ever tried to paint the landscape of his poems? No? Well, I have. I composed it. The new world. I am the new Columbus; I discovered a new continent for music. Lassie," he said, forgetting Dupont just as abruptly as he had approached him, "lassie, I'm afraid I won't take you home tonight. I'm going off with some fellows—celebrate, you know. It's strictly a man's party. Kant invited me, it's very important. He wants me to play Paumanok for him. D'you think you could manage to get home without my assistance for once?"

"Don't be silly," I said. "When will you stop babying me around?" "I'll take care that Marion gets home safely," Charles said politely. Shani gave him a quick glance from under the thicket of his eyebrows, suddenly alert, sober, appraising. "All right," he said. "All right then." He marched off, not quite steadily. "Lassie," he called back at me before he reached the exit, "if you should step on a rainbow by accident, be careful not to trip—they are damned slippery."

"Poor boy—so talented, and so jealous!" Charles said after Shani had disappeared. "I would like to paint him; as a clown, a sad, grotesque clown, with a lot of orange for the background and no eyes in his face at all, just circus paint and mask and utter resignation. Come now, let's go. I'll take you home—and I hope to God you live at the other end of town."

I did some very fast thinking. If I told Charles that I lived in the next block, this evening was over. The mere thought of it made me feel as if a taut string inside of me were tuned too high; it broke and snapped and hit the walls of my heart with a sharp pain.

"I do, in fact," I said. "Way out in the nineteenth district. Braganza Gasse 14, Braganza Gasse." That address, all of a sudden, slipped out from the purple bag of my subconscious where it had been stored away for many years. It was the address of my granduncle Heinrich, whom I had visited once as a little girl. The bus trip had seemed to me a very long, never-ending journey.

"Nineteenth district. Good," Charles said. "We'll look for a fiacre with very old, very tired horses and a very sleepy coachman, and we'll tell him to make a few detours. Oh, Marion, now that I have found you I'll never, never let you go again."

It's a funny thing about progress. We live in it, it's all around us, we are carried ahead by it and when we look back we can see how much ground we have covered, what strides we have made. But while progress progresses we really don't feel it or notice it or know anything about it. Do you remember the first time you saw an automobile? No. The first time you rode in one? No again. The first time you encountered an airplane, a motor yacht, a radio? No, not at all. They weren't there when I was a child and then suddenly they were there. I close my eyes and try to recapture the time before the war, when I was a young girl. Yes, there were motor cars on the street and we went to the movies which seemed very marvellous and dramatic and our daring young officers fiddled around with dirigibles and airplanes and predicted a great future for them. It all seems to have sneaked into our lives behind our backs and there it was. But the only real great step toward progress which I can definitely remember was when we got that water faucet in our kitchen.

I remember our ride in the fiacre that night; the sleepy cloppety-clop of the horses' hoofs on the cobblestones of the empty, quiet streets, the dreamy cracking of the whip, the weary back of the coachman in front of us. Although the night air was brisk and cool, Charles had the hood of the fiacre taken down, almost demonstratively, as if to assure me that he had no bad intentions. Riding with a man in a closed vehicle was called a porcelain ride and stamped you a fallen maiden; therefore I was grateful and relieved when the hood folded up behind our heads and I could see the wide, open sky above us. Cloppety-clop, cloppety-clop went the two horses. Charles put his arm around my shoulder and we tilted our heads back, looking up to the stars—which were much brighter than they are nowadays because the streets were so much darker.

John once said that happiness is like radium; it is an article that is bearable in infinitesimal small amounts only, but whose force and light and power regenerate themselves on and on. I don't mean that slack humdrum happiness which consists of not being unhappy; I don't mean contentment or satisfaction or having fun. I mean really being happy, with that full, transparent, sharp happiness that lasts for a few minutes sometimes, or for half an hour at most. If we should add it up at the end of our life, all of that real happiness we have had would not even fill a day. But then I also think that every human being is given an almost equal amount of that happiness, and whether you find it in the church or in the gutter, in sex or in thought, in sacrifice or in crime, doesn't make any difference.

That ride through the cool, new night was one never-forgotten long stretch of being happy.

We rode on and on. It took us a little eternity to get to the address I had given Charles, but in the end we arrived in the exclusive district and I had the fiacre stop at the corner of Braganza Gasse and asked Charles to let me walk to the house alone. Uncle Heinrich's swank villa stood white and clear in the moonlit night, with sharp black shadows. All windows were dark, and I thanked God that no one was about. A lamplighter in his white coat came down the street, turning off every second lantern. Midnight. The air tasted sweet and green. I stood there wondering how I should ever get back from the outskirts of the town to the heart of it where we lived. I had never been out by myself at night. I did not know altogether how to pick up my former life after this night of falling in love with Charles. My shadow on the sidewalk was joined by another shadow, and when I turned around I found Charles at my side. "I just wanted to say good night once more," he said.

"Thanks," I said. "Good night."

"Good night," he said. "Good night. It's been an enchanted evening."

"Charles," I said, "I've lied to you. I don't live here. I only wanted to be a bit longer with you. Can you take me back to town?"

"Good!" he said, laughing softly. "I would not have let you go anyway; do you know that I haven't even kissed you? It's much too early for parting."

We went back into the carriage and rode on. The night grew

thin and light and dreamlike. I was very tired, but I did not want to sleep for fear of missing some of these precious minutes. Reality had gone out of everything. The coachman slept and the horses slept, yet the fiacre rolled on in its sleep. Cloppety-clop. Cloppety-clop. We stopped in front of a low, rambling structure with green shutters. "I want you to come for a minute into my studio," Charles said. "Just to know that you have been here will make it a different room. Tomorrow when I go to work I'll feel your presence, in the air, in the atmosphere. Now that I've found you I'll become a great painter, I promise you."

Love feeds on words like these. I was scared and I hesitated. "Wait here, we'll be back in a few minutes," Charles told the coachman as he helped me from the carriage and took out his key. The man grinned knowingly in his sleep. "You must not be afraid," Charles said, letting me in. "I'd rather die than do you any harm."

I swallowed the smell of paint and turpentine, which was to become so familiar to me during the following weeks. There was a puddle of moon on the skylight. "We won't turn on the electric light, it makes everything so cold," Charles said, putting a match to a candle. Paintings without frames sprang from the walls, a sketch stood on the easel, canvases were rolled up and stacked in a corner. There was a low, wide couch, and a little round iron stove, and there were black pipes like angry serpents crawling up to the ceiling and a huge antique cupboard with roses painted on its doors.

"Don't look around, it's messy," Charles said. "It's really an old stable that has been converted into a studio. I only wanted your imprint on the air I am going to breathe."

"Do you still want to paint me?" I asked shyly. I had wild ideas about bringing a great sacrifice, letting him undress me, look at me, and paint me, and somehow by this very process inspire him and make him the greatest artist among the living. I felt my body shiver inside of my black dress, and I was aware of the smallness of my breasts and hoped he would like them, new and little as they were.

"No, Marion. I'll never paint you," he said, standing away from me.

"No?" I said, disappointed. "I know I'm not very pretty, but I thought——"

"I cannot paint a woman I love. I love you, Mignonne. Have you ever heard that a surgeon would operate on his own wife or sweetheart? Well, it's the same with painting."

"Yes, but operating is dangerous," I said.

"So is painting—if you are in love. You don't know how dangerous," he answered curtly. I suppose I looked crestfallen in the flickering light of the candle. "How young you are, my sister, my bride," he said softly. Only later did I remember that this came from the Song of Songs. "Do you want me to kiss you?" he said. "If you don't want me to kiss you, I won't do it." He did not move, he waited for me to cross the space between us. I stepped over the beams of shadow the easel threw onto the floor and into his arms. Of all the kisses I have given and received in my life, this first one stands out the clearest and most unforgotten.

"Let's go," he said huskily as he released me. He almost pushed me away and went to the door, ahead of me. The floor creaked under his step, there was the rustling of loose plaster trickling down in the dark, and then the coolness outside touched my face like a hand. We woke up the coachman and rode on. The moon was not quite full but very bright. It had left the haze behind and etched fine, Japanese shadows of branches with little buds onto the whitewashed garden walls of the old park we passed. Later we stopped at a little café that snuggled up to a small church and went in. A sleepy blonde woman enthroned there between two potted palms counted lumps of sugar on tiny nickel saucers. In a corner four men played cards and a fifth one kibitzed. A badly washed waiter went through the motions of cleaning the marble top of a little table for us and brought us coffee and brioches. Blue stubbles were coming out on his cheeks because it was so late in the night. Charles spoke of his childhood and of a dog he had liked as a boy and of a fig tree in his parents' garden. The bells in the little church next door struck four. The night began to wilt. We left the place and rode on. The moon was waning; the first street cars rumbled through the quiet town. The coachman woke up and told us that his horses needed a rest. We got out of the fiacre and took a walk. My ears sang with fatigue, and I remember that I talked and talked, handing over my whole soul and reaching out for his. It got lighter, a thin mist hung from the trees, the pavement began to shine with moisture. The first workmen came through the dawn, and in some distant barracks a bugle blew reveille. We went back to the fiacre and rode on. We sat on a wet park bench. We wandered across a bridge. We stopped and looked down upon the flat boats at their moorings, softly creaking in their sleep. We rode again. We went into an old little chapel filled with the stony scent of cold incense. A priest curtsied before the altar and mumbled his morning Mass. When we came back onto the street the horses were munching hay from feedbags tied around their ears. We had another palaver with the coachman, and he took us to a little hamlet at the bank of the Danube. We had breakfast in a little place filled with fishermen and fat, shrill market women. The kerosene lamps were still burning, the day was not up yet. Charles said we had to see the sun rise from the top of the Kahlenberg. It was all very crazy. We rode uphill between the chilly-looking bare patches of dormant vineyards. The air was fraught with the scent of millions of violets from the meadows of the Vienna woods. I told Charles about Putzi and our spring expeditions. He cupped his hands around my face and kissed me, very gently, very carefully this time. "Your lips taste like strawberry ice cream," he said. The horses gave up as the grades became steeper, and the coachman grew recalcitrant. We told him to wait for us and climbed on.

At sunrise we were near the crest of the mountain. We saw the treetops turn pink and the cupola of the monastery on the next hill pierce through the mist, green with patina and catching golden sparks under the rising sun. We saw the Danube slither across the hazy plains down there like a big, fat, glittering yellow snake coiling up alongside the city. We heard the bells in the hundred churches wake up and usher the morning in. Charles said something that was very much the fashion then and impressed me greatly: about closing your eyes and giving yourself up and Feeling One with the Universe.

At last we rode back to town and took an endless farewell in the green little square while Schiller glared fastidiously down on us from his high black marble pedestal. Charles, at the last moment, told me that he would not be able to see me for a week because he had to go to Paris; he made it sound staggeringly casual, as if Paris were just around the corner, and I floated home, feeling as if I had sails or wings or some new organ to keep me off the ground.

It was almost nine o'clock in the morning when I slunk past Herr Jerabeck's janitor's cubicle. Somehow during that endless, enraptured night I had dimly conceived the hope that I would manage to sneak into my room before my parents were up for breakfast and that, with some expert lying and with Vefi's assistance, I might be able to cover up my sinful doings. But the moment I let myself in with my key and tried to creep to my room I realized that everything had gone wrong. First of all there was the smell that accompanied the nervous fits to which my mother was subject. Camomile. Ether, faintly sweet. A horrible concoction called Hoffman's drops. Rubbing alcohol. Even carbolic acid. All the depressing odors of a hospital ward combined. Through closed doors I could hear my mother sob, or so, at least, I imagined.

Vefi had swollen eyes and was in the midst of a crying spell. Kathi, my friend, turned her glance to heaven and muttered some strong Bohemian curse at me as I went past her through the kitchen—for, to make things worse, it was laundry day. Aunt Caroline had suffered a nervous breakdown and was flung down on the couch in my room, having hysterics. My mother was in bed, looking smaller than I had ever seen her. Our sticky family physician, Dr. Popper, was hovering over her with a spoon in his hand. She looked at me as if she had pains recognizing me, but she did not say a word.

But in the front room my father sat at the table, his head in his hands, in a pose of deepest despair. Putzi, my Little grandfather, apparently summoned during the night, stood behind him with his hands consolingly on my father's shoulder. It was a group that would have done honor to the second-act curtain of a Sudermann play. At the table opposite my father sat the Law, behind a jigger of brandy: a policeman in uniform, with a little book in his hand, licking a pencil and taking notes for a report to the bureau of missing persons, I suppose. It was the return of the fallen daughter, complete, well staged, and well executed.

Thus my first real love began with a scandal, and it ended, five months later, with a scandal, and it kept on being a mess and a scandal and unmitigated hell all the while it lasted.

I DON'T KNOW how Vienna ever got its reputation of being gay and carefree if not through its busy industry of saccharine operettas full of sweet waltzes and fake hilarity. The truth is that Vienna was a sad and depressing place as far back as I can remember. A beautiful town, yes, with a vibrant, sensual air, but a town that had grown too old and disillusioned. Spent and tired, dissatisfied with things as they were, yet unable to do something about it, Vienna had outlived itself, with no hope and little future. People were oversensitive, sad, even though they danced and made love, extremely sorry for themselves all the time. We all carried our suicide with us in our pockets and pulled it out and waved it in front of everybody at the slightest provocation. The step from life to death seemed very small and easy for anyone born in that dying town, and suicide a natural and elegant exit. The vibrant air of Vienna hung heavy with this ultimate tiredness, with an ironical, graceful, yet boundless self-pity. It was the Weltschmerz of people who had been pampered and softened and spoiled by too much security and soft living. It took a lot of beating to awaken them from their inertia and make them tough and brave. It is amazing to think that many of those were the same people who are standing up so well today under the endless tortures of concentration camps, exile, flight, and war. But then, between 1914 and 1920, we all went through a good training for the present inferno. . . .

As for me, I went out and bought myself a pistol before I had known Charles Dupont a fortnight. I had entered into open rebellion against my parents and anything they stood for. I pursued my course, I loved Charles, it was the only thing worth living or dying for. Home had become an unbearable chamber of tortures, or so it seemed to me. Whenever I returned from my high, soaring flights into those realms of beauty I shared with the beloved, I bumped my head hard against the ugly walls of reality. My parents called me all sorts of names and treated me as if I were a streetwalker. "You don't understand me," I cried desperately. "You make everything dirty, you have a dirty mind. I love him and he loves me." "Yes," my parents screamed back at me, "but is he going to marry you?" Marriage, oh my God! On the enchanted planet I inhabited with Charles there was no marriage. "That's all you know, marriage," I sobbed. "Making a filthy nasty habit of something that must be kept free and mysterious. Marriage, indeed. Quibbles over the household money, gas bills, diapers on the laundry line, the sour smell of respectable muck. Never, never, never will I get married."

They locked me up like a prisoner, but I broke out. My father beat me up, and I stopped talking to him. My mother watched me with tearful anguish for any signs of being pregnant. To be pregnant was the thing to be expected from a daughter who carried on with a man. But I didn't get pregnant because Charles, against all expectations, did not seduce me. He wanted to want me and to desire me and to long for me and never to get me. He wanted to suffer and to make me suffer too. It was an exquisite, subtle frying in oil. To kiss me for hours and then bundle me up and send me home, still a virgin, was his approved way of keeping us at a pitch all the time. It was not a very healthy way of being in love but a very intense one, Love with a capital L, Love in italics.

It was at this point that the family produced Cousin Hermann, in the hope of bringing the fallen daughter back on the right path. Cousin Hermann was the fattish, pinkish son of one of my mother's sisters. As a child he had been a good boy, the sort of boy who brought home prizes from school and who never caused his mother an unpleasant hour. I had met him occasionally at a children's birthday party or one of the frequent family weddings and had always detested him. I had lost sight of him for several years, and now I found him suddenly at our dinner table, rubbing his hands over the soup plate and telling bad jokes in the manner of a great raconteur. I sensed at once that something was wrong, for my mother had powdered her little red nose, the table was laid with the good damask table-cloth and with the better set of china reserved for honored guests. Cousin Hermann had been in Paris for a year, and great stress was put on his beautiful Parisian French. "Ma petite cousine, me voilà, embrasse-moi!" he said when I entered our front room.

"Hermann, you're an ass," I replied.

My parents and his parents smiled at us benignly. After dinner Cousin Hermann offered to accompany me on the piano if I would give him the honor and pleasure to play the violin for him. "Dear Hermann, he is so musical," his mother announced. My own mother gave me a little kick in the shin when I remonstrated. I decided that playing was better than making conversation. I picked the easiest things I knew, and the ones I loathed most. Serenade by Tosti. Chant sans paroles by Tchaikovsky, transcribed for violin and piano. Cousin Hermann put his fat hands upon the keys. They looked like the upholstered furniture covered with pinkish satin in my old doll's house. There was a little shrub of blond hair growing on each finger. Before we had finished playing, both sets of parents had sneaked from the room and left us alone, and I found those hands and fingers around my waist. It was pretty obnoxious, and I resorted to the methods of our childhood. "Let go or I'll spit," I whispered. Cousin Hermann let go. "I'm patient," he said meekly, "and you will get used to me. We have always liked each other, haven't we, Marion? No reason for you to be on a high horse, is there? You should be glad if I'm crazy enough about you to close both eyes about certain happenings, don't you think so?"

Behind the obnoxious little fellow I felt the mighty pressure of the whole machine called The Family. In Cousin Hermann I found concentrated everything I hated about my own background: the smugness, the fat, saturated self-satisfaction of the bourgeoisie, the lack of imagination and generosity, and not a trace of the entire vague complex which we called Beauty. Marry Cousin Hermann? I'd rather have died.

I badly needed a little rest in Charles's studio. To be made comfortable on the couch in the corner, to be covered with the soft old, moth-eaten, faded red cashmere shawl, to have tea brewed for me on the little iron stove, to have a cigarette started for me and put into my mouth—oh, lovely intimate little gesture! —to cry, to sleep, and to forget. But Charles was in Paris. He had friends there and business to attend to, an exhibition had to be arranged, an art dealer had to be coaxed into buying, he had to paint the portrait of a cabinet minister who looked like a crossbreed between a baboon's behind and an overripe watermelon. Charles wrote me many letters whenever he was in Paris, sometimes two or three a day. I picked them up at the poste restante window of the post office—an enterprise that made me asthmatic with embarrassment—and carried them with me, hidden in my stockings. Every hour or so I would lock myself in the toilet, pull them out, and read them; they were sweet and tender and passionate and amusing, and they kept me precariously afloat on a raft of hope in an ocean of loneliness.

After an eternity he was back and began painting my portrait as a sort of remedy for his creative power. "I have to get you out of my system," he said (or words to that effect). "I can't have your little face haunt me day and night, I'll have to get over this madness or I'll never paint a decent piece in my life. Maybe if I analyze you, cool and detached, and put you down in paint, it'll break the spell." He sounded like a poisoned man grabbing for an antidote, and I felt wonderfully devastating. I posed for him all during June and into the heat of July. The sun beat down on the roof of the old stable; the air was thick with turpentine. I sat on the little platform, wrapped in the smoldering red cashmere shawl, smoking too many cigarettes, losing pound after pound. Behind his easel Charles groaned and moaned; the portrait or study, or whatever it was to be, did not come up to his expectations; he cursed the brush, the canvas, the paint, the heat; he cursed me and he cursed himself. "You have made me impotent," he lamented. "Here I am now, an idiotic castrate with an emasculated brush and eyes that see everything out of proportion. Oh, holy Matisse!"

One evening, coming home after an especially hot and miserable sitting, I fainted in the midst of our front room. It was Wednesday; a card game was under way; I smelled the cigars of the men the moment I let myself into the entrance hall and heard the exalted voices of the ladies doing a post-mortem. "You're late again," Vefi whispered to me as I crossed the kitchen on the way to my room. "Holy Mother of God, where are you keeping yourself all the time? Your mama asked for you at least ten times. Come, brush your hair. Jesus, and how you smell of cigarettes! Clean your teeth before going in. I really don't know what's going to become of you. Here, take the cookies in to them."

Reluctantly I took the silver plate with the cookies and went into the front room. They all looked up as I entered; there was a sudden silence, and the green felt covers on the two card tables became greener and greener, with a sharpness that stabbed my eyes. "Good evening," I said. "It's very hot, isn't it?"

Then the green turned black, everything around me grew soft and cloudy and pleasant, and I thought, What's this? and I also thought, Why not give in, it's so soft? and I heard my mother scream. The next thing I knew I was sprawling on the carpet and somebody put a spoon between my teeth and poured brandy into me. It burned my throat and I began to cough. "I'm all right," I said. "Must be the heat," I said, collecting myself from the bed of crumbled cookies. "Yes, the heat, that must be it," my aunt Caroline said, much too eagerly. My mother stared at me, and her lips quivered. The guests looked stupid with shock. It made me feel miserable. Fainting is pleasant, but coming out of a faint is a very nasty sensation. "Excuse me," I said, wading through a pond of silence toward the door.

That evening, after the hurried, embarrassed, and scandalized exit of the guests, my parents put me through a cross-examination. I, the culprit, had fainted. The conclusion was that I must be pregnant. They sat at my bedside all night long and let all the tortures of the Inquisition loose against me. I was young and all wrapped up in myself. I didn't understand that they were at least as miserable and bewildered as I was myself. The next morning my father put on his Prince Albert coat and his silk hat and marched off on some sinister errand. My mother, her eyes swollen with the lack of sleep, dragged me to Dr. Popper's office to have me examined. With soapy smoothness he invited me to lie down on a leather couch, to relax, not to be afraid, he wouldn't hurt me. I can still feel the coldness of the leather touching the skin of my thighs as the doctor pulled up my skirts to find out the truth about me and my cursed virginity. When this is over I'll kill myself, I thought. When this is over I'll kill myself. "When this is over I'll kill myself," I said aloud. My mother sat on a chair in a corner, with downcast eyes and folded hands, as if in silent prayer.

"It's all my fault," she whispered. "I should never have let you play the violin."

Suddenly I could see that this was funny, outrageously funny, and I began to laugh, to Dr. Popper's deep consternation. It is one of the great gifts of life I have salvaged from the debris of my silly, high-flying, and futile first love. There is nothing in the world so tragic, so pathetic, so horrid that it may not be funny at the same time. If it were not for the laughter behind it all, humanity could not have survived.

Neither could I.

When I was pronounced undamaged and intact, I got up and marched out of the room without speaking another word to my mother. The last thing I heard was the gurgling of water at the old-fashioned washstand where Dr. Popper washed his hands of the whole unsavory business.

I went home and hurriedly packed my suitcases; the one-night stands on my concert tour had given me quite some practice in it. "What's the matter? You going away?" asked Vefi.

"Yes, I'm going," I said. "It's time I lived my own life."

"Jesus, child, Marion," Vefi said. "You aren't running after that man? No man is worth running after, believe me."

"You're not the one to tell me—you, with a lover on each finger," I said, snapping my suitcases shut.

"Ah, with me that's something different. I'm a little bastard myself—no father, see? And as soon as August has served his twelve years, we'll get married anyway. Say, is this man you're after going to marry you? No. Not if you come to him with your suitcases. Leave it to me to know men!"

"I'll have Pepi Jerabeck take my luggage downstairs," I said rather grandly. "And tell my mother not to worry, I'm going to let her know my new address soon. And give August a nice kiss from me."

I put my arms around Vefi's neck and kissed her. She gave a few dry, awkward sobs, and I let go of her for fear of getting soft in the warm kitchen smell that clung to her. I didn't even look around. I made myself stiff and hard as a board as I marched off. I closed the door and turned my back to a petty, mean, safe little world that revolved around one thing only: whether a girl was a virgin or not.

THE MOMENT I had myself and my bags installed in a one-horse cab, I began to shrink until I was very small and lost while the world around me grew into a nightmarish size. I hadn't been brought up to find my way alone. I didn't know how to hire a cab, how to enter a restaurant and order a meal, how to rent a room, and for the first hour of my new freedom my greatest problem was how much to tip the driver. Up to that moment I had been handled like a neat parcel; wrapped and stamped and addressed and delivered and picked up again and taken by people wherever they wanted me to go. Now I was independent, I had to move on my own strength and to make my own decisions. It was so frightening it took my breath away.

There was first the problem of money. I had some of my pocket money in my handbag—eleven kronen and some pennies, to be correct. Moreover, I had two hundred and twenty kronen in my savings account in a bank. That much I knew. What bank and how to get it out of there I did not know, for my father had handled all financial matters for me. However, I was certain I could always ask Charles for money. To me Charles seemed a very wealthy man. He wore a silk hat and a Prince Albert coat for every day, which was the mark of the truly elegant gentleman in the Vienna of those days. Whenever we took a ride we did it in great style, not in a one-horse cab like the one that now took me bumpingly away from the street where I was born, but in a swank fiacre with rubber tires. He had given me many presents—books, flowers, little gadgets of one sort or another. He traveled to Paris with no more ado than other people going on a Sunday outing to Grinzing or Hütteldorf. And he never talked about money, whereas my parents talked about it incessantly.

In spite of Vefi's warnings I went directly to Charles's studio. I didn't realize exactly what I expected, but it was something dramatic, something like: Here I am, I belong to you, I am free, take me and keep me, forever. I was not even seventeen, a most dramatic age. When I arrived in front of the green shutters I told the cab driver to take my bags and bundles down; my violin case I carried myself, as always. The door to the studio was open, and Susanne, the model, came out as she heard us rumble in with bag and baggage.

"Oh, it's you, Fräulein Sommer," she said. "Monsieur isn't here." She had the silly habit of calling Charles "Monsieur"—I never found out why. I had only seen her in the nude when Charles painted her, but now she wore an apron and a cloth tied around her hair and she looked like a gray, colorless chambermaid.

"I'll wait for him," I said, entering with the cabman behind me. I paid him; the fare was almost three kronen, and he kept the palm of his hand waiting for more. "How much tip does he get?" I whispered to Susanne; she counted my baggage with a glance and advised thirty pennies. It seemed too skimpy an amount, and I gave him fifty. The man thanked me sourly, not even calling me "Your Grace" as cab drivers usually did, and left. I was alone with the girl who scrutinized me with her nearsighted, slightly protruding eyes.

"You going on a trip?" she asked.

"No—that is, yes—in a way," I stammered. "What time do you think Dupont will be back?"

"I couldn't tell. You know how unreliable he is. He might come home late this evening and he might stay out all night.

He told me I could clean up a bit, he wouldn't be back soon. D'you want to leave a note for him?"

"No, I think I had better wait," I said, flattened out considerably. I sat down on a wobbly antique chair, and Susanne returned to her business, pottering around the room, shaking little bits of rugs, blowing dust from the tops of cupboards and tables and rustling among the rolled-up canvases that were stored up in a corner.

"Cigarettes are on the little tabouret," she said after a while. "If you'd like a cup of tea, I could make you some."

"Thanks, no," I said. "I thought Dupont would be here. He said he would do some detail work on the shawl today."

"Yes," Susanne said from behind the easel, where she was dusting something. "That's what he told *you*." It sounded mean, and I decided to ignore it. She came up from behind the easel and folded her arms. "I've often thought I'd like to talk to you," she said. "Alone."

"Well——" I said. I felt that something unpleasant was coming and had no power to stem it.

"And don't you think that I'm jealous of you. I'm not," Susanne said. It had never occurred to me that Susanne had any feelings at all. She seemed like one of the necessary props of this studio, like the wooden dummy in the corner. Suddenly the full meaning of what she had said arrived in my brain and I felt myself blushing hotly.

"Why should you be jealous?" I said.

"Yes, why should I? I'm married, ain't I? I have a husband and a baby and I'm making a living here, ain't I? Well, I'm telling you I'm not jealous. But I've often wondered why a nice girl like you should let herself in for this. You're too young for this sort of thing, don't you see? Mark my word, you'll get hurt if you hang around this studio for too long."

"Thanks for your advice," I said pompously. "I don't think I need it."

Susanne gave me a wry little smile. "You're still riding high and mighty, ain't you?" she said. "Well, Fräulein, I've been just as crazy about him, just as crazy."

She went to a wardrobe, knelt down, and opened it. A load

of dirty underwear tumbled from it. I turned my eyes from the sight. Somehow I had never thought of Charles having dirty underwear like other people, or any underwear at all, for that matter. I pulled myself together and answered as heroines in the books I knew would have answered in my case.

"Look here, Susanne," I said, "if you want to indicate that you—that he—that you were—that Dupont had a—a liaison with you before he knew me, it doesn't impress me at all. In fact, he told me so himself."

"Oh, he did, did he?" she said, bent over a heap of crumpled socks. "Well, and with you it's the great love. You won't get a kick in the pants when it's all over—and two kronen a sitting for pity's sake. With you it's eternal, is that it?"

"With me it's something quite different," I said.

Susanne began to chuckle; it sounded not mean, rather good-natured. "That's what every one of us thinks, every girl who falls for a man. Different, my arse. I haven't seen anyone in love yet who did not believe that with them it was different. Well, Fräulein, let me tell you: The music box plays only one piece, and it's always the same one, and it's short, and it's over much too soon."

I remembered the music box in the album at home, and all the faces in that album were coming toward me in a sudden rush, with the tinkle of its forgotten music and the stiff, honest smile of my ancestors: the whole fenced-in world I had thrown away and left behind. It made me dizzy, and for a second I was afraid I might faint again, but I sat very straight and stiff and it passed. Susanne had stepped to my side and looked at me curiously. "I didn't mean to hurt you," she said. "I really mean quite well, Fräulein. It would be a shame if such a nice young girl should come to harm."

She gesticulated feebly with her hands; the right one was covered with one of Charles's socks, which she had pulled over it to look for holes. Her forefinger was peeping through one, and she lifted it to her nearsighted eyes and examined it with a smile that had grown soft all of a sudden.

"He always makes holes with his right big toe," she said, shaking her head and twisting the damaged sock back and forth.

I had to turn away and bite my lips to prevent myself from bawling right then and there. The little gesture had suddenly opened long vistas of an intimacy between her and Charles of which I understood nothing. We had spent our time in a castle of clouds, beautiful yet unsolid ground. But here was the other side of love, the down-to-earth, the run-of-the-mill side: the sock-mending, meal-cooking, button-sewing, nursing, caring, prosaic housewifely love.

"D'you mind sitting over there?" Susanne said. "I want to make his bed before I go home."

I watched her bring out some sheets and pillows from a closet and spread them over the couch. The pillow slips were crumpled, a bit soiled. She dived into the closet once more and returned with a pair of pajamas, blue silk with red stripes. These were the first pajamas I saw in my life, and they made a great impression upon me. Susanne unfolded them and laid them out on the couch. "That's the newest thing," she said proudly. "He brought them from Paris." She stroked them with an entirely unconscious gesture and then she turned to me. "If it's all right, Fräulein, let's go now. I have to lock up the studio," she said.

I looked at my suitcases and bags helplessly. "You go, don't mind me, Susanne," I said. "I'll wait here."

"Oh no," she said. "Oh no, I can't let you wait here. I have to lock the studio, see? I'm responsible for it, see?"

I fumbled around for some bright argument, but I found none. "I don't know where to go," I blurted out. "And I have not much money."

Susanne took this in absorbedly; her nostrils quivered like a pointing bird dog's. "Look here, Fräulein Sommer," she said, "this ain't none of my business, but if you are clever don't you stay here and wait for him. He might come home and bring company along, see? And where would you be then? Better you go to some little hotel, there are plenty along the Währingerstrasse. You can get a nice room for one krone. Just look out so you don't get bedbugs."

"What do I do about my bags?" I asked, completely at a loss. "I can't carry them around. And I can't afford another cab. What do I do now?"

"Leave 'em here and pick 'em up tomorrow," Susanne said. "Tomorrow at ten he's expecting you for a sitting and everything will be all right. But believe me: Never surprise a man; it don't do you no good. Not with a man like Monsieur."

I did have bedbugs that night, and I paid three kronen for the room, and it was in a hotel where couples would go for an hour of illicit lovemaking—but this, of course, I discovered only afterward. I found this small hotel after a long search and only after having been turned down by many fastidious hotel clerks. My hotel had a chicken-breasted, high-shouldered look; it had five stories with only three windows front, and a huge sign: Hotel Garni. Even here I had a little tussle at the desk before they gave me a room; there was no clerk but an ample-bosomed lady with more teeth in her mouth and blonder curls on top of her head than I had ever seen before. She gave me a brash look and said evasively that there might be a room free, perhaps. "How much does it cost?" I asked timidly. I was discouraged and very tired, and I wished for nothing as fervently as to take off my shoes and stick my feet into a bowl with cold water. I had almost given up hope of finding any room and I was ready to pay all of my remaining eight kronen for a chair, four walls, a bed, and a wash. "For how long do you want the room?" the lady asked me. "Only for tonight. That is, if I like it I might stay longer," I added hastily to win the lady's favor. She gave me another look, as if taking my measurements for a complete set of petticoats, camisole, corset, and garters. "Three kronen," she said. "To be paid in advance."

When I took out my purse she seemed surprised. "Are you going to pay for it yourself?" she asked. "Why, yes," I answered, just as surprised. She shrugged her shoulders as if to say: Well, there are all sorts of people coming to this place. "Plus ten per cent for service," she said, raking in my money. The change came careening toward me across the desk. "Do you want to wait here for your escort or do you want to go upstairs right now?" she asked me. "I would like to go to my room as soon as possible; I am alone," I said, afraid that this admission might yet spoil it all. "Alone?" the lady asked. "You mean you want the room for yourself alone? Say—you haven't been in Vienna before, have you?"

"I was born in Vienna," I said, afraid again that she might demand some documents of legitimization. But all she said was, "All right—just sign the name here," as she crossly shoved a guest book toward me. "Police orders, you know." I was interested to note that only people with very ordinary names frequented this hotel. Meier and wife. Huber and wife. Mueller and wife. My own name looked lonely and forlorn between all those coupled ones, although I affected strong, bold letters. "Franz, take her up into Seven. If anyone should still come for you I'll send him upstairs," the woman said with a wink and a grin that shocked me, they sprang so unexpectedly from her gloomy face.

The winding stone stairs were polished with age, and an ugly design crawled along the walls. The corridor was narrow and smelled of cheap, perfumed soap; so did the room I entered. There was a big bed that took up most of the space, a little washstand with bowl, pitcher, and an oversized chamber pot in the corner, a clothesrack next to the door, and a huge mirror on the wall next to the bed. A few names were cut into its glass as a sign that some of the girls who had occupied this room must have been in the proud possession of diamond rings. I saw all this in the light of a bed lamp with a red-beaded silk shade. The heavy curtains were drawn close, and the air was stifling.

"Anything else the Fräulein wants?" Franz inquired.

"If you could open the windows and draw the curtains back," I said. Franz gave a little whistle. "But you gotta pull 'em close when you undress," he said. "The people across the street peep with opera glasses, and then there is trouble with the police."

He pulled the curtains back, and the sun painted a yellow shaft of dancing dust particles across the room. "How late is it?" I asked, because this was before the invention of the wrist watch, and the little gadget I had pinned to my front was only an ornament and never showed the time. "About four o'clock," Franz said. "We are not half filled up yet. But wait till after business hours." He gave me a quick look. "You've never been here before, have you?" he said. "No, I thought so. I never forget a face." He dawdled around some more until I had a flash of comprehension, brought out my purse once more, and gave him a tip, fifty pennies again. I still can't give tips without getting embarrassed; it must be a remnant of that first day of my independence.

Alone, I took a deep breath and looked down into the narrow street. Children played hopscotch, and two tough-looking guys with caps were leaning at the door of a basement opposite. A policeman stood firmly planted at the corner of Währingerstrasse, a main thoroughfare from where the rumble of street cars, horse-drawn vehicles, the frantic honking of horns, the ringing of bicycle bells, the buzzing of the town wafted in little gusts of noise. A crooked old little woman crouched near the hotel entrance with a basket of flowers in front of her on the pavement.

I turned back into my room and began to undress. In the midst of it I remembered the warning Franz had given me; with many contortions I sneaked up on the curtains and pulled them close. In the choking dark I groped for the electric switch, stubbing my toe and almost falling over my violin case. When the light was finally on, I proceeded to wash myself. I even found a half-used piece of soap with a few dark hairs sticking to it. After I had rubbed my face and hands with that soap, I emanated the same cheap perfumed smell that filled the whole house. As I flung myself down on the bed to rest and contemplate my situation, a new wave of quite another smell enwrapped me. Acetic acid, the acrid odor which all over Austria and the Balkans testifies that an eager pursuit of bedbugs has taken place. I did not care. Bedbugs should be the least of my difficulties and worries. While I was still lying there, undressed and only slightly refreshed, there was a knock at the door, a key was turned, and before I had the presence of mind to say anything, a brisk chambermaid buzzed into the room. I quickly pulled the blanket over me, but she did not even give me a glance. "Towels," she said and deposited two of them on the washstand. "If you want more, it's twenty pennies apiece." She emptied the washbowl into the pail, peered into the emptied pitcher, shook her head, disappeared and returned soon with the pitcher filled. "If you want hot water, ring the bell," she said. She too waited for something. "I brought you towels," she said impatiently. I wrapped myself in the blanket, picked up my purse and paid my tribute of fifty pennies. The chambermaid left. "I'll tell the gentleman that you are in Seven," she said before closing the door. It sounded cryptic.

It was almost five o'clock, and I had not slept all night; I had gone through the nightmare of an examination at the doctor's and I had not eaten anything since the cup of tea Charles had brewed for me the day before. I was not exactly hungry, but I had a headache and a flighty, light-headed feeling all over and a gnawing pain in my stomach. You can't think on an empty belly, Putzi always used to say. I knew that I should have been happy to be free and on my own, but I felt depressed and afraid instead, and I concluded that what I needed was food. This was a problem that kept me pondering for quite some time, but finally I found the solution. I got up and washed once more, because I had a funny feeling, as if that bed had made me unclean. Then I dressed, rang the bell, and sat down on the only chair.

"I'm hungry," I told the chambermaid as she came buzzing in with a preoccupied air. "Could you tell me where I'll get something to eat?"

"I'll send the waiter," she said and disappeared. The waiter was an old man with the air of a pater confessor. "Well, what can we do for the young lady?" he asked, pulling a pencil from behind his ear, licking it eagerly and poising it over his pad. "We have very good champagne, Veuve Cliquot or Mum, if the lady wants me to chill a bottle; there's nothing to make you feel better, that's what I always say—or would the lady prefer some Tokay? We have also——"

"I'm hungry," I said. "Could I have something to eat?"

"Of course, of course, we can send out for a dinner. Grager's Restaurant is right around the corner; there is no better food in the whole of Vienna. To tell you the truth, Herr Grager was chef at Sacher's for many years, and since he left, Sacher's has never quite been what it was before—so shall we say a nice dinner for two—and shall we leave it to Grager to suggest the menu——"

"It's too early for dinner," I said, hot and desperate. "All I want is a cup of tea—and some sandwiches—or ham—or sausage and bread—or something——"

"Oh!" said the waiter. "Oh! Well! I see! Of course! Of course, it could be arranged. But we don't serve any refreshments without drinks. Maybe some port with the repast? Or some sherry? And we'll leave the champagne for later . . ."

The end of it was that I gave him a tip, just to get rid of his confidential false-teeth smile, and he folded his face up like an accordion with all the air gone and left in a huff. I swished past the lady at the desk, muttering that I would be back soon, and went to the Währingerstrasse to look for a place where I could eat in peace—something not too expensive. I did not dare to enter a coffee house or a restaurant without a male escort, but at last I found a dairy shop. It was familiar and cool and clean inside, and I drank buttermilk and ate black bread with butter, which was Good For You, musing all the while that I wouldn't have needed to run away from home to end up at one of those chaste, familiar little marble tables.

The late afternoon had begun to settle over the town when I left the dairy shop. On the way back to my hotel I meditated how I should go about letting my parents know that I was alive and well. I scouted around for a redcap messenger, but although these men usually sat at every street corner waiting for customers, there was not a single one to be found. Besides, I had a dim notion that sending a messenger from the ninth district, where I was, to the first, where my parents lived, would be too expensive for my shrunken funds. I would have to telephone, and I had never telephoned in my life.

Telephone to whom? Telephone how? Families and simple private people did not have telephones, not in Vienna, not in 1912. My father had a telephone in his office, but office hours were over, and I would not have dared to talk to him personally in any case. Herr Krappl had a telephone, but Herr Krappl had gone to Karlsbad for a cure. Szimanszki had a telephone, but to talk to him would result in a hopeless Polish-French-Szimanszki muddle. Shani had no telephone. Putzi had no telephone. The Balbis had no telephone. And there the list of friends stopped.

I might, however, telephone to the opera. It seemed a desperate and hopeless enterprise, but I might succeed in getting one of the Balbi tribe to the telephone, providing they were on duty.

"Still alone?" the lady at the desk said to me when I returned to the hotel. A tense, quiet couple had entered with me through the door. A loud, giggling couple was just in the process of signing "Meier and wife" into the book. Both couples looked at me. Obviously, to be alone was not the correct thing in the Hotel Garni. The red electric bulbs of the sign in front were turned on by now, shedding a glowing light into the narrow street. The sky was clouded, and although it was not dark yet, the day was over and everything had assumed the wilted aspect of a sultry July evening. Suddenly it dawned on me in what sort of a hotel I had happened. And just as suddenly I calculated that it was too late now and that I could not afford to move out and pay for another room in another hotel. "May I use your telephone?" I asked the lady. There was a big contraption hanging on the wall; I eyed it with fear and distrust. "Twenty pennies," the lady said, giving me another wink. She thought perhaps that I was going to summon some company by phone.

To find the number in the book. To crank the handle. To get the connection—first a wrong one and then a wrong one again and finally the opera. To penetrate through walls of departments and secretariats and offices and shouting, disturbed dignitaries, until at last someone understood what I wanted and promised to look for Clara Balbi. To wait through an endless silence, with the operator asking in intervals: "Are you still talking?" And with the lady at the desk, Franz, and the old waiter watching me and wanting to listen in: it was one of the minor hells, and I felt cold perspiration collect on my upper lip and in the nape of my neck and stream down my spine. And then, just when I wanted to give up, there was Clara's voice.

"Hello? . . . Oh, it's you. I didn't quite get the name," she said as casually as if telephoning were the simplest thing in the world.

"Listen, Clara," I shouted into the telephone, standing on

my toes and trying to cover all the distance with my thin thread
of a voice, "I've run away from home."

"You have what?" said the telephone. I threw a haunted look
at the lady at the desk; her mouth had fallen open, and the
waiter cupped a hand to his ear to hear better. "I've left home,"
I yelled into the phone. "I'll tell you everything about it, but
not now. Listen, Clara, send a message to my mother. . . . Yes,
to my mother, right now. Tell her that you talked with me and
that I'm fine . . . I'm fine, I said, yes, sure . . . I'm fine, and
she shouldn't worry, and she'll hear from me, and listen," I added,
defying the whole Hotel Garni, "tell them if they send the
police after me I'm going to kill myself."

"You're crazy, kid," the telephone said. "Plumb crazy. Where
are you now? At Dupont's studio?"

"No," I shouted, "I'm in a hotel. Will you send my mother
the message? That's all I want from you."

"All right, Mony. I'll send my mother to your mother, not
that she'll like it," the telephone said. "But I wish you hadn't
run after your Pied Piper. What are you going to do now?"

That I did not know myself, but I didn't feel like acknowledging it. "I'll see you tomorrow and explain it all to you," I
yelled. The telephone murmured good night, called me a fool
and a lunatic, and subsided. I hung the receiver into its hook
and dried the sweat from my face. My knees had gone wobbly.

"Makes forty more pennies," the lady behind the desk said.
"You talked nine minutes."

Spent and exhausted, I returned to my room. I undressed,
washed in the bit of water that was left in the pitcher, and went
to bed. I turned out the light, closed my eyes, and tried to sleep.
But I was too tired, and the air was so thick I could not breathe.
I reached out of my bed and pulled the curtains back. The red
light of the sign painted a pool of magenta on my bed sheets.
A few of the glaring letters were reflected in the big mirror
on the wall, and I stared at them, dimly disturbed. I lifted my
arm and dropped it. The mirror doubled the movement. I sat
up and looked at myself in the glass. How crazy to hang a
mirror so that you can watch yourself while you are asleep, I
thought in my innocence. Well, Marion, I thought, closing my

eyes, not a very successful day altogether. But we'll learn, we'll learn to be on our own and free and independent. Relaxing, I began to laugh. Quite a day, I thought. In the morning Dr. Popper poked his dirty rubber fingers into me to find out that I am still a virgin. At night I am going to sleep in a dirty place, in a dirty bed that has seen all sorts of vice. Going to sleep— alone. Good night, Marion. What an absurd person you are.

The walls had begun to sigh and to giggle, there was a thump on the ceiling, the splashing of water next door; someone with rustling skirts whispered along the corridor, and then a signal was whistled in the street. I closed my eyes, and when I opened them again it had gone almost dark outside. A little later it began to rain with an even, calming, swishing sound, and the sign "Hotel Garni" grew brighter as the evening became night.

I thought how it would be if the door should open and Charles should come in and lie down beside me. My skin felt lonely and was craving for him. "Some night I'll carry you over a marble threshold," Charles had told me, "and there will be candlelight in the hall of an Italian palazzo and an ocean of roses. You are so young, Marion," he had told me. "We have time, everything will happen at the right moment, at the right place, in beauty. . . . "

It was at this point that the bedbugs commenced their nightly revelry. I began to scratch and to itch and to hunt them to no avail, and I got angry, and at last I beat my retreat. I moved out of my bed and left the battlefield, stained with blood, to my bedfellows. I was very tired. I wanted to sleep. My eyes were drooping. I wrapped myself in my coat and sat down on the chair. I sprawled my legs and propped my head against my violin case on the little table, and after a short while I was asleep: an innocent stranger in the cheerful Babylon of the Hotel Garni.

WHEN I CAME to see Charles the following morning he was waiting outside on the street for me, looking pale and anxious, and he told me that he had worried himself sick about me. He kissed me and he told me how much he loved me and he had a lovely breakfast prepared for me, for Charles belonged to the race of perfect lovers who always know when you are hungry or thirsty, when tired, when gay, when you want to be kissed, when to be silent, and when to discuss the Higher Things. After he had fed me and put a cigarette between my lips I felt fine, until he told me that my father had visited him and demanded that he should marry me. "Is that what he told you?" I said feebly. "That's horrible, Charles. What did you say?"

"I told him the truth. I gave him my word of honor that there was nothing between us but the most beautiful friendship. But I don't think he believed me. He insisted that I had seduced you. Unfortunately I couldn't promise him to marry you. But I promised to send you home posthaste."

"You know that I'll never go back, never, never. I'm through with all that. I am free at last," I said.

Charles began pacing up and down nervously, a strand of hair coming down over his forehead, half covering his right eye. He looked like a decadent son of Wagner's Wotan. "Look here, Marion," he said, "I'm no Sir Galahad. I've always despised damsels in distress, especially if I've got them into it. You seem to have illusions about me to which I can't live up. I refuse to be burdened with your problems or trapped into any obligations. I don't want you to run away from home on my account, and I don't want to be responsible for something so silly and childish. I have been careful not to touch you, haven't I? I haven't done you any harm so far——"

"Wait," I said, "don't go on. You sound like a damned book-keeper or a lawyer or something. You've been careful—Jesus, how careful you've been! All right. I didn't ask you to be held responsible for anything I am doing. I am I, and this is my own life. I am free, I love you, and I want to stay with you. You can do with me what you want—except send me back."

"What do you want from me?" Charles shouted. "What did you think when you ran away and came to me with your suit-cases? What do you want me to do with you? Keep you here, make a habit of it, get it all drab and dirty? Kill the butterfly and pin it to the others in my collection? Blot out the colors, clip the wings of a bird of paradise? Make another Susanne of you? Free love—I had so much of it, it spoiled my appetite forever. Free love, indeed! What a mess!"

"Well then, let's get married. It's only a formality. It wouldn't make any difference," I said bravely. Mind you, we were the mauve decade and the flaming youth, and Free Love with capitals was one of our pet causes. But if marriage was the only way to stay close to someone you loved, I was ready to compromise.

"Oh yes, you would mind," Charles said. "You would mind horribly having a husband and being a wife. Cooking meals and washing diapers and nursing babies—you? Marion? Make me paint rich, fat, ugly ladies so I could pay the market bill? Give up your career and mend my socks? Never." He sat down at the table and absent-mindedly began to poke his spoon into the empty eggshell. "Besides," he said after a moment's hesitation, "besides, I am married."

They say that people who are hanged die with a grin—and people who get tangled up in a high voltage, or people who are killed by a stroke of lightning. I think I grinned.

"No," I said, stupefied.

"Oh yes," Charles said, and he too grinned. "I told you so the first time I met you. Don't you remember? It's the first thing I tell a girl when I feel that I am falling in love. It's only fair that the girl should know what chances she takes with me."

I had been drowning for a few seconds, but I came up to the surface and gasped for breath. Quite incoherently I suddenly remembered the sock with the hole pulled over Susanne's hand.

"Is it—Susanne?" I asked.

"Susanne? Of course not. You must have no great opinion of my taste. No, my wife is a very mondaine, very well-dressed lady, très chien, as they say in Paris. You want to see a photo of her? With the children?"

"Thanks," I said grimly. "I'm not curious."

What made the whole scene slightly ludicrous was the fact that Charles had a tiny bit of eggshell sticking to his lip. I couldn't help staring at it fascinatedly. I wished he would wipe it off.

But you can't say in the midst of cataclysm: "Please wipe your mouth, you have eggshell on it." Charles sat down at my side and put his arms around me. I shrank back, and yet I felt better, my body felt better the moment he touched me. There is a strange sort of constancy, of loyalty, in our bodies. They keep on yearning and being in love long after our lovers have left us or have died, long after our conscious mind has turned away and given up and even begun hating instead of loving.

"Look here, Marion, my darling, my love, you can't say that I lied to you. I never did. To remain silent is something different from lying, isn't it?" he said. (There it was again, his queer pedantry and lopsided logic.) "What good would it have done to spoil our few hours by drawing my marriage into it? They are in Paris, Antoinette and the children." (So her name is Antoinette and she is très chien, a mondaine French lady.) "I see her maybe once a month, and it's all very smooth and polite and it doesn't mean a thing in my life. A burnt-out volcano. A mountain of ashes, that's all it is. Can I help it that I knew her before I knew you? You see, she gave me my first break; she had me paint her portrait when I was still a pupil of Legandre, she has been married before, she left her husband on account of me, she helped me a lot in my career, she comes from an old French family and has very important connections, we are friends, that's all—friends, companions. You can't be jealous of an old friendship, it wouldn't be like you." (You don't make babies with a friend, I thought bitterly.) "All that takes place in another world, on a different planet, it has nothing to do with us, Marion, please, please, you must understand me, you must be broad-minded, don't look so stony, come, give me your hands, they are cold, poor little paws, and you look like an old-fashioned mermaid by Boecklin, with all those cold colors in your face, greens and blues only, you don't want me to change my palette, do you? Marion! I love you, I love you so. . . ."

Men always demand from girls that they be broad-minded. It's one of the hardest tasks in life, and you can't be trained early enough for it. I suppose I should have turned my back and left Charles right then and there. But love is not like that. Love is to do the wrong thing and to know that it is wrong and keep on doing it just the same. Besides, there was a good deal of submission under man's wishes bred into me, as a good nose is bred into a setter and speed into a thoroughbred. It will take a few hundred years to uproot it in the females of the future—and then I am not sure whether they will be happy about it or not. We are funny plants, we women, and we need a few spells of frost to make us bloom.

And so I cried a bit and then I pinched my cheeks to get color into them and I climbed obediently onto my little platform, wrapped myself in the red cashmere shawl, took on my pose, and sat for two hours. I felt rather proud of the enormous amount of broad-mindedness I was capable of producing on such short order. I also promised to return to my parents, although I was resolved to do nothing of the sort. I had my pistol and I was going to put an end to a life that had turned out to be a very disappointing and disgusting business. There was an embarrassing little moment before I left, when I had to ask Charles to lend me some money. He was embarrassed too; he dug into his pockets and drawers and into the little flower pot where he used to keep a few gold coins. Finally he unearthed twenty kronen and put me on my way, suitcases, violin, and all. It was the first time that I had asked him to let me go home alone.

Charles stepped back on the sidewalk when the fiacre began to move. "Tomorrow then? The same time?" he called after me.

"Tomorrow!" I called back. I was blown up like a balloon with scorn and irony. Tomorrow at this time I'll be dead, I thought. It was a sharp, cutting thought, and it made me lonelier than I had ever been before. I was going to commit suicide, and my lover had not the faintest premonition of anything. There he stood, smiling and waving and perfectly at ease. That was how little people knew about each other. I kept on looking back at him until we turned the corner and a sudden stinging rush of tears blotted him out.

But I did not kill myself that day. That is, I made all sorts of preparations. I went to the best hotel on the Ring, wrote my farewell letters, put the muzzle of my pistol to my temple, and pulled the trigger. But my gun did not go off. Click. I was still there.

I suppose the friendly old gentleman who had sold it to me was a good psychologist. I suppose he had read the threat of suicide in my much too young face and given me cartridges that didn't fit or something. I've never touched a gun since, and I am no expert in firearms. I wouldn't know why the contraption didn't work; but praised be the old gentleman, for it is fun to be alive.

I got up as soon as my feet would carry me, dressed myself, threw my farewell letters into the toilet, and flushed them down. I was through with it. I could take a deep breath and begin to live all over again.

Love is over when we see our partner as all the world sees him: not the enchanted vision we carried in our heart, but the plain, flat person he really is. As long as I was in love with Charles he was the man who had stepped out of a dream landscape, the eternal stranger, mysterious and full of danger. He had been a genius and I his inspiration. He had been one of the great lovers of all times and I had been the one he loved. Our love had been greater and higher and deeper and more indestructible than anybody else's love. But now I wasn't in love any more and I knew better.

He wore socks with holes in them. He slept on grayish, crumpled bed sheets and he rubbed his scalp with nettle oil because his hair had begun to get thin. He was a flamboyant but mediocre painter. He had a wife and children like anybody else, and there was no mystery about him at all. He was a calculating, cautious opportunist at heart. He had charm, yes, and he had been in love with me for a while as he had been in love with many others. It was over and I was through with him.

To amputate a first love is a painful operation and takes time. For a while I still missed him, and then it was only my skin, my blood, my body that kept on being hungry, and then I only dreamed about him. And then that was over too. I woke up one morning and my ears were wet because I had cried in my sleep and the tears had streamed down my face. But I could not remember the dream or why I had cried. And I promised myself that love should never hurt me again, never. And a few months later I went to bed with the conductor Kant—par dépit as the French call it—just to get rid of that cursed virginity of mine. I daresay Kant was rather unpleasantly surprised to find me as innocent as I turned out to be. But he handled the situation with tact and experience. When it was all over I lay in bed and looked up at the ceiling, and, like millions of girls before me, I thought: Is that all there is to it? And that's what they are making all that fuss about?

SOMEONE ought to have gazed into a crystal ball and told me that 1913 was going to be a tough year for me. Come to think of it, it was the last year when one could have bad luck individually. It seems to me that ever since bad luck and misery of all sorts have become a collective experience. If an organism is sick, each and every cell will be part of the sickness. After that year the world entered its drawn-out illness and we stopped suffering singly and did it by the millions, all from the same ills at the same time, and what happened to us individually became insignificant and without any weight.

It began as an unsuccessful season with unfriendly write-ups and half-empty concert halls. That was bad, because Herr Krappl had got me tangled up in a meshwork of contracts that burdened me with high risks. When I signed them I had only a vague idea what they meant, and in my whole life I've never learned to read a contract to its bitter end or to get any enlightenment out of it for that matter. I was left working hard without pay, and I used up my little savings on top of it, what with hotel bills and taxis and tips and evening gowns and hairdressers.

It was in Amsterdam that they handed me a telegram just before I went out on the platform to play Mozart's Concerto in A Major:

MAMA VERY ILL AFTER OPERATION WANTS TO SEE YOU PLEASE RETURN AT ONCE URGENT YOUR FATHER.

I rushed home as fast as possible—which wasn't very fast in any case. When I arrived my mother was dead.

"Why didn't you let me know about the operation?" I whispered.

"She didn't want to disturb you on your tour," my father said. I felt a sharp, stinging sadness, and for a few seconds I hoped I would be able to cry. But no matter how hard I tried I felt stunned and empty.

The funeral took place on a cold, clear, sunny morning, and during the night there had been a frost. The grass on the grave mounds and the evergreen of the cypresses was covered with a fine silvery film, and all mourners breathed little puffs of steam into the air. There was something gay and even hilarious in the riot of sunshine and blue sky and glittering foliage over the cemetery. The funeral was absurd as most funerals are, and the speeches contained much nonsense about my mother and no truth at all, and when all silk hats came off in one gesture I couldn't help being reminded of the chorus of a musical comedy. The Dobsberg-Sommer clan was assembled in full force and did not quite know how to treat me: as the black sheep of the family or as the dark horse that had made good.

"What are your plans now?" my father asked me when we were back home and the last condoling handshakers had left.

"If you want me to stay with you for a while I will be able to arrange it," I answered politely.

"No—er—I did not count on that. You have given me no reason to count on you in any situation," my father said querulously. "In fact, I have made dispositions of some sort and I will need your room for the lady who is going to be my housekeeper. She is a lady. I can't let her sleep in the table-bed."

"So much the better," I said. "I'll pack my things."

And that was that.

In December Putzi died of what he had treated as a little cold but what was pneumonia. By and by I'll get used to trekking out to the cemetery and not being able to cry, I thought grimly. I looked around me and I was very lonely. A month later I was in the great train wreck of Wolzinje in which thirty-eight people were killed and more than two hundred wounded. I was among the wounded ones, but the funny part is I don't know how it happened.

I had played that evening in Warsaw, had rushed to the station after the concert and barely caught my train. Dog-tired as I was, I had undressed, wrapped myself in a kimono to avoid too close a contact with my pillow and blanket, and had fallen asleep almost at once. The last thing I remembered was the narrow strips of light gliding by through a chink in the window blinds as we seemed to pass lantern after lantern in leaving the boundaries of Warsaw. There was the usual feverish after-concert confusion of music in my mind; scraps of the Mozart concerto bobbed up and vanished in the darkness. Phrases I had played were repeated again and again inside of my exhausted head, and a full symphony orchestra had installed itself behind my temples and played there in fierce fortissimo. The next thing that happened was that I woke up and someone seemed to hit me over the head. There was a white flash of pain or light or heat and I knew that someone had killed me. Then I was dead for a long time.

When I returned into a dim state of half-consciousness I felt very cold; so cold that for a few minutes I thought that I was burning. There were torches moving in the night, the crackling of flames, the hissing of steam, the moaning of many voices. The white around me was snow that bit into my flesh with its icy coldness. The black was a looming embankment over which the twisted shapes of smashed train cars had spilled. I tried to take a deep breath and couldn't. I wanted to get up and walk away. I didn't like it where I was. An enormous hand, black and big like a giant's, appeared in front of my eyes and gently pressed me down to the cold, snow-covered ground. The voice of someone I could not see said something to me I could not understand. "I want to go, I'm all right," I said. I had no pain and I did not know the meaning of all this. I tried to get up, and then the torches went out as everything turned black. I was dying a second time. It was very pleasant. I remember the tremendous relief I felt as I let myself fall into the blackness. But it's wonderful to be dead, I thought. An echo came from somewhere. Is that what they are making all the fuss about? A line from a

poem I had read once: I opened the gates and passed through
them and closed them behind me. The face of an old lady who
had sat in the third row of the auditorium. A scrap of music.
And nothing, for a long time.

I was still cold and I still felt no pain when I came to once
more, and I still could not take a deep breath. There was the
jingling of bells as I seemed to be gliding through a soft, velvety
nothingness, with the clear, dark sky of the night above me. The
stars were big and close. Drifting along the Milky Way, I
thought. The rough surface of a fur tickled my chin, and a sour
smell rose from it and stung my nostrils. I tried to lift my hands,
which were inside the cover, and touch the fur, but I could not
move them. My fingers were glued together by some sticky substance. The small, abortive effort zigzagged through me with a
lightning stab of pain. After that I lay very still, careful not to
move. There was wet straw under my head. There was the
bitter smell of burned and charred things and the brassy sweetish
odor of blood. There were four other people lying with me in
the straw, covered with peasants' lambskin coats. One of them,
an old Russian, kept on moaning in regular intervals: "O my
God. O my God. O Boje moy." Much later another voice joined
his in French: "Regina, where are you? Regina, où est tu?"
There was no answer, and the first voice went on and on:
"O Boje moy. Boje moy." The clouds around my mind thinned
out, and I realized that we were driving on the sleigh through
the night. Then it began to snow, without a sound, and the
snowflakes clung to my face and melted there and froze to ice
again. The tops of trees were gliding by, white against the dark
sky. I lay very still, so as not to awaken the pain that I felt
lurking behind the thin wall of numb half-consciousness. Once
more the voice asked for Regina. I was sharing my lambskin
with the woman who asked. We were close and cold beneath it.
Suddenly her hands grabbed my shoulder and a new stab of
pain went through me. The hands relaxed and went limp. After
a while I turned my head toward the woman. I saw that she
had died, with broken, wide-open eyes. And then, all of a sudden, in the midst of all these nightmarish goings-on I had a blinding, piercing feeling of reality, as if nothing I had known up to

that moment had been real. This was real and nothing else, this pain, this fear that began to shake me, this utter misery, this helpless being-cut-to-pieces and carried off.

I don't know how long it took the sleigh to reach the little town of Wolzinje, but during that ride I learned one of the most important lessons of my life: to make yourself empty, to extinguish yourself like a light, to step outside of yourself whenever pain or hardship becomes too great to be endured. The moment you give yourself up, everything becomes easy and bearable. It's some sort of a mental anesthetic, I think. Or it is the trick all small, defenseless animals know by instinct: to roll up and pretend to be dead, until the danger is over.

Wolzinje was a small town that existed only on account of its military garrison. The tiny military hospital whence we were taken was in no way equipped for the emergency. It was dingy and damp, the walls were sweating, it reeked of urine and men and leather boots. It did not even have electric lights, and what was called the operating room was a good fifty years behind the times. We were lined up on mattresses and stretchers on the floor of a corridor and taken in, three and three, to be examined and treated. We were an amazingly quiet lot, except for the old Russian who kept on moaning to God. Out of the night the male staff had conjured some Catholic sisters, who walked among us and bent down, murmuring little consoling words in Polish. One of them had a syringe and gave hypodermics to those who insisted on being noisier than the rest. But on the whole it is surprising how well people will behave in a catastrophe. I suppose that I was a comparatively slight case, for I was among the last group taken into the surgery, and while the doctor attended to my injuries the white dawn began to rise from the snow-covered grounds outside of the windows.

They had run out of anesthetics by that time, and the doctor set my broken wrist without the soothing help of any. It was a pretty grim business, but I was not quite clear enough to feel it to its full extent. I had a cut across the head, and the doctor thought my skull might be fractured, but owing to the lack of X-ray equipment he could not make sure of it. I had a concussion in any case, and a few ribs were cracked. They shaved my hair off and poured iodine into the cut and stitched it up, and they wrapped me in bandages and put my right arm into a cast.

Dr. Blumenthal was very proud of himself. He was a swarthy, bony, dangling structure of a man, stuffed into an ill-fitting uniform and with a pair of burning Jewish eyes behind glasses. He spoke something that resembled German and told me that he had studied in Vienna for some time. Considering that only four patients died of the fifty the train crash had dumped into his lap, he had a right to be proud of himself. But I often thought what my life would have been like if a better surgeon than Dr. Blumenthal had set my broken wrist. Or if I had missed that train. Or if I had not gone on that concert tour at all.

It was the beginning of March when I returned to Vienna. My violin had not been found in the wreckage, and I had missed renewing the insurance. I could have used the money, but I could not have played on the instrument anyway. My right wrist was stiff and would remain stiff. My career as a violinist was over. I was poor and I was alone.

Well, Marion, I thought to myself, we've behaved pretty well so far. What are we going to do now?

I WAS YOUNG. I was strong. I was alive. I had lived through a disaster, and it had neither bent nor broken me. I was myself. That was something, wasn't it? I felt it in every vein, that I was I, Marion Sommer, who could take a blow standing up. I've often experienced it since: there is a great part of satisfaction mixed into any catastrophe that befalls us. It means measuring our strength against some power without us, and with every challenge we discover how much fortitude and courage has been buried in us. I looked into the mirror and had to laugh. With the hair sprouting over the scar on my skull I looked like a crossbreed between a nun and a porcupine. My face had grown harder; there was less prettiness and more character in it. I was satisfied with this face; it was my own and it suited me all right.

It felt good, having to start life all over again; there was a drive in it like the strong, swift current of a river.

I looked around for some new way of supporting myself, because I knew one thing for sure: I would not ask anyone for help. I had to pull through on my own strength or I would never trust myself at all.

There were of course the traditional, respectable occupations for young ladies of good families: teaching, being a governess, or a companion to some old lady. I saw myself hanging around strange people's houses, like a ghost of my aunt Caroline, and it made me shiver. I ended up by doing what all the other girls did who had to support themselves without much delay. I would enter a business school and learn to write shorthand and simple accounting and typewriting. The course took six months, and it cost sixty kronen to take it. That left me with one krone a day to live on for the time being. It was quiet and clear now inside of my head, and no symphonies were played behind my temples. To get rid of that eternal Mozart Concerto in A Major alone was worth going through a train crash, six months of great poverty, and the preparations for becoming one of a million stenographers. I took a deep breath and stretched and rolled up my sleeves and I discovered with surprise that I felt happy and contented and filled with an inner peace I had not known before.

Spring came and early summer, with the chestnut trees lighting their pink- and cream-colored candles and the Persian lilacs hanging out their purple plumes.

I lived in the back of a house, where the cobbler Matauschek took in boarders. I shared the room with two other girls, but as one of them worked in a cabaret and came home only in the morning to go to bed, we were not too crowded. We had breakfast together and then two of us left for our work, leaving the room to Minna, who went to sleep. She was, as far as I could make out, entrusted with the ladies' toilet at the cabaret, and she amused us with many shrewd observations about her lady customers. The other girl, with the fancy name of Maja, was a mannequin and had a beautiful figure according to prewar standards. Today, I am afraid, she would be a plump number eighteen.

The house where I lived was respectable and honest, filled with little people and their bustling lives; the butcher, the baker, the candlestick maker. It was a little community all by itself and everybody knew everything about everybody. There was a lot of gossip between the kitchen balconies and a lot of jealousy and begrouching each other's private possessions. But at the same time we all stuck together and leaned on each other and helped each other, and that was something entirely new to me. There was a constant stream of borrowed flour and sugar and lard flowing from kitchen to kitchen; the children who played in the court or on the street were watched and taken care of by all of us, they were community property in a sense. If you were sick, some neighbor would nurse you. If you had worries, the neighbors would give you advice and moderate assistance. If someone died in your family, the neighbors would sit up with you and cry with you and come to the funeral in their best black finery. If you gave birth to a baby all women would be there to help you, to hold you, to boil water, give the newly-born a bath, make coffee for the midwife and console your desperate husband. If you got married, the whole house would take a strong interest in it and adorn your wedding. If your sweetheart let you down, they would take your side and call the curse of heaven down on him.

I felt strong and proud of myself and almost happy. All the mauve hues had gone out of my life, all the febrile beauty and exaltation, but I felt firm ground under my feet. I shared the existence of all the little people in my little street and it gave me a new, warm feeling around my heart. To stand in line takes a lot of loneliness away.

In business school I turned out to be a shining light. After the rigid discipline of becoming a violinist, all this was almost too easy and simple. If one is trained to learn one thing really well, one is trained for all learning. For the first time in my life I had enough spare time left to enjoy myself. There was, first of all, the importance of eating. I was hungry, I had to plan my meals, and every one of them was a feast. I began to think about them when I got up in the morning. During the noon intermission at school I would go to the market; I would walk along the rows of stands, scanning them for the best and cheapest thing there was to be had. The market women sang out their goods, they made jokes and called compliments to you, trying to lure you to their stands and away from the others. Just to look at all the mounds of cherries and new potatoes, of green parsley and crisp lettuce, would make you hungry and gay.

Papa Matauschek was a widower. There was no woman in his household, and he gave us boarders permission to cook our own meals. It was an important part of the deal, for on one krone a day you certainly can't go to a restaurant, and there were no drugstores in Vienna. "What have you got tonight?" Matauschek would say, when I began cooking. "My, what a nice cauliflower. Me, I'm just frying the potatoes left over from yesterday." The kitchen filled itself with the smells of frying lard and onions from Matauschek's cooking, and I got hungrier by the minute.

"Do we need light?" Matauschek would ask every evening. "No, we can move the table to the window," I would give my routine answer. I liked to eat there at the window. It was not quite dark yet, and we had red geraniums in a box outside. In the court somebody played the accordion, and the children were at a game of hide-and-seek. They swooped by with keen little chirps, like swallows learning to fly. Minna bustled into the kitchen, grabbed a bag of cherries she had deposited there, called "Good evening," and bustled out again, to go to work. Maja seldom came home before ten o'clock because she had a boy friend. I set the table and Papa Matauschek brought his fried potatoes over. I lifted my cauliflower from the pot and sat down opposite the old cobbler. Cobbling is one of the less nicely smelling trades, what with glue and leather and old much-worn shoes, but I got so used to that smell that I almost liked it. Papa Matauschek told me interesting things about the feet of people, and I reported about my progress in school. But the moment we began to eat we stopped talking and it was as quiet as at a children's party when everybody is stuffing cake. It tasted good. My, how good it tasted! Sometimes we swapped some of our food, which elevated it at once into a two-course meal. When everything was eaten, I dipped the last bit of butter and bread crumbs from my plate, Matauschek gave a deep sigh, and he went to the sink and washed the dishes. The accordion stopped and began again. Mothers called for their children, and the evening sank swiftly from the small square of sky that closed over our court like the lid of a box. I took my schoolbooks and went into my room to do my homework. Oh for the deep peace of those evenings! For the happiness of the filled stomach and the dreamless sleep! For the contentment of being alone, and not in love, and not wanting anything from anyone!

Have you ever seen the Chinese tumblers at the circus do their tricky Great Pyramid, when the music stops and only the big drum rolls on? There is the groundman, all bulging muscles and strength; there are three men on top of him, two on his shoulders and one standing on the back of his neck. They balance two girls in Chinese costumes against their hips and two younger boys on their heads. The boys hold up a girl by her stiff, straight legs, and the girl balances a chair in one hand. On the chair sits a man who juggles with three golden balls. Well, my budget was a structure like that, tricky, dangerous, and ready to tumble down at the slightest mistake. The golden balls I juggled on top of my financial Great Pyramid came under the term of "extras." Extras were all those unforeseen expenses that bear down so heavily on a tight budget. New soles for my shoes. A new pair of stockings. A book I needed for my course. A bottle of aspirin to keep my regular sore-throat spells in check. Cleaning fluid to keep my gloves and dresses in order. A little gift for Maja's birthday. Two new plates for the ones I had dropped and broken in Matauschek's kitchen. This and that. The obligations that my sort of genteel poverty brought along. I daresay it was still easier than it is for girls today. There were no cosmetics and no permanent waves. We washed one another's hair and dried it in front of the open window. We had a box of rice powder among us, but hardly used it. The worst difficulty of being poor and having to look nice today was still an unknown quantity; namely, a run in the stocking. We wore black cotton stockings with a perforated design called à jour and felt ourselves most alluring in them. They were as hardy as if made of cast iron. And so, with much planning and juggling around, I was able to balance my budget, at least most of the time.

A bad wisdom tooth was enough to bring the whole structure down and plunge me into bankruptcy and ruin. It began during the first week of August with an unpleasant sensation in my jaw. It disturbed me when I worked, took the zest out of my meals, and did not let me sleep. I played around the swollen, throbbing spot with my tongue. I took aspirin. I tried to forget it. "What's the matter with you, kid?" Maja asked me in the morning. "Have you been in a draft or in a fight?"

"Why?" I asked, chewing my bread with the left side of my mouth only. "Look in the mirror," Maja said. I looked, and I saw that my face was so swollen it looked like a lopsided moon. My right eye watered and was small, pinched in by my cheek. My cheek burned and my mouth was gushing with saliva. I touched the funds marked "Extra" and bought myself something the pharmacist recommended for toothache. It cost fifty pennies and did not help. After four days of this I was ripe for the dentist. Minna knew one who was said to be inexpensive and efficient. She even gave up her morning sleep to take me there and talk to him about the price. The dentist was a sleepy-looking man with an Italian organ grinder's sort of mustache. He told me that it was a wisdom tooth and that we should wait. He treated me for a week and then he cut my gums. The second week he found that the tooth had to be dug out from the jawbone and extracted. The tooth broke, and something happened to the jawbone. From then on everything was a throbbing, aching mess, and I had to stay in bed. When violent chills began to shake me, the dentist turned pale, put me into a cab, and delivered me at the hospital. The verdict was blood poisoning.

And so this period ended as it had begun: in a hospital ward. The whole thing convinced me that it is easier to go through a major catastrophe than through a real bad case of toothache. The great pains are always easier to bear than the small ones, and people who would cry about a bee sting will get themselves shot like heroes.

Papa Matauschek cooked outstanding meals for me. Minna and Maja nursed me in shifts. The whole street sat at my bedside, told me the latest gossip, made jokes, comforted me, and worried about me. Suddenly the world was full of friends and kindness. I looked for my loneliness and it was gone. The world was good. The world was a very good place in which to live, to get sick even, and to recover. To make things still better, the door opened one afternoon and Clara entered my room. I had missed her badly all the time while she had been away, startling the beer-drinking audience of a cabaret in Munich with her New Dances. She still looked like the angel with the sword, and just to see her again gave me that peculiar warm tickling of joy around my heart that I had felt when I had met her for the first time, ages ago, in the dairy shop.

"The things that happen to you the moment I turn my back!" she said. "If that isn't the shits."

"Clara, darling!" I cried. "How come you are in Vienna?"

"Great things have happened, great things," she said with mock gravity. "I have come home to pack my bundle for good. I have a three-year contract—three years, baby, three years' work and pay and everything. I finally got hold of the button on Fortuna's cap, as the poet calls it."

She sounded a bit drunk, and she was so alive that it made me dizzy. I could not stand so much vivacity yet. "Tell me," I said feebly. Clara took my hands and turned my wrists, careful, as if they were made of glass. "Show me your paws," she said. "Do they hurt a lot?"

"Not much. Not all the time," I said. "I've got them pretty well used to typing, for instance. Of course I am a living barometer. You could use me for coming out of my little house with a red umbrella and saying 'Cuckoo!' before it's going to rain. I feel it twelve hours ahead. I'm very reliable at that."

Clara had begun to rotate my wrist with a gentle movement. It hurt, and I bit my lips. "You shouldn't have given up your fiddle, you bungler," she said. "All you need is doing this a few hours every day and your wrist will be as good as new. If I make it well again, will you have guts enough to start with your fiddle all over again?"

"No," I said.

"I didn't think you would give up so easily," Clara said sternly.

"It's not that. I have been sick and tired of my fiddling for a long time. I'm glad this happened."

"Ah—that's different," Clara said after she had digested this. "So you think you are cut out to be somebody's stenographer?"

I did not answer, and Clara kept on moving my wrist. She had good hands. "Tell me about that contract," I said.

"Well, baby, you see in me the appointed and acknowledged ballet master of the celebrated Hof-Theater of Bergheim," she said, very dignified.

"Where the hell is Bergheim?"

"It's in southern Germany, you ignoramus, and it's a lovely little town, the sort we cut out and pasted together when we were children. There is an Old Castle and a New Castle, and funny streets and high-gabled houses and a park with black swans on the little lake. And the whole works belong to the Grand Duke, who they say is crazy. He must be crazy, because he saw me dance in Munich and sent one of his baboons with the contract, and I made my debut in his theater and he seems to think that I am the answer to a crazy Grand Duke's dream as far as dancing goes. And his people like best to eat a soup they have kept boiling on their stoves since Napoleon's time; it's called French soup, and the corps de ballet consists of eight old ladies with bunions and gout and eight adenoidal children under sixteen. I mean, you add a bit of water and meat and vegetables each day but you never take the pot from the fire. It tastes divine."

I groped my way through this maze of new information while Clara kept on revolving my wrist. "You mean you are going to leave Vienna and stay away for three years?" I said sadly as I had come to a conclusion.

"Exactly. Don't you wish me luck?" Clara said. It had never occurred to me that one could live elsewhere but in Vienna. You could go on tour, yes, you could work in a cabaret in Munich for a few weeks. But to live anywhere but under the chestnut trees and baroque roofs of Vienna, to breathe any air but the vibrant air of Vienna, which was fragrant with violets, fraught with music, and full of the hard dust that came from our granite cobblestones—it seemed fantastic.

"There," Clara said, putting my hand down on my blanket. "Does it feel better now?"

"It hurts like hell," I said. It had taken all my control not to yell and yelp under her treatment. "Good!" she said contentedly. "When do you think you'll be out of bed?"

"Next week at the latest. I've tried to catch up with my course so that I can take my examination at the end of the summer term and get my diploma—that's two weeks from now. Then I'll have to look around for a job. It's easy to get one. The want ads are full of demands for efficient stenographers." It sounded surer than I felt. I could write shorthand pretty well, but I was unable so far to decipher what I had written.

"No, you ain't," Clara said.

"I ain't what?" I asked.

"Looking for a job," she said. "I've got a job for you. You've got to come with me to Bergheim and help install me there."

"You're crazy," I said.

"I've two railway tickets, paid by my Grand Duke. I need a chaperone, don't I?"

"I am no charity case," I said. Clara smiled at me, amused and very friendly.

"Maybe I am one," she said. "I don't want to go to Bergheim all alone. And the tough luck is that little Salvator has the measles and my mother must stay with him. It's a mean trick of his, getting the measles just when his parents are to be married. It'll spoil their wedding no end."

"Are they?" I asked surprised.

"Yes. Nicki has been disowned by his parents because he refused to marry the young lady they picked out for him. So now it's up to my sister to take care of him, isn't it?"

I contemplated this bit of news and moved it aside as unimportant. "I don't want favors from you," I said stubbornly. "I want to be on my own. I've learned something, and I want to get myself a job, that's all. Thanks all the same. It's sweet of you to try to help me."

Clara got up and patted my hands. "I daresay they will need stenographers in Bergheim too. But do as you please. I don't want to press my point. I'd like to have you along, though; it would make it easier for me to go away from Vienna."

If Shani hadn't proposed to marry me and if it hadn't rained the day I began looking for a job, I might never have gone to Bergheim. But Shani did propose, and that was one reason to get away from Vienna. When I had seen him last he had been on top of the world. He was about to finish his opera Touggourt, and there was even some talk that the Imperial Opera might be interested in it. He had had a haircut. He had a new suit that looked just as crumpled and uncouth as his old one. And he was in love. He clamored for a public telephone to make an urgent call, covered the marble top of the table in the café with sketches of a girl's face, made up of notes. He hummed a sentimental melody. Suddenly he popped the name Susie at me like a gun.

"You must meet her," he said. "You'll like her. She is so sweet and so small, you have never seen such a small girl in your life. She is no heavier than something a little bird would drop in the palm of your hand. That's how small she is, but she is strong all the same. She has the loveliest coloratura voice in the world. Sing a high D flat? That's nothing to her. Sing a high E flat? That's nothing. You must hear her sing the first aria of the Queen of the Night in the Magic Flute. Now I'm coaching her to sing Madame Butterfly. There won't be any Butterfly like hers in the world, whatever you say. I give you Lehmann. I give you Bellincioni. I give you Selma Kurz. You give me Susie. That's all I want. Susie. You must meet her soon, you'll laugh how small she is."

"Well, Shani," I said, delighted with his delight, "this time it really got you, old boy."

"I'm happy, Marion," he said, sweating big drops of embarrassment. "Do you mind?"

I met Susie and I liked her very much; there was a birdlike chirping quality about her, something very blonde and very light, something that was the perfect complement to Shani's clumsy, grave being. Like Adam, he was made of clay and you could see it. But it was the very finest of clay, prime quality. I was glad that Susie seemed just as crazy about him as he was about her. They had secret little names for each other and they could not bear to sit at opposite sides of the table, they had to be close all the time, and as lovers do, they lived in a perfect, round cocoon spun of memories and mutual experiences and of a thousand insignificant things that meant all the world to them. I was locked out, the disturbing, superfluous third, and I let myself gently slip away and out of Shani's sight. There goes a good, nice friendship, I had thought to myself, happy for Shani yet with a tiny sting of jealousy, as we all feel when our best friends fall in love or get engaged or marry. But I had been wrong. He came to visit me two days after Clara, and he looked as browbeaten as if the score of Touggourt had been destroyed in a fire.

"How are you?" I said. "Nice of you to look in on me, Shani."

"How are you yourself?" he said. "Not as strong as the Rock of Gibraltar exactly, eh?"

"I'm fine," I said. "I'm perfect."

"Well," he said, "well—I'm glad you are."

He looked at his feet in his new shoes and at his fingers, and then he shot a quick glance at me, and then he looked away again, and then he began plucking hair from his bushy eyebrows.

"How is Susie?" I asked.

"Oh, Susie. She's all right, I suppose," he said listlessly.

"What's the matter with you, Shani?" I asked him. "Did Susie let you down?"

"Look here, Marion," he said, using my full name instead of calling me a stinking little rabbit as usual, "look here, we've been friends for a long time, haven't we? Yes, we've been friends, always. Do you remember that time after the graduation concert when I tried to kiss you? Well, I did it because I was in love with you. Don't you know?"

"Well——" I said, not knowing what to make of it.

"I am still in love with you," said Shani. "I have been in love with you all these years. I have a steady income, I can take care of a wife and a family now. I want you to marry me."

It sounded as if he had learned it by heart. There was not a spark of life in it. My mouth fell open with surprise.

"What about Susie?" I said.

He played a chord into the air. "Oh, Susie," he said. "It's all right with Susie. She was just an—just an episode."

Poor Shani; he was the worst liar in the whole world. He took out his handkerchief and dried the sweat from his forehead.

"She knows that I am asking you to marry me," he added. "It's quite all right with her."

Bless little Susie, bless her tiny great heart of a canary bird! In a flash I understood it all, the whole, crazy magnanimity of it. Susie had agreed to give up Shani in order that he should save my life because I had a broken wrist and couldn't play the violin, see, while she had the best coloratura voice in the world.

"You're crazy, Shani," I shouted. "I'm sorry, but you're stark, plumb crazy. I like you very much and I think you are almost a genius, but I can't marry you."

"You can't?" he said with a glimmer of hope in his voice. "Why can't you, lassie?"

"I hope I was a better liar than Shani, but I don't remember exactly what stories I told him. It was something magnificent, such as that I was in love with a wonderful man, a wealthy man and a fine man, and that I was almost engaged to him and that I would leave Vienna—this came to me in a flash—to get married to this man who lived in Germany. I could see Shani coming back to life; it was as good as bringing a man his reprieve the evening before his execution. He tried damned hard to act disappointed, but it just did not come off. "Well, lassie, if you don't want me, I guess I'll have to take Susie after all," he said, forgot his hat, ran away, came back for it, kissed me, stumbled over a chair, reached the door, and was gone.

It rained the day I went out to look for a job. The streets were as dirty as only streets in Vienna can be, the town where the Occident ends and the Orient begins. There was a cold wind, flinging wet, dirty pieces of paper into my face, and my shoes, which for lack of money were not resoled, were soaking and made sucking noises at every step. I waited in many lines, introduced myself to many unpleasant people—for a day like that one makes them all seem unpleasant—and was refused at every place because I had no office experience. I was wobbly and weak and exhausted and, to make things worse, I met Cousin Hermann in the rain. I stood there under my umbrella, from which my private torrent rushed down on me, and waited for a bus, because I had given up and decided to waste ten precious pennies for a ride. It was there that Cousin Hermann saw me and stopped his car at the curb. "Why, if it isn't Marion," he said. "Come, I will take you along if it isn't too much out of my way."

He was pompous as ever and he was sorry for me. He said so and kept harping on it. "I really felt sorry for you when I saw you standing in the rain," he said. "I felt very sorry. You looked so forlorn and unhappy. I simply could not drive by in my own car and let you stand there. You know, I almost drove by without recognizing you? This can't be Marion, I said to myself, this bedraggled, poor creature. Well, well. I suppose you've got what you wanted. You've made your choice, and if things did not turn out as you hoped they would, you have no one to blame but yourself. I am sorry for you all the same, I don't hold anything against you. By the way, did you hear that I am engaged to be married? Yes, yes, that's life. But I could not let you stand in the rain and just drive by——"

"This is my corner," I said. "Let me get out, and thanks for the ride." I stepped out and directly into a deep stream of muddy water. It came way up over my ankles. I stopped to open my umbrella, and the wind gripped it and turned it upside down, with me sailing after it. Such things will always happen to me at the appropriate moment. Cousin Hermann drove past me, waving an upholstered hand and spattering me with mud. I wanted to cry for a moment, but, as always in such situations, something snapped inside of me, I could see myself like a funny figure on a movie screen, and I began to laugh instead.

When I came home Clara was waiting for me. "I'm leaving for Bergheim next Monday," she said. "Are you coming with me or not?"

"Did you say they have black swans in the park?" I asked feebly.

"Yes, they have black swans and little high-gabled houses, and the streets are so clean you could eat from them, and the Grand Duke's coat of arms is laid in at the sidewalks around the palace, sort of like mosaic, it's very cute. And they cook French soup——"

"How is the weather there?" I asked. Clara looked at my soaking countenance and began to grin. "Beautiful," she said. "They have the most beautiful weather you have ever seen, sunshine always, every day of the year, so help me God."

So that is how I happened to leave my town and my country and the little bit of a past I had accumulated between fourteen and seventeen and how I started life all over again.

3

AFTER MICHAEL HAD GONE to see Christopher off, Marion sat around for some time with limp hands, confused and rather unhappy. The sun had lapped up the last puddle of mist, and the mountains across the lake stood clear against the noon azure of the sky. She tried to get some peace from the familiar sight, some consolation, some assurance, some of the things her grandfather had called the equilibrium. But things didn't want to make much sense just then. Everybody seemed just as confused and unhappy as she was herself; even wise old Hammelin, pottering around his cold bellows and cleaning his venerable old rifle, had seemed to stand on wobbly ground lately. Marion had a notion to go into the village and visit the old man in his forge, lean against the half-door and have a nice little chat with him. But she gave up the idea. She didn't want to meet Christopher there by any chance, and she was afraid Hammelin might have nothing to offer that would make her feel better about things in general.

She got up with a deep sigh and stretched a few times as she had learned to do from close acquaintance with cats. For God's sake, let's do something, not just sit and mope about, she told herself. She wandered aimlessly out onto the gallery and back into her room again until at last she stumbled onto the right idea. I'll carve a little likeness of Nero, she thought; it will please Michael.

She went downstairs and into the little barn that served as her workshop to look for the toolbox she had not used for quite some time. At last she found the piece of pearwood that she had kept there for just such an improvisation. She began weighing one knife after another in the crook of her fingers until she found the one that suited the mood of the pearwood and her own, and then she began to whittle away.

Marion knew nothing so soothing as the feel of a familiar tool in her hand. Her fingers touched the wood to test it for its grain, its texture, its hardness, its willingness to submit to the knife without breaking and to let a new form be created from it. It's a good piece of midwifery, she thought: extracting from the shapeless womb of the material the little creature that lives in it. Give birth to the lovely, the funny, the abstruse, the fantastic shapes that are concealed in every rock and stone, in every stump of wood, every lump of clay, on the face of every empty gray canvas. It's satisfying and exciting, like that dream game all children play when they look at clouds. There are bodies and animals and sailboats and turreted towering castles hidden in every cloud, and faces and birds and flowers in the cracks of every wall. She turned and tested her piece of wood, eager to bring it to life.

It was an old custom between Marion and her children that she would carve something funny for them whenever they had got hurt. So, now that Nero was dead and Christopher was going away, it was the right moment to make a tiny St. Bernard dog for Michael. She pictured him coming home after saying farewell to his best friend and from Nero's funeral, trying not to let her notice how blue he felt. He would make a few poor jokes and then he would mutter something and disappear into his room under the roof. That was when he should find her little gift and begin to feel much better at once. Marion was eagerly bent on making something funny and amusing out of Nero. A tender caricature of all St. Bernardish qualities: broad heavy paws, big head, drooping jaws faintly reminiscent of Queen Victoria, coarse, shaggy coat, and a brandy keg tucked under his double chin; a piece of pearwood turned into that canine essence of clumsy and embarrassed kindness: a St. Bernard. She might have carved a caricature of Christopher as well—but that would be too obvious, Marion thought.

At a certain turn of her life and quite incidentally Marion had made a career for herself and a name as a wood carver. For her, each little piece of wood had its own inner life, its own texture, its own secret, its own scent. The pearwood was light of color, like the sun-bleached hair of country children, rather soft, and it had a summerly, fruity smell. This mingled with the brisker fragrance of the simple furniture in her room, which the village carpenter had made of aspen wood. The love and understanding of wood was about the only thing Marion had inherited from the Dobsberg clan.

The chips splintered away under Marion's busy fingers, and she smiled as she thought that this was the last trickle of the great stream that had been her family's love and livelihood: wood. Her mind, released of much weight, drifted off again, way into the past. Funny how many little things I can remember, she thought, while Nero slowly took shape under her fingers. I didn't even know I had them stored away in some corner of my memory, each one in its place, each one wrapped in cellophane, and as I unpack them they come to light, one by one, looking as good as new. I didn't think of all that for many years, I suppose I never had time to go so far into my past. Somehow all this together must make some sense; it can't all have been planless, haphazard living. Still it looks to me like Michael's box with the cat. When he started to study biology in Heidelberg his professor gave him a box filled with numberless little bones. "This, my young friend, is a cat," he told him; "I give you the parts, you put them together"—and a cat it was in the end.

That's what I mean. In the end it all must make a whole, even if it looks like a puzzle game just now.

BERGHEIM was a picture-book town sitting smack in the center of a picture-book country. The air was blue with autumn when arrived there. The fields around the town were a tiny, checkered patch in the bigger patchwork of the many small states of which Germany was made. It took a moderately fast train three hours to cross the whole state, and across the border there was another just such little country belonging to another just such paternal grand duke, residing in just such a high-gabled little town. The hills were fuzzy with forest, beech trees and oaks, burning with the warm colors of sherry and port wines. The Rhine wound its way along the edge of the town, and the old bridge leaped across it, planting gray strong feet firmly in the midst of the river. The statue of St. Francis stood in the middle of the bridge, and there was always a bright bold bunch of flowers in front of it, brought by the peasant women who came from the outlying country into town. An old cathedral was mirrored in the river, and it was fun to look from the bridge down into the water and watch little boats row through the reflection of steeples and rose windows. One tower was high and beautiful; the second one was only a stump with a dull slate roof slapped on its top and never finished. The people of Bergheim were gay, cheerful, and happy by nature. Most wine-growing people are, I found out. There were many orchards too, bearing heavily when I saw them first and surging, wave after wave of white and pink frothing blossoms, against the town when the spring came. There had never been a spring like the spring of 1914; at least that is what the old peasants told us. There was such an abundance of bloom as never before, a glorious jubilation on every branch and twig, a promise of wealth in the tiniest garden patch as well as in the Grand Duke's parks and crown farms. After the blossom time was over, the trees were so heavy with the green little buttons of unripe fruit that every one of them had to be supported and made secure. They looked like an army of peglegged men marching on crutches toward the town. Meanwhile the haulms came up in the fields and there was much talk of raising the best crop anyone could remember. The Grand Duke drove proudly around in his new automobile, inspecting his own fields and those of his subjects, and the people stood at the roadside, took off their caps and shaded their eyes, cheering and smiling back at him. As the automobile disappeared in a dun-colored cloud they felt elated and honored to swallow the dust of the royal car and to have their ruler share their hopes: There would be fine apples and good wine and plenty of potatoes and rye and wheat.

It is difficult today to recall the perfect contentment of those days and the general feeling of being one happy family. True, the Grand Duke was on top and the little tenant farmer at the bottom, but still they were molded after the same cast and essentially not very different. The Grand Duke had the round head, the high cheekbones, the blue-gray eyes, and the dark hair prevalent among his subjects. He had their sort of humor and spoke their dialect, a good-natured, humorous, soft dialect, good to make fun of oneself or to make love in. On Rhine Street stood the high column on which the royal ancestor Grand Duke Hugo the Kind was perched, wearing the outfit of a Roman emperor and covered with pigeon droppings. East of the center of the town the old parts of Bergheim sloped down toward the Rhine. West of it there was the new town with the New Palace, the New University, the New Theater, and the hillcrest of Oden-berg, where a colony of modern architects had scattered an odd assemblage of flat-roofed, vile-colored public and private build-ings.

Beyond Odenberg, where the hill ran down into a sandy flat that was said to be the bottom of some prehistoric ocean, the less attractive and more utile parts of the town were hidden. The gas and power plants, the big chemical plant of Heil & Warburg, Hewa for short, the barracks and the training grounds. The settlements of the workers, the freight depot, and another one of the Grand Duke's toys: a military airfield with hangars and a small fleet of rickety-looking planes in which young officers juggled around.

It was known that the Grand Duke hated any military display and endeavor and that he disliked his cousin, the Kaiser, from the bottom of his heart. There occurred a little scandal that spring, when the Kaiser came for a visit and the Grand Duke was too late for the military parade because he had missed the time, watching a ballet rehearsal in the theater. His surprised subjects saw him sprint down the street, dressed in a general's uniform, his chest covered with cutlery, catching a street car for the parade grounds and then fumbling in his pockets for a coin to pay his fare. As grand dukes habitually carried no money with them, butcher Wiegele, one of the passengers, offered devotedly to help him out. "Why, that's very kind of you," the Grand Duke said. "You are butcher Wiegele, aren't you? I have often enjoyed your liverwurst. It's the best in town."

"At your service, Your Royal Highness," butcher Wiegele replied. "May I take the great liberty of submitting to Your Highness a little sample of my new sausage called Bergheimer Delight?"

He did so and was awarded the title of Royal Court Butcher and the permission to paint the Grand Duke's coat of arms on the sign over his butcher shop. The local papers told the little story, and the subjects loved their Grand Duke the more for it. They did not like the Prussians and their big-mouthed fool of a Kaiser, and they were pleased that Hugo had let him wait on the hot, sunny, dusty parade grounds.

The Grand Duke was comparatively poor, although the country was rich and fertile. The people paid their moderate taxes without too much grumbling or cheating, and the tax authorities, in return, were lenient with delinquent payers. It was said also that the Grand Duke used for the good of the country every nickel of the appanage appropriated to him and his family. He gave the university a new wing and a well-equipped laboratory, for chemistry was one of the things in which he took a little boy's burning interest. He bought a painting by Dürer for the museum he had installed in the Old Palace. He had roads improved because he himself loved to drive his car at the breakneck speed of thirty-five kilometers an hour, and he founded a public library because he believed in books. Though he spent money only for those things which interested him and which he liked, so that the whole town and country reflected his own personality and moods, he still spent it freely and generously on anything he believed worth while and kept nothing for himself. His own life was simple, and he covered his personal expenses, like any other country squire, from the output of his farms and forests. He was a lovable, tall, smiling fellow in the middle of his thirties, followed by a shy, scampering, inconspicuous shadow, his wife. Grand Duchess Eleonore had been a little country princess; she had a pinched face and a bad complexion, like most princesses she was badly dressed, and the intellectuals of the town chuckled over the bloomers she pulled when the Grand Duke introduced some of his artists or scientists to her. The simple people on the streets and in the market stalls liked her, though. They said that Helena was kind and, in her unobtrusive way, did a lot of charity. Also she had done her duty by giving the country two little princes who were just as headstrong, amiable, and handsome as their father.

I saw the Grand Duchess for the first time at one of the many balls that were given between New Year and Lent in that pleasure-loving town. Clara showed her to me.

"Look—that's her," she said, nudging me with her elbow.

"Her—who?" I asked.

"The Grand Duchess. The one over there—with the old black velvet dress and the cotton gloves. Why in heaven's name does she wear those bedraggled aigrettes in her coiffure? Couldn't somebody tell her personal maid that they need steaming up to bring them back to life?" Clara said, keeping her eyes glued to the little figure.

"What do you care how her aigrettes look?" I asked, surprised.

"I wonder why he ever married her," Clara said instead of an answer. There was an expression on her face I had never seen there before, but I forgot it in all the fun we had that night and only recalled it many months later.

The ball took place in the old Assembly Hall, a fine rococo building with yellow damask hangings and huge crystal chandeliers. You had to keep on dancing all the time because there was no heating system in the ancient edifice, and the cold wind of a January night blew through the high french windows, billowing the hangings and turning you into an icicle the moment you sat down. My dancer of the evening was Howard Watson, a young Englishman whom I had met a short while ago. He had the perfect, just a little flat beauty of a young, blond Apollo and had come to Bergheim to study German literature or something. Bergheim was full of young Englishmen, because the Grand Duke's mother had been an English princess. He himself loved anything British, and his frequent travels in Scotland, Ireland, and England were good propaganda for his little town, whether he knew it or not. Howard's German was limited, and I did not know a word of English. But we got along fine, with laughter and glances and signs and little sketches he drew on my fan. He took me in a close grip and taught me the sensational new dance, the tango. It was shockingly intimate, yet there was a spiced, floating pleasure in the new rhythm that no waltz had ever given me. After dancing three tangos with Howard I felt that I had fallen in love with him. I was happy about it, because I had been not-in-love for too long.

"Du gefällst mir," I said in German.

"That means, 'I love you, darling,'" he said. "Come, say it in English: I love you, darling."

"No," I said. "That's more than I want to say."

It was my first lesson in something rather important to know: that love repeats itself, and once you have learned the routine you never forget it, like swimming or horseback riding; and that you soon know all the cues beforehand and the answers too. We kissed a lot, and I was proud of Howard because he was so good-looking and well bred and an Englishman and wealthy as, to our mind, all foreigners were. There exists no greater inferiority complex than that of the Germans, and all the overcompensations Hitler has pumped into them won't get rid of it. It is part and parcel of the German mind and the German soul. Whatever they write and speak and scream in all their manifestoes, deep within themselves all Germans believe that they are of a lesser grain than the French, the British, the Americans, the Russians, the Italians, and sundry other people. There is something pathetic about the unreturned love and admiration that Germans squander on anything not German. They know all foreign literature, they study foreign languages, they travel, they make pilgrimages to foreign places of art and worship before foreign shrines, and they dig deep into the psychology and philosophy of every nation on earth. And all that it gets them is enough understanding to go and make war on them, destroy what they admired, kill what they loved, and conquer those whom they cannot force to like them. . . .

After that night I saw Howard every day. He would stop his car in front of the little cottage where I lived with Clara, would honk his horn and take me riding in his car into the country. Or when the weather was bad he would come in and drink tea with us. We would laugh a lot and kiss a lot and dance a lot. We would see movies together and go to the theater, and after the show we would pick up Clara and eat in the little restaurant where all the actors and singers of the Grand Duke's theater gathered for a late snack. We would swap knowledge, Howard teaching me English and I typing pages and pages in German for his thesis.

When he first found out that I was a stenographer he was taken aback.

"I can't believe it really," he said. "You're simply joking."

"Why shouldn't I be a stenographer?" I asked, exasperated as I sometimes was about a certain English denseness in him.

"Because you are so definitely a lady," he said. The stupidity of it made me laugh.

"I am a lady who has to work to make a living," I said.

After I had convinced Howard that I was a stenographer he became, if possible, still a shade more polite and attentive to me, which was very sweet of him. But he never touched the subject again, as if it were something embarrassing for both of us. I was worried, because I was without work and for two months I had been unable to pay Clara my share of the rent and the household. Clara worked very hard with her ballet girls and gave lessons to an amateur group besides. Since the Grand Duke was interested in her style of dancing, many a daughter was delivered at her doorstep in the hope of attaining beauty, grace, and litheness. When Clara came home, thin and tired, hoarse from shouting commands, dropping into a chair and massaging the muscles of her legs or inhaling pine oil to soothe her exhausted throat, I felt small and ashamed. I had done nothing but fritter away the time, flirting with Howard or answering help-wanted ads in the two papers.

The trouble was that my wrist had got me out of the two jobs I had held so far and hampered me in getting another one. Surgery before the war was by no means the wizardry it became later, especially not in Wolzinje. If you broke a joint it was pretty probable that it would remain stiff ever after. My wrist, instead of improving, got stiffer and stiffer as the time went by. If I worked for a while my fingers got cold and numb; I dropped my pencil, I missed words, I pretended to have no pain while it spread into my arm, into my shoulderblades, into my whole body.

"Is anything the matter with your hand, Sommer?"

"No, not at all, it's nothing, really. I had a little accident once, but that was long ago. I can do a hundred words a minute easily."

"You look as if you hate taking dictation, Sommer. I like cheerful faces in my office."

"But I love taking dictation, I really love my work, Herr Simons, please, don't pay any attention to my silly face . . ."

When I got fired the second time I sat gloomily in my room and wondered what profession I could learn in which a person wouldn't need a right hand. To get fired was something pretty awful in those days and did not happen to decent people. If you got fired it put you into the same class with bums and loafers and good-for-nothings.

Clara came in and stood behind me with her fingers on my shoulder. She had the touch of a dancer, vibrant, alive, and very light, different from that of any other person who ever touched me.

"Are you moping, baby?"

"No. Not exactly. It's just that getting fired is no fun."

"So what do you want to do? Go around with a stiff wrist for the rest of your life and be sorry for yourself?"

"It's not a question of what I want to do—it's what I am able to do, Clara."

"Listen, baby: one can always do what one really wants to do. I mean *want*. Trouble with you is you haven't really wanted to get straightened out yet. I've worked out a set of exercises for you, and I'll do them with you twice a day. It's going to hurt like hell, and if you skip them once I'll kick you out of this house and never talk to you again. Come on, get up, you loafer, quit blubbering and do something about your goddamned wrist. I've had enough of this."

Bless Clara, she gave me the only medicine that would help. I

did my exercises and they hurt, not like one hell but like ten
burning, stabbing, aching hells; they hurt so much that it became almost a pleasure to accept the challenge and go through
the torture without a squawk. After three weeks my wrist was
just as stiff, but my fingers didn't get so numb and cold any
longer, and I had more courage and self-assurance. I put an ad in
the papers and I received three answers but came too late in two
places. The third letter sounded quite definite. It ordered me to
introduce myself on Thursday at ten in F 12, Giessheim. It was
not inviting, for Giessheim was the sandy flat beyond Odenberg,
the proletarian quarter where the streets were simply marked with
the letters of the alphabet, as if they weren't worth the trouble
of choosing pretty names for them. However I had no other
chance and took the trolley car, and with much tooting and ringing and swerving we went up and across the hills, past the new
library and down into Giessheim. I had never been there before
and I sniffed into the air, loaded with chemical smells from the
Hewa plant, chloride and something acid and something bitter
and something plain bad. The streets were nude and sober like
their A B C names, the settlement houses looked clean and antiseptic, hundreds of houses built after the same pattern, each
one housing four families. There were trees planted along the
streets, but they were still small and thin, leaning against thin
stakes for support. It was a cold, sunny morning in February,
and all the sand of the prehistoric sea bottom seemed to whirl
around, prick my face, and settle in my eyes. The whole district
looked sanitary and well planned, but it lacked the warmth and
disorderly friendliness of the older parts of Bergheim. In back of
every house was a small vegetable patch, and in every patch a
laundry line fluttered in the wind, whole families of laundry:
father's shirts and long woolen underwear, mother's bloomers
and coarse petticoats, and then the children's underthings, getting
smaller and smaller, down to baby's diapers and flannels. People
had many children in Giessheim, and lots of washing.

F 12 was a two-story house of red brick, two blocks off the
freight depot and opposite a new school building. I stopped
there and hesitated; I pulled my jacket down and put on my
clean, white suède gloves. I belonged to a period when suède

gloves were indispensable for a nice girl. Yet I dimly felt that they were not quite suitable in these surroundings. At the curb opposite the street three little boys were standing and having a peeing contest. They called something to me which I didn't understand and then they ran away, laughing, the flies on their patched panties gaping. I entered F 12.

There was a new smell inside. Printer's ink. Through an open door to the right I looked into a room where an old man with a green visor over his eyes worked on something while a boy kept a hand press moving. To the left there was another door with a cardboard sign: Editor. I knocked and entered. A young, Jewish-looking man looked up from a book he was reading and stared at me with absent-minded eyes. He was in his shirt sleeves and did not sit at his rickety desk but on a battered, overstuffed chair near the window.

"My name is Marion Sommer, I received a letter from you——" I began.

"You the typist?" he said, and by the way he looked at me I felt that everything about me was wrong. My trim black suit, my freshly washed white gloves, the ribbon on my hat. I nodded and pulled out the letter.

"Upstairs," he said, pointing an ink-stained thumb to the ceiling. He dropped his eyes and went back reading. I closed the door, quickly took off my gloves, and went upstairs.

I HAD LIKED Howard Watson at first sight. His clean, good looks. The way his gray flannel suits hung loosely from his broad shoulders. The way his tailcoat clung impeccably to his tall athlete's body. The way his blond hair grew in a whirl into his forehead. The way he smelled of Yardley. The way he got all bungled up in his German sentences. The way he laughed. The way he danced. The way he kissed.

I disliked Walter Brandt the moment I set foot into his room. He was the sloppiest-looking individual dwelling in the sloppiest-looking cave I had ever seen. There were stacks of books and magazines and old manuscripts everywhere, on the floor, on the sofa, on the chair he offered to me. He brushed some of them off and they fell down in a cloud of dust; on the rest I sat—it was slippery and uncomfortable. The floor was littered with sheets of paper and pages torn from newspapers and cigarette stubs. A fat gray cat slept on the blotter in the center of the desk. While Brandt spoke he had a habit of absent-mindedly pushing the cat aside, but she always crawled back without so much as opening an eye. The sofa had only three legs; an empty fruit crate was shoved under it to hold it up. The windows were grimy and rattled in the Giessheim wind. In the corner a round little stove spat heat, red in the face, glowing with labor. A water kettle stood there, boiling over and spilling little gushers of water onto the stove, where they went up in steam with an angry hiss. I felt like turning around and going home. But I needed a job and I did not go.

"My name is Marion Sommer. I received this letter from you——" I began once more, waving my document in front of the man who sat behind the desk. He was in shirt sleeves and without a collar. A jungle of auburn hair grew on his head, and two deep lines were clefting his cheeks.

"You're ten minutes late," he said. "Sit down." There was no clock in the room. Later on I discovered that Walter used the school bells across the street instead. "I'm sorry," I said. "I did not find the street right away. I have never been in Giessheim."

"I can see that," he said, and my black suit began to burn on my back as if it were on fire. I slid uncomfortably on my pedestal of old manuscripts. "I'm sorry," I said again.

"I'm Walter Brandt," he said. "You've heard of me?"

"No—not that I remember," I stammered. "I haven't been in Bergheim long," I added.

"I can see that. Where do you come from?"

"Austria. Vienna," I said, wondering if this would be something wrong again.

Brandt looked at me. "You're a long way from home," he said. What funny eyes he has, I thought. They were amazingly alert and round, like the eyes of a bird. A black pupil in a circle of yellow agate. "Say, if you are from Vienna, do you know Victor Adler?"

I quickly thumbed through my memory. "The socialist?" I said with relief. "Yes, I met him several times."

"Ah, now that's interesting. Where did you meet him?"

"We had a Society for Modern Art——"

"Modern Art!" said Brandt. It sounded like a guillotine dropping and executing Modern Art; I heard its poor head fall into the basket and I got angry. "Yes, Modern Art," I said. "Very good art at that."

"You didn't belong to the party then," he said.

"What party?" I asked blankly.

"The Socialist party," he said. "The Socialist party, Fräulein. Or aren't you aware that such a thing as the Socialist party exists?"

"I am not interested in politics," I said. Brandt gave a whistle and a deep sigh. "That's nothing to be proud of," he said. "Nothing to be proud of, Fräulein. But we'll wake you up, all of you who are living with feedbags tied to your noses and wax in your ears and blinkers before your eyes——"

"Look here," I said, very angry now, "I didn't come here for a political examination but because I want to work. Politics is a business for politicians. My business is typing. If you'll excuse me, I think I had better try to get the eleven-o'clock trolley."

"Easy, easy," Brandt said. "I did not mean to hurt your feelings. You see, my business happens to be politics, and it's a pretty tough business if you sit on the wrong side of the fence. I thought you knew that you were in the lion's den. I am no Victor Adler, but I run a socialistic publication. Now, if you don't want to work for me because it's dangerous, I'm not holding you."

I had gotten up from my precarious seat, but now I sat down again. After all I was the girl who had wanted to put her head into a lion's mouth.

"Is it dangerous to work for you?" I asked quickly. Suddenly Brandt gave me a big grin and a wink.

"Moderately so. Moderately and most unromantically so,

Fräulein," he said. I began getting used to the rhythm of his speaking. He spoke the soft, humorous dialect of the country, and he had a habit of repeating every point he wanted to bring home. It slowed down the conversation, but it was most effective on the platform, I found out in months to come. "We don't get hanged and we don't get boiled in frying oil. We are the biggest legal party in Germany after all, with 110 seats in the Reichstag; in fact we hold more votes than any other single party, even if the Kaiser has officially called us sons of bitches. But we get beaten up once in a while, or people storm the office or the paper gets suppressed after we have worked sweat and blood over it. In fact, the reason why I want a lady secretary this time is the deplorable circumstance that my men always end up in jail. The last one got arrested on Tuesday, and we are lagging behind with our work."

This was good. This was marvelous. I could see myself in a prison cell; my hair that had just grown to my shoulders was shorn once more, I wore a blue prison suit, and the sun painted the shadow of the prison bars onto the floor. . . .

"Why do they get arrested?" I asked happily.

"Oh, for anything. Getting into a brawl, or insulting a police officer, any flimsy pretext will do. They can always find something against a person who works for me."

"I want to work for you," I said.

Brandt fumbled around on his desk, took the cat, put it on his lap and began stroking its neck. The cat stretched, opened its eyes, and cuddled up to him. I was surprised to see that this sloppy, unkempt socialist had remarkably beautiful, well-groomed hands. They were strong and sensitive and, as he buried his fingers in the gray fur, they struck me as being lonely hands. Later on I found out that stroking the cat was his gesture of escape whenever he felt embarrassed or moved by something. He put the cat back on the blotter and became once more alert and businesslike.

"Why did you leave Vienna?"

"For private reasons."

"Worked there?"

"Yes. Yes, I worked there," I said. It wasn't exactly a lie, was it? "And here too. At the Simons bank and at a bookstore," I added quickly.

"References?"

I grew hot. Both references had stated that I was fired through no fault of my own but because of a defective right hand. I had torn them up and flushed them down the toilet. "No. No references," I said.

Walter Brandt got up, went past me to the door, opened it and shouted down the stairs: "Fritz! Come up for a moment." Then he sat down again, pushed the cat off the blotter, and looked at me with his steady, round yellow eyes. The young Jew I had seen downstairs came rumbling in a minute later.

"Coffee ready?" he asked.

"Look here, Fritz," Brandt said, "we'll have to get along without a secretary until Bürger gets out of jail. This one won't do. She is everything all wrong. And you've seen the others. D'you think we can get along without?"

"No, we can't," Fritz said, getting busy with the water kettle and a coffeepot he produced from under the sofa. "What's wrong with this one?"

"Wrong background. Wrong upbringing, that's obvious. Never heard of us. No experience. No references. Probably never did a stitch of work in her life. Probably she thinks we're playing cops and robbers here and that it might be fun to play with us."

"If you want to look into my mouth, it's quite all right with me," I said furiously. "You know they do it when they buy horses."

Fritz burst out laughing; but Brandt kept his steady glance at me without moving his face. "And you think you are good in French?" he asked. Fritz pushed a chipped cup without a saucer into his hand, and he lifted it to his mouth without taking his eyes from me. "We have a lot of correspondence with our French friends," he said. "Can you take French dictation?"

I had spoken French since I could remember, like any well-brought-up child in Vienna. "Why not try me out?" I said. By now I had become stubbornly resolved to get this job. "All right. Why not?" Fritz said. "Where have you that article by

Hervé?" I was amazed to see Brandt dive into the mess of sheets on his desk and with one grip produce the thing he wanted. I began to grasp that there was method and order of some sort in this jungle. I caught my breath and sat up.

"Shorthand or typewriter?" I asked.

"Typewriter, so we can read it," Brandt said. He pulled one from under his desk and put it before me. I took off my hat and jacket. "Want a cigarette?" he asked; he might have noticed that my hands were shaking. It was the worst stage fright I ever had, worse than in my first concert with the Vienna Philharmonic Orchestra. I took the cigarette and perked my ears. "My name is Fritz Halban. I'm the assistant editor around here," the young Jew said with a feeble attempt at being polite, and then he began dictating to me. He walked up and down the small room, kicking up the litter on the floor and spouting a fast and easy flow of the funniest French I had ever encountered. I played my typewriter with as much velocity and care as if it were a piano, trying to give my fastest speed. My wrist hurt and behaved like a bucking horse. Brandt got up from his chair and watched me over my shoulder. I began to perspire. "Enough," he said when I took out the first sheet. "What's wrong with your right hand?"

"Nothing," I said. "Nothing is wrong with it, really——"

"Listen, Fräulein," he said, "what's wrong with you altogether? You don't look like a typist, you don't talk like a typist, you have a crippled hand, and your past smells something awful."

"Her French spelling is good, though," Fritz Halban said from the background.

"I have to know and to trust anyone who works with me," Brandt went on without paying any attention to him. "To know and to trust. We are no sissies this side of town; we are used to strong tobacco; you don't have to hide anything from us. But I have to know you thoroughly before I can put you to work. Have you been in prison? Have you killed somebody? Stolen? Embezzled? Your prison haircut gives you away the moment you are without a hat. Or are you someone's agent? Did anyone pay you to worm your way into this office? Speak up."

When I saw how furious he got while he shouted at me, my whole tension blew off in an explosion of laughter. "Who's playing cops and robbers now?" I said. "It's too bad that my story isn't half as interesting. I've been in a train crash, broke my wrist and almost split my skull. That's all. I ran away from my family and I got fired twice because of that damned stiff wrist. The trouble with me is that the only profession where a stiff wrist won't disturb a girl isn't exactly in my line. Good day. Sorry I took up so much of your time."

I pulled my hat down over my ears and grabbed my incriminating gloves. "Wait," Brandt said. "Tell me more. Why did you run away from your family?"

"They were too bourgeois for me," I said. I didn't mean it in any political sense, rather with the contempt the Modern Art people had taught me. But unknowingly I had given Brandt the right cue.

"There you are," he said happily. "A wealthy family, eh? Bourgeois; I can smell it. I come from such a family myself. How come you were in a train crash? How did it happen?"

"I was on a concert tour. I played the violin," I confessed reluctantly. "You may have heard of that crash. Near Wolzinje, in Poland."

Brandt whistled. "Didn't the railway company compensate you? You have a pretty strong claim, don't you know?" he asked. "The lawyers are still bickering about it," I said. "Anyway, I owe my impresario whatever money I may get and more."

"There you are," Brandt said, getting more and more cheerful. "There you have the whole story, Fritz. Look at the girl. She hasn't heard anything about socialism, but she has an instinct that drives her away from the parasitic morass her family is living in. She is made an invalid by an accident for which capitalistic enterprise, a railway, is responsible. They put her out of work, they ruin her. But they don't even pay her any compensation. To make things perfect, there is a bloodsucker of an agent who takes her last nickels away. And when the poor thing tries to find a different sort of work, she gets fired time after time—fired without warning, thrown out on the street. No social security, no social conscience anywhere. A perfect example of the working of the capitalistic system. Let me look at your wrist, Fräulein, will you?"

There was something lopsided and unjust about this version. "Herr Krappl is no bloodsucker, he did a lot for me," I said lamely.

"You worked and he got the profit," Brandt said. "You played the violin and he got paid for it. That's as plain as two and two."

"Well——" I said. I needed the job. I couldn't afford to contradict this angry prophet.

"Listen," he said. "You'll have to work hard here, and I can't pay much. Sixty marks a month. But I can assure you that you won't get fired because of a stiff wrist. It's the other way round. Take off your hat, and Fritz will show you what you have to do first."

And thus I had a job again, not in spite of my stiff wrist but because of it.

I AM NOT one of those people who reverently tote around chests and trunks filled with tokens of memories. My attic isn't cluttered up with them, and the drawers of my desk are comparatively empty. But I do still possess a few numbers of the Morning Call. The last time I ran across them was when I gave up our New York apartment; cleaned out anything that clustered up my life and packed the rest into a steamer trunk to go back to Europe to see if Michael's eyesight could be saved. They looked very faded, for we used the cheapest paper; the print had turned gray, and the contents seemed oddly trite. It was the sort of stuff to make you sigh: Good heavens, here they go again! Struggle of the classes. Eight-hour day. Social security. Universal vote. Distribution of wealth. This and that. The same old slogans. I read a few lines, and it all came back to me, the whole setup in F 12. I smiled down at the old numbers of the Morning Call and showed them to my stepson Johnnie Sprague, who had returned from Spain, still full of civil war and Falangists and all that. "You see," I told him, "your train has just arrived at the

same station where we stopped more than twenty years ago."
But Johnnie has little sense of humor. "What train? What are
you referring to?" he said in his most fastidious voice. "The
same old issues, teacher," I said. "The things you are fighting
for just now. We fought for them in those prehistoric middle
ages, before the World War; we even got them after the war was
over—and look what happened." John looked me over with his
grave owl's eyes as he said: "These issues are as important today
as they ever were. Karl Marx lived and preached sixty, eighty
years ago yet the world still hasn't caught up with him. It speaks
against the world and not against Karl Marx."

"Maybe that's what's wrong with it," I said. "I mean with
Karl Marx. Maybe if he would live today he would write differently and more up to date, or am I an idiot?"

"Yes," John said and I could see he liked me. "You're an idiot
and a pain in the neck when it comes to any political or social
discussion. You still believe that having a social conscience
consists of cluttering up your kitchen with a bunch of colored
brats and nursing your cook personally when she comes down
with typhoid fever. You're a bloody individualist and a stinking liberal and people like you are more dangerous for the
achievement of any radical progress than the out and out re-
actionaries." Yes, I thought, but it's the individual who feels
the toothache and the hunger and the beating. But I didn't
say anything because those young Lefties are so intolerant and
dictatorial and I didn't want a fight.

I went on reading the old papers. May 7, 1914. May 14, 1914.
It was as if Walter Brandt's voice came to me across the years:
"There will come the time to bring an end to the injustice by
which humanity has been split in two classes throughout the
ages. Masters and Slaves. Lords and Vassals. Landowners and
Tenants. Nobility and Serfs. Capitalists and Workers. Exploiters
and Exploited. Oppressors and Oppressed. It is up to us to
create the new economic order on a socialistic basis. By evolution
if it be so. By revolution if necessary." His editorials were ashes
now, but still they had been fire, and even the ashes felt burn-
ingly hot.

I did not throw the old numbers away; I folded them up and

put them at the bottom of one of the drawers in my trunk. I cannot help being a bit sentimental about Walter because I think he was the only man I really loved, with the good love, the great love, what Michael calls "the real thing." Maybe I would feel differently about Walter if we had married and grown old together. It's hard to think of Walter being old—older than he was in 1914. We would have married and lived in Bergheim ever after and would have had children. He would have become something important under the German Republic, mayor of the town or cabinet minister or something like that. And later, when Hitler came to power, he would have been thrown into a concentration camp, they would have beaten him up or killed him. Or maybe he would have escaped and become one of Chiang Kai-shek's advisers, as Fritz Halban is now. Or maybe he would have made a face-about like so many of the socialistic vanguard and become a big shot with the Nazis. In any case, I would be just where I am today. What's the use of all these maybe's, anyway? Maybe if men like Walter had survived the war there would have been no Hitler.

March, April, May, June 1914. The first weeks at F 12 were horrifying. I felt as I had felt once when I turned a rock around after sitting on it for half an hour, enjoying the sun and eating berries. To find all the squirming, writhing, sunless life beneath that stone, the worms, spiders, larvae, sawbugs, gray, eyeless creatures, crawling over one another, an ugly, repulsive sight that spoiled my appetite for the rest of the day! Did I say Bergheim was as pretty as a picture? Did I say there was perfect peace? Did I think the people were happy and loved their grand duke? Well, I learned to look under the stone, and what I saw was not nice.

". . . Sommer, I advise you to read the statistics about T.B. among the tenant farmers." . . . "Sommer, don't you know that we are having a little epidemic of meningitis in Giessheim every year? They don't let the news pass through, but eighty or ninety children die all the same this side of town. Not in Odenberg, where the rich people live, mind you, but among the workers." . . . "Sommer, give me the figures about accidents in the chemical industry." . . . "Sommer, don't talk sentimental pap, better read up on your Karl Marx." . . . "Sommer, what do you think is the average income of a skilled laborer in this state? Eighty marks a month, a ten-hour day. How do you think a family of six people shall live on eighty marks? Do you know how old coal miners get in the average? Forty years, and they are sick and twisted with rheumatism long before that. Who, do you think, supports those invalids? The mines where they worked themselves crooked? No, Mäusle, our so-called social insurance is the bunk. . . . What do you say? Why do they have so many children? Don't you know that making babies is the poor man's cheapest pleasure—or so at least it seems at the moment he makes them? I've fought for birth control and sex advice for years; there should be an office for it right next to the gate of every factory. They've preached in church against me because of it— as if I were the Antichrist. Yes, I know, the Grand Duchess has founded a home for illegitimate babies, the confounded amateur! But don't you understand? Charity is an insult. People who work have a right to live decently and get old decently and die decently. That's all we are asking for. Decency. A fair distribution of everything. I have not told you about the lead sickness in Faber's factory, have I? . . . "

For a while I was utterly bewildered and desperate, as only a youngster can be after finding out that the friendly image of the world she had made herself was completely and hopelessly wrong. It was not easy to readjust myself, but after a while I found my stride and swam happily along in the stream of socialism wherein the Morning Call was but a tiny wavelet. I found out that there was a right wing and a left wing of socialism and many shades and hues in between. I got entangled in the theories of radicals, orthodox socialists, revisionists, syndicalists, communists, anarchists, of English laborites and Russian bolshevists, and of the German Social Democrats with all their disputes among themselves. I found out that Brandt did not quite agree with the party and followed his own course. In some respects he was more of a revolutionary, in others he believed that the party went too far and made only trouble for the workers. Altogether he didn't like the party leaders, whom he called the Big Baboons.

The writings of Karl Marx were given to me like a sort of Bible, to learn the fundamentals of socialism from them. Like the Scriptures, they were deeply absorbing in stretches and absolutely barren in others. Like the Scriptures, they contained much intentional or unintentional darkness. Like the Scriptures, they contradicted themselves and, as with the Bible, it was a hopeless undertaking ever to get through reading it all. I often wonder how many of the sworn believers and followers of Karl Marx have ever read every word he wrote, have pondered over it and tried to get down to the real meaning of it all. As for me, the more I read the more confused I felt. I am a hopeless case as far as theories go. I can understand only what I can see and touch and feel. I saw that much was wrong with the people in Giessheim, and I wanted to do anything to help make them happier. It was not that they were poor. The people in Kandl Street had been poorer, yet happier. It wasn't that they worked hard. The farmers around Giessheim worked harder and still they were happier. Yes, maybe if the tools and machines and the factories where they worked belonged to the workers, they would be happy too. Maybe promising them a revolution was as good as the heaven other faiths promised their believers. Anything to give them a soul and a hope and a flag to follow and a light to carry and a fulfillment to look forward to.

Not one of the rules Brandt demanded for the regulation of work was applied to us who worked for him; no maximum working hours, no minimum wages, no consideration of any kind. Brandt at work was as ruthless as a hurricane. Yet, Brandt in his meager spare hours was gentle, considerate, and shy. He had two pet subjects on which he harped in every one of his editorials. The one was local and concerned Faber's paint factory, where working conditions were unsanitary and precautions against lead sickness were unsatisfactory and did not conform to the laws. The Morning Call battled along in every issue demanding inspection, demanding that the airless building be condemned, demanding a fair deal for the men and girls who worked there. The other subject concerned the whole world. Internationalism. Brotherhood of men. Hands across the borders. Sacred unity of all workers of the world.

In spite of all my enthusiasm for the cause of the workers I don't think I ever became a socialist. I am not born to be a member or a joiner or to belong to an organized group; I just have to blunder along in my own way, and probably Johnnie is right when he calls me a bloody individualist. Sometimes I even wondered if Walter Brandt was a real socialist, he who had never done any manual labor, he with the sensitive white hands, he who was shy and embarrassed when he talked with workers privately and only got his wind up when he spoke from a platform to a meeting. I don't know whether I believed in the confusing, complicated, and entangled issues of socialism. But I did believe in Walter Brandt and his blazing desire to make the world a better place; or, if not the world, at least Giessheim and Faber's paint factory.

It was one of my duties to read the French and English socialist publications, draw red frames around articles I thought important and sometimes to make a raw translation of them. My French was tolerably good and I wrestled successfully with Hervé and Jaurès, but my English did not live up to Ramsay Macdonald's style. Once I took an article home and asked Howard to translate it for me. We had our first fight over it.

"What filthy nonsense!" he said after he had read a few lines. "It's the sort of rot one shouldn't even touch with a barge pole!"

It made me furious, and I gave him a dose of the statistics Brandt had fed to me.

"How awful to put such rubbish into your pretty head!" he said. "If you had any consideration for me you would leave that place tomorrow."

"What has it to do with you, where I work?" I asked angrily.

"But don't you see, my dear? It reflects on me if you are known to be a socialist or, at least, to associate with that sort of people. It's a beastly situation for me."

"Now you sound like Cousin Hermann," I said and left him standing on the street.

I took dictation, I wrote shorthand, I typed and retyped Brandt's and Fritz's articles, I copied other articles from the papers and pamphlets that came in. I helped with the proof-reading, I cut clippings, pasted them into scrapbooks, I registered

and filed things away, I telephoned, talked to visitors and ped-
dlers, kept Brandt's schedule in mind, I lied for him and protected him, as is the duty of a private secretary. Each week had
a climax, a torrent of work, when it came to the distribution of
the new issue. Folding every one of the three thousand we
printed, pasting crossbands around them, typing the addresses,
putting the stamps on, stacking them up in piles, and finally
helping the boy to carry them downstairs to take them to the
post office; it made me stiff in my back for two days after. But
the office work was only half of it. There were the meetings I
had to attend, taking shorthand notes of the speeches; the trips
into the outlying villages for discussions in some smoky beer
hall, the late, sleepy returns on local trains, the cajoling of reluctant party members, the invitations to smaller committee
sessions, the evenings we spent in the Workers' Club making contacts and keeping abreast with the party. It was fun, though. It
was fun not to be treated as a girl but as a comrade. It was fun
not to be alone but part of a group, a black sheep of a unit
within the greater unit of the party. All my life I had loved
meeting people; I had a sort of cannibalistic hunger to absorb
lots and lots of them. Now a new dish was set before me, and I
devoured it with great appetite. Workmen and their shapeless,
tired-looking wives. The old, monosyllabic, reliable foremen. The
young boys with raw voices and banging fists. The philosophers
who sat in the reading room of the club and studied Darwin and
an enlightening magazine called Kosmos. The sons and daughters
from the farms who had come to town, preferring the Hewa to
the fields, the meeting hall to the tedious Latin mumblings in
church. I was happy during those few months of spring and early
summer 1914. I could feel the pulse of the world under my finger.
I was proud the day our Morning Call was suspended. Prouder
still when a group of farmers broke up one of the meetings in
a village and a fight with fists, chairs, and beer glasses took
place, with me crouching under a table where Brandt had stuffed
me the moment the fun began. I watched him from down there
and was surprised and strangely elated to see that he was a quick
and astoundingly strong fighter.

"Mäusle, I wouldn't give you this evening for a thousand

marks," he said happily when we were back in F 12 that night and I helped him put iodine on the scratches he had got. Fritz had been taken to the emergency ward of the hospital with a bad cut on his forehead, and we were alone. We cooked coffee, and Brandt dictated until the street outside went gray with dawn and the sky beyond the school turned green like a hard, unripe apple. "How do you like marching ahead of the parade instead of behind it, Mäusle?" he asked. "I like it," I said. "I'd like it still better if I were a boy, though, and didn't have to be stuck under a table when the fun begins."

Brandt took the cat from the desk and cuddled it to his shoulder. "Yes, sometimes I too wish you were a boy," he said. "Sometimes I wish it. And sometimes I am glad you are just as you are."

He went over to the window and stood there with the twilight on his face and the cat's head cuddling in the hollow between his chin and his shoulder bone. "Come here, Mäusle," he said after a while. "Look at the sky. Looks nice, that color, doesn't it?" Then we stood there together and said nothing and watched the green turn orange and we heard the clanking of the milk train as it pulled in at the freight depot. I was jealous of the cat. I envied her—that's the only way I can describe it. I was tired and sleepy and I would have liked to put my head where the cat's head was and rest there and have Brandt's hand stroke me with that absent-minded, lonely, tender gesture of his. A little later he put his hand on my shoulder and repeated: "Yes, Mäusle. I like you just as you are."

That was the beginning; being jealous of the cat. Feeling restless. Wanting to cry for no reason. Wanting to play Schubert on the piano. Wondering how he had looked when he was a baby. Wanting to plead with him: "Please, don't drive yourself so hard. Please stop for a moment, to breathe, to look, to see a flower, a smile, a color. Taste the tart sweetness of the first cherries. Smell the clean rain on a dusty street." He was like a man closed in by high walls. He was like a convict walking in a circle, with other convicts in front and in back of him. When he had called me to the window and showed me the green at the horizon, I had felt my eyes sting. It was so rare that he saw anything outside of his circle. How he had said it: "Looks nice, that color, doesn't it?" As if he had never seen anything green before.

"What's the matter with you, kid?" Clara asked me. "Are you sleepwalking?"

"It's the spring," I said. "Maybe I have a little cold coming."

"Your wrist is better though, isn't it?" Clara said.

"Oh yes, it's much better, thanks."

"Wouldn't you like to have a fiddle again? I heard in the theater that one of the violinists would like to sell one quite reasonably."

"Thanks, Clara. You're a fool. I don't want to play the fiddle; never again. I like this work much better, much."

I had more quarrels with Howard, and I saw him only once or twice a week. I still liked him and his looks and his kisses, but sometimes he seemed tedious with his polite and innocent way of being arrogant. "You are a snob," I told him. "You're a prig, you're smug." He would pull snapshots of his family from his wallet and he would repeat little scraps of conversation in which he bragged about his relatives in an unostentatious British way. "My uncle, Lord Crenshaw," and: "You know what Lady Ellevyn said to my mother? 'Lady Watson,' she said, 'if you knew my husband as I know him . . . ' " He tried to explain to me what all-important difference there was between a solicitor and a barrister and again between a simple barrister and a king's counsel like Sir Frederic, his father. It bored me to tears. I even grew tired of dancing with him. Dancing, indeed, while the workers at Faber's got slowly poisoned with lead!

I had visited some of the sick men with Brandt when he gathered new material on his old theme. The white of their eyes was yellow and they seemed like ghosts; the way they hung their shoulders and told about the burning in their stomachs and the slow stiffness creeping up their legs . . .

In May, Brandt went to Frankfort for a week to visit his mother, and it came as a shock to me to discover that I could not be without him any more. "Baby, you're running around like a poisoned rat," Clara told me. "What's the matter? Did anyone put some pepper in your behind by mistake?"

"Oh, leave me alone, for God's sake," I shouted at her. Clara looked at me, but she didn't get sore. She put her arm around my neck and patted my head. "It's all right, Marion," she said. "It's all right, I know how it is. I'm afraid I've gone and fallen in love myself."

"With whom?" I asked, surprised.

"With a man you don't know."

Well, Marion, there we are, I told myself. In love again. In love with a man who thinks of you as an appendage to his typewriter, a piece of office equipment. In love like a crazy, senseless fool. This is a new hell to explore. Please, will somebody show me the way, I haven't been here before. In love with a person who is infatuated with several millions of underprivileged and to whom sex means a birth-control office at every factory gate. He is ugly, I told myself, but I remembered the line from his chin to his shoulder, where the neck rose sparse and perfect, like carved polished wood; the jungle of auburn hair and the keen white forehead that came in sight when he brushed it back before he went on a platform to give a speech. He is cold and has no emotions, just a brain and an obsession, I thought. But I remembered the day a little boy had been hurt by a motorcycle and he had carried him into the office and attended to him and told him stories to make him forget the pain. He had been a different man then: tender, soft, gentle. And thus, in a circle, I came back to the cat. Please, please, couldn't you like me as much as you like the cat? Couldn't you take me into your hands and give me whatever little warmth you have to give? Then I remembered that the cat had no name. It was called The Cat, and that was that. Walter Brandt could not be bothered with finding a name for a cat. He had to attend to humanity, hadn't he? He could not be bothered with a secretary who was an ass and a fool and who got jittery when she only heard his voice or his steps on the stairs or saw the muscles of his back move under his shirt. A nice comrade you have turned out to be, Marion, I told myself. So now you are one of the million private secretaries who are in love with the boss and try not to show it. . . . "Mäusle, where the hell did we put the report on the grape pickers' wages I brought from Frankfort?" . . .

I stopped and gasped. He called me Mäusle. He had given me a name all of my own. In that respect I was far ahead of the cat. Come to think of it, I was the only person in our little group whom he called by a nickname. He had also brought me a little present when he came back from Frankfort. It was a silly piece of yellow silk, a shawl or something, quite cheap and tasteless. That was something, wasn't it? That was a lot, coming from him. Unrequited love feeds on little things like that. . . . "Here is the report. I have underlined the figures, and I wrote to the Vine Growers' Association of the Ingelheim district so that we may countercheck them. Anything else you want?"

I evaded calling him Herr Brandt, and he had not asked me to call him by his first name as the other comrades did. A secretary in love with the boss has to do a lot of juggling and tightrope walking. But I managed.

June 28. It was a Sunday, but we had urgent work to do and stayed in the office until seven; then I changed into a fresh white batiste blouse I had brought along, and Brandt went under his shower and came out slipping his arm into his coat and with his hair neatly combed back with water. Fritz Halban waited downstairs with three of our friends: Adolf Hausman, a foreman in the oxidation plant of the Hewa, his son Louis, and Louis's girl friend Paula. There was a friendly gathering of party members at Heinzel's beer garden scheduled for the evening, a shindig with speeches, music, and dancing. Brandt was one of the speakers, and he took it for granted that I would come with him, as on similar occasions, and take his speech down in shorthand. He rarely prepared a speech because he was much better in informal improvisations, and he wanted to be able to read afterward in black on white what he had said. As for me, all I wanted was to be around him for another few hours. I would have happily followed him to the bottom of the sea if he had invited me to go there. The evening was warm and mild, shining with the peculiar glow of early summer; the sun had disappeared behind the crest of Odenberg, but it was not yet dark. The sky was clean, with a heap of feathery pink clouds swept together in the west by a broom of wind. The moment I came out I saw Howard's car standing at the curb across the street, with him sitting behind the wheel. It was an unexpected sight and made me gasp, for he had never come to this part of the town. In fact I had never told him the exact address of our office. He honked the horn, left his car, and came toward me, taking off his hat. "Hello," he said. I stopped. "Hello, Howard," I said. The two Hausmans with Paula, who had been ahead of me, stopped too and waited for me. "Go on," I said, "I'll meet you at the trolley station." I was embarrassed. In back of me I heard Brandt fiddling with the key and Fritz asking in a screaming whisper, "Who is this young Siegfried with the automobile?" The Hausmans had planted themselves at my side. "We have time, the trolley car won't be there for another ten minutes," Paula said. Howard had reached our side of the street, and I shook hands with him. "Hello, Howard," I said. "This is a surprise."

"Hello," he said once more. "Yes, I thought I'd come for you and take you home. It's a shame you have to work on Sunday; it spoiled our day. But it's a lovely evening, isn't it?"

"Lovely," I said, looking and feeling silly. They all stood around me and waited. "This is Howard Watson, a friend of mine," I said in German. There was handshaking all around. "Glad to meet you," the Hausmans said with the grave correctness of little people. I introduced them one by one. "How do you do," Howard said. "How do you do. How do you do." He put up his sunniest front for them, but he obviously felt ill at ease. So did my gang. Their hands were black around the base of the nails, where no scrubbing will ever get workers' fingers clean. Fritz had inkstains on his as usual. Only Walter's looked like a gentleman's. Paula felt Howard's glance and hid her hands in the folds of her skirts. "It's that damn silver nitrate," she said. "It sticks."

"I know, I am dabbling in chemistry myself," Howard said, showing his own finger tips. His conspicuous being-a-good-fellow irked me.

"Get rid of them and come with me, darling. I have to talk to you," he said to me in English. "I don't think I can do that," I answered. "If I had known you were coming——" I turned around and faced the others. "Howard is here to study German, he doesn't speak it very well yet," I tried to explain. The

Hausmans stared at him with benevolent curiosity. Fritz had a glint of irony in his heavy eyes, and Brandt unexpectedly said in very good English: "Watson—Watson? Didn't I meet your sister at the Engelmanns' in Frankfort? . . . Yes, I thought so, she told me she had a brother studying in Bergheim. You resemble each other. We had a nice chat about Florence. We seemed to have a lot in common in our ideas about Italy."

"Yes, my sister was in a school in Florence for a year," Howard said. "I think she loathed it. And you? You don't like Italy either?"

"I would not generalize," Brandt said. "But it did not live up to my expectations. I did a sort of sentimental journey. I hiked from here to Venice, and some of my experiences were rather amusing. Rather amusing. And informative too."

"You hiked?" Howard said, flabbergasted. "You mean to say you hiked all the way from Berkheim to Venice?"

"Yes, indeed, and why not? I followed the route of the German Wanderburschen of the olden times. Across the Brenner and through the Puster Tal. It was most educational, and I am sure I saw more than I would have seen from the windows of a train. The slower the journey the richer the harvest."

"And you have met my sister?" Howard said, dropping the subject, which was too much for him. (Imagine, my dear, I met a German who walked on foot from Bergheim to Venice They are rather potty, aren't they?) "How is she? How did she look?"

"Charming, if you will permit my saying so. She told me that she plans to visit you in July. She promised to let me know her arrival so that we might exchange more Italian impressions."

"Yes, Helen might come and stay here with Lady Diana for a few weeks before going back to England," Howard said. "Lady Diana is my father's cousin and invited her, you know."

I listened with utter amazement to all this amiable patter. I expected any moment some Oscar Wilde aphorism to pop from Brandt's mouth. Instead Howard's face turned suddenly serious, as if an electric switch had been turned off, and he said, "Of course this horrible thing that happened in Sarajevo might change all our plans. You have heard of it, of course."

"Yes," Brandt said. "One of my friends in the Bergheim Press office called me up and told me. He was asthmatic with excitement. It's the greatest sensation that has come across their way in many years."

"What happened?" I asked in German, to break up their flow of English. Brandt looked at me over his shoulder. "Oh, I forgot to tell you, Mäusle. Your archduke Franz Ferdinand and his wife have been assassinated. The Hapsburgs are a hapless family, aren't they?"

"Heavens, Marion, darling, you don't mean to say that you did not know about it? They printed extras, the town is full of them, and they say the Grand Duke ordered a special session of the crown council."

"What are extras?" I asked. I remember that so clearly, because I had never seen or heard of extras before. "They sold some at the depot," the elder Hausman said. "I think I have one in my pocket." He was a silent man, and when he spoke his voice sounded like the creaking of an oar in a rusty lock. He produced the sheet; the printer's ink was still wet on it, and the letters were smudged. I read it in the last light of the day. "Well," I said, "maybe it's better so. Nobody liked them in Austria."

"Are you or ain't you coming?" Paula asked petulantly. "We're going to miss the trolley."

"That's why I came for you," Howard said to me. "This is horrible. You don't seem to grasp what it means. I am all rattled; I had to come and to talk with you about it. Come, darling," he added in German, "say good night to your friends, they are in a hurry."

"But I have to stay with them. I'm on duty, don't you see?" I said. "I have to take shorthand notes—it's important."

"I say—there is such a thing as overtime, or whatever you call it," Howard said with sudden sharpness. "I am sure Herr Brandt does not demand more than ten hours' work from you, especially on Sunday."

"We did not plan to work tonight but to have fun. A friendly get-together. Wine, music, dancing. It's entirely up to Fräulein Sommer whether she wants to come along or not," Brandt said, his round amber eyes glancing just a fraction past my head.

"There you are, darling," Howard said and took my elbow to lead me across the street.

"Make up your mind," Paula said, pulling Louis's sleeve. "We've got no time for standing here and quibbling."

"I want to go with them," I heard myself say. There was a tiny silence and then, before Howard could say anything, Brandt spoke. "Why not compromise?" he said with more elasticity than I had ever known to be in him. "If Mäusle wants to be stubborn, why don't you come with us too, Mr. Watson? You might like the change from Lady Diana's garden parties."

"All right," Howard said after a moment's hesitation. "All right. Thanks for the invitation. I'll be glad to come along. Too bad we can't all ride in my car—unfortunately it has only space for three at the most. Shall we meet you there—wherever we are going?"

"I'd be scared to ride in that thing anyway," Paula said bitterly. "Come on, you two, let's run for the trolley." Howard took me across the street. I did not have to look around to know that Brandt was following us. I felt him close, as if he threw out rays or vibrations or whatever it is people do to you when you are in love with them. The moment Howard opened the door for me, Brandt was at my side. "Thanks," he said. "I think I shall accept your invitation and ride with you. The air will do me good after the day in that little stinkhole of an office." I saw Howard bite his lips at the intrusion, but he kept up his countenance. He handed me the veil, cap, and goggles he always had in his car for me. "You can have my goggles," he said to Brandt in an ultimate exhibition of English fair play. "I'm used to driving and you are not." He went around the car and began cranking the handle. Then he came back and coaxed the vehicle into an explosive start. I sat between the two men, wondering which side of me felt more of an electric prickle and why it was that I had to fall in love with the one who was nasty with me and did not care and why I had to hurt the one who was kind and considerate and liked me a lot.

"Yes, Mr. Watson, you will like it at Heinzel's," Brandt called over the noise of the sputtering, bouncing, rattling car. "We will show you a good time as simple people understand it."

"I'm afraid I'm too perturbed to enjoy myself tonight," Howard shouted back. "This is not the time to be gay."

"You take this episode of Sarajevo too seriously," Brandt shouted.

"You cannot take it seriously enough," Howard shouted back. I turned my head from one to the other, as if I were following a tennis match.

"I am surprised that the death of some Austrian archduke or other should mean so much to you," Brandt shouted. "If I am informed correctly, he was a man without talent, without even the easy charm the other Hapsburgs had, unpopular with his people and very much under the influence of a man you British have little reason to like—the Kaiser."

"It's not a question of what his death means to me. But what does it mean to the world?" Howard answered.

"To the world it means probably that another stone has crumbled down of an autocratic and monarchistic order which has long outlived itself. I can't possibly feel alarmed about it. I expect that many more potentates will be assassinated or forced to abdicate before this century gets much older, and that the world will be the better for it."

"Heavens, do you Germans close your eyes to all realities?" Howard shouted, more excited than I had ever seen him. "Let your diplomats—or our diplomats—commit the smallest slip and there will be war."

"There won't be war; never again," Brandt said. "Never again war. Never again will the workers of one country fight against the workers of another country. Not because some decadent fool of an archduke got killed by some fool of a crazy chauvinist. Not to pull some king's or kaiser's chestnuts from the fire. Not to furnish opportunities for advancement to officers and bloody militarists and profits to the ammunition makers. No, there won't be any war. That is how we will save the world, we, the international social democracy."

The street lamps were on, and we had reached the crest of Odenberg. I saw the muscles move in Howard's face as he prepared the right answer, like a schoolboy memorizing for an examination. He seemed pale to me in that last dusky gleam; his hair was blown away from his forehead, and the dust of Giessheim clung gray and heavy to his eyebrows and lashes.

"If there is to be a war," he said, forming the sentence in careful German, "if there is to be a war, I put my hand in the fire that not a single British workman will stay behind. I don't know what your German workers will do; you have a big army, and your kaiser is a braggartish little fighting cock, and you are a nation of militarists at heart; but it is barely possible that your workers would refuse to take up arms. Our king is a peaceful man, and we are a peaceful nation minding our own business. But if there is to be war, every British man will be in it, and you can take your international social democracy and chuck it in the river."

The car rolled down toward the town with much less noise than before, the motor steaming after the climb and resting now. The two men were silent too, and not another word was spoken until we came to Heinzel's beer garden. It was in the oldest part of the town, and a terrace with a dance floor was built on poles over the bank of the Rhine. There were garlands of Chinese lanterns reflected in the water, and people in little boats floated down the river, arrested for a moment in the darkness as they stemmed their oars against the current to listen to the muffled *m-tata, m-tata* of the music. The air was sweet and fresh, full of the scent of wet planks and freshly cut grass and dripping wax candles and wilting, sun-tired roses and the smoke of wood fire. The world was a lovely place, Brandt's eyes shone like amber, his speech was exciting, and who cared what had happened way off in Sarajevo?

I often remembered that conversation in the car, later, when they had been killed in the war, both Howard Watson and Walter Brandt.

How UNBELIEVABLY ignorant we stumbled into that war, how little we knew and still how much less we were told! I don't know what went on in the mind of the Kaiser and his generals and sycophants. But I do know that I never encountered a single soul either in Germany or Austria who contemplated making war on any neighbors or invading foreign countries, or who even believed such a thing to be in the realm of the faintest possibility. When the order of mobilization was given in 1914 we were told and easily convinced that the archenemy, the French, would overrun Germany, bomb the cities, burn up the fields, rape the women, kill the men, and put the children through unspeakable tortures if our men could not stop them. And so our men, with shining eyes, their chests inflated with noble emotions, went out to defend our fatherland; it was as simple as that. Still, today, I don't know who wanted the war—if anybody anywhere in the world really wanted it—and how the strings of deception were pulled that moved millions of little marionette soldiers of all nations into the battlefields. It was not true what we were told about the French. Neither was it true what the French, the British, and the Americans were told about the Germans. The Germans are quiet people, by nature hard to arouse, but with a passionate obsession for doing their duty, blessed with the power of endurance, and with a great talent for suffering. Suffering brings out the best in them, whereas success easily makes them a bit obnoxious.

Maybe in recent years they have had just a trifle too much success for their own good and that has made the present top layer so spiteful. Beneath it, I am sure, are millions of Germans; even today, as they always were; diligent, frugal, quiet, peaceable, sentimental, and honest to the core. Germany is an unhappy country with gray skies and unfriendly rainstorms; the lamps have to burn all day long throughout the winter months, and the soil is poor and yields sunless, joyless crops. Rye. Potatoes. Cabbage. Germany is squeezed in and pinched from all sides. Germany is like a man who goes around in too-tight shoes all his life. Tight shoes make you moody and unfriendly, and tight shoes are bad for your sense of humor, and there comes a moment when nothing seems important but to get out of those tight shoes.

I am afraid we know as little today as we knew then. I do not trust the arguments of either side, and I think that all warn-

ings against propaganda are propaganda of some sort in themselves. War is a low business and it is made for low reasons, and
no high-sounding speeches and deeds will convince me otherwise. No soldier would give his life to gain or keep a market;
not for all the oil of China, not for all the rubber of the East
Indies, not for all the steel of Sweden, and not for all the profits
somebody is making out of it. Soldiers want a flag to follow and
a good cause to fight and die for. A place in the sun. Lebensraum.
Defend your country against aggression. Protect your children.
Help us keep democracy. Freedom. Liberty. Our way of living.
This and that. Sales slogans. The great, murderous swindle. How
magnificent, how childish, how basically and pathetically good
is humanity that it will never make war for the mean little things
that are real but only for the fine, great, glowing words that are
lies! . . . I do not know who is winning the wars or gaining
by the victories. But I do know that the soldiers, all soldiers,
and the people, on any side, must always lose.

On a Monday in July when I came into the office, it was
strangely quiet there. Our old printer, Anton, was not there, and
the printing press looked like a tired sleeping animal. "Good
morning, Fritz," I called into the room across the hall, but there
was no answer. I opened the door. The room was empty, the
windows open, and the desk almost shockingly neat. I went up
the creaking stairs and into my cubicle. I heard Brandt pace up
and down in his little bedroom, thumping things to the floor,
slamming the doors of his wardrobe, and making all sorts of
noises. "Mäusle, come here," he called as soon as he heard me
working on the typewriter. I brushed my hair back and went in.
"Good morning," I said at the threshold of his private room. "I
made a rough translation of Jaurès' speech at the Chambre for
you, if you want to see it."

Brandt was throwing things into a fiber suitcase. "Good
morning, Mäusle," he said. "Sit down." This was only a friendly
gesture, for there was not an inch of space to sit on, as usual.
"I don't need the speech," he went on, stuffing some underwear
into the suitcase, "but you could hand me my shirts one by one."

"Are you going away?" I asked.

"Yes."

"To Frankfort?"

"Yes."

"What about the number for next week? We should have an eight-hundred-word editorial from you before you go. Fritz and I can do the rest if you will look at the dummy we prepared."

"There is no next number—suspended for six weeks," he said. "You can take a vacation."

"What about Fritz?" I asked.

"Gone. Called to his regiment. Wiesbaden," Brandt said, taking a coat from his wardrobe and shaking it out.

"Seems everybody is going away but me," I said.

"Who else?" Brandt asked. He put the coat down on his bed and knelt in front of the cupboard to pull out more things. It was a uniform coat.

"Howard Watson, for instance," I said. "He left yesterday for England. He sends you his best regards."

Brandt came up with a pair of military boots in his hand. They were blind with dust and had the pitifully human expression that unused shoes frequently assume.

"So, so," he said. "Young Lochinvar is on the run. Well, that's fine. That's good, Mäusle. But the ship isn't sinking, even if the rats are leaving it."

"He was called home," I said. "It's not nice to talk like that about an absent person. Howard wouldn't do it."

"Well, I've often felt that I would like to kill him. Maybe I'll meet him somewhere in the war; it would be a relief to shoot a rifle at him, besides being patriotic."

"As a joke this isn't up to your standards," I said. "And he won't be in the war. Our war is with France. England is our friend."

He laughed angrily. "Did it break your poor little heart when he left?" he asked.

"No, it didn't," I said. "What do you have against him anyway?"

"Nothing. I just don't like him. I don't like his class and his kind, and I despise everything he stands for: their whole damned system, their hypocrisy, their smugness, their cant, their imperialism, what they did to China during the opium war, what they did to India, what they are doing every day to oppressed people all over the world, just so they can feed their five-per-cent Moloch, the sacred Bank of England." He put the boots down with an angry crash.

"You really can't make the poor boy responsible for all the sins of the British Empire," I said. "He is such a harmless creature and so nice."

"Damn him," said Brandt. He is sore because they suspended the magazine, I thought.

"Damn his being nice," Brandt said. "Give me my shirts. You know very well why I would like to shoot him. Not that you care."

There was nothing I had to say. Brandt brushed his hands, took my face between them, and tilted it back. "Or do you?" he asked. His eyes were almost black all of a sudden, all amber gone and the pupils big and fluctuating with a strong life of their own.

"Do I what?" I said. I had to clear my throat.

I don't know what Brandt saw in my eyes or in my face or what the huskiness of my voice told him. But his hands left my chin, his arms closed around me, and time stopped.

Maybe someday science will find out what it is that makes two people click, as they call it in America. Why one embrace only skims the surface while another one will be of a deep and strong perfection, reaching down to the core of our being, making us feel that we have been but one half of a whole; that here is completion, in the union with this one person and nowhere else; every nerve stilled, every want satisfied, every unrest calmed, every wandering, erring urge at home at last. There must be currents of vibrations or rays, some cosmic rhythms exactly tuned to each other, to bring about the platitude of two lovers feeling as one.

I think it is a very rare thing to happen, and many never experience it. If I had been late in the office that morning and had missed Walter Brandt I would have never experienced it myself.

When he released me the world had changed, and what I had lived up to that moment was blotted out: Charles Dupont,

Kant, Howard, ridiculous little shadows, were making their bows and taking their exits.

"I didn't know," I said.

"Neither did I—not for a long time—or maybe I did not want to give in," Walter answered.

"Your hands——" I said happily.

"What about them?"

"Nothing. I like them. You fed the cat and let me go hungry."

"I was a goddamned fool. I did not know. I saw you careening around with your snobbish young god—I bit my nails and thought I could not have you."

"When did you know it first?"

"I think the day you came here. With your stiff wrist and short hair and so frightened and so impertinent. And you?"

"I don't know. Wait. When you had been under the shower and there were drops of water in your hair. When you were angry about some blunder the party made—yes, I think I love you best when you are angry."

We sat on his bed that was littered with the things to be packed, reciting the old, old litany of all lovers.

"Your eyebrows—they are shaped like wings," he said, following them with his fingers. "And you've got two lines on your forehead—I like them."

"They come from reading Karl Marx," I said. "And from being in love with a blind, eyeless, senseless rainworm of a man——"

"Hang Karl Marx!" he said. "Hang the whole goddamned bloody Social Democratic party plus the fumbling, blundering, disintegrating Second International; hang Bebel and Liebknecht and Rosa Luxemburg and every one of them!"

He pushed the hair back from my forehead and seamed my hairline with a fine thread of kisses. "Mäusle," he said, "my girl, my friend, we have four days left before I have to report to my regiment. We'll have to make an eternity of it."

I looked at the blue uniform coat he had flung over the counterpane of the iron bedstead. Arms limp, collar crumpled, buttons dull, it hung there with the imploring gesture of a desperate beggar.

"You? To your regiment?" I asked, stumped.

"I am a reserve officer, you see, Mäusle. I have to report on August first. If there is no war it simply means six weeks' training like every year. If war should come I'll have to go like everybody else and beat the hell out of the French. In any case, four, five days is all we have at the moment."

"What about the International?" I asked. "Surely they won't let it come to a war? They'll call a general strike, they'll make the workers refuse to take up arms and fight. Isn't that what you always said?"

"Let's hope to God there won't be a war," Walter said, just as Howard had said the day before when he had left. (Funny, how atheists of Walter's caliber will call to God in a pinch; out of an atavistic habit, I guess.) "But you can be sure it won't be the International who will prevent a war. Not after that congress. Not after Jaurès' orations. Watch them scurry around like mice who can't find their hole. There will be proclamations and speeches, they will tell you that war has to be prevented at any price, and then they'll all take their rifles and go and shoot one another—Germans, French, Russians, and the whole confounded rest of them. Unless some blasted, old-fashioned diplomat has better sense and finds some solution at the last moment."

I did not know what to say. So now Walter was to slip into his old blue uniform and drill goose step into soldiers and give commands and be an officer. I didn't know whether I should feel proud or disappointed about it. On the one hand I was a zealous young convert to international unity. On the other hand I was far from being unimpressed by an officer's rank and uniform. After all, I had been brought up in a world and age that believed in officers as the ultimate flower of manhood.

"It doesn't add up," I said timidly.

"Listen, Mäusle, don't let it confuse you. I was a man and a German before I became a socialist and I still am a man, first of all. Even Karl Marx was for the participation in the war in 1870–71. Would you like me to behave like a coward? Would you like me to run away and desert my country when it is in danger? Escape to Switzerland, sit in cafés and theorize with other conspirators? Enjoy myself while the French invade Germany and murder my brothers? I have an old mother in Frankfort—I have you—you don't really think I wouldn't fight for you and your safety? Don't let's talk about it any more, I have made my decision and know that I am right. Besides—let's hope there won't be a war. Come, sweet, don't let's waste time."

Paradise is a secluded inn, bedded deep in the beech forests of the Odenwald, and that is where we spent our last days before the execution. I remember the sound of the latchkey; the pattern of clumsy birds that ran around the whitewashed wall of my room, five birds and a nest and five birds and a nest again; the bunch of jasmine in a brown earthenware jug on the window sill. They had dripping yellow pollens in the depth of their four white petals, and in the middle of the night Walter had to get up and carry them out to the balcony because their scent was so heavy. I remember the peaceful morning sound of the gardener raking the gravel under our windows, the shadow of a branch moving on the blinds, the sound of a voice calling for Franz. I remember that I had honey on my buttered bun for breakfast and that Walter washed my sticky fingers with his napkin as if I were a baby. I remember the twisted shape of an old oak tree on the road, the cracks in the wooden floor of the veranda, the rough feel of the stair rail under my hand. I remember the color of the sunset, the shape of an evening cloud above, dissolving into mauve fluff while we kissed, the damp country coolness of the bed sheets. I remember the atmosphere, the scent, the flavor, the melody of these days. I remember every silly little detail. But I do not remember what we spoke, or what we did hour after hour, or how we crossed the bridge of shyness that makes new lovers hesitate and fall silent and stall another five minutes before turning the key and entering the room, not daring to look at each other, and saying good night and pretending to part. And then at last rushing into each others arms. Eyes closed, lips searching, hands getting bolder, skin to skin, bodies fitted into each other, falling through rainbows, through a whirl of stars, now through jungles, now through a leaping fire, now through a blue silvery nothingness deeper than death, now on the crest of a wave, wave after wave, till they are swept ashore by the last one. . . .

I felt the fine, long muscles of his back under my hands and I felt our heart beat, hard and quick at first and then slower and slower. Our heart, not mine, not his. And, like a million girls before me, I thought: I didn't know love could be like this, God, I didn't know it. . . .

We had two rooms, with a balcony running along both of them and a bathroom between them. Our toothbrushes standing in the same jug looked married, as did our morning robes too, hanging from two hooks on the same door. We had not registered as Herr and Frau, but quite correctly as Walter Brandt and Marion Sommer. I was grateful that Walter would not lie about us, it seemed so petty and bourgeois. When we had breakfast on our balcony, the owner of the inn came to say good morning. She was an ample-bosomed, friendly creature with a sort of Charlotte Corday bonnet over her lanky hair. "Good morning, good morning, Herr Brandt," she said. "It's good to see you again, and how have you been? And how long are you going to stay with us this time? Oh, only four days? And the Fräulein? Well, I'll tell the cook that you are here and she'll try and put a few pounds on you in a hurry. My, aren't these disturbing times? But we won't get a war, that's what I say; let the Austrians do their own fighting with those dirty Serbs down there."

After she was gone I sat silent, feeding bread crumbs to some sparrows that had come and asked for them. "You have been here before?" I said finally, all of a sudden lost in a black cave of misery.

"Oh yes," he answered. My throat began to hurt. "With another girl?" I said, and felt that I might have to cry.

"No, alone. God, how alone I was at that time, Mäusle! It was after my wife had died. I needed quiet and healing. This is a good place to get well again."

"I did not know you were married," I said after that had sunk in. "I know so little about you altogether."

"Yes, I was married when I was very young, only twenty-two. She worked in my father's factory; that's how I met her. She had consumption and she died a year later. Undernourished when she was a child. No proper care, no treatment—a good example of the evil of child labor. Anna was her name. She had hair so ash blonde that it looked almost gray. God, and how she loved to be alive!"

It sounded dry and casual, like any of the statistical reports he dictated to me.

"So when she—when she left you, you became a socialist," I said.

"Yes, sort of. It brought the shortcomings of the present order home to me with a bang. You know, the cat was hers. I gave it to her for company. It's a very old cat. You must take care of her in case I'm away for long."

"Sure," I said. "How come the cat has no name?"

"Oh, she has a name, but it's too silly for daily use. Anna called her Countess Yolanda. She liked dime novels. She thought the world was like that: Countess Yolanda. I think it's more honest and flattering to call a cat a cat, don't you? Poor Ann, she believed rich people ate whipped cream with every meal and slept in diamond-studded nightshirts."

"You must have loved her very much," I said, foolishly jealous of the past.

"I thought I did," he said, and I felt much better.

The hours went by, a slim procession, too soon to be over. We walked through the tunnels of beech trees, our shoes kicked up the copper flood of last year's leaves, we sat on a rock in the midst of a little stream with the cool scent of mint around us and the tendrils of wild hop spinning a net above our heads. We took off our shoes and hung our toes in the bubbling rush of water. We picked big, juicy wild raspberries, we found mushrooms in the deep cushions of moss. We stood at the edge of a meadow on the mountain slope and watched a man mow it in big swaths. The grass made a silky sound under his scythe. He said it would take him two days if the weather held out, and I thought I would have to part from Walter when that meadow was mowed. I picked up a little bunch of the freshly cut grass and hid it in the pocket of my coat. I carried its fragrance with me through the evening, and it dried in my pocket and I forgot it. And when I took out the coat a year later and found it there, it made me cry. The dusk came with the swift little calls of birds and the noiseless velvet flight of bats and with the gurgling of an invisible spring alongside of our path.

During the next two days I had an experience that ever since has repeated itself over and over again: that, while the great events of history happen all around me, I am never there, in the center of things, but just out for lunch. I wonder if most women are like that. The World War started the day I wore that new summer dress, blue with a cherry-colored sash. It ended the day little Martin had a bellyache because his third back tooth broke through. The Anschluss happened while I had dinner with Clara and we ate Apfelstrudel. And the fall of France in the second World War will always mean that silly day I wanted to run after a boy fifteen years my junior. Fiddling while Rome burns seems to be a predominant occupation of humanity, and we never understand the bitter jokes of history at the time they are told to us, but only some twenty years afterward. . . .

And so, on that momentous, pregnant July 31 I put on the new blue dress with the cherry-colored sash and went for a day's hike with Walter, happy as a skylark. We discovered a hidden little lake, a delightful thimbleful of water with the sky reflected very blue in its depth, with reed on one end and pine trees marching down the slope of the shore, their bark almost purple with sun, their trunks swaying sleepily, their tops clanking together with a singing sound that made me think of my lost fiddle. The peace of this day was round and flawless like a precious emerald. We swam in the cool clear water that had a keen tang to it, we lay in the sun and let the dry brown pine needles trickle through our fingers as if they were sand; we still had one day and a half ahead of us, an ocean of time. We unpacked our hard-boiled eggs and sandwiches and fruit and had a magnificent picnic. Later I pretended to sleep; I kept my eyes closed and inhaled the smoke of Walter's cigarette, which floated in little gusts against my nostrils. I felt his shadow falling upon me and I knew that he watched me. I felt the warmth from his body close to mine. I felt that he put something light next to my hand and I wondered what it was. When he got up and tiptoed away I blinked at it. Flowers, wild yellow iris, with a fine scent of sandalwood. "Like a Japanese print,"

I murmured. He had plucked them clumsily, with much too short stems, as little boys pick flowers for their mothers. I sat up and looked after Walter. He was walking down to the lake, his skin golden with afternoon sun. I smiled because now I knew his skin. I liked its texture; it was warm and fine, but not as soft as mine. I could still not quite understand the miracle that had happened, the eternal miracle that changes the strangers of yesterday into the lovers of today. Man, I thought, man-arrow. He was tall and sparsely built, and there was nothing slack or soft about him; a slim, erect purposeful structure of bones under a thin layer of muscles. He darted into the lake, and I got up and ran after him into the cool water, which left a thin line of froth where our arms cut through it.

When we came home, war had been declared.

Someone had telephoned the news to the Paradise, and in the evening, while we had supper, a boy came from town and brought a few extras along. I remember that I said, "The second extra within one month, imagine!" and then we smoothed out the wet, smudged sheet and read it three times. Frau Müller, the owner of the inn, came to our table and said: "What does it mean, war? What does it mean?"

"We'll show them," Walter said, "we'll show them home all right. Don't you worry, Frau Müller. Not a single Frenchman will set his foot on German soil. They are braggarts, but they don't know how to fight."

"My older son is in the army, it's his third year," Frau Müller said. "He'll have to go to the war right away."

"The quicker we get it over, the better," Walter said. "Don't worry about the boy. We'll make a little promenade to Paris and in a few weeks the whole fun will be over."

I wondered if he meant it or if he only talked so big to comfort Frau Müller. His eyes were black again, and I knew that he was excited. He ordered wine for us and filled my glass. "Let's drink to it," he said. "To what?" I asked. "To the better world that will come after this war," he said, watching the tiny golden bubbles that rose in the sparkling Moselle. "To the future —of the world—of Germany—and ours."

"I wonder if he got his meadow all mowed," I said.

"Who, in heaven's name?"

"It's two days, isn't it? When he began mowing it there was peace. Before he has it finished there is war. It's funny to think of. Maybe he has to go away before it's all done."

"You are drunk," said Walter. "Come on, I'll take you upstairs."

Our shoes were wet from walking through the dripping dew of the meadows, and a wilted daisy had got caught in my shoelaces. When we crossed the little lounge a white-haired old lady who seemed to be one of the permanent fixtures of the Paradise came up to us. "Did you hear about the war?" she asked us. "It's hard for you young folks, isn't it? The young gentleman will have to go into the war and the young lady will stay behind and cry her eyes out. Yes, I know how it is. I'm an old woman, I remember the war of 1870. I was engaged at the time, and my fiancé was with the Königs Ulanen. He did not come back. War is a bad business. Well, I shouldn't tell you such sad stories. You will come back, young man, you will come back. There is nothing we can do but fight if those Frenchmen get fresh again. They have to be taught a lesson from time to time. Well, good luck to you, young man, all the good luck, and may the Lord bless you."

I saw Walter squirm under the old-fashioned benedictions and pulled him away. But the old lady came after us. "Listen, young woman," she said, taking me aside. "I want to give you a little bit of advice, because I know what war means and you don't. Take all the money you have from the bank, exchange it into gold pieces and keep it under your mattress. And buy all the split peas you can get to make soup from. Split peas, you understand. Knorr's split-pea soup. In France they ate rats in 1871. You don't know what's coming. Take two hundred, three hundred marks and buy split peas with it. Then nothing can happen to you. All you need then is hot water. Or, if things should get real bad, cold water will do if you soak them long enough. That's what you need in a war. Gold and split-pea soup. Good luck, my dear. And don't think I am silly. I am just old and I have seen a lot."

"What did good old Cassandra want from you?" Walter asked me as I came back to him.

"She seems to be a little off her head," I whispered. "She has the split-pea-soup obsession. But quite harmless."

How often in the years to come have I thought of her! A hundred pounds of split-pea soup might have helped us through the famine. A hundred gold pieces would have saved us in the inflation. But that evening I went giggling up the stairs, singing a duet with Walter, a cannon over the theme: "We don't want split-pea soup, split-pea soup, split-pea soup, doodledoo." I suppose we really were a little drunk, not with the wine so much as with the summer air and the sun and the excitement that now there was a war. We said: War. But we did not know the meaning of it. War, to us, meant flags and bugles, and a general on a prancing white steed and a cavalry attack with sabers glittering in the sun and drums rolling and men marching and victorious troops parading through Rhine Street. There were no dead or wounded in our war, not even dead or wounded Frenchmen.

This was our third night, and we never had a fourth one. Walter had become restless and absent-minded, and we spent the morning on the veranda, waiting for some long-distance calls to get through. The telephone lines were jammed, but after a few hours Walter managed to speak to his brother in Frankfort—there was, all of a sudden, a solid, settled family of Brandts —and to get some information. "Come, Mäusle, let's go for a walk. We have to talk business," he said quietly when he hung up.

"Look here," he said, as we strolled across the clearing in back of the river. "This may sound a bit abrupt. But you know me a little better now than you did two days ago. Do you think you could cope with me? Do you feel as I do? That we belong together?"

"Yes, I do," I said huskily.

"You know how I mean it. For better, for worse——"

"Till death do us part," I said, and tried to look as if I smiled.

"Yes, Mäusle, till death do us part. We will get married as soon as I come back if you don't change your mind while I am gone. Meanwhile you can look around for an apartment and some furniture; I leave it all to you. I'd like the old part of town, with a view over the river. We'll keep the office in F 12 for the time being, and you must attend to all the loose ends I am leaving behind. I'll send you a credit letter, you pay the rent and three months' wages for Anton, and take out three months' wages for yourself. When the three months are over we'll see further; most probably I'll be back by that time. I'll keep the magazine suspended for the length of the war. I think the party will present the government a bill for the loyalty it is showing in this critical moment. I expect everything to be different and much better afterward. Mäusle——"

"Yes, sir?" I said.

"Do you think you'll be happy with me?"

"Don't you know it yet?"

"My brother advised me to get to Frankfort at once. It seems to be difficult to find any transportation, all trains are reserved for the troops. It might take me longer than I thought, and I have to be there tomorrow at noon. What shall I do?"

"Well—if you must go, then go, go quickly. I would not like to keep a lieutenant from doing his duty in wartime."

We still tried to make it all sound funny. "I love you," Walter said suddenly, "I love you, Marion, I love you, do you hear me? I love you so." It is a great word, very seldom spoken in German, and there was a desperate urgency about it.

"I hate to go, Mäusle. I want you so, I haven't even begun to be with you. There is another night due to us, isn't there? Isn't there, Mäusle? The regiment can wait, but this is urgent."

Women are an unreliable race by nature. We are created thus, and there is nothing we can do about it. We can become fliers and arctic explorers and acrobats and stunt riders and simply refuse to pay any attention to the goings-on in the female department of our body. But as lovers we can't keep schedules; things have an exasperating way of happening to us just at the wrong moment, and more girls have remained virtuous because they "had their days" when it was most inappropriate than through their strength of resistance. I had watched the drawing familiar pain accumulate in my back and loins for several hours. I did not know how to explain it to a man; I was not even sure if men in general were informed about the biology of women. I stopped, kicking up the turf with my heel; I bent down to pick up a ladybug and sat it into the palm of my hand and pretended to be most absorbed in its antics.

"Look here, darling, about this night: Maybe you had better go to Frankfort today after all—I don't know how to explain it to you—it's something very silly—but I could not be with you tonight anyway—maybe the excitement—— We'll have credit for one more night when you come back from the war."

Walter blushed slowly; even his ears got red. "Oh," he said. "Well—that is—naturally, I understand—my poor little Mäusle— what a brute I am to bother you all the time! Shall we sit down?"

The ladybug stuck out a flimsy, tiny little black train under its red-lacquer wings. "It wants to fly," I said, to get over our embarrassment. Walter leaned his temple to mine. "Can you make it fly?" he said. "I never remember the words."

"Certainly I can make it fly," I said. It was an old nursery rhyme:

> "Flieg, Käfer, flieg,
> Dein Vater ist im Krieg,
> Deine Mutter ist in Pommerland,
> Pommerland ist abgebrannt,
> Flieg, Käfer, flieg."

And with the last line the little bug spread its wings and took off as expected.

"See?" I said proudly.

"You know, it goes back to the Thirty Years' War, that rhyme," Walter said. "Pretty cruel, isn't it? Your father went to war, your mother stayed in Pommerland, Pommerland is on fire, fly, little flier! Let's hope no songs like that will be born in this war."

THIS WAS A GREAT TIME. We had so many victories we couldn't keep track of them. The bells pealed from the steeple of the cathedral, the flags came out day after day, the bulletins pasted on round little kiosks all over town were glorious, and no one told us that we had lost the Marne battle. We did not even know there had been a Battle of the Marne. The first wounded soldiers came home and were celebrated around. When you asked them how it was on the front, they said, "Fine." The first mothers and widows of fallen heroes were seen in mourning on the streets, and old gentlemen stepped aside and doffed their hats with a fine show of reverence. The war created its own conventions; we all were clad in them as in protective steel. If you were worried about your man you were not to show it. If you could not sleep for tormented visions you were to keep it to yourself. If you got the message of his death on the field of honor you were not to lament but to smile and to be proud. If you felt like screaming and fighting when they took your father, husband, lover, son from you, you were better off locked away in a prison. Praise be to those conventions that keep people in wars, air raids, and retreats from stampeding into screaming, frothing, insanity.

The cat died nine weeks after the war had started, and I was afraid to write Walter about it. I could have saved myself the worry, for by that time he was dead himself. I learned of it with great delay, because I was no relative of his, and the letter Fritz Halban wrote me about it took a long time to reach me. Even after I knew for sure that Walter had fallen somewhere in Flanders, I kept on worrying about him, thinking of him, yearning for him, waking up with a start in the middle of the night and calling his name, because I had dreamed that he was in danger. The wounded soldiers said that a hand or foot would keep on hurting them long after it was amputated. This was the same thing. All women experienced it, and no one spoke about it. In a way I was worse off than the legitimate mourners. It would not have been proper for me to wear mourning, and nobody treated me with special reverence. Nobody but Clara, who sensed many of the things I had not told her.

Why, Fräulein Sommer, you have no one at the front? No brother? No fiancé? You are a lucky girl.

No—only a friend of mine got killed in Flanders. My former boss, you remember? Walter Brandt.

Oh, him, well! What do you know! They say some of those socialists show more gumption before the enemy than many others. Well, he fell for his fatherland; that makes up for many mistakes he made. Don't you worry, you'll find a better job any day.

The more men were sucked into the vortex of war, the more jobs were left to the women. Clara went in circles around me, sniffing keenly to find out which way I was to go. "Don't you want to go back to work, little monk?" she said. It was her newest name for me and contained all the brisk unsaid tenderness that only exists between woman and woman.

"Yes, I want to work. But not in an office. It leaves you too much time to think——"

"You are right. What you need is hard work," Clara said. "Baby, I'll look around and find you something that'll make your bones crack and'll let you fall into bed like a ton of lead."

She herself drove at a furious pace. Rehearsals all morning, calisthenics with professional and amateur groups all afternoon; before the evening's performance an hour's workout for herself. The theater was crowded as never before, and giving the populace good performances had become part of keeping up the morale at home. There were not more than two evenings a week without a ballet. In between, Clara did some work for the Red Cross, went with her prettiest dancers to the hospitals to perform for the mutilated invalids, spent every spare hour training for the Red Cross. And then there was The Man. She seemed to meet him every day, if only for a few minutes. When she was too tired to keep up her barriers she would talk about him and her hard, willful face would soften. "He has funny eyes," she would say. "The left one is smaller than the right one. It looks ridiculous. I like it, though. He is such a babe in the woods. He knows nothing of life, only the things he has read in books. But I'll shock him out of his rosy dreams. It's good for him. He has been born a few centuries too late. He would do well in tight silk panties and lace cuffs, let's say in Florence, let's say during the late Renaissance. There is nothing so appalling as a six-foot-two man who has to be fed with a spoon. Someday I'll be sick and tired of pushing him around in a spiritual sort of perambulator. He'll have to get around by himself." From such snatches I had made myself a picture of The Man and Clara's relation to him, but it was incomplete and there were holes in it, like in an unfinished jigsaw puzzle.

When the war had lasted four months and the people began to say that it might last another half year, The Man seemed to be very depressed. He seemed to demand more of Clara's time than ever, and I felt slightly exasperated about the way she pampered him. "Little monk," Clara said, "there are things you don't understand. If I leave him alone he will drink himself blind. It's his way of running away from himself and from everything, sort of." The term "escape mechanism" hadn't transpired yet.

"Does your man drink because he is afraid of the war?" I asked Clara.

"He is not afraid of it," she said. "There is not a grain of physical fear in him. But he hates this war; he was against it from the first moment——" She stopped and bit her lips, for such things were not to be expressed. There was an uncomfortable pause. "How come they have not clapped him into a uniform yet and sent him to the front?" I asked. "He is not sick, is he?"

"Sick? He? Oh no," Clara sang out, and I could hear how crazy she was about her Man. "He has some business to attend to for the time being, it makes him ineligible. Important business. But he'll go to the front eventually, like everybody else."

There is no fabric as tight and firm as a woman's discretion. Men are babblers and gossipers by nature and instinct. You have only to watch a canary bird announcing in high coloratura that he is in love; a rooster crowing from his pile of manure that he has slept with all the hens of the barnyard. Or a club car filled with traveling salesmen discussing their conquests. And then look at the girls keeping men's secrets locked in themselves as if they were little fireproof safes. The little whores, the companions of one night, the mistresses of married men, the girl friends of bankers and politicians, the slim-legged secretaries, all those cohorts of fluffy-looking females who could ruin men, families, industries, countries if they would talk. But they don't talk. There are two sides to this special, female brand of discretion. Not to tell. And not to ask questions. I didn't ask, and Clara didn't tell.

Since Walter had fallen there was no sense in keeping the office in Giessheim, and the three-months'-credit letter had been exhausted for a long time. Liquidating the Morning Call was my last duty as a secretary. I did it, all stiff and numb and dry inside. Around New Year Clara found the right job for me. It appeared that the Grand Duchess had made an appeal for social workers and nurses to be trained, as all the trained ones had to attend to wounded soldiers in the hospitals at the front and in the hinterland. Looking after the old and decrepit at home, after the rickety illegitimate babies, controlling the whole wormlike life in the slums of the old quarters, was much less glamorous than nursing Our Heroes. We were a scant group, hardly a dozen, rushed by a tough middle-aged lady doctor through the necessary preparations for our improvised duties.

Dr. Süsskind looked and talked and acted exactly like the caricatures of feminist leaders and suffragettes in funny magazines. She never called the war anything but a big pigsty, and she maintained stubbornly that woman suffrage would do away with all the evils in the world, with wars, injustice, child labor, executions, and all the other cruel nonsense men had slipped into their laws and habits. To her all men were nasty boys who liked nothing better than to make dangerous noises with firecrackers and didn't care if an innocent bystander got hurt. In her own order of the world everything was beautifully and serenely organized, except that she had forgotten to put in a little nook for the sexual relations between men and women, for the disturbing, ruinous little something which she definitely refused to call love. It was good to be trained by Dr. Süsskind, for she was hard and tough to herself and there was no cuddling us or our charges. For some time I still hugged my loss and grief to my heart before I fell asleep, but soon I was so tired that my eyes closed the moment I turned off the light. And still a while later it seemed natural that Walter was gone, because he was only one in millions, and you could not expect any special treatment from fate, could you?

I had an edge on my fellow workers because this was not very much different from some of the work I had done for Walter. When certain districts were assigned to us I begged to be put into Giessheim. "You'll have to talk to the Grand Duchess about that," Dr. Süsskind told me. "She is the organizer of this work, I'm only the drill sergeant. Great woman, our Grand Duchess." I was surprised to hear such soft and loyal praise emanating from Doc's faintly mustached lips. I was even more surprised when I discovered that the Grand Duchess seemed to know me. We had been given two rooms in the Assembly Hall for our training; the big hall, where the balls of happier winters had taken place, was converted into a hospital ward. One morning when we came there we found the Grand Duchess sitting behind a little table with the Doc, busy with maps and charts and files and case histories. A lady-in-waiting yawned in the background, because she and the Grand Duchess had been at the depot all night long taking over the transports of wounded soldiers. There was no formality at all about our so-called graduation. Doc barked a few words at us, and then the Grand Duchess, obviously embarrassed, said in a low voice and with a lisp that she thanked us for offering our time and assistance. "This is no charity work but a very necessary, very legitimate part of the order we have to maintain at home," she said. "You helpers will get paid—very badly paid at that, because there are too many causes that need financial support and our means are limited. You will be expected to give your whole heart and soul to your work and not to get tired or discouraged. I hope you don't start out with false, romantic ideas about the social work we are doing. It's hard, gruelling work and most ungratifying. The only satisfaction is to know that it has to be done and that you are doing it. And now, if Dr. Süsskind agrees, I will give you your first assignments. If you will step up one by . . ."

It did not sound at all as you would expect a shy, embarrassed, shadowlike Grand Duchess to sound; but while she spoke she seemed to become surer of herself, even if she did not raise her voice and we had to perk up our ears to understand her. She had a little lisp that made everything she said slightly funny, and she spoke the rustic dialect of the district where she had been brought up. She was dressed in an abominable sort of moldy green, and she had pinched a most unbecoming pince-nez onto her nose through which she scanned the files that Dr. Süsskind shoved into her hands.

"Marion Sommer, Marion Sommer," she said when I came up to the table. "So you are Marion Sommer. And you want to work in Giessheim, Dr. Süsskind tells me. Why?"

"I know the district and the people there," I said. "Your Royal Highness," I added lamely.

"It's a difficult district. Did you work there before?"

"Yes," I said. "I was Walter Brandt's secretary for a while."

"Oh," she said, taking off the eyeglasses and looking straight at me. "He fell in Flanders, didn't he? I am sorry. He was a good man, and he stuck to his convictions. Well, then. There will be a lot to do in Giessheim. Many of the girls working at the Hewa are—er——"

"Pregnant," said Dr. Süsskind.

"Yes. I would like a list of them with the presumable dates of their confinements so that we will be able to provide beds for them in the hospitals. Furthermore there is an increase of diseases—er—I mean——"

"Venereal diseases. Syphilis. Gonorrhea," said Dr. Süsskind.

"Exactly—to be expected, and we should like to keep a certain control over it. We have handbills printed that tell when and where free treatments can be obtained. Let's see what else. According to reports I received there is a new district coming up near the barracks—a district which——"

"A red-light district," Dr. Süsskind assisted.

"That's it. You will have to keep an eye on it. We won't allow any girls under twenty there. Dr. Süsskind will also furnish me with a report about the health of the girls who work in the new explosives plant of the Hewa. I want you to collaborate on that too. That is all for the moment. Dr. Süsskind will give you your detailed orders for this week. Your wages are seventy marks a month. Thank you and good luck, Fräulein Sommer."

"Thanks—I'll try to do everything to your satisfaction," I said "—Your Royal Highness." She was the sort of person you would always forget to address by her title. She put the pince-nez back on her nose and rustled in her documents. "Fräulein Sommer," she said, just as I made a poor attempt at a curtsy and turned away.

"Yes—Your Royal Highness?"

"Aren't you from Vienna?"

"Yes, Your Royal Highness."

"Can you talk with our people? I mean, do you have trouble with the dialect?"

"I don't think so. I pick up dialects rather easily. I like this one."

"You are a friend of our ballet master, aren't you?" the Grand Duchess said. "Yes, I thought so. I saw you together in the theater—or was it at the Assembly Ball?"

God, what a small town this is, I thought. For a second that incredible gay night bobbed up from the past. Howard. We had gone up to the gallery and kissed in this same building, it wasn't a year yet. Gott strafe England.

"Yes, Your Royal Highness."

"She is a great artist, Clara Balbi is; I admire her greatly."

I didn't know what to say.

"Well—that's all, so far. Thank you, Fräulein Sommer." The Grand Duchess discharged me.

"At your service, Your Royal Highness."

Times kept on being great and glorious and studded with victories; there was an exultant, slightly febrile gaiety everywhere. The theater crowded, with handsome officers on leave in the orchestra seats and a row of boxes reserved for wounded privates who were herded in by good-looking, tender nurses. Celebrations with wine and music. Bazaars for every conceivable purpose. People fell in love, got engaged, and married within a week while on leave from the front. Spring came like a fever, and the park and the orangery at night resembled the groves where ancient Greece had celebrated its Orgiastic Mysteries. On every bench, behind every shrub and bush, a man in uniform lying with a girl. May, June, and July. The first crop of war babies was born and given patriotic, high-sounding names. About thirty per cent of them had been made fatherless orphans before their birth, for the waste of human lives during the first unexperienced year of the war was stupendous. In Giessheim the number of pregnant girls was staggering to a young welfare worker like me. Also, my statistical curves of venereal diseases looked like the Himalayas. Dr. Süsskind shook her head and prescribed the new miracle remedy, Salvarsan. The Grand Duchess gave us the gate lodge in the little summer palace to be used as a home for illegitimate babies. We worked there in shifts between our outside work. There was hardly a week that we did not discover the ugly, shiny blisters of the disease on the tiny soles of a newly-born's miraculously perfect feet. I liked the work in the baby home best of all; my hours of duty there seemed like a holiday and a relaxation. The Grand Duchess seemed to feel the same way. She would visit us many an evening before going to the depot, where she had organized the service for taking over the badly wounded soldiers, who were mostly brought in during the night. She would walk with with me from crib to crib, watching me giving the ten-o'clock bottle to my yelling charges, who suddenly grew silent and cross-eyed with absorption.

"Do you think you would have a glass of lemonade for me before I go to the depot, Marion?" she would ask.

I made the lemonade, with some white, synthetic powder instead of lemons, which we did not have since the war began. Sugar too had been rationed lately and the country began to be short of this and that. But people said it would surely all be over before winter, and the bulletins from the front were better than ever. The Grand Duchess drank her lemonade in the little office that was partitioned off for the baby nurse on duty, while her lady-in-waiting took a little ten-minute nap in the car outside. It was during these brief quiet pauses that we became acquainted at first and later almost friends. The Grand Duchess seemed of an insatiable curiosity. "Tell me something, Marion," she would say, "tell me about Vienna and about your life there. You went to school? How many children were in class with you? . . . Fifty? How interesting! It must be marvelous to grow up with such a bunch of children. You had many friends among them? And Clara Balbi? She is your best friend, isn't she? . . .

Oh, you know her since childhood? How interesting. Tell me about her—was she a beautiful child? And talented? How is she? Very delicate? Whimsical? She is as fluffy and charming as a Dresden china doll, isn't she?"

It made me laugh. "Clara? Fluffy?" I cried. "Your Royal Highness, Clara is as straight and strong and springy as a rod of steel. She swears like an army sergeant, works like a Turk, and eats like a shark. I wish we had a midwife in Giessheim with the strength and endurance of Clara. You have been tricked by her gauze skirts—Your Royal Highness."

The Grand Duchess seemed to pore for a long time over my description. "Interesting," she said absently. "Give her my regards, your strong friend—I would like to meet her sometime. . . ."

I told it to Clara, and Clara shut up with that peculiar deaf-mute expression on her face that meant: Closed road. "Her Royal Highness is at liberty to command me to the royal box any time Her Royal Highness desires so," she said. And later that evening, as she sat under the lamp and mended her tights: "You seem to be all charmed that she condescends to talk to you like a normal human being. A fine socialist you have turned out to be, my girl!"

"She is a good sort, that's all," I said, blushing all the same; for it was true that I felt impressed and honored by the special attention the Grand Duchess bestowed on me. It's amazing how firmly planted such prejudices are and how hard it is to shake them off.

I am afraid there is something wrong with me. It's always been my trouble that I see both sides to everything. As long as people thought of the world as a flat slice swimming on top of the universe with God above and the devil beneath it, everything was much simpler. When you find out that it is a round globe—that one side is dark when the other one is bright, that the two halves are not simple black and white, but that they take their turns at it—things become much more complicated. That's why I could never be a partisan or a real fighter. All I can do is to be sorry—for the oppressed as well as for the oppressors. For the ones who carry the flags in front as well as for the stragglers

who are left way behind. That's why Walter never made a real
socialist out of me and Kurt didn't turn me into a conservative,
and John Sprague couldn't talk me into becoming a Republican,
nor his son into going communist, nor Michael invoke my
sympathies for the Nazis. And why all the isms which were
preached to me one after the other ran off like water from a
duck's tail. There is a leak in my character, I'm afraid. I simply
can't take sides.

And so, although I had loved Walter, I could still become a
friend of the Grand Duchess. And though I grew very fond of
her I did not give up looking upon the little court of Bergheim
as on a silly and expensive masquerade. As for the people in my
district in Giessheim, they were real enough, and I was sorry
for them and wanted to help them as best I could. But it was
not an easy job to like them, and they made it rather hard for
me. The names I've been called in the course of it, and the lies
I've been told, and the things they did to spite me! But that is
the common experience of all welfare workers, and I had been
warned.

"How come you don't prefer being a nurse in a hospital and
taking care of soldiers like the other girls?" the Grand Duchess
asked me some other time.

"I don't know," I said. "It seems so much of a trade, or
whatever I should call it."

"What do you mean, a trade?"

"Oh, all that petting and flirting that goes with it, and it's
so damn becoming to be a nurse and wear a cap; most soldiers
can't help falling for it."

"I didn't know you were a prude, Marion," the Grand Duchess
said. "I think the nurses in the field lazarets are admirable, and
what we can do at home is absolutely nothing compared with
their heroism."

"Yes, but in the field lazarets they have the good, old, ugly
ones. Our hospitals in town are marriage markets."

"Is that bad? Wouldn't you want to get married to some nice
officer with the E.K.I.?"

"No. Not yet," I said. "You see, the man I was in love with

was killed in Flanders. Maybe that's why I shrink back from bandaging wounded men—I can't quite explain it, but I'd rather stick to babies and prostitutes for a little while yet—Your Royal Highness."

"Oh. I see. Look here, Marion, could you keep the 'Royal Highness' for those occasions when my lady-in-waiting is around? It's so much bother when we are alone. Agreed?"

"Yes—I—thanks, Your Royal Highness. I mean—I wouldn't know how to address you otherwise."

"Well, Marion, the few friends I have call me Pimpernel. It's a funny name, but that's what they call me. Will you remember it?"

"Yes—indeed—Your Royal Highness. I'm—I'm very fond of you—Pimpernel. So are most of the poor people in Giessheim. . . ."

In September the Grand Duke decided to go to the front and stay with his glorious regiments, as the Bergheim papers put it. There was a solemn ceremony as he handed the reigns of the country over to the Grand Duchess. He also made a speech that was printed in the papers and in which he proclaimed his good wife, the Grand Duchess Helena Doris Malvina Eleonore of Zuche-Bergheim, would take over the regency during his absence and that she would be a mother to the country, head of the crown council, ruler over the people of the town and state of Bergheim until the time when he would return with his victorious troops. That evening there was a torch parade, and the Grand Duke came out on the balcony with the Grand Duchess and the two little princes and the military band played the Dutch Thanksgiving Prayer which, for some reason, had become another German anthem during the war. People said that this war would last three years; meat, bread, butter, and eggs were rationed, and there were many cripples on the street. The Grand Duchess installed those who had lost their eyesight in the summer palace where we had our baby home and had them trained in Braille and basket weaving. She dropped the last pretenses at court etiquette, left her yapping ladies-in-waiting at home, and could be seen trotting along Rhine Street, her hat awry, her suit impossible as ever, in a great hurry to get to a session of the crown council, while her car took a load of invalids for a ride along the Rhine.

"People say you are wonderful," I told her, proud as if Pimpernel had been my own creation. "They say the country has never been run so efficiently as just now, in spite of the war and the blockade and the lack of food. In comparison to the other states of Germany——"

"That's nothing," she said, wiping the beads of perspiration from her face—she was always perspiring now and always in a hurry. "Every woman can run a country efficiently. It's just like running a household, only on a larger scale. Look at Catherine and Maria Theresia and Victoria. But I am. glad I can prove to the Grand Duke that I am good for something."

Poor Pimpernel, ever since her second cousin had been a visitor for the hunting season at her parents' castle ten years ago, she had lived in his shade; married to him yet unhappily in love; he was so charming, so brilliant, so artistic, so beloved by everybody. No wonder she had grown an. inferiority complex and nursed it along through the years until it had become as heavy as an oversized pumpkin on a thin stem. Since he had gone to war she unfolded herself, she began to bloom in her own unobtrusive way; she still was badly dressed, her complexion had gone rather worse, she took no time to groom her hair, and her lisp was what it had always been. But she had dropped much of her shyness and baffled her cabinet ministers by the amount of solid knowledge she had accumulated in her quiet way. "Other women may be like flowers," she once said to me, "but I am like a potato. I've got my shape and coloring from growing underground. Not pretty but useful. I'm not any better than I was before, it's only that people prefer potatoes to flowers just now."

What worried me a bit about her was that she grew thinner and thinner and that she had acquired a nervous twitch. of her left eyelid. Sometimes she would close the eye and press the lid down with two fingers and hold it. there for a while. Yet as soon as she opened the eye there was the twitch again. "You don't get enough sleep, Pimpernel," I would tell her, galloping at her side through the corridors.

"Oh, but I sleep plenty, I catch a catnap ever so often," she would answer. "I bet I sleep more than you and your friend Clara Balbi. I notice she is on hospital duty almost every night after the theater."

The truth was that Clara recently seemed to have more spare time than she had afforded herself ever since the beginning of the war; that beginning that seemed to lie somewhere in a dim and almost mythical past. We all had adjusted our lives to the war. It seemed natural, as if there had always been a war and always would be. Life was normal in an abnormal way. Any terror, if it lasts long enough, will become a routine, and there is nothing so amazing and reassuring as the human ability To Get Used To It. But we sometimes sat up in the middle of the night, torn from sleep by a sudden terror, and listened as if we could hear the roar of the battlefields somewhere in the west, where the great killing and dying went on day after day.

During the summer, when the theater had vacations, Clara passed her examination as a Red Cross nurse, and one nice day she startled me with the announcement that she had volunteered for service in a front lazaret. "And what about me?" I asked. "Am I to stay behind, all by myself?"

"You are all right. You have a lot of work to do, and you like the sort of work you are doing, or don't you?"

I said yes, in a way I did. "Well, that's the point," Clara said. "I hate the work they have settled on me in the theater. I am sick and tired of all the silly flag-waving, patriotic little ballets they make me do for Our Heroes. Moreover I have a good idea that Our Heroes are just as sick and tired of it as I am. I simply don't feel like dancing a goddamned idiotic rose or a peacock or some such blinking nonsense for the entertainment of our audiences. For God's sake, Marion, don't you feel we are not living in these times but outside, preserved in a jar and put away on a shelf? Jesus, when I think of the things I would *like* to dance and of what I *am* dancing, I feel like puking at myself."

I sat quiet and listened to the outburst. I thought I could guess what was behind it all. Clara grabbed her hair in both her hands and pulled it hard, as was her habit when she tried to get hold of herself. "Anyway, as long as I can't dance what I like, I want at least to be where things happen. Not just sit safely behind and go insane by and by," she said, calmer. I waited a moment, wondering whether I might cross invisible boundaries. I had never asked questions, but it worried me that Clara had stopped talking about her Man.

"Has he gone to the front?" I said. "You don't have to tell me if you don't feel like it."

"Yes, he has. What about it?"

"Is he—I mean—is he all right? Or haven't you had mail for a while?"

"Oh, he is all right. He is behind the lines. Near Brussels."

"Well, that's fine then. What is he doing there?"

"He's writing sonnets," Clara said to my utter amazement. "Sonnets about little wooden crosses and about the stumps of shelled willow trees which look like praying hunchbacks, and similar trash. And I suppose he's getting drunk a lot or maybe he has started on dope. Anyway, they keep him well fed and out of danger and as ignorant of the real things as a goldfish in his bowl."

"Who are They?" I asked, bewildered. I had worked out a little idea that Clara's Man might be a doctor in one of the lazarets near the front.

Clara got up and knelt down in front of the corner cupboard where we kept our china. She took out the plates for our supper with a great rattling and clattering of dishes.

"You mean to say that you are dense enough not to know who he is?" she said. "Of course, it's him, the Grand Duke. Hugo the Feeble. Hugo the Out-of-Step-with-the-Times. And of all blasted idiots I have to be the one to be in love with him."

It took a time to sink in. "Well, say something!" Clara shouted at me.

"There was never even the faintest gossip about you and him," I said stupidly. "You must have been wonderfully discreet."

"Oh yes," she said, "I've been discreet till I got blue in the face. This is not exactly the court of Louis XV and I'm no Du Barry. He was so mortified lest his wife should get hurt. But I think she is the only person who has an inkling. Wives always have. Poor pimple-faced nuisance. Mother of the country! Haw!"

"She is good," I said loyally.

"Oh sure. She's much better than he is, I suppose. It's no fault of hers if she bores him so he is all molding and rotting away inside. If he only weren't so helpless I wouldn't have to love him so."

I was sorry for all three of them, every one of them unhappy and lonely in his own corner of the eternal triangle. "She loves him too, the Grand Duchess," I said.

"Yes. I know. But she is impotent," Clara replied.

"For God's sake! Don't be absurd. She has two children," I cried, exasperated.

Clara came from her corner, stopped in front of my low chair, cupped her hands around my face, and looked down at me with her old, amused expression, which had not changed since our first meeting in the dairy shop.

"Don't you know, little monk, that there are millions of women with children who have always been frigid?" she said.

It was just like Clara to say such a thing, and I could hear that she was sorry for my innocence and also for all the frigid women on this earth.

I'VE SOMETIMES WONDERED whether Kurt Tillmann and I would have been a happily married couple, with children and grand-children, with a silver anniversary and a bridge party every Friday evening and a nice annuity for our old age and two lots, side by side, in the cemetery. It would necessarily have been a German cemetery, because with Kurt I would have lived and stayed and died in one and the same place, and there would have been none of my own restlessness and itinerant living and packing up and going elsewhere. Or maybe I would have packed up anyway and gotten a divorce and left him with a great crash and noise, unfit as I am for marital bliss. Or maybe, with Kurt, I would have lost that rebellious, nomadic strain in my character and would have become calm and serene, a good Hitler-worshiping German hausfrau. And I wouldn't have made a fool of myself at forty-four, falling in love with an Englishman hardly older than my own sons. Kurt certainly had the making of a good husband, a good, solid, home-loving, peaceable, well-providing husband with shoulders extremely restful to cuddle up to and go to sleep on. Clara once told me that men can be divided into two classes, those with cold and those with warm feet. She claimed that it takes a great love to go to bed with one of the cold-footed race, especially in such a rough and freezing country as Germany was when coal was rationed. But she maintained that even a little spark of passion was sufficient to slip under the blanket with a warm-footed man, and, once there, you would feel cozy and tender and delightfully relaxed very soon.

Such a man was Captain Tillmann.

However, it is all idle speculation how our marriage would have turned out in the long run, for although we were married for almost two and a half years, he was on leave not more than six weeks at the most during all that time, and, like hundreds of thousands of war wives, I kept on being married to a stranger.

I met him one night in May 1916 at the depot when he came in with a transport of wounded. He wore a tattered infantry captain's uniform, with his right arm in a sling and the coat thrown over one shoulder. He limped a bit but he could walk; obviously he was a slight case, and he was pleasantly brisk but not loud. As far as I could make out, he had escorted twenty of our wounded men to Bergheim while he himself was to go on to Hahnenstadt in North Germany. He had a little beard, much lighter than his hair, deep-set blue eyes; he was short and stocky and looked like every other slightly wounded infantry captain. "You are a Prussian?" the Grand Duchess asked him, lisping with embarrassment as she always did when she had to talk platitudes to the wounded. "I should say, my little one," he answered pleasantly. Somebody nudged him, whispering into his ear that he was speaking to Her Royal Highness the Grand Duchess of Zuche-Bergheim, and for us, who had been on duty with her through a hundred weary nights, it was funny to see how terrified he snapped to attention, stuttering worse than Pimpernel herself.

How well I remember that night—or any of those nights when we did station duty. The light of the arch lamps seemed dim, for the waste of electric power had been cut down greatly and sometimes it was more merciful to keep the trainloads of wrecked men in darkness. The stale breath of coke and coal and steam under the glass roof; the blurred, pale-looking faces of soldiers peering out from passing trains which went back to the front; the strangely mute procession of wounded men emerging from the lazaret trains. Some walking alone, some supported by their comrades, some carried out on stretchers. We had to sort them out: the slight cases, the helpless cases, the hopeless, the dying, the dead. Some had bundles of bloody gauze instead of faces, some came without their arms or legs, with a queer smarting emptiness under the grayish blankets thrown over the stretcher, some delirious, some unconscious, some swearing so as not to groan. On the whole though they were rather quiet; I don't know if the nurses kept them under morphine for the arrival, if it was resignation or even a pathetic sort of swagger. All the slight cases had the same fixed grin as they piled out of the train, glad, I suppose, to be away from the front for a while, glad to be alive and to have two feet, two hands, two eyes, all still complete. There were no pretty young girls ready with flowers and kisses any more, only two determined, middle-aged women ladling out coffee and handing cigarettes—patient and enduring left-overs of the exuberant cohorts which had been there in the beginning of the war.

I remember that we were short of doctors that night, for our army surgeon had come down with typhoid fever (there was a slight epidemic in town under the official heading of Intestinal Flu) and Dr. Süsskind had taken over—to the amused surprise of the slight cases who had never been treated by a lady doctor. She looked like a badly shaven old gray-haired man in her uniform anyway, and only when she walked from one stretcher to the next could you see that she wore skirts. "Well, Captain, what seems to be the trouble with our arm?" she asked Kurt. "I'm supposed to get my bandage changed," he said. "But I can wait; take the others first; this is really nothing."

Although it was a warm night he looked chilly, as most of them did. Lost too much blood, I thought. I took him into the second room, where we had tea and coffee for those who had to wait. I don't remember a word we talked while I took off his bandage and prepared him for Dr. Süsskind's inspection. The usual stuff, I think. I asked him if he had pains and he said no, and I asked him how things were at the front and he said fine, and I asked him where he had been last and he said at Donaumont. The same conversation we had with all soldiers. I did not like the looks of his arm, and I went into the other room to Dr. Süsskind and told her. When I came back he had begun to perspire but he still looked chilly, and I knew it was cold sweat. It didn't mean anything to me, because when you do this sort of duty you have to get callous or you are of no use. "Want some more coffee?" I asked him, and he grinned and said, "Brandy would be better." We had no brandy at the station, and he snatched my hand and said, "Or holding onto you for a moment." I stopped, balancing my bandage tray in one hand. "Don't act like a baby," I said, because he was really a slight case and I could not spend too much time on him. "Tell me, do you have one?" he said, hanging onto my hand.

"What?" I asked. "Brandy? I'm sorry, but——"

"No, a baby," he said.

"No. I'm not married," I said.

"That's good," he said, and with that he let go of my hand and I went on. When Dr. Süsskind examined his wound she told him that he could not go on but would have to stay in one of our hospitals. He remonstrated weakly; he seemed very anxious to get to Hahnenstadt, where his family lived. "Listen, Captain," Dr. Süsskind said brusquely, focusing her eyeglasses on him. "You don't want to get gangrene and lose that arm, do you?"

"Hell no," he said.

"That's fine," she said. "Because some do. Some would rather lose an arm than be patched up and sent back to the front. But I wouldn't think you were one of them."

"Assembly Hospital," she told me, writing out his blank. I flung his coat over his shoulder, as his teeth had begun to chatter, and took his good arm to lead him out.

"I'll have to send a telegram to my sister," he said.

"Sure, sure," I said.

"She'll be worried to death," he said. "Will you do it for me?"

"Certainly," I said. "Now come on, the bus won't wait for you. You'll feel much better in your hospital cot."

"I feel better already," he said. "You're wonderful. You're a wonderful girl. What's your name? I'd like to marry you."

Before we had reached the door he keeled over. They had to keep him three weeks in the hospital, but then he was perfectly sound and well again and he still had both his arms.

THIS IS HOW IT WAS toward the end of the second year of war: we still had many victories, not as great and important ones as at the beginning, but enough to keep us happy and proud and safe. The French had not invaded Germany, whereas the Germans stood deep in their country. The papers harped on it and we told it to one another whenever we felt a little downhearted. The flags were still brought out occasionally; they looked a bit washed out from sunshine and rain and too much use. Life still went on as usual, and we were as gay and cheerful as ever. Also there seemed to be more people more in love and more married couples more deeply devoted to each other than in peacetimes, and this alone should have given a heightened glow to life. On the other hand, whereas in the beginning we had believed in war as something beautiful and great, in fact the greatest thing there was, we now knew that a lot of ugliness was mixed into its heroic fabric, and we began to dream of peace as a prisoner dreams of freedom. Too often had the church bells of the old cathedral pealed for a victory. Oh that they would ring for an armistice soon!

Food was strictly rationed, and most of us felt tired and fagged most of the time. If vitamins had been discovered at the time, we would have known that we suffered from lack of vitamins, but as we lived in ignorance, anyone who had farmer relatives remembered them with a great physical urgency and visited them in the hope of extracting a scrap of bootlegged butter or a little piece of meat. There was no leather for shoes, and the knitting orgies of 1914 had stopped for lack of wool. Milk was reserved for babies and pregnant mothers, and we had a lot of trouble with our teeth. The so-called love parcels that were sent to the men at the front contained books and games and saved-up cigarettes instead of ham and cakes and woolen socks as before. There were very few men who volunteered for military service, but many who tried by hook and crook to become ineligible and stay at home. We all had learned a thing or two: That not all generals were strategic geniuses. That not all French, Russians, Italians, and British were cowards. That not all Germans were good and not all enemies were bad. We still believed that ours was the good cause and that God fought on our side—and didn't realize that the enemies believed the same on their part. We also began to notice that the war did not have the cleaning, purifying effect on our characters as generally believed. There was a lot of bootlegging and bribing and racketeering and profiteering all around us, all done by our co-patriots. We also found out that our soldiers had no hatred for the enemy, rather a sort of respectful compassion and sympathy. They are good guys, just like us, was their contention; we are fighting for our country and they for theirs. Still we liked to read the high figures of people killed by our armies in battle. There was the same gloating, itching satisfaction in it as in winning at the races or catching big fish. We did not think of them as human beings who had been young and strong and alive and who were dead now, fouling corpses, bodies blown to bits, cadavers caught in shell holes and hanging from barbed wires. A few thousand dead enemies was something abstract to be glad about. Also it never came to our mind that any of the soldiers we knew personally had killed. Nor did the soldiers ever mention it. And all of us had the feeling, though no one expressed it, that something would snap in us if the war were not over by winter.

As Captain Tillmann got better I saw a lot of him. I found him loitering around the baby home when I left. He rode on the trolley car to Giessheim with me, escorted me on my errands from house to house, waiting outside. Usually he was seen surrounded by children, for their curiosity never got tired of wounded soldiers. He told them tall stories, showed them new figures for playing cat's cradle, and presented them with little bits of shell fragments that had been taken from his arm and thigh and made wonderful souvenirs.

Soon Kurt Tillmann had become My Captain. Most females had a soldier of their own, a possession dangling between being a helpless, pitiful invalid to be nursed and pampered and fussed over and a strong, gallant, brave protector to look up to and be proud of. "How is Your Captain doing?" the Grand Duchess would ask me. "Your Captain will be dismissed from hospital on Monday," Dr. Süsskind would tell me. "Your Captain is a fine fellow; he gave my Willie a piece of chocolate," the women in Giessheim would gratefully remark. "Your Captain is the first nice Prussian I've met," the girl who was on duty with me in the baby home would say when she found him waiting for me. Kurt seemed to think of himself as being My Captain too. He had handed his whole person over to me. He claimed that he had to be taken care of, that I had to walk him in the park, that I had to visit him on the terrace of the Assembly, that I had to write his letters for him until he could use his right arm again. Eager as he had been to get home to Hahnenstadt, he kept hanging around Bergheim even after he was dismissed and given four weeks' leave for his full recuperation. During the second week we became engaged.

Since Clara had left for the front I had been lonesome. She had not become a nurse after all, but had been commanded by the Grand Duke to give performances with four of her ballet girls for the Bergheim regiments at the front. She swore fiercely when she packed her trashy costumes. Captain Tillmann was the first bit of personal warmth that came my way after a long time of emotional frustration. (I kept on thinking of him as Captain Tillmann even after we were married.) It felt good to be kissed again, to watch him smoke his pipe, to listen to the masculine sound of his knocking it against the ashtray and to help him fill it again, for he was still awkward with his hand. It felt good that the room smelled of tobacco and leather and shaving soap and man. For too long had I been in the sole company of women who were soft and sad and frightened, yet who pretended all the time to be strong, gay, and cheerful. Men were strong by nature, they needed no make-believe, and I think Kurt was brave also. At least he never gave any sign of being afraid or of not wanting to go out again after every one of his injuries, and he seemed not to be aware that he could be killed. Maybe this too was only pretense and a convention—I never got close enough to him to find out.

We had a little tift before our wedding, because Kurt wanted me to give up my work and join his family in Hahnenstadt and I refused. "What a pighead you are!" he said. "Worse than Pulke." Pulke was his sergeant, and he spoke of him all the time —telling little anecdotes, making fun of him, complaining about Pulke's constantly disobeying orders and knowing everything better—and altogether giving me a faint idea of the unspoken, infinite fondness behind his words, the sort of fondness that might spring up between men who share endless dangers and the raucous brief respites between them. "And you like Pulke more than me," I answered evasively. In the end the Grand Duchess settled this problem for me. She talked to Captain Tillmann and begged him not to take me away from her. He bowed and scraped and stuttered nonsense, clicked heels, and stood to attention. It amused me to see him so utterly impressed by royalty, even by Pimpernel's unimpressive, badly dressed, shy sort of royalty. Probably Captain Tillmann was a snob. Probably under normal circumstances he would have been just another Cousin Hermann. Probably he would never have married me under normal circumstances and maybe I wouldn't have been able to live with him for six months. But it was during the war, and we never found out.

We were married on the running belt, along with another dozen war couples. Kurt's train left at four o'clock in the morning. We got up in the middle of the night, doped with sleepiness and not quite aware that our parting would hurt. It was like the queer twilight condition you pass through before an operation when you are nicely filled up with scopolamine. "Where did you put my shaving things?" Kurt said, standing in the door of the bathroom, in his underthings. I would have liked to kiss the scars on his arm, but I was afraid it would seem sentimental. We had been sentimental at the beginning of the war, but now we had left sentimentality way behind us. I gave him his razor.

"Won't Pulke be surprised when he sees my face as smooth as a baby's behind! The old blighter," Kurt said and dived back into the bathroom. I folded our marriage certificate away. He came back into the room, shaved, and I saw that he wore his identification tag again, which he had taken off during his leave. "Here," he said, rummaging in the pocket of his tunic. "You can have my bread tickets for this week, I don't need them. I'll get mine on army rations." I took the sheet of perforated stamps and automatically counted them. "Thanks. It's a great help," I said.

"This is a God-awful hour to go away from one's wife," he said. "Come, give us a kiss before I put on my coat."

"Take good care of yourself," I said. And then I stood stiff and silent for a moment, because I had seen a ghost. "Take good care of yourself," I had said to Walter Brandt. He had gone away and never come back, and I had piled huge boulders of forgetfulness over his memory. There he was all of a sudden, the only second in my being together with Kurt that he had made an appearance. I wanted Kurt to come back.

"And don't cheat me with one of those cute French girls our soldiers always fall for," I said hurriedly, because it was very necessary to make a joke.

"Pulke wouldn't let me even if I wanted to," Kurt said. I don't want you to get killed, not you, was what I thought. Don't look so pale and desperate, I won't get killed, not if I can help it, now that I have you, was what he probably thought, what every soldier thought when he left his wife. But those were forbidden words, never spoken, never expressed. The conventions held tight. Good women did not cry when their men went off, and that was that. I sometimes wondered whether our men were grateful for it or whether they thought us hard and callous and thoughtless; if it wouldn't have been kinder to them to let them know how afraid we were for them and that we would have preferred a living coward to a dead hero. As it was, women seemed all to confoundedly eager to send their men to the lines, as if they didn't know what was going on out there.

We took a taxi, we went to the depot, we stood around on the platform and spoke nothing but nonsense, the train pulled in, punctual as trains were in Germany even during the war; it was not a military train, just a train like any other train, half of it filled with civilians and some compartments reserved for officers. Three minutes' stop.

"Well," Kurt said.

"Well," said I.

"Good-by, my little one," he said.

"Good-by, my captain," I said. He boarded the train, appeared at the window, let it down, and held out his hand for me.

"Give my deepest respect to the Grand Duchess," he said; I don't know whether he meant it or whether it was for the benefit of the other officers in his compartment. "I will," I said. "And tell Her Royal Highness not to work you to a frazzle," he said. "I'll want you complete when I come on leave next time."

"When are you coming?" I asked. The train began to move, and I walked alongside, holding onto his hand.

"At Christmas, I hope," he said. The train moved faster, and I began to trot.

"There we go," Kurt said. "Good-by." I ran along for another few yards, and then the pull became too hard and I let go of his hand. The engine spat a thick ball of gray steam into my face, and when it dissolved I saw the train disappearing into the tunnel behind the depot, with its tail lights gleaming and gone. I don't know how it happened that I suddenly thought of my Fine grandfather then. I hadn't thought of him or of any of the clan for years. When I had been a little child he had been sitting on a cloud next to Godfather and put in a good word for me whenever it seemed necessary. Putzi was up there too. Wonder if they still call each other Herr Sommer and Herr Dobsberg.

Please, I thought, please, you, up there, take care of Captain Tillmann: he is my husband.

AFTER A FEW WEEKS my wedding and my marriage and my having been with Captain Tillmann took on the queer, in-

tangible quality that dreams have when you try to tell them.
Certainly it didn't seem as real as the cases in Giessheim, and the
babies in ther cribs and the mothers who did not want to nurse
them, and the transports of wounded coming in during the
nights, and Pimpernel's homely twitching face and the pale
countenance of Anna, the girl who came to me once a week to
clean our cottage and whose boy friend had been lost on the
field of honor. And it all became real only six weeks later, when
I began to feel sort of funny and when Dr. Süsskind pronounced
me with child.

God, how wonderful I felt with that child growing inside of me!
Never before had I felt so strong and healthy and complete and
in harmony with everything and everybody. During the first
three months I had to spit a little every morning; I rather liked
that. It was little Erika's way of saying good morning to me
and assuring me that she had not got lost during the night. Erika
is the German name for heather, and I had always liked it; my
favorite doll had been called Erika too, and there was no hesitation about the name and no doubt for me that my child would be
a girl. I had also very definite ideas how she would look, how I
would dress her, and how I would save her many of the detours
I had taken before growing up. Maybe my feeling so full of pep
and cheer and enterprise also had something to do with the fact
that half a pint of milk was added to my daily ration, according to my new station as a pregnant woman.

To prepare a trousseau for a coming baby was not an easy
undertaking at that time, because the six diapers and two layettes
ascribed by law were made of ersatz and fell to pieces after three
washings. I had enough of that trouble in our baby home and
among the 1916 crop in Giessheim. The Grand Duchess had given
us a few dozens of her own sheets with the crown embroidered
on them, and we had cut them into pieces and washed them into
rags, and after that there were no more sheets. On the strength
of my marriage certificate I had also received my lawful ration
of three bed sheets; the idea was to use two while the third one
was laundered. I cut them up and made them into tiny baby
shirts; they were rough and coarse, and I wondered if Erika

would like them. But this was a rough and coarse world, and she had better get her skin hardened right from the beginning.

And then we had the explosion in Giessheim. It happened on a Monday morning in November when I was down in K 36, attending to the three Moller children.

They had whooping cough and the germs came floating into every house, having taken passage on the dust clouds of Giessheim. I had just lined them up on the kitchen table to wash them, clean their noses and dose them with Thymol when something hit us. Many things happened at the same time. Something knocked the breath out of my lungs and my ears seemed to burst, not with the huge muffled noise in the distance and the crash all around, but with the pressure. Something lifted me off my feet and hurled me against the stove where I burned my hand. The pain pulled me out of my stupor or a second of unconsciousness, or whatever the blackness was that had come down on me like a curtain. The windows were broken, the mirror, pride of the Mollers, had crashed down and hit the baby. I found myself holding the youngest Moller boy in my arms, he was silent for a minute dumb with fright and then he began screaming wildly, kicking his feet into my tummy as if it were a tom-tom. Erika, I thought desperately, but this was not the time to think of her.

It was a black day for Giessheim. We never learned the exact number of the victims. The papers spoke of twenty-four and called them heroes who had fallen on the Field of Honor. By and by we could not bear reading their bromides or hear the Field of Honor mentioned without a twitching pain all over and a desire to kick somebody in the face. Because the truth was kept from the public on principle, wild rumors spread through the town. Four hundred were killed, no six hundred, no twelve hundred. Mostly women who worked in the ammunition plants, and children too, in the packing rooms. There was a lot of muffled talk in Bergheim. Some spoke about the millions of damage the Hewa suffered and others, hitting the air with their clenched fists, asked how many millions profit the Hewa had made in this war so far. Officially the explosion was an accident as they are inevitable where huge amounts of explosives are manufactured. Unofficially people whispered of British spies, of socialistic sabotage of anarchists, of a pacifistic plot for blasting all ammunition plants and putting an end to the war, and for weeks to come the town was holding its breath, expecting another blast to tear us all into bits.

There was a solemn funeral ceremony with the Grand Duchess lisping a few stilted words which were obviously composed by one of her cabinet ministers. The people stood there, a black mass of women with a scant sprinkling of cripples and old men among them, their faces shut, their eyes empty. Pimpernel spoke into a void and I knew how agonized she felt whenever she had to use the vapid swollen words of the official lingo.

Funny, how strong and clear and sharp these memories have returned to me since there is war again. They have been buried under years of easy, carefree living, under the certainty it could never happen again, drowned out by the cries of "No More War," asleep in the false security of a pacifism that seemed to embrace the whole world. Now there is war again, with people starved, with soldiers killed, villages burning, churches bombed, women lonesome, frightened and stupidly brave, with the same God claimed by all parties to fight on their side: and all we did was walk in a circle for twenty years.

Remember the camel we saw in Jerusalem? It worked in an oilmill, it went round and round and round on a shaft, to turn the millstones that pressed the oil from the olives. It was an old camel, with the exaggerated eyelashes of a movie actress and an especially stupid expression in his face, stupid even for a camel. It had walked on and on for years, it must have covered thousands of miles, enough miles to have marched around the globe several times. "Doesn't it ever get tired?" I asked the Arab who was his master. "No, it is blinded, lady," he said with dignity. "It does not know that it walks in a circle. It believes it will arrive at an oasis at the end of the journey."

That's us, that's humanity. A stupid, blind, old camel walking in a circle, turning the millstones and hoping for an oasis.

Shortly after New Year Clara came back in a hurricane of kisses and questions and laughter and funny stories about the front theaters. It was good to have her back, and there was no end to the fun we had together after the long separation. But she still wanted to become a nurse.

"They don't send ballet girls where the real things happen," she said. "All we had was a little shelling once. It's a funny feeling. You should have seen us scramble for shelter. I'm going to get a medal for it. Imagine me with a medal, baby. But war is the shits, absolutely. For a while they kept us in Brussels and we gave performances in the Theater de la Monnaye. It has a stage as big as a depot, with the goddamned lousiest old-fashioned backdrops you can imagine. I was always afraid my four girls would get lost on that stage. But the soldiers liked it. The proposals and the propositions we got! I liked Brussels least of all, though. It's full of French whores; you should see them hanging around the hotel lobbies, all ages, all classes, expensive ones for the officers and discreet, reliable ones for the General Staff and the scum for the soldiers. They have to stand in line for their bit of fun like we do here for bread. And the men behave like devils on the loose. You see, three days' leave in Brussels means that they will be thrown into an attack when they get back in the line. No wonder they snatch what they can before they are blown to bits. And then there are the Belgian women. They all wear mourning, but I mean mourning: long black widow's weeds; and they don't look at you when they pass you on the street. Gives you the creeps. I was ashamed every time I saw one of them. I felt like saying: 'Forgive us, we have not chosen to do what we are doing. It happens to us just as it happens to you.' Well, you can't do such a thing. But I didn't like being in Brussels."

"And how is he? Your Man?"

"Homesick as a loon," Clara said. "I just hope this war will be over before he gets to see pink snakes. Seems sixteen generations of royal ancestors give you a very thin skull which is apt to crack much easier than such plebeian noodles as mine and yours. But I think I straightened him out, for a little while at least." She shut up; I could almost hear the mechanism click, and I knew that I was not to ask any more questions.

"I understand Clara Balbi has come home to us," the Grand Duchess said one evening, soon after Clara's return. "She must have interesting things to tell."

"She is not very talkative, Pimpernel."

"I should like to talk to her all the same. Do you think you might bring her along some night? I should like to meet her, quite unofficially, you know. Do you think she would mind?"

"Why should she?" I said fumblingly. I knew in my heart that she would mind, but if Pimpernel was foolish enough to be so eager about meeting her rival, it was up to me to bring Clara along. We had a little tussle about it, but I found Clara getting mellow and easier to handle since she was so undernourished. Also I could get all I wanted from her if I threatened that Erika would acquire a prenatal bellyache if she made me nervous.

And so, after not even a week of persuasion I brought Clara with me to the depot and we played our little comedy neatly, with all the correct cues and retorts.

"Your Royal Highness, may I take the liberty of presenting to you my friend Clara Balbi?"

"Fräulein Balbi, I am very happy to meet you. I am a great admirer of yours."

"Thanks, Your Royal Highness. Your Royal Highness is too gracious."

"You have given several performances for our troops. Did you enjoy doing it?"

"Certainly, Your Royal Highness. It was a wonderful experience."

"How did you find the spirit of our good soldiers?"

"Splendid, Your Royal Highness."

Long pause.

"Did you happen to see the Grand Duke while you were at the front?" Pimpernel asked, with twitching eyelids.

"Indeed, Your Royal Highness. His Royal Highness gave us the honor to be present at some of our performances in Brussels."

"How did you find him? How does he look?" the Grand Duchess asked, taking a run and jump over a few ten-foot hurdles.

"His Royal Highness seemed to be in perfect shape. He appeared to be somewhat slimmer, but maybe the uniform makes him appear so. He is sun-tanned and he seemed to enjoy himself; he laughed frequently about our little caprioles."

"Did he speak with you?"

I looked at Clara, who had her angry angel's face, and I was afraid she would say: "Now look here, what's all this bunk? You know and I know that you know, so let's speak straight from the shoulder." But Clara, my little diplomat, held onto herself. "Yes, Your Royal Highness," she said. "His Royal Highness came on the stage after the performance and spoke a few words to our troupe. We felt greatly honored."

The Grand Duchess gave a deep sigh. She had tried to climb over a high fence and had been pushed down to her own side of it again. Clara's face melted a bit and she added: "I had a letter from Baron Zwerchsattel a few days ago. He tells me that His Royal Highness feels exceptionally well. He seems to do much horseback riding since he moved to Château Branquet, and he has taken up aquarelle painting for his relaxation. Zwerchsattel sounded quite cheerful."

The Grand Duchess took a deep breath. "You know Baron Zwerchsattel well?" she asked. Baron Zwerchsattel was the Grand Duke's aide-de-camp, a handsome young lad, son of the court marshal.

"Yes, Your Royal Highness. He is a good friend of mine. He is a great letter writer, Zwerchsattel is. If Your Royal Highness should be interested in the news I get from him quite frequently——"

"Did Zwerchsattel write anything about the losses our infantry regiment suffered in Flanders?"

"He indicated something, Your Royal Highness, but he gave no details."

"Did he say anything about the impression it made on the Grand Duke?"

"Yes, Your Royal Highness. He says in his letter that the Grand Duke did not want to see his staff for two days and had his meals served in his room. I'm sorry, Your Royal Highness, if this should worry you——"

"No, no. Not at all. You have to expect such ups and downs in a war. Of course the Grand Duke feels the loss of every one of his soldiers very deeply. He is very sensitive."

"Yes. Very sensitive. All thoroughbreds are, aren't they?" said Clara. I cleared my throat as a warning, and Clara shut up.

Pimpernel gave her an anguished glance, and Clara smiled at her, consoling, comforting, as if to say: "Don't worry too much, somehow we'll get him through all this mess and muddle; you can take care of the throne and I'll take care of the man."

"How do you like the Grand Duchess?" I asked her on the way home.

"She's all right in her own way, I guess," Clara said. "But, for God's sake, what's the matter with her complexion? Can't you tell her to use castile soap for her face?"

It made me laugh. "Do you still remember how castile soap looks?" I asked her. The one gray piece of soap a month that was our ration broke into small crumbs of clay when it came into contact with water; it gave no lather and felt like sandpaper on the skin, and it played havoc with our complexion and our ersatz fabrics and linens.

"Well, you can be sure Her Royal Highness can have all the good soap she wants," Clara said angrily.

"I don't think so," I said. "She lives strictly on rations like everyone else as a principle."

"Strictly on rations, with milk and butter from the crown farms thrown in with game and fowl from their forests."

"No, that's the funny part of it. She gives all that to the hospitals. You don't think she lives like a Kriegsschieber, do you?"

Kriegsschieber were a new race, the war profiteers, maggot-like, growing on the decay of the country. They had money, they bought up the food, there was a bootlegged traffic of edibles for those who knew how to get it and who were able to pay the exorbitant prices. They were like worms in the wood, or like termites; they bored and undermined, breeding distrust and hatred and envy. There were only two classes in Germany: those who went hungry, and those who knew how to fill their bellies: the Kriegsschieber.

At home Clara rummaged in her things and produced a cake of soap. I can still see it; it was a Roger & Gallet violet soap, wrapped in a mauve paper with a little gold-and-violet vignette on it. It smelled of violets too.

"There," she said. "I got it in Brussels. I saved it up for some great occasion. I wanted to take a bath and smell divinely when the war is over and The Man comes home—sort of a song of victory. Give it to her and tell her to get the hell rid of her confounded pimples."

In February I had my baby, exactly as I had planned it, in my own bed and without a doctor. It was good though to have Clara there; Clara, my darling, my friend, my Rock of Gibraltar; she stayed with me through the twelve hours of the ordeal and enjoyed every minute of it. I clamped onto her, I beat her and punched her and bit her, and she kept on laughing and saying: "What fun it is, Jesus Maria, what fun it is! Come on, baby, work, do something, there, there, give! Hear me, give! Lord, this is better than doing a new ballet—and much easier—and you know what you've got when it's all done. Come on, just another ten minutes, come on, my little monk, you've got to help Erika!"

The mouse of a midwife, scurrying in and out somewhere in a dim background, wrung her hands about our vigorous duet, with me screaming and Clara encouraging me to make all the noise I wanted if it made me feel better. It must have looked more like a wrestling bout than like a childbirth, and I too felt that it was huge tall fun. The pains so strong and so natural and so healthy, as if my body had waited for them and was satisfied at last to dive down to the roots of being a woman.

The sun was just about to come up and it was a pink mother-of-pearl morning when the baby was born. There was the fraction of a second, very sharp, very penetrating, when I thought of Kathi, the washerwoman. I lifted myself up on my elbows and looked at my child that was lying between my thighs, wet and red and wrinkled and unbelievably alive. "So. Now you may call for Dr. Süsskind," I said. The child was taken away from me; it gave a funny quacking scream; it had a voice, it had fists much too big, it had little feet and toes and little dots of nails on them. Clara held it up; she looked stupid with surprise.

"It's a boy," she said. "Look, it's a boy."

"Sure it's a boy," the midwife said with a chuckle, manipulating the umbilical cord. Clara held the baby close to me so I might see its brave, well-formed little sex equipment. My little man, I thought, we'll see to it that there is no war when you grow up. The midwife took him away and wrapped him in a sheet of thick white crepe paper. I lay on the same paper, to save linen. We still had four sheets, but they were thin and threadbare and full of holes. Then Clara came in with a steaming pot of cocoa. "It's made with milk, not with water," she said. "And there is real sugar in it. Drink it. You've deserved it." It was the perfect climax to little Martin's glorious appearance in this world.

Funny to think of Martin just now. What a miracle he was when he was born! And now he is a traveling salesman, solid and average as his father was, drumming up the trade in the Middle West, and there is a war again, worse than the last one, and it looks as if he would be in it before long. And I am still on my way to a station to see a man off who wants to fight for his country, and it is like a bad dream in which the same things happen over and over again. . . .

SPRING 1917 came, and if there was an offensive we didn't hear about it. We had lots and lots of victories but we didn't care. The bells did not peal and no flags were brought out. The last men in the country were scraped together and sent out, old fellows and young schoolboys. In the hospitals the wounded were patched up in a hurry and pushed back into the lines. By now all the soldiers called the war "the great mess," and we sucked in a deep distrust for big, noble words, a distrust that the whole world hasn't overcome during all the years since—the whole world with the exception of the dyed-in-the-wool Nazis. We did not send many parcels to the front any more because there was nothing left in the country to be sent. On the contrary, soldiers on leave brought food for their families in their packs, canned army rations, hard, dry crackers, a sausage, a cheese, a pair of shoes they had bought or stolen from some French girl. All we thought of was how to get food; there was a beastly urgency about it, and we began to hate our stomachs, which insisted upon being filled at regular intervals if we wanted to stay alive. Our days were broken up into busy, futile errands, into standing in line, registering, picking up food stamps, swapping this week's herring against next week's margarine, running to some place where—rumor had it—potatoes were to be had on the sly, going into the forest and digging up beechnuts under the dry leaves, because there was a mill that would press the oil from them and you could grease your turnips with it. There were a hundred and one such absolutely important activities to be pursued, crowding our lives so much and seeming so utterly important that we almost forgot the war.

When the U.S.A. joined the Allies there were no extra papers in town and no headlines. It was slipped into the news like a bitter medicine in a slick capsule. To us it seemed that one enemy more or less didn't make much difference one way or the other. The Americans were far away, and what could they really do to us? They hadn't even an army, and they were crazy millionaires, that much we knew. Also, our submarines did miracles on the seven seas, and the idea of transporting troops across the Atlantic seemed perfectly fantastic and ludicrous. But we were tired; God, how tired we were in spring 1917, and the word "peace" took on a sound like angels' singing, like the golden trumpets of heaven. "Great Lord, if there would only be peace again!" people said everywhere. "Only peace, why can't we make peace?"

Well, you can't make peace. How do you imagine peace is made? You wave a white flag and everything is over?

But if we would stop fighting, wouldn't there be peace?

You can't stop fighting.

Why not?

Well, you just can't, that's all. What do you think would happen if we would stop fighting?

All right. Suppose we do stop fighting. What would happen?

I don't know. Nobody knows what would happen. Suppose we stop fighting and the French and the British don't? We would be just where we were when the war began. They would invade Germany, burn down the towns, rape the women, torture the children, kill the men, poison the water, choke us with poison gas, bomb us with their infernal planes—do you see why we can't have peace?

But the Russians stopped fighting. Why can't we?

Pshaw, the Russians. They were cowards to begin with. Now they are killing each other with their revolution. You wouldn't want a communistic revolution in Germany, would you? Now that we don't have to keep an army in the East we'll lick the Allies, lick them good and quick. That's the only way to get peace, and we'll get it. Soon.

At three o'clock one afternoon the bell sounded from the old cathedral, the big bell that had been silent for a long time; the one bell that was left after all the others had been turned into cannons. People stopped and listened and went to the kiosks to read the latest war news, but there was nothing about an important victory. Crowds stood on the bridge across the Rhine, their chins lifted as they looked up and listened to the bell. Then, all of a sudden, the rumor was all over town: The war is over. An armistice. The Kaiser has made a peace offer, and the Allies have accepted it. Peace. Peace. Peace. The streets went crazy. People embraced and kissed one another, people cried, people knelt down and prayed: "Thanks, O Lord, peace, peace, peace!" The statue of St. Francis was swamped in flowers; in front of the New Palace they had begun to sing the Dutch Thanksgiving Prayer: "Wir treten zum Beten vor Gott den Gerechten." There were many invalids among the crowd; they sang, loud and flat and deep, and their chins quivered with the strain of not starting to cry. They waited for the Grand Duchess to come out onto the balcony, but she was not in town that day. She was out in the country, where she had to organize help for the farmers so that there would be a crop in the fall. War prisoners had been distributed all over the country to do the labor in place of the men who were lacking. "Peace, peace!" the people told one another. Our men would come back, the prisoners would be released, the war was over. A procession formed itself, a stream of women surging across the Rhine bridge and into the cathedral. The bell kept on ringing for a full hour and then it ceased, with a few lost, last, straggling metallic notes.

The bell had been tolling for the death of the archbishop. That was all. There was no peace. There would never be peace, never. The people crept back into their houses, silent, not looking at one another, ashamed, as if they had been caught in a drunken debauch. That day left a little wrinkle in our souls, and a week later there was some talk about riots in Giessheim and secret meetings of some communists who wanted to bring about a revolution as they had in Russia.

As a result the rations for the ammunition workers were increased, at the expense of those who didn't make ammunition. I had taken up my work again, but there was not much I could do. Everybody had enough money, and there was nothing you could buy with it. Some of the girls went around with yellow-greenish faces after being poisoned with picric acid; then half of the face would return to normal while the other half still looked as if somebody had painted it green just for the hell of it. The people shifted their Sunday-afternoon outings to the prison camp behind the training grounds in Giessheim. They would stand outside the barbed-wire fence and stare at the war prisoners inside as if they were animals exhibited in a zoo. There was no hatred or malice in it, though, just a dull curiosity. "Look at the poor devils," people would say, and: "It's a shame we have to feed them. They should have been shot without pardon." And then some woman whose son was a prisoner somewhere in Russia or France would speak up and say: "We've got to treat them well or they'll take it out on our boys in their prison camps."

I too went out there several times because I had an idea that someday I might discover Howard Watson among the prisoners. But then Clara told me that he had been killed in a dogfight. He had been an aviator, one of those gay, cold-blooded English boys who kept up the tradition of chivalry in the midst of mechanized slaughter into which war had deteriorated since the advent of tanks and poison gas. Clara had it from her Man, who had written her also that the German fliers had given Howard a funeral with honors and had dropped his belongings over the enemy lines as a token of their respect for him as a good fighter. Clara told us about it one night when we were at the depot for duty. She told it as news that Zwerchsattel had sent to her.

The canteen at the depot had given up work because the coffee for the passing soldiers had become too much of a luxury. The arrival of wounded men, the sending off of patched-up soldiers, the passing through of trains going to and coming from the front had become a drab and casual affair. The Red Cross helpers had given up the night duty. Only Pimpernel sat there almost every night, all alone, not even wanting her ladies-in-waiting to sacrifice their sleep. I suppose it was a stupid gesture of hers, or maybe she couldn't sleep and would rather do something than toss around in her royal bed in the empty palace. Or maybe she thought that, by being kind and stubbornly doing her duty and some more, she would be able to hold up a system that was about to topple over. The men who came from the battlefields didn't care any longer if a Grand Duchess smiled at them or spoke to them. There were many who swore under their breath and called her names as soon as she turned away. Sometimes I felt like crying about that smile she carried around like a useless shield. It touched me when, recently during the last year, I seemed to recognize that same smile of hers once more, this time on the face of the Queen of England. Smiling while she ate hot dogs in the hope of getting the United States into the war. Smiling at the retreat from Dunkerque, smiling at the shambles of her country.

We were a queer trio, the Grand Duchess, Clara, and I, who was the friend of both of them. Many nights we would sit there and play a game Pimpernel had invented. "Let's think of something nice," she would say, and we would try to think and remember and talk about the good things we knew. It was like carrying a light into darkness.

"A summer day," Clara would say. "I am very hot and I have a bit of a sunburn. I stand on the diving board at the shore of the lake and test its springiness. I feel the roughness of the coco-fiber mat under my soles and the air is cool on my arms and shoulders where I have the sunburn. It smells of wet planks and water, and there is the splash and the little shrieks of children in the water. I stretch and tense and hold to the edge of the board with my toes and hesitate for a second. And then I jump and sail through the air and feel that the dive is perfect, and then I hit the water, not hit it but cut into it, and am in the heart of a big roar and open my eyes and everything is green. I float up again and then I swim out into the lake."

"Yes," Pimpernel said. "Or come into the stables in the morning and during the night a colt has been born. It's still wobbly on his legs, and they are much too long, but it has bright eyes and looks at you with that funny newborn look, and there is the clean, good smell of horse dung, and the stableboys go around and fill hay into the hay racks and you dig your hand into the oats and bring a handful of it to the mother. The noise as the horses crunch it; they stomp their feet and turn around and look at you as you walk by their boxes. And the stableboy slaps their haunches with the flat palm of his hand, and you say: 'This morning I'll take Schneewittchen,' and you are all pumped full with anticipation, because you are only ten years old and your father has promised to take you on a cross-country ride, over all the fences, and you are proud and afraid, and cold in the pit of your stomach."

"Did you ever go out and search for mushrooms?" I asked. "I did, with my grandfather; we went into the Vienna woods and gathered basketfuls of them. Their little heads stick out from under the moss, and do you remember the smell? You must go after the rain, before the worms and snails get at them, early in the morning, before the sun comes up. Your feet get wet, and there are little hammocks of spider web hanging in the grass, full of dew. Sometimes squirrels will nibble the mushrooms; you can find the marks of their teeth, especially on those redcaps you find under birches. We call them Franciscans, like the monks."

"To drive in a sleigh on a cold, blue winter morning and arrive at the Waldhaus and drink Glühwein, hot and spiced, with cinnamon and clove in it . . ."

"To lie in the tall grass of a mountain pasture and hear the bees humming over my head and make myself as small as a cricket . . ."

"To sit in the theater before the curtain rises and hear the tuning of the instruments . . ."

"To walk along a field of wheat and let the ears glide through your fingers, and there is a fat, white cloud in a dark, blue sky . . ."

"To skate on a sunny ice rink when the music plays a waltz and you are in love and you wear your new outfit and you are only fifteen . . ."

"To listen to a brook . . ."

"To see a cherry tree in full bloom . . ."

"To watch two little kittens play . . ."

"To be thirsty and drink a glass of cold milk . . ."

"To be hungry and bite into a piece of bread . . ."

"To be tired and take your shoes off and stretch and fall into bed . . ."

The good things. The warm, rich, lovely things that are life. We dug up our little treasures and polished them and showed them to one another. There were so many of them we would never run out of supply.

Those were funny nights when we three sat together and unwrapped our surprise parcels of happiness and waited for another trainload of human debris to be swept from the battle fronts into this western outpost of Germany.

4

ARION PUT DOWN the little figure of the St. Bernard unfinished. She looked at it with unseeing eyes while she roped in her thoughts, which had wandered far off during the last half-hour. Down in the village the clock struck with the whining sound of an old woman's voice. Marion brushed her hands and got up. Two small blisters had begun to form, caused by the pressure of the knife upon her index finger. I'll have to do more work and get my good old honest calluses back, she thought absent-mindedly. She shook the chips off her skirt and swept them with her foot under the table. It was twenty-five minutes to one when she stepped out onto the gallery and screwed the telescope down so that it pointed toward the lake. She waited for the hotel boat to appear in the small segment of glittering water that she could see between the fir tops, the blue-white motorboat that would probably take Christopher across the lake. The day was warm and cloudless by now, and a humming non-stillness had settled over the valley. The sky was round and of a glassy, old-fashioned blue; it reminded Marion of the sugar bowl on her grandparents' breakfast table. After a while she heard the asthmatic noise of the motor chug-chugging in the distance, but she could not see the boat. The sound faded away and stopped. Marion took a very

237

deep breath. Now he is gone for good, she thought. She pointed the telescope toward the distant zigzag mountain trail that led up the Kees. After a few minutes she thought she could discern a tiny figure moving up that trail; it could be 'Christopher. Yet it could be anyone, the postman, the boy from the Kees Alm; it could even be a trick of her sun-blinded eyes. If he is gone, Michael will be home soon, she thought as she went back into the house, tired and empty all of a sudden. Then she heard the children sing down at the mill and she remembered that Michael would stay with them to help with Nero's funeral.

"What nonsense!" she suddenly said aloud, standing stiffly, staring with wide-open eyes into some nowhere for a moment; and then, all of a sudden, she hurled herself into a waterfall of action. Going into a trance, Clara had called such fits in the old times. It was true that Marion had always made the most important decisions of her life during such queer, abrupt attacks of semiconsciousness. She might plan and reckon and think clearly and calculate carefully, weigh everything, and be cautious and sensible for a long time. And then, all of a sudden, she would go off like a skyrocket and always in the wrong direction. "You should be the lady who gets shot from a cannon at the county fair," her son Martin had told her more than once.

Chris, my darling, Marion thought, I want to pluck the stars from the sky with you tonight.

The next moment she was in her room, flinging her dress off, lacing her hobnail boots, pulling on her hiking pants, throwing her night things into her rucksack, tearing her leather jacket from its hook, and rumbling down the stairs in breathless haste. She stopped for a moment to scribble a little note for Michael: "Milky! I'm going to see Christopher off. Will be back either tonight or the day after tomorrow. You can phone me at the Arli Hütte. There is cold meat and salad in the larder. Tomorrow you can eat at the hotel. Money is in the top drawer. Take good care of yourself."

She put the fountain pen into the pocket of her pants and slipped the note under pearwood Nero's unfinished paws, right in the center of the table so Michael would be sure to find it. The clock struck one.

There was no rhyme or reason to Marion's sudden exodus. It was only that suddenly the fifteen years that separated her from Christopher had shrunk into nothing and that all her scruples seemed ridiculous and petty measured by the things happening in the world at that hour. She stopped for another second in front of the mirror, and now she seemed to have only very few wrinkles and very slight ones. Probably Christopher has never noticed them, she thought, and if he has he is possibly even fond of them, as all lovers are fond of the imperfections of the beloved. She parted from the mirror with a fleeting grin, rushed off, turned back once more to grab the ice ax that hung next to the two gas masks, together with the rope, in the small hallway; she shouldered the ax, slammed the door, and was off.

When Marion left the house she had a vague notion that she could possibly catch up with Christopher before he crossed the lake. He had spoken about leaving at one o'clock, and it was hardly fifteen minutes past when she arrived at the hotel. But there she learned that Mr. Lankersham had left about half an hour ago with the motorboat, which had gone across the lake to pick up some tourists and had not returned yet. It was the only motorboat in Staufen, and all Marion could do was to let herself be leisurely rowed across by old Hammelin. She hollered for him and his boat, and the old man came creeping out from the dimness of his forge and blinked into the sun.

"Going over the Kees?" he coughed when he saw the ice ax hanging on its leather strap from Marion's wrist.

"Yes, and I'm in a hurry," she said.

"Want to catch up with your Englishman?" Hammelin asked her. Shoeing horses during a long lifetime had made him something of a mind reader.

"Yes—more or less," Marion answered vaguely, and the old man gave her a sly wink. He always referred to Christopher as "Marion's Englishman," and she usually derived a faint pleasure from it.

"Your Englishman is gone for good," Hammelin coughed. "Said good-by to me this morning. The good ones go and the bad ones stay."

Marion watched impatiently how the other shore came nearer

and grew distinct with every rock and tree as Hammelin's long, flat strokes drove the boat across the green clearness.

"It's going to be a nice sunset tonight and good weather to-morrow," he said after scanning the weather corner between the Seven Brothers. He handed Marion his prognosis like a present, and she accepted it in the same spirit.

"Thanks, Father Hammelin," she said as the boat jarred, land-ing on the sandy bank. She leaped ashore before the old man had time to pull it upon the sand.

"Haste makes waste," he said calmly. "If you run like that you'll never catch up with him. In the mountains it's easy, easy and steady, steady."

"Yes, thanks. I know," Marion said impatiently. Hammelin took his time in handing her rucksack to her.

"The guide from the hotel is taking two tourists up to the Arli Hütte; they're going to start out within half an hour," he said. "Maybe you'd better wait and hang onto them. Eh?"

"No, I think I'd rather go ahead," Marion said, quivering with impatience. "I'd rather hurry and catch up with my English-man, see?"

"Not afraid of the Grauhorn Glacier, are you?"

"Certainly not," said Marion. "It's an easy one, isn't it? I've been up there so often I know every crevasse and sérac and schrund on it."

"Sure it's an easy one," old Hammelin agreed at last. "Well, I'll tell the guide to look out for you anyway. Berg Heil!"

She slipped her arms into the straps of her rucksack, shouldered her ax, and was on her way. She marched quickly across the stretch of sandy grass at the shore, which was humming with bees, alive with the dance of hundreds of tiny blue butterflies, and full of the pungent breath of thyme. Only when she reached the trail and began the uphill grade did she slow down, giving her-self over to the steady, rhythmical pull of her heavy hobnail boots. At the third turn of the trail she stopped to look down and wave a farewell to old Hammelin, whose boat from up there looked like an insect creeping across the green glass of the lake. He waved back at her and yodeled. The clock in Staufen struck two.

Marion strode on quickly. If Christopher had started at a slow pace, as he usually did, she could still catch up with him in the shade and fragrance under the firs below the timber line. But after ten minutes she had to rest and regulate her breath and slow down. She gave herself a grin of sympathy. Maybe he will stop at the Kees Alm, she thought. Maybe he will stop at Camp Arli. Maybe he will rest at the spring where we stopped to fill our flasks the last time we made this trip.

The boy at the Kees Alm had seen him pass a while ago, but he was very vague about the time. He had not stopped at Camp Arli, the men there said. The firs receded; there were still some windblown creeping pines, and then Marion had crossed the timber line and the trail was hardly visible on the stony, rocky ground. She wiped the sweat off her face and marched stoutly on. She pictured how she would meet Christopher at the spring. He would sit there on a rock, smoking his pipe, and he would look up when he heard her fast steps. The sun would glitter in his eyeglasses and he would shade his eyes, and as soon as he recognized her he would slowly get up. "Hello, Marion. So you have come after all. I knew you would change your mind," he would say, trying to keep his voice unemotional. And then he would hollow his hands and let the water from the spring collect in them and lift them to her mouth and let her drink. He had done it before, and it had seemed a lovely gesture to her, even if drinking water like that was very uncomfortable.

But when Marion arrived at the spring there was no one. She allowed herself a few minutes to rest, to cool her hands and to wash her hot face. Her ears had begun to get numb, the blood sang in her temples, and her heart ran riot as it always did when she crossed the 8,000-foot line. As she bent down to tie her shoelace, her eyes focused on a tiny glittering object on the ground; she picked it up and examined it carefully. It was a scrap of tinfoil such as Christopher would peel from his Swiss chocolate, which he always took along on mountain trips. While Marion was still standing there with this bit of evidence in her hand she discovered a little mound of ashes, a miniature volcano with a wisp of smoke clinging to it. It smelled of Christopher's pipe. She bent down and touched it. Yes, it was still warm. It could be only a few minutes since he had left this place, and it could only be a few turns of the trail before she would overtake him. Hastily Marion picked up her rucksack, swung it over her shoulders, grabbed her ax, took no time to rest or drink, but walked on through the sun-drenched silence of the Kees, faster as before.

Two buzzards in love were playing in the still air above; the shadows of their wide wings moved ahead of Marion over the rocky ground. It was a beautiful sight, but Marion did not permit herself to waste any time on watching them. The trail grew steeper now, tracing its herringbone pattern up the Kees. Soon she left the two buzzards below, and as she stopped to regulate her breath she saw them writing the soft dark circles of their flight against the sweeping fall of the mountainside.

COME TO THINK OF IT, it was a simple louse that brought me back into the lap of a family and made me give up my independence; a body louse such as our soldiers imported from the front in the hair of their scrotums; a simple pediculus pubis and nothing else.

Captain Tillmann came home in pretty bad shape this time. A bullet had hit him beneath the right ear, and only by a miracle had it avoided passing through the jugular vein. Also he had been buried in the destruction of the trenches and had been found only days later, delirious and with pneumonia. However, here he was, with two weeks' leave for recuperation after they had patched him up in some hospital behind the fighting lines; a bit wobbly, a bit quieter, his eyes sunken and his expression furtive, but otherwise still a good man, ready to go out and fight some more. I introduced Martin to his father, and they took a great liking to each other at first sight. Little Martin's eyes almost fell out of his head, he was so interested in his father's beard, medals, and Prussian voice. As for Kurt, he naturally behaved as if he were the first man to have worked the miracle of making himself a father. The two of them could spend hours and hours of tranquil contemplation together, just staring at each other and being completely happy. Outside of being a very hungry baby, little Martin had the pleasant, even disposition of his father, though just before Captain Tillmann's arrival he had taken to crying more than usual. He would dig his little fists into his eyes and cry till he was blue in the face. I felt apologetic because he disturbed Captain Tillmann's sleep, and, by God, my husband needed all the quiet we could possibly cram into these two weeks of respite. But Captain Tillmann didn't seem to mind.

"What's the matter with his eyes?" he asked me after two days. "Aren't they a little red?"

"Yes, I know," I said. "Many babies have that sort of irritation now: Dr. Süsskind gave me some drops, but they don't help much."

"The old battle ax!" Kurt muttered; he didn't like her at all. I left my two men alone and went out to hunt up some sort of food. When I came back I found Kurt in great agitation. "Come here, Marion," he shouted at me. "Look at the boy. Look well. Can't you see what it is? It moves, that's what it does. It moves. It's some sort of vermin. It's some goddamned sort of filth he got into his eyes. You and your Dr. Süsskind—two blind idiots, that's what you are!"

I stared at the red-rimmed eyelids of my baby. There was a brownish scab, and the scab moved. Kurt, without another word, handed me a magnifying glass. Yes, now I saw it too; something like tiny crabs, drilling their legs into the tender skin around little Martin's eyes. I was horrified. God damn it all! was what I thought when my husband rushed me and the baby to a doctor of his own choice. Somehow someone must have smuggled his pediculus pubis past the delousing stations and into Giessheim; I must have carried them home and given them to little Martin. The lice searched his nude little frog's body for some hair, some cozy place to dwell in, and as the only hair they could find was his eyebrows and lashes, that was where they had settled down.

No wonder I was absolutely crushed. Captain Tillmann told me that I neglected my own child, his child, our child, while taking care of the filthy communists and criminals of Giessheim. "You're right," I said, crestfallen. He told me that he would not permit me another hour of welfare work. "You're right," I sobbed. Not another day in Bergheim. "You're right," I cried. He told me to pack my bundle and join his family in Hahnenstadt at once, so that his son would be brought up in decent surroundings. What could I say or do? I packed my bundle, said good-by to Pimpernel, and the next morning we were on our way, all three of us. What made it a bit easier was the fact that Clara had left for the front again, this time as a full-fledged nurse, and I had been lonely. Maybe they'll have more to eat in Hahnenstadt, I thought. But this was an entirely unjustified optimism.

To move from Vienna to South Germany had been nothing. To move from South Germany into Prussian North Germany was like being shot to the moon by some fantastic missile. The people were different, their voices, their speech, their manners, their way of life. The soil was different, the sky, the light, the very air. Of all the foreign countries to which I came during my life, not one was as completely alien to me as this province two hundred miles north of Bergheim.

My husband installed me in the apartment of his sister, and for a few days I felt so homesick I could not eat or sleep. Irmgard Klappholz was a thin, straight, prematurely gray woman with a monotonous voice. Her mouth was pursed as if from suppressed pain, and she smiled incessantly. After a while my own face began to hurt with the strain of looking at that smile. Irmgard was kind and friendly to me—what people in Hahnenstadt would call friendly. They had some dark superstition that showing any emotions or warmth would stamp you a sissy. "It's time you came to us," she said. "After all, you belong to our family now and we have to stick together. Yes, yes. Oh, dear Lord!" Every one of Irmgard's sentences ended with that sigh. My brother-in-law was much older than Kurt, and his trousers fell in those characteristic loose folds which meant that he had lost one leg in the war. He made sour little jokes about it and proudly exhibited the artificial limb they had made for him. It was a very fine artificial leg indeed, and I paid him all the compliments about it that he seemed to expect. They had lost their oldest son in the war, and their second one had been missing for so long that they had given up hope that he would ever be found. Recently the third one, merely a schoolboy, had been called to arms too. He was at the training camp and would go to the front within two or three weeks. Irmgard installed me in the room that had belonged to the two older boys and asked me not to touch or change anything. She indicated that it was quite a sacrifice on her part to let me use this chapel of memories, and I understood it well enough. I would sit at the edge of my bed and not dare to move, trying to reconstruct the personalities of the former owners of this little sanctuary. The older one would have become an officer like my husband—"In our family the oldest sons have usually been soldiers," Irmgard told me. There were photos showing him among groups of cadets in their tight-fitting uniforms. A snapshot of a young girl stuck to the mirror. Swords and sabers crossed on the wall above the bed. Books of military science and history on the shelf. He also had a corner with pictures of Frederick the Great, whom he seemed to have worshiped. I wondered if he had never discovered what a cynical, skeptical devil of a Prussian-hater the great king had been. The second boy seemed to have dabbled in astronomy. At least there was a primitive telescope, apparently pieced together after the prescription of some boys' magazine, and there was a stamp collection. There were also some books by Nietzsche, which rather surprised me in these surroundings. Over his bed—which now had become my bed—there hung a nightmare of a color print, Wagner's Wotan standing among tongues of fire and holding the swooning Valkyrie in his arms. After Kurt had left for the front I dared to turn this horror toward the wall, at least during the night and when I was left alone in my room, but I was constantly afraid I might forget to turn it back and be caught committing such a sacrilege.

This is where I will have to live when the war is over, I thought, sitting on the edge of my bed. I'll be somebody's wife and somebody's daughter-in-law and somebody's sister-in-law. Didn't you rush into this marriage with blinkers on, Marion, my girl, as a horse is rushed through flames? Well, maybe I'll be somebody's mother, won't I? That's better. That's much better, isn't it? I like Kurt. I like him an awful lot. With him it'll be safe and peaceful, like in Abraham's lap. That's what Fritz Halban always called it: Abraham's lap. Imagine Fritz being an aviator now and a war ace with the Pour-le-Mérite, the little Jewish bookworm! How come he could become an aviator with his eyeglasses? Maybe he was farsighted; that must be rather good if you are a flier. If I had wool I would knit a scarf for him. . . .

The apartment itself looked like millions of other better middle-class apartments at that time. The entrance hall was a black, windowless worm whose guts were clogged up with a big chiffonier, the hat-and-coat rack, the umbrella stand, the boys' bicycles, and other odds and ends. On top of the chiffonier the family's suitcases, hatboxes, and empty fruit jars lived a gloomy existence. The kitchen smells hung forever in this appendix, unable to find a way out. Also from the kitchen came the more or less protesting sounds that Elizabeth produced in one of Her Moods. She was a stern and loyal gem, walking through life on hard and squeaky shoes and looking upon the family as upon her property, which, at the same time, made her responsible for our morale, health, and social standing.

The rooms had high, dark ceilings and imitation wood panelings, the furniture was dark and heavy, and there were huge Dutch stoves standing in the corners, grinning at us with black faces when we ran out of coals. There were four of such flats on every floor, and when you entered the house the starvation smell of boiled turnips was so thick on the staircase it took your breath away. The house stood in the old-fashioned but decorous district called the Riede, as was proper and befitting for a family of our standing, and there were hours when I felt like screaming and breaking out of the bleakness of this respectable prison.

I would have persuaded Kurt to let me move out and have my own apartment, but around this time a new calamity had begun, which grew and grew during the years to come. There were not enough homes, houses, or apartments anywhere, and new laws were passed that rationed the rooms. It took high amounts of bribery if one wanted to find a place; yet, for the first time in many years, I did not earn any money but was supported by a man and, consequently, had to do what he told me. That this man was my husband did not make much difference to me. I felt cramped and uncomfortable, because supporting oneself becomes a very luxurious habit, hard to break.

"Is your name really Marion?" Irmgard would say. "I thought only circus riders have such a name. Oh, dear Lord! You won't mind if I call you Maria, it sounds more decent, don't you think so?" Inside I still was Marion Sommer. But on the surface I had become Maria Tillmann; quite a metamorphosis, my girl, I told myself. My father-in-law would come to town for a visit from his hunting lodge near Detfurth and bring some partridges along. He and his dachshund Manne would inspect the new grandson with severe sniffings. "He looks exactly like his father," the old gentleman would declare at last. "Not a bit like you, Marion, not a bit." Thank God, I could almost hear him sigh.

My brother-in-law would stomp into the room and rummage among his boys' things. "I thought I'd go through the compositions Hellmuth wrote in school," he would say. "His professors adored him. Stay where you are, Maria, you don't disturb me. And, if you don't mind, don't squabble with Irmgard about the feeding of little Martin. She has brought up three, and you are such an inexperienced young woman——"

"I took care of a station of forty," I said, but he waved them aside. "Forty bastards," he said. "Forty young prolets to make more trouble in the future." To call proletarians "prolets" and make it sound like something utterly disgusting was another custom of the Riede. "It's incomprehensible why you did it," my sister-in-law would say. "Now, if you had nursed brave soldiers, that's something else, but to mix with that rabble, oh, dear Lord, dear Lord!"

"Pimpernel asked me to do it," I said pompously.

"Who? Pimpernel? Another one of those circus names," said Irmgard.

"The Grand Duchess of Zuche-Bergheim. My best friend," I said, putting down my only trump, and then there was silence for a while.

Still, after a time I found out that these disagreeable people were kind and decent in their own harsh way and that they even began to dislike me less, although such an emotion could not be displayed. Irmgard presented me with her boy's baby trousseau, a miraculous wealth of soft little linen shirts and diapers and knitted caps and jackets and tiny woolen socks for the cold times to come. My brother-in-law would cheat on his own bread ration so I should eat more, because I still nursed little Martin. My father-in-law would go on complicated expeditions in the country and, with the air of a great lion hunter, he would bring three pounds of potatoes and a rabbit to town, putting them down in front of me like a tribute. As for Kurt, he kept on writing jocular letters from the front in which he described his new dugout as an elegant French château and called Pulke his major-domo. Obviously he was much relieved to have me away from Bergheim and with his family. And little Martin, having got rid of pediculus pubis, was hungry and contented as before and put on weight and looked at his fingers and admired the wonderful sounds he could make with his throat and his tongue and his silly little pink jaws.

The youngest boy, called Martin like my own son, came to say good-by before he went to the front. He was a thin little fellow with eyeglasses, really only a child, and I liked him very much. There was a great to-do over how much he had grown during the six weeks' training, and there were some pained little jokes about how he would lick the French and how the war would soon be won, what with Martin Klappholz in the army. Irmgard smiled to the last minute, and then she went into the bedroom and locked herself in for three hours. But at dinnertime she was up and around again, presiding stiffly over the table with its abundance of fine old china and almost no food. It took only three weeks until we got the message that Martin had fallen on the field of honor. Also, the family was advised that Hellmuth, the missing son, had to be given up for dead.

Scientists will tell you that people don't turn white overnight. But I have seen it happen. Irmgard was gray when Martin left, and after he had died she was white. She was an old lady of forty-two with white hair and a crinkled parchment skin, and she kept on smiling with her pursed, strained, down-turned lips. "He fell for his fatherland," she said monotonously. "He did his duty and we have to do ours. Oh, dear Lord!"

I was yearning to take her in my arms, relax her and make her cry, break that stony smile and tell her that I admired her. But you couldn't do such a thing in Hahnenstadt. My hair didn't turn gray, but from one day to another there was no more milk for little Martin. I scurried to the town house and stood in line for his baby milk ration, and we sent a frantic telegram to his grandfather to try and get some carrots or spinach for him. Old Herr Tillmann came to town with a scant supply of vegetables for little Martin's benefit, but the ingrate made a terrific rumpus and went on a hunger strike for two days before he would take the bottle or eat his mashed carrots, of which the whole family was so proud. I think all this excitement helped Irmgard to forget her own boys, at least for a few minutes at a time. My brother-in-law seemed to take the latest blow rather well. The only change I could notice was that he stumped into the cellar every day and brought up one or two bottles of heavy Burgundy, which he emptied in the course of the evening. Like most Prussians he knew and loved good wine, and he had a store of the best down there. "That's good," he would say, "that warms those chilly old bones." He was a man of forty-seven and held some high post in civil service that had to do with the state salt mines in the province. He had lost one leg and his three sons and. altogether, he appeared a bit too cheerful, considering it all.

Well, then the fall hunting season began. My father-in-law invited my brother-in-law to come to the lodge and have a good time. I suppose the old man wanted to help him get over his grief and loss. Herr Klappholz put on his hunting clothes and looked for all the world like the caricatures of East Prussian Junkers in the Simplicissimus, which was our most progressive satirical magazine. He took his rifles from the glass cabinet in the living room, gloated over them, cleaned them, oiled them, and played with them all evening long.

Then he took the late train for Detfurth and never came back. "An accident," old Herr Tillmann said as he arrived two days later with the bad news. "He must have released the trigger when he tripped over some tree roots." We all knew that he had committed suicide, but we stuck gallantly to the official version. The nerves of a Prussian civil servant had no right to crack, a father was not allowed to kill himself because he had lost three sons, and members of the Tillmann tribe had the obligation to die honorably. Only once in all that time did Irmgard admit that her husband had made an end with himself. That was in November, when a letter from Hellmuth arrived.

It came from some prison camp deep in Russia and sounded just as cheerful as Captain Tillmann's epistles from the front. The same sort of heavy-footed, crackling, manly humor. Hellmuth wrote that he was well, that he had learned carpentering, that he had grown fat, and that his parents shouldn't worry about him. It had taken this letter more than half a year of meandering through the civil wars of Russia to arrive in Hahnenstadt. After Irmgard had read it twice she stopped smiling and she said: "If his father had had a bit more fortitude he would not have gone and shot himself. He would have waited and hoped and trusted. But he gave up. Do you think I should write the boy about his father's accident or should I save it until he comes home?"

"MAY I bring a friend for coffee?" I asked Irmgard one day in November.

"Coffee?" she said, raising her eyebrows.

"He'll bring the coffee and a little can of condensed milk; I thought we could make a bean cake . . ."

We had all sorts of wonderful recipes at that time. You could make a magnificent cake if you had beans. You would boil them and mash them and knead them with water and put saccharin into the dough and bake the concoction. You could be extravagant and fill in some jam made of carrots. If you had carrots and beans, that is. I happened to possess half a pound of them, which I had hoarded away for just such an occasion.

"Who is this friend of yours?" Irmgard asked suspiciously.

"Fritz Halban," I said.

"You mean the real Fritz Halban? The flier?" she said, awed. "And he is a friend of yours?"

"Yes. I used to know him in Bergheim, and we kept up some correspondence," I said.

"Of course. It will be a pleasure and an honor to have him for coffee," my sister-in-law conceded.

If I had met Fritz on the street I wouldn't have recognized him, he was so changed. But he had announced his coming to Hahnenstadt in a letter, and I had talked over the telephone with him. He looked smart in his gray aviator's uniform; he carried himself differently, spoke differently; he did not wear eyeglasses, and he had received the Pour-le-Mérite, which was the highest distinction for bravery you could get. His name had become popular as belonging to a man who had done the outstanding. As was the fashion, he made jokes about his heroic deeds when Irmgard pumped him, hungrily devouring every word of his. It was the new way of being boastful, and there was a trace of Jewish skepticism in it that was alien to her straight, unbending mind. "You are joking," she said finally. Fritz shrugged his shoulders and turned his palms up in a deprecatory gesture which in one flash brought back the times of F 12 to me.

"How does it look out at the front?" I asked him when Irmgard left the room for a minute.

"Oh, it's fun for us fliers, but otherwise it looks pretty bad," he said. "The troops don't want to fight any longer. They have to be driven into the fire by our own guns. On the other hand, they pay back for it by shooting their officers from behind."

I was shocked. Such things were always told about the enemy, but it had never occurred to me that they could happen in our own army. I also thought of Captain Tillmann and hoped to God that his Pulke would protect him in the back. I was glad that Fritz hadn't made his remark in Irmgard's presence. "You're a bloody defeatist," I said. "And mind you, in this house you're expected to talk and act like a national hero."

"I'm only speaking the truth," he said. He looked around the room. "Well, Mäusle, this is a far cry from F 12, isn't it?" he said. "We live in a great time, that's what they tell us; but wouldn't you wish times were still small?" He had shrunk a bit and looked quite Jewish, but when Irmgard entered with the bean cake he pulled himself together and straightened up and became a snappy, smart officer again right there in front of my astonished eyes.

"How did you like him?" I asked Irmgard after Fritz had left. She had a bit of color in her bloodless cheeks, and her eyes were bright with the excitement of this visit. "You can feel that he is a great man," she said. "He is so modest and so unobtrusive about the things he has done! As long as we have men like him to keep the vigil in the west . . . "

I winced when Irmgard expressed herself in the bromides she picked up from the daily editorials. But she was wholly innocent about it.

"You don't think Colonel Halban could be a Jew?" she asked me unexpectedly.

"Why not?" I said.

"He almost looks like one," she said. "But Jews are cowards. He couldn't be one."

I was a coward myself at that moment. Instead of saying, "Yes, he is a Jew, though certainly no coward," I faltered, muttering something like: "I really don't know. I've never asked him."

I had good reasons for wanting to preserve Irmgard's good opinion about Fritz. He had come to Hahnenstadt for a definite purpose. He was visiting with a younger cousin of his who had been very ill and about whom he seemed rather worried. Manfred Halban was one of the actors of our civic theater; I had seen him play and had liked him very much indeed, not knowing that he was related to Fritz. Maybe it was a faint resemblance in his gestures or in the sound of his voice that gave me the vague though pleasant impression that I had known him before. Fritz wanted to install the boy in a nice home, and in this he counted on me. On the other hand, the apartment where we lived had become too big for us two women, and the law would compel us soon to take in a boarder. Zwangsmieter such forced-on-you boarders were called, and if you couldn't produce one of your own choice, the authorities would put anyone they liked into your home. The air was full of funny and horrible stories about the experiences refined persons of Irmgard Klappholz' standing would have to undergo with such Zwangsmieter. To me it seemed a pleasant solution for a double problem if we would take Manfred Halban into the apartment. But to make this possible I was not to let her know that Manfred Halban was a

Jew. Jews, in the opinion of the Klappholz family, were unclean, they did not wash themselves properly, they cheated you
all the time, and they had a peculiar smell. And so I shut up
when Irmgard asked me if our ace flier was a Jew.

I met Fritz and his cousin in a café the day after his visit, and
two days later he brought him to our place and introduced him
to Irmgard. Manfred had an eager face and expressive hands, and
there was still a trace of the South German in his clear stage
enunciation. His eyes were a bit too big and a bit too bright, and
there was a slight huskiness in his voice, rather attractive. He had
light brown wavy hair, soft as a baby's, and a high, white
forehead.

"How come you are not in the army?" Irmgard asked him
in her straightforward manner and with the lack of tact customary in Hahnenstadt. "I admit the theaters should be kept going,
but young men like you should not be made ineligible. We could
make out nicely with our old guard of actors."

I saw the blood shoot into Manfred's cheeks and the muscles
of his jaw tighten.

"I wish you would tell that to the army doctors," he said.
"They are the ones who would not let me go to the front. I
have offered myself for military service again and again since
the first day of the war. You don't think it's fun for a man
to sit at home and knit stockings with the old ladies while the
others are out in the trenches, fighting?"

"My cousin has been rather ill," Fritz said. "So far he has
been unable to convince the medical board of his fitness."

"Oh, but you look so well," Irmgard said, putting her foot
into her mouth as usual. "What is the matter with your health?"

"A little trouble with my bronchia," Manfred said. "But I am
quite well now. In fact, I hope they will take me next time, when
they call up the 1918 classes."

"I am sure he will be sound as a brick if you two ladies consent
to take him in and watch a bit over him. What he needs is a
home and some regular feeding hours. Besides, he gets some
extra rations—on account of not being quite well," Fritz said
diplomatically.

There was some wrestling back and forth during the following days, but in the end Manfred Halban became our boarder and Fritz returned to the front, somewhat easier in his mind. He was very fond of this cousin of his, for Fritz was a single child and had adopted the boy like a younger brother, with the exaggerated attachment that can be found in Jewish families. "His bronchia, my eye," he said when he gave me my instructions about the care and feeding of the actor. "The poor devil lives with the tail end of his last lung. They cut out some ribs and operated on him last year, after he had one pneumothorax after another to no avail. You see to it, Mäusle, that he has a good time as long as it lasts, won't you? He should be kept quiet, and he is such an excitable chap. I daresay, acting is not a very healthy occupation for him either, but it's the only thing he knows how to do. He eats his heart up anyway because he can't go to the front. Imagine anyone being enough of an ass and a fool to still want to get into the big mess before it's all over. Well, I know you'll take care of him—for old times' sake, Mäusle. Thanks."

I had qualms to smuggle a man into our home who was a Jew and a consumptive. Maybe if Fritz hadn't called me Mäusle, and if he hadn't reminded me of that short spring in F 12—— But what's the use of speculating on what would have happened or not happened if some of the if's had been different. Fritz furnished a doctor's affidavit that Manfred Halban's illness was, in its present stage, not contagious at all, and I took good care to keep him away from little Martin. As for his being a Jew, I told myself that Irmgard's prejudices were simply too silly to be considered. Some of the best people I had encountered in my life were Jews. Herr Krappl, for instance. The conductor Kant. Walter Brandt too, I suppose—even if I had never thought about it. Jews had been in Germany as far back as Charlemagne, and during all those centuries they lost all marks of their race and became just plain Germans.

"Manfred, will you do me a favor?" I said to the young actor the day he moved in with us and I helped him to arrange his books in his room. "Don't tell my sister-in-law that you are a Jew. It's silly, I know—but it would complicate matters unnecessarily."

Again I saw the blood rush into his face and the muscles tighten under his skin. "But I am no Jew," he said.

"Oh—I'm sorry—I thought as you are Fritz's cousin——" I stuttered.

"If my parents were Jews that doesn't make me a Jew, does it?" he asked jerkily. "I was baptized and brought up as a Catholic; you want to see my certificate?"

That was before the theory of racial purity had become popular; "Jewish blood" was not a slogan yet, and the Jewish grandmothers in German families were not treated as foul branches on the family trees. I muttered some apologies and let it go at that. But I soon found out that Manfred was all tied up in knots about these two shortcomings: that he came of Jewish stock and that he was not in the war. He would drag it into the conversation whenever he met anyone; getting tense and taut and flushed, he would complain about the army doctors who refused to let him become a soldier, and he would talk in a querulous voice about his going to church every Sunday and going to confession and taking the Holy Communion, as if to convince himself that he was a good, genuine Catholic. To be a Catholic was the normal thing in Austria and in South Germany. In Hahnenstadt it made him almost as much of an outsider as if he were a Jew. After a while I discovered that Manfred was not only a Catholic but a fierce anti-Semite. There is no anti-Semitism so sharp and biting as that between Jew and Jew, I found often. "That's because we know one another too well," Manfred said when I asked him about it. "Don't you know how the members of a family despise one another? Well, Jews have been one family since Abraham's time. That's why."

The winter was hard, and Germany ran out of coal. Before the war she had had a surplus of it, just as she had had a surplus of sugar. No one could explain why and whereto one necessity of life disappeared after the other. But during this winter of 1917–18 we discovered that going hungry is much easier than going cold. I went out and brought home our coal ration in a little market basket. The hot-water stoves in the bathrooms were sealed by a commission that went from house to house, and there was no difference between Jew and non-Jew as to cleanliness and smell. The use of electric power and gas was cut down to the last limit. You could cook only at certain brief hours, and the rest of the time you were supposed to let your meals simmer in a padded chest or under the heavy German feather pillows of the beds. The streets were dark and not too safe. There was always the danger of being robbed of your food basket or the food stamps in your handbag. In the empty shop windows hung one sad dim bulb, and only a few swanky stores had delicacies on display; they were made of painted cardboard, and yet they caused your stomach to tighten in a funny, futile little cramp. We sealed the windows to keep the cold winter air out and, unable to feed our hungry monsters of Dutch stoves, we installed one small iron stove in the dining room, in which we nursed along the bit of warmth we could coax from the coke briquettes allotted to us. In the bedrooms the water froze in the washbasins, the water pipes in the walls cracked and broke, and the plumbing went constantly out of order. We went to bed, dressed to the gills, wrapped in old coats and shawls and yet shivering for hours before we managed to get warm enough to fall asleep. The genteel people of the Riede took to living like the "prolets," a whole family huddled together in the one room where the stove stood. There were ingenious devices by which we hoped to lead some of the precious warmth into other rooms. Long stovepipes meandered through the wall, crossed Manfred's room (he was installed in the den adjoining the dining room), pierced through the next wall into the former bedroom of the Klappholzes, where I slept with little Martin, and ended in the boys' room, which Irmgard had taken over. You could lay your hands on the pipes; they were alive with a feeble warmth in Manfred's room, tepid in mine, and completely cold in Irmgard's. Although she, the Spartan, stubbornly professed to prefer sleeping in the cold, she had attracted a chronic catarrh. During the night I was sandwiched between her and Manfred's coughing spells. Hers were explosive, whereas Manfred only cleared his throat in a queer manner, never permitting himself to really cough: as if suppressing it would make him a healthier man than he was.

Only little Martin seemed to thrive on whatever food we could get for him; the good little boy grew fat and apple-cheeked, as if the cold and the want and the harsh winds blowing from the marshes nourished him. Little Martin was my own private warming stove during that bad winter. Dark as things might be, I went around with my own little glow inside. There were days when I was so happy that I felt like bursting. Miracle after miracle happened before my eyes. Little Martin getting his first teeth, for instance. They came in pairs, first the two lower incisors and then the upper ones, and he went busy on his consonants after that, practising for hours. He learned to squeal with laughter, not just grinning at the funny things that went on all around him, but making himself really heard in his delight. The day he discovered that you could play peekaboo I was convinced that I had given birth to a genius. One day he could sit up and, four weeks later, he could stand on his wobbly sausages of legs, holding onto the side of his perambulator. (We had inherited the old contraption that had served the Klappholz boys many years ago.) The jubilant animal yells with which he greeted the yellow cup in which his milk came; the deep absorption with which he dived into it; the tender gurgling and babbling when he tried to make conversation with this beloved cup: I would have given you all the symphonies by Beethoven, with a good part of Bach thrown in, for the music of my baby drinking his milk. Little Martin was the only one who could melt Irmgard's iron self-control and wrangle some human emotions from our dragon Elizabeth, who had served the family for twenty years and never forgave me for being married to Kurt.

Altogether Manfred Halban's presence in our ménage turned out to be rather a blessing. First of all there were his extra rations, a bit of milk, a bit of meat, a speck of margarine, which helped our cuisine considerably. There was his share of coal. There were the free passes to the civic theater, which enabled us to spend many evenings in comparative warmth, saving fuel at home. And there was something vaguely pleasant in the feeling of having a man in the house. Manfred was quiet and tactful; he would sit in his cold den and never enter the one warm room where we all lived without being asked to do so. He never took advantage of this forced being-together and never disturbed us.

He would read a book and become invisible, so that we almost
forgot his presence. Or, if he felt that we were in the mood for
it, he would tell us funny stories. He knew a lot of them and he
told them well. He could, miraculously, make Irmgard laugh—
not only make her press the corners of her mouth down in her
strained smile, but make her really laugh. It was a priceless gift
of his, and I was grateful for it. On the stage he was not half so
effective as in a small circle. He only played supporting parts,
played them quietly and correctly, but never outstandingly. But
when he received one of Fritz Halban's letters and read it to us,
he came to life. Fritz wrote interesting letters, and in some of
his phrasings I seemed to recognize Walter Brandt's influence.
I would sit back in my chair, warming my feet on the stove,
with little Martin asleep in his pram at my side, and close my
eyes. It was like withdrawing to a hidden small island of which
nobody knew. Manfred's soft, husky, consumptive voice with the
slight trace of the South German accent I had come to love; the
things Fritz had to tell; the way he expressed himself and the
way Manfred would interpret his letters: it took me away from
Hahnenstadt on a magic carpet and carried me across those
war years, back into a past for which I was sometimes terribly
homesick.

And everything would have gone smooth and well had not
Manfred taken a notion to fall in love with me.

TOWARD the end of February we had a very severe cold spell and
that was bad. Old Herr Tillmann fell ill out there in his hunting
lodge and wrote us a miserable letter. Irmgard scraped up whatever coal and food we had, Elizabeth wrapped herself in her old
black shawl, and the two women went on an expedition to join
and nurse the old gentleman. I was left alone in the apartment to
take care of little Martin and our boarder.

Manfred was an actor and could be two different people
very easily. With Irmgard he played the quiet, polite, correct
young gentleman. Alone with me he was cynical, moody, witty,

pleading. He never said in so many words that he was in love with me. He took it for granted that I knew it—and I knew it indeed. His hungry eyes followed me wherever I went. When I undressed in my room I had the queer feeling that he could watch me through the walls. I didn't dare to turn around in my bed because I felt that he listened to every sound I made. I felt uncomfortable and I felt terribly sorry for the boy. He was such a poor dog; he was a sick and dying man and he carried it well. There was that constant drive in him to be like all the others. Go out and do things. In winter 1918 the country was full of men who had had enough of the fighting, men who would do anything to be left at home. Swindle, lie, bribe, buy their ineligibility at any price, with any humiliation. Mutilate themselves, ruin their hearts with strong drugs, desert in danger of their lives to some neutral country, or hand themselves over to the enemy to be taken prisoners. Anything, anything to keep out of the war. But to Manfred it was an open sore that he was refused to be let out there with the others and fight.

"The stupidity of keeping junk like me at home and sending sound, healthy fellows into the lines!" he would say bitterly. "They are the ones that want to live; they have a right to be kept alive. But I? Just good enough to be sold to the glue factory. For what do they preserve me here? To eat the food they could give to women and babies? Extra rations, indeed! It's a bloody, outrageous shame."

I could see that he was running a temperature and I tried to calm him down, but he went ranting on: "If it comes to being brave—there is no man so brave as the one who has carried his own death with him for many years. What have I to be afraid of? God, it's people like me whom they should send out on their most perilous tasks. Form a suicide squad of guys like me and let us loose on the enemy. There must be a few hundred thousand moribund candidates of my sort in the country. Why don't they build a division of us and let us win the war for them? It would be the only sensible thing, don't you see? The fun we could have! And how much every one of us would prefer to get an honest finish than to lie in bed and spit his lungs into a nasty little blue bottle until he croaks."

"Come, come," I said, "don't let your imagination run wild; you are much better and you want to get entirely well, don't you? All you need is a bit of patience. The war can wait. It'll go on forever and there will be plenty of time for you to get there after you have recovered."

"It'll be nice when my son asks, 'Papa, where were you during the war?' 'I played Mortimer in the civic theater of Hahnenstadt, my child. I kept up the morale at home,'" he said, grimly fighting the air with his restless hands. Then he folded them tightly and put them down and stared at them. "Only I won't have a son and I'll be dead and buried before this war is over," he added miserably.

"Manfred, my boy," I said, "if there is one thing I detest it's self-pity. Stop being so damn sorry for yourself and go to bed."

"Yes, go to bed like a good boy. And don't you dare dream of Frau Captain Tillmann," he ended the conversation. We sat in the cold dining room, into which some of the living-room furniture had been squeezed, since it had become the only livable room in the apartment. There was a feeble fire flickering in the stove, and we had pushed a bench close in front of it to catch some of the thin, insufficient warmth. As Irmgard had taken our coal ration to my father-in-law, we kept that stove going by desperate means. We bought stacks of old newspapers for an exorbitant price. We had used up every wooden crate we could find, and we began contemplating which pieces of furniture we might use for fuel. The trouble was that wood fire was short-lived. If we had had a layer of fat over our bodies we might have felt warmer; but we were so thin, both of us, that the bones stuck out under our skin. "You are the prettiest skeleton I've ever met in my life, Marion," Manfred said to me. He was the only one to call me by my circus name, and he did it only when we were alone. In front of Irmgard I was decorously Frau Captain Tillmann to him. Out of such tiny, intangible trifles he had spun a net around me, as if we shared some secret.

"You don't like me, do you?" Manfred would ask some other day, watching me while I prepared Martin's oatmeal.

"But certainly I like you," I said impatiently. "Now, please, will you get out of my way?"

He sat down on Elizabeth's kitchen stool. "Why don't you like me, Marion?" he went on stubbornly. "Why? Will you tell me the truth?"

"I told you the truth. I like you and I am glad Fritz brought you to us. Now there."

"Is it that you don't like me because you think I am a Jew?" he asked.

"Now you are being plain silly," I said. "Please, hand me Martin's plate."

"Or is it that you don't like me because you think I am a useless cripple and a coward?" he persisted. "You know it's not my fault."

"I don't like you when you go off on those exhibitions of self-flagellation," I said angrily. "Otherwise I like you well enough."

"But you don't think you could love me, do you, Marion?"

"For Christ's sake!" I said, exasperated. I took Martin's soup plate and carried it into the room. The baby was sitting in his pen and greeted the food with his usual jubilant squealing fanfare. Manfred had followed me like a dog. I picked up the little boy, sat him on my lap, and began shoving the spoon with the oatmeal into his greedy wet snout.

"If I were away in the trenches like Captain Tillmann you would love me," Manfred said. "Those absent heroes have all the advantage over us poor guys at home. Tell me, what sort of a man is he? If he is anything like his sister I can't understand why you should have picked him. You seem to fit into this family like a bottle of perfume into a tub with dead fish. Don't say anything. I know. I know you much better than you know yourself. Jesus Maria, how lonely you would be if you couldn't talk to me at least."

"Someday I'm going to slap your face, Manfred," I said. I was very angry, more so because there was a shade of truth in what he said. The baby on my lap snorted with the strain of getting as much food as possible into him in as short a time as possible. "If he is not the hungriest baby there ever was!" I said; the spoon clinked against his new teeth, which was our newest joke, and little Martin began to howl with laughter.

"All right. No love then. But you could give me pity at least.

You could be good to me out of pity. Or is that also asking too much?" Manfred said.

"You wouldn't want pity, Manfred," I said. I felt damned sorry for the boy. I would have liked to take him on my lap or something to calm him down.

"Listen, Marion," he said, "didn't you buy some horse meat last Wednesday? You went all across town and you stood in line for five hours, didn't you? And you were so afraid all the horse meat would be sold out before it was your turn that your hands were shaking—like that, see?" He held his trembling hands under my eyes, and I shrank back instinctively. "And when you brought home a piece of horse meat you were as happy as if your life were saved. Well."

"Well?" I said.

"If horse meat is good enough for you, pity is good enough for me," he said. "We all must learn to compromise one way or the other. As the Great Crooked One says in Peer Gynt: 'Go round about!' Compromise!"

Then something happened two days later, and it didn't seem important at the time—only afterward, in the dark years to come. . . .

That morning the papers announced that anyone who would come with a pushcart to the civic market could buy fifty pounds of cabbage. Slightly frozen it was, but still edible. It was an offer of dizzy magnitude, and after I had fed little Martin and put him to bed for his afternoon nap I set out enthusiastically for the civic market. As Irmgard and Elizabeth still stayed in Detfurth with old Herr Tillmann and I knew no one to do such errands for me, I had borrowed a pushcart from the janitor and went happily on my way. It was a cold day, the streets were covered with ice. There was always a strong wind blowing from the northeast into Hahnenstadt; it came from the distant North Sea, and people had a habit of leaning against it automatically the moment they emerged from their houses. I pushed my cart the long way, across the bridge that spanned the narrow river, through the poor quarters on the other side, and farther on, to the edge of the Hahnenmarsh, where the market was situated.

It was a bleak, depressing sight with its empty stalls; you felt like a scavenger, sneaking around there, trying to hunt up some food. Sometimes that market gave you the feeling that the world had come to an end, that all growing had stopped and that soon there wouldn't be any trees or pastures left on the face of this ravaged earth. Sometimes again you would dream of a market with meat and fowl, with eggs and fruit and pyramids of bread and hams and bacons hanging from the rafters. Even today, in a well-supplied market, sometimes this dreamlike feeling over-comes me—as if I might wake up any moment and be back in Hahnenstadt and hungry. Maybe that's where we all are headed anyhow: back to the starvation and miserable hopelessness that goes before the end of a war. . . .

There were the usual lines in front of those few stalls where the legal rations were sold that day. The quarrels, the excitement, the grumbling. Some people pushing, some resigned, some selfish, some kind and helpful. You certainly get a good idea of human nature if you stand in food lines for a few years. The early dusk settled over us while we slowly advanced, and the frost bit into our fingers and toes. But finally I received my unbelievable treasure of fifty pounds of cabbage. They threw it into my pushcart and happily, if somewhat tired, I pushed on home. Whenever I stopped for a brief rest I would tenderly touch my load and feel the lumpy roundness of my cabbage. There was a funny smell about my precious load, but I told myself that it was the pushcart that smelled and not my cabbage. I pushed on, for it had become late and dark; during the last hour I had begun worrying lest little Martin should awaken and fall from his cot or smother himself with his pillows. At last I arrived at the Riede and asked our janitor to help me upstairs with my load.

"What have you got there, Frau Captain?" he asked. "Cabbage? And such a lot?" He sniffed. "Good Lord, and how they stink!" he said. "I don't think it's worth taking them upstairs, if you ask me. They'll only stink up your kitchen."

I looked at my load, I touched it. It felt wet and clammy and it stank like nothing on earth. My treasure was nothing but some filthy, foul, rotten slush. The janitor helped me throw it into the garbage can. "There you are, Frau Captain," he said.

"Fine people like you and Frau Oberinspektor go hungry and give their men to the fatherland while those dirty Jews on the third floor stay home and fill their bellies." The Kriegsschieber who had recently moved into the flat above ours were a sore spot and a target of contempt for the whole house, but cursing them didn't help me in my abysmal disappointment. I think I cried a little as I crept up the dimly lit stairs. But when I let myself into our entrance hall I stood arrested on the threshold. There was another smell, one I had almost forgotten. A happy smell, sweet, wintery, and homelike. One of the smells of which we had talked in Bergheim, Pimpernel, Clara, and I, when we recited the things made for happiness: apples baking on the stove.

I heard Martin crow and babble in the dining room and Manfred talking to him. I tore open the door and stood on the threshold of fairyland.

The room was warm. A good lively fire crackled in the stove, and Martin was peeled of his woollies and played in his shirt, which gave a full view of his round little behind. On the stove six apples were baking, filling the whole world with their aroma. The table was set; there was a pat of butter and a glass with honey. Half a ham, a whole loaf of bread, four eggs, and three packages: coffee, flour, and sugar. It looked for all the world like one of those hunger dreams. I felt the saliva gushing in my mouth and for a second I could not speak.

"Good evening," Manfred said. "I gave the baby a bath and let him romp for a while. It's warm here, isn't it?"

"Yes. It's warm," I said.

"I have four scuttlefuls of coal in reserve. If you want to have a bath you can heat some water. It's warm in my room too and you can use my rubber tub." I looked around; the door to his room stood open and the pipes in there were glowing with heat.

"How come you are not in the theater?" I said, stupid with astonishment.

"That's over. No more theater for me. From now on I'm nobody's monkey."

"What does all this mean?" I asked. "Have you become a Kriegsschieber?"

"No, but a soldier. They have taken me. Marion, they have taken me. I am off for the war. They have taken me at last. Tomorrow I am going to camp. This is my farewell party for you. How do you like it?"

"Where did you get all this?"

"Oh, you still can get anything if you pay the price," he said nonchalantly.

"Where did you get the money?" I said. "This must have cost a fortune."

He laughed softly. "You know I don't need my savings any longer. You know that I won't come back," he said. It hit me so that I stood stiffly for a moment, and then I went over and gave him a kiss.

"You are drunk," I said, "and you have a fever and you are such a fool, such a crazy, foolhearted fool—what am I going to do with you?"

I have never told anyone that once I went to bed with a man for no better reason than that he gave me a good meal and because I had a hot bath and because the room was warm. And maybe also because it was so little and so unimportant, what I could give him in return, and it meant so much to him. You did not tell such things after the war was over and people wouldn't have understood them. Perhaps they will understand them now again, the refugees on the highways of Europe, the crowds huddled in air-raid shelters, the women who are cold and hungry and frightened and lonely, the men whose lives are in danger.

It happened in Manfred's room. Through the open door I could hear the soft roaring of the fire in the stove and see its reflection dance on the ceiling, and there was still the sweet scent of baked apples in the air. The pipes that came through the wall kept on glowing for a while, and then they turned dark and shrank into the night with a gentle clanking. Manfred's body was hot with fever and very thin and utterly unfamiliar. I held him politely close to me and thought all the time of the cake I would bake. I hadn't baked a cake for a long time, and I tried to remember the recipe. I would take half a pound of flour and one egg and some soda bicarbonate to raise the dough, and I still had some raspberry jam hoarded away for a filling

I would bake it myself, without Elizabeth's strict supervision, and send it to Captain Tillmann.

I heard Manfred give a little sigh in my arms, and I felt sorry for him and began to stroke his soft, silky hair. And it was all so without weight, as if I had kissed the empty air and allowed a cloud to embrace me.

SUDDENLY it was spring: a procession of sunny, warm days came marching from the heath in the south into the town, an early vanguard of better months to come. Old Herr Tillmann had recovered, and Irmgard had brought him with her to stay with us. His dachshund Manne came with him, a sentimental creature who seemed ashamed that he was always hungry. Irmgard took the news of Manfred Halban's sudden departure coldly. "I am glad he has moved out; it saves us trouble," she said. "I would have given him notice anyway. You know, my dear, that he is a Jew after all? He and his celebrated aviator cousin too. Father is absolutely certain about it, aren't you, Father? General Pritwitz told it. I really don't understand the world any longer, if they take Jews into the flying corps and give them the Pour-le-Mérite. Do you, Father?"

"I used to know several Jews who were quite nice people," the old gentleman said with the limited liberalism of his generation. We installed him in the den, after Elizabeth and Irmgard had given the room a thorough scouring, as if to clean out every trace of poor Manfred. I went into the kitchen and baked my cake for Captain Tillmann, but fortunately I had not sent it off yet when a telegram arrived, announcing that he was on his way home. Like all women whose men came unexpectedly on leave, I buzzed around like a horsefly, I dolled up the baby, washed my underslip, did my hair, rubbed glycerine into my hands and the last bit of eau de Cologne behind my ears, and felt ready and alluring like the Queen of Sheba waiting for King Solomon.

This time Captain Tillmann was not wounded, only shell-shocked and slightly gassed, though he was very eager to explain that he had accidentally swallowed a few mouthfuls of our own gas, as if he would begrudge the enemy the ability of using poison gas too. I could see that his nerves were shot to pieces. Under normal circumstances he would have been put into an asylum as slightly crazy, but during a war there was nothing extraordinary in his behavior. He would scurry for cover every time a street car whizzed by in the street below. He had entered another period of vegetarianism, and at the sight of meat he would turn green in the face and leave the table. And he could not sleep in a bed. It cramped my heart to see what the last winter had made of this good, brave, calm, and enduring man, and I would have given my right hand to make him as he had been when I met him first.

I'll never forget the first night after Captain Tillmann's return. We spent it like strangers, or like a patient and his nurse. I had always loathed the furniture in the Klappholz bedroom. It was big and heavy, a load of that horrid Hahnenstadt Gothic with a bit of Tudor thrown in. The chiffonier looked like a castle, with turrets and parapets, and the counterpane of the beds too, especially if you were tired and looked at them for a while. "Do you mind if I sleep on the floor?" Kurt said when we entered the room and closed the door behind us. We had hardly been left alone all day long and we felt a bit like strangers. He gave a short embarrassed laugh. "I'm not used to sleeping in a bed any more," he muttered. "It sort of chokes me. I had a devil of a time with one in an inn on the way home."

He turned the light off before he began undressing. I sat on the edge of my bed and heard him rummage around in the dark, dragging some of the bedding onto the floor. Then I heard him stop for one of his deep, bellowing coughing spells. "Let me fix it for you," I said. "No, thanks," he said in the dark. "You don't know how." I undressed slowly, not knowing how to handle the situation. If only Clara were here, I thought, grinning in the dark, because it was a funny idea. She is so clever about everything that goes on between men and women, I thought. After a while I felt that he stood at my bedside and bent down to kiss me. He had taken off his boots and his tunic but had kept

on his shirt and pants. He pressed his lips to mine and his beard
scratched my chin. A street car went past on the street and I
felt him flinch and shrink away. "It's all right," I whispered,
clasping my arms around his neck. "It's nothing." But he
wrestled himself free and crouched down, holding his breath
and listening. "Crazy," he said, "but it sounds exactly like those
trench mortars."

"You'll get used to it. It's only the street car," I said.

I heard him sigh and stretch out on the bed he had made for
himself on the floor. "It's nothing," I said again. "You're home
and safe. Forget your trench mortars and go to sleep."

"Silly," he said. "Out there, in the trenches, you dream of it
all the time. You think of it every night: I'll take a bath and
shave off my beard and I'll take off my uniform when I go to
sleep, and I'll have a bed. I'll have a bed, you think; I'll sleep
on clean sheets and I'll have a pillow and I'll smell that good
clean smell that clings to clean linen, and there will be no shooting and no alarm and I'll sleep in a bed. That's what you think.
And then you are sent behind the lines for a rest period and
you get a good billet and there is a bed. And the first thing you
know, the Parlez-vous is shelling the village in the midst of the
night and you are caught without pants. And after that you can't
sleep in a bed, the devil knows why. But you keep on thinking
of it every night. I'll shave and have a bath and undress and sleep
in a bed, that's all you can think of. Are you asleep, little one?"

"No, Kurt, I am listening."

"Are you tired?"

"No, not really. Are you?"

"Yes, very tired. But I can't sleep. Let's talk a bit, shall we?"

"Do you want me to turn on the light?"

"No, don't. Let's talk about Martin. He is wonderful, isn't he?
There is so much talk in the lines that our babies at home are
starving. But he certainly doesn't look starved, does he?"

"Oh, but we have plenty to eat. Don't let that worry you."

"And he knows me. Did you hear him call me Papa? He is
bright. Imagine such a mite, just one year old, who can talk and
walk. What a boy young Herr Tillmann is!"

I heard him laugh down there on the floor, and then the laughing turned into another coughing fit. "Little one," he said when he was through with it, "could you let me have your hand?"

I let my hand hang down, and he took it and tucked it under his cheek. "That's better," he sighed. I heard him breathe steadily and thought that he had fallen asleep. My arm got numb and I tried to take my hand back, but he was still awake and held onto it. "Listen," he said. "Did you miss me?"

"Oh yes. Very much. All the time."

"I missed you too," he said. "Lord, how I missed you!" He lay silent for a few minutes and then he said, "I missed myself impotent out there. It happens to many of us."

"Why do you say that?" I said into the darkness. "You are just tired out. It's natural, isn't it? Just rest and relax, that's all you need."

"Are you mad at me?" he asked when I pulled my hand away.

"No, why should I be?" I said. "But my arm has fallen asleep."

"Poor little thin arm," he said. "Come, let me rub it. There, that's better. Now I'll let you sleep."

"Good night, my darling," I said into the darkness. "Sleep well."

I heard him toss around for a while, and then another street car went by. He sat up and listened. My eyes got used to the darkness and I could perceive the outline of his body. He sat there hugging his knees to his chest, his face upturned. "It's all right," I said. "It's nothing."

"I thought you were asleep," he said. "Aren't you?"

"Yes, I am asleep," I said, smiling in the dark. He stretched out again.

"Marion," he said after a while.

"Yes, dear?"

"I love you so."

"Yes, I know. I love you too."

"I want you so. I want you so just now."

I thought it over. "Shall I come to you?" I whispered.

"Yes. No. Wait. Lord, I want you so. Do you mind lying on the floor with me?"

"No, it's fun on the floor. Wait. I'll bring my pillow down to you."

"You know, it makes me nervous to be in a bed."

"Yes, I know. There now."

"It frightens me to be in a bed."

He had begun to tremble, and I took him into my arms. I held him so tight that it must have hurt him, and after a few moments his tremor stopped. We kissed hard, and then a street car went by below and his body shrank away from me, limp and powerless. "It's all right," I whispered. "It's nothing, it's all right." He slid down a bit so that his head came to rest on my shoulder, and I felt a sharp pain as he dug his teeth into it, and then I felt him shaking in short convulsive fits and I understood that he was sobbing about himself and did not want to sob. The floor was hard beneath us, and the night began to grow cold. I held him in my arms, with his scratchy beard on my wet shoulder. I stroked him and caressed him and did what I could to help him mend his broken pride. It's a funny, primitive sort of pride men have; it sits right in the center of their sex, and I am afraid what they call love consists, in good part, of their need to assure themselves again and again that they are strong and well-functioning machines.

As for Kurt, he healed as quickly as a lizard's tail, as my grandfather used to say, and after a week he was almost normal again, tender and quiet and considerate. We even spent a honeymoon of sorts together, escaping the turreted bedroom in the Riede and going to my father-in-law's hunting lodge in Detfurth. What he called a hunting lodge was really only a small shed under pine trees, the remnant of some old farmhouse, four whitewashed walls with dark brown oak beams enclosing one room. We kept a log fire burning in the big tiled stove and watched the snow falling outside, for the short, early spell of spring weather was over, and we were very happy. The nights were long and I was filled with a deep, floating fondness for my husband, and after a week he had learned to sleep in a bed again and there were no street cars. . . .

But even before his leave of absence was over he grew very impatient to get back to the front. The Army had made great preparations for a decisive spring offensive all along the front, and everybody was sure that the French lines would crack and the war be over in no time at all.

As for Manfred Halban, he was killed in battle in the beginning of April, just around the time when I found out that I was pregnant again.

IN SPRING 1918 it was almost like the beginning of the war, because we had such great victories every day. We all felt that if we could only make a little effort and hold out a few more weeks the war would be over and we would have won it. We were so full of hope and courage that it seemed to us as if we had more food and less hunger than for a long time. Had we ever complained about anything? It was really ridiculous even to mention the insignificant privations or sacrifices that were inflicted upon us. It wasn't cold any more, the sun shone over the heath in the south of the town. The marshes in the northeast were yellow with wild ranunculus, and the world was a fine place. Then, after a while we stopped having victories and the bulletins went back to their old song: no news from Verdun. We felt hungry again. Fall came, and all summer long there had been dark rumors everywhere, but not one had told us that we had lost the war.

I came down the stairs on a gray morning in November, and the janitor stopped me. "I would not go out on the street if I were Frau Captain," he said. He had a broom in his hand, but he didn't sweep the stairs.

"Why not?" I asked, surprised.

"Just so. Not today. I would stay at home. It's safer," he said with an air of secrecy that irritated me.

"I have to go to the town house for my food stamps," I said. "In fact I should have been there yesterday."

"Why doesn't Frau Captain send Elizabeth? I would recommend sending her. No one will hurt her," he said.

"No one will hurt me either. Elizabeth is in bed with the flu," I said. "I'm afraid Frau Oberinspektor Klappholz is getting it too. What's the matter with going out anyhow?"

"Doesn't Frau Captain know what happened?"

"The paper didn't come this morning. What happened? Did we lose a battle? Or are there riots in town?"

There had been riots off and on. There had also been strikes in the industrial districts across the bridge. A few times a mob had stormed the bakeries in the poor parts of the town and taken away the bread, which was one third sawdust anyway. In fact, lately machine guns had been posted in front of the town house and at the bridgehead as a warning to rioters. But the unrest over there reached the Riede only as a faint murmur.

"Riots?" the janitor said. "No, not exactly, Frau Captain. But the war is over."

"The war is over? What do you mean, the war is over? It can't be over from one day to another, can it?" I cried. "Did we win it?"

"No. They just stopped fighting," the man said. "And now there is a revolution."

"You mean we have peace?" I cried. "Is it true? Or is it only another one of those rumors?"

"Yes, we have peace," he said. "The war is over and the revolution is on. If I were Frau Captain I wouldn't go out on the street."

I brushed him aside and went on my way. I felt as if a brick had fallen on my head. I could not think. The street looked no different from any other day. The same old lady I saw every other morning took her dog from street lamp to street lamp; the same straggling school children hurriedly trotted on wooden shoes toward school. The same chimney sweep passed me, black and cheerful under his layers of smudge. I let him pass to my right side, for that meant good luck. I took the street car at the corner and demanded a ticket to the town house. "I don't know if you can get in today," the woman conductor said as she punched the ticket. "But you might try anyhow." That was all. Never has the world seen a quieter and more respectable revolution than that German one. And never a more futile one.

The machine guns stood at the bridgehead as before, with a group of bearded soldiers in tattered gray uniforms around them. They had red badges on their sleeves. There were also some marines with them. They were friendly and good-natured in a gruff way and willing to give anybody all the information they had to impart. People of all ages had formed a circle around them, with the little ragamuffins of the district closest to the soldiers, eager and curious, some of them with soldiers' caps on their unkempt heads. I didn't see anybody belonging to the Better Classes among the crowd. I myself didn't feel or look as if I belonged to the Better Classes. In my delicate condition I looked like a telegraph pole with a bag tied to its front. By and by the rumors crystallized into some shape: Yes, the war was over. The men had stopped fighting, the Navy first and then the Army too. Hindenburg was dead. The Kaiser had committed suicide with all his sons. Our men would be home soon and there would be plenty of food for everybody. No, you needed no pass to get through to the town house. Everyone was free to do what he pleased. Free. There was that word which had such a ringing sound. We were free. The war was over. We had peace and we were free and the offices of the town house worked as usual and I got my food stamps, including the extra ration of milk for Martin and for myself, who happened to be in my ninth month of pregnancy. It was almost impossible to grasp the full meaning of it within the first hours. The people who stood in line for their food stamps exchanged the funniest ideas. They were happy and they made lots of jokes. It seemed Germany was going to be a republic from now on. It looked as if a revolution were the best thing that could have happened to us. It also seemed that we had lost the war. Nobody cared. Nobody knew what it meant. Nobody shed a tear for the Kaiser or Hindenburg. Nobody could envision what had happened to bring this sudden peace about or which shape the future would take from now on. If you have been buried in a collapsing mine and are saved and by a miracle brought to the surface alive, you don't care how the weather is up there. That's how we all felt.

That's what Walter Brandt fought for, I thought on my way

home. A better world. A free country. Free people. A republic. If he could only have lived to see this day! There would be food for everybody. Free schools and universities and education for all. Theaters and concerts free for anyone who liked to go. Maybe they would abolish money altogether. I was almost sure they would. No more poverty and no more wealth. What a wonderful world to hand over to a newly born baby! This was better than winning a war; oh, infinitely better. I saw white pillars rise from the heath like Greek temples, and a happy throng dancing in the sunshine, and there was a roar of mighty music, a song of peace and freedom, overwhelming in its beauty. I came floating on a cloud into our apartment. "The war is over," I shouted, bursting into Irmgard's room. "Kurt is on his way home. Maybe he will be back before the new baby is born. Aren't you happy?"

Old Herr Tillmann sat near the door with a rifle across his knees, ready to shoot any intruder. He had even pinned two old-time medals to his coat. There was an expression of sinister resolution on his face, and even his mustache stood up like the hackles on an angry old boar's back. Manne sat alertly at his feet, ready for whatever sort of hunt this one was going to be. Irmgard, dressed in her deepest mourning, stood at the window and looked down on the street from behind the heavy curtains. She was gray in the face, and her beginning flu made her sniffle. Both stared at me, unbelieving.

"Happy? I don't understand what you mean to say, Maria," the old gentleman said. "This is an hour of deepest humiliation. It is the end of Germany. And you are happy?"

"I can't help it. I am happy. The war is over, that's all I know. And Germany will be a better country after this, you'll see, Father. Aren't you glad too that Kurt is on his way home?"

"If I know my son he would be rather dead than defeated," the old man said. "As for me, I am sorry I have to live to see this day."

"Oh," I said, abashed. "We don't seem to understand each other."

"No, we don't. We never did," Irmgard suddenly broke in. "But whatever I thought of you, I would never have expected to find you on the side of the traitors, the communists, the scum, in such a moment. My poor brother!"

I had never seen her so excited. Her pale eyes blazed and her hands trembled. The whole scene was so ludicrous and the big words seemed so funny to me all of a sudden that I broke out in laughter. The pent-up fear and tension of all those months came up in a blast of bubbles that burst in my throat, and I couldn't stop laughing. Steady, my girl, steady, I told myself. Now we are getting hysterical. I swallowed myself full of air and tried to keep myself in hand. "You Austrian!" Irmgard said. It sounded like "You dirt!" She came up to me and stopped so abruptly that, for a moment, I thought she was going to hit me. But she gave only a muffled sound and rushed past me from the room. It sobered me up. "I'm so sorry, forgive me, Father," I said. "I have no sense for high-grade tragedies, I am afraid."

"You seem to forget that my daughter has sacrificed two sons and a husband in this war," the old man said. "Sacrificed for what? To save the country, to help us conquer the enemy. To uphold our glorious traditions. But not to prepare the road for a bunch of criminals and mutineers. Oh, what a waste of life for such an end! But let them come, let them come. They won't get me alive. I'll shoot anyone like a mad dog who dares to lay hands on me."

For a few days they locked themselves in their rooms and treated me like an outlaw. Even old Elizabeth, stewing with fever in her room in the garret, would only reluctantly speak to me when I came to bring her some soup or medicine. I, together with Martin and the unborn baby in my pouch, represented the revolution in the household. Only the janitor, trying to sit on both sides of the fence, was friendly and even confidential with me, at the same time obviously losing all respect for me. He stopped calling me Frau Captain; if I didn't mind the communists I was just plain Frau Tillmann to him.

By and by the muddle and stunned surprise that we called revolution began to clear up a bit. We had no peace but an armistice that might be terminated at any moment. The Kaiser hadn't committed suicide but had run away. Hindenburg wasn't killed but, in his plodding, reliable way, tried to get his armies home; and the soldiers respected and obeyed him as before, mutiny or not. Soldiers-and-workers' councils shot up overnight and gave out manifestoes, new laws, and promises. We also learned that it was the Spartacists who had ended the war and saved the country and ruled it now—whatever Spartacists might be. It took me many years to realize that well-organized underground work had prepared the soil for this poor imitation of a revolution; in fact, that a revolution needs as much systematized organization as a war. Taken all in all, it was a highly diverting time, and I learned a lot about the adaptability of human nature. My father-in-law didn't shoot anyone but began scouting around for old acquaintances among the new men; anyone who might be obliged to him, any poor devil whom he had treated nicely during his time as Oberamtsgerichtsrat in Detfurth. If they were now the ruling class it would be better to come to terms with them. On the other hand the soldiers-and-workers' councils were too inexperienced to take over the reins; they wanted to keep order and were afraid of their responsibilities. Therefore they left the conservative old officials of the imperial regime in office; gratefully they shook their hands and felt honored to win their cooperation. Everything turned out different from what anyone had expected. Our heroes, the officers who began drifting back into the country, didn't kill themselves when their epaulets were torn from their uniforms. On the contrary there were many who quietly and neatly took them off themselves to avoid trouble on the streets. Also, they didn't dream of starting a counterrevolution. They were tired of fighting and killing. All they wanted was to rest and relax and make up for their lost youth. Get married, dance, and drink and try to forget that they had been through all the hells of a world war. And, most surprising of all, the poor people didn't kill the rich people as in other revolutions. They killed those who were just as poor. There they were again, my old friends from F 12; the left wing and the right wing and the middle of socialism. Independent socialists and just-so-so socialists; the Spartacists, the communists, the radicals and not-quite-so-radicals. There they were, unable to agree and fighting like hungry dogs over a bone for the domination of Germany. Whatever serious shooting and killing was done in those days and for years to come occurred between socialists and communists, and if they ended up by getting Hitler, I sometimes think they deserved him.

One day I got caught in a little shooting bout myself, as I had taken little Martin out for a little airing. I had tied a big, red bow to his perambulator and everything went fine, but on the way home I suddenly found myself caught between two firing groups. People rushed by, screaming and yelling. Some pointed up to a housetop and shouted that they had machine guns up there. There was a funny clatter and noise which I had never heard before and then I saw two men in front of me topple over and lie sprawling on the sidewalk. I scuttled away, frantically searching for an escape, like a mouse for a hole, but behind every house door and every window I suddenly saw men ready to shoot. You don't think much in such moments. I simply broke into a good canter, pushing my perambulator ahead of me, with the red bow bobbing lustily and Martin squealing with glee, because this was obviously all done for his entertainment. It's funny how puny things like a revolution appear when you are in the midst of them. That's because you never see the whole, only the tiny fragment that hits you personally. On my way home I decided not to tell a word of the incident. Before I had reached the house in the Riede I had convinced myself that I had been panicky about nothing at all. It turned out to be a complicated day, though.

The flu finally and seriously caught up with Irmgard, and she had reluctantly put herself to bed. My father-in-law paced up and down, with Manne behind him, his long dachshund nose glued to his master's heels in an expressive display of grief and sympathy. I fixed some lunch for the old gentleman and stole some oatmeal from little Martin's ration and cooked soup for my two patients. Irmgard had turned her face to the wall and would not talk to me. I carried the tureen for old Elizabeth up to her room under the roof. It was a dismal little hole, like all servants' quarters in the good houses. Her bed was squeezed into a corner under the slanting roof, and it was cold and drafty there, in spite of the stale, old, unaired breath of the place. On the way downstairs I felt some pain collecting somewhere in my back, pain I refused to recognize. It was not the time for the new baby yet, not for another three weeks at the least. I telephoned for Dr. Mayer, the old family relic, to come and have a look at Irmgard. He promised to be over soon.

However, half an hour later he called back and informed me that he could not come. They had built barricades near the railroad crossing, blocking the connection between Wrangel Platz, where he lived, and our quarter, and there was fierce fighting— I didn't quite understand between whom. I ate the soup that Irmgard had not touched, but shortly afterward my stomach rolled over and gave it all back. I could no longer cheat myself about the sort of pains I had, and they came at shorter and shorter intervals. This is a nice mess we are in, I thought. I began to call up the hospitals to find myself a bed in one of them and a nurse to come and take care of Irmgard. It turned out that our fine district was cut off from the rest of the town, and they doubted if even an ambulance could get through. They would do their best, they promised. I sat down and waited. The pains came every five or six minutes; it seemed to be a very impatient baby, this new one. I went into Irmgard's room; the old man was sitting at her bedside, pretending to read some old magazine. Irmgard's cheeks were flushed with fever; the red spots stood out like paint in her gray face. She didn't smile exactly, but she still looked as if she did.

"How are you, Irmgard?" I said timidly.

"I have a very high temperature," she said querulously, as if to make me and the revolution responsible for it. Her lips were dry and cracked. I felt sorry for her. "What do you want?" she said. "Why can't you leave me alone?" I braced my back with my hand and waited until the next pain had passed, because you can't speak while it stiffens you in that peculiar way. "Look here," I said, "this is really too silly—but I think the baby is coming and I might have to go to a hospital. I'll see that you get a nurse. If the worst comes to the worst, Elizabeth will have to get up and take care of you."

Then our bell rung and my father-in-law went heavy-footed to open the door. The patter of Manne's claws on the bare floor of the entrance hall sounded loud and cheerful. The young man who stood outside was a doctor whom the hospital had hunted up in our district and sent to me, because there was no way to get me through the barricades. He seemed pitifully inexperienced and frightened. He might have been wonderful at abdominal shots or other such war casualties, but I wondered if he had ever even heard how babies were born. No sooner had he ordered me to bed and dispatched the old man into the kitchen to get water boiling than Irmgard and Elizabeth put in a simultaneous appearance. Both had left their beds in great commotion, ready to do their duty by me. I doubted if two such good Samaritans, staggering around in clouds of influenza germs, were good for me and the new baby. But, God, how glad I was to see their stern, concerned faces and feel some women near me!

It had been huge fun to give birth to Martin. But this new child tore me through an inferno of pain and took its time to do so. Every minute of it felt like the cutting of a butcher knife. To make things worse, the electric power was cut off in the middle of the evening on account of the revolution, and I had to go through with the show by the flicker of meager candles and as much kerosene as my father-in-law was able to collect from some of his friends who lived near us. My young doctor sweated streams of anguish and I had to console him whenever I had a breathing spell myself.

Wasn't it just like Michael to be born too early and to come out wrong end first, so as to make everything as difficult as possible, and to take such a long time for it, and finally to enter the world as a stillborn blue lifeless little something that had to be desperately coaxed into breathing! And to do all this just when a revolution was on and the light was cut off and the crackling of machine guns seamed the edge of the night.

5

CHRISTOPHER always claimed that one could traverse the Grauhorn Glacier in one's bedroom slippers; he called it a little before-dinner promenade. It was the sort of glacier where the guide took his amateur tourists to give them something to brag about back home: a maximum of thrill with a minimum of danger. Where the trail reached the crest of the Kees, Marion stopped to look down at the glacier and survey the terrain. The fun of climbing up to the crest had almost blotted out her disappointment of not having caught up with Christopher yet. It's hard for forty-four to catch up with twenty-nine, she thought apologetically. Christopher on a mountain trip seemed so slow that he looked almost funny, yet somehow he left everybody behind, taking every obstacle and difficulty in his easy stride as if they were nothing at all. "He climbs mountains like Heifetz plays the violin," Michael had said of him only recently.

There is nothing in the world as silent as the mountains. Marion looked at her eagerly ticking wrist watch. It was ten minutes past three. She dried her perspiring face and she heard her own breathing like a big noise; there was a faint, rasping pain in her windpipe as the air brushed in and out. The glacier was spread below like a softly curved river of ice flowing in a bend around the sturdy, massive cone of the Grauhorn. The shade of the

Kees that fell over it cut it sharply into two. It was of a cold blue this side and of a golden, glaring white over there, where the full impact of the sun hit its corrugated surface. As soon as Marion's eyes got used to the hard reflection of that mass of ice down there, she discovered a little black spot creeping along in all the shadowy blues. Christopher, Chris, my darling, she thought happily. She took a deep breath and made one of her unsuccessful efforts at yodeling. It was an art she had never learned to master. I sound like a young rooster trying to crow, she thought, laughing at herself. Then, as she strained her eyes, which were not so young and sharp as they used to be, she discovered another little figure somewhere else on the glacier, and then three more, in single file, roped together most probably. They looked like flies crawling on a birthday cake.

The trail that had taken her so far ran on along the ridge, and Marion had to leave it for the short steep descent to the glacier. She remembered the two characteristic rock formations that marked the easiest starting place for the route across it, and also the best way for climbing down the moraine. As she approached the frozen flow of ice it grew colder and she stopped to slip on her jacket and cover her face with zinc-oxide cream to protect it against snow burns. She was very impatient now to get across; she was not afraid of traversing the glacier alone, but she would have loved to do it in Christopher's company. The last fifty feet she came sliding down the moraine, with rocks and stone rumbling away under her feet and leaping down to the glacier. She caught herself and steadied her knees and her breathing. She felt somewhat shaky when she arrived at the mouth of the glacier, where the ice was soiled, streaked with brown and several shades of gray and looking altogether like a cut through an enormous old and rotting cheese. With the automatic gesture of the experienced mountaineer she gripped her ax to have it handy for testing the ice and cutting steps into it if necessary, and then she set slowly out to cross it.

The first part of the glacier that lay in the shade of the Kees was easy enough. It was what Christopher called a promenade. The people who had crossed it before her had left a clear route on the flaking ice of the surface, and all Marion had to do was follow these traces. She bent down to search for Christopher's foot tracks among the others. It so happened that she knew the traces his hobnail boots left, and he knew hers. The pattern of nails was as definite and easy to recognize as a face. But it looked as if too many people had traversed the glacier that day; it looked, in fact, as if a herd of elephants had stampeded across this part of it, and Marion straightened up with a sigh and tramped on. But where the shade of the mountain ended, pinnacles and ridges of ice rose up, with narrow crevasses between them, and to bend over and peer down into their unreal green-and-blue crystal depth was not without risk. Before Marion ventured out into the glare she took down her rucksack to bring out her snow goggles. She fumbled among the few things she had thrown into the bag but she could not find the goggles. Suddenly she remembered where she had left them. At this moment they were lying on the balcony at home, where she had last used them when she took the first sun bath of the season. "Hell and damnation," she muttered, for this was a bad break. She looked across the glaring, glittering expanse of ice before her and wondered how she was to get across without goggles. It's nothing, she thought. Twenty minutes of discomfort, that's all. She pulled the rim of her old felt hat down over her eyes and ventured out into the glare. She advanced carefully and slowly, balancing on the ridges, which were sometimes hardly wider than her boots. She was deeply attached to her hobnail boots as one is attached to an old and loyal pet. She trusted them to take her safely across the glacier and to Christopher. She felt them grip the ice and get a firm hold of it with every step. Once in a while she stopped to use her ax, cutting a comfortable way for herself into the surface. After a while the two blisters on her right hand split open and some new ones began to form. Also she had to stop again and again, plant her feet firmly in the ice and close her eyes to rest them from the strain. Once she tilted her head back to look up the Grauhorn. It was a beautiful mountain, gray and heavy where its flank rose from the schrund at the edge of the glacier but getting lighter and almost transparent where its summit bit into the deep azure of the sky. A cocky little cloud was rakishly slapped over the highest peak, blazing in ten different shades of gold. To Marion's eyes, blinded by the merciless radiance of the glacier, the sky seemed almost black, and the snow up there not white but of an unreal flamingo pink. Even as she closed her eyes once more this pink remained inside of her lids and she felt the blood pulse heavily in them.

There came a moment when Marion, skirting a high pinnacle of ice, was suddenly quite certain that the dark figure moving ahead of her across the glacier must be Christopher. She stemmed her ax against the ice wall at her side to gain a firmer hold, hollowed her left hand around her mouth and called his name, long-drawn, as the Alm boys would call each other. The call came back to her in five echoes. She called again. The little black figure ahead of her stopped. Marion called once more. The little black figure answered with a yodel that sounded familiar. It must be Christopher, she thought happily. I'll wait until he turns around to get me. Only at that moment did she realize that she was tired, that her eyes were getting unreliable from the strain, and that she was afraid of making the ascent to the Arli Hütte alone. Traversing the glacier was easy, but afterward, when the rock climbing began, there was one chimney she did not quite know how to tackle without a rope or a companion. She waited, called and waited again. Then she saw that Christopher—if it was Christopher—made no move to turn back. Steadily the small black figure crept on, disappeared behind a ridge, and was gone from sight. Marion gave a sigh and went on. I can always wait for the guide and beg him to take me through the chimney, she told herself. The shade of the Kees began spreading out like thin, blue ink on a blotting paper. She was rather glad about it. The sun glare was a nuisance, and there was always the danger of treacherous, rotting ice on the warm side of a glacier.

To REMEMBER is one thing and to know is something else. We all know what happened in 1918 and what was wrong about the

Versailles Treaty and how the germs for future strife and war and endless trouble were part and parcel of it. We have read about it and been told and lectured over and over again, and oceans of printer's ink have gone into all the explaining. But the things I remember are just funny little things; a patchwork; broken fragments of colored glass that don't even form a kaleido-scope.

For instance, there was the feeling that all walls stood lop-sided and were about to fall down on us. I don't know why we all felt like that. You would walk through a street and look up, and the houses didn't stand straight. They looked as if an earth-quake had shaken them from their perpendicular center. It was a dizzy upside-down world in which we lived. The painters tried to paint it and the writers tried to write about it and the whole thing was called expressionism.

It was cold in the homes and dark on the streets. Only every third street lamp was allowed to burn; the two others had their burners screwed off. They looked like headless soldiers in gray, marching down the street. Trucks and delivery cars made a shattering noise because there were no rubber tires to be had, only some sort of wire spiraling around the wheels to absorb the bumps. If you went to the dentist you couldn't get a gold filling in your teeth except when you brought your grandmother's golden brooch along. Yet you had given your grandmother's old brooch to the fatherland long ago, and the dentist put some-thing into your teeth that tasted and behaved like a full-fledged electric battery, God knows why. There was less food than before because the men had to be fed too. The town was crowded with crippled soldiers and the sidewalks were seamed with beggars who didn't beg but demanded.

Remember the little burlesque tragedy of the American bacon? I don't know whether we got it as a present from the United States or whether we had to pay in gold for it. But there it was, salted American bacon in a country which hadn't seen fat for years. I suppose the Americans, loving their bacon for break-fast and feeling sorry for us, had the sensible and kind idea to push a lot of it into Germany to feed us first of all what we needed most. It was the one thing every one of us could afford to buy and it was sold freely. But, God, how we hated the Americans for it! Their bacon had no resemblance whatsoever to our own bacon. Before it reached us it had gone rancid, and it tasted salty like the Dead Sea to us. We had no way of keeping it fresh, I am sure; no proper refrigeration, not in the warehouses nor on the railways, and certainly not in private households. Millionaires might have possessed such luxuries as iceboxes, but then, millionaires didn't need to eat that repulsive bacon. It got more and more rancid from day to day; we had never heard that bacon could be fried, and no one told us. We boiled it in water and tried to swallow it in big hunks. It didn't taste good. It made us throw up. Then someone had the idea to cure it in boric acid to preserve it better. It tasted like hell and we gorged it down and threw it up, cursing the Americans all the time. It ranked together with cow fodder and dog meat as one of the most despicable things we had to eat to stay alive.

In 1918 everybody hated everybody. The Army, which had been fighting at the front, hated the Navy, which had done nothing all the time but mutineered in the end. The former front soldiers hated those who had managed to stay in the hinterland. The socialists hated the communists and vice versa. They killed off each other's leaders and brains, and then they were left as headless as those street lamps. The dethroned nobility hated the new order, naturally. The intellectual middle class, backbone of Germany, hated the workers, who earned three times as much money as any lawyer, professor, or scientist. The workers hated the intellectual upper crust for their stubborn cultural arrogance. The Reichswehr hated the police force. The police force, split in Schupo and Sipo, hated itself. And everybody hated the profiteers, who had their bellies filled, who drove in well-cushioned cars and led their womenfolk around on diamond leashes.

There were riots and strikes and street fights and minor killing bouts of one sort or another all the time. But we had what was called peace.

As for me, I had my own problem during that time, five and one-half struggling, quaking pounds of it. Michael was a difficult baby from his first reluctant breath. He had to be kept alive with hot-water bottles all around him, and he was pitifully small. But he survived with the greedy, urgent eagerness of all small creatures concentrated on this one, foremost instinct: to stay alive. Michael was designed in some sort of El Greco lines: everything on him was long and stretched, as if I had looked too much upon the Hahnenstadt Gothic while bearing him. In spite of it, old Herr Tillmann was inordinately proud of the little boy and thought him exceptionally well formed. "Look at the little shaver," he would say, cuddling the tiny head in his wilted hands. "Look at the shape of his skull. A real Nordic longhead." It was the first time I heard this expression, which later on was to become so unpleasantly familiar, and it startled me. Old Herr Tillmann looked me over and nodded, satisfied that I had not been able to disturb the line of good breeding in the Tillmanns.

It seems strange altogether that I had no qualms or apprehension during all the time while I expected Michael and even after he was born. For a long time it didn't occur to me that he could be anything but Kurt Tillmann's child. I had pushed that fleeting weightless hour with Manfred Halban way down into the purple bag of my subconscious, out of my waking, conscious life. It hadn't meant anything to me, if not a little kindness toward a sick poor devil about to die. And he had been so careful and had remained a stranger all through it. The morning after, when I gave him his breakfast and saw him off, we hadn't exchanged a single intimate word.

"Good-by, Frau Captain Tillmann, and thanks for everything."

"Good-by, Manfred, and good luck to you."

Babies weren't born out of such detached relations—or were they?

Michael was an excitable, nervous, sensitive, problematic child. He cried much and had a pitiful way of sobbing, not like a baby, more like a very weak old man. There was one or another sort of trouble with him all the time. Out of a clear blue sky came short but frightening spells of running a temperature. Cramps. Bellyaches of various descriptions. Getting his first teeth was like the outbreak of a major illness, and the same rumpus repeated itself every time a new tooth broke through. He remained long and thin and frail, and to put a bit of weight on him took every trick I had learned in the baby home.

"A war baby," Dr. Mayer said. "He will outgrow it."

"What can you expect? He was born during the revolution," his grandfather claimed. "You were frightened and excited, don't forget that."

Elizabeth dug up forgotten reminiscences from the babyhood of my husband. It seemed he too had suffered from bellyaches and little fevers. They showed me his faded baby photos and crowed happily over them because of the resemblance. In a way all babies look very much alike—as they say the Chinese do. But not if you know the Chinese—or babies. As for me, I had learned in the baby home to recognize the sharp differences in the tiny personalities. No, I didn't think that Michael looked like his father or even like his brother. I thought that he was much more beautiful, made of a finer stuff than the Tillmanns. He had been born with a reddish flock of hair over his forehead. Then came a period when he was a bald-headed little old man, and then he grew the finest, nicest pelt of white silk. His eyes were big and his eyelashes dark and long; they gave him a melancholic look, as young monkeys sometimes have. Long eyelashes had given Manfred Halban that soft, pleading expression, I remembered.

Born in the midst of famine, Michael had an almost arrogant way of not caring for food. He demanded a lot of company, though. He was an exhibitionist. He had to have an audience, and he would eat, go to sleep, or play with his toys only if he knew that somebody watched him. "Putting on a show like an actor, he is," Elizabeth said. I stood arrested, with the milk bottle in my hands. Like an actor. I think that was the first time that the idea occurred to me. Michael was seven months old. For a few weeks I did a lot of thinking, and then I made a decision.

I didn't trust old Dr. Mayer much in the way of bringing up a baby of problematic strength. In August, when Michael had a cold and a fever that was out of proportion with the cause, I was resolved that something had to be done. There were only two good child specialists in the Riede, and if I went to either one of them I was certain he would recognize me or find out by some gossip who we were, Michael and myself. I wrapped him up and packed him into his pram and set out with him, across the bridge, into the poor quarters and to the town house, where they had opened a baby clinic, almost like the one we had had in Bergheim. Waiting among the other women on the hard benches; reading the popular illustrated posters and statistics about baby welfare that hung around the walls; smelling once more the familiar smell of poverty and much-washed diapers; it made me sentimental. Here too they had a lady doctor, not a manlike fighter of Dr. Süsskind's mettle, but one of the young, slick-haired, clean-cut women of my own generation; her name was Dr. Merz.

"Marion Sommer?" she said, reading the card the nurse had filled out. "No father's name? An illegitimate child? . . . All right. What's the matter with him? . . . A bit underweight, eh? Nervous? Well, they all are and no wonder. What do you feed him? . . . Good. You seem to take good care of him."

"I worked as a baby nurse myself," I said timidly.

"Well, then, why are you worried? He has a little cold, but that's nothing. Otherwise he is as sound as a tree. Fine little fellow."

Michael stared at her in fascination. He was quiet for a change. I think he enjoyed being the center of interest.

"His father had some trouble with his lungs," I said. "In fact, he had a far-progressed tuberculosis. I worry lest the baby may have inherited something."

"Oh! Well. No," the doctor said. "No, you don't inherit tuberculosis, as far as we know. But I wouldn't let the father be around the baby too much. I would keep myself away from him too if I were you. You know that it is contagious in a high degree, don't you?"

"The father died before the baby was born," I said.

"Oh, did he? Well, I'm sorry to hear that. But maybe it's better for everyone concerned. Look here, I'll prescribe a bigger milk ration for the boy. Half a liter a day, how's that? And let him have all the fresh air and sunshine possible. Let him sleep with all the windows open; in winter too. That's about all."

"Thanks, Doctor. I'll see to it," I said while a few ton loads of worry rumbled off my chest. I picked Michael up; he pushed his little fists into my face and crowed.

"Listen," said Dr. Merz, writing out a card for me. "I would like to see the little fellow once a month. Better to keep him under control."

"Then—you think there is danger that he might still get it?" I asked her. She didn't look at me but kept on writing.

"My dear girl, anyone can catch T.B. I don't have to tell you that," she said. "In the case of our little boy we might do well to watch and be careful. He can't inherit the disease, you understand. But he may have inherited the disposition. Here is the prescription for his milk. Pasteurized, of course. Don't worry. There is nothing wrong with him."

"Thanks. Thanks a lot, Doctor," I said. She looked at me, clear-eyed and strict. "It's all right," she said. "But it's the devil that you girls can't be more careful. It isn't exactly necessary to have a baby with a consumptive man. There is such a thing as birth control, after all. Here, read this little pamphlet. It's contraband, you understand? We're making our progress at a snail's pace, and I'm not allowed to advise you how to use contraceptives. However——"

I sailed out as happy as if someone had given me the crown jewels of the Hohenzollerns. The talk with someone who spoke my own language and belonged to my own kind and generation had braced me up immensely. It hadn't been easy to haul up my secret guilt from the dark bottom where it had sunk, not easy at all. What had sounded like a casual dialogue between the doctor and myself was the outcome of many sleepless, tormented nights. But the result had been worth it. Michael was sound, and I would see to it that he would never get sick as his father had been. If Manfred Halban was his father. If. If. If. When I crossed the bridge which led me back into the Tillmann realms I wasn't sure of it at all. When I put him to bed that night and his temperature was gone, I looked at the two heads of my sleeping little sons, and they seemed so much alike all of a sudden that I called myself a neurasthenic fool. The crazy idea that he was anything but Captain Tillmann's child!

It was like that for many years after. There were periods when all went well with Michael, when he was healthy and behaved normally and gave no trouble and I was convinced that he was Captain Tillmann's true son. And then, out of a clear, blue sky, he would fall ill and do crazy things, filling the air with his problems and showing the flickering temperament of my forgotten boarder. And then I took a deep plunge and felt guilty for it all and hated myself for that brief meeting with Manfred Halban's feverish, hungry, rotten body.

Maybe if my husband had stayed alive and Michael had been brought up by him and had taken after him by that mysterious process which shapes children after the image of their elders with whom they live—I would never have floundered through those murky fogs of doubt. But Michael was hardly four weeks old when I received the message of Captain Tillmann's death. It came close on the heels of Irmgard's funeral, after she had quietly and without much struggle given in to the flu, and it hit me the harder because it came so unexpectedly.

I had not heard from him since the revolution, but that was only natural and rather common during the retreat. If any officer would stick to his troops and bring them home in good order it was Captain Tillmann, of this I was certain. I was impatient for his coming. I sat at the window and watched the street and waited for the doorbell to ring; there would be his voice and his footfall in the entrance hall and he would be home —and only then would the war really be over. Then, on a foggy morning in December, the doorbell rang and Elizabeth ushered in a man in the gray, ragged uniform they all wore, men and officers alike. He was about forty years old, he had a round head with close-cropped hair, he seemed embarrassed and was sweating profusely, and he introduced himself as Otto Pulke, Captain Tillmann's sergeant. We had some polite small talk; I offered him wine, and he drank to the health of the new baby. I asked him what I could do for him, and he answered that the shoe fitted the other way round. The men had elected him their delegate—

he wore the cocarde of the soldiers' council—and he offered to get me food stamps from the new authorities, with whom he seemed to be on good standing. After we thus had been polite for a while I took the plunge. "When did you see my husband last?" I asked with a flutter of apprehension inside of me. "Do you know how he is?"

Pulke cleared his throat. "That was a week ago, no, nine days, to be correct," he said. "Yes. I didn't know how bad off he was. You know Captain Tillmann. He wouldn't show it. It's a shame it should happen to a man like him."

"What?" I asked, feeling my hair grow cold at the roots.

"That's what I came to tell you. I talked to my wife this morning. 'You go there yourself and tell it to Frau Captain Tillmann, sort of careful like,' that's what she said. But damn it, it's not so easy to do it. I don't know by what end to tackle it, see?"

"He is dead?" I said.

"Oh—so you know it anyway?" I heard Pulke say through the big roaring of a waterfall or something.

"Excuse me," I said. "I'm still a bit weak after the baby. It's all right. Thanks."

I held onto little Martin and drank the wine that old Elizabeth forced into my mouth. "You know, I'm getting to be an expert at it," I said, wondering why I should be giggling. "This family has a funny way of dying wholesale. You want to tell me how it happened?"

"Yes. At your command, Frau Captain," Pulke said, snapping to attention. He seemed to be glad that I had not fainted, and I was glad too. As he began to unreel his story I could hear that he must have told it before, to his wife probably and to his friends at home, and that, for some reason obscure to me, telling it gave him a queer satisfaction.

"You see, the captain had a fever and dysentery even before the armistice, or maybe it was typhoid. He would not take the time to be laid off in a lazaret, and I can't blame him. He just wanted to get home quick. So we got him a horse and he just kept on riding along with our men. God almighty, the roads in France! We lost men all during the retreat; they just fell down at the roadside and croaked right there, in the mud. It was raining most of the time, and we got Herr Captain some blankets or hangings or whatever it was; we found them in one of the houses. They had pictures woven into them, and we wrapped him up in them because he had bad chills. He said it felt fine and warm, he didn't care how it looked. Looked funny, though. All those pictures of naked women wrapped around our Herr Captain! So we come to a village in the evening and find out that the bridge ahead of us had been blasted. They must have done it by mistake after the armistice, our own men. It had been raining all day long, the sort of rain that's colder than snow, and we all were pretty well pooped. So I talked to Herr Captain and he gave orders to camp in that village for the night. Of course, there was not a rat hole in that place that wasn't taken up by soldiers, and there wasn't much discipline left, as Frau Captain can imagine, and maybe it would have been better to go on, pooped or not. But Herr Captain looked as if he wouldn't hold out much longer. All day long we had to lift him from his horse, and he would crouch down at the roadside and the blood and water would just run from him. And there's nothing to make a man as weak as that damned trouble with the guts, if Frau Captain will forgive. So I told some artillerists of the 14th who slept in the church to make place for Herr Captain. We had a little argument about it, and I had to show them my gun, but then they squeezed together and even let him have some hay. I think he felt quite cozy that night. 'This is fine, Pulke, you old camel. This will make me a new man,' he said, and then he was dozing off and I went outside to look after our company; what was left of it, that is. Only twenty-six out of two hundred, and not a single officer except Herr Captain. It's a shame he should get through the whole mess alive and then pop off in some lousy church in France with not even me around. But we gave him a decent funeral the next morning; the men were good about it and took their time. They were all sorry for him. Well, I've made a little map of the place in case Frau Captain wants to visit him after we have peace and can go back there as much as we like. It's on that little hill just north of Vernerouge; there are more crosses, but I had his name cut into his. And I brought some of his things home too; I left them outside. I thought it might give Frau Captain too much of a shock if I rumbled right in with them . . ."

That is what was left to me after the war was over: A crude map of a village somewhere in France. Captain Tillmann's wallet with my letters and snapshots, his army revolver, his belt and sword. His medals and a small pension. His old father to take care of, and my two little sons.

I took stock of it all, and, like the rest of the world, I set to work and started all over again.

IN FALL 1919 Hellmuth Klappholz came home from Russia, where he had been a prisoner of war, and we made great preparations for his arrival. Especially Elizabeth had worked herself up into a state and went around smelling of rosewater and glycerine like a bride on her wedding night. We had scrubbed the two little boys until they shone with cleanliness, and a magnificent meal had been prepared. Though Grandfather was so chock-full of arthritis that he had to give up hunting, some loyal soul from Detfurth had provided us with venison. Elizabeth had cured it with roots and herbs and spice—"the way Frau Ober-inspektor used to do it"—and the entire flat was filled with that German holiday smell of roast game. She had also baked a cake—"plum cake has always been Hellmuth's weakness"—and the saved-up eggs and sugar of weeks had gone into the making of it. The old man had put on his best regalia early in the afternoon, wearing his long, black coat with the medals, and every half-hour or so I went in to him and brushed the dandruff and the cigar ashes from his vest and lapels and then I looked at Martin's pants, in case they needed changing; for although he was a man of two and a half, little digestive surprises would still happen from time to time. As for Michael, in his pen, he had for this exceptional occasion permission to play with Manne, the only creature that could keep him quiet and content for any length of time. Grandfather nursed two bottles of Burgundy along to keep them at the correct temperature, warm enough yet not too warm, and altogether there was a faint glow of the former good life spread over the flat. We couldn't meet Hellmuth at the train because he had been vague about the time of his arrival, and I felt impatient and nervous. Cold hands, a headache and, as I played with the tip of my tongue over my lips, I even found a budding blister. Stage fright, in a word. I wore a black dress and a strand of seed pearls that Irmgard had left to me. As I passed the high mirror between the windows my reflection looked one-hundred-per-cent Tillmann. Perfect camouflage, I thought, amused at myself.

The bell rang. I heard Elizabeth open it and pour out a sparse trickle of welcome. Grandfather hoisted himself from his chair, straightened up, and marched out into the entrance hall. I thought it more tactful to stay behind. But then, after a few snapping words, I heard the old man whimper, and that gave me quite a turn. I went out and found him hanging around the boy's neck, rubbing his face against his shoulder and crying. The boy whom he hugged was about three inches shorter than his grandfather, though still tall, and he looked over the bent head of the crying old man with an expression of embarrassment and even contempt. He had his mother's clean-cut face, the long chin and the narrow temples and a pink skin. He waited, disgusted but well mannered, until the old man had found his countenance, blown his nose, and muttered something about getting old and soft. The moment he was released, Hellmuth walked straight up to the bicycle that stood in the back of the long, narrow entrance hall. "Oh, you've still kept my bicycle," he said. "No, Hellmuth, it's not yours," Elizabeth said. "This one belongs to Pulke."

"And who, pray, is Pulke?" Hellmuth asked arrogantly.

"It's our Zwangsmieter. We'll tell you later," Grandfather said. "Come here, meet your aunt Maria."

"Welcome home, Hellmuth," I said. It wasn't exactly what I should have said, considering the circumstances of this homecoming. He clicked his heels smartly as he snapped: "My special pleasure to meet you, Aunt Maria." It made me smile to observe how intact he had kept his manners through the war and the Russian prison. He did not wait for me to take him into his room but went there ahead of us. I had put a photo of his parents on the dresser, next to his childish telescope, and stuck a few ivy leaves in its frame. There were also his father's medals displayed in a little glass box, which I had taken from a butterfly collection I had found in the attic.

"Well—this at least hasn't changed much," he said, standing at attention in front of the photo, his hands at the seams of his trousers. When I closed the door to leave him alone I saw him pick up the telescope.

After a while Hellmuth came from his room and had himself introduced to his little cousins; he admired Martin's red cheeks politely, but it was obvious that he immediately took a greater liking to Michael. It was a common trait of all men of this family that they loved babies and knew how to handle them. I suppose they were born to be chiefs of some Nordic tribe rather than simple fathers of one or two children. Hellmuth insisted on having Michael perched up in his high chair at his side during dinner. Michael's eyes were so big and bright that I thought he might have a slight temperature, but as he grinned happily and behaved quieter than was his habit, I gave in. Elizabeth brought in the soup, and we had hardly begun eating when the phonograph started playing behind the wall.

"For God's sake, are we having a concert?" Hellmuth asked.

"It's the prolets," Grandfather said. "They like making a racket at all hours."

"What prolets?"

"The Zwangsmieter. The people whom the Emergency Home and Housing Board compelled us to take in. Frau Pulke has a deplorable preference for vulgar music."

"I think it's an outrage. No government has the right to break into the privacy of your home. These are dirty Russian practices. I didn't think I would live to find them in my own house," Hellmuth said, pushing back his plate.

"They cope with the problem as well as they know," I said, trying to appease him. Elizabeth had taken so much trouble to cook this soup, and our entire meat ration had been boiled in it to make it strong and tasty, and now he didn't eat it. "It's a transition. Until homes are found for all the people who have returned——"

"How come there is not enough space now if there was enough space before the war? What about those who haven't returned? They were the better ones, millions of them," Hellmuth said. "Couldn't you at least choose whom you want to take in?"

"We did," I said. "Pulke was your uncle's sergeant all through the war. I feel an obligation toward him, and also, they are nice people."

"Except for the smell," Grandfather said sarcastically. "And that Frau Pulke feels a frequent urge to drown her sorrow in strains of phonograph music. But you'll get used to it. You'll have to get used to many things, my boy—to many, many things."

The phonograph had ceased playing, and after the pause it took to rewind it, the same song began all over again. Elizabeth came in, threw a hurt glance at the unfinished soup plate in front of Hellmuth, and carried it off. "Bang," said Michael. "Bang, bang, bang." It was his first word, an imitation of the sound Martin's toy rifle made when it plopped off. Martin had been dispatched to the kitchen, where he learned the difficult art of feeding himself with the aid of a cunning spoon which was bent at a right angle and landed directly in your mouth, however clumsy you were.

"What sorrow has Frau Pulke to drown?" Hellmuth asked. "Her husband has come back, hasn't he?"

"It's something about her brother. He got a shot in the lungs during the last street fights and has been in the hospital ever since," I said.

"A communist," Grandfather said.

There was a pause. And then, at the worst moment, the chandelier began to sway and a burst of piano music broke through the ceiling, screeching chairs were pushed around, and a herd of elephants seemed to stampede through the apartment above.

"There they are," Grandfather said. "The Jews. Dancing. Every night the same racket. Two years ago they peddled the

East Side with a pack of old clothes on their backs. Now they are
dancing over our heads. There you have it in a nutshell."

Hellmuth seemed to have gone pale under his nice pink skin.
The muscles played tightly in his long, narrow face.

"Why don't you call in the police and have them arrested for
the disturbance of public peace?" he said.

"Police? You know what would happen—or don't you? They
would give the policemen eggs and butter and liquor and the
police would scrape and bow and lick their boots. Police, indeed!
All socialists. All paid by the Jews."

Elizabeth came in and served the venison. She waited and
watched until Hellmuth, absent-mindedly, shoved the first bite
of it into his mouth. Then, when no admiring remark came from
him, her old face fell and she crept to the door. Hellmuth didn't
seem to notice the food at all. His eyes wandered, and I could
see that some ideas took shape behind his narrow forehead.

"*We* should have been here," he said.

"Of course you would have stopped the revolution," Grandfather said with a cold, constrained fury. "You and who else?"

"I can't understand what's become of all of you if you take
every outrage and humiliation as if it were a God-sent punishment," Hellmuth shouted. "Punishment for what? For giving
our life and blood! I don't know what has happened to this
country. I don't know what has happened to all of you. Have
you no guts? Do you allow a bunch of dirty socialists to rule
over you? *We* should have been here. But wait, just wait until
we all are home again, all the officers who are still in the prison
camps. There will be a reckoning, believe me."

Michael had watched his excited cousin with open mouth. I
saw his little face twitch and quiver, and I knew what was coming. The moment Hellmuth finished his speech and dug his fork
into the venison as if it were the body of an enemy, Michael burst
out in a wailing, ear-rending shriek. He was a frail, thin baby,
but, by God, he could make a better and louder noise than anyone around. Martin, in the kitchen, must have heard him and
came shuffling in, all hurry and revenge. From the first moment
he had accepted this little baby brother as his property and his
responsibility and he wasn't going to let anyone hurt him. "You

—bad man!" he yelled, beating with his little fists against Hellmuth's thighs. He still held his tricky spoon in one hand, and the oatmeal dripped from it over Hellmuth's trousers. Michael, inspired by this sight, screamed only louder, the phonograph played, the Jews were dancing, and Grandfather shouted for order and silence.

Michael stopped screaming as suddenly as he had started and stared terrified at the old man. Before he could go into another rumpus I got up and took him in my arms. "I think I had better put them both to bed before they get too excited," I said hurriedly. "If you will excuse me. Elizabeth, will you serve the cake and coffee in the living room? Please, Father—Hellmuth, you too—go ahead with the coffee. I'll be back in a few minutes."

When I came back to the living room I found the two men quarreling.

"What has become of us?" Hellmuth was shouting. "A nation of slaves, beggars, serfs? You don't understand what it means to come home and find the country as it is; out there, in Russia, all I could think was: Deutschland, Deutschland. I slept with the horses, I worked in the fields, I got beaten up, kicked around. I didn't mind, I didn't care. I was a prisoner and I was proud to bear it without a sound. That's the only pride a prisoner has left. Not to show them that they can hurt you. And then the way back—it took me four months to get across Russia. The filth, the hunger, the hardship. The Reds, the Whites! Today they pulled this side and tomorrow the other. And all the time I thought: Deutschland. We were four of us and we stuck it out together: Heinz Arnheim, Joachim Sarvitz, and Andreas. You remember Andreas, don't you, Grandfather? All we dreamed of was to get home. But, by God, if we had known how it would be in Germany, we would have joined the White Russians. We would have joined anyone. Nothing could have been so humiliating as this sort of life to which you have lowered yourselves. How can you, how can you bear it, Grandfather, a man like you, how can you compromise? Here—there are my father's rifles and yours. Why don't we take them and go out and shoot anyone who dares to tell us to knuckle under? One thousand men—give me one thousand men who are not afraid, one thousand men resolved to change it for the better or die—and this country full of deserters and mutineers could still be saved."

"Shut up, now I've had enough," old Herr Tillmann shouted. "You are talking like the stupid young pup you are. Where were you when we went through our blackest days? In Russia! A prisoner! You are not the one to tell us what courage is! Valiant men aren't taken prisoners. Valiant men die, like your brothers, like your father, like all my other sons and grandsons. You— you——"

The old man shook with anger; he looked like a brittle old tree in a storm. Hellmuth came up against him, and for a moment I was afraid he would raise his hand. But suddenly he snapped to attention. With great effort he clicked his heels and put his hands to the seams of his trousers. "At your command, Grandfather," he said. "I beg your pardon. It is an upsetting experience——" He had allowed himself to sag a bit but straightened up again. "And now, if you'll permit me, I'll take leave," he said, snapping back to his military manners. "I have an appointment with some friends. Good night."

He left, and I went out into the kitchen, where Elizabeth was spread over the shattered remnants of our splendid meal in a fit of sobbing. "He didn't eat anything, Hellmuth didn't," she said, staring at me with her red, old eyes.

"It's because he was so happy to be home," I told her. "Don't you know that great happiness spoils the best appetite? That's at least what my grandfather always used to say."

Elizabeth began to scrap the leftovers together.

"How should I know?" she said. "How should I know?" And then, pulling herself together, she added: "If we could get a bit of flour somehow, we could make a game pie tomorrow, doesn't Frau Captain think so?"

WHEN Michael or Hellmuth became too much of a problem for me, each one in his own way, I would turn to little Martin for support, for he was born to be the head of the family, a calm, good-natured, responsible sort of fellow and a good provider, even at a time when he had still trouble to keep his pants dry. He would save little bits of his own meals and generously smuggle them into my bed as his contribution to my upkeep. Whenever I threw back my blanket I would find little scraps of potatoes, carrots, a green speck of spinach, or a blob of meal mush on my pillows. I appreciated these gifts deeply. "Martin gives," he would tell me. "Martin good little boy." He also tried to teach Manne to eat with the trick spoon that had been so helpful in perfecting his own table manners. "Manne is dumb dog," he would complain. "Milky is dumb child." He had converted Michael's name into the best word his vocabulary knew: Milk. Milky. Still today he calls him by that name. Martin was overeager to share every one of his new linguistic achievements with his brother and make a housebroken gentleman of him. Milky, on his part, would go into a rage of kicking and screaming when Martin called him dumb. He knew he wasn't dumb and he wouldn't take any insult, even if he wasn't able to express himself yet in that intricate babble humans call their language. If, thank God, he hadn't inherited Manfred's T.B. he certainly had inherited his inferiority complexes, complete with overcompensations. He would sit there in his pen, ears perked up, eyes alert under the heavy dark lashes, and would collect sounds. He could imitate almost any sound he heard: Manne's growls, sighs, moans, and short, joyful barks. Grandfather clearing his throat. The door squeaking, the thud-thud of Elizabeth's felt slippers, the squeak-squeak of her shoes, the whistle of the water kettle on the stove. Long before he could say "Mama" he could sing in his thin, trebling baby voice every one of Frau Pulke's five records, and I began wondering what sort of child this one was turning out to be and what sort of man would grow from this strange little bulb.

Later, as the boy grew up, you had to tell him stories. A swarm of locusts couldn't eat up a crop as fast as Milky could consume stories and stories and yet more stories. First the simple ones Martin handed down to him, in his own abbreviated versions: "There were seven dwarfs and Snow White said, 'I want an apple,' and the dwarfs said, 'You can't have an apple, we are no

Kriegsschieber, we have no apples.' " (This was an insert from Elizabeth's teachings.) And so Snow White boughted the apple from the bad queen and she said, 'Yumyum, what an apple!' And she throwded it up and the prince said, 'Marry me.' And now they eat apples every day."

Milky contemplated the story. "What is an apple?" he asked. "I don't know," said Martin. "You are dumb," said Milky. "You are dumb yourself," said Martin, and the fight was on. Hellmuth came from his den and asked irritably: "What's up this time? I have to think. Is there not a moment's quiet in this house?"

"They have never eaten apples," I said. "That's what they're fighting about. They have still a great treat coming."

Hellmuth would go back into his room and bang the door behind him, raging against a world in which little boys didn't get apples. Pulke would take them both on his lap, one on each knee, and tell them about the apple trees and that next fall there would be a hundred apples for each of them. Grandfather would rummage in his stacks of old magazines and produce pictures of apples and orchards. And I would go out and try to dig up anything in the shape of fruit at the empty stalls of the civic market to feed it to my boys.

Still later the stories would grow up together with the boys; Grandfather, Hellmuth, and Pulke, every one of them, would have his own department of storytelling. Grandfather told them about the times before the war, those wonderful, those unbelievable times, when the Kaiser rode in an open carriage and there were parades and everybody was rich and happy and everyone could eat as much as he liked and do as he pleased. I didn't cherish much that he filled the little brains with resentment against their own way of living, and I had fights about it with the old man. "It's all right for you to be bitter about it, Grandfather," I said. "But they are born in different conditions; this is their period and their time, and it's no use to make them yearn for something that's gone and past." Still the boys liked Grandfather's stories best. Pulke counteracted his effects by telling them stories about the wonderful things they would get within a short time, with just a bit of patience. They would have an automobile when they grew up, each one an automobile all to himself, and maybe they would even learn to fly. All people would live in bright, clean, big houses, and the schools would be huge fun: playgrounds and games and trips into the country. There would be theaters and movies and concerts for children, and for grown-ups too, free of charge. And they wouldn't have to work hard for a living, just enough to like work because no work at all becomes very boring and makes you fidgety. And there wouldn't be one Sunday a week but two or even three, with cake and whipped cream for every one of them. I recognized the brand of these tales. Pulke worked at the railway and was a sworn socialist Giessheim F 12. They were still sounding the morning call.

The boys listened to Pulke but, good as it sounded, they grew restless after a while. There was too much theory in it and nothing to put their fingers on. "Tell us about my father," Milky would demand. "And about the war. When he wented out with four men and caughted twenty-three Frenchies." Pulke gladly obliged, and this was much better. There was flesh and bone to it; you could smell the night they went on patrol and hear the frightened voices of the Frenchmen, whom they surprised at their campfire in back of a village by the name of Moulin-sur-Crute, and you could almost see and touch Our Captain Tillmann, your father, bless him, who was the bravest man in the whole 26th Division.

"I like my father," Martin would say with a deep sigh, when such a story came to an end.

"I like my father too," Milky said. "I like him more. I like my father mostest of the whole world. When he had a bullet in his leg and he walked and he walked and he said, 'It's all right, Sergeant, it doesn't hurt, it's just a fleabite.' He likes me too."

"How do you know he likes you?" Martin asked, hurt because he found himself incapable of producing such keen statements.

"He told me so. He came into the room and he said, 'Milky, I like you, you are my coddlepop.'" (Taken from Elizabeth's vocabulary.)

"That's not true."

"It is, too."

"When did he come into the room? He can't come, he is dead—

isn't he, Uncle Pulke?—and when we are bigger we'll visit him and bring him flowers, but he can't come to us."

"He came when I was in bed and he said he liked me."

"You *dreamded!*" Martin said with contempt, relieved to have a materialistic solution for the unbelievable.

"I didn't. Mama, tell him I didn't dreamded it. He came to my bed and he said"—and here Michael had one of his sudden mean flashes of sheer genius—"he said, 'I like you much better than Martin.'"

This floored Martin for a moment. I saw him clench his fists and knew that the inevitable fight was coming. "Look here, Martin, he is just a baby," I said hurriedly. "He doesn't know yet whether he is dreaming or not."

Martin relaxed and Michael sulked. "Mama, please forbid him to dream that my father likes him more than me," Martin begged. "My father walked and walked with a bullet in his leg and he said, 'It's just a fleabite,' but Milky is a cry baby and when he bumped his head he screamed so much Uncle Hellmuth had to slap him."

And after that it was Michael's turn to slink away in shame, because it was true that he cried easily. Not only when he bumped his own head, but he cried about a hundred smarting little things that Martin, with his more robust nature, wouldn't even notice. Because Manne was sad. Because of the unhappy mouse Elizabeth had caught in a trap. Because the prince was hexed into a frog and begged to sleep in the princess' bed. Because it rained. Because Milky's guardian angel, with whom he had a lively mental intercourse, wore no shoes, not even in winter when it snowed. Because he simply had the blues, the sad, mysterious, tearful, and inexplicable baby blues of an oversensitive three- or four-year-old.

Not that Milky simply gave in to his own weakness—not by any means. He fought hard battles between himself and himself, and once in a while the Tillmann part won over the alien, Jewish, and disgracefully soft side of his nature. In this he had the full support of his uncle Hellmuth. How deep Hellmuth's influence went I found out only much later. I don't know what sort of stories Hellmuth told the two boys, because they were not told in public but remained a secret between the three. But I saw my little boys emerge from Hellmuth's den with red cheeks and over-bright eyes, rebellious, unwilling to go to bed, and announcing that they were men and would have uniforms and rifles and shoot at everybody, bang, bang, bang. After such sessions Michael was apt to run a bit of a temperature or to scream in his sleep, and I had a serious talk with Hellmuth and begged him not to excite the little fellows too much.

"On the contrary. You coddle them too much," he answered ungraciously. "You and old Elizabeth would make pampered softies of them. They need a man's hand, they need spanking, they need to be hardened. Make them strong and brave, that's what they need. Don't you understand, Aunt Maria? They are the coming generation, they'll have to bring Germany back; they'll have to fight their fight and it'll be a hard one."

Maybe he is right, I thought; I did not believe in being pampered either. Still, while Hellmuth proclaimed Spartan ideas for my boys and overexercised their little minds and bodies, he him-self lived in a strange inertia and seemed unable to do anything worth while. Officially he was catching up with his law studies, which the war had interrupted. He would withdraw into his room and remain there as on an island. Hour after hour and day after day he would lie on his bed, his feet in the old army boots propped up on the counterpane. The lawbook would fall from his hand and he would fitfully fall asleep. When I came into the room he would wake up with a start and stare at me as if I were his worst enemy. Slowly recognition would spread over his face and he would sit up and become correct and polite again. I felt sorry for him. There was something decadent about his narrow, long face and his thin, neglected hands, as if this last branch on the old family tree had no sap and strength left. Surely his grandfather was of a tougher grain, in spite of all his arthritis. Sometimes the boy seemed to me like those thin, puny stalks of asparagus which sprout from the soil after all the good, thick, juicy ones are harvested. "Are you tired?" I asked him. "Don't you want me to open your window? Why don't you take a little walk in the park? It will refresh you, and you'll not fall asleep when you should study."

"Study—what? Study—what for?" he would say with a gesture as if throwing something disgusting away, a worm, a bug, a sticky bit of dirt. "Ach, it's all so hopeless. Leave me in peace, Aunt Maria, will you?"

The moment dinner was over he would roll his napkin and put it into the little metal ring with the inscription "Gold I gave for iron," would politely click his heels, and disappear. "Pardon me, Aunt Maria, I have an appointment with my friends," he would say and be gone. I knew some of them slightly. They came once in a while and sat in his den, and afterward we had to air out a lot of infernally smelling pipe smoke. Or they would whistle for him from the street, a bright, keen signal, the sword motive from Wagner's Nibelungenring, and he would hurry off with them to secret meetings and mysterious doings. "These stupid young pups with their childish games!" the old man would grumble after him. "Shooting peas from toy cannons! Who are they, anyhow, those so-called friends?"

Heinz Arnheim. Joachim Sarvitz. Count Andreas von Elmholtz. Three of the thousands who couldn't find their way out of the war and back into peace. You could see them everywhere on the streets; the same young and yet lined faces. Their swagger and their poverty. Their military manners, their expression, pregnant with dark resolution, a mask to disguise their bewilderment. They looked alike, they talked alike, they thought alike. They all wore the same windbreakers, old army trousers, army boots or leather puttees; it was almost a uniform. They were no soldiers any longer, but certainly they had not become civilians either. They were a dangerous in-between. They huddled together in secret societies because they couldn't bear to be alone. They had been boys when they were sent into the war, and when they came back their own world had been pushed out from under them. They had no ground to stand on and they didn't know what to do. They hadn't learned anything but to shoot and to take cover, and they couldn't live without their daily dope of fights and thrills and danger. In the midst of a country that wanted and needed nothing so much as peace to heal its wounds they kept on living like soldiers camping in a hostile land. They stuck together to talk the old war slang, play the old game, take solemn oaths, build their rank and file, take and give commands, and keep up their discipline of blind obedience. They wanted to fight. For what to fight, they didn't quite know. It was an attractive setup for people who were proud and unhappy, young and narrow-minded; who didn't want to do honest work and had that confounded German passion for suffering and martyrdom, handsomely dressed in a flashy uniform, if possible. After a while they had even a name if not a cause: National Socialism.

In the United States, thank God, they are having their football games.

There is no love lost between me and the Nazis—certainly not. But I have seen one of them grow up right under my nose, and I know how it all came about. I have never forgotten that evening when Hellmuth came home after five years of war and prison and found nothing but a photo of his dead family and his father's medals in an old butterfly box. And I understand only too well that a few thousand who came home like that made a neat culture from which to breed the malignant germs of future armies.

It was toward the end of 1922, if I remember right, when I saw Clara again. The walls still looked as if they would come falling down, the young artists painted more expressionistic paintings than ever, and the young writers wrote in an explosive style about condensation of space and the virtues of patricide. On the crest of this wave of expressionism Clara was swept to fame and into our town.

We were in the midst of something people began to call an inflation; it was a process no one could understand or explain, and it felt like being caught in a landslide. Prices went up and wages followed. Then wages went up and prices followed. It was like climbing, hand over hand, on a ladder that had no end. The workers would get one thousand marks instead of one, and next thing the bread would cost two thousand. The workers would go on strike and the troops would be called out to drive them back to work. There were more and fiercer street fights than ever, and the lines in front of the food stores were longer and hungrier than during the war. Somewhere somebody made a fortune out of it; we all felt that never before had there been a generation as disillusioned as ours. And if some psychiatrists had taken the trouble to examine the whole population, they would have found that we all were slightly insane, every one of us.

On an early morning in December I stood under the dirty glass roof of the station, with the hollow tickle of expectation in my stomach, and then the train came in and there was Clara, whom I had not seen in all those years. We would have liked to cry, but we didn't belong to a crying generation; we just smoked our cigarettes a bit hastier and looked at each other with that strict feminine scrutiny which asks without words: How are you, my friend, how did life treat you, are you still beautiful, in love or not, what made those little shadowy hollows under your cheekbones, it makes you look older than you are, I am fond of you, I missed you, and how about you?

Clara was still a hurricane as she tore into the sedate Hahnenstadt hotel, grabbed the telephone, shouted her wishes about matters of rehearsal, lighting effects, staging to some bewildered official of the theater, arranged about her trunks, costumes, and settings, gave two interviews, posed for some bewildered press photographer, ordered breakfast for both of us, at last threw everybody out, and then flung herself upon the hotel bed, kicking off her shoes and laughing at me with that deep, husky boy's voice of hers for which I had been so homesick many times. Taking photos in a room was still a fussy business which left a lot of unpleasant magnesia fumes behind and made you look, on the final print, like a corpse just hauled up from the bottom of a river where you had stayed too long for your own good. Clara opened the window and bit off a hunk of fresh air.

"What a life! It's really and absolutely the shit," she said conclusively. "And Anna couldn't come along to make things easier for me on account of Black Ignominy——"

"Who's Anna?" I asked.

"Oh, she is my everything: maid, dresser, secretary, conscience, or what have you. Don't you remember her? She used to clean house for us in Bergheim."

I had a faint recollection of something pale and spindly and young crouching on the floor and battling with the dust under some piece of furniture. "Oh, Anna, of course. So, she is with you now. And, what's that about Black Ignominy?" (Black Ignominy—Schwarze Schmach—was the newspaper cliché for the colored occupation troops.)

"Well, when Bergheim got those African niggers for occupation troops, Anna had a baby from one of them. That's why I keep her with me; no one else wanted her, and you couldn't just let her jump into the Rhine, could you?"

"Did she get raped?"

"Raped? Hell, no. She's crazy about that black fellow of hers. So am I, for that matter. He is the handsomest, most childish piece of ebony you could lay your eyes on. Black Ignominy unfortunately didn't turn out so favorably. I don't think black and white blood mixes well; it's rather a problem, bringing up that baby. She looks sort of grayish, like the coffee we gave the soldiers on the depot, remember? And she's very shy and also she's sick a lot. Right now we are having the measles, that's why I have to struggle alone with all these things. Well, you've been on tour yourself, you know how it is."

"It's not been like this," I said; I had to grope way, way back to remember that I had played the violin in concerts. "I have never been a real celebrity, you know?"

"Celebrity, phooey!" Clara said. She looked at me, long and seriously. "Let me look at you, little monk," she said, holding out her hand to me and pulling me to her bed. "Have we changed much? Or just a little?"

"I wouldn't know," I said. "I think we have, Clara. But how and when it happened, I don't know. I don't even know how we were before."

"Before what?"

"Oh—before all that——" I said vaguely, sure she would understand. "Remember when we thought our antipodes would stand on their heads all the time? Well, we have become our own antipodes, sort of, that's how I feel. I think I have been dizzy ever since that war stopped."

"Maybe you don't get enough to eat, that's what makes you dizzy," Clara said. "Come, let's have breakfast."

It was a great, glorious breakfast, which, according to our currency, must have cost several thousand marks. It gave us time to munch and to look at each other and to get acquainted all over again. Yes, we had changed; we wore short skirts, and Clara's hair was cut shorter—"It's so much bother when you dance," she said. So far as I know she was the one to start the fashion of short hair, in Germany at least, but we other women still wore our demure buns. We moved differently too, and we spoke in a still tougher slang than we had done in the past. Our men had imported this lingo from the trenches, and it stuck.

"You know, I've to bring you regards," Clara said. "I danced in Vienna last month. I saw a lot of our old friends. Those that have come back, I mean."

I wondered what old friends she could have seen. I knew from her infrequent letters that Mama Balbi had died and that Clara's sister was a widow with a little millinery shop. I knew that Clara's Man had been forced to abdicate and that he and Pimpernel were running an experimental farm at Rheinhalden. When he had left he had given Clara a handsome amount of cash with which she had started a dancing school in Munich.

"Regards from Shani?" I said.

"Shani's all right. He went over with his whole company, you know. He was with the Czechs. Good for him. You'll hear a lot of good new music as soon as he gets going. No, not from Shani. Regards from Charles Dupont. God, wouldn't he hate the way you look now. No 'BEAUTY,' eh?"

"How is he?" I said mechanically.

"Mushy as ever. Successful. He's making a lot of money painting the portraits of nouveaux-riches. Come, have more butter. Honey too. Tell me."

"What?"

"How do you live? Alone?"

"You know I have two boys."

"Yes, yes. I mean—no man? No love?"

"No. No man. No love."

"Funny. Why?"

I thought it over. Yes, why? Those heavy, cramped dark rooms in the Riede, Hellmuth brooding behind closed doors, my father-in-law, very old, very grouchy, full of arthritic pains and prostatic trouble. Maybe it was the beginning of cancer, Dr. Mayer thought. Milky didn't seem to be in very good shape either. I would have to take him to Dr. Merz soon and have a serious talk with her.

"I think I don't have the time for such luxuries as love," I said. "You know, I have a job. I only got myself a day off today because of you."

"Good. What are you working at?" Clara said as lightly, as if getting a day off in the middle of the week were the simplest thing on earth.

"Oh—anything that comes along. At the moment I am in a florist's shop. It's one of the jobs where they won't use men. There are too many of them unemployed as it is."

"I'll say there are. Do you have to work? What about your pension?"

"It's practically nonexistent. They always promise they are going to revalue it but they don't. I couldn't buy one week's bread for a month's pension. It's all crazy."

"Hm," said Clara.

"What about you?" I asked.

"Well, what about me? Sometimes I make lots of money and sometimes I am broke."

"No. I mean—about men. You have everybody at your feet—or is it still the same?"

"Me? I can't be tied down. Men are so much bother," Clara said vaguely, wriggling her toes in the silk stockings. She sat up, rolled down the stockings, and looked seriously at her legs. Only Milky could be so deeply absorbed in the sight of his own feet as Clara was. She stretched out her hand, found her cigarette case, and lit herself a cigarette. "Catch," she said, hurling it to me. Clara could make a bed look like the tent of some nomadic tribe in a jiffy. It was littered with books, magazines, letters, and telegrams; there was a little paper bag with cheap candy—cheap in a relative sense—two shiny apples, a manicure set, a scarf, a brief case from which photos, costume designs, and silk samples tumbled over the bedspread. It looked sloppy and cozy and turned the hotel bed into a home.

"Tell me. How is he, your Man?"

"Oh, he is all right, I guess," she said, and from the sound of it I knew that he was as dead for her as Charles Dupont was for me. "God, isn't love the most unimportant thing there is? And the most ridiculous too?"

"Yes. Especially when you happen not to be in love at the moment," I said wisely.

"That's it. Or when they bring the man you happen to be in love with to your lazaret with his guts hanging out like macaroni and all you can do for him is to give him a huge shot of morphine—enough to get him out of his misery in a hurry for good."

I didn't say anything, and after a while Clara added: "He was one of our stretcher bearers. I think I was what's known as being madly in love with him. He had refused to fight but, by God, he would get you any wounded man, from whatever hell it was." She sat up and slipped her feet into her shoes. "Bury the dead and forget the war," she said almost cheerfully. "It happened some thousand years ago. Now they say I am a Lesbian."

"What's that?" I asked, stumped by the new word, and Clara gave me a brief explanation. "Well, are you?" I asked. I had two children, but once more I felt inexperienced and shamefully innocent compared with her.

"I haven't tried to seduce you yet, have I?" she said with a short, deep laugh. "And you are what they would call 'my best friend' in quotes. Come, let's go. I have my rehearsal at ten."

I was in for a hectic day, the most hectic day I had experienced for a long time. Rehearsal until three, with Clara swearing and shouting up to the flies and down into the dark house and making a row at the office and shaking the entire sleepy civic theater like an earthquake. More interviews and more photos to be taken—slow, arty ones this time. Lunch with a group of ultramodern young artists who called themselves the Black Steeds. In the afternoon I coaxed her into a brief visit in the Riede to show her my boys. Martin, as usual, behaved beautifully, his eyes glued to Clara's handbag in the expectation that something edible might emerge from it. Milky made an instantaneous hit with Clara. He crawled onto her lap and offered to tell her a story.

"I like you," he said, fondling her face with his chocolate-stained paws. "You smell fine. I'll let you sleep in my bed too." I could see him falling in love with her at great speed. In these skyrocketing passions for people or pets or things he was very much my child. Hellmuth came wandering in to have a look at the celebrity; he tried to seem arrogant, but he was shy and almost scared of Clara. But after a while she went into his room to look at some relics he wanted to show her. I heard them talk seriously, and Clara pried him open and discussed his problems with him, and he told her about dances he had seen in the Caucasus. In the end he asked her if she could give him a free pass for the theater; he would like to see her dance. "You know, I couldn't buy myself a ticket," he said with a tortured, crooked smile. "We are practically beggars."

I remember that day and evening so well, because it was so different from my daily life. I saw Clara dance, and though I liked it very much it didn't excite me as much as it did the rest of the audience because I had grown up with her and her ideas, and everything she did, new and original as it was, seemed deeply familiar to me. There were all the creatures she had wanted to shape into dances, there was our time and our life, stark, sometimes cruel, sometimes comical, sometimes fathomless and vague like the substance of which dreams are made.

After the performance Clara took me along to some party given in her honor in the house of some rich people, Kriegs-schieber, obviously. There were rooms and rooms, the furniture was dazzling, the carpets too thick, the supper table creaked under the load of precious imports, in the library they had books which they seemed to have bought by the yards, bound in leather which made me conscious of the holes in my shoes, the champagne was too good and the hospitality choking. It looked as if they bought everything wholesale, grand pianos and automobiles and food and liquor and jewelry, bolts of silk and fabrics, fur and linen, tapestries and strawberry preserve, pheasant and rice, nightshirts and glass chandeliers, paintings and crates with soap.

I didn't know that Clara had invited Hellmuth to come along. But suddenly I discovered him standing there with a champagne glass in his hand and looking so green in the face that I was afraid he would get sick and make a public spectacle of himself. I suppose he had fallen in love with Clara and had simply followed her around, not aware of the sort of party this would turn out to be. "Did you drink too much?" I whispered to him, "Do you want to get some fresh air?"

He looked at me as if he wouldn't recognize me and then he laughed. "Fresh air is right," he said. "They stink to heaven, these dirty Jews. Doesn't it make you sick? See how they stuff themselves while we—great God—what I should have brought along are a few hand grenades, that's all! Well, next time I'll be better equipped when I go to a party."

"You shouldn't have taken us along," I told Clara after he had left. "It's all right to read jokes about those things in the papers, but when you see it with your own eyes it burns you up."

"On the contrary. It's good for you to be taken out of your rut and learn how other people live," Clara said. I drank more champagne and things began to have softer edges. Later we piled into a magnificent car—or so it seemed in 1921—on cloudlike rubber tires, and drove through streets which were wide awake that late at night. I hadn't known there was a nightlife in Hahnenstadt. The word in itself was new. But there it was, bars and dancing places and taverns and more bars, all of them crowded with well-dressed people, throbbing with American jazz, overflowing with sweet, strong, iced drinks. While I had slept in my chaste citadel in the Riede a whole new world had shot up in the side streets of the town.

I had the first cocktail of my life and I was floating in a happy vagueness when we arrived very late at Clara's hotel, where I had decided to spend the night.

We walked up the stairs in silence. I was still tipsy and happy and in a floating condition, but I had also begun to worry because I had to be at my job at eight in the morning. Clara's room was cold, and she turned on the heater; the pipes said clunk-clunk-clank-clank but remained cold. "No heat during the night," I said. Clara wrapped me in a heavy, padded kimono. She lit a cigarette and put it into my mouth before she took one for herself. Then she produced a little primus stove from her trunk and began to boil water.

"What's that?" I asked.

"Coffee," she said. "You need sobering up." She took some brown cubes, dissolved them in the boiling water, and filled a water glass. The good, bitter scent filled the room and made it seem warm. "My own invention," she said. "You never get coffee in a hotel when you need it most, between four and five in the morning."

She sat down next to me and put her arm around my shoulder. "I can't bear to think that you should go on living as you do. I didn't know it was like this, not from your letters. But now that I've seen it—little monk, you're in prison! It's not like you! Why do you do it? Why do you tote that grouchy old misanthrope and that sinister young conspirator around on your back? It's worse than a prison. It's being buried in the family vault."

"You don't understand it," I said. "I have obligations and I'm going to fulfill them."

"Obligations, my foot! You had obligations to your own parents too and you left them without as much as batting an eyelid."

"This is something different," I said. "I didn't pick my own parents, so I felt free to leave them. But this is a soup I have cooked myself and I'm going to eat it."

"The hell you have!" Clara shouted at me in exasperation. "When you married your captain you didn't marry every god-damned relative he might have chosen to leave behind. You are talking plain bunk."

"That's not it. I must tell you something, Clara. I don't want you to think that I am a repenting Magdalene, but I have made a mistake. Everyone makes mistakes. The difference is only whether you have the grit to bear the consequences. There you have my whole credo, and that's what I'm doing. Basta."

"Nothing, basta," Clara said, smiling faintly at the old Viennese word which had cropped up in the midst of Hahnenstadt. "What, if I may ask you, is the mistake you made? I don't like you being mysterious."

"All right," I said. "I have never spoken about it to anyone.

I've hardly admitted it to myself. But here it is: I think that Michael is not my husband's child."

Clara wasn't exactly shattered. She looked at me as if she were amused, as if she would have liked to laugh or to whistle.

"Hm," she said at last. "You think so. You don't know it for sure?"

"Well—you see——"

"Of course. It's a wise mother who knows the father of her child," she said.

"Listen, this is no joking matter," I said, hurt.

"You bet it isn't. Well what's the matter with him? Can't you marry him? Is he married? You love him, don't you?"

"He is dead, and I wouldn't marry him if he were alive. I didn't love him at all. I hardly knew him. And two and two doesn't always make four."

"So that's it," Clara said, more gently. "You've gone through lots of trouble, haven't you?"

"You don't know the worst yet. He was a Jew and he was consumptive, and I get into a panic whenever Milky as much as sneezes. God, I have made such a mess of things that I don't know how to make up for it. Don't you see that I owe that family something? That's why I stay away from love and men and all that. It's all I can do to make up for what I've done."

"You musn't dramatize yourself, little monk. Don't take yourself so damned important. How many millions of married women do you think are in the same fix? Millions of girls who have no idea who their children's father might be—their husband, or their lover, or that nice man they met in the bar and never saw again."

This had never occurred to me.

"Are there?" I asked, stunned with this new revelation.

"You bet your sweet life," said Clara. "All the stuff that's been written about men never being certain whether they are their children's father or not! Well, what about the mothers? How should they always know? It's the bunk!"

"If he only hadn't been sick——" I said.

"Tell me," Clara said, lifting my chin and looking into my eyes with a queer, strict scrutiny, "do you like the child less because of this?"

"Less?" I said, flabbergasted. "Less? More, of course."

"Why do you think he is from that—from that man you hardly knew?"

"He seems so much like him; more and more so, the older he gets."

"Well then, I would say this man must have had great charm. The boy is so lovely it gives you that little cramp around the heart that you get when things are almost too perfect."

"No. I don't think Manfred was charming. He was—you know—I wouldn't have drunk from the same glass with him. And here I have a child that is most probably his. I don't know why such funny things should happen to me."

"To you and to everyone else. Just look how people live all around you. They certainly make up for lost time and have no inhibitions. And it's all so unimportant, what happens between men and women. Did you ever look through a microscope at a drop of filthy water? Well, it's about the same. The whirl, the hurry of some of those infusories to permutate, how they swarm, how they split, how they fuse—someday I'm going to make a dance of it. And I'll call it 'Polygamy'—you silly, chaste little monogamist."

GRANDFATHER died early that summer; I kept up his self-respect through those infernal last months of his cancer by keeping him nicely doped and cheating more morphine out of Dr. Mayer than this old-fashioned, strait-laced gentleman was willing to allow. Only in the end the old man took to crying in his weakness and cursing himself for it. He had become transparent like a lamp-shade, but he died as well as one might expect from a Prussian Oberamtsgerichtsrat of the old school. He worried a lot about his unfinished memoirs, I Served My Country, and I had them put into the coffin with him. I like to think that he met my two grandfathers somewhere on some solid, nice cloud reserved for old gentlemen of the Better Classes, so they can play some heavenly bridge.

Hellmuth sold out the apartment, lock, stock, and barrel—I don't know how many millions in inflation money he received for it, but I do know that two months later he could do nothing with it but flush it down the toilet. Elizabeth gathered up her belongings and disappeared on the horizon like the grumbling of a distant thunderstorm. As for me, Hellmuth told me to ask the Emergency Home and Housing Board to put me up somewhere. The same held for Pulke and his family. It was easy for Pulke, for he had joined the police force, where men of his caliber were highly valuable. I think it was his happiest day when he put on a real uniform once more and went out to haze and drill green, soft, abject young police recruits. For me and the children things didn't look so sunny.

"Look here," said Dr. Merz, "it's nothing to worry about, but the fact is that the boy runs a bit of a temperature every evening. He is lymphatic and he is anemic and we simply have to put a stop to that whooping cough."

"You are sure it's only whooping cough?" I asked her.

"It's whooping cough all right; the whole blasted town has it, but I wouldn't call that 'only.' It's a nasty thing, and it takes his appetite and his sleep away. As long as we have this epidemic in Hahnenstadt he'll never get rid of it. And with his disposition, you know——"

The word "tuberculosis" was never mentioned between Dr. Merz and me, but it formed the background to all our councils.

"What the boy really needs is good, clean mountain air and a lot of sunshine, not the black murk they call a sky in this town. Make him sleep outdoors, summer and winter, and give him plenty of good, simple food and you won't have to worry. It's only that I don't like his running a temperature all the time . . ."

So that is how we moved to Einsiedel.

It's not so easy for me to conjure a clear picture of Einsiedel out of the past, because it was so similar to Staufen, and the two places have a way of fusing and superimposing and blending into each other in my mind. It was in the Bavarian Alps, and it certainly deserved its name, which means, in German, "hermitage." To get there you had either to row across the lake or take the narrow trail that serpentined along the shore. Where the Upper

Lake ended, turning at a sharp angle and petering out into the dark pool of the Lower Lake, a tiny peninsula jutted out into the green water. That's where the chapel of Maria Einsiedel stood, in memory of a boat with young folks that had been smashed some two hundred years ago in one of the angry storms that sometimes churned the lake. A few farmhouses scattered here and there nestled against the mountainside, each one as far away from its neighbor as possible, because the sort of people who cared to live in Einsiedel were recluses, whether they knew it or not. This was lucky for me, because somehow the Emergency Home and Housing Board didn't seem to care a hoot about Einsiedel and therefore allowed us to lease a whole house all for ourselves. It was a deserted, ramshackle edifice with a low overhanging shingle roof which it pulled tightly down over its ears; rocks were piled up on the roof to keep it anchored when the storms came. The roof leaked constantly and we always had pots and pans on the floor to catch the drip, drip, drip. There were wooden balconies running along two sides and a leprous-looking St. Florian was painted over the door with the legend:

Holy Patron St. Florian,
Protect my house, burn others down.

In the dialect of the country this made a perfect rhyme, and what it lacked in human kindness it made up in faith. The balconies were of great importance, because that is where Michael slept, summer and winter. I made some padded sleeping bags for him and bundled him in, warm and safe. On clear winter nights the stars were close and big and the jagged cone of the Watzmann stood high and white across the frozen whiteness of the Lower Lake. The air was so cold it hurt in your throat and so lovely it made you want to yodel. A glittering drapery of icicles hung from the eaves, and off and on one of them would break and drop and splinter into silver dust, with a fine, singing, crystal sound. On sunny days the sky seemed unbelievably dark against the glowing snow peaks. In spring we heard the avalanches rumble down, and sometimes we could see one loosen itself from the side of the mountain and burst into a rocket of white powder. Some looked like waterfalls of snow and some were compact,

mean, and menacing, breaking down fir trees and killing whatever came into their way. The mountain walls fell steeply into
the Lower Lake, and in summer they were burning with the
deep healthy red of alpen roses. Nature was large and untamed
in Einsiedel, and I felt pretty small and scared, alone with my two
little boys in the dilapidated lonely house. In summer some people would come from Munich, to row across the Upper Lake and
picnic around the chapel. In winter we were snowed under
most of the time, but the lake would freeze and you could ride
across it on a sleigh. Boat and sleigh belonged to the house. The
boat leaked and the sleigh had something wrong with the left
runner. Trying to make myself over into a strong, unafraid
mountain woman wasn't a simple experience altogether. My first
weeks were a struggle against four thousand mean, tough, invincible obstacles. To Get Away From It All is a pretty desolate
business, and no one is going to tell me how wonderful it must
be to live on a desert island. How to make a fire without choking the house in smoke. How to chop wood, how to keep it dry,
how to fill the kerosene lamps and keep them from smudging.
How to organize my transports of provisions, which I had to pick
up in Anzbach and row across the lake. Expeditions through the
snow to get my daily supply of milk from the Gabel farm and my
eggs and chicken from Guggl-mother, way up the mountain trail.
The mountain people don't like to talk and are not given to
friendliness toward a foreigner. They were deaf and dumb and
hostile. To them I seemed a half-wit. I didn't know how to bake
bread, how to kill a pig, make sausages, smoke ham. If a swarm
of bees chose to hang itself to my balcony like a humming brown-
golden bag (which was a sign of great good luck), I wouldn't
know how to haul them in and put them into a beehive. If one
of the Guggl boys took pity on me and did it for me, I would
be scared to take the honeycombs out in fall. If the people of
Einsiedel had been a little less locked into themselves they might
have stoned me for forcing my boys to sleep in the cold. As it
was, they settled down to the contention that I was crazy but
harmless. What help they gave me they gave unwillingly, and
what small money I paid them for it convinced them the more
that I wasn't quite right in my mind. Small money, in those

years, meant at first million- and soon billion-mark bills. My back hurt all the time, my hands grew as hard as wood, and I was often scared out of my wits for loneliness.

But, God, how beautiful it was and how clean and wide and free! Milky grew strong and healthy and tall and, of all the places, Einsiedel was probably the only one where I could support myself and the children on my devaluated officer's widow's pension during those mad years of inflation.

Of course, it had been Clara again who had found this place for me; she seemed to be always on the spot when I needed her most; better still, she came up to visit me for prolonged week ends in summer and for skiing trips in winter, and once, when she had torn a ligament and needed rest, she spent a whole month with me. Also from time to time I packed up my boys and we careened across the lake, took the train in Anzbach—for so close was civilization to our lost wilderness—and stayed for a few days in Munich, under the pretext that Michael had to be examined by the doctor. But the doctor only laughed when I presented him for inspection. "Sound as a tree and, you'll see, he'll outgrow his brother," the doctor told me every time. Martin was still the man in the house and the head of the family, chief of the tribe and master of the manor. A placid little fellow, much more practical than I was. Each one of the boys had his own little chores to attend to: collect kindling wood, water the little garden, feed the cat, keep the oars oiled in their rowlocks, the chickens fed in their pen, set the table for our meals, watch the rain barrel so that it would not flow over. After a few months we received a new boarder, Black Ignominy. Clara brought Anna along and Anna brought her little colored girl along and they left her with us while Clara went on tour. Black Ignominy, three years old, with her black brambleberry eyes, her blotchy brown skin, her sudden, untamed torrents of tears or laughter; Black Ignominy, dressed in a Bavarian dirndl, her African hair plaited into four tiny pigtails, attending Sunday Mass in the little chapel, was a sight to behold. Clara paid for her board and room; I guess she used Black Ignominy as an excuse for bracing up my finances during those worst years of the inflation. My boys were insupportably proud of Black Ignominy. Why, everybody could have white babies or brown ones like the Guggl children. But no one had a black one, real black through and through. That Ignominy was black through and through seemed to be a point of greatest significance to them. I found them scrubbing her with fierce determination, working with my scouring brush and some of the sandpaper I used on my copper pans. There was great jubilation: the paint didn't come off. I also found them investigating her insides. Martin pulled her mouth open as far as he could, and Michael fairly crawled into it to see if Ignominy was black everywhere. She wasn't, and the boys sulked for two days. I had an idea that they would like to take Ignominy to pieces to see how she looked inside and if she was really and truly black through and through, and I had to give them some good talk along with a basic explanation of biological facts. The funny part was that Ignominy submitted willingly and without as much as a squeal to any torture the boys would deem necessary in the course of their research. I had an idea that her tiny three-year-old soul felt honored and flattered by so much serious attention. Martin took over her education, just as he had helped me to get Milky housebroken and treatable in every way. She inherited Milky's sleeping bag after he had outgrown it and I had made a new one for him.

Oh for the deep, serene calm of those winter nights, when I had put the three children to bed on their balcony, listened to their prayers, and tucked them in once more! They would roll up like three little pretzels, and soon I would hear them breathing softly as they fell asleep. I would stand there for another minute and listen to the quiet. It was so still you could hear the stillness sing. It was as if the world would breathe and sleep, with me and my children, safe and becalmed, in the palm of God's hand. . . .

IT WAS about ten minutes later when Marion discovered that she had lost the tracks of those who had crossed the ice before her. She gave an angry little laugh and turned around to go back, retracing her own steps until she came to the spot where she had deviated from the beaten trail. It was much more difficult to clamber back the same way she had come. Once she slipped and caught herself, biting the ice ax into the ground and gaining a precarious hold. Steady, steady, she thought. Her heart was pounding way up in her throat. This is crazy, she thought, I'll never make it. It'll get dark before I'll get to the Arli Hütte and what then? Let's turn around and go home and forget the whole adventure, she thought. But when she looked back over the expanse of ice she had crossed up to now, an endless stretch seemingly, the Kees was very far behind, while the wall of the Grauhorn appeared very close ahead. She regulated her breath, called once more and listened. Nothing answered but the five echoes. She closed her eyes because she needed them clear and sharp to find the trail she had lost. Inside of her closed lids a lovely vision waited for her. She saw Christopher walk across this same glacier as she had seen him when they had crossed it together. He strode ahead of her with so much ease and confident balance, as though he were not going over slippery, treacherous ice, with deep blue crevasses falling away to the right and left, but over the velvety lawns of his native England. So real and pleasant was this vision that Marion smiled at it with closed eyes and kept on smiling even as she opened them and clambered on. She herself tried to relax and to ease the tension of her muscles and her breathing. Looking around from a higher pinnacle, she discovered, narrow as a foot, the beaten trail which she had lost. It couldn't be more than twenty yards off, but two pinnacles with steep crevasses between them separated her from it.

It was when Marion stepped across a bridge of ice that she suddenly felt the ground give beneath her. What happened occurred so rapidly that she hardly understood it. She felt herself break through. Dropping as through a trap door, she groped for some hold; ice splintered under her fingers, she was still sliding, dropping; something cold and white like snow gushed around her face, and there was a burning pain everywhere. The ax was wrested from her hand by some obstacle stronger than her grip. She was still falling, falling, it seemed an endless trip down into the depth of the glacier. At last her fall was stopped by a hard wall of crystal that pushed itself up against her. There was a last bump and a pain, and Marion rolled over and sat up.

"This is idiotic," she said, loud and very strict with herself. She needed to be strict now and not let the shock of her fall get the better of her. Her heart pounded a crazy rhythm and she was shaking all over. Deep breathing! Marion commanded and obeyed herself. After a few minutes—or maybe it was only seconds—she gained control of her nerves and began to take stock of her situation. Meanwhile her eyes had got used to the queer twilight of these regions, and she looked around. It was funny—and it was one-hundred-per-cent Marion—that the first thing she thought was: How beautiful. How unbelievably, unreally beautiful! The next thing was to thrust her hand into the pocket of her jacket and, with a sigh of relief, find the cigarettes and the lighter. She inhaled the smoke and began to laugh. "This is the funniest thing that ever happened to me," she said aloud. "You're badly rattled, my girl," she said. "You're talking to yourself. Don't do that. Pull yourself together."

She pulled herself together and examined her situation. It was not quite so bad as she had believed while she was breaking through. It had felt like falling from the uppermost floor of the Empire State Building. But as she looked up she found that the rim of the crevasse was not very far away. The distance from the tier of ice that had stopped her fall to the surface of the glacier was not more than the distance from the floor of a room to the ceiling. The sky was dark and close above, and the sun reached down into the crevasse, hitting the ice wall opposite and catching glittering sparks in the blue transparency. There was something strongly assuring and comforting in this bright layer of sun that she could almost touch. However, it was less pleasant to look down into the darkening depth of the crevasse that sank away beneath her precarious throne.

Marion winced as she saw her ax way down there; it had caught with its spike on some protruding ice formation about thirty feet below, where the crevasse broadened into an impenetrable bluish blackness. There was no hope whatsoever of retrieving this ax. Let's kiss it good-by, Marion thought, trying hard to make slight of her accident. She smoked her cigarette to the end and squashed it on the ice before she dropped the butt into the crevasse. This, obviously, was very funny. Marion grinned. She wriggled herself into a more comfortable position and contemplated the next move. It was good luck that her crevasse was only a few feet off the trail that anyone traversing the glacier would take. If she kept calling for help, someone was bound to pass by and hear her. There were five people on the glacier right now, one of them must hear her, and one of them was Christopher. It seemed to her the most natural thing that he would eventually come and get her out of this place. If not, Marion thought, if not I'll have to get out by myself. It wouldn't be easy without a rope, but it could be done. Automatically her eyes noted every knob and knoll in the ice that promised a foothold or a grip for her hands. It would be child's play if I had my ax, she thought. She could clearly see where she would cut steps into the slanting wall if she still had her ax. Not even ten feet of ice, that was all that separated her from being safe. Yes, but we don't have the ax, my girl, and that's that, she told herself. Let's try and call.

Her voice sounded small and terribly insignificant. We'll have to sing louder; this isn't exactly bathtub acoustic, Marion thought. She filled her diaphragm with air and let go. Suddenly the most perfect yodel rose from her throat. She listened to it with surprise and appreciation. The things you can do when you have to, she thought. She held her breath and listened for an answer. Yes, it seemed as if she heard another yodel, very faint, very far above, and without the resonance of an echo. She yodeled again.

It was very cold down there; Marion was glad her rucksack had stayed with her. It formed a good insulating layer between the ice wall and her back. Not quite so lovely was the sensation underneath her bottom, where it felt as if she were freezing to her pedestal. Her mouth was dry, her hands were skinned; so was her left cheek. One pain after another woke up in her body after the numbness of the first shock had left her. What worried her most was a queer blunt ache and stiffness in her right ankle. She tried to move it, but it kept on behaving suspiciously. She wedged herself into a safe place, between the side wall of the crevasse and a small pinnacle that, forming a barrier in front of her, was friendly enough to conceal the depth below from her sight.

She called again and again; she seemed to hear an answer, closer and more distinct this time. Well, we've been in worse situations, she thought. Wolzinje was much worse. When Michael was about to get blind it was much worse. She lit herself another cigarette and called again.

It's beautiful down here anyway. Too bad I didn't bring my camera along. Remember Andersen's fairy tale of the Snow Queen? This is it. A palace of ice. A cave filled with emeralds and diamonds. In a way I'm glad I fell into this crevasse, it's an experience few people can brag about. I'm as glad about it as Kathi was about her wooden leg. I just hope my fanny isn't going to freeze to my throne. I wonder how Andersen's Snow Queen handled this delicate problem. I'm cold now, but I'm not upset or unhappy and certainly not frightened. It's natural to feel cold when you are down in a white, blue, green crevasse of ice. I'm one hundred and twenty pounds of frozen meat, have you any use for it? It's the funniest thing that has happened to me in all my funny life. I wish I could walk now as I walked this morning. Careful now, Marion, careful, or we'll slide down the deep drop

. . . like on a roller coaster. Well. All we can do now is sit and wait. Christopher will be here soon.

Marion sat and waited and smoked and called at regular intervals and waited again. She tried to recollect every scrap of advice Max Wilde had given her. Max Wilde had been a great mountaineer and had taught her everything she knew about mountains and rock climbing and ice craft. She had not thought of him for years, but now she thought of him. She thought of him with great urgency while she waited and scanned the ice wall for an exit and watched the sun creep inch by inch higher up toward the rim of the crevasse.

MAX WILDE came to us during one of the worst storms we ever had. It was spring, the late spring of those high altitudes, and a hot wind from the south had suddenly melted more ice on the glaciers than the narrow beds of the mountain streams could hold. It was avalanche weather, and the waters came roaring down from the heights, bowling timber and boulders before them and piling them up on the flats of our peninsula. There had been heavy clouds marching up from behind the Watzmann, and when they burst it was something on the scale of the Deluge. The lake churned and boiled and frothed madly. It rose and licked at the trail and swallowed it up. We couldn't row across those angry waters, neither could we hike along the shore. Farmer Gabel, when I waded up to his stable that morning for my milk, muttered something about a landslide further down the trail. Our house stood on a knoll and was safe from the flood but rather desolate otherwise. To say that the roof leaked was a bold understatement. There were, however, a few small islands where it didn't leak, and I crammed the mattresses of the children into those corners which seemed safe and dry. Martin and Milky, breathing hard and snorting with important work, were about to lay boards for gangways across the room, from the stove to the table, from the table to the cupboard.

Ignominy, sitting on a footstool and splashing with her bare little feet in the water, played one of her favorite games. Each dark little toe was an animal, Anky, Panky, Lanky, Manky, and Sanky, and they all took a bath. The rain roared and the evening came riding on the storm, and I felt like Father Noah in his ark. It was cold and we had used up all our wood, and there was nothing I could do but take the stable lantern and wade out and cross the back yard to the lean-to where we kept our wood-pile. Martin and Milky had spent the better part of one week piling it up along the wall outside of the shed, where it was usually protected by the overhanging roof. Like Ignominy, I took off my shoes, threw my raincoat over my head, and splashed through the rain. The yard had turned into a groundless morass, and I had to pull my feet from it before they got sucked in too deep. The wood was soaking wet, a solid sheet of water ran off the roof and over my woodpile. I took the key and opened the lean-to where I kept my store of canned food under lock. The door had warped, and I had to give it a good pull to get it open.

"Good evening, Mother," said an unexpected bass voice in the dark. My heart stopped, because there was always talk about robbers and bandits in those mountains—not that there was anything to be stolen in my house! I turned my lantern in the direction of the voice and found a bundle of old clothes lying on the shelf, between my cans of vegetables. We all had learned to can our own provisions; it was one of the tricks hard times had taught us.

"Don't be scared, Mother," the bundle said. "I don't mean no harm. It's raining, see? You won't begrudge me a shelter?"

"How did you get in?" I said, dumfounded. The bundle sat up, dangling two bare feet from the shelf. They were covered with mud, and there were three toes missing from one of them. There came a chuckle from the other end of the bundle, where the head was. "Mother, if you don't want no robbers to get in here, you have to do better than that. I did it with my pocketknife, see?"

I collected some cans in my apron. "I didn't steal nothing," the man said. He was an old man, though his voice was strong and young. He had long white hair and a brown face, a map of a face, full of rivers and mountains. The eyes were lakes in that map, they were of such a hard blue and banked steeply by the deep eye sockets. "I'm all hollow with hunger, but I didn't steal nothing," the man repeated. "I wouldn't promise, though, that I ain't going to grab myself some chow before I get much hungrier," he said, laughing straight into my face.

"Where did you come from?" I asked him. He made a vague gesture toward the northwest. "From over there. Across them mountains," he said.

"You don't mean you got across the Watzmann in this sort of weather?" I said. He had come down from the shelf, and a puddle collected around his muddy feet as he stood there, with the water running from his drenched rags. "The Watzmann or any other man, Mother," he said cheerfully. "You never been to the Himalayas, Mother. Them is mountains, not molehills."

"What do you know about the Himalayas?" I asked, arrested.

"Been there up the Karakoram in '98, with the Whitley expedition. I know what you're thinking now. You're thinking, 'What a liar!' Well—look." He opened his shirt, or what he called his shirt, and fumbled with a chain he wore around his neck. A wild growth of gray hair tumbled through the rags on his chest, and his arms were tattooed. "Look," he said, as he brought up a strange-looking leather bag that he wore on his body. He crouched down on his haunches, opened the bag, and spread some papers and documents on his knees. I could see that he had a Wanderbook (remnant of the German craft guilds and colorful and adventurous predecessor of today's union cards), and finally he produced a faded, yellow, much-fingered clipping. It was a woodcut in the innocent yet fussy style of the family magazines of long ago, and it showed a group of men in ridiculous mountaineer outfits. "This one, that's me," he said, pointing with his dark, gnarled finger at one of them. "Fine young fellow, eh? Well, that was in '98, and much water has flowed into the sea since then."

He stored the clipping into the bag and the bag under his shirt. In the years to come I learned to understand what an enormous treasure this bag seemed to Max and what a flattering sign of confidence it had been for him to show it to me so soon after we made each other's acquaintance. Also it was this bag that in the end gave Max Wilde away and delivered him to his fate. . . .

The children came out on the balcony and yelled for me: why did I stay so long and should Martin come and help me? "No, for God's sake, stay where you are, I'm coming," I yelled back. Max listened with obvious pleasure to the trio, who sang out: "Hurry! Hurry! We want dinner!"

"Your'n?" he asked me.

"Two of them," I said. "We have—we have a little black girl with us—you know how it is since we have had the black occupation troops."

He grinned at me amiably. "Black, white, all the same," he said. "Mother, if you had seen the colors I have seen on God's earth, you wouldn't be surprised about anything. Underneath the skin they're all alike. Stick a knife in them and they bleed red, hurt them and they cry salt and tears."

"You seem to have gotten around a lot," I said. The art of conversation wasn't highly developed in Einsiedel, and it was fun to talk to the old tramp. I went to the door and looked at my soaking wood. "What a mess!" I said desolately.

"Where's the farmer?" Max asked me.

"Who?" I said. "There is no farmer. I'm alone with the children." As it was said I bit my lips. Maybe Guggl-mother was right to think me a half-wit. To tell this bum that there was no man in the house meant inviting trouble. In the uncertain light of the lantern it seemed to me as if an ugly gleam had come into his eyes. "No man?" he said. "That's too bad. No one to warm your bed? Come, let me carry it." He picked up the wood with one quick grab and stepped ahead of me.

"Listen," I said. "Even if there is no man in the house, there is my husband's good army pistol. So don't you get funny ideas."

He stopped and turned around. "Jesus Christ Maria! Mother, you mustn't be so scared," he said pleasantly. "I tell you something. Never be scared. Never. And if you are, don't show it. Come. Here. Step on this. So."

He threw the logs in front of us one at a time and picked them up as soon as we had stepped across them. When we reached the back door of the house, where the three children stood waiting, he stopped. "I'd like to show you how to make wet logs burn," he said. "But as long as you are so scared I won't come in. Maybe you put a bowl of soup outside for me, Mother, so I won't have to steal."

I felt silly, and while I still hesitated, Martin came over, pumped Max's hand, and said in his clear, high boy's voice: "You like dumplings? My mother makes the best dumplings in Einsiedel. Come in and watch her. We like guests. Don't we, Mother?"

So that's how Max Wilde came into our house to stay with us for two years.

Men are transients by nature. They meet you, they stay with you for a little while, and then they leave you and go away. They go to war and kill and get killed. They go bankrupt and shoot themselves in the men's toilet of the stock exchange. They fall for another woman and divorce you. They may even remain at your side, but so changed that it is worse than if they had gone away. They may keep on being married to you, and still you feel that they have traveled on, as if they had left only a dummy behind to sleep in the other bed and read the paper across the breakfast table and pay the household bills. But each man, however short or long his stay with you, leaves something to remain with you before he wanders on: His children, his money, his reputation; his phonograph records, his telephone number, his recipe for Planter's Punch; some little memories, another bit of knowledge, another experience; a lingering nostalgia for his hands or his voice or his kindness; a little bitterness, a line in your face, a sharpness in your laughter. Max Wilde, an old tramp, a bum and something worse, gave me more good and lasting things than any of them, although he never as much as touched the tip of my finger. But he too went away and got himself killed in the end.

God, how easy and pleasant life became after Max Wilde had come to us! He loved the children and the children adored him. He mended the roof and there were no leaks any more. He fixed the chimney and our wood burned well, whether it was dry or wet, and we weren't choked with smoke but only the good, fine scent of burning logs remained in the house. He made new locks for our doors and painted a new St. Florian on the wall. He cultivated the fallow land that belonged to the house and planted berries and vegetables and herbs in the little garden, and he could cook stranger and better dishes than the chef of the

Four Seasons in Munich. Our hens laid big brown eggs, and after a while we had our own pig too. At the right time and moment he took it across the lake for breeding, because he didn't believe in the reproductive qualities of the Guggl farm's boar. We had two pig litters that year, one of twelve and one of fourteen little pigs, and he made the children watch how they were born, earnestly pointing out to them the importance of the event. We had sausages and hams and bacon and our own cabbage and potatoes to go with them at a time when you couldn't buy such food for billions. We also had a goat with two kids; the milk was supposed to be Good For You, but Michael claimed that it tasted like old shoes and I didn't force the matter. We ventured out and it didn't take long until we had a cow in a nice clean stable, which Max built from the driftwood the flood had swept into the flats at the edge of the lake. The cow was called Amalia, and the children treated her as if she were the Queen of Sheba. There was nothing Max could not do and no profession he hadn't learned at one time or another. He carpentered furniture and painted roses and forget-me-nots on it. He patched up my copper pans and resoled the boys' shoes. He boiled sirup from the wild raspberries the children brought home and he made bows and arrows for them and taught them to shoot. He had blessed hands; they were always dirty, black, knobby like roots; they smelled of glue and pig's entrails and gunpowder and a hundred other smells. But everything grew and blossomed and thrived under his care, from the bees in their hives to Black Ignominy, who worshiped Max; from the rabbits in their cage, who, unlike other people's rabbits, never, never had colic, down to Michael, who during these years shot up and became a handsome, strong, sound boy, with sun-bleached hair and a brown face, with cheeks as deep red as the cheeks of an Indian peach and a good hold over the flickers in his character. I think even today his picture of the world is still colored with the high colors of the stories Max told him before he could read. My children needed no books during those years and no school. Max was better than any book you could buy.

It wasn't as if he had settled down for good, the old tramp. He had only stopped for a little while, and there came periods when he got very restless, and three times he left us and stayed away for a few weeks. But he always came back because he had forgotten something important. He worked out some good alibis for his staying. Amalia had to be bred to the Gabel bull, for instance; it was a great event and had to be done just right. As at the birth of the little pigs, it was important that the children should be present and learn early and seriously about such matters. It certainly gave them a good, clear idea and saved me from such stuttering coy explanations as other parents had to work out for their brood. Then again Max had to wait until the calf was born. It was a fine calf and he had to watch its upbringing, had to take it to Anzbach in time and sell it to the butcher. Meanwhile fall had come around and it was a bad season for going away. And so Max stayed on the year round, making me wonder if he felt that he had given up adventure for a place behind the stove, with three children cuddling up to him.

Of course there were some difficulties also with Max, and it wasn't all honey and sweetness. There was, for instance, the fact that he tried to dodge the police, obviously and plainly, and that he tried to talk me into siding up with him. He wouldn't do his duty as a citizen and row over to Anzbach and report to the local authorities. The gendarmes had to come and question me about my new boarder or handy man or whatever he was, and Max disappeared and didn't come back for three days. Finally I collared him and took him to the Anzbach office myself. Out of his bag Max produced some documents, which were found in the best of order, were duly stamped and registered, and then we rowed back home. The only trouble was that in these documents his name wasn't Max Wilde but Emil Hacker.

"Well," I said as we rowed back, "what was all the fuss for? They didn't chew an ear off you, did they?"

"I just hate their guts," he said. "Mother, you don't know them coppers as I do. Them in the offices are the worst. Troublemakers."

"Now what's your real name?" I said. "Are you Max or are you Emil?"

"I'm Max," he said with his usual grin, "but Emil was a better guy than me, bless his soul." I deduced that he must have stolen

Emil's documents, or maybe Emil had died in some out-of-the-way adventure and Max had kept his papers for good reasons.

"You don't ask questions, Mother. That's what I like about you," Max said, and I felt oddly honored. "Women ask you questions and then they give you away, because they're too dumb to keep things to themselves. But you don't."

"I didn't assume that you were a white little lamb when I found you in my shed," I said. "And I don't care to know why Max has to keep away from the coppers while Emil can see them eye to eye."

The tattoos that covered his dried-up brown body and came into sight when he stripped to the waist for work would have made the madame of a Port Said brothel blush. But we got so used to the scenes depicted around his navel that we didn't notice them at all. He had many scars, and then there was also the matter of his missing toes.

Ignominy brought it up first. "You have no Anky-Panky," she said. "What did you do with them?"

"I bit them off," Max said. It was the sort of joke the children adored.

"I know, let *me* tell," Milky cried eagerly. "You fell into a trap and the iron made click and there you were. So you bit them off and you ran away."

"Well, sort of. That's about it," Max said. "Only it wasn't a trap. It was up in the North of Canada, a few years ago. We were prospecting—not for gold, mind you, for radium. They call it pitchblende; it looks just like nothing, just like a piece of dried-up horse apples. Well, as I said, there was this camp, it was called Devil's Chimney, and we had thirty-five below zero. You know what that means? So then my Anky-Panky gets frozen and I says to myself, 'Brother,' I says, 'if you don't get rid of these here tootsies quick you're a goner.' So I take my pocketknife and cut them off. You don't feel it when they are frozen. Nothing to it. Only afterward, in spring, when they thaw up." And he took his knife out and looked at it thoughtfully. It was his other great treasure and seemed to have shared all his adventures. The blades had gone thin from years of use, and the leather sheath was shiny with age.

As for the toes, I was sure that he had told a fib. They might have been frozen and he might even have cut them off himself, but it couldn't have been a few years ago. When he came to us and after he had given his muddy feet a hot bath, his feet had turned out to be a filthy, infected mess where the toes had been cut off. It took all my old tricks from the times of the Red Cross to get them free of pus and make them heal cleanly. I had my own theory about those missing Anky-Pankies. A man who would rather hike across the Watzmann with such pains than go to a hospital and have himself treated, such a man must have very good reasons to keep away from official observation and files. But, as Max said, I didn't ask questions and I didn't want to know the answers. I had no noble reasons. It was simply that I needed him. I couldn't afford to find out something about him that would have compelled me to turn him over to the police.

He went to Anzbach and came back drunk. I didn't want the children to see him like that, and I dragged him into the lean-to and left him there to sleep his liquor off. It was a disgusting business, dragging that smelly old man around, and I hated him for it. I was surprised about the desperate moral hang-over Max suffered afterward. "Mother," he said (he kept on calling me "Mother" in spite of his white hair), "Mother, if you ever catch me drunk again, take some chains and lock me tight somewhere. Because when I'm drunk I don't know what I'm doing, and that's terrible. I can't tell you how I feel when I come out of a drunk. I am scared—it's the only time I'm scared. I look at my hands and I think: Hands, what have you done while I was drunk? If you have done bad, I wish I was dead. See? Once I came out of a drunk and my hands were bloody and I thought: Hands, did you murder somebody? It's the most awful feeling; the cold sweat pours out from you as if you had fountains all over you. That time it was nothing. I had broken a bottle and had cut my hands. But, God Almighty, Mother, don't let me get drunk again."

I remember something he said to me some other time: "Some people are born with one drop of black blood in them. And sometimes that black blood comes up in you and everything goes black. All the blood goes black from just that one drop. It's like when one of them squids pours out its ink. All black. All black!"

The worst fight we had was when the Gabel farmer came to complain that Max had molested his youngest daughter and swore that he would break his neck if he ever went near the girl again. I took it upon myself to talk to Max about it. "How could you do such a thing? It's awful," I said. "If it's true, it makes me sick to even think of it."

"What's so awful about it?" he said. "I'm a man and she's a woman. What's all the fuss about?"

"She's hardly twelve. She's a child," I cried.

"She's a woman all the same," he said. "It's not the years. She's of age and she's itching for a man. If a cow gets hot you take her to the bull, but if a girl needs you-know-what there is a big to-do about it. I found her crying on a Sunday because all the other girls were with their boy friends and she had none. So I fondled her a bit and made her feel better. That's all."

"All right. If she wants a boy friend, let the young boys take care of her. You're an old man and you should be ashamed of yourself," I said, realizing how prim I sounded, preaching to that old reprobate.

"If it comes down to that, old men know better than those young bucks what a girl needs," he said with that ugly gleam in his eyes. "And I'm not as old as all that. I'm fifty-two and that's a damn good age."

"You are not," I said, flabbergasted. To me Max had seemed somewhere past seventy and way beyond sexual exploits.

"Want to see my passport?" he said, snorting at me.

"Yours or Emil's?" I said. He spat artfully and hitched his trousers up.

"You need a man yourself, Mother," he said. "It's against nature to live as you do, and that's the greatest sin there is."

It made me furious, and I yelled at him and shook my fists under his nose. "You stay away from the girls or I'll kick you out!" I yelled. "I want my peace here, and it has been hard enough to get it. I won't have the Gabel farmer kill you or one of the Guggl boys shoot you, understand? If you have hot pants at your age, go to Anzbach and grab yourself one of the waitresses at the hotel, that's what they are there for, but leave the girls in Einsiedel alone." I went on saying several unpleasant and obscene things to him, to make myself clearly understood, and he listened sulkily. "All right, all right, Mother," he said finally. "I didn't do nothing wrong. Someday I'm going to tell you about some islands where the girls come of age when they're ten and there is a great feast and every man of the tribe has a go at them, from the chief down to the youngest boy. That's fun, see? That's natural. All right, so here they have different customs. I've got along fine with Eskimos and Zulus, I'll get along with old sour-puss Gabel too. Don't you worry no more."

But I kept on worrying, and I had a talk with Clara about him when she came up for one of her flying visits. Clara was crazy about the old man, and he, obviously, was highly impressed by her. He would take a bath and scrub himself clean before she arrived, even shave his beard and invest a lot of money in new shirts, embroidered suspenders, and an expensive pair of shorts made of the soft gray leather of a mountain goat. Clara was delighted about the growing account of his sins. "The old trespasser," she said, "the old heathen, don't you love him? What would you do without him? Show me, did he do any new carvings?"

The money he needed for schnapps, for his visits to the waitresses, and for his sartorial excursions, Max made with the toys he carved and sold. Toy carving was an old traditional craft in those hidden mountain valleys. I had seen many of those bold little figures and liked them, but I didn't dream how important they were to become in my own life. When Christmas drew near, Max took out his precious pocketknife and began to whittle away on bits of wood he brought home; harder wood than the pine logs of our woodpile; walnut, wild-cherry wood, the wood of the asps which grew down in the flats and looked like slim white-bodied girls walking through the evening mist.

"What are you doing?" I asked him, interested.

"Making a Child in the Manger for the kids," he told me. "It's going to be a surprise. Don't tell them and hide it good." He whittled and carved during the evenings, after the children had gone to sleep on the balcony, and I watched him. It was

fascinating to watch him, and those evenings stand out in my
memory as something still and good and pregnant with joy, like
watching flowers grow. The fire crackled in the stove, and later
in the evening there was only a glow and we heard the logs
rustle when one fell down on the grate and the others adjusted
themselves, like living creatures turning in their sleep. Sometimes
an icicle would break from the eaves outside and fall onto the
frozen ground with a small sound, like that of a glass bell. There
was a smell of baked apples and pine cones, and the dog would
sigh in her sleep and yelp and move her paws, dreaming that
she was running after a wild bird. I could see the brown scalp
shine under Max's silky, thin white hair and the muscles move
under the indecent tattoos of his arms. The chips would fly
from his knife and the thing he carved would gain shape and
smoothness. He lined up his little creatures on the table for me
to play with them. First the little Jesus Child in His manger,
then the kneeling Mother Maria, looking very surprised, Joseph,
with the face of the Gabel farmer, the Wise Men, the shepherds,
the angels, the sheep, the oxen, the stable, the palm trees. By and
by he filled the cupboard where we kept the surprise with a whole
crowded world of colorful humanity, and while he carved them
he would tell me about the people he had seen and how he had
met them and why he had left them behind. I listened with a
little tightness around my chest because I wondered when and
why he would leave us. Life had become so much smoother and
richer since he had been with us that I dreaded to imagine that
we should ever again have to manage without him. Sometimes
he drifted off and carved some strange-looking tokens. "This is
how them Maori in New Zealand carve their figures," he would
tell me, and some wild-looking creature would take shape under
his knife. "They always have only three fingers and their tongues
are sticking out. The Maori believe you can frighten your
enemies by sticking out your tongue. Imagine a tribe of goddamned fierce cannibals running away from another tribe of
cannibals just because they stick out their tongues at them!" . . .

"This is what some African tribes make up for their hocus-
pocus," he would say, presenting two primitive human forms to
me. "It's a man and a woman, see?" It was impossible to overlook

their sex, because there was hardly anything else to be noticed about their wooden bodies. Max began to chuckle. "There was a missionary down in the Cameroons who hunted up every pair of them he could find to burn them, year after year; he must have burned hundreds of them. So then along comes an expedition and they ask him if he ever ran across such figures. They wanted them for some museum and they would pay a thousand dollars apiece. Well, by that time my missionary had converted every black soul along the upper river and not a single figure was left. He tore his hair and cried, the old boy with his religion. A thousand dollars apiece—and he had burned them all, he had burned a fortune! Mother, was it fun!"

"So what happened?" I asked, because I knew Max's narrative technique and was a willing stooge.

"So I carved a few for him and we split the money," he finished, taking the two figures into his hands and pushing them together in a most obscene position. His was an amazing talent. He could imitate any style he had ever seen. He populated my cupboard with Gothic, baroque and Victorian figures, with Javanese rococo and primitive Negro plastic. He carved figures that you couldn't contemplate without blushing and others so delicate and tender that you hardly dared touch them.

"I want to help you," I said after I had watched him hungrily for several weeks. "I makes me restless just to sit and look and do nothing."

"Got itching hands, eh, Mother?" he said. "Well, why don't you take the paintbox and paint them? I'm not so good at that."

First I painted them, and a little later I carved my first figure. Max brought me a knife—the same one I used today for carving Nero—and a special selected piece of wood; not as soft as pine and not as hard as cherry wood. He spent a whole day testing among the driftwood down in the flats, and I can still feel the knobby texture of that first piece of wood I had to carve. It was washed to a silver gray by the water and smoothed down by time and bleached by the sun and yet it was alive. "Watch where it wants to go," Max told me. "It'll tell you if you listen carefully. Wood has sense, just like you and me." I felt its springiness under my fingers, and I was afraid to cut into it, almost as if I could hurt it if I made one wrong move. "What am I going to carve?" I asked Max. "Try and find out what's in it," he said. "In the beginning you have to give in to its will. Later you can force it and make it obey you. Try something simple at first. Something you know, something you like. Say an apple. How's that for a beginning?"

Clara still has that apple. She uses it as a paperweight, the silly girl; she took it along when she had to run from Vienna for dear life in '38; it's not much of an apple either, but I was as proud of it as I had been after Martin's birth.

After three months of wood carving I felt as if this were the only thing I had ever wanted to do in my whole life. My violin playing had been a painful, frustrated effort. My secretarial attempts had remained amateurish. My social work had been more of an escape than anything else. But this here was what I was meant for. "You have wood in your blood, Marion," Clara told me, teasing me about my ancestors, the respectable firm of Dobsberg & Sons. There was some truth in it. Soon I went out on expeditions to find my own pieces of wood, lugging home roots and stumps and cut-up trunks and cherishing them like pure gold. My hands seemed to develop some sense of their own; I was glad that they had grown hard and strong during my time in Einsiedel, or I wouldn't have been able to fight it out with the wood. I made it obey me all right. Soon I discovered that I too knew lots of creatures I wanted to shape, even if I hadn't been a world traveler like Max. I carved me all the babies I liked in all the funny positions and occupations I had watched them assume. I carved me all the animals I wanted: cows and goats and dogs of any description and an old fat cat, called Countess Yolanda, for sentimentality's sake. I ventured out into the fairy tales that I used to tell the children, and carving became more and more fun as I left reality behind and formed fantastic little creatures; Zwerg Nase and the Bad Queen and the Hare and the Tortoise. I would catch myself laughing out loud, all to myself, when another funny figure came to my mind that I might carve from that little piece of birchwood I had put aside. The children took a burning interest in my efforts. They leaned against my knees and watched me, giving helpful criticisms and ample encouragement. Max seemed to be proud and yet a bit jealous. There were wild competitions between us, and he whittled away like mad to keep one step ahead of me. By and by we had filled every shelf and board with figures; they fell down and broke, and even the children had enough and grew tired of them. Summer had come and they had a new pleasure: Max taught them how to make flies and fishing tackles, they grubbed for rainworms and went out fishing. The first summer tourists showed up and a snake appeared in our paradise: Commercialism. I began to sell my figures to the tourists. They didn't care much for the flights of my fantasy, but there were two babies that sold like hot buns. One was fat and rosy and fair-haired and tried to stuff its big toe into its mouth. The other one lay on its belly and presented a round, blushing behind to the world. Every damned tourist wanted to buy the same babies, and I could use some money. Someday, soon, I would have to give up this place where we felt safe and content and go back to some town where my boys could go to school. I turned away from the lovely creatures that crowded my imagination, made me smile in my sleep, and wanted to be born, and I bent myself to the task of carving the same stupid two babies over and over. Max joined me in it, and between us we fabricated enough toe-sucking and behind-showing babies to make millions and billions of inflation money. And then, during that summer, several things happened and changed it all.

First Clara came for a visit and announced that she would stay for two weeks and then take Anna and Ignominy with her and move to Berlin. I felt as if she had dropped a hammer on my head. "Away from Munich? To Berlin? Leave me behind in Einsiedel? Why, for heaven's sake?" I cried unhappily.

"Because Kant has offered me everything I could dream of," Clara said. "Remember Kant? 'Pierrot Mélancolique'? The man with the demonic beard and the persuasive baton? He has become the head of the Academy of Music in Berlin, and the first thing he did was to introduce some classes for modern dance and to appoint me as the leader of it. I am the big cheese, Mony, don't you see?"

Shani Kern too was in Berlin, head of the State Opera and a

famous composer. Susie, his wife, had become a prima donna
and put on weight like the best of them, Clara told me. Everybody seemed to be in Berlin, while former art centers like Munich,
Dresden, and Vienna fell behind. "How come they are all on top
now?" I asked Clara.

"Baby, it's our turn," she said. "The world has caught up with
us at last. We are the generation that runs this show."

I felt a bit bewildered as she went on flinging new names
and new ideas at me. I was a peasant woman, I had a cow, and
my sow was going to throw another litter soon. Also, Max had
grafted some of the wild-cherry trees; it was a momentous
experiment, and if it turned out well we would have big sweet
cherries next summer. Yet somehow my talks with Clara seemed
to have touched something in me that had been asleep for a long
time. She was working on a new dance, and I asked her if I
might watch her. "Wait, till it takes more shape," she said.

"What are you going to call it?" I asked her.

" 'Pietà,' " she said. "It's about a woman holding her dead son
on her lap."

A week later Clara called me down to the threshing floor that
served her as a studio. It was cool and dusky in the barn, and
there was the smell of hay from the loft and the moist scent of
freshly cut grass, which Max had carted in for our Amalia's
supper. I watched and Clara danced. It was a great dance and
it made us sad, both of us. To break the sadness she threw in
another dance, a caricature of all the gauze-skirted, empty, brilliant sweetness of the old-fashioned ballet, and this one was
so funny that I couldn't help laughing out loud at every turn and
pirouette and attitude. After Clara had left and taken Ignominy
with her, the sadness returned to me, because Einsiedel didn't
seem the same with Clara so far away. To drive the sadness out
of my house I began making little figures of Clara. I called one
"Pietà" and one "Ballerina" and sent them to her new Berlin
address as a birthday present. Max scoffed me about them, and
Clara didn't write whether she liked them or not, and I forgot
all about them.

Next came the stabilization of the mark. The towering billions
toppled over, the world went back to normal, and the sobered

people drew their purse strings tight. I went back to carving Baby Toe and Baby Behind, but there was no one to buy them, and in this new, orderly, stabilized world you needed some money. Suddenly there was a short and hurried, almost incomprehensible, letter by Clara with a newspaper clipping pinned to it. I couldn't make head or tail of it for several hours. It seemed, however, that Clara had entered my little wooden figures in some Art and Craft Exhibition and that they had made a hit. Art and Craft appeared to take itself very, very seriously, and the write-up treated my figures as if they were the next thing to the sculptures on the portal of the cathedral in Chartres. It was the very exaggeration in those statements that stamped the whole thing as something ridiculous, but it made me feel good all the same. Look here, Marion, my girl, I told myself, patting my shoulder and shaking my hands, there you have been tucked away behind the mountains, learning how to milk a cow and how to churn butter, and all the time you have kept in step with the rest of the world, whether you knew it or not. Let's see, what do they say about you? "The fragile beauty and innocence of these carvings ranks them with the oeuvres of the anonymous primitive masters of old, and while 'Pietà' is soaked in the deep wisdom that springs from the soil of Bavarian Catholicism, 'Ballerina' is of a bitter and final sophistication that makes it almost unbelievable that so wide a range should be given to one and the same artist!" Oh, shucks, the pigs have to be fed! "Max! Get me the buttermilk for the pig mush and tell the kids to get the hell home from the lake."

A little stone had been thrown into the still pool of my life. I felt it ripple; little air bubbles rose from the ground and burst, and the surface was disturbed by waves so shallow they were almost not noticeable. Still it might all have passed and calmed down, had not the cabinet minister been killed.

The cabinet minister had been a quiet, retiring sort of man, not much of a fighter. A dreamer, maybe, a thinker, a bookish sort of fellow, respected by many, loved by few. The German government of the twenties couldn't or wouldn't use fighters. It needed quiet, levelheaded men to clean up the debris, clear the financial mess, somehow raise the enormous amounts necessary to pay the war debts, build up the good will of the victorious countries and work toward an easing of the burden, soft-pedal at home in the hope of preventing the people from clashing too hard, class against class and opinion against opinion, and, altogether, carry the load the Kaiser's rule had brought about and settled on them. So now the cabinet minister had been shot on a train near Munich and, though he hadn't been popular, no one doubted that it was a great loss for Germany. A few arrests were made, a few nests of some childish secret societies were raided, and a new minister was appointed to carry on. Ever since the war, political murder had occurred so frequently that this one did not cause much of a stir. To us in Einsiedel only the faintest echo of it all reverberated, carried by newspapers that were four days old before they reached us and by some rumors from the political debates in the taproom of the Anzbach hotel.

Two weeks after that murder, Hellmuth Klappholz came for a surprise visit to Einsiedel and things began to move. I found him sitting on the corner bench of the main room, suspiciously eyed and watched by Max. The two boys were crawling all over him, and Milky especially seemed out of his mind with joy and excitement to see Hellmuth again. This surprised me, because the boy had only been a baby when we left Hahnenstadt, and I hadn't realized that he could remember him at all. But here he was, choking him with his embraces, telling tall tales and bragging loudly about his achievements as a great hunter, farmer, and fisherman. "Good day," I said, flabbergasted, putting down my two pails with the blueberries I had picked along the trail. Hellmuth got up and saluted with his old, ridiculous snap. "Good day, Aunt Maria," he said. "You didn't expect me, did you?"

"I could have kept him outside, but I wasn't sure you'd like me to have a fight with him," Max reported sulkily.

"No. It's all right, Max," I said. "It's my—it's my nephew."

"Nephew, eh?" Max said, with a world of insinuation in the one word. "And he's going to stay here?"

"It's none of your business," I said. Max whistled and left us alone without another word.

"Who is he?" Hellmuth asked nervously. It seemed queer

that he should have nothing more important to say after so long a separation and such an unexpected appearance.

"Our hired man," I said.

"Has he been in the war?"

"No. I don't think so."

"A deserter then?"

"Don't be an ass, Hellmuth," I said. "He's an old man and he was stuck somewhere in Turkestan when the war broke out. What is it to you anyway? He was in the Foreign Legion for a while, if that means anything to you."

"It's easier to come to an understanding with former comrades," Hellmuth said. "Frankly I didn't expect to run into some dubious stranger when I came here."

I looked him over. He still wore the same old windbreaker, the uniform trousers and puttees; his face was thin and strained, which made his chin appear still longer than before. He was badly shaved and a bit too rigid.

"Are you hungry?" I asked him.

"Yes. Thanks. Thirsty too."

I sent the boys down to the cellar, where our milk was set out in flat bowls to collect cream. I went to the cupboard, cut a few heavy slices of our home-baked bread, and fixed it with butter and sausage. The boys came pattering back on their bare feet, each one carrying a bowl of milk. Hellmuth's face relaxed somewhat as they climbed on the bench, rested their elbows on the table, and watched him eat and drink. Michael poured the milk from the bowl into a jug; there was a trick to it, but he didn't spill much. Hellmuth began to draw absent-minded figures with his forefinger in the rings of milk on the table.

"Well, Hellmuth," I said, after he had eaten, "what brings you to this corner? It's a bit out of the way, isn't it?"

"We are on a hiking tour," he said, "and we thought it might be nice to stop here for a few days. If we are not intruding, that is, Aunt Maria."

"You and who else?"

"Andreas—remember him? Count Andreas von Elmholtz. You met him in Hahnenstadt. We came from Russia together."

"Where is he?"

"He went up that trail," Hellmuth said, with a vague gesture toward the window. "If you agreed to keep us here for a few days I was to give him a signal."

"What signal?"

"Never mind what signal. Of course we didn't count on that man you have hanging around. We sort of wanted to get away from it all," Hellmuth said with a taut little laugh.

"Look here, my boy," I said after I had taken it all in, "are you in some sort of a mess? And do you mean to say you want to stay and hide in my house?"

"Not exactly. We are on a hiking tour, that's all. We are a bit low in funds and need a few days' rest before we go on—if you want to call this a mess——"

"You know what I mean," I said.

"No, I don't," he answered.

"Michael, Martin, will you go and get me today's eggs?" I told the boys, who ate up every word we spoke. "You must search for the brown hen, she has run away and hidden her eggs. She might be up on the rock again, like last time."

"I have no secrets," Hellmuth said after the boys had gone. "I didn't think there would be so much fuss about a simple visit. After all, you and the boys are the only relatives I have left; it's only natural I should want to see you once in a while, isn't it?"

There was something desperately urgent behind his words, and I felt once more the old mixture of emotions toward him—dislike and yet pity. I suppose I stared at him absent-mindedly and forgot to say something, while I tried to figure out the correct interpretation of his cryptic words. I was certain he hadn't said what he meant; neither did he expect me to take his words at their face value. Suddenly he threw his head back and said with his strained laugh: "All right. Some of our friends have been arrested, and we think it's better to keep out of harm's way until the stink has blown over."

"Still playing cops and robbers," I said, exasperated. He seemed childish to me, but you couldn't blame him for his shortcomings. He had been sent to the war before he was grown up, and he had just stopped at that point and never developed further.

"Did you have anything to do with the murder of the minister?" I asked. Living in Einsiedel had made me awfully simple and direct. He looked straight into my eyes with a queer sort of challenge.

"Naturally not," he said.

"On your word of honor?"

"On my word of honor," he said. I took a deep breath.

"Because I wouldn't feel very enthusiastic about shielding any political killer of any shade or hue," I said.

"Naturally not," he said again.

"All right," I said. "You can give your friend your signal."

He went to the window, and with a little shaving mirror that he took from his knapsack he flashed a signal toward the Lower Lake. The reflection of the sun bounced sharp and compact from its surface; Hellmuth repeated his signal several times, and then he tucked his mirror away again. "You might use it for shaving off and on, you know," I said. I almost hated the boy for breaking into the peace of our quiet corner.

Andreas was a dark-haired, dark-eyed boy, dressed in the same sort of outfit that Hellmuth wore but otherwise a very different type from him. He looked so exhausted that he seemed to be near a collapse, and he had, frankly and openly, the jitters. I installed the two in the room under the roof that had been reserved for Clara's short visits and told them to stay at home if they wanted to keep out of trouble. Andreas went to bed right away and remained there for several days because he was footsore. It made me smile to think how weak and soft those two heroes appeared in comparison with the hard stock of mountain folks to whom I had become accustomed. "If you really wanted to hide, you have picked a bad place," I told them. "Two fellows like you might easily disappear in a city like Munich; but you can be sure that by now you are the main topic all over Einsiedel, Anzbach, the Upper and the Lower Lake."

Andreas answered with a little groan, and Hellmuth kept on pacing his room hour after hour as if it were a prison cell. Both of them got more and more jittery from day to day. I didn't know what they feared or expected, and I didn't want to know. "This is worse than a jail," Hellmuth yelled at me as I brought them their food. It made me angry. "The doors are open. You may go any time you like," I yelled back. "I didn't ask you to come here and I'll praise the day when you leave." There was no answer to this, and the next day the papers said that the man who had killed the minister might have sought refuge in one of the mountain cabins of the Watzmann range. The papers described the killer as a man in his twenties, middle-sized, of military bearing, rather slim and wearing a windbreaker, uniform trousers, and boots or puttees. There were thousands and thousands who fitted that description. Andreas and Hellmuth grinned crookedly when they read it. I was sure that they knew more than they would tell me, but I was also sure that they had nothing to do with the killing directly. I felt, rather, that they gave themselves an undue importance and that their hiding was a pose to impress—I didn't know whom. I simply couldn't take them seriously, but they certainly were a nuisance around the house.

One afternoon Michael, who had been down to the lake fishing, came racing up the trail and burst into the room, breathless, with cheeks so hot a drop of water would have sizzled on his face. "They're coming," he cried. "They're coming, they're going to get Uncle Hellmuth. What are we going to do now? Shoot them? Mother!" He clasped his arms around my knees and shook me furiously. I could see that he was going to cry. He hadn't cried for a long time, but now his brave little pride was breaking into shatters.

"Come, come," I said, unfastening his grip. "What's all this nonsense? Who's coming?"

"Police," he said with a sob, "police, and they're after him. I know it, they're after him. I heard him say so when I listened at the window. Mother, don't let them get him, don't, please!"

I had great trouble in calming the little fellow, and that night I had to go out on the balcony twice and cover him up, because he screamed in his sleep and was fighting some nightmare. The police posse that had come with the official motorboat from Anzbach passed our house and the Gabel farm higher up and disappeared on the mountain trail that led around the Lower

Lake and toward the ski hut on the Watzmann. A wake of whispered gossip trailed after them.

"That young fellow who came first, is he your sweetheart?" Max Wilde asked me that evening as we sat together, painting the commercial blush on our babies' behinds.

"You're a fool," I said. "He's my nephew. He's the only one left of my husband's family, that's why I have to stick to him."

"You're taking too much of a chance for just a nephew," Max said; he had taken a stubborn dislike for Hellmuth from the first moment, and it was heartily reciprocated. "He'll get us the police on our neck before we can say 'Ludendorff.' If you had a grain of sense you'd kick him out good and fast."

"He is a summer tourist like any other," I said. "He has studied hard and he needs a rest and a lot of good milk. The police have nothing to do with him."

"No? Why would he telegraph his friend that the air was clear? I smell a rat if you don't."

"Who telegraphed whom?" I asked, pretending to be more stupid than I was.

"Heliographs," Max said. "We used them all the time. In Uganda. I tell you something, Mother. It's him or me. If you don't kick him out, I'll go. I don't like staying under one roof with him. He looks too scared. Scared men make all the trouble in this world. It's scared men who start wars, and scared men's guns go off too easily, and scared men shout loudest and step hardest on those who aren't scared; because scared men need showing off to themselves all the time so you'll believe that they ain't really scared."

"Have you never been scared?" I said. "You're just a show-off yourself."

"I sure have, Mother, sure have been scared," he said, and a queer expression came and went in his lined, parched face. "You don't know how scared I've been once or twice—that's how I know what might happen if you are. It's bad, Mother. It's the worst thing, being scared. I tell you something: There are a million ways of being scared but only one way of having courage. Courage is when you come to a point where you say to yourself, 'Nothing can happen to me.' Nothing. Hear that?

Nothing can happen to you. That's all you've got to know: nothing can happen to you. That's all that counts."

He put down the baby he had been working on and reached for his knife. I thought that he was beginning to carve another baby, but he just whittled a good piece of wood down to nothing, and I could see that his thoughts were far away.

"What do you mean, nothing can happen to me?" I asked. "I know a lot of things that could happen—and very unpleasant things too."

"Unpleasant! That ain't what I'm talking about," he said, impatient with my feminine denseness. "I mean, once you know that nothing can happen to you, life gets very simple. It's like this, Mother: Whatever happens, there are only two ends to it. Either you live through it, and that's good. Or you die—and that's almost better. Get me? Nature is kind that way. No one gets a heavier load than he can carry, see? Let's say you are sick, you have such pain you can't stand it. So what happens? Either the pain goes away and you get well and you stay alive and you forget all about it; or you die and the pain is gone for good. Suppose you get a beating—I mean a real beating, like they beat people in China. You stay alive or you die. In a war, or when you get shot, or when your house burns down with your children in it, or when you get under a car, or when your love lets you down, or whatever pain and grief and loss and hell there is to go through. Well, either you can stand it or it's too much. Either you live through it or you die. Now, Mother, that makes it simple, don't it? That's what I tell the kids every day: 'Never be scared, nothing can happen to you.'"

It was as good a speech as I had heard for a long time, but in spite of it Max got scared when another troop of police came and searched every house in Einsiedel. He got very scared and hid himself, first in the milk cellar and then, in an outburst of panic, he went away and off into the mountains. Meanwhile Hellmuth and Andreas, two nicely shaved, arrogantly calm gentlemen, were examined by the police, their papers were inspected and found without fault, and their visit seemed the most natural and harmless thing in the world. It was quite a comedy, because the policemen were former army sergeants or corporals and my two unwanted guests were former officers. All of them had been in the war, and they spoke a language of their own. There was much clicking of heels and saluting, and it was funny to see that the policemen looked upon Hellmuth and Andreas definitely as upon their superiors. They left with apologies, and afterward Hellmuth lugged Andreas up to their room because he had not enough strength left in his knees to get there by himself.

So far I had allowed things to drift, and what else could I have done? You don't deliver people who seek shelter with you to the police—or do you? It was hard to decide what was wrong or right in a case like that, but when the police left I was covered with cold sweat and felt like a criminal. The children rumbled in for supper; they were so excited I had no power over them.

"Why did they want to take Uncle Hellmuth away?" Michael asked, breathless. "But they didn't, did they? I wouldn't have let them take him, I would have shot them with my bow and arrow, I'm a good shot, ask Max."

"Yeah, but I'm better with my sling, tell him, Mother, aren't I? And they don't put people in jail just for loving their country, do they, Mother? Uncle Hellmuth says they do, but I don't believe it," Martin said, levelheaded and sensible even though excited.

"Uncle Hellmuth is going to be a general, and when I'm grown up I'll be a soldier like my father was and we'll kill every Frenchman, every one of them, and—and I'll carry the flag—and the band will play—and—and——"

"Don't talk, Milky. Eat," I said, tired. . . . "Why don't they build a division of us and let us win the war for them?" I could hear a husky, feverish, consumptive voice speak out of the past. It was a dangerous mixture, the quick, burning Jewish ambition of Michael's father stirred together with the family pride of the Tillmanns and Hellmuth's fanatical, unadulterated nationalism. I felt it as a faint breath of anxiety that evening, but it took me years to realize how deeply Michael had been impressed by his uncle's brief, mysterious stay in Einsiedel.

Hellmuth came downstairs later in the evening, quiet and not quite himself. "You were a brick, Aunt Maria," he said. "Thanks for covering us. You've done a good service to a great cause." His face was green under the superficial tan; the whole boy was green, inside and out.

"It's all right," I said. "And now, I think, it would be better if you and your jelly-kneed friend left."

"Right. At your command," he answered, snapping to attention, and went upstairs again. That's all you know, I thought. Click your heels and get yourself and other people into trouble.

I stayed up late that night and waited for Max to return, but he did not come back. I searched the cellar, the shed, the stable, and every nook and cave down in the flats, but I could not find him. Our boat was on its moorings, but Captain Tillmann's Mauser pistol was gone from the drawer where I usually kept it. I tried to sleep, but I was too disturbed. Before dawn I took my coat and my mountain boots, filled my rucksack with food, and went up the mountain trail. If he was hiding from the police he might get hungry, I thought. It was a senseless expedition that led to nothing. The morning came up, the peaks of the mountains grew pink, and the lake lifted itself out of the dawn with its dull pewter shine. I turned around and went home, and for days we waited for Max to return. But he never did.

Hellmuth and his friend joined a harmless group of young folks and marched off with them across the mountain passes, led by a mountain guide. Two weeks later Count Andreas von Elmholtz was trapped in a mountain cabin and shot himself. He left a note saying that he and he alone had killed the cabinet minister and that he was glad to pay the price for it with his life. The case was pronounced solved and dismissed, though I personally believed that he hadn't done it at all but had been ordered to take the rap for some more precious member of his society. Hellmuth, together with a few others, was arrested in Nuremberg, put through a trial for conspiracy or whatever they called it, and sentenced to one year of honorable confinement in a fortress.

If Hellmuth hadn't set the police loose in our quiet corner, Max might have stayed alive and become a mild, mellow, toothless old granddaddy. As it was, they hunted him up some-

where in our mountains and took him to Munich on grave sus-
picions. The leather bag tied to his neck, from which he wouldn't
part, gave him away. They identified him as the long-searched-
for murderer of two young girls.

Both murders were sex crimes; the one had been committed
six years ago and the other about half a year before I had found
Max in my lean-to. There was a grim irony in the thought that
this man with the blessed hands, who had been kind and helpful
and unselfish every minute he stayed with us, had also been a
ruthless, senseless killer. But then, I think sometimes, there is a
drop of death and murder at the bottom of every love and every
kiss.

I still have the smudgy postcard Max wrote me the night
before he was executed:

"Dear Mother don't worry about me I'm content as it is
and remember I'm not scared. Don't tell the kids what I done
they wouldn't understand. You do because we were friends
and I always liked you. God have mercy on my soul he will
wash out the black spot and make me like new Amen."

GOD HAVE MERCY ON ME, thought Marion, down in her crevasse. Wonder if old Hammelin will make one of those little crosses for me with a tiny roof over it as they do when someone had bad luck in the mountains. Here lies Marion Sprague who fell into a crevasse on Grauhorn Glacier, June 14, 1940. God have mercy on her.

She could see the little cross; the shingles of the tiny roof looked like gray satin, what with age and the weather of many years that had beaten down on them. Wake up, Marion, my girl, she thought and shook herself out of the drowsiness that had made her almost fall asleep. This is neither the time nor the place for a nap. It's goddamned cold down here and my hands are getting stiff. She blew into them to thaw them out. I can't use stiff hands if I have to try getting out of here without assistance. She still called and yodeled from time to time, but there hadn't been any answer for quite some while. It's too silly how one loses all sense of time in a situation like this, she thought. She looked reproachfully at her wrist watch. The glass was broken and the watch had stopped, showing an obstinate forty-three minutes past three. She shook her wrist and wound the watch, but it did not go. Marion focused her eyes on a black crack in the ice wall on the opposite side. I'll wait until the sun has crept past this crack, she thought. If no one comes for me until then I'll have to try getting out all by myself.

For the next few minutes she concentrated hard on sketching her way out. She planned every step, every grip, every hold. Ice climbing without an ax and a rope was no trifling task, but if it was a matter of life and death it could be done. It took the sun much too short a time to pass the crack and leave it in the shade, which slowly but resolutely spread toward the rim, like a stem of darkness sprouting from the darkness below. All right, let's try then, Marion thought. She had dreaded this moment and postponed it as long as possible. But if she wanted to get anywhere before it was dark she had to begin now. A ten-foot distance to cover. If everything went well she would be out of here within five minutes and be able to forget the whole idiotic interlude. Although she had kept on moving her body, her legs were stiff and cramped, more from the cold than from crouching behind that pinnacle. Good, solid, reliable pinnacle, she thought with a queer sort of affection. She used it now as a support on which to draw herself up to a standing position. The crevasse had begun to fill with weird little sounds, with glassy sighs and a thin musical crackling here and there, and once or twice there was a loud detonation like a shot, amplified by the depths below. Carefully, cautiously Marion straightened up. She stood there for a moment, her hand stemmed against the pinnacle for support, and then, just as carefully, she sat down again.

This is bad, she thought. This is pretty damn bad. I knew it all the time, didn't I? I just didn't want to admit it.

Her right ankle was fractured. She had recognized the sensation the moment she tried to rest her weight on it. Once, skiing, she had fractured the left ankle. It was a feeling one didn't forget. As if there were nothing inside of her boots. A trembling impotence, no pain, no; no real pain, but an absolute inability to stand on this broken leg of hers. "What a mess!" she said aloud. "What a silly, confounded mess! Such things always happen to me. And it serves me right, too."

She sat very still, thinking hard. There was nothing she could do now but sit and hope for something to happen. She took out her cigarettes, lit one, and counted how many were left. Fourteen. Enough to last her through the night if necessary. Now let's see what our chances are, she thought. People don't do it. People generally don't fall into crevasses, to be left there to rot and die. What are the odds? Pretty good, I should think. Better than the odds were at Dunkirk, aren't they?—and yet those English troops got home. I'll get home too. In a way we are all stuck in a crevasse, the whole blasted humanity, and we don't know exactly how we'll get out again. But out we'll get. We've got out every time so far; it's just a matter of not giving up too easily.

There is, for instance, old Hammelin. "Going up to the Arli Hütte?" he'll ask the guide from the hotel, who is taking up the two tourists. "Would be a good idea to take a look how Mrs. Sprague is making out on the glacier. She went up alone, running after her Englishman." The guide will grunt and forget about it. But, crossing the glacier, he will find my tracks going off into the wrong direction. That's why he is a guide. There is not a grain of ice those mountain guides don't see and watch and understand. He'll grunt again, will tie the rope with his two tourists to some firm piece of ice, will tell them to stand still and wait while he follows my route, sniffs around where I made the loop and retraced my way. He will come to the bridge that broke through and then he'll haul me out of here. He will scold me terribly in his Swiss Dutch and I won't understand half of it. And then he will shingle my ankle, tie me to his rope, and either lug me up to the Arli Hütte or back into Staufen.

Then there is Michael. He will read my note and grin leniently, but he will be pleased that I went after Christopher. He will look through the telescope and be proud as hell that he has eyes to see me, a tiny point, scrambling up the Kees. He will figure out at what time we will be at the Hütte—Christopher and I (of course he will believe that we will arrive there together), and he will telephone around suppertime. Christopher will tell him that he did not see me, and Michael will tell Christopher that I went after him. First they will both think the other one is joking. Then they will agree that I'm crazy. Then they'll get very serious and very silent. Then there will be a huge and most embarrassing super-de-luxe fuss with a rescue expedition and torches and flares like that time, three years ago, when they had the avalanche; and Staufen will have something new to talk about until the next accident.

No, I know what will happen. Christopher will receive a little telepathic message from me. Something will pluck his mind or whisper to him. After all, lovers should be able to give as good a performance as a twelve-dollar portable radio. I'm sure there is something like an antenna in our system and we're able to send out and receive rays. Hello, this is Marion. Can you hear me or feel me, Chris, my darling? Please, turn around and go back. You want to see me once more, don't you? You want to be with me tonight, just as I want to be with you. You must turn back and find me. The hell with old Grauhorn summit, you must think; I'm going back to Marion to be with her every minute that's left until my plane takes off. You will stride down the glacier, easy and free and in a hurry to get back to Staufen and surprise me. Then you will stop and bend down very low and with your shortsighted eyes you'll trace my tracks in the soft, flaky ice. These are Marion's hobnail boots, you will think. You told me once that you would recognize my tracks among hundreds, didn't you? Well, this is the time to prove it, Christopher darling. You will frown and contemplate what these tracks mean, and you will gasp and understand and be happy. So it was Marion after all whom I heard yodeling, you'll think, and not a hallucination; she followed me, she loves me. Where is she now? You'll come to the edge of my crevasse soon, very soon. You'll call out: "Marion! Marion! Where are you? What happened to you?" And your voice will sound very anxious and not at all English and restrained. I'll answer—very cool, very collected: "Hello, Chris. I've been waiting for you." Then you'll let down your rope and haul me up artfully and I'll laugh and say: "I've put myself into the refrigerator to keep fresh for you." And then you'll set my ankle and kiss me and rub me warm and lug me home somehow. And you'll stay the night with me and we will laugh about all this.

That's a lot of whistling in the dark, Marion thought, watching the little puffs of steam that streamed with every breath from her mouth. She moved her arms and rubbed her hands and slapped her thighs to coax some warmth into her body. A while ago she had taken her heavy sweater from her rucksack and slipped it on, using the rucksack itself for a cushion to sit on. She was installed as comfortably as conditions permitted, safe at least and with enough space to keep her back off the ice wall. She would have liked a piece of wood to splint her leg, but wood didn't grow on glaciers or in crevasses. There still was not much of a pain in her ankle, only a growing pressure and stiffness. The main thing now was not to fall asleep, not to let the heaviness of her eyelids get the better of her, and to keep on calling so that she could be found. She remembered once more the game they had played during those weary nights at the depot in Bergheim. She recalled all the lovely and good things of life and built them around herself like a hedge to protect her from the cold and the fear and the lonesomeness. The strawberries Michael had brought her that morning. The feel of Christopher's rough tweed coat when it brushed against her shoulder on some narrow trail in the woods. The piece of pearwood from which she had carved Nero's image. Her thoughts meandered off in a crazy crisscross pattern. One moment she thought so intensely that she could almost see and touch the grandchild she would soon have; and the next moment she met Christopher, but she was not forty-four, a woman with eyes too weak to discover the failings of an ice bridge and with bones so brittle they cracked from a slight fall. She was sixteen again, and the man she met was not Charles Dupont but Christopher Lankersham, and there was so much happiness to squander that the crevasse grew warm from it. It is amazing what a lot of thinking one can do, Marion thought. The sun had crept a bit to the left, and the shade reached not even a foot higher up than before. Marion gave herself a pitying smile. A lot of thinking, eh, my girl? They say it is a bad sign when your thoughts race off with you like that. They say drowning people can see their whole life in one last minute, and people who freeze to death too.

All right, all right. Let's have another cigarette and think of something funny. Of kangaroos, for instance. First thing when

I get back to New York and begin to work again I'll carve a set
of kangaroos. What was it the old kangaroo said to its baby
kangaroo? "I'll teach you to eat crackers in bed!" Funny, yes?
Funny enough. How warm it must be in the pouch of a mother
kangaroo! . . .

My IDEA of complete happiness is a mother kangaroo; to carry
my young with me, safely tucked away in my pouch, while
I go off in leaps and bounds, with just enough time off for nib-
bling the greens from tree and bush. That's the best thing I
know, and that's exactly what I did during the years between
1925 and 1930. Bad times were over, for me and for Europe.
We did a good job of forgetting in a hurry that there had ever
been a war, and there was friendliness and good will all around,
food in the market stalls and solid, stable money in our pockets.
That's the great thing we learned in the last war: that troubles
come and go and that nothing is so horrible it cannot be forgotten within an amazingly short time.

Berlin was a good place during those postwar years. It had a
brisk, invigorating climate for work and play, and the people
were bright, quick, humorous, and tolerant. In its character
the Berlin of that period resembled New York as much as any
European town might resemble any American town. But then
all big cities had begun to look alike, much more so than ever
before. Before the war America, to us, had been a far-off continent, where noble Indians went around scalping brutal gold
prospectors and whither good families sent their black sheep of
sons to sell newspapers and end up as fabulously rich though
eccentric magnates. Now we discovered that we all were Americanized. We were not quite sure if this was a process to be
lauded or lamented.

In the war we had learned that there was not such a thing
as friends and enemies. Soldiers were pretty much alike, whether
French, British or German; so were mothers and victims and
children and people generally. As for their corpses, why, there

was hardly any difference at all. And so, with this new wisdom, we edged up closer and became good neighbors. For a while at least.

I think each period is wildly in love with its own style and taste and Clara was right: Now it was our turn. In America these might have been the Roaring Twenties. In Europe the Twenties were only smiling, with the mellow, wise, somewhat feeble, somewhat hectic smile of a patient who has undergone a dangerous, almost hopeless operation and, coming out of it, finds himself still alive. We brushed our hands and looked around and were pleased with this, our new, small, friendly world. Also, it was a women's world, and we girls were allowed to help clean up after the men had made a mess of things. They gave us the right to study, to work in any profession, and to vote. Just now I can't see that it got us anywhere or made us any happier or gave us more influence than our mothers had; not even that it made us stop our men from getting themselves into a mess once more. But during the Twenties we felt that we were the absolute apex in accomplishments, every one of us a little savior of the world. Being women, we went first of all into a jag of thorough housecleaning. We took off the curtains, looked under the beds, and swept out the old, old dust; we took the skeletons from our closets and gave them a good airing, and we threw some of the more blatant lies into the garbage can. Our houses became bright and our lives comfortable, with a bathroom and a radio and a victrola and a car for everyone—or at least with the hope of having them someday—and no more messy nonsense about double morals either, please. This done, we looked into our mirrors and decided to become beautiful. Because we had missed the years when we had been really young and shining, we permitted ourselves a delayed, artificial, hectic sort of youth. In a hurry we invented the beauty parlor, the cosmetic industry, the rouged cheeks, the painted lips, the permanent wave. For the first time disappeared the enormous advantage which Bad Women held over Good Women through the centuries—not a small achievement in itself. Meanwhile our men discovered the calories, the vitamins, the hormones. It was a great relief to learn that our most hidden and sinful desires had nothing to do with morals or ethics and were not brought about by the devil but by our glands. It was the best news we had had in a long time. Now let's just have organized birth control, we said, and the world will be perfect. . . .

Michael told me once that the cultivation of rubber on a big scale is hardly more than thirty-five years old. It was a piece of information on which I chewed a lot. I liked to think of some little rubber tree planted somewhere in Sumatra some forty years ago and what drudgery and sweat and ingenuity had gone into it before it began supplying those useful gadgets that are sold discreetly across the drugstore counter. My, how that little rubber tree has changed the ethical, moral, philosophical, social outlook of the world! The courage it gave us to love and be loved, the freedom to end a relation when it was over and come out of it unscathed and without consequences! The blessing that no more unwanted, unwelcome, unhappy children were hurled into being! The suicides it helped to avoid, the child murders it prevented, the misery it stopped, the oldest, tritest theme of literature it cut clear off! Good, brave little rubber tree in Sumatra, there is still a great mission ahead of you, but even up to now you have done as much for the world as all the moral theorists together!

On this streamlined new planet I found my own little nook, and maybe I wouldn't have been so pleased with those years hadn't they brought me so much success. But there I was, Marion Sommer, creator of streamlined toys. Career woman, provider for a family, money earner, friend of interesting people and chief designer and head executive of the toy department of Eichheimer & Co.

Eichheimer & Co. was a big plant, catering to many aspects of modern living, like bathroom fixtures and sliding doors, garden furniture and awnings, and scores of other whatnots. Its toy factory was only one of its many departments, though I daresay the company made good money with it. German toys were an export article, paid for with good, hard foreign currency, and the new trend in child psychology, together with a certain importance that such minor arts and crafts had assumed after the war, made the fabrication of toys quite important. I had a crammed twelve-hour working day, with six assistants and a staff of apprentices working for me. I had little to do with the factory itself where my designs were put into mass production. Once in a while Karl Buttner, an excited and gloomy old foreman of gnomelike appearance, would be dispatched to tell me that it was technically impossible to reproduce such and such a figure on a big scale. But I had known how to treat old foremen since those prehistoric ages in F 12, and most of the time I could wheedle old Buttner into an extra effort and appease him by some minor changes in my design. Also I had hurriedly and secretly acquired the technical knowledge necessary for my new profession. The rest was easy. What was needed was ideas and the stamina to put them through by hook or crook against old Eichheimer's resistance.

We lived in the quietest part of a quiet residential district; the house stood in the midst of a big garden with old trees that sloped down to a little private lake. House, lake, and garden belonged to a family who had been great and wealthy but had become small and poor. It was a ghost of a family, dying out in silence and dignity, surrounded by black porphyry pillars, outmoded paintings, dry bread for supper, unpaid water bills, and subpoenas for delinquent taxes. I had rented from them the former servants' quarters in the uppermost floor and rearranged them. They made a lovely flat, in spite of a few slanting roof corners. I also found a gem of a woman to run my household and take care of the boys during my working hours. Gertrude was thin and sour-faced and unfriendly, though efficient in a terrifying way and devoted to us with the fanaticism of a one-man dog. Gertrude had one weakness, which she shared with most domestic employees of those enlightened, progressive, socialistic years. She wasn't to be thought of as a servant and she had, under all circumstances, to be addressed with her full and right title, Fräulein Household Assistant Bieber. I suppose only God was permitted to call her by her first name.

My clock would scream at me every morning ten minutes to six and I would roll around and stretch and yawn and bask in the knowledge that I had an eternity of time before getting up. I would grab the paper that the treasure Gertrude pushed under my door, scan the news, yawn once more, play a little with an idea that had come to me last evening while dancing. It was something about a penguin by the name of Sebastian who looked to me like a funny fellow to throw on the market. Then I would get up and begin dressing. After my long, luxurious beloved bath it was just time for waking up the boys. I would tiptoe into their room where it was always fresh and cool, even in summer, and would wait another minute, contemplating them. Michael always slept on his tummy and in great disorder. He looked as if sleeping were a very strenuous task, an athletic feat, a race against some dream competition. He had kicked his blanket to the floor and his body was long and had the marks of a thoroughbred. He didn't look like a child but like the small edition of a handsome man. On his night table he had a pile of books; he was an avid reader and passed various periods of enthusiasm for one thing or another. The Indians; the Jungle stories; the Bees; the Crusaders; the Sky and the Stars; Richard the Lionhearted. On his desk he had a microscope and in the corner on the floor he had an old pot in which he nursed some filthy water along for his research. Quite incongruously he also had a sleeping companion clutched in his arms. Nibble, the one-eyed rabbit that he took to bed with him ever since he had received it as a present on his fifth birthday.

I touched his neck and his temples slightly. It was an automatic gesture, I was so used to testing his temperature. Since Einsiedel there was no more danger that his lungs might get affected, but he had had a mastoid, and the operation had left me a bit jittery. Martin claimed that I spoiled Michael and made a sissy of him and Michael, to prove that he was no sissy, had beaten up his brother in a highly convincing way. Michael always awoke the moment I touched him; he popped out of his slumber like a shot and was wide awake at once. But it took a lot of noise to wake up Martin. He slept as tidily as Captain Tillmann had slept and sometimes, when I looked down at the sleeping boy, I got homesick for his father. He was shorter and sturdier than Michael. The blanket was neatly tucked around him, and though he didn't exactly snore, he breathed noisily and I could imagine that he would be a snorer at thirty-five. An obnoxiously pretty calendar with a lovely pink lady was pinned over his bed, and on his night table he had a little furnished doll's room, cut from cardboard, folded up and pasted together. It was a rather shameful hobby for a boy his age, but it went well with his adroit and reasonable character. I called him and shook him and slapped a wet wash rag into his face before he crawled out from the deep cave of sleep where he spent his nights.

"I should tell you not to forget that we have to call a man about the gas stove," he would say as soon as he was up and about. He looked into his notebook, worried and serious like a little accountant, seeing to it that we wouldn't forget anything concerning the household. He loved his notebook and scribbled it full with odd scraps of information, which he avidly collected. There would be such items as: The speed of light is 186,000 miles a second. A wet poultice of tobacco on the stomach of a man can kill him with nicotine acid. To keep boiling spinach green add a pinch of soda bicarbonate.

There were also some deadly dull jokes that he had picked up somewhere and duly registered. I asked him once why he preserved all those jewels of fact and fancy, and he explained to me very earnestly that he wanted to become an interesting and entertaining young gentleman. Bless his heart, I just hope those old jokes are helpful in his efforts at getting contracts with farmers in Iowa!

During breakfast we held an important conference about the commercial possibilities of a penguin by the name of Sebastian. These breakfast talks were the best fertilizer for my brain, and Michael gave such a lively imitation of a penguin—not that he had ever seen one—that we were howling with glee when we piled into Old Whooping Cough. A model 1926 car is not very impressive if you look at it today, but, Lord, how proud we were of it then! It derived its name from the strange and persistent sounds of its backfiring, which no remedy could cure. Driving to school in a car was huge fun, but it acquired a lot of diplomatic handling. A decent boy would rather be seen dead than driven to school in a car; it smacked of being rich and spoiled. Rich people were still something contemptible; you didn't touch them with a barge pole. And so we approached the school district with cunning detours and I let the boys off on some street corner, looked after them until they had galloped off around the corner, and then I drove Old Whooping Cough to the bustling heart of the city where I had my office.

My old stand-bys, the baby with the toe and the baby with the behind, kept on selling steadily all over the world. They were called Hanky and Panky, and I had given them a black little sister, modeled after Black Ignominy's cuddlesome image. We called this one Bamba, and it did well, especially in England. Then came a big success with the cow Amalia and her long-legged, stupid-looking calf. We cut them with the band-saw by the thousands, put them on wheels, and sold them very cheaply, and for a while the parks were full of them. I took a flop on the pig and its family, but made up for it with a Bavarian farm, with the gnarled figures of farmer Gabel, the Guggl-mother, and her yellow-haired children. Then came the zoo, which was great fun and got us big orders from England. Especially the hippopotamus and its offspring became very popular, because they looked so silly and everyone seemed to know someone who looked just like them. After my trip to Africa I made a Zulu kraal and an expedition of white men in pith helmets, with their tents and porters and the wild beasts they had captured, and the little boys of all ages liked it. I had long, deep discussions with the psychoanalyst we had on our board, who explained to me that toys were a substitute for missed experiences and a fulfillment of something or other. Maybe so. I just went on designing and carving what I thought was fun and what Herr Eichheimer doubted would sell.

Like any career woman's, my day consisted of brief hours for real creative work and a succession of minor nuisances, conferences, and hagglings with people under and over me. There was also the perpetual big problem of when to get around to having my hair shampooed. You can skip your lunch, munch an apple, and drink a glass of milk while working, and then use the saved-up lunch hour for fittings at the dressmaker, for getting a manicure, buying a new hat, going to a gym, for all sorts of small errands that are part of being a career woman and having to look your best. But getting a shampoo is, as far as I know, one of the problems that no working woman has solved entirely satisfactorily yet. Another is the way home after working hours, whether you make it by car, bus, or the subway. You are tired and irritable and impatient—and so are a few hundred thousand others going home from work. A whole population of straphangers and horn-honkers stepping on one another's toes and trampling on one another's nerves. There is a stiff little pain between your shoulders and another at the inside of your legs and, maybe, a bit of a headache from the day's strain and those damnable things that are persistently going on in the female apparatus inside of you. It's usually this chaffing, buffeting half-hour between work and relaxation that takes out a lot of strength and delivers you at your doorstep in the shape of a shipwrecked neurasthenic.

And then the magnificent resurrection brought about by a hot shower and another dress and renewed make-up and a flirtation with yourself in the mirror and perhaps a drink. I'm sorry for men, because all they can do in the way of making themselves new is having a shave, and even this they don't like. No wonder so many of them are so dull in the evening.

My evenings were rich and full. Most of my friends had come to live in Berlin. There was, first of all, Clara with her flock of dancers: short-haired, long-limbed creatures exploding with joie de vivre. Shani Kern, very funny, very famous, still in love with his wife Susie, who had begun to look like a real two-hundred-pound prima donna. Kant, a little old, a little shriveled up and slightly bewildered by the new generation of girls who did not have to be seduced but did the seducing themselves—and without great ceremonial. There were actors I had known in Bergheim, painters I had known in Vienna. Once in a while Fritz Halban would dash into town and take me up in the air in his ludicrous Birdie. He was something big in the government's air department and he was the only person in the world to call me Mäusle. . . .

Funny to think of them just now. Clara a masseuse in New York. Kant an old man just good enough to conduct the second string summer concerts in Scheveningen—if he didn't by any chance happen to be in Rotterdam during the bombardment. Shani? In which prison camp, on which road are you just now, best friend of my early days? Fritz Halban training young Chinese in Chungking to fly. And Charles Dupont painting slick portraits of the Nazi big shots and making them look as they would like to look. It's a funny upside-down world in which the grain flies away and the chaff remains. . . .

Lately there has been so much shouting and writing and Hitler-advertising that it has become a generally accepted belief that it took the Führer to save Germany. But that's not true; cross my heart it isn't. We were doing fine during those years, thank you. In fact, we were doing amazingly well, considering the things we had gone through and the debts we had to pay and the war we had lost. There was a happy air of reconstruction and rebirth about those years, and with a bit of patience and a bit of assistance and a bit of magnanimity from the French and a bit of understanding from the Anglo-Saxons and a bit less stubborn selfishness on the part of the rich and a bit less interference from Moscow and a bit less stupidity all around, the world could have been a good place and Germany a pleasant cooperative part of it.

Berlin was a center of cultural life during those years, and artists and intellectuals are a resilient lot. They are a sturdy lawn that can't be harmed by being walked on; after the war and inflation had tramped over them they stood up and were as good as before, and better. The stage was alive, plucky and sizzling with experiments. The schools were full of new ideas, the concerts many and of unsurpassed quality. The art exhibitions were amusing in a knowing, hard-bitten way. Lectures and discussions, week ends at the many lake shores around the town, trips into the disappearing slums, fancy-dress parties in crazy studios, which were veritable orgies of steel furnitures and potato salad. First we all ate as only half-starved people can eat. Then we began to diet, to reduce, to cut our hair, to pluck our brows, to take off the fatty tissue of body and soul. We swam, we played tennis, we danced. We danced and danced, at any time, any place, and never had enough of it. We danced the way sick dogs eat grass—to get the poison out of our systems. There was a lot of casual love-making and also a new queer twilight of the sexes. Women wore monocles and men behaved a bit too gracefully, and both swapped symptoms and psychoanalytical terms. I don't know what brought about that sweeping wave of homosexuality that was openly accepted with a sort of Greek naturalness. I suppose men and women had lived too long in enforced separation, making a habit of their own sex in the proximity of trenches and war prisons and the huddled feminine loneliness of the hinterlands. Also we had become so damned tolerant and understanding that it was almost a disease.

As for me, I traveled a lot during those years, and, like many of us, I dropped my narrow local, provincial, national shells and became a cosmopolitan. I had to go to the metropolises of Europe, make new contacts, rake in new ideas, see what other people liked and how they reacted. I found women of my own kind everywhere: an unwritten sisterhood of girls who knew work and ambition and independence and who took it for granted that we all were acquainted with various sorts of hells and had left them behind without ever talking about it. Sometimes I remembered with a smile that awkward first time when I had ventured out alone, not knowing how to hire a taxi, tip a porter, or keep my heart from breaking. Now I had a good feeling of myself, on entering a dining car, coming down the stairs into a ship's lounge, going out with a man. There was that new sureness that comes with success. To be right, dressed right, groomed right, made up right, poised. Not a chicken any longer, to be sure, but still attractive enough to choose whom I wanted to be my companion, for a year, a month, a night.

I met John Sprague the way people meet in musical comedies, with the bleak, gray Moscow of 1928 for our backdrop. Moscow was bleak and gray because the Soviet government had declared bourgeois all colors but gray and red. Therefore the new buildings were painted gray—the color of the proletariat—and the red streamers with party slogans strung across the streets and the red flags fluttering over Lenin's tomb were not enough to brighten up the town. They had even removed the paintings by Renoir from their galleries because of the soft pink bourgeois flesh of his women, and in the theater all characters dressed in blue, green, or pink were easily recognized as bourgeois and to be hissed at.

Once more Clara was responsible for my going to some place where I had no real business to be. She had put the bug into my ear. She had been to Russia herself to study their school of dancing, and ever since she had pestered me to spend my next vacation in Moscow. "It's different from anything you know," she had told me. "It's an experience you can't afford to miss. It's the beginning of something great. It's like watching the first Christians creeping out from the catacombs or something of the sort. You go there, baby, and you'll be exploding with new ideas. And don't forget to take food along, because that's the one thing they don't have."

Different it was, and a beginning of something too, but I cursed Clara fiercely when I found myself without a room on the evening of my arrival. Intourist, their government's travel agency, had got me smoothly across the border and dumped me with only eight hours' delay at the dismal station. It was cold and dark and strange, and there was no one to meet me; no guide, no representative of the agency, and no car in sight anywhere. Some Russians I had met on the train took pity on me and packed me into the vehicle that had come to pick them up. They had something to do with the young Soviet Picture Industry, and therefore the outstanding luxury of a car was allotted to them—an ancient open truck without rubber tires. Even after the brief rocky ride through those Moscow streets, the lobby of the Grand Hotel had an unreal quality—something freakish and incongruous, like a museum with wax figures, where the grandeur of former days was preserved. There were marble pillars though the floor was bare and dirty, and there was a desk as in any other hotel; there was even a clerk who spoke several languages. There was, however, no room for me, in spite of the reservation the Intourist had promised, and all my remonstrations were met with complete indifference. That people had no room was too usual an occurrence for anyone to be bothered about it. First I laughed, then I pleaded, then I got very angry, and at last I was desperate. The Intourist office was closed for the night, and the clerk wouldn't go into any discussion. No room, was all he had to say. Absolutely no room? Not a corner, not a couch, not a bathtub where I could stay overnight? No. No room. I was bounced back by a rubber wall of disorganization and apathetic smiles. Maybe in the Metropole, someone suggested. A man in felt boots let himself be persuaded to carry my suitcases through the snow, and in his wake I trekked to the Metropole. I felt my ears freezing so that I expected them to drop off my head and splinter on the pavement, as the icicles had splintered in Einsiedel. In a hole torn into the pavement I saw a group of little boys huddled together, asleep or dead, frozen under the snow. "Bez Prizornye," said my guide, grinning, nudging them with his felt boot, and walking on. I had never seen into such fathomless misery, and it frightened me, the sight as well as the complete indifference with which it was accepted. It was late, and at the desk of the Metropole the scene at the Grand repeated itself. No room. Any other hotels in town? No hotels, no rooms. Well, what in the name of Lenin was I supposed to do? Could I stay in their lobby and sleep in a chair? No, not permitted. Sleep in the waiting room of the station? Closed for the night. Well, what then? Go back to the Grand the clerk suggested, and gave up talking to me. I looked around; my man with the felt boots had left. My wet suitcases stood next to me on the dirty floor and looked frozen too. Well, what now? I can't sleep on the street, can I? It's below zero. A smile, an apathetic shrug, no answer. I felt like crying.

That's where John Sprague stepped into my life.

"Do you speak English?" he asked, for my haranguing had been partly in German and partly in French.

"A little——" I answered. He was a tower of a man, heavy-looking in his raccoon coat. I had never seen such a coat before, and it impressed me as something extremely magnificent. I told him my plight and he listened thoughtfully. "Say, tovarich," he said to the clerk, "can't you put the lady into Ferber's room? He's staying in Leningrad until Saturday; he told me so himself."

"We have eight people in Ferber's room already," the clerk said. "A delegation from Kiev."

"Hm——" John said, rubbing his chin. It's funny how such little gestures become so familiar when you live with a person that you don't even notice them, but when I remember our first meeting I always see him like that: standing at the desk of the Metropole with a filthy gray light trickling over his fur coat, rubbing his chin and wondering what to do about me.

"It's an outrageous situation," I said. "If they are not capable of handling tourists why do they take our money and advertise their blasted Intourist tours all over the world?"

"Come, let's sit down for a moment and see what can be done," he said, dragging me into a deserted dining room or whatever it was, where a few people were sitting at one table and two sleepy waiters dreaming under potted palms didn't give them any service. Looking around at the old-fashioned, anachronistic splendor of the room I felt again like a remnant of a lost world. Capitalism is just a dinosaurus, I thought.

"Are you alone?" my tall American asked me as we sat down.

"Yes. I prefer traveling alone," I said.

"What's your line?"

"Beg pardon?"

"I mean, what's your business? Or are you here for the sheer pleasure of it?" I heard the irony and balked at it.

"Both," I said. "I am a maker of toys." I had some trouble understanding his broad American pronunciation and still more trouble digging up my half-forgotten English. He grinned at me. Maker of toys, eh?" he said. "You look like Orphan Annie to me. Waiter!" he shouted and banged his fist on the table. "Excuse me, but they come only if you yell at them. You are cold. What you want is tea and a good shot of vodka. It will take us an hour to get it, but never mind."

I looked around. "It doesn't seem quite real, the whole setting," I said.

"But it is. Darn real," he said. "That's why I took you away from the desk. You might have got the man there into trouble—and yourself too. Didn't you see how frightened he was when you started to kick against their organization?"

"I'm not a Russian, I can say what I want, can't I?"

"Well—no. Better not. Don't forget that the G.P.U. hears every word you speak. You don't want to get anyone in trouble. Better take it all as a good joke."

"It's no joke to arrive in the middle of the night in zero weather and be sent to sleep on the street."

"Look here," he said. "You can have my room for tonight. I—I was just going out anyway. Playing poker with the boys. I can double up with a friend of mine for one night. It's no trouble at all, really not. Don't let's have a long discussion about it. Here comes the vodka now."

Run down as the Metropole was, it still showed signs of former splendor. The corridors were long and wide; the room where John took me had a high ceiling. Everything smelled of broken sewer pipes and the toilets turned out to be in an appalling condition.

"All their plumbers must have been White Russians," John said speculatively. "Not a piece of plumbing intact in the whole town."

One electric bulb was shedding some grayish light. The only furniture was an iron cot, a tiny washstand, two chairs, and a little table, all suffering with the rickets. "Did you bring your own foodstuff along?" John asked me. "Good. Put it outside on the window sill; that's where I keep mine too." He began packing his night things while I still stood in the middle of the room, choked with grateful embarrassment.

"You are very kind," I said.

"Don't mention it, kid," he said. "Tomorrow the Intourist will take care of you—maybe. Well, good night. The light switch is next to the door. Sometimes it functions." He came back once more. "Do you know anyone in Moscow?" he asked.

"I have a few letters of introduction."

"That's okay then. Otherwise I'll be glad to introduce you to the boys. Newspapermen, you know; they know the ropes. By the way, the telephone is tapped; be careful in case you talk to any of the natives. Do you have a flit gun?"

"No——" I said, stunned.

"You can have mine. You'll need it. Well, good night."

He left me alone, shivering, tired out, and slightly dazed. Look out, my girl, where you have got yourself this time. Lost in Moscow, in a huge friendly American's bed. The pillow sheets smelled of him, unfamiliar but not unpleasant. Cigarettes and rubbing alcohol. Let's hope he was just friendly. Let's hope he won't come back in the middle of the night and try to be funny. No, he seemed casual about it all, just eager to help me. I didn't know Americans were friendly. We all thought they were hard, calculating, ruthless, and money-crazy. This one wasn't, though. Come to think of it I had never met anyone to whom being helpful seemed as natural as to this stranger in his fur coat. Come to think of it I had never met any American at all. If there are many Americans like this one they must be nice people. In Europe it's everyone for oneself and against all the others. . . .

Bedbugs. I hadn't had bedbugs since that remarkable first night of my young independence in Vienna.

I got up in the strange room, stubbed my toe, padded through the cold to the light switch, found the flit, and used it profusely. I was tired but I couldn't sleep. Someone opened the door—there was no lock—peeped into the dark room, and closed it again. I grinned into my blankets. The G.P.U. I thought. Going to take me to Siberia because I have kicked against the Intourist. Their bedbugs were strong and lively though. . . .

The next day was still colder, and I kept on struggling against the countless obstacles that beset every step in Russia at that time. Their inefficiency and lack of organization was appalling.

The public toilet was a place of horror. The public bathroom had a rusty, leaky tub, dreaming under layers of dirt, and naturally there was no hot water. The cold water came after a while as a sputter of brown sauce. The bell did not ring and the door did not close. I made my American bed and cleaned the room with my own towel and then I ventured out onto the street. There were few street cars, and I saw people standing in endless lines, fighting tooth and nail to get in. I gave up and, somehow, asked my way to the Intourist office. I waited there two hours for a certain tovarich who had handled my reservation. When he came at last, a smiling, friendly little man in a filthy Russian shirt, he seemed sincerely hurt that I had gone to the Metropole without official consent. When it turned out that I did not know in whose room I had spent the night I felt that I was precipitating a major state crisis. They knew, however. Their system worked, and I had been under observation from the moment of my arrival. First of all I was furnished with an interpreter, tovarich Amphiteatroff. She was a woman of my own age and kind, but obviously something had turned her into stone. I deducted that she might have belonged to the former intellectual class and that she was frightened out of her wits lest some word or even an unintended expression on her face might give her away as not one-hundred-per-cent bolshevik. I never succeeded in coaxing so much as a smile upon her broad, bland features. If, in the course of our endless tramping from sight to sight, I would ask her: "Aren't you tired?" she would shrink and shake her head. "Would you like to have a glass of tea with me?" And she would flinch as if I had invited her to commit an act of high treason. Good bolsheviks, I perceived, were not allowed to feel either tired or hungry. They had to be enthusiastically happy all the time. The explanations Amphiteatroff gave me were learned from a book; so were the answers to any questions I might have asked. Questions she did not want to answer she claimed not to understand, although her German and French, though slightly tinged with a Yiddish accent, were perfect.

At the Intourist they were most friendly and urbane, but when it came to giving me a room I ran up against the same old rubber wall. A smile, an apathetic shrugging of shoulders. No room. I pleaded with them. I showed them the bill I had paid in advance, including a first-class room at the Grand. No room. Well when will you have a room for me? A deprecatory gesture: Who knows? I got roaring mad. "If you have no room I am going back to Berlin tonight," I told them through my Amphiteatroff mouthpiece. There was a discussion in Russian and I bumped into a second wall. Not possible. Trains sold out. Your reservation made for February 9th. Cannot change.

"I have letters of introduction to various people," I told my interpreter. "Ask them if I am permitted to visit them and sleep there in case they invite me." More Russian discussions. They looked at the letters Clara and some of my leftist friends had given me. They grinned; they nodded; I was told to see whomever I liked and do whatever I liked. They practically handed me the keys of the city. They gave me a little booklet with food stamps and sent me on my way with their blessings. There began a relentless pilgrimage under Amphiteatroff's stern supervision, a cast-iron official program of things I was to see and a strict avoidance of things I was not to see. They never said a direct no to any of my demands. Sights not meant for tourists simply faded farther and farther away and disappeared at last in a vague vacuum. I felt like treading water all the time, never feeling ground under my feet. I visited a factory and factory schools and a baby home and a home for former prostitutes and Lenin's tomb, with the little man in his glass case, looking like a minor number at Madame Tussaud's, and barracks and workers' clubs and another factory. Their political organization was staggering and their actual output negligible. I began to see what Clara had meant by comparing them with the first Christians. What they had built up was impressive only because it had grown from complete destruction. It was clumsy and insufficient, and primitive like the early Christian art had been after the perfection of Greek art and the technical marvels of Roman colonization had been destroyed, buried, and exorcised. They had torn down their civilization to the lowest level of their illiterates so that they all could start together from the bottom. There was only one sight worth while, and I never grew tired of it. That was the pride the simple people felt in their achievements, the enthusiasm of those ragged, hungry masses, their conviction that they were chosen to save the world. A world of which they knew very little, I must say, and of which they had a highly cockeyed conception.

The people to whom I had letters of introduction were kind and hospitable to me from the first moment; only when I had told them about my difficulties in obtaining a room, they coiled up and pulled in their horns like frightened snails. Obviously they were not allowed to invite foreigners to stay with them overnight, and there would have been no place anyhow. What made it complicated was the fact that they were not allowed to tell me that they were not allowed to invite me. It was all rather confusing, because the most important things remained always unspoken, between the lines. Meanwhile I was taken around on a leash by Amphiteatroff who sat in a corner and listened to every word I said. After a while I felt as though I were in a prison whose ceiling was so low I couldn't stand up straight. That first day in Moscow gave me a breathing sample of the atmosphere that people in totalitarian states inhale. A queer mixture of enthusiasm, fear, and voluntary self-annihilation.

I was packing my things when my American came home that evening.

"I'm sorry I'm still here," I said. "People are very unpunctual in this place."

"You're telling me," he said.

"Beg pardon?"

"Forget it," he said "Skip it. So they didn't give you a room."

"How do you know?" I asked.

"Found out at the desk. Anyway, I almost expected something like it."

"They agreed to put a mattress into another room for me. Where that delegation sleeps."

"Have you ever slept in the same room with eight tovarich?" he asked. "No, I thought so. You wouldn't like it."

"I haven't much choice, have I?" I said. "You were so kind last night——"

"Look here," he said. "Provided it is okay with you I told them to bring that mattress in here. I mean it's the best you can do—stay here until you get a room for yourself. I might not be good company, but I'm better than eight tovarich. I wash every day and I don't snore. I mean, this is Russia, people have different ideas about bunking together——"

"I noticed," I said. "I was visiting with a family today; there were forty-nine families living in a one-family house, a dozen in one room——"

"Exactly. That's what I'm talking about. It may seem sort of funny somewhere else to share a room with a stranger, but it isn't funny in Moscow. We don't have to disturb each other at all. Okay? Okay. I'm John Sprague."

"My name is Marion Sommer," I said stiffly and slightly overwhelmed. It was the name under which I was known professionally. I examined John Sprague surreptitiously, and he gave me a nod and a grin. It felt good to be taken in charge, and this was no place or time to act coyly.

"I am harmless, trustworthy, forty years old, and happily married—this is Mrs. Sprague——" he said, pointing to the photo of a very beautiful woman standing on the rickety table. "I suggest you keep the bed and I take the mattress. The bed is too short for me anyhow. All hotel beds are. I'll see that the mattress gets here before midnight. Meanwhile I'm going out with the boys and you'll be asleep when I come home, I guess. Just pretend that I'm not there at all. Or would you care to come along?"

"No, thanks," I said. "I'm tired. It's my first day in Moscow, you know; it sort of overwhelms you. Of course, you seem to have lived here a long time——"

"No, only five weeks. In fact I hope to go back to the States next Monday, and then you can keep the room to yourself. I am a salesman, you know. I have to stay here until I have sold them my stuff." He began to grin. "I am a maker of tools," he said. "Yes, I guess that's what you would call me: a maker of tools. That's what I'm going to have printed on my cards from now on: John W. Sprague, maker of tools," he chuckled as he left me.

I came from a country where they liked titles and big, puffed-up words. I was not acquainted with the understatements of the Anglo-Saxons. It took me years to find out that Sprague was among the great machine manufacturers in the United States and that the tools John sold to the Soviet government were not nails and hammers, as I had thought, but complete drilling equipment for the plants, factories, railways, mines, and power works they were going to build.

For a few days I lived in the same room with John Sprague,

hardly ever noticing him. He would tiptoe in late at night, undress in the dark, and lie down on his mattress with a suppressed
little sigh; a loose board of the floor would creak, and then there
was only the quiet breathing of a tired man falling asleep. In
the morning I sometimes caught a glimpse of him, wrapped in
a green bathrobe, brushing his teeth or shaving. I would close
my eyes again and turn toward the wall, and when I woke up
once more he was gone. During the days I was taken around
by Amphiteatroff and shown the sights of the town. On returning in the evening I noticed that Sprague had been home during
my absence, had used his typewriter, eaten a bite from his
provisions, smoked some cigarettes, and splashed some water
on the floor, as if he had treated himself to a real good wash.
Sometimes I would find little messages tacked to the wall, telling me where I might find him in case I needed something or
asking if I would care to go to the theater with him or meet
the boys. One morning he came back to pick up a brief case he
had forgotten. "Good morning, maker of toys," he said merrily.
"How are you doing?"

"Thanks, fine, Mr. Sprague," I said. "I hope I am not too
much bother to you. The Intourist has entirely given up finding
a room for me."

"Well, and how do you like Moscow?" he asked.

"I am most impressed by it," I answered in my stiff, earnest
English.

"You are, are you? Well, you aren't doing business with them;
that makes all the difference. Or are you a parlor pink? You
don't look it."

"What is a parlor pink, please?" I asked. He explained it to
me, and I told him that in Germany they were called salon
communists. "I don't understand anything about politics; it's a
closed book to me," I said. "It's like mathematics; either you
comprehend it or you don't. But many of my friends are parlor
pinks."

"Yes, there is a deplorably low sense of self-preservation in
the intellectuals of most countries," John said. "They get dazzled
too easily and forget that freedom of thought is the base of
all decent living. Why are you laughing?"

"It is funny that you should quote Schiller," I said.

"I didn't quote any of your big-mouthed German classics," he said. "I quoted the constitution of the United States, and it's a darn good constitution if you ask me."

"And you know it by heart?" I said mockingly, because it struck me as something funny.

"Sure. Don't your kids learn your constitution in school?"

"I have never heard of anyone outside of our professional politicians having even the faintest idea of what's in our constitution," I said, dumfounded.

"Well, that's the difference between us. You people know a lot of highbrow stuff by dead writers and we know the simple basis of our daily life."

"Still I can't see that you have more sense of self-preservation than our intellectuals. They, at least, don't supply the bolsheviks with goods."

He laughed good-naturedly. "Well put, tovarich," he said. "But listen, kid: I am a salesman. All I have to do is sell my stuff. I would sell it to the devil if he would meet my price, see?"

No, I don't see it, I thought though I didn't say it. Sprague surveyed my breakfast, which I had spread out on the little table, right under the alert eyes of Mrs. Sprague's photo. "Look here," he said, "wouldn't it be a good idea if we pooled our foodstuff and had breakfast together once in a while? Having breakfast downstairs hasn't been any fun for me, to tell you the truth. And I know where to get better bread."

From then on I got domestic, tidying up my bed and the room a bit in the morning and setting the table while John Sprague foraged for food. We had caviar with our breakfast and whatever else he could get in the special shop for foreigners. I also found out that his offer to share his food with me was another unobtrusively kind gesture. He seemed to think that I had not enough to eat; he himself kept on moaning for the fleshpots of America. Scrambled eggs. Bacon. Hot cakes. Orange juice. However, he had a big store of condensed milk and hard frozen butter and he seemed to enjoy watching me eat.

"So Moscow has got you, kid," he said a few days later. "Now tell me, what's so wonderful about this filth and squalor and mess here?"

I tried to put it into words and gave up. "The people——" I said. "They have something to live for. They have their great idea; that's all that counts with them. Look at their faces! They are proud; I have never seen people so proud and happy as those Russians in their utter poverty. They don't live for today. They have the faith that their children and children's children will live in a better world——"

"That's a lot of hot air. That's all their leaders have to give them: promises for the future—instead of bread today."

"That's just it. They don't care for bread; they don't need it. The whole world has gone materialistic. But an idea is more important than bread, and the people here are proof of it."

"Well, that's still the question. I am a materialist and I come from a hundred-per-cent materialistic country, as your pink friends will tell you. I believe in good plumbing and a car for everyone and decent food for the children of our workers and a few little luxuries thrown in like equality and the pursuit of happiness for instance. There—that's another sample from our constitution."

"And what about their souls?" I said, not wanting to give in.

"Their souls? Let them go to church," John answered promptly. "Don't tell me they have no religion in the Soviet Union. They have kicked out their saints and ikons and hung Lenin's picture in the same corner instead. They've closed the churches and built Lenin's tomb. Did you see the people standing in line and marching in, in long processions, to look at their dead saint? If that's not acting like Catholics, I don't know what is."

"Yes, they are naïve, they haven't been atheists long enough," I said. "In a workers' club they showed me a little embryo in alcohol and told me that in that glass jar they were holding the proof there could be no God."

"There you have it," John said. "They showed me a tooth-brush in one of their barracks and asked me if I had ever seen anything as wonderful. They treated it like a piece of strong magic. They demonstrated for me how it could be used. The poor beggars!"

"Still, when you are in Russia you feel as if the rest of the world were wrong and dead, just good enough to be put into a museum. Even I cannot imagine that I will go back and live on normally as before. But, I suppose, when you are back home you can't imagine anything like Russia."

"What I would like to do is to send a few thousand of our reds over here and let them have a taste of the blessings of communism," John Sprague said. It sounded smug and commonplace and flat after the inspired preachings I heard every day in the gatherings of my Russian acquaintances.

"That is no argument," I said impatiently.

"Arguments, arguments, that's all you get here all the time. Party slogans and arguments! It gets so dull I could scream. What I want is a hot bath and a talk with free people who are not scared stiff of getting liquidated. God, will I be glad to get home!"

"If someone could give the people bread *and* an idea to live for —faith without terror—the world would be saved," I said. John Sprague got up and grinned at me.

"You aren't asking for much, are you?" he said. "Well, so long, maker of toys. I've got to go to the Kremlin and spring another high-pressure sales talk on the saviors of the world."

"That's a nasty cold you've got yourself there," John Sprague said to me the next morning.

"I am so sorry—does my coughing disturb you during the night?" I said, embarrassed. "I must have caught it when I went to the steam bath."

"It takes more to disturb my slumber," he said. "But it sounds nasty. Here, take this and rub it on your chest, tovarich——"

My cold got worse and I knew that I had a fever, but I did not want to admit it to myself. My teeth were chattering and I felt miserable. I told Amphiteatroff that I would have to stay in bed for a day or two; she shrugged her shoulders and accepted it as if it were an insult to the cause of the bolsheviki. I crept under my blankets, shivering, and drank a gallon of hot tea with a gallon of vodka. After a while I had to stagger to the washbowl and throw it all up again. As I made an expedition down the long, wide corridor, to clean the washbowl in the public bathroom and get fresh water, the walls were reeling around me and I wondered how, in the name of heaven, I would ever get back into my bed. Marion, my girl, falling ill in Moscow would be a bad joke, I thought. Sternly I told myself that I had no business getting ill, fell back into my bed, and pulled the blankets over me. In the middle of the night the light was turned on and someone bent over me. It took me some time to penetrate the drifting green and black shreds with which my fever filled the room.

"What's the matter with you, kid?" John Sprague asked. "You are not getting sick, are you?"

He contemplated me seriously for a little while, and then he brought his raccoon coat and spread it over me. "There, there," he said. "This will get you warm."

I still have that old raccoon coat. I took it along to Staufen and spread it over Michael when he had to lie on the balcony during those long, cold, anxious winters. That coat, to me, means warmth, safety, kindness, protection: It means John Sprague. I am very sentimental about that coat, as sentimental as I can ever get about anything. That night in Moscow I went to sleep under that coat, with John sitting at my bedside, watching me like a good, reliable nurse, while warmth and quiet spread through me. I wish I had that coat here, now, this very minute. Wrapped in John's old raccoon coat I could stay the whole night in my crevasse and never feel cold and never come to harm. But the raccoon coat is hanging behind the door in our house in Staufen, and John went away and died and left me alone.

The good thing about pneumonia is that you don't have to wait a long time for your verdict. As Max Wilde had told me: Either you die or you live. During the crisis that occurred on the seventh day I thought I would die. It seemed rather absurd to die in a filthy Moscow hotel, with the bedbugs doing acrobatics all around me, and it appears that it struck me as funny and I laughed a lot in my fever. There came clear moments when I remembered that I had two little boys at home and couldn't afford to die. I told it to John Sprague and he said: "Right you are, kid. Don't take it lying down. Stand up and fight." I fought and I won. I couldn't have done it without John. He stayed in Moscow until I was well out of danger. He got me an American doctor and he nursed me and took care of me and he was there whenever I needed him.

"Don't you have to go and sell tools, John?"

"You let my business alone and see that you get well in a hurry. I've sold all the tools I wanted to sell them this time."

I thought this over. By and by I learned to understand his American way of expressing himself by implications.

"Do you mean to say that your business is finished and you have remained in Moscow because of me?"

"Well—in a way, yes, and in a way, no. I couldn't simply have left you alone here in your condition, now could I? I didn't trust you to pull through in one of their filthy tovarich hospitals."

"I can never repay what you did for me."

"Oh nonsense. You're a swell kid. Some day when I am in a fix you'll help me out. Now close your eyes and take a little nap while I get some caviar from the store."

After he was gone I had a silent little dialogue with Mrs. Sprague's photo. She looked poised and smart and so intolerably beautiful that I suspected the photographer of a very flagrant piece of retouching. A boy was leaning behind her, sulking and humiliated, as children will look in photos. John had introduced him to me as Junior. During the days of my convalescence I had pumped him for some details of his life in the United States, but I couldn't make myself a picture of it. They lived on Long Island, some sort of suburb of New York but not exactly suburban, he explained, and I didn't know what he meant. His wife was the best girl in the whole world. He had met her during his sophomore year in college and married her immediately after his graduation. This too sounded Chinese. He was crazy about her, he told me. She was wonderful, fine, and helpless, like a flower, sort of. She spoke French like a native, and there was no book she wouldn't have read and no Philharmonic concert she would miss. She liked the South of France. She went there every year and met the most interesting people. The week ends in their home on Long Island were famous among their friends. She had a way of attracting celebrities like no other girl he knew; that was because she could discuss with them any topic they might bring up. By and by I had begun to loathe this perfect wife of John Sprague's. A lion huntress, I thought. One of those shrill, brittle, over- and underdressed Americans I had seen at the Côte d'Azur. It was obvious that John had a very humble opinion of himself compared with this wonderful wife of his. "Me?" he said. "I'm dull. Just a run-of-the-mill business man. I can play mediocre golf and fix a moderately good mint julep. There you have all my assets. It's a wonder a girl like Sheila doesn't get bored with a fellow like me."

Listen, I told Mrs. Sprague's photo, I just hope you are as crazy about your man as he is about you. I hope you have no silly ideas about celebrities. I know them; I live among them; in a way I am some sort of celebrity myself. And I am telling you there is more adventure and sweep in a real man like John, who goes out and sells tools to a dangerous bunch of punch-drunk rulers, than in all Quartier Latin, Montmartre, and Soho together.

The boy pouted at me from the silver frame and Mrs. Sprague paid no attention to me. She kept on looking straight ahead with the arrogantly empty smile of a goddess. Suddenly I knew that I couldn't bear the thought of saying thanks and good-by to John and never seeing him again.

"What have you got up your sleeve? You look too darn bright," he said, rubbing his freezing ears when he came home.

"I just decided that I'll spend my next vacations in New York," I said.

"That's it, that's the spirit. Maybe Sheila will be able to dig up a few parlor pinks for you. And I'm sure you'll like our materialistic bathrooms," he said. I could see how pleased he was.

He managed to commandeer a real automobile to transport me to the station and saw to it that I was comfortably placed into a compartment of what the Soviets called the "soft" coach. "Let me hear how you are getting along," he said. "Here is my address. Let me have yours too."

He wrote it down. "And your telephone number?" he asked me.

"What for? You are not going to call me up from New York," I said.

"Why not?" he answered.

And he did.

THE TELEPHONE OPERATOR in Berlin was almost as excited as I was myself. A call from New York was no trifling matter, indeed. My knees shook and my voice trembled.

"Hello—this is John speaking—John Sprague, remember me? We met in Moscow."

(Silly, as if there were more Johns to call me up from New York.)

"Yes. I remember you, John. How are you?"

"I'm fine. And you?"

"I'm fine too."

"That's good. And your two boys?"

"They are standing right next to me. They are very excited. So am I."

"Let them talk into the telephone. Might give the kids a thrill."

There was some scuffling and whispering. "You must speak English," I prompted them, and one after the other said gravely: "How do you do," just as they had learned it in school. Then they stood aside and watched me talk to the American about whom I had told them so much.

"They sound like swell fellows. Speaking English too."

"I can hear you as clearly as if you were in this room," I shouted into the phone, stupid with excitement. "How late is it in America? How is the weather there? It's raining here."

"The sun is shining here and all our tulips are out. Do you like tulips? Listen, kid, I'll be in London the week between the fourteenth and twenty-second. Why not hop over and have lunch with me and Mrs. Sprague?"

"Oh——" I said. "No. I can't do that. I would like to see you again. But I can't simply go to London. That is no hop. That is a long journey."

"Well, try and make it anyhow. And when are you coming to the U.S.A.? You promised, remember?"

"Yes, John, but I won't get a vacation for another year."

"Okay, next year then. Three minutes are over. So long, maker of toys. It's been swell hearing your voice again."

There came cablegrams from time to time, and once in a while even a letter. I was amazed how easy and amusing those letters sounded. It's another American quality of which we Europeans knew nothing, this sparkle and polished brightness in their letter-writing. The year 1928 went by, and 1929. I worked hard but with little success. Eichheimer & Co. had trouble, and so had everybody else. They had to lay off more and more workers, and there was constant talk of giving up the toy department altogether. We had left inflation behind, but had stumbled into that new thing called depression. By and by we found out that we had lived in a fool's paradise. Other generations grew up behind us, shouting their demands. The lost generation, which had come home with shattered nerves, bitter, cynical, and jumpy. The fifteen-year-olds asking us what sort of a mess and muddle we were going to hand over to them. The ten-year-olds, like my own brood, serious-eyed children with the privations and undernourishment of their early years in their bones, who seemed to think that they would have to save the world once more, at whatever price; only they could not agree among themselves how it was to be done. Because Michael had come too much under the influence of a young communistic teacher, who was homosexual on the side, I had taken the boys away from the progressive country school where they had stayed during my travels. But no sooner had I installed him in a school in Berlin than he joined a group of pathfinders, made a full face-about, and became a Hitler junge. He spat at a Jewish boy in his class and painted swastikas all over the walls of his room. Martin beat him up for it, and I had to have the room repainted. The perpetual riots and street fights between communists and Nazis reverberated in my apartment, and whenever I came home from work, tired out by the constantly growing difficulties there, I found the devil loose among the boys. Fräulein Household Assistant Bieber sympathized with Michael and the Nazis. Martin, out of sheer opposition, threatened he would grow up and become a communist. I held my head, in which a headache drummed on its tom-tom and shouted that what they both needed was a good spanking. "Frau Captain should marry again," Pulke advised me when he came for one of his Sunday visits. "The boys need a man's hand, that's what I say." He himself had begun to incline toward the Nazis. "At least they have guts and discipline," he said.

"Yes, yes, Pulke," I told him. "But it isn't so simple to catch a husband nowadays, is it?"

"That's true," he agreed. "And Frau Captain isn't exactly a spring chicken any longer, if I may say so. It's a shame Herr Captain didn't live to bring up his boys."

I thought so myself. Sometimes I was very homesick for Captain Tillmann, and once I dreamed of him, but he wore John Sprague's raccoon coat. Michael had built a little shrine of worship for his dead father. There was a faded photo, the iron cross, the sword and the belt, and he held silent hours of reverence before them. "Like a Chinese, like a heathen," said Martin, and the fight was on. Then I caught my problem child having secret meetings with his uncle Hellmuth, and we had a very serious talk about it.

"You know that I can stand anything but lies and secrets," I told him.

"You will be glad if uncle Hellmuth will save you when the day comes. You should thank me for keeping in contact with him," Michael replied grandly.

"You're talking like the pompous stupid little boy you are," I shouted. "If your uncle Hellmuth wants to keep contact why doesn't he come to us openly?"

"Because it's dangerous. He is persecuted," Michael said pompously. "The Jews want to kill him."

"It's catching up with me," I told Clara. "The sins of my youth."

"I didn't know you committed any," she said. "What is it about?"

"Michael," I said. "Remember, I told you I think his father was a Jew? Now the child wants to be a Nazi."

Clara grinned amiably at me. "That's just it. How many Jews do you think would like to become Nazis? It fascinates them, it's romantic and theatrical. Like music by Richard Wagner. Well, what are you going to do about it?"

"There is nothing I can do. That's just it."

"Why don't you tell him the truth?"

"Because he wouldn't understand it. Don't forget, he is just eleven. Besides—I am not sure what the truth is."

"Or maybe you are a little coward, baby."

"Yes. Maybe. I'm afraid—it would break him. He is not very well balanced anyway. I'll talk it over with him when he is old enough."

Clara scrutinized me and gave a sigh. "You don't look your best," she said. "Sort of oldish like."

"Pulke informed me so last Sunday. Well, I am not so young, am I?"

"It's not that we are not young. It's that we have lived so much," Clara said. "How about having some fun for a cosmetic. They say love will do wonders for your complexion."

"Love," I said with contempt. "I haven't been in love for ages. Not even for one single evening."

"Yes, I know. Not since you came back from Russia. Could it have anything to do with that big American you met there?"

It had never occurred to me, and I pondered the question seriously. "No," I answered sincerely. "It has nothing to do with him. Except—except, maybe, that I use him as a sort of yardstick. I didn't notice it, but now that you ask me—I measure men by him and they all seem somewhat skimpy in comparison. And dull too. He has so much life. I guess it's because he's an American. Their springs haven't gone slack like ours over here."

"Hm——" was all Clara said.

Late one evening the telephone rang: long distance call from

London. I hadn't heard from John Sprague for many months. My knees went wobbly again.

"Hello—may I talk to Frau Marion Sommer?"

"I am speaking, John. How are you, John?"

"Fine. How are you yourself, maker of toys? Still traveling alone?"

"Yes. Oh yes."

"That's good. How about hopping over to London for the week end?"

"I don't know—I don't think it is possible—really——"

"Why not?"

"I have no leave of absence—and I am broke for one thing——"

I had taken lessons in English from an American girl in the meantime and was proud of my slang.

"Broke—as who isn't! Can't we put it on the expense account? Please, Marion, come."

"But really, John——"

"Look here: I am the man with the gas bill. I told you I would cash in some day. Remember? You promised you would help me whenever I was in some fix?"

"Are you, John?"

The telephone was breathing hard a few hundred miles away.

"Yes. I think I am."

"What is it, John?"

"Oh, this and that. We are having a depression among other things—I don't know if you've heard about it——"

"Certainly. We have it too."

"And also—my wife died."

I stood frozen, with the receiver in my hand, and didn't know what to say.

"Oh John. How did it happen——"

"Automobile accident. I can't talk about it over the telephone. But I do want to talk to you. Are you coming?"

Of course I was coming. I had saved some money for a new car. But if I kept Old Whooping Cough for another year I could afford this trip. I had my eyebrows plucked in frantic haste and my hair set; I had a tussle with Herr Eichheimer; and on a foggy April morning I went ashore in Southampton.

I hadn't seen John for more than two years, and he looked quite differently from the man I remembered. Either my memory had tricked me and glorified him or he had changed a lot. He was tall, but a little stooped. His hair was of a dull, listless gray as he stood there with his hat in his hand, searching the gangway with a bewildered expression on his face, and his skin had become too large for him and hung in loose folds.

"Hello, maker of tools," I said. I had prepared myself to say it. It seemed bright and witty to me and friendly too, though not too emotional. With all the slang I had studied I still felt that I could not express myself as easily and amusingly as Americans did. In all these years I've never overcome this feeling. As if we Europeans were made of lead while they consist of a much lighter, more buoyant, resilient substance.

"Hello, maker of toys," he said. He came down from his height and kissed my cheek, which was wet with mist. There was an odor around him that I did not know then but which I learned to know rather thoroughly; the morning smell after a night spent in the company of a whisky bottle. His eyes were bloodshot, with little bags underneath, and his hand was not quite steady. But then neither was mine.

"It's sweet of you to have come," he said. "I didn't believe it until I saw you walk down that gangplank."

"I am glad you forced me out of my routine. I needed a little change anyway," I said. He took my elbow and we went over to the train, both rather embarrassed. John installed me behind a little table in the compartment and ordered breakfast. Our conversation consisted of nothing and ran aground every few minutes. We were very close friends—or why would he have called for me?—and at the same time we were complete strangers. "Remember the toilets at the Metropole," we said, and "Do you ever in your life want to eat caviar again after Moscow?" and "Wonder how their five-year plan is going to work." I asked how business was and he said lousy and I said so was mine. And he asked had I been in London before and I said only twice. And then we just sat and looked out of the window until we arrived at Waterloo Station.

John had taken for me a two-room suite at the Savoy; his own room was on another floor, which I thought rather tactful. I was dazzled by the elegance of my living room, satin draperies and a fireplace with a pleated paper fan in it, and a bunch of very beautiful, flaming tulips in a vase on the table. John seemed very concerned about pleasing me. He told me to take a rest after the bumpy crossing, while he had to see the boys. There was always an anonymous bunch of boys romping about in the background of his life. This time they were the men who worked in the London offices of Sprague. Before he left he bent down again and I thought he would kiss my cheek once more, but he lifted my hand instead and kissed it. It didn't make any impression on me at all because I came from a hand-kissing race, but I found out about a year later that it meant a lot to him.

"Thanks, Marion," he said at the door. "I'm glad you came."

I was left alone, wondering why he had chased me all the way to London and whether I was crazy or he was. We had lunch, we had dinner, we went to a show, we had a nightcap in the lobby of the hotel. John said good night to me at the door of my rooms and kissed my hand. "I guess you'll want to have breakfast in bed," he said, and I said: "No, thanks, breakfast in bed is one of the things I've hated all my life." We met for breakfast downstairs and then we went to the zoo and looked at the young bears and at an expressionistic ape with a blue nose and a purple behind. The day went by with a lot of small talk, and in the afternoon I packed my things to catch the night boat, still wondering what the hell I had come for. We had tea in my sitting room and John mixed himself what he called a highball and I felt like a complete fool.

"Look here, John," I said. "Why did you ask me to come to London? I thought you wanted to tell me something."

He looked at me with his eyes of a sick dog. "I guess I was crazy when I called you up," he said. "It was after a few drinks with the boys and it seemed the most natural thing to do."

"Well now I am here," I said. "And tonight I'll be gone."

He emptied his glass, poured himself another one, and sagged a bit in his chair. "It's sort of hard to talk about it, but I thought if I get it off my chest I might feel better," he said. "Marion,

please, don't leave me alone now. Stay another night. I have
to get my steam up first."

"Is it—is it about your wife's accident?" I asked, groping my
way.

"Yes. That's what I wanted to tell you, but damn it, it's not
so easy. You know, back in New York I ran across a magazine
article about you, with pictures of you and your boys and the
toys you are making. I didn't realize you were famous, you
seemed such a kid! I was very proud of you. Look, that's Marion,
I thought. Maybe if I talk to her it'll clear up some of those
things I can't get straight myself. She's a swell kid. I cut that
clipping from the magazine, I must have it somewhere. I'll show
it to you, I think it was in Vanity Fair——"

"Well, John——" I said, not knowing what to make of it all.

"Let me exchange your ticket; you can take the morning
plane and be home in the afternoon. What do you say?" he
suggested, getting into a frantic spell of activity. After much
telephoning and rearranging we had dinner in my room and
he still had not told me about his wife's accident. I watched him
drink and come to life. My girl, I told myself, this is becoming
a taut situation. I did not understand the first thing about it.
The men I had known on the continent did not drink like the
Americans. I suppose theirs is a different chemistry. I did not
know that many Americans need drinking in order to be able
to dance or to be brilliant or to clinch a deal or to make love
or even to talk about themselves. In order to overcome their in-
born shyness and humility and their inferiority complexes. In order to endure unhappiness, disappointment, desperation, and
several other varieties of human misery. Neither did I know
anything about the mute and lonely and valiantly desperate fight
against drinking and the smarting victory called: Thanks, I'm on
the wagon. . . .

We sat there, not two people but two continents, with an ocean
of miscomprehension between us. It took me years of living with
him before I grasped that John Sprague in the evening, after a
good dose of alcohol, and John Sprague in the morning, sobered
up and full of Alka-Seltzer, were two entirely different men.

"I told you that Sheila died in an automobile accident," he began late that evening when he had his steam up. "But I didn't tell you how it happened. There are lots of things I can't understand. That's why I thought I wanted to talk it over with you. I can't talk about it with the boys, see. Though I daresay there is not a sordid detail they haven't read in the papers and there is not a club or a speakeasy in New York where it hasn't been the juiciest bit of gossip they had in a long time. That's the worst of it—all that publicity. You're different from the girls in my own set. I couldn't discuss Sheila with them. They are bitches, most of them. You know, I don't know much about women. We Americans are not sophisticated like your European men. Maybe you'll think it funny, but I had never anything to do with any girl but Sheila. That is, only a bit of necking while I was at college, before I knew her. And once during the War I spent a night with a French girl. Well, I guess that doesn't count. But all the time that we were married I never so much as looked at another girl. Maybe I should have. All I thought of was to keep her happy, give her whatever she wanted. You should have seen the emerald ring I gave her for our tenth anniversary. Well, I've never seen a more perfect lady than Sheila. Poised, quiet, smart, not a hair out of place. Now I'll tell you how it happened. She had gone down to Miami with some friends of ours, as far as I knew. Then one night the police called me up on Long Island to tell me that she had been in a collision. I took a plane; she was still alive; she looked horrible, and she never came to. Here is what happened. She had been at the Lagoon. It was a pretty bad place, a joint with a nude floor show downstairs and gambling upstairs, sort of a gangster hangout. She had been there with a playboy who has a very bad reputation, and they told me that everyone knew he had been her lover. Everyone but me of course. On the way home their car had collided with an oil truck. The truck driver lost both his legs. A kid he had with him, a hitchhiker, was killed. That playboy I spoke about got well though, thank you. What made it so nasty was that they both had been senselessly drunk when it happened. They had won huge money at the Lagoon. Sheila's purse had sprung open and hundred-dollar bills were scattered all over the road. It was a golden mesh purse, I had given it to her for a Christmas present. That drunken scoundrel's pocket too was full of money, right along with his hip flask. I am a proud guy in my own way, Marion. There has never been anything people could hang on to the name of Sprague. And then that scandal! There were bottles in the car, all smashed of course, puddles of alcohol on the road, and the hundred-dollar bills soaked with gin and blood. Great mercy, I don't know how I lived through it all. The headlines. The way people look at you. And the boy, Junior. He's fifteen. What do you think he must have felt like when he read those stories in the papers about his own mother? I sent him to a school in Wyoming, as far off as possible, but still——

"I've tried to wipe her out of my memory. I've told myself that the woman I adored was not the woman I was married to. Just a figment. Wishful thinking, that's all it was. But, great God, you can't wipe out sixteen years of your life. I remember her as she was when I met her: She wore a white dress, one of those fluffy affairs; you have never seen a more angel-like creature. And our honeymoon and later, when the boy was born, she was so sweet and childlike. I can't understand it. Sometimes I think I'll go crazy. When did she start to lie and to cheat and to change? Why didn't I notice anything? And, Marion, tell me, what mistakes did I make? She was my wife, after all. I must be responsible for whatever went wrong with her, mustn't I? If I hadn't let her down in some respect, I don't know when and how, maybe she wouldn't have let me down either. Maybe she wouldn't have had to end up like that, as a dirty headline in the yellow sheets——"

He reached with his unsteady hand for the bottle and poured himself another glass of straight whisky. "I always need a few drinks before I can go to sleep——" he muttered apologetically, and then he held out his hand over the side of his low chair like a man groping in the dark and I gave him mine to hold on to. From the heap of human debris I tried to sort out some un-damaged pieces and some bright little scraps and rags. He seemed so pathetically innocent about the complexity of all relations be-tween men and women that I didn't know how to start consoling him. I think I talked a lot of commonplace trash, but it seemed to do him good. Or maybe he had come to me only for some animal warmth, to hold a woman's hand, to hear a woman's voice. Poor John, I thought, I can't mend your broken pride in one night. It would take a lifetime.

I WENT TO NEW YORK early that fall, after Eichheimer & Co. had given up the manufacturing of toys, and I joined the brigade of unemployed. There was a general feeling of breaking camp in the air all over Berlin. The house where we lived was auctioned off, after the owners had died one by one and the heirs had paid neither mortgage nor taxes. I stored my furniture, dismissed my Fräulein Household Assistant Bieber, boarded the boys with Clara, and sold Old Whooping Cough, and with the money I bought myself a tourist round-trip ticket for the United States. I had a very thin and threadbare alibi: a small selection of my wood carvings was to be exhibited in New York; I might get some publicity, I told myself, and, on the strength of it, even a job. But in the back of my mind I knew that I really went out on a live-saving expedition. We women are fiends about saving lives, and I had never had as attractive and worth while a broken doll as John Sprague.

I was headed for a surprise. True, there were still the fumes of yesterday's whisky around him, as he bent down to kiss my cheek, but he was a changed man again. Straighter, more buoyant, a bit surer of himself.

"John, you look swell," I cried, proud of my up-to-date slang.

"You don't look so bad yourself, kid," he told me.

"What have you done? Got a few monkey glands implanted?" (This too was still highly fashionable in 1930.)

"Took up a bit of horseback riding. You like to ride horseback?"

"I never tried."

"Never mind. We'll play golf."

Golf! In Berlin the one and only golf course belonged to a millionaires' club, and it was a most expensive, snobbish, and exclusive sport, totally inaccessible to a simple career girl of my own brand. I felt like a leaden duck in deep water, whereas John Sprague was at home in this strange new world. I stumbled into it, floundered, stubbed my toe, bumped my head; every minute was a muddle of new discoveries and profound misunderstandings. I said and did all the silly things you do when you fall in love with a man as sweepingly, as greedily, as passionately as I was in love with this country. I had never dreamed of a city as beautiful and exciting as New York. I took Vienna, Berlin, Paris, and London and threw them into the ashcan. Here was the new beauty, the fantastic, throbbing, pulsating, streamlined beauty of my own time and age. Here it was Today. Here I was at home at last.

I walked around as in a dream, where everything looks strange and fantastic and yet you know all the time that this is where you belong. I had never noticed how much energy we wasted in Europe in countless little everyday frictions. Between people and people. Between people and rules, conventions, authorities. Between people and obstinate, badly designed objects. Between people and outlived traditions. Here everything seemed so free and easy; life was a well-oiled machine and a soaring song and a fabulous bird on widespread wings. And then, one day, it came to me as a great and blinding revelation. This land was free. These were free people. Freedom. That was it. I felt as if I had dragged chains with me all my life and now at last they fell off and clanked to the prison floor. Freedom was what I had been searching for, ever since my rebellious childhood days when I had wanted to put my head into a lion's mouth. No wonder I felt like coming home after a long voyage full of detours.

How do you like America? everybody asked me. It's swell, I answered.

I have become a pretty good American in the years since— for, while you have to be born English or French or German, you can become American, and that is one of the lovable secrets of this continent—and many of my memories are blurred by later experiences, slackened through habit, but I still remember the sharp delight, the boundless wonder of those first days in the U.S.A.

The sky was bluer, the air was brisker and clearer, the clouds had more silver, and all outlines were more precise than anywhere else. To live in this atmosphere felt like a constant, invigorating massage. You touched a door handle and you felt electricity tingle in your hand. You turned on the tap in your bath and the water itself seemed effervescent.

I went drunk with the abundance around me. The food, the shop windows, the lights, the sights. How rich they are, I thought dizzily, how rich, how rich! A phrase from the Bible repeated itself over and over in my mind, like the refrain of a song. All the kingdoms of the world in a moment of time. That was it: all the kingdoms of the world.

And then the people. I had thought—though hardly admitted it to myself—that John was one of the best looking men I had ever encountered. Here they all looked just as handsome. They looked like men; there was a definite masculine charm about them that our men didn't possess. They were loose in every joint, and behind the ease of their walking, standing, bending, you sensed great reserves of strength and power. I felt my hand itch for the chisel to carve and hold my impressions of those strong, pleasant male creatures. As for the women, they were so beautiful and perfect that I stood gaping. As if some breeder had taken endless selective pains to create them long-legged and exquisitely slim, like fashion plates. They had small hands and feet, shining hair, even teeth, and their skin was as smooth as polished metal. Sex appeal (another fashionable concept) seemed to burst from every one of their movements, openly and unmitigated.

I had crushing hours. I took my bedraggled self-assurance before the mirror and put myself through a severe examination. There I was, dressed in the uniform of the well-groomed European woman: Black suit, Oxford shoes, white kid gloves, a restrained little black hat from Paris. I preened my modest feathers. A sparrow among birds of paradise, that's what I was. Let's see, are there no faults we could find with these perfect beauties? Aren't they dressed a bit too flashy, aren't their voices pitched too high, their smiles fabricated; and what about their jewelry? Ten-cent-store or Tiffany, they had too much of it, dangling from their wrists and necks, covering them to the elbows, even gleaming from their pretty ankles. Only in the Hottentot kraals of Africa had I seen such innocently primitive exhibitionism. Still they were lovely and I couldn't compete with them, could I? So what? I told myself, it all boils down to the fact that they had orange juice and cream and plenty of vitamins at a time when you lived on acorns and sawdust. They became pretty and you became wise. And then I went to the best beauty parlor in town for a five-hour session and had myself made over.

My exhibition in one of the galleries on Fifty-seventh Street was a nice little success that appeared like a big success to me because there was so much noise about it. Interviews, press photographers, invitations. What a funny world this was! I made mistakes all over the place. All around me people talked about things I didn't understand and asked me questions I didn't know how to answer. Everybody spoke first of all about the depression, apologetically and still a trifle stunned. You should have seen this town before the depression. You should have known this family before the depression. What will happen to this country if we don't get over the depression soon? It made me laugh; to me they seemed as grave and concerned as children playing patient and doctor. Babies, I felt like shouting; you babies, what do you know? You and your ridiculous depression! You have never suffered, you complain about your misery while you are in the midst of plenty, you have no perspective at all, you are on the top of a high mountain and you moan about the low altitude.

Their second important topic was drinks. How to get them, what to pay for the case, which speakeasy was the best. I was offered everything, from dry French champagne vintage 1911 to bathtub gin, and although I accepted politely, I couldn't understand the importance of it. Also it seemed a funny sort of freedom that would encroach upon such perfectly private matters as drinking a glass of beer. What vexed me next was the relationship between the sexes. I might spend a whole week end with a crowd and never find out who belonged to whom and who was married to which. They romped and joked, they called one another darling and sweetheart, the girls sat on the men's laps or danced with them in the most erotic fashion; and then they said good night, picked up their indifferent legal partner at the other end of the room, and retired into the respective guest rooms, leaving me completely baffled. I wondered whether they were so innocent or so depraved.

John Sprague's lawyer, a much-traveled wise old gentleman by the name of Mr. Farrar, gave me a little explanation. "The law of the pendulum," he said. "They were puritans up to the war. Then they skipped the stages in between and swung too far to the other side."

I spent most of my week ends on John's place, Elmridge, which was always filled with guests; they brought their tennis rackets along, their golf clubs, their bathing suits, and their eager, twittering gayety. They crowded around John as if to show him that they liked him and did not blame him for his wife's disgraceful exit. He was a pleasant host, took part in every game, laughed about every joke, was as gay as the rest of them and seemed not at all like the mangled man I had met in London. There were only fleeting moments, when I watched him sitting in front of the fireplace, his old cocker spaniel asleep at his feet and the highball glass at his right elbow, that I felt him wrapped up in an impenetrable loneliness. That he was inarticulate and did not seem to be conscious of it made him the more pathetic. He would catch my eyes and come to life. "How about another drink, Marion? No? Want to play ping-pong? How about a little plunge in the pool?" I was crawling along through those week ends like a turtle in a greyhound race. Hard drinks made me sleepy. My tennis was deplorable and my ping-pong not much better. I had never had time to learn bridge, and back-gammon bored me to tears. I still swam breast stroke, as I had been taught in old Vienna, and felt as dated as last year's coffee. My talk was not snappy and my comebacks had no punch. I could not even make John laugh let alone make him forget. The only thing I could have done was go over to him, stroke his fore-head, ask him: Are you tired, my pal? Sad? Lonely? Do you want to talk to me about the woman you still love? I am fond of you and—my friend—I have gone through a lot and understand many things. I tried it only once. "You are a bit lonely, aren't you, John?" I asked him. He looked at me, faint surprise in his eyes, rather amused.

"Lonely? With sixteen week-end guests? What do you mean?" he said. "Aren't they making enough of a racket for you?"

I was Europe and he was America and there was an ocean between us. John would empty his glass, look at the bottle, pour himself a quick jigger straight, and would walk out onto the terrace, to join the others, who had called for him. A second later there was a burst of laughter, and he was laughing the loudest. I would slink upstairs into my guest room and lie down on my bed. I wonder how Stanley felt when he finally found Livingstone and discovered that the doctor did not want to be rescued, I thought bitterly. You don't need me to save your life, Mr. Sprague, I presume. All right, Marion. Your six weeks are almost over. Pack your things; go back to Berlin and scramble for a job. Now you've been in America. It's a swell country. People are swell. Everything is swell. Except that no one needs you over here.

One evening my old friend Mr. Farrar sidled up to me. "I'm rooting for you," he said with a friendly chuckle under his white mustache.

"You're what, Mr. Farrar?"

"Rooting, you know. Betting on you. You are my little dark horse and I bet you'll win the race in the last stretch."

"I didn't know I was in a race," I said.

"That's just it," he said. "Listen, Marion, did you ever watch the sea gulls when the ship's cook pours the garbage from the porthole? Well, just look at the girls. Just as shrill. Just as greedy. Only John is no garbage; he is the prize catch of the season and, mark my word, you'll get him."

"I have no competitive spirit like the American girls," I said. "And I don't feel equipped to enter the Grand National. You must have seen too many movies in which the old horse from the milk cart is rushed into the race and wins."

"But you do like John," Mr. Farrar said.

"Yes," I answered much too sincerely, "I do like John."

My boat was to leave on Saturday. On Thursday John called me up. "How about coming out for dinner tonight? I can take you back to town tomorrow morning on my way to the office."

"Who else is coming?" I asked.

"Nobody. Just you and me. Okay? Okay. I'll pick you up around five."

It was raining when he came, but shortly after we had crossed the Queensborough Bridge it stopped and a rainbow stepped out from behind the trees and clasped the sky to the shining road. It was the first time that we were alone in all those weeks, and we had a quiet, lovely drive. I played a little game with myself, betting if I could recognize the road marks by now and find my way. Well, what good would it do me to know my way on Long Island when I was back in Berlin?

"Why are you so quiet, kid?"

"Oh, you know me. Rancid with sentimentality. Sorry for myself and all that."

"Sorry about what?"

"Oh—you know. I'm saying good-by to every gasoline station and hot-dog stand on the way. I always squeezed the last drop out of farewells, even as a little girl."

"But you are coming back," he said, cutting a curve, and then we were on the open road. The rainbow was gone and the evening closed swiftly in on us.

"If you don't come back I'll come over and get you," he said a long while later.

We arrived in the big house, which seemed very still and empty without guests. John turned on the radio and Lindquist, the butler, brought in the drinks. We had our dinner served on a little table in front of the fireplace in the maple room. I thought that Sheila must have had very good taste. I liked this one best, with its early American furniture and hobnail glasses. Topper, the old spaniel, kept us company, and after a while he came over and put his head on my knee. I felt honored, as you always do when someone else's dog seems to like you. "He likes you," John said. "The choosey old fellow." I patted his head and John patted it too, and then our hands met on the warm, fine coat of the old dog. John spread his out, palm up, and I put mine into his. The smoke of our two cigarettes spiraled to the ceiling and the fire held its breath for a moment to listen how still it was.

"I'm glad you could come tonight. I wanted to have you to myself, at least once, and the hell with all your admirers."

"I didn't know I had any."

"Sure. You're the toast of the town. Everybody is crazy about you."

"It's much nicer to be alone with you. I'm no shining light in a week-end crowd. Why didn't you ask me for dinner like this before?"

"I didn't want to get you into any gossip. I wouldn't have stood for it," he said. I did not know what to make of it. "Come, let's go out on the terrace for a moment, there's a moon coming out behind the clouds," he said, getting up. I noticed that he had drunk some wine with the dinner but no whisky afterward. "It'll be a bit chilly outside, but I'll bundle you up," he said.

"Do you still have your fur coat?" I asked him when he came back from the hall with some coats.

"The old raccoon I had in Moscow? That relic? Yes, I guess it's still somewhere around. Why?"

"Oh, for no reason. I always liked it."

"Then I'll ask Lindquist to take good care of it and put moth-balls into the pockets."

The moon was up, playing a tremolo on a silver string across the Sound. The air was fresh and moist and smelled of freshly dug-up earth.

"I must tell the gardner to put some snail poison out," John said. Then he took me and turned me toward him and bent down to me. He searched in the dark and kissed first my hair and then my cheeks and at last my mouth. He did it so quietly that it made not even a ripple in the tranquillity of the night.

"But why?" I asked him, astounded.

"Just so," he said. "Because we belong to the same generation."

It was one of those surprising answers when, in a flash, I realized how much more insight he had than he usually let me guess. Everything was in his answer—understanding and ex-perience, companionship, a little pity for ourselves, and a dash of humorous self-irony. I found it often, that Americans were thinking in short cuts while my mind was still crawling along the old cow paths.

"You are clever, aren't you?" I said.

"Clever? No. I'm just feeling good. Maybe you don't know how much good it has done me to have you around."

"I'm glad about it. I like to be—what do you call it?—your pal."

"Tell me," he said as we turned back toward the house, which stood still and expectant in the night with the warm yellow light of its french windows. "Tell me, do you like it here?"

"Oh yes. It's swell," I said.

"Think you would like to live here?"

"Sure. It's lovely," I said lightheartedly. John studied my face for a moment and gave a sigh.

"Sometimes I wonder if you really understand English," he said. "I meant: Would you like to live here?"

I caught my breath. For a second I was on a fast merry-go-round with my life revolving past me in dizzy streaks. The boys. Michael. Martin. My work. My profession. My career. My past, all of it. My future. My independence. Michael again. And there was this house with Sheila's shadow in the fold of every drapery and a man with gray hair of whom I was very fond and whom I hardly knew. . . .

"I don't know, John," I said. "I'll never learn to play backgammon."

ARION PASSED three different stages during the time it took the sun to creep up another two inches toward the rim. The first stage was all courage and action and great hope and rational thinking. This is too silly, Marion thought. I can't just sit here and wait and let things happen. I never did things that way, did I? I'm not the passive type. I'll just have to get out of here, broken ankle or not. How do you think wounded men survive in the war? Not by just giving up. Remember the pictures you saw of the men returning from Dunkirk? They had worse things than a puny broken ankle. Never be scared. Nothing can happen to you. All right, Marion, let's go!

The ankle had begun to swell, and she did not need to lace her shoe tighter for support. She got up, slipped her arms into the straps of her rucksack, and shoved herself along the side of the crevasse toward a place she had chosen as a starting point for climbing out. By now the crevasse had lost much of its weird and frightening aspect. Marion had made herself familiar with it and was not afraid any more. She tried to keep her weight off the broken leg and concentrate all her strength in her hands and arms, using her knees to stem herself against the ice, her chin even to pull herself up. If she had any pains she did not feel them, or maybe the cold helped to numb the sensation. She heard her own strenuous breathing and it rather reassured her. I'm a good old machine, she thought appreciatively, almost as good a machine as the ones Sprague's used to build. Now if this little peak of blue diamonds will hold——

It did not hold. Marion had climbed about six feet of the ten or twelve she needed—for the distance to the edge of the crevasse had proved a bit more than she had calculated—when the peak broke. Instinctively she angled for some hold with the broken leg, but it folded up under her; that's at least how it felt—like one of those deck chairs that fold up under you if you don't put them up correctly. Spouting a good, rich flood of curses, Marion slid down a second time and landed, not unpleasantly, somewhat lower down than where she had crouched before. The advantage of this place was that there was more room, an almost comfortable little cave in the ice, with a flat floor at least six feet wide.

And that's that, Marion thought after she had caught herself. If I try a few more times I can be sure to break my neck too.

It was then that she passed through the second stage, and among the samples of infernos whose acquaintance Marion had made in her life so far, this was the worst one. It began as a chill and grew into a convulsion that shook her shoulders and pressed the breath from her chest. It was panic, pure and unmitigated. I don't want to die, Marion cried, I don't want to die, please, please, help, help, help! I don't want to die, come and help me, Chris, Michael, John, Martin, help! Mama, please help me, Mama——

It left her spent and hoarse from calling and shouting, covered with cold sweat, which felt like sleet on her back. Come, come, let's be rational about this, she told herself. This won't do, my girl, this won't do at all. To live halfway decently is simple. But to die decently is the one test that really counts. Yes, but life is lovely and I love to live. All right, Marion. How do you know that death won't be a hundred times lovelier? Maybe to be alive is only a narrow little prison and the great freedom lies outside, in not being alive. Remember what Max Wilde told about the jubilation and frenzy they work up on some faraway island about their dead? They burn their bodies and put the ashes into coconut shells and stick candles into them and let them float out into the ocean; and they believe that those freed souls are happy beyond human happiness. Marion could see the little flames float away into the distance; it was a lovely sight and stopped her from trembling. Her own soul sailed away to new horizons, sheltered in some shell as between folded hands, safe and calm. She blinked a few times to chase the friendly vision off, because this was no time for daydreaming. Let's think this through to the end. Is there much sense in life? Not much sense, except the sense to live. There are many people who keep on thinking they are alive long after their life is spent. I wouldn't like to be one of them. In a way this may be the right and ordained moment for me to take my exit. My job is done, Michael is well, and soon Renate will take him over. All my men have gone ahead, and Christopher is going too. I don't know if it will be much fun to live through the next few years. Oh yes it will. To live is fun, whatever happens. Remember Olga Wasmuth?

Olga Wasmuth had been a prostitute in Giessheim, and Marion had written down her case history like many others. It had made a fleeting impression on her at the time, and then she had forgotten Olga Wasmuth completely. Now, all of a sudden, that cursed decrepit creature put in an appearance down in that cold crevasse. Look at the things I have stored away in the purple bag of my unconscious mind—Marion thought with a surprised smile.

These were the regular questions she had asked Olga Wasmuth, and these were the answers:

When did you have your first sexual intercourse?

When I was twelve.

Did you like the man?

No, he was my stepfather. He raped me.

Did you have children?

Yes, three. The first one when I was fifteen. They're all dead.

Did you have many sweethearts when you were young, before you became a prostitute?

Yes, many.

Did you enjoy making love with them?

No, never.

Were you ever married?

Yes, twice. My first husband beat me and the second was a drunkard. I hated both of them.

Ever had anything to do with girls?

Yes, we all do in those houses.

Did you get any satisfaction out of it?

None whatsoever.

Do you drink a lot?

If I can afford it.

Does alcohol give you a lift?

Not at all. Just makes me sick after a while.

Ever used any drugs?

Of course. Cocaine. Heroin. Whatever I could get.

Did that satisfy you or make you happy?

Not that I know.

Marion had written down that history point by point. She remembered the hospital ward where she had visited Olga, who was not young any more, and sick in every organ of her wasted body. She had shuddered a bit when this picture of utter squalor and misery and vice and numb passivity had unfolded itself. She had hesitated to ask the last question, which had to be filled in on the form:

What do you think about life in general?

"Life?" Olga had said, sitting up in bed. "Life? Why—life is wonderful."

Marion chuckled as she remembered it. Sure, Olga, you're right, she thought. Life is wonderful—and full of surprises. It's full of good, timid, little things that no war and no eclipse can take away. A book, a fiddle, a flower, a glass, a piece of wood. The tiny slipper of a baby. The new hat. Even the cigarette stub someone we love has left on the ashtray. Difficulties are good too; they are among the best things I know. All my life I had to have at least one joy and one difficulty each day or I wouldn't have felt alive. True, sometimes the joys and the difficulties got somewhat out of proportion, the difficulty consisting of losing a husband or having a child given up by the doctor, and the joy not more than a bed to sleep in or a hot bath.

My bed, Marion thought longingly, my good, faithful bed, warm and soft and ready night after night to make me sleep and forget. Thank you, my dear bed, best of friends, place of peace and of ecstasy, for giving birth and for dying. It wasn't in my schedule that we shouldn't be together in my last hour, you, my bed, and I. Well, never mind, I'm not dead yet; in fact I'm very much alive and I'm feeling fine, thank you. A hot bath. Who said a hot bath was a small joy? If I had the choice now between being in the cold with Christopher and being alone with a hot bath, good, soft, fragrant hot bath, I would take the bath. I would stretch in it and melt my frozen fanny and watch tiny air bubbles cling to my skin and raise to the surface; I would let the hot water run and steam myself like a Japanese fanatic. I'd give everything, but I mean everything, for a hot bath just now.

Thinking of her bed and her bath kept Marion warm for a few minutes, and then she was back in her cold crevasse again. All right, she thought, at peace now and almost cheerful. No bath then. We still have cigarettes. We still have chocolate. We have just what we always wanted: a joy and a difficulty. She first ate the chocolate, chewing it slowly and deliberately, to derive the greatest possible amount of pleasure from it. Then she lighted her cigarette and swallowed a few chunks of smoke. After a while she began to try blowing smoke rings. It was an art she had wanted to learn all her life, but she had never been patient enough. I learned to yodel today, why not to blow nice neat smoke rings, she thought. She rounded her cheeks and knocked the smoke from them with her finger. It came in white little balls but not in rings. Marion concentrated hard. She felt much better. She had not given up yet, not by a long way.

I WAS married to John Sprague and John was married to the Dinkley Pneumatic Water Drill! It was a typical ménage à trois, American version. On the whole I liked Dinky, though I was often jealous of her. Dinky, on the other hand, had hardly any reason to be jealous of me, for, although she influenced every phase of my life, I never had anything to do with that part of my husband that was entirely devoted to her. You can fight another woman but you can't fight a thirty-horsepower machine with a Diesel motor. Dinky sucked the last drop of pep out of my husband. No mistress could have been so strenuous, so inconsiderate, so exacting, or so expensive as Dinky was. I suppose most married women in the U.S.A. have some sort of a Dinky to cope with. Men are eternally in love with their insurance companies or their dry-goods shop or their hardware store or their lawyer's office or their workbench.

Dinky went to bed with us and joined us at breakfast. She sat down for dinner with us and she broke into our quietest hours with telephone conversations, wires, and urgent cables. John's every mood depended upon Dinky's whimsies. Sometimes John would have the blues about her, and even my best jokes and capers would only get me a preoccupied smile from him. Sometimes he would bring a brief case full of calculations and statistics into bed and prop himself up in his pillows for a few hours of good work. I would get tucked in with an absent-minded kiss and a pat. I would hear the sheets rustle as he turned one page after the other, and I would feel locked out. Hard as I tried, I never learned to understand the intricacies of constructing and selling Dinky.

"—you see, kid, the basic difference between a percussion drill and a pneumatic drill is the same as between an ax and a chisel and a hammer. Now don't you think it would seem more logical to dig your way through rock by means of a chisel and a hammer than with a battle ax——?"

"Yessir," I would say from my abyss of uncomprehension. But essentially John did not even care for my sharing of his troubles. My conception of a good marriage and his were different. I had dreamed in great seriousness of being his pal and companion. I felt like someone diving into a pool, trusting it to be deep, and finding it a shallow affair indeed. I came up with bumps on my head and a slight concussion. All John wanted me to be was another Sheila. A lady with not a hair out of place, an asset to show off to his friends, a sort of a one-woman harem, ready and willing to entertain him and ask no questions.

"How's Dinky doing, John?"

"Oh, she's okay. As soon as this matter of our patent is

straightened out we'll go to town with her. Now be a good girl and take your shut-eye."

"Well—good night, John. Don't work too long."

But he would not hear me any more, and after a while I would fall asleep, feeling left out of the main part of his life. Sometimes, again he would crush me, smash me, burn me to cinders in a blast of passion. At first this made me quite happy, until I found out that it was a bad sign. Something had gone wrong with Dinky, and John's kisses meant flight and escape and wanting to forget Dinky, if only for the short moments of our embrace. To keep a marriage happy means persistent work and some talent and, above all, an endless amount of tact. It's a full-time job, and I was glad that I had held jobs before. Sometimes I remembered what Clara had told me. "Baby," she had said to me, "if wedded wives would just take as much trouble and be as tactful about certain things and put on as much of an act as every three-dollar whore, there would be fewer broken-up marriages and divorce cases in court."

Depending upon Dinky made life a perpetual roller coaster. Up and down and up again. The little drop and the big drop, and every minute the mixed feeling of elation and danger and the great sweep and the little nausea. Of course Sprague's manu-factured other things too: grinders, jack hammers, riveting ham-mers, and other incomprehensible contraptions, all on the pneu-matic side. But Dinky's pneumatic water drill was the star of the Sprague outfit; she was our livelihood, she was the apple of John's eye, and she gave bread and work to about 400 men. During the time when John stubbornly followed up his dream and had his staff experiment with a new huge Dinky who would be driven by her own motor like a tank, there was a lot of trouble, and John needed great quantities of whisky to lubricate his mind. When it looked like a successful innovation and he had presented Dinky with a few new patents, there came a few good weeks and John was down to one or two highballs a night. He would take time for playing golf, for romping with my boys, for looking at the garden and taking me to see the new shows. He almost went on the wagon, almost took a vacation, almost sailed for Hawaii with me. Only just then it so happened that he had to go to Utah to sell Dinky to the Bingwood Copper Mining Company people. After he had sold well, he bought me a ring with a big diamond. I detested the coldly flashing thing and felt like sitting on my hands as I had done in my childhood to hide my dirty fingernails. When, a year later, the deal with the Sonoma Valley Project fell through, John's hair turned a bit grayer and, quietly, he gave up his two horses.

I made Dinky's personal acquaintance shortly after our wedding, when John took me to the Sprague's factory in Albany to introduce me to her. She was a big, handsome and overpowering creature, slick with oiled bearings and more wheels than I had ever seen on anything, but she scared me out of my wits. All my life I have been rather frightened by anything mechanical. I would be less afraid of an untamed gorilla than I am of a simple telephone. But then, no gorilla has ever done me any harm while the telephone has lashed out at me at various occasions, shouting bad news and harsh words at me from its inhuman, gaping black mouth, so that I still feel the scars when the weather gets bad. John beamed with pride as if he were the father of quintuplets and a bunch of his boys stood around us and grinned at me with the leniency of technical wizards for the ignorant little woman. Suddenly John made a grab under Dinky's skirts and she began to move, giving a shriek of steel, that sounded as if an ill-mannered giant would scratch his plate with his fork.

"How do you like her, kid?"

"Oh—I think she is wonderful—and so big, isn't she?" I said, knowing at first sight that we could never be friends, Dinky and I. Cautiously I patted what I supposed to be her shoulder. I would have liked to feed her sugar lumps as I did to John's horses. "Now be a good girl and run along," I was told. "Beecher, why don't you take Mrs. Sprague around and show her the plant while I look into those new blueprints."

Beecher was a boy with damp hands and eager eyes and he showed me the plant. There were hundreds of cars parked outside. There were hundreds of milk bottles stacked up for the workers' lunch hour. There were flowers on the tables in the commissary and it did not smell of yesterday's cabbage. There was a counter with malted milk and ice cream and fruit juices. There were huge windows everywhere and the workers had as much fresh air and light and comfort for their work as possible. The girls in the packing rooms wore bright, becoming uniforms. There was a dentist's office and a shower room and on the roof an outdoor gym. Look here, my girl, I kept on telling myself, this is no Giessheim. This is no dark, dismal Eichheimer & Co. dump. This is the Promised Land, undiluted. In the old days in F 12 we had sometimes wondered why the United States had no real militant socialism. Now it came to me in a flash. You have to suffer before you want to fight; revolutions don't grow from theories but only from blood and sweat and bitter tears. These workers had not suffered. It was the first thing you noticed everywhere in America: this people did not know real sufferings like other, more mature nations.

"How do you like it here, comrade?" John asked when he joined me, a bit disheveled and out of breath.

"I like it. I think it's grand, John."

"You should have seen it before the depression, kid——" He sighed. That's what they all said all the time. They simply didn't know how rich they were and how poor one could be. John perked up. "You know what I'll do if we get that Turkish contract? I'll put in a plunge and a tennis court for their sports club; sort of a wedding present from you to them. How would you like that?"

"Yes, John, thanks. I couldn't think of anything nicer."

A shadow, dear and unforgotten stepped out from the dark and walked along at my side: "It is up to us to create the new economic order—Masters and slaves—Capitalists and workers—Oppressors and oppressed——" Walter Brandt spoke, soundlessly, as ghosts speak out of the past. I took John's arm and gave it a little squeeze. So now I was the wife of a capitalist. Not for the life of me could I think of John as an oppressor.

Like distant lightning, Dinky's name had flickered across my horizon as far back as Moscow. At that time he had sold twenty-four to the Soviet government, and he had hoped to sell them more for their five-year plan. He even went there a second time, but he would not take me along. Wherever a country would wake up, stretch, and yawn, and begin to modernize, to industrialize, to build new settlements, John would be among the first ones on the spot.

"How about a little hop to Ankara, kid? How about a little hop to Helsinki? How about a little hop to Nanking?"

I would pack my things and be off for a little hop, happy as a lark. I took my portable typewriter along, and John could never get over his delight that I was capable of doing service as his secretary. "Take a letter, Miss Crump," he would say. "How are your sniffles today, Miss Crump? Now how would you say we have to address Mr. Soong? Your Excellency? Dear Son of Heaven? Or plain Mr. Soong?"

Miss Crump was another tiny wrinkle in my life, a bit uncomfortable as most private secretaries are in the lives of most wives. She was oldish and looked as if she had never been young. She was despotic and possessive and Knew Everything Better. She had a chronic head cold and always gave the impression of just coming out of a good crying jag. All the tributes of flattery, aspirin, chocolate candy, and asking her for advice that I layed at her feet were to no avail. Crump was not to be reconciled with the fact that John had married me instead of a lady that she had picked out for him: a certain Miss Boyd, of the Philadelphia Boyds.

In a sense all the places we went to were more or less like Moscow; there was the same feeling of a beginning, of a laborious dawn. The streets were the same jumble of beautiful ancient buildings and dirty, crooked lanes and high new structures made of steel and concrete and glass. The people seemed the same, grave and proud under their load of a new ideology, impoverished, keyed up and working hard on being reformed. In the hotels you met always the same men, a tough and colorful crowd, men of John's kind and grain, watchful, alert, brutal if necessary, coming from the four corners of the world to sell their goods and make their profit. I had been told by some of John's engineers that he was a very fine engineer himself. But I think that he was a salesman at the core of his heart. I never found him more happy, more alive, surer, calmer, more himself, than when he went out to sell. All his knowledge, all his charm and

wit, all his power and personality he compressed into those conferences and when he had succeeded and brought home a contract he did it with the swagger of a conquistador.

Altogether those selling jaunts took us into an immensely
masculine atmosphere, with heavy drinking bouts, endless poker
parties, long-distance calls with the home office at all hours of the
night, with typewriters clattering in every hotel room, and with
a delicately balanced system of rumors and diplomacy, graft and
double-crossing. I often wondered why John would take me
along on those hops: he claimed that I was his mascot and
brought him luck. "I'd never have sold those Dinkleys in Moscow
without you," he told me over and over again. "And look at the
nice contract we clinched with Kemal Pasha. Now don't tell me
that I don't need you."

But I think he needed me to bolster up his self-assurance. His
pride was still a convalescent and had to be nursed and pampered
day and night and given hot poultices and strong injections. The
pride of the male is a fragile article anywhere, but the American
variety of it is as thin and as easily and irreparably damaged as
the bloom on a butterfly wing, I found out.

Twice a year we would get into our car, and drive through the
United States to inspect the contract work our Dinkies were doing
all over the country. To me, this made it John's country, as if it
all belonged to him. I had a faint idea that he was embarrassed to
take me along on such business trips; at least he kept me hidden
from his rugged foremen and crews, tucked away in some hotel or
auto camp. But this was a question on which I was stubborn. I
wanted to see every corner of this, my new country, which I
loved so much, and Dinky was kind enough to take us sometimes
into the most extraordinary places, where no streamlined trains or
airplanes stopped and where the water tank was the center of
the town. I got a taste of the last frontiers as well as of huge industry centers, of Minnesota farms and dreamy Louisiana planta-
tions, of the overwhelming dam constructions in the West and
tight-lipped New England villages; I saw the plains and the
mountains, the highways and the bridges, the mines and the oil
fields, the gardens and the high corn. I saw the smokestacks and
the silos and the canneries and herds of cattle and the small fish-

ing craft and the citrus groves and the universities and the deserts and the lazy yellow giant Mississippi in the South.

"My wife never heard of Columbus," John told his friends. "She's trying her darnedest to discover America."

Discovering America was not an easy task, and I worked hard turning myself into a good American citizen, worthy of being Mrs. John Sprague. In Europe, life had been narrow but deep. Here it was wide though shallow. We had been taught to save and scrimp and scrape and survive. Here, you were not called thrifty but stingy. The country lived on waste, on extravagance, on buying and using up as quickly as possible and throwing away and buying something new. It gave me the same stab, whether I saw bread and butter thrown into the garbage can or whether I found the soil of Oklahoma bled dry and the timber of the mountains in the Northwest ruthlessly slaughtered. The idea of conservation hadn't yet penetrated to this continent. Sometimes I was frightened by the general trend of creating new demands and greater demands all the time. There was a policy of keeping the customers dissatisfied, wanting this and that, in order to keep the money rolling. All around me I watched people working their souls off to make a dollar and then squandering it as easily as if it were dirt. John tried to explain their economical system to me. I understood some of it but it remained alien to me. Still, the more I saw of the United States and its people the more I liked it. My first infatuated flare of passion for my new country burned down to a steady, warming flame, and after a while I was really married to America just as much as I was married to John Sprague.

I remember how bewildered I was when, shortly after my arrival in 1932, the country took a deep slump and there was a lot of hysterical excitement, outweighed by a still bigger lot of common sense (and these two qualities—extreme excitability together with perfect common sense—seem to me the main ingredients of the American character), and a new president was elected. And how delighted and overwhelmed I was when the wild clamor of the campaign didn't end up in a civil war as I had expected—judging from my European experiences—but in a sort of honeymoon. Blue eagles everywhere and We Do Our Part pasted on every car, shop window and outhouse. There was also a beer parade and no more prohibition, which, as far as I could see, meant that people went on drinking as before; maybe a trifle less. Meanwhile, Germany had its Reichtagsbrand and its revolution and I complimented my good old nose, which had smelled the coming disaster and had warned me to take myself and my boys out of that doomed country in time.

When I think of Elmridge I always have the fine scent of burned wood in my nostrils. The fireplace in the maple room where we usually sat in the evenings did not exactly smoke but its draft was not perfect and the smoky smell of our fire lingered in the house. There was also a fireplace in our bedroom and I loved watching the reflection of the glow moving on the ceiling when the lights were turned off and I was not asleep yet. It made me feel small and safe. In spring and fall the wind would howl fiercely around the corner of the house where we slept and the fireplace made it twice as cozy to be at home. I loved our bedroom. I had been stupid to be afraid of Sheila's shadow in its chintz curtains. John had turned over the old bedroom to my boys and had ours installed at the other end of the hall and radically done over in plain modern style. Bleached walnut and red leather and chromium gadgets and mirrored walls, as if to underline the contrast between me and the first Mrs. Sprague.

"Like it, tovarich?"

"Love it. I just hope I won't be too messy a girl for all this shining beauty."

"You can mess around all you want in the little workshop I fixed for you on top of the garage——"

Dear John, thoughtful John, it was good being with you. I'm often homesick for you, though I am glad you died before I fell so stupidly in love with Christopher. But then, if you hadn't died I wouldn't have fallen in love, nor would I have tripped into a cold, green crevasse: no, I would never have gotten myself into a jam again, if you had stayed with me, dear John. . . .

I remember the deep pleasure when a party was over and the last guests were gone, the last high-pitched flurry of voices faded away, the cars rolled down the driveway and the house seemed to breathe and stretch and regain its peaceful every day face while I went around and emptied the ashtrays and Lindquist picked the cocktail glasses off the piano and John took Topper out for his little evening pee.

I loved Elmridge and I was very happy there. The wide sweep of lawn sloping down in front of the terrace and the shadows of clowds gliding across the green. The voice of a morning bird in the elm trees. Rain on my roof. To come home on a winter day and stand with my back to the open fireplace and feel the warmth seep into me. My little workshop on top of the garage, with its smell of wood and paint and turpentine. My herb garden with the brick walk, with dill and sage and rosemary, tarragon, and thyme, a concert of pungent scents. And the west porch, where I brought my cut flowers every morning to arrange them in all the pots and vases. Yes, I think nothing made me feel so rich and happy as going into the garden and cutting flowers. My hands were wet and cold and scratched, the knees of my slacks were wet too, and I could never keep my hair in order. I had to creep under shrubs and through hedges to chase up the one particular flower I wanted. I pressed the whole freshness of the morning between my fingers, charmed by the profusion of shapes and colors and scents piled up on the table in front of me. I would dig into them and feel a tingling, sublime pleasure when I picked up the right flower to match an old hobnail glass or a vase by Lalique or the old pewter jug from the entrance hall. I had found a rather coarse earthenware pitcher for John's desk in the maple room and I liked to arrange some bold splashes of flowers in it. Sunflowers with centers like deep, dark brown carpets, hollyhocks in all shades of naïve purple. Delphinium like a burst of blue skyrockets, and some red geranium for contrast. Silvery green lace of wild oats and a tumble of many-colored ranunculs.

Hunting up new combinations for my husband's desk was my way of showing him how fond I was of him. I wonder if he ever noticed it. Not when things went wrong with Dinky, I am sure.

THERE COMES A TIME when your own life begins to appear less important and the weight shifts to your children. The colors get dimmer, as in the backgrounds of old tapestries. There are lots of things going on in those backgrounds. People hunting, people making love, people harvesting, fighting, or just standing around in a vegetative sort of contemplation. But all this background life forms only a pattern, and the real action is vividly and romantically enacted by the big young figures in the foreground.

You still can be happy, though not as sweepingly, penetratingly, floatingly happy as when you were young. You still can love, though not with the all-excluding, all-consuming love of youth. You still can suffer, but not suffer with the excruciating, insupportable torment of before. And only then, when even the pains have blunter edges, do you know that you are not young any longer. You stop and think. Does it make sense, this vague transitory stage called life? No, not much sense except that there are children. I don't know why having children seems a satisfactory answer to many cosmic questions. Maybe to love is the deepest urge in our nature—and you can always love your own children.

The monkey cage—that's what John called the wing where the three boys were installed, and it certainly was fun to watch them grow into their own form and shape, sharply defined and unchangeable as crystals. John had a good hand at handling boys, and Martin and Michael must have been hungry for a father and a man in the house, for they took possession of John so eagerly. On the other hand it was not quite so easy for me to win Johnnie Sprague's confidence, but after watching me for a few weeks with disdain and distrust he seemed to come to the conclusion that I belonged to his corner of the ring and accepted me as an ally.

Johnnie—John Sprague IV—was a gangling boy of eighteen when I saw him first; he had nice, clear brown eyes, which he kept hidden behind obnoxious hornrimmed eyeglasses, and he had the loud and boisterous manners of a young person who is not sure of himself. Wherever he went he left a track of back issues of the New Masses behind. John picked them up patiently, chuckled, and put them on the shelf with the other magazines. It made Johnnie pretty furious that he could not make his father really angry. "This is a free country," John would tease him. "Everyone is entitled to his convictions. In fact it might be a good idea if you would join the union and start working in the plant. I always maintain you can't be a good communist if you haven't worked hard. You have to learn on your own body how your back aches after eight hours behind the workbench before you can talk about a forty-hour week. Your great-grandfather did, you know."

Johnnie would slink out of the room with the sulking expression I had seen first on that photo in Moscow, and John would keep on chuckling.

"Those young monkeys," he would say. "Aren't they fun? I guess it takes a lot of growing up before you have the courage to be yourself and give up acting. He's still in the polliwog age. He has legs *and* tails and lungs *and* fins and he feels damned uncomfortable being neither fish nor frog. Well, I remember when I was his age I wanted to become as rich as J. P. Morgan and build my own railway. So he wants to be America's little Trotsky. It's a fashion like any other."

The issue between them was that John wanted Johnnie to go to Yale and join his old fraternity, Psi U, and later on take over the plant, whereas Johnnie insisted on going to Columbia and becoming a journalist. That he would write for the leftist press only and hand over the plant to the workers as soon as he would have the power to do so went without saying. "If you want to work your way through college, you have my full consent to study where and what you want," John told him rather reasonably. "But as long as I support you and pay for your upkeep and tuition I feel entitled to have you do things my way. What do you say, Marion?"

"I don't know," I said uncomfortably. "I don't understand the difference between one university and another. Psi U sounds pretty awful to me; like a stamp on cattle. Anyway, I never believed in telling boys what to do. If I can't convince them I give up."

"Ah you—tovarich," John said good-naturedly. "Poor me, all alone in a house full of reds!" He stretched his hand out, palm up, in that characteristic gesture of his and waited smilingly for me to put my hand into his. I liked his hand. It was warm and dry and large and deeply familiar to me in every fold and wrinkle. It was as much of a home to me as I had ever had in my life. "Don't you turn on your public relations charm on me——" I said happily, and for a while we forgot our youngsters.

The next morning, as I was arranging my flowers, Johnnie came strolling into the porch. He picked up some of my sweet peas, played with them, and put them down again. "Mind if I watch you?" he asked.

"On the contrary," I said. "It flatters my exhibitionistic instincts." I took some dogwood branches and stuck them into a big pewter jug. Their pale pink looked lovely against the dull grayish shine of the pewter. Some raindrops had collected in the hollow of the petals. When you looked closely enough you could see a tiny picture mirrored in every drop. The door frame and a milky piece of sky outside and the Japanese maple that grew in front of the porch, fine red leaves on delicate branches. The sweet peas filled the air with their almost too-sweet perfume and there was the cool fragrance of crushed, moist leaves and the bitterness of green wood cut with a sharp knife. There were tulips too, John's favorite flowers, to go on his desk in the maple room. They seemed slightly affected and somewhat over-dressed.

"So that is how it's done," Johnnie said. "I often wondered. Now where does this jug go?"

"On the table in the hall," I said, surprised at his sudden friendliness. He carried it out while I began sorting the tulips. I had an idea that two tendrils of yellow jasmine might take some of the stiffness out of them. Johnnie returned and went on watching my hands.

"Don't they look like subdebs?" I said. "As if their governess had always prodded their backs and said: Watch your posture, dear."

"You know a lot about flowers, don't you?" he said. "I never saw anyone so handy with them as you are."

"That's because I worked in a florist's shop for a living," I said. "It's the professional touch."

"Martin told me you met my father in Moscow. Is that true?" Johnnie said abruptly.

"Yes, why?"

"What did you do there?"

"Oh, I just looked at things. I wanted to know how it was there. I'm a rather curious person, you know."

"That's where I want to go. Moscow. Russia," he said, blowing his cigarette smoke through his nostrils. He seemed to smoke for the benefit of the spectators rather than for his own pleasure.

"You would be disappointed, I'm afraid," I said. "It will take them many years to arrive at the point where America stands today. If they ever get there."

"I won't be disappointed," Johnnie said. "Not me. I have many friends who have been there. They all think what's happening there is so wonderful it makes them sick to look at this country."

I had nothing to say, and Johnnie picked up my scissors and played with them.

"You don't mind that I am a communist," he said and put them down with a clank.

"I suppose I was one myself at your age," I said. "It's all right for young people to be radical."

"Something you said last night was the first decent idea that's ever been expressed in this house," he said heatedly.

"What did I say?" I asked, surprised.

"About production for use and not for profit. That's all we demand—production for use and not for profit. But try and make a man like my father see it. To say it stamps you a criminal in this wonderful free country."

"Now you're exaggerating, Johnnie."

"Oh, am I? What about Sacco and Vanzetti? What about Mooney? What about all the people who were hunted down and put out of the way, so the capitalists and fascists won't be disturbed. But the day will come——"

He embarked on an editorial and I went on arranging my flowers. It's a disease, I thought, and it has spread across the Atlantic. You have to be either a communist or a fascist, as if there were nothing in between. What a dull, boring place the world would be if there were only two kinds of people, and both regimented. But go on, talk, Johnnie, I thought. Get it off your chest, if it makes you feel better. . . .

He tagged after me when I took the pitcher with the tulips and carried it into the maple room. I always cleaned John's desk myself; I suppose it was a remnant of my secretarial days. Johnnie stopped talking as abruptly as he had started and watched my scratchy hands handling the dust rag. "I suppose you would think it not quite loyal to take sides against my father," he said suddenly.

"Oh, Johnnie," I said. "I am not much of a side-taker. Your father has lots of trouble, and I just hope you are not going to make more trouble for him. He is very fond of you."

"In a way I'm fond of the old man too," Johnnie said with the grave fairness of the very young. "I don't say he is wrong. It's the system that's wrong, and he happens to be part of the system. But you could make him see our side of it too."

So now it's our side, I thought, amused. "I'll do my best, Johnnie. Just now is a bad moment to make decisions. Wait till your father comes back from Washington. He's there to get some contract work for his Dinkley drill——"

Johnnie gave a deep sigh, from which I deducted that he too was familiar with Dinky's little moods and tricks. At the door he stopped. "Well, thanks anyway for listening to me," he said. "Mind if I call you Marion?" He blushed, kicked the door open with his foot as was his habit, and was gone. Poor young polliwog.

I suppose Johnnie had been rather lonely after his mother's unhappy death, in spite of all his leftish comrades. Maybe he had locked himself up in a voluntary isolation. At least he accepted Martin's friendship and admiration as eagerly as it was offered to him.

Martin had but one wish and goal: to make himself over into a hundred-per-cent American boy as quickly, as thoroughly, as completely as possible. He wanted to forget Germany overnight and become part of this new country, which seemed to him paradise. The metamorphosis took place at top speed before our astonished eyes, and I watched my older child change, as by a miracle, not only from day to day but from hour to hour.

Johnnie, far from being a Regular Guy himself, was leniently willing to initiate and dominate the boy. He simply could not resist Martin's enthusiasm, his zest to learn from him the language, the slang, the finer points of football, baseball, and crawl stroke; his eagerness to be taught everything a regular fellow ought to know, from the way sweaters were worn that particular season to the preference for banana splits as compared with hot fudge sundaes. Soon Martin was everybody's friend. In his easygoing, calm, practical way he fitted into our new world like a peg into its own hole. To me he was an enormous help during the first years of adjustment. I wonder how I would ever have managed to run the Elmridge household smoothly without my daily conferences with the boy. He was a reservoir of useful information and advice. The first gift he asked from his stepfather was a subscription of Consumer's Research; he read it avidly, made notes, stored facts and figures away to pull them out all of a sudden and amaze our guests with them. Soon he knew the sordid secrets in the manufacturing of some expensive cosmetics. He knew which brand of coffee was the best and why; which car to prefer and for what reasons; what whisky to give John for his birthday, how to make a real good steak and how much duty was paid on English Tweeds. His mind was a neat filing cabinet full of miscellaneous knowledge. He devoured every magazine he could lay hands on; he believed every word he read in them, never got confused by their contradictory opinions, but somehow managed to blend them into a pretty correct and clear picture of the world. "It's like with a three color print," he explained to me once. "If you listen to one side only you get it all in black and white. Now you print the same object in green and in red and combine it. In the end it'll look pretty true and good, won't it? Well, that's my way of looking at things I guess, it's the American way. That's what a free press is made for. Gee, Mom, think how stupid we've been kept over there." His speech was full of Gee and Gosh and he changed his linguistic trimmings faithfully, according to the code of the year and the school. I remember one day when he had been on a full day's excursion with his high school class and came home, his nose red with sunburn, his hands scratched and his shirt extremely dirty. "How was it, sonny?" John asked him. "Gee, it was swell," Martin said. "I hope you guys didn't get drunk on your allowance," John said. He had given him a dollar for extra expenses. "I brought back the buck you gave me, John. Thanks, all the same," Martin said and clapped the bill down on the table. "I didn't need it. I made some money of my own."

"Oh, you did, did you?" John asked. "How come?"

"Caught a few butterflies and sold them to Pat. A nickel a piece. He collects them," Martin said nonchalantly.

"Well, son," John said and he didn't even laugh. "You go and get yourself some education in a hurry so you can help me selling my contract for Dinkley. I'll need a good salesman pretty soon."

As the years slipped by it so happened that Martin became more and more John Sprague's son, the less Johnnie seemed inclined to take over where his father would leave off. Johnnie went to Columbia and took the courses the boys called snaps or cinches, drifted off after two years of fitful learning, and was swallowed up by a crowd of leftist friends. At twenty-one, when he came into the possession of his mother's money, he founded a magazine called Life and Labor, which lived and labored for not quite six months and then folded up, leaving Johnnie with empty pockets. I had visited him several times in his editor's office, sniffed the well-remembered smell of wet printer's ink, stale cigarette smoke, and perspiration caused by strenuous flag-bearing. We were good friends, Johnnie and I. I did not mind him boring me with his written and spoken editorials, and he forgave me for being a stinking liberal.

"Now that he's broke he'll crawl back to the fatherly fleshpots," John said to me when the magazine was finished. But Johnnie did nothing of the sort. I was glad that he did not knuckle under and, I believe, so was John. "Maybe he hasn't got much sense but at least he has spunk," he said when a daily paper began to run a series of articles by John Sprague, dealing with the conditions of the workers in the oil fields of Mexico. That summer we went to Mexico City ourselves—one of our little hops in the interest of Dinky. We met Johnnie down there, had dinner with him at Sanborn's, and I could see that John was pleased with Johnnie. Johnnie had dropped his eyeglasses and some of his mannerisms. He looked sun-tanned and wiry and he seemed to know what he was talking about.

In the end it was Martin who went to Yale and became a Psi U as John had done in his time. The trouble with Martin was only that he had not much talent for any of the exact sciences and least of all for the things he wanted to do most. In his freshman year he flunked in mathematics and physics, and some soft-spoken student adviser hustled him into economics and accounting. Even there he was no shining light. Poor regular guy; my good, reliable Martin! Never would he understand the intricacies of a complicated creature like Dinky. Never would he be the head of Sprague's, nor would he be capable of selling millions of dollars of machinery to the Kemal Pashas and Chiang Kai-sheks of tomorrow. He would be a good husband and father, a good citizen, a fairly successful salesman, chairman of some committees, acting secretary of his club, well liked by everyone though envied by nobody.

Martin would be the right company in a shipwreck. But as soon as my raft was swept ashore on a desert island I would prefer Michael for company.

Martin has never given me an hour of trouble, bless him. But Michael had meant trouble from the minute of his birth, and he kept on being lots of trouble all the time. And yet, even during those years in Elmridge I knew that I had no better friend in the world than this problem child of mine. Michael and I, we looked at most things the same way. We laughed about the same things and felt sorry for the same things. With Martin I could discuss all my troubles, from the cook's regrettable habit of putting sour cream into every dish to John's hardening arteries. But with Michael I could share all the luscious fun of being alive.

He spent hours with me in my little workshop on top of the garage, watched me carving my little figures and criticized them seriously while everybody else in Elmridge treated my carving just as a little whim and hobby. Together with Michael I kept up the European habit of taking long hikes and never mind that the people thought us crazy and the cars stopped and offered us lifts, because no one could understand that two people would walk just for the fun of it. We would snoop around the waterfront villages, have talks with the fishermen, watch the hauling up of oysters, collect shells and pebbles and especially attractive tangles of seaweed. We would go on ski trips at a time when no one in New York seemed to have heard of such a goofy enterprise, and from every one of our expeditions we brought home some secret little store of common memories. But all the time Michael seemed to live in a state of suspense, as if all this were only temporary, as if he were waiting for something, I didn't know what. Meanwhile he accepted with an arrogant and slightly bored expression the agreeable things this new life had to offer. Riding lessons, the permission to drive the car, the private swimming pool, the visits at the Great Neck drugstore soda fountain, and the blind devotion of Topper. Whereas Martin, in his plodding way, worked hard on becoming an American, Michael soon talked and looked like one; it came to him all by itself. His father was an actor, I thought, and he comes from a chameleon race which easily takes on every protective coloring.

Michael grew up to be a remarkably handsome boy, and although he sometimes was troublesome he never was dull. Even in high school the old lady teachers spoiled him and the little girls made a fuss about him; they twittered around him and painted their lips and wrote him little notes. But Michael paid hardly any attention to them. "They look artificial," he told me. "Mass production. Like the cheap dolls you made at Eichheimer's." He was full of memories, and little references to the past cropped up in our conversations all the time. "Remember Amalia?" he would ask me. "Not the toy. I mean the real one, in Einsiedel. Remember the smell of her stable? When we would go there on a winter morning, five o'clock; it was so dark outside even the new snow looked black. How warm it was in that stable, remember? I would put my hands on Amalia's flanks and warm them as if she were a stove. I think I still know how to milk a cow, or do you think one forgets it? Remember how the milk tasted, warm from Amalia? There was foam on top and it made a fine little noise when the air bubbles burst and the foam disappeared. It tasted a bit like very fine leather and like wet straw and like Amalia. I bet there were millions of germs in that milk, and it wasn't so very rich, and I doubt if Amalia was what you would call a contented cow. But, God, Mony, how that milk tasted! Look at their celebrated milk here. It looks and it tastes as though it were made in a factory. It's not milk to me. It's something artificial. Just like the girls. Just like everything. Please, Mony, promise me one thing. You'll send me back to Germany for my first love. I don't want my first love to be antiseptic. That's what I feel here all the time. It's perfect and it's empty and it's antiseptic. I want to go back to Germany."

That was the refrain and that was his daily song. I want to go back to Germany. Please, send me back to Germany. Once, when he had a cold and a fever and I felt him being soft and pliable, I asked him: "Are you homesick for Germany, Milky?" He stiffened as he looked at me from under his much too heavy eyelashes and he said: "One can't talk about those things, can one?"

And then came the scandal when I found out that Michael, my little friend, had a conspiracy with Hilda, the upstairs maid. Her brother Erich, our German gardener, told it to me while I was cutting roses and he was spraying the ramblers.

"Mrs. Sprague," he said, seemingly quite absorbed in his work, "You may say dat it is none of my business, but I do not tink it is right dat Michael goes to the Bund meetings. I do not tink Mr. Sprague would stand for it if he heard about it."

I stood arrested with a rose in my hand. "Is that what he is doing?" I said.

"Yes, Mrs. Sprague. He goes dere with dat crazy sister of mine. Now I do not vant to say a ting; Hilda is a good maid and all dat. But I just feel I have to tell you about it. It just does not seem right that she would drag the boy dere. Noting good will come of it, that is vat I say. If it were my boy I would give him a good spanking, just so it learned him that he has to tank God to be in a good country and it is a shame he should be monkeying around wid dose krautfressers. Dey are nuts, dat's vat dey are."

We had a most unpleasant scene about it, Michael and I; he was posing theatrically in front of his little shrine of ancestor worship. There was a snapshot of Captain Tillmann, his sword, his belt, his medals, and a few dry, crumpled ivy leaves.

"I remember having been told that this was a free country—or does your celebrated freedom of thought not hold when it comes to ideas you don't share yourself?" Michael said arrogantly.

"I hoped you had outgrown your diapers by now, that's all," I said hotly. "I thought we were friends. I didn't think you would act like an ass and keep silly, childish secrets with my upstairs maid."

"Hasn't everyone some secrets?" he asked. It hit me between the eyes, and I wondered if he knew how right he was.

"Besides, I'm glad you know it now. I'm not one of your wishy-washy immigrants. I am a German and I'm proud of it. Someday I'll go back to Germany and I don't want to lose contact with my own country. I think Hitler is great. He has given us faith and dignity and unity and something to live for and die for. That's what we young people need and that's what America is lacking. Faith. Faith and discipline and the readiness to sacrifice. You can have your U.S. and your ice-cream sodas and ten-cent movies. You can have it and keep it."

"Michael——" I cried, startled. "Don't you like America?"

"Why should I like it? They killed my father, didn't they? When we were bled white, starved, in rags, after four years of war, they came over as though for a football game, strong and full of food, and trampled on us and thought it was fun and good clean sport. They sold us out at Versailles. They spat in our faces. They put nigger regiments into our towns and starved our babies to death even after we had peace. I haven't forgotten what Pulke told me and Hellmuth and Andreas. I haven't forgotten Black Ignominy. You thought it was a joke calling her that. Well, I didn't. I didn't forget. Why should I like the Americans, say yourself!"

He sounded as if he would break into tears. I think he did. He made a sharp turn and retreated into his room. Later I heard him hammer and knock, and the next morning I found out that he had nailed a photo over his bed. It was clipped from some magazine and showed the Führer bending from a car and with a pained smile accepting a bunch of flowers from a little girl with blond pigtails and in a dirndl. Among the S.S. officers who surrounded the car in a half circle I discovered Hellmuth Klappholz' blurred portrait. He looked smart and trim in his uniform and stared not at his leader but straight into the camera.

I tried to laugh about it, but it kept bothering me. Well there we go, I thought. Now we have two boys talking editorials in this house. But this is more serious than I knew. I'll have to talk to John about it.

That was always my last resort, and it made me feel much better. I'll have to talk with John about it.

WHAT I REMEMBER best just now thinking of those years before the Great Eclipse is the cigarette box on John's night table. It was a tricky contraption made of handsome red morocco leather. Inside there was a little rack, and when you pushed a button a cigarette jumped out right into your hand. The small click of that box, the short glow of the electric lighter, the luminous little ghost face of the clock next to the box, and then the spark of the cigarette in the quiet dark room and the little waft of bitter smoke in the still air. How often was I awakened by it and watched the spark grow a bit brighter as John took a puff; and then it wandered from his lips to his hand, hung over the edge into the black miniature abyss between our beds, grew dimmer, almost extinguished; then it arched into the darkness as it went back to his mouth and came back again between our beds. John was careful not to move, not to sigh, not to rustle with his pillow when he could not sleep. The curtains were drawn close and I could not see the night outside, but I could hear it. Sometimes the wind came whistling around the corner, sometimes the rain brushed softly against the lawn. Ten minutes past three. An owl would complain bitterly in the elm trees. A tomcat would bring a raucous spring serenade. In the chauffeur's flat a baby would cry, and then a young rooster down at the gardener's lodge would awkwardly begin his vocal training. John would squash his finished cigarette in the ashtray on the night table, and I would try to breathe as steadily as if I were asleep, waiting for him to go back to sleep too.

Sometimes he began stirring, sighing, making little animal noises, and then I knew that he was falling asleep, because he was so careful to keep himself quiet as long as he was awake. Sometimes though he would lie motionless for a while and then take another cigarette, and I felt sorry for him.

"Can't you sleep, darling?"

"Oh! I didn't know you were awake. Did I disturb you?"

"Not at all. May I have a cigarette too?"

"You know, my father always used to say that old men need less sleep. I never believed it."

"You're too young for an old man, John."

"Are you making a play for me, kid?"

"I'd like to put you to sleep. Can't I count sheep for you or something?"

"How about counting my deficit for a change?"

"Want to talk about it? Sometimes things look so big and bad at night when you think about them. When you talk about them they get much smaller. Anything you want to get off your chest?"

"Nope. Nothing. You count your own sheep and I count mine."

It was not easy to make him talk. He was brought up in a cast-iron tradition that ruled that troubles and worries had to be kept away from the little woman at home. Sometimes I wrestled a few dry reluctant hints from him. Most of the time it was Dinky and the depression and the plant and the taxes. Once in a while it was Johnnie. If it was money—which it most probably was perpetually—I never heard about it.

"Well, let's try and catch a little nap now, shall we? How about letting me have a hand?"

His hand would come across the Grand Canyon—that's what we called the space between our beds—and I would put mine into it, and after a while we would be asleep. Sometimes again I would spread my troubles before him in the quiet of the night, and my troubles usually meant Michael.

"Now Michael insists on going to Heidelberg to study medicine, John," I would tell him. "It worries me sick. As if there were not enough good universities over here."

"Well if he has made up his mind to go, let him go, kid. I let Johnnie go too, didn't I?"

"I loathe the idea," I said unhappily. "I don't want to hand my boy over to them and have him made into a stupid robot without a thought of his own."

"Didn't you say you had to convince your youngsters or give up? You won't convince him as long as he hasn't been there. The boy is bright; he'll look through the whole mess pretty soon. He doesn't know himself how much of an American he has become. Don't tell me they are going to make a goose-stepping Nazi of him over there."

"I am no shareholder's meeting," I said. "For me you don't have to paint things brighter than they are."

"I mean it, kid. The only way to cure him is to send him abroad. I bet you anything he'll be back before the second term is over. How about some sleep now. How about letting me have a hand?"

The worst nights I remember happened when they had a strike at the Sprague factory. In Giessheim I had seen strikes from the workers' end. Now I was in the other corner—the wrong corner, I felt. I was not much use to John in those nights, I'm afraid. I pleaded and quarreled and behaved stubbornly like a mule. That's what John called me. "God damn you, Marion," he would shout at me in exasperation. "Can't you see eye to eye with me?"

"I'm so sorry, John, darling. I just can't help it. I'll always stick up for the underdog. Now, look here—couldn't you cut down your profit and give them what they demand?"

"Profit, my eye! Want me to tell you how much deficit Sprague's had during the last two years? If we go on like this we'll have to close down, and what then with your underdog? They'll be out of work entirely."

There were meetings and conferences and John went to Washington and to Albany and back to Washington; he did not come home for two weeks, and then he met the workers halfway and the strike was over, but it had been another blow to John's pride that he had to give in. A year went by and there came another night, when it snowed and we had a fire in the fireplace and there was still a little glow in the embers when I woke up at half-past two and there was a patch of dim red reflected on the ceiling and here and there a little high light in the slick red leather of our smart bedroom.

"Marion—kid? Are you awake?"

"Yes, John. Anything the matter? You seem so restless."

"I wanted to tell you something. I just don't know exactly how to put it. All right, there it is: I am going to give up the plant."

"Give up the plant? Oh, John——"

"Yes. I'm going to sign it tomorrow. No more Sprague's. I'll be just a little sidekick of Ingersoll's. They call it a merger. What do you say now?"

"I don't know—it's a bit sudden——"

"Sudden, hell!" he said, and it gave me a faint vista of all the weeks and months of agonizing struggle he must have undergone before it came to this.

"Well, John, if it makes things easier for you——"

"Much easier. Much. I'll have an easy job. They are very nice to me; they'll make me the vice-president of something or other. One of their vice-presidents, that is. Yes, sir. Mr. Throttlebottom, the vice-president, that's me from now on. What was the name of that funny show we saw a few years ago?"

"Of Thee I Sing?"

"What? Yes, that's it. Of Thee I Sing. Remember that funny guy? Victor Moore, wasn't he the one? Mr. Throttlebottom. It's the perfect part for me. I'll be a scream."

He began to laugh, and I was afraid he would get hysterical. But he caught himself and held out his hand and I took it and held it very tightly, and after a while we both pretended to be asleep. And then again a night in spring and there was a crazy persistent bird somewhere in the shrubs singing like mad; the windows were open and the curtains billowed and the night-blooming jasmine down at the end of the terrace was running amuck with its wild, untamed perfume.

"Marion, I have to ask you something."

"It gives you a headache, doesn't it? That jasmine and that bird."

"Listen, kid. Would you—would you feel very bad if we had to give up Elmridge?"

"Give up Elmridge?"

"Yes. Give up Elmridge. Rent a smaller house or an apartment or whatever you want and maybe we could get along with just two servants?"

"I think that's grand," I said as firmly as I could manage. "That's swell, John. Now that all three boys will be gone soon, this house seems much too big for us anyway. I was afraid of it. It would feel awfully lonesome, wouldn't it? To be rich means only carrying a lot of excess baggage."

"You're a good scout, kid. I was afraid there would be a big fuss. I'm sorry I let you down like that. A nice husband you've picked yourself, Marion, my girl. A failure, that's what I am. A failure and no mistake about it. Think you could let me have a hand?"

Funny, I can never think of John as if he were gone now and of myself being a widow. When I think of him he is very much alive and very close to me and I catch myself thinking ever so often: I must tell this to John, he will laugh about it. And: I must ask John whether I should do this and that or not. And when I fell in love with Christopher I thought first of all: He is the sort of man John will like.

THE GUIDE PUSHED the two tourists in his charge into the main room of the Arli Hütte. He looked like a piece of wood covered with tanned leather. He also had a little goiter, which should have made climbing hard for him but did not seem to disturb him at all. "S'Gott," he said, putting down his own rucksack and the one of the smaller tourist, who had given up on the way and who now sank exhaustedly onto the corner bench. The guide hung his rope on a nail and leaned the three axes into the corner next to Christopher's ax.

"Two for tonight" he said to the hütten warden. "I'll make over to the Alm. Them will go down to Arlingen with the funicular tomorrow morning." There was so much contempt in his voice that Christopher put down the letter he had been reading and gave the two crushed mountaineers a consoling nod. They had rumbled onto the bench like two parcels the guide had deposited there. One was squat and heavy; the younger and smaller one, who couldn't carry his own rucksack, was green in the face.

"It's a rather stiff climb if you are not in training," Christopher said, to help them gather up their self-respect. He spoke his slow deliberate Swiss Dutch, which is a comical language anyway, but sounded still funnier when Christopher wrestled with it.

"Stiff? Not at all," the squat one said boisterously. "Not to be

433

compared with the Zug Spitze or even with an easy mountain like the Gross-Glockner. If we had started out in the morning, as I wanted, there would have been nothing to it. In the afternoon, of course, the ice gets soft and you have the sun against you. Ever made the Zug Spitze?"

Christopher turned back to his letter without giving an answer. There was never a hütte without a braggart of this sort. The green-faced younger tourist said tremulously: "It was only that chimney. When that rock broke and I slid off, down and down, God almighty, down and down——"

"I had him on the rope. He slid down a foot or two," the guide said to the warden; he never addressed his tourists directly, he was so fed up with them. "Skinned his hands a bit and tore a hole in his pants."

"I could have died. I could have smashed my head. When that rock broke and I went down and down it was a feeling I'll never forget. Never."

"It's all right, Georg, it's all right," the squat one said. "The guide should have used pitons, that's what I say. When I made the Gross-Glockner——"

"If he's such a hero why isn't he in the war?" the guide asked the warden, a merely rhetorical question. The two tourists spoke a hard Prussian German.

"I am thirsty," the younger one said querulously. "I am terribly thirsty. Can I have a beer?"

"You would do well to wait a little while," Christopher said without lifting his head from the letter. "You don't want to get a stroke or pneumonia."

"Two beers," the squat one said. "And one for the guide too. Makes three."

"Milk for me," the guide said, separating himself with finality from his charges and sitting down on the bench next to Christopher.

"When did you get here?" he asked.

"Five to four."

"Made good time."

"Rather," Christopher said. "I like to watch the view around this time of the day."

In front of the window there was the immense panorama of the Valais Alps spread out before them, with the Fischerhörner to the north and the peak of the Aletschhorn craning its neck to peer across summits and summits, a newborn world of ice and snow melting bodiless into the afternoon sky.

"Old Hammelin told me you're going away," the guide said.

"Yes. It's time for me to go home."

The guide spat into the corner. He grabbed the mug with milk, which the warden had put down in front of him, and drank. His goiter moved up and down with every gulp. He wiped his mustache, set down the mug, and then said: "We'll all be sorry to see you go. But as you said, it's the right time for a man to stick to his country." He raised his voice and added: "Are enough big-mouthed, cowardly bastards running around who'd do better to go where they belong too."

There was no one else in the room because the funicular had taken the last load of fashionable tourists down to Arlingen, and the few who were staying overnight to climb to the summit early in the morning had mostly retired. There were only Christopher and the guide in one corner and the two German tourists in the other; between the two corners there lay the whole second World War.

"Come, let's go outside and look through the telescope," the squat one said to the green one. "I'll explain the panorama to you."

The warden threw a glance after them as they tramped out.

"Nazi agents?" he said.

"What else?" said the guide. "Those cockroaches are everywhere. I should have let him drop down a few hundred meters, the stinking little cheese."

Christopher took out his pipe and filled it. "Want to try mine?" he said, shoving his tobacco pouch toward the guide, who had also produced his pipe.

"I'm taking the liberty," he said, stuffing it into his pipe bowl, which had a lovely picture on it: a young forester kissing a girl, with an astonished stag looking on.

"Going up to the summit tomorrow?" he asked between puffs.

"Yes. Giving myself a treat before leaving Switzerland."

"It's a good idea. You never know if you'll come back," the guide said casually. "The lady going up with you?"

"Who?"

"The little lady from the miller's house. The American one."

"No."

"It's just as well. She's not young enough for the strain."

"She's much tougher than one would think," Christopher said.

"She must be. I started out only fifteen minutes after her and rushed those two flour bags across the Kees because Hammelin asked me to look after her. But I couldn't catch up with her; I wonder how she made the chimney all by herself."

"Who?"

"Her. The American lady who lives at the miller's house."

"You mean she wanted to come up to the hut?"

"Yes, she left around two o'clock. I saw her traversing the glacier when I looked down from the Kees but I couldn't catch up with her."

"She didn't arrive."

"She didn't arrive?"

"No! She didn't arrive!" Christopher said, and the corners of his mouth grew taut.

The guide threw a quick glance through the window. The dales and glens began to fill with gray and blue haze. Strings of clouds had assembled toward the east; they were so compact that they looked like another range of mountains. But all the summits stood clear above, swimming in yellow sunshine.

"If we hurry we can make it before sunset," the guide said. "Take your rope and crampons. The warden can telephone to Arlingen in case we don't find her before dark. It's a goddamned nuisance to search the whole glacier. There should be a law against women running loose in the mountains. Not a season without one or another getting lost."

He grabbed his ax, rope, and rucksack and rumbled out of the door. Christopher heard him call for the warden. He stood for a moment, stiff and bewildered, biting on the stem of his pipe. Then he picked up his own things in the corner and followed without another word.

The two tourists were peering into the telescope screwing it back and forth, while the older one gave the younger one a ponderous lecture. They looked like people Marion had known, but she could not remember. She struggled hard. The young one with the green face was Count Andreas Olmholtz. I thought he committed suicide, Marion thought. How come he is now in Switzerland? She watched the guide and Christopher striding past the platform of the funicular and past the engine house. There were about two hundred yards of almost even ground and then the descent began. I knew they would come for me, Marion thought as she saw them disappear behind the rocks. She felt unbelievably easy and well. He must have got the goiter when they executed him, she thought. It's funny I did not recognize him when I met him in Staufen. I knew Max Wilde would not let me turn into frozen meat, she thought happily. It was a wonderful relief to know that Max Wilde was now a mountain guide in the Walliser Alps and on his way to rescue her.

She awoke with a start as her head sank forward. She could have dozed off for a few minutes only. The stripe of sunshine up there had hardly grown any narrower. Marion tried to sort out what was only dreamed and what the truth. It all had been so perfectly logical and clear and only toward the end it had slipped off into cloudy regions. She could not shake off the feeling of easiness and relief; they're on their way now, she thought. Or why would I dream it?

Her ankle had begun to throb and ache. She had lost all sense of time. It would be a good joke if I hadn't spent more than five minutes down here, she thought. Maybe there is not such a thing as five minutes. Maybe there is neither time nor space and we have only invented them as crutches for our little minds. Maybe there is no life, nor death either. Let's have another cigarette and try to stay awake.

I WILL NEVER FORGET the exact moment when, for the first time, I was irrevocably certain that Michael was Manfred Halban's son. It was when the train pulled into Heidelberg station, glided past him, and came to a stop with a gentle jolt. Michael was standing on the platform, a tense smile on his sun-tanned face as he tried to find the coach from which I would disembark. I had not seen him for more than a year, and it seemed to me as though I had never seen him as clearly and completely as during that one brief moment. He wore no hat and his hair was very fair, almost white. He had grown a bit and he seemed thin, older than his nineteen years. He shaded his eyes with his hand, although the station was anything but bright. He looked quite different from Halban, as much as I could remember him, but there was something in the strained expression of his face, in the slightly stooped way he carried himself, in his hesitant walk and the abrupt turning of his head, which answered for once and all the question I had never dared to decide in all those years.

"Hello, Milky——" I said, touching his sleeve. He reeled around, took both my hands, and shook them awkwardly. I held an umbrella in one and my handbag in the other. "Hello, there," he said. "Hello, Mony. Well, here you are at last. Hello. So you kept your promise and came. How are you?"

We both were a bit breathless with joy but careful not to appear too emotional.

"How are you, Milky?" I said. "You look a bit thin."

"Ever seen a mother who would think her baby fat enough?" he said, squeezing my arm and taking me down the platform toward the exit. Two porters trailed after us with my luggage.

"What do you want to speak? German or English?" I asked him. I did not want to make any faux pas and I had the feeling that anyone might be a Gestapo man.

"Better stick to English," Michael said. "Better wear an American flag on your lapel. Only a foreigner will be forgiven for the way you look."

"I took off my mascara and nail polish before I left Paris," I said. "Do I have to wear red flannel bloomers to be accepted here?"

"You won't see many mink coats around, and your high heels are definitely bad style," he said teasingly. "Altogether you look much too slick and young for my mother, and Anneliese won't approve of you."

"Who is Anneliese?"

"My landlady's daughter. You'll meet her soon."

Aha! I thought. The old Heidelberg tradition is still alive, even if everything else has changed.

"Is she nice?"

"Very nice. Very, very nice. You'll see. Come, let's take a taxi," Michael said, shoving me into a contraption that looked as if it had been waiting there ever since I had been in Heidelberg last, twenty years ago. I saw him fumbling with some coins in the palm of his hand, which he held close to his eyes and examined with a strained expression that was new to me. "Let me take care of it," I said, but he got it straightened out, paid the porters, told the taxi driver to take us to the Neckarhof, and we rattled off.

"How's Topper?" he asked.

"Thanks, he's all right. Getting a bit old and wheezy, though."

"And the old man?"

"He's fine. A bit restless, but fine otherwise. I hoped he would come to Europe with me for a vacation, but you know how it is. Something came up the last minute. He sends you his love."

"I can't imagine John being restless. He always seemed such a rock to me."

"It's just that American disease. Driving too fast. I have an idea he also worries about Johnnie."

"Is he still in Spain?"

"Yes, and I think he was quite sick for a while."

"If I were mean I'd say it serves him right. Our little Babbitt is okay, I hope?"

"Yes, Martin is doing well. I have an idea he plans to get married as soon as he is through with college."

"Good for him. I had a few very nice letters from him but I've been a lazy skunk and didn't answer yet."

Michael had spent the summer in Heidelberg, using the term to catch up on his Latin and Greek. He was younger than most of the German students, and what he had learned in the Great Neck High School had proven a pitifully insufficient preparation for Heidelberg.

"How are you coming along in the university now?" I asked.

He shrugged his shoulders. He shrugged them skeptically like Manfred Halban. "Oh I guess I'll catch up by and by," he said without enthusiasm. He rubbed his eyes with his fists, like a sleepy child. "There are of course Max and Moritz, they are a lot of bother to me."

"Who are they?"

"Well, Max is a box with the bones of a cat, which I am supposed to fit together, a million little bones. Moritz is a dog in a tank with formaldehyde. I have worked on him for almost three months, and he didn't get any prettier or any more fragrant by it."

He shaded his eyes with his hand and looked out onto the street. "We'll be there in a moment," he said.

"What's the matter with your eyes?" I asked. "They are red."

"It's all that work with the microscope. And I can't stand the glare of the snow without goggles," he said. "This is the earliest snow they have had here in eighteen years. We've been skiing for two weeks, and it's only the third of December."

There was some snow, not much. It was swept into little heaps along the curb, not a bit glaring but soiled and gray, ready to be sent to the laundry. The taxi stopped and the driver opened the door and helped us with the luggage. "How much?" Michael asked him. "One twenty," I said, reading the meter. Again Michael fumbled with the small change; some coins dropped to the ground, and the driver searched for them. Michael stood by with the rest of the money in his palm, looking flustered or arrogantly impatient, I could not decide which. Before there was too much confusion I paid the driver myself, and the porter carried my bags into the lobby.

The Neckarhof was the best hotel in town, and I had been there before; for dinner and dancing with Howard Watson and also with Captain Tillmann, when he was a convalescent in Bergheim. Heidelberg had always been a favorite spot for little pleasure trips from Bergheim, and in those dim past times the Neckarhof had seemed the apex of luxury to me. I looked around while I registered at the desk, but I could not remember having been in that lobby before. It was cozy though somewhat cramped and shopworn. Ever since crossing the German border

I had that odd feeling of being unable to recognize things and places I had known well. Even a few hours earlier I had almost passed through Bergheim without recognizing the station where I had spent so many weary nights. "That's Bergheim," the old lady in my compartment had said just as the train pulled out again and I had looked out of the window and felt nothing at all. Since I knew the Mississippi the Rhine seemed an insignificant trickle. Their mountains were only hills and their towns were much too close to each other. Their streets were narrow and crooked, filled with an impoverished-looking crowd. Only the many men in uniforms were trim and smart, especially the black elite guards. They appeared theatrically sinister to me, as if just getting ready for a dramatic entrance at the second act finale. Throw bombs into a nest of conspirators, form into a firing squad and perform an execution, precise and without any human regrets. But maybe I was prejudiced and had read too many sensational magazine articles and probably those black guards were simple boys like any others who collected butterflies in their spare hours and went bowling and had silly little quarrels with their girl friends.

My room was nice and agreeably old-fashioned, except for a vicious wall paper with a lattice of bloody-looking tomatoes. Also I didn't care for Hitler's portrait, which hung over the tiny writing desk; in the old days it had been Bismarck or the Kaiser in just such a glorified version. I hadn't liked them either. The windows gave out onto the snow-patched lawn in front. In the center stood a little bird shelter; the snow had melted beneath the little roof where crumbs were scattered on the moist, dark ground. Somehow it was reassuring that they still fed their birds in Germany. Well, here we are now, I thought. Let's hope everything will be all right.

"The people here are very friendly, aren't they?" Michael said.

"Yes, I noticed it on the train too. They go out of their way to make you like them. They want so desperately to convince you how wonderful everything is with them and that they really don't care for cutting up Jewish babies limb by limb."

"You mustn't believe all the nonsense you hear. It's mostly anti-Nazi propaganda."

"You still like it here?"

"Why shouldn't I? I love Heidelberg; it's a beautiful place. Next term I will start on Groonemann's course of histology; he is one of the greatest teachers you can find in the world——"

"Look here, Milky," I said, "I came here on a hunch. Your last letters sounded funny. We got worried, John and I. We thought there might be some things you couldn't write, what with the censorship and all that. Is there anything the matter? Any trouble? Any danger?"

Michael threw an instinctive glance at the door. "Danger? Nonsense," he said. "If my letters sounded funny it's possibly just because I'm a poor letter-writer. Usually I fall asleep in the middle of it."

"It worried me," I repeated. It was a meager expression for the weeks and months of murky, vague suspense and the shapeless fears that had emanated from reading those letters. Michael rubbed his eyes with his fists.

"You look tired," I said.

"I am tired," he answered. "Premedical classes are no joke, and they make you work here, not play, thank you."

"Come, let me look at you. Do you get enough to eat? And what's the matter with your eyes?"

"Nothing. A little irritation, I guess. Most of us get it in bacteriology. Just try to peer through that microscope into that glare for a few hours. Next term it'll get better, when I start working on a dark field." He blinked at me and covered his lids with his fingers.

"I don't like it," I said. "Did you ask a doctor about it?"

"Sure. I asked Dr. Tillmann. A very good doctor, Ma'am. He prescribed boric acid solution."

"I'll take you to a real doctor. I don't like you to go around looking like Nibble with the red glass eyes."

"Okay, okay, I'll go to a real doctor. You don't have to come along and hold my damp little hand. I'm quite a big boy now, really."

I don't know exactly what I had expected when I crossed the border of Germany. It was like that trip when I had crossed the equator for the first time. I had known there wouldn't be a red line, like in the atlas of my school days, and yet I was faintly disappointed that nothing at all parted the endless grayish-green reach of waves. There was no definite line to cut off the totalitarian confinement of Germany against the outer world. Not at first and not to be seen on the surface. People were cheerful and lively, and if I had expected them to walk around like the living death, like the zombies of Haiti, I had been grossly mistaken. True, there was an overwhelming number of soldiers and uniforms on the streets, but so far the whole continent had seemed to bristle with them; even traditional islands of anti-militarism like Switzerland and the Netherlands were full of them. The daily tramp-tramp of marching cohorts at five in the morning was a nuisance, and chains of trucks loaded with soldiers rumbling down the streets of the dreamy little university town gave me a queer feeling of being back in the war. So did the flags that fluttered from almost every house for no visible reason at all—if not as a shield and an assurance: Behold, here dwell good Nazis! That's what I noticed first: That mostly everybody seemed overanxious to tell me how wonderful everything was, as if they all hoped their enthusiasm would be noticed and rewarded by some invisible but ever-present higher instance.

It was the things that were not said. The sentences that broke off in the middle and were never finished. The furtive glance toward the door, this new and most characteristic movement of the Germans; the glance of prisoners to see if the guard was watching them through the spy hole of their cell. The different ways in which the unavoidable party salute was given. Some did it perfunctorily, and you knew that they were powerful and had nothing to fear. Some did it shy and embarrassed, almost apologetic, as if they still had not got used to it. Some did it loud and trumping, because they had a bad conscience or because they hoped to be noticed and advanced. Some did it like a bad joke in which you had to join if you wanted to survive, and some, especially the young ones, did it as casually as youngsters in America shouted "Hiya!" at you. They did not know any other way of greeting, and it had lost its meaning to them.

After a few days of acclimatizing, I met Michael's friends,

who called themselves The Thundering Herd. Most of them were boarders of Frau Streit, like he himself. They were a nice bunch of young people, well-behaved, not very bright, and almost boastfully insensitive, as if some of their nerves had been deadened. Being used to the constant clatter of political discussions in our New York living room, in women's clubs, American schools, newspapers, and magazines, it struck me as something strange at first that these young people talked about anything under the sun but politics. But they were so frankly pleased with themselves and in such complete accord with their surroundings that every attempt at criticism was disarmed. Michael was obviously an alien among them in spite of his fair hair and his mimicry. Too mobile, too skeptical even when he admired. But then he had been an alien in Great Neck too, and he would remain an alien almost everywhere. The German youngsters treated him a bit too politely, as though they were on guard with him all the time. Among themselves, in the inner sanctum of their companionship, they were rude to one another, which is the German way of showing fondness. But they never called Michael "swine" or "ass" or "beast," and he was left somewhere outside.

Anneliese was one of The Thundering Herd. Her skin had that well-scrubbed shine that is so charming on seventeen-year-olds, and her round head was heavy with real blond hair. This was quite a distinction in a country where most females went around with badly peroxided or home-bleached tresses, trying their darnedest to live up to the Aryan ideal of womanhood. Poor German women, having lived along a main thoroughfare of Europe through the centuries, they had consorted with every race that came marching by. Romans, Slavs, Celts, Italians, Frenchmen, Spaniards, and Jews. They all had left their traces, and it was tough on the girls when they were commanded by their Führer to be of a pure, superior, and blond race. But being women and accustomed to changing themselves in compliance with their lords' demands, they did their best to look wholesome and Aryan, and I suppose the hairdressers did a thriving business of touching up and bleaching. Anneliese had spent the summer doing Arbeitsdienst; some tan was still left on her face, and her arms were strong and freckled. She and Michael behaved like two colts in a very green pasture. They would banter and tease, measure their strength, and kick each other; sometimes they would be quiet for a few minutes and stare at each other in an astounded, dumb contemplation, or put their hands together, side by side; they would arrive breathless, eat great amounts of cake, giggle a lot, have some secrets that I was not to know, and suddenly with a loud neighing they would be off again, two long-legged awkward young animals. Under Anneliese's stern scrutiny I felt uncomfortable, too young to be Michael's mother, too old to be his companion; and yet I was both. But after a while Anneliese's curiosity got the better of her and she came to visit me quite unexpectedly, asked me a hundred silly questions, and played with my dresses, shoes, and make-up things.

"America must be a funny country. They get married dressed in nothing but cellophane so you can see their brassiere and panties underneath. It's shameless."

"That's nonsense, Anneliese. You mustn't believe such stories."

"It's true too. I saw a photo in a magazine. The bride wore a bridal veil and a dress of cellophane. You could see *everything!*"

"That's some silly propaganda, Anneliese, I assure you."

"That's what you always say when you don't like something. Propaganda! Our new roads are propaganda too, are they? And our schools and our sport stadiums and everything. I think you Americans are just jealous. You have lots of trouble I understand. I saw a picture of thousands of people standing in line for food——"

Sometimes she would hold my dresses in front of herself and caper before the mirror, and once I caught her experimenting with my lipstick and rouge and making a mess of her pretty young face.

"Do you think Michael would like me better with all that goo on my snoot?" she would ask me seriously. She had a stern, absorbed, straight way of looking into one's eyes, as little children do.

"No I don't think so, Anneliese. Here, take some cold cream and wipe it off."

"But he told me all girls in New York are made up, and they are much prettier than we are," she said.

"He was just teasing, I guess. He likes you as you are."

"I was only twenty-three seconds behind him in our last slalom race," she concluded. "Michael says American girls can't ski."

In a way I liked Barbara better, a fat, ugly, dark-haired girl, Anneliese's foil, faithfully following her around. Anneliese's adult babbling bored me. She was a little parrot, fed on slogans and propaganda. Besides, forty-three and seventeen do not mix well. I had given up smoking in Anneliese's presence and had bought myself a rather ugly pair of flat-heeled shoes. It's funny the humiliating things mothers will do to please the puppy loves of their sons.

Michael came wandering into my room and flopped down on the chaise longue.

"If John were here he would offer me a pick-up," he said petulantly.

"Are you tired?"

"No. Just pooped. Like the New York stock market: listless. Moritz didn't behave, and I'm afraid I'm going to flop in bacteriology."

I went over to him and with an old, old gesture I touched his temples. His hair felt exactly as Halban's hair had felt, silky as a baby's. His forehead seemed dry and warm. "Aren't you a bit warm?" I asked him.

"No, your hands are cold," he said. He took my hand and put it over his eyes. "There, that's better," he said. After a while I went to the window and looked down on the lawn. The snow was almost gone and the grass had an unappetizing color, like yesterday's spinach. The sparrows fought bitterly for crumbs under their dripping little shelter. I thought that I should soon go home to John, but I couldn't leave Michael behind as some problematic and utterly unfinished business.

There had been great commotion in the Streit family when I invited them to celebrate Anneliese's seventeenth birthday at the Neckarhof, because it was an elegant and expensive and even international place frequented by foreigners, English and American students and a few tourists. Anneliese's mother immediately began to worry over her old black silk dress and her broken fingernails. Frau Streit had the pursed lips and the frown and the mechanical smile which are the result of taking in boarders. She had gray hair and a gray skin and fine fragile hands with broken nails. Looking at her hands I knew her whole story; the genteel breeding, the slow and dignified decline; that she could not afford a hired maid and cleaned house herself, wearing her old suède gloves for the rough work, and that she gave her boarders the best food she could manage and ate what was left, warmed over and rehashed. To worry had become a habit with her and she could extract a few bitter drops of trouble from every flowering joy. She belonged to the puzzled, bewildered and submissive German middle class, and, like all of them, she suffered perpetually from fear and a bad conscience. To make her feel easier I had disguised myself in a much too solid black dress, which I had bought in Heidelberg. I felt uncomfortable, as in a cheap masquerade, and once more I realized how quickly and completely I had Americanized myself.

Anneliese had been in feverish anticipation and she looked lovely that evening, intoxicated with herself as young girls will be when they suddenly discover how pretty they are. I had taken her to the best dress shop in town and given her an evening dress for her birthday present. It was blue and stiff, with a naïve pattern of red roses woven into the silk and a little collar of real lace, and she looked like a young peasant woman out of a German folk song and also, I thought, like an astonished young swanlet crossing the lake for the first time. Her hair was parted in the middle and pinned up in the nape of her long neck. From time to time she pushed a hairpin into place with an unconscious and very old-fashioned gesture. The headwaiter had reserved for us a long table with flowers on it, and we marched in a bit too solemnly, as though down the aisle of a church.

Frau Streit had brought one of her boarders along as an escort, an elderly baldheaded professor of boastfully timid manners, who sat uncomfortably between us two black-silk monuments. There were also a few members of The Thundering

Herd in their stiff, dark suits; but the high light of our table was Anneliese's brother Hans, a nice-looking young fellow in the trim uniform of an officer aspirant or whatever they called it. Michael in his tuxedo and with his new dark eyeglasses, which the doctor had recommended, looked as alien as ever, like a movie actor in disguise. To break the ice I started them off on sherry and followed it up with champagne. Anneliese, who never had champagne before, wrinkled her nose and said it tasted like mosquito bites, but before she had her glass refilled she had begun to giggle and to loosen up. The baldheaded professor whispered Hitler jokes into my ear. They were old and had been known in New York for years, but I laughed gratefully, because it took a lot of daring to tell them in a public place. Hans Streit got up, clicked his heels, and in well-mannered succession asked first his mother, then me, the hostess of the evening, then his sister, and at last the fat girl, Barbara, for a dance. I remember passing Michael and Anneliese on the floor; they were bantering as usual; Anneliese reached up and tried to take the dark glasses away from him, and he slapped her freckled little girl's hand. Her hands were much younger than the rest of her; I had never seen a palm so without any lines, as if she had not lived yet at all.

"Nice going!" Michael called to us, and Hans took a firmer hold of me and we careened off. When we came past Michael the next time he was without his glasses and it gave me a slight shock to notice how red his eyes were and how strained the unsmiling expression on his face. He did not look like a boy steering a pretty girl around a dance floor but like a captain piloting a battleship through a dangerous zone. There are many ridiculous details I remember about that evening. The pattern of the dance floor for instance: an abundance of salt and pepper shakers, shaped like Dutch boys and girls, with the salt and pepper coming out through their caps. Frau Streit stepped into the seam of her dress and made a big fuss about it. The trumpet player of the band was a megalomaniac who tried to look like Hitler. The band leader, who also played the fiddle, wore a moth-eaten toupee, and from time to time he remembered his sagging tummy and pulled it sharply in. The whole band was dressed in some sort of a fancy uniform.

At the end wall of the room, to the right side of the bandstand, a cardboard sign was hanging, printed in rather discreet letters: JAZZ VERBOTEN! I had seen it without actually being conscious of it. It should have been hard to dance jazz to the homespun robust music the band supplied. However, some of the guests, obviously foreigners, experimented with a few timid fox trot steps.

"Look what they are dancing," Anneliese said to Michael. "Can you dance like that too?"

"Of course. So can you. Don't you remember, I showed you those steps?" Michael said.

"I remember it," Barbara cried eagerly. "I do! When we were at the ski lodge, after the race, don't you remember, Anneli? Let's dance it together, Michael."

"Yes, do," Anneliese said. "I want to see you dance it. Go on. Don't be a frog!"

The professor wagged a finger at Michael when he got up to lug the fat girl onto the floor. "Jazz verboten," he whispered into my ear. "Everything verboten. Fun verboten. To think verboten. To talk verboten. To die and rot permitted." Obviously he had drunk too much champagne and had cut the barbed wires around his inhibitions.

Michael brought out his glasses again; he put his arm around the fat girl and they were swallowed up in the swaying crowd on the floor. I smiled after them.

"Barbara shouldn't do that," Frau Streit said. "It's all right for Michael—he is an American—but if anyone would see Barbara dance jazz—there might be trouble—and he is our boarder—it reflects on us——"

"Oh, Mother, don't fuss so much," Hans said, and I could see that he was embarrassed. "What will Mrs. Sprague think of us? Mother always worries over nothing," he added, turning to me. "If I weren't so clumsy I would try it myself. It looks as if they were having great fun."

He moved his feet under the table and hummed the melody.

I'll never forget what they played. Rosen aus dem Süden, by Johann Strauss. I did not see how one could dance jazz to it. Hans got up and took Anneliese onto the floor, and I saw them edge up to Michael and Barbara and bump into them just for the fun of it, and then they danced alongside of them, watching their feet.

"Did you hear the story when a certain person went out in a rowing boat?" the professor said, embarking on another old Hitler joke, and I turned my attention to him. When I looked back to the dance floor I saw Michael manipulating that "verboten" sign without interrupting his dance.

"He's turned it around," the professor whispered. "That's right. We are here for our pleasure, not to get more discipline beaten into us."

The next moment the bandleader gave his percussion man a sign, and he put down his drumsticks, reached out, and turned the cardboard back. JAZZ VERBOTEN. Rosen aus dem Süden went on. The headwaiter served us the black coffee and brushed the bread crumbs from the tablecloth. When he came to me he bent down to my ear and whispered some throaty English. "If Madame would not mind telling the young gentleman not to make fun of that sign," he said. "The management has to request our guests to respect orders; I am sorry, Madame——" There was a load of cauliflower on his breath, and I shrunk away from him. He gave the tablecloth another perfunctory swish and avoided my eyes. I had the definite feeling that he detested that sign and the unpleasant task of reprimanding a guest who paid well and gave ample tips.

There was some applause on the dance floor, although the piece was not finished but just approaching its end. When I looked up I saw Michael reversing the sign a second time. A little circle of dancers had formed around him, and some of them applauded. Hans, in his neat, slim uniform, stood among them with Anneliese, and both of them watched Michael with a happy grin on their young faces. Michael brushed his hands as if he had done a good piece of work, and one of the foreign students patted his shoulder. Then I saw Hans and Michael exchange their girls. Hans took Barbara in his grip and waltzed off with her, and Anneliese tried not very successfully to dance with Michael. The bandleader smiled benevolently over the bobbing heads and without a pause went from his waltz into a hybrid fox trot-march. By now almost all the dancers on the floor had adapted their steps to it.

"What fun, what fun," Anneliese cried when they returned to the table, out of breath and exuberant, as if they had been off on a wild and vicious escapade.

The headwaiter popped another bottle open and filled new glasses. When I looked at the sign it had been turned back again. JAZZ VERBOTEN. The band was leaving for a pause, and the music stands looked lost and deserted.

"I propose a toast," Hans called, drying his happy flushed face. Hear! Hear! came from The Thundering Herd further down the table. "To the ladies! To our mothers and our sisters and our sweethearts and to all the women we love——"

It was at that moment that the gentleman from the other table came over. He was a man in his forties, dressed in a double-breasted blue suit. His trousers were tight and rather short, as most German trousers are for some reason. I thought at first that he was one of Michael's instructors. He had the face of a fish of prey, of a pike as they fill the German rivers.

"Heil Hitler," said this gentleman. "Heil Hitler," murmured The Thundering Herd. "Good evening," I said. I had an idea that he knew the Streits and might want to ask Anneliese for a dance. But he turned to Hans and said, softly but clipped, "Will you come outside with me, please."

Hans put down his glass sharply. "At your service," he said. "Excuse me, Mother. Excuse me, Mrs. Sprague." He made a military turn and followed the gentleman.

I heard the headwaiter click his tongue in a discreet exhibition of sympathy, for what we had witnessed was the traditional opening for the challenge to a saber duel between students in Heidelberg. But then, one did not challenge young officer aspirants, and a startled silence settled over our table.

"Maybe he was a bit drunk——" the professor ventured at last.

"Shall I go and see what's the matter?" Michael asked Frau Streit. She had crumbled up all of a sudden, a pitiful ruin in black silk. "I knew it, I knew it," she said monotonously. "I knew something would happen. I knew it, I knew it."

"Nothing has happened. Nothing is going to happen," Anneliese said. "Don't be such a rabbit, Mother."

No one said another word. We just waited. The champagne went flat in our glasses. The band returned and began playing again. "Want to dance?" Michael asked. Anneliese shook her head and bit her lips.

"You, Barbara?"

"No, thank you," said Barbara. Michael pushed his glasses up to his forehead and rubbed his eyes. "Mourning becomes Electra," he said, and they didn't know what he was talking about. Then I saw Hans entering the room. He walked stiffly and with too much deliberation, as though he were drunk. When he approached our table I saw that his face was white, his lips too; even his ears looked as if they were made of wax, and sweat was streaming down his forehead and temples.

"Hans——!" his mother whispered. He started twice to speak, but gave up as if his tongue had gone dry. He picked up someone's glass and gulped some champagne. "I have to go to the barracks at once," he said finally. "Something has happened. I can't talk about it here."

I saw the pike gentleman return to his table and sit down with a thin smile. My own party was breaking up in a restrained sort of panic. The Thundering Herd stampeded off. The professor supported Frau Streit as if she were a mourner about to break down at an open grave. "Come, come, Hans, what's all this?" Michael said, patting Hans' shoulder. Hans jerked his hand off as if it were dirty. "Let me alone," he hissed at him. "It's all because of you." Anneliese let go of Michael's arm and hung onto her brother. "Hans," she whimpered, "Hansel, my Hansel, what is it, tell your sister." They were gone, and Michael was left standing alone. "Mother——" he said. "It's all right, Milky," I said. "It'll all straighten itself out. They are a frightened lot——"

The headwaiter blocked our way as we wanted to follow them into the lobby. "The bill, Madame," he said urgently. "The bill, if you please——"

"I'll sign it——" I said. But this was not New York. You could not simply sign a bill. "Go—find out what happened," I told Michael. "Don't let them run away in a panic."

"And the flowers," the headwaiter said fussily. "Doesn't the young lady want to take her flowers along? We put them on the bill too; they belong to you. If you put them in water with half an aspirin they will last a long time——"

When I had finally straightened out my bill and reached the lobby, everybody had left except Barbara. Michael was just about to help her into the sportscoat she wore over her dinner dress; he looked as if someone had hit him over the head. "What is it? Where are they? Can I do anything?" I asked, unacquainted as I was with the sudden catastrophes that might befall a family in Nazi Germany. "You tell her, Michael," Barbara said, tearing her coat from him and rushing to the swinging door. "Don't go with me, please. It only makes it worse. I don't want to be seen with you." The door swung against our faces, there was a rush of cold air, and we were left alone.

"I don't understand it——" Michael said. "I don't understand it. I am not a leper, am I? Dancing a fox trot doesn't make me a leper, does it? O God, Mother, what am I going to do now?"

When Michael called me Mother I knew that he was in serious trouble. He was shaking all over when he told me in a few words what had happened. The gentleman with the pike face was Major Vitztum, an artillery officer in mufti. He had reported Hans Streit to his superiors for publicly making fun of and disobeying official orders, for associating with foreign and subversive elements ("That's us, Mother," Michael said), and had announced that he would insist on having Hans Streit dishonorably dismissed from the Army.

"That's absurd," I said, completely stunned. "Major Vitztum must be drunk. Or maybe somebody is playing a practical joke on Hans."

Michael looked at me through his dark glasses. "They don't play practical jokes in this country," he said. "Hans knows it. He said he would kill himself if he gets dismissed. I am sure he will do it, too, if he can't become an officer. And Anneliese! I thought she would spit into my face. Frau Streit asked me not to come back to their house. She said I had ruined them all.

And it's true, Mother. It's all my fault, but great God, how could I dream that dancing fox trot would be treated like high treason?"

"Shall I go and talk with the Streits? I am sure they exaggerate it all," I said. "Things are not handled like that, not even here." But I was not so sure any more. There it is now, I thought. The menace behind the friendly blond front. The fanaticism, the insanity, the sudden killing blow.

"For Christ's sake, don't," Michael said. "Let them alone. Hans went back to his barracks. Major Vitztum told him to stay in his room until further orders. Frau Streit and the professor are trying to appeal to some people of influence. I think the professor knows the sister of the Gauleiter——"

Suddenly Michael was a little boy again, young and silly and helpless. "Come, we'll have to talk a word with this Major Vitztum," I said. "He seems to be a sadistic maniac, and we'll have to try and bring him to his senses." Michael's lips were white and thin; it looked queer in his tanned face of a skier. "Take off those silly glasses," I said. "This is no time to play Greta Garbo." He took them off, and I saw that his red, strained eyes were full of tears. Suddenly I remembered that he had always had wet knees when he had cried as a baby. The tears would roll down his long eyelashes and he would sit with his head unhappily bent and then the tears would unfasten themselves and drop on his knees. It made me smile to remember that and I could not be really mad at him. Do mothers never get through changing their children's diapers? I thought.

"May I disturb you for a moment, Herr Major?" I said when we had arrived at Major Vitztum's table. I tried to sound as submissive as any major of the Nazi army might expect any woman to be. "I feel responsible for the little disturbance that seems to have caused you some annoyance and I want to apologize."

The major got up, clicked his heels, bowed, muttered his name, smiled, went through the complete ritual of being polite and well-mannered and even chivalrous, and for a moment I thought: It's all a silly misunderstanding. Nothing is going to happen.

"Shall we sit over there for a few minutes?" I said, pointing to the long, deserted birthday table with Anneliese's flowers in

the center drooping their wilted heads. A champagne cooler with
a half-empty bottle was still standing there, the ice had melted
and all the gayety had fizzled out. The band played the Blue
Danube, and the dance floor was bobbing and swaying.

"If you please. Thank you. Please," the major said, waiting
for me to sit down first, bowing once more, and then sitting
down too. Michael was standing behind my chair, his hands
clutched to the back of it.

"Herr Major," I said with my best smile, "we want to humbly
apologize, my son and I. We are the real culprits, the only culprits, in fact. I encouraged the young people to dance some
steps that are customary in our country. We are Americans, as
you possibly know; we have a different sense of humor. My son
thought that turning around that little sign would be accepted
as a harmless little joke. He is sorry, aren't you, Michael?"

"Yes. Very sorry," Michael said behind me with a dry, small
voice. The major listened with a polite and interested smile on his
narrow fish face, and I ran out of words, but I took a second
run and jump.

"Hans Streit, that young officer—he had nothing to do with it
at all. On the contrary. He reproached my son for it and
warned him not to do it again. Didn't he, Michael?"

"Indeed, he did," Michael said, and I was glad he helped me
to lie.

"I don't know what you, Herr Major, told Hans Streit, but I
know that he was terribly upset about it," I went on. "You will
understand that I and my son would feel awful if an innocent
bystander like Hans should be punished for the mistake we made.
A mistake, I want to add, which seems so small, so innocent, and
so excusable, especially if committed by foreigners like us——"

There we go, I thought, listening disgustedly to myself drib-
bling apologies. The major rocked his head in a display of
regret and surprise. He plucked a flower from the basket and
thoughtfully began playing with it. It was a lily-of-the-valley,
a frail hothouse creature pierced by a piece of wire. A tiny
crucifix with a pale green body and drooping head. The major
pulled the wire from it and began stabbing every one of the
little bells.

"There seems to prevail a profound misunderstanding," he said. "A profound and regrettable misunderstanding. What I as Streit's superior officer choose to decide about him has nothing whatsoever to do with you and your son. You are guests in this country, you travel on American passports. You are at perfect liberty to behave according to your own taste and tact. We are hospitable people, as is known the world over. If your son thinks it amusing and witty to make fun of the rules of a country whose guest he is, a country, I may point out, that gives him all the benefit of its rich sources of science and educational institutions—no one is going to stop or even reprimand him. We realize that you Americans have a different code——"

"Herr Major——" I tried to interrupt him, but he stopped me with a slightly affected movement of his hand, like a conductor silencing an orchestra.

"Just one second," he said. "You Americans get a certain decadent sensation out of dancing nigger dances to the accompaniment of nigger drums. You don't mind being carried back to the grotesque abandonment of the nigger kraal. Good. The decline of a civilization always announces itself in similar spectacles. I remind you of the fall of Rome. Of the unhealthy orgies that were the forerunners of the French revolution. But that is America's business and America's concern. You can keep your jazz. We are satisfied to be the country of Beethoven, Bach, Wagner. We have the inexhaustible fountain of our folk songs and folk dances. We don't want this fountain contaminated, that's all."

"Herr Major," I said. "Is it really necessary to bring down the whole weight of the Nazi Weltanschauung for such a simple little accident? This was a birthday party. The children were happy and gay—they are only children, don't you see? Maybe they had a little more champagne than was good for their manners—but I insist: Hans Streit did nothing that would ask for punishment."

"That is up to his superior officers to decide," the major said, and I recognized the old Prussian nasal voice of command, which could only be answered with a self-annihilating: "At your command." "At this moment we are not talking about Streit. We are having a friendly little conversation on the ideology of the Americans as opposed to our own ideals. You are Americans——" he said, and suddenly he jerked his head up and looked past me at Michael, who was still clamping his hands to my chair. "Or aren't you? Isn't your name Tillmann? Yes, I thought so. A good German name, if I am right. You speak our language amazingly well too. I just remember having heard rumors that you are German by birth, even if you call yourselves Americans now. You left this country in its darkest hour, you and your sons, and now you come back with a bagful of dollars to shop for some real culture and to make fun of us and to implant anarchistic ideas into the minds of our unsuspecting young people. But you will not succeed."

I knew all the time that they were keeping our secret dossier, I thought; I bet they know what's in my suitcase, what paper I read, and if I take a laxative. . . .

"You will not succeed," he said, giving the lily-of-the-valley a last stab and then dropping it to the floor. "Because there are two different worlds, which can never be reconciled. You Americans with your money and your decadent eccentricities, with your slackness and mushy tolerance. And we, welded in common battle, hardened and disciplined, a young, strong nation——"

"Exactly, Herr Major," I said; I felt an explosion coming on and hoped to God I would not take that champagne bottle and pour it over his head. The desire to do so was almost too much for me. "Exactly," I said. "Hans Streit is a very fine example of this new German youth. He is hardened and disciplined. He did not do anything wrong, he did not dance any prohibited steps, and he told my son he would beat hell out of him if he ever danced the fox trot with his sister again."

"He stood by and laughed when Herr Tillmann insulted the Reich by making fun of one of our rules. By tolerating this abuse he made himself an accessory to it. He has clearly demonstrated tonight that he is not worthy the honor of being an officer. Our army is made of sterner stuff. And now, if you'll excuse me, I won't detain you any longer."

The major got up; his face was pale with anger, and all

politeness had gone out of it. He pulled down his coat and buttoned it. Suddenly Michael began to speak, still holding on to the back of my chair.

"Herr Major, just one more word," he said, his voice shaking with excitement. "You are right, I was born here and I have come back to this country because I love it. It is my country. My father was a Prussian officer and my grandfather and my grandfather's father. I know of what stuff officers are made. I'm made of that stuff myself. I want nothing more in the world than that Germany shall be strong and rehabilitated and on equal terms with the other great nations. That's why I came back. That's why I gave my allegiance to the Third Reich and its Führer. But, Herr Major——" he said, and I felt his fists tremble on the back of my chair, "if a few dance steps seem so dangerous that you have to convict people just for watching them—then, Herr Major, this country is not strong. In America—in school—we estimated a guy by the way he could take it. If he couldn't take it we knew he was a weakling or a coward or a sissy. You can't take it, it seems. You can't take a joke because you're afraid of it. You are scared of laughter, you and your Reich, and of criticism and of contradiction. You are afraid of your subjects and you keep your subjects afraid of the state. You can beat fear into people but you can't beat strength into them or courage, let alone love and loyalty. I didn't know I liked America, not till just now, when you got nasty about it. Well now I know; I like it, thanks to you, Herr Major. I'll go back there and tell the American people that my best friend had to shoot himself, that he got kicked out of the German Army because he saw me dancing a lousy fox trot and the mighty German Reich couldn't take it. I'll write in the papers about it. I'll make a hell of a noise about it. It'll make a wonderful impression over there, I assure you, and we'll feel terribly slack and decadent, Herr Major—and now, if you want to put me in jail, just go ahead."

There we go, I thought. Now he'll get arrested. What will I have to do then? Call up John. Contact Washington. Telephone the American Embassy in Berlin. Maybe they'll arrest me too for being the mother of this impudent youngster—and didn't

he sound exactly like Manfred Halban in a Schiller drama?
Wonder what has become of Fritz Halban. He simply disappeared. Liquidated? Or what do they call it here? I was
riding dizzily on a fast merry-go-round. But then I saw to my
amazement that the major seemed to be thrown off balance. He
did not answer Michael's astonishing tirade but turned to me
and became polite again.

"I appreciate it that you and your son are worried about
your young friend," he said. "You are good advocates of his
cause, I must admit. Unfortunately the case is out of my hands
by now. I made my report by telephone and the procedure will
have to take the official course. I might, however, suggest to
Streit's superiors to be clement on account of his youth and
inexperience. I wish you a pleasant night. Heil Hitler!"

He clicked his heels and went back to his table with a funny
stiffness in his back, as if he expected Michael to kick him in
his behind.

"Phooey!" Michael said, still trembling. "Did you see him
duck the moment I showed him the fist? What do you think
he is going to do now?"

"It's all right. The whole stink will blow over," I said. "Major
Vitztum is just an ass of a busybody. Let's take a taxi and see
how Frau Streit is coming along."

BUT IT DID NOT BLOW OVER. It took what Major Vitztum had
called the official course. Frau Streit sent Michael's belongings to
the Neckarhof and refused to see him. Once he managed to
see Anneliese, but she made him so horrid and nasty a scene
that he came home shattered and I had trouble putting the
pieces of him together. We sat in my room, Michael and I,
and stared at the bloody tomato pattern of my wallpaper until
I thought we would go crazy. People shrank back from us as
if we were contaminated. The only connecting link between us
and the other camp was Barbara, who came and gave us reports. I think she was in love with Michael, in the pathetic,

intense, and hopeless way fat, ugly friends of pretty girls usually are. Once the baldheaded professor sneaked into the Neckarhof, under cover of night and with the air of a conspirator, to assure us that he was not entirely in sympathy with the Nazi regime and couldn't I help him to get a visa and a job in America. It was the ever-recurring refrain in my conversation with everyone; they thought it pretty wonderful what the Führer had done for Germany, but meanwhile they would have given anything to get out of the country. My old headwaiter clicked his tongue in sympathy when he served us at our lonely island of a table. The sulky chambermaid who came to clean our rooms would sometimes gaze at Michael with a speculative absorption. Only by undercurrents, by a twitch of an eyebrow, by the indication of a smile, did all those people dare to communicate with us and to hint that they were not in full accord with their rulers. I thought of Max Wilde. Never be scared. Here I could see what fear did to people. It tore every shred of dignity from them and made them at home in their shivery abyss of humiliation until they had forgotten that one could live on a different level.

"What are we hanging around for?" I asked Michael when we had gazed for a week at the tomato walls of my room. "Why don't we take the next boat and go home? The trip and the rest'll be good for your eyes and it's still time for you to catch the second semester in some university over there."

"Didn't you teach me to eat the soup I've cooked myself?" he said. "I'm not used to running away from trouble. And you wouldn't want me to. I have to stick it through here until we know what's going to happen to Hans. Maybe I'll be called as a witness. Maybe I can still get him out of this mess. They can't all be nuts, can they?"

We didn't know exactly who "They" were and how the machine worked and who decided about the future of a stupid little officer aspirant. We told each other that all this was absurd, ridiculous, and impossible. It frightened me the more because there was nothing sinister and secret about it. This was no concentration camp Schrecklichkeit, no muffled cries of tortured victims in the cellars at night, no beating up of Jews and communists and enemies of the Reich. This was the simple, soulless everyday annihilation of a good, clean young Nazi boy, and the worst of it was that he himself accepted it as something that was coming to him. As far as we knew, Hans Streit was still under confinement, waiting for the verdict. Barbara reported to us his unbending intention to shoot a bullet through his head if he got cashiered. By and by I grew pretty weary of his constant suicide threats. I didn't think it very manly of the young warrior to scare the daylights out of his mother and sister. It exasperated me also to see that he was so blindly devoted to the system that he could not perceive of a life without complete submission. "After all, there are millions of men able to endure life without being officers. Even in Germany," I told Barbara. Her wide, flat face was flushed, because she had been crying.

"It's a matter of honor. I don't think you can understand that, Mrs. Sprague," she said pointedly. Michael left the room, banging the door behind him. He had given up going to his classes and looked miserable. "They treat me like a murderer," he had muttered. "Soon I'll believe I am one."

The day Anneliese came to us, secretly, against her mother's consent, in a fit of desperation, to cry in Michael's arms and ask me if I couldn't do anything to help them, I decided to go to Berlin and talk with Hellmuth. They expected the final verdict for the next day, and they all seemed out of their minds with fear.

"Try to sleep tonight," I said as she left. It sounded as if Hans Streit were in the death house by now, and I caught myself. I'm getting just as goofy as the rest of them, I thought. It was difficult to keep your common sense under the pressure of ever-impending menace, danger, and disaster.

"Let's telephone Hellmuth. He is a big shot and I am sure he can iron out this whole nonsense with one word," I told Michael. "I loathe asking him a favor; that's why I didn't do it before. But on the other hand, I have done him favors too—and he likes you a lot——"

"You can try it," Michael said dryly. "But I don't think Uncle Hellmuth will permit personal emotions to influence him."

"For Christ's sake! Don't talk like Der Voelkische Beobachter!" I cried. "Give me his telephone number and put some drops in your eyes. They look awful."

Long distance calls in Germany are complicated matters that take much time, and when I finally had penetrated to Hellmuth Klappholz's office in the Ministry of War in Berlin, he was in a conference and could not be disturbed. I left my name and number and asked him to call back on an urgent matter concerning his nephew Michael Tillmann. The telephone seemed politely yet stiffly surprised at this very private request. Then I sat and waited for Hellmuth's call, which did not come. Fortunately Michael found Hellmuth's private number in his address book, and an hour later I started the whole business all over. It was past seven o'clock when the connection finally came through. A maid, speaking the hard Berlin vernacular, announced that Captain Klappholz had gone out and was not expected back before late that night. By that time it had become an obsession with me that putting the whole, senseless affair into Hellmuth's hands was the only chance we had. I called up the desk and made a reservation on the morning plane to Berlin. Michael paced up and down my room, his head bent as if he were walking against a storm.

"You want to go into the dining room?" I asked him. He shook his head and I ordered coffee and cold meat into my room. The clatter of silver spoons on china in front of our door broke the dismal tension and the floor waiter rolled in the small table.

There are always some such small comforting things lined up along the weary road, ready to console, to make everything bright and warm and easy in the midst of cold dismay. A cup of hot coffee after a funeral. A cigarette for the murderer in the death cell. A gulp of whisky in life danger. A warm water bottle for the bereft, a nap for the hopeless, a book to read for the sick, a hand to hold for the dying.

Berlin was the same gray, wintry town it had always been. So this is where I was happy and successful, I thought when the taxi drove me from the airfield to the center of the city. It had not changed much except for some new buildings here and there. They had got rid of their beggars, but the crowds on the streets looked altogether a bit down at the heels and seedy. Yet, somehow, when I heard that hard, quick, humorous dialect again, and looked into those bland closed faces, I felt assured that this town still made deadly jokes about the authorities and that somewhere in its factories and depots, in its slums and proletarian quarters, the next revolution was being brewed.

I had sent Hellmuth a telegram announcing my arrival and called him up from the hotel. Again I could not talk to him in person, but a clipped voice told me that Captain Klappholz would meet me at one-thirty sharp in such and such a restaurant. I had been in that restaurant often enough in the old days, after the theater and before going out dancing. I smiled when I recognized the raspberry-red carpet and the pillars of imitation marble and an atrocious Flora strewing flowers from a cornucopia just in front of the men's toilet.

"I am looking for Captain Klappholz," I told the headwaiter, and by his submissive scraping I knew that Hellmuth had become a big shot indeed.

"Herr Captain is expecting the lady; I have instructions to show the lady to his table; this way, if you please," he said, walking ahead of me on the raspberry-red carpet. "Herr Captain's table is in the blue room, it's quieter there." When we entered the blue room I saw Hellmuth getting up from a small round table in a corner and coming toward me with obvious pleasure. I would hardly have recognized him if I had met him unprepared. He had grown heavy, and there was something un-young in his face. He reminded me of somebody, I tried to remember of whom. The bandleader in the Neckarhof in his fancy uniform, I thought. Hellmuth too had a sagging stomach, smartly held in check by his tunic and his tight belt. He too remembered it from time to time and pulled it in with an almost audible snap.

"Aunt Maria! Looking younger and smarter than ever," he said amiably. "What a pleasant surprise! Will you have some sherry first? Oh I forgot, you Americans prefer cocktails. I personally think it a trifle barbarian. It blunts the palate, don't you think so? I admit I have become somewhat of a gourmet since you saw me last. Will you leave it to me to order your lunch? I know their specialties. How about roast duck with sauerkraut? It's delicious here; they make it with champagne you know——"

I could see that he was happy to show off for me. He gave a demonstration of being a great man yet worldly and simple and entertaining and human, all for my benefit. I tried my best to supply the second voice in our duet of friendly patter, and all the time I searched my brain for an acceptable transition from the roast duck to Hans Streit's desperate plight. I tried to synchronize this blooming, ripe, saturated, and good-natured man with the thin, hard, embittered boy I had known.

"Thanks, Martin is doing fine," I said, and, "Business is rather slack in the U.S.," and, much too eager: "Yes, I think it's wonderful what's happening in Germany."

He told me that he was not married but that he had a very beautiful friendship with an actress of the State Theater. He spoke about Bayreuth, and his tummy sagged as he lost himself in dreamy reminiscences of Wagner's music. I remembered the horrid picture of the Valkyrie swooning in Wotan's arms, which had hung over his bed and which I had always turned around. This brought me back to Michael, who had also committed a sacrilege by turning around something that was not meant to be turned around. Sure, Hellmuth knew that I hadn't come to Berlin to discuss Wagner with him. I wondered whether he let me sizzle in hot oil because it amused him or whether he did not want to discuss my problem in a public place like this. We had reached the black coffee and the cigarette, and I had not yet said a word. When Hellmuth threw a glance at his wrist watch and announced that he would have to see the Field Marshal at three o'clock, I took the dive.

"I telegraphed you that I needed your advice in something concerning Michael," I said.

"Of course, of course," Hellmuth said. "You can absolutely count on me when it comes to Michael. No doubt, you have heard that we Germans have had to resort to substitutes? Well Michael is my substitute for a son—a very good substitute I must say."

Well, well, I thought. This is going to be a cinch. Hellmuth had made an almost unnoticeable sign, and the two servile waiters had disappeared like the jinn in the bottle in the Arabian Nights tale.

"Michael is in a jam," I said. "And you are the only person to get him out."

"I hope it is nothing serious?"

"No. Not at all. That's just it. It's something so unserious and childish and unimportant that you'll laugh about it," I said. "It has been blown up to a terrifying size, but it's really nothing. All it needs is a pin-prick and it'll burst like a soap bubble."

"Well—let's hope so," Hellmuth said. "Would you like some brandy with your cigarette? Or our own Kümmel?"

It was easy to tell Hellmuth my little story. I told it like something to amuse him. A silly little anecdote. The children had champagne and it went to their heads, I said. The band-leader wore a toupee, and you could see he was afraid it might slip off, I said. You know how Michael likes to make little jokes, I said. He thought it was fun; he didn't think of any consequences.

When I had told it all, Hellmuth said nothing. I emptied my jigger of Kümmel; it burned down my throat, but I had taken Kümmel to please Hellmuth. You do such silly things when you are a supplicant. I gulped some water and took another cigarette. Hellmuth lighted it for me, all good manners and eager politeness.

"Look here, Aunt Maria," he said when he was through thinking it over. "You said Michael is in a jam. But if I understand you right, nothing has happened to him. No one even treated him roughly. He is free to do what he wants and to go where he likes. What is his trouble?"

"But, Hellmuth, you know Michael. It is much worse for him to know that his friend has to suffer for a mistake he made than if they had put him in jail himself or beaten him up or something. You must understand how hard this is for both youngsters."

"Yes, I suppose it is worse. But possibly this is an experience that is good for his character. I remember that Michael had something flickering, something impish. I think this is a good cure for him. Yes. I am convinced it is," Hellmuth said. He gazed at the smoke rings he blew artfully into the air, and his face slackened in a queer sort of pleasure. "You remember what happened to Frederick the Great," he said. "His father made him watch the execution of his friend Lieutenant Katte, to punish him and to make a man out of him. Cruel? Perhaps. But effective, you must admit."

"But, Hellmuth—Michael is not going to be a Prussian king," I said, baffled by the queer logic in Hellmuth's conclusion. "He doesn't need such drastic education. Moreover, he is no Frederick the Great; that means he is not worth the sacrificing of his friend. Forget Michael for a moment. Consider Hans Streit. He is perfectly innocent. He is as fine a young German soldier as you could wish for. And his mother, his sister—it is impossible they all should go through such an inferno just because this fool of a Michael made a poor joke."

"How can you say this—what's his name?—Hans Streit is innocent? How can you say such a thing, Aunt Maria? You can be convinced that his guilt will be investigated and proven beyond a doubt before he gets dismissed from the Army. I agree completely with his superiors. He might be a fine boy, but his behavior made him unworthy of wearing the uniform of an officer."

"Because of a ridiculous piece of cardboard? Forgive me, Hellmuth, but this borders on insanity. It's like those insane girls carrying an old brush around and believing it to be their baby. This is not healthy; it's a weird sort of fetishism."

"I read recently a very interesting study about symbols in the world of schizophrenics," Hellmuth said with a thin smile. "When their whole mental outfit goes to pieces they still will recognize symbols. Why? Because the symbol answers and satisfies some deep indestructible urge of the human soul. Granted, that piece of cardboard is only a symbol. The sign 'verboten' is only a symbol. So is the cross. So is the swastika. So is the crown that makes a man into a king and the flag that leads a regiment into battle and victory. You can't say that a cross is only a piece of wood, a flag is only a piece of striped cotton. There are concepts that are so great and sacred that we can only compress them and show them in a symbol. That explains the explosive power and strength people sense behind those symbols. That's what makes the swastika strong enough to conquer the world. Do you follow me?" They are doped, I thought, all of them. Their ecstasies are not human and they copulate with hosts of strange incubi, like the sorcerers of the middle ages.

"Yes. In a way——" I said feebly. Hellmuth moved his hand, and a waiter appeared from nowhere and filled his glass again. He drained it with closed eyes, not as if he were drinking Kümmel but like a man lost in an orgasm.

"That sign 'verboten' is a symbol of law and order," Hellmuth went on. "To respect it is a symbol of obedience. Obedience is the first duty of any soldier. How will an officer enforce obedience if he has not learned to obey himself? Remember Kleist's Prinz Friedrich von Homburg? He wins a battle by disobeying orders and he is convicted to death for it. What was true a hundred years ago is just as true today. You say this Streit had drunk too much and did not know what he was doing? That is the proof that he would make a bad soldier. A soldier has to keep control of himself, sober or drunk, hale or wounded, in battle, in danger, in death. It is much better that he failed on a dance floor than if he had failed in the barracks. Or in a maneuver. Or on a battlefield. I think you have become a bit slack in America, Aunt Maria, or you should know that as well as I do. Uncle Kurt was an officer and a good one, and you yourself made a perfect soldier's wife."

It was funny that I had to stop and think for a moment before I realized that Uncle Kurt had been Captain Tillmann, my husband. Yes, maybe I had been a pretty good imitation of a Prussian soldier's wife, but I had gone on from there and they had crabbed backwards. I felt unable to counter Hellmuth's Nazi dialectic, and his examples taken from Prussian history and literature took the wind out of my sails. He looked at his wrist watch.

"All right, Hellmuth," I said hurriedly. "I can see all your arguments. But for my sake and for Michael's sake—won't you use your influence and see that an exemption is made in this one case?"

"There are no exemptions," he said. "There is no place for exemptions and pampered individuals in a strong state. Even if this young man is no good material for an officer he must have grit enough to accept his punishment without flinching."

"He does. He accepts his punishment. But I don't. And Michael doesn't."

"I'm disappointed in Michael if he doesn't. I counted on him to take the gist of our philosophy back to the United States. There is an enormous field for a German-American of his upbringing. But I see that he has much to learn yet. This is his first lesson, and if it hurts, so much the better. The idea of hiding behind your apron and sending you to sob for mercy doesn't appeal to me."

So that's what you want to make of Michael, I thought, cold with anger. A Nazi agent!

"Look here, Hellmuth, speaking about hiding behind a woman's apron——" I said. "You might be a very great man and a man to be feared and to be admired. But to me you'll always be the boy whom I had to hide from the police when he had got himself into a mess. Remember that big, blue apron I wore in Einsiedel? And how footsore you were? And how scared? I hate to remind you that I helped you when you were in a jam, but you force me to do it. I don't like cashing in old debts and I wouldn't do it if it were for myself, nor even for Michael. But it's for Hans Streit, and I tell you that you'll have to do something for him, whether you believe in exemptions or not. I made an exemption in your case and it was just as much against my grain and my ideas as this may be against yours."

I don't know what Hellmuth thought about it, because his face shut off every expression except a sleepy and dreamy sort of curiosity as if he were to say: What sort of a crazy bird are you, Aunt Maria, to flutter so impertinently into a lion's den?

"Don't let's get sentimental," he said, and with this he left the subject suspended in mid-air and jumped into a conversation about art, the new, German art, almost classic in its beauty, he told me. He advised me not to miss a certain exhibition, brought me to a taxi, and stood smiling and saluting at the curb, a fine monument with a beginning double chin and a sagging stomach smartly held in check by a uniform.

HELLMUTH'S INTERVENTION came a bit too late, for Hans Streit's nerves, worn thin and brittle, cracked, and he shot himself. He did it badly, as people will who do not really want to die. The bullet was taken out of his left lung and the doctors gave him a fifty-fifty chance. However, this harakiri, combined with Hellmuth's powerful appeal, seemed to have appeased the gods above. They decreed that if Hans survived he would be reinstated to his former honorable station in the Army. Anneliese came to tell it to Michael, and Frau Streit wrote me a letter full of thanks and respect. Obviously Hellmuth's glory reflected a faint glow on us, and we stopped being treated like outcasts. All we had to do now was to wait another few weeks to see whether Hans would live or die. I felt almost ashamed that we had remained unharmed and safe through it all, with our American passports shielding us. I called up John and had a compressed three-minute talk with him, wished him a Merry Christmas, and told him that we had to stay on for a while yet but that I hoped to bring Michael back to New York with me. I was filled with boundless nostalgia for New York, for John, even for silly little things like my kitchen sink and my icebox; and for Columbus Circle where people could make as many soap box speeches as they liked.

There is no doubt that those anxious weeks of waiting, first for the military verdict over Hans Streit and then for the decision over his life and death, precipitated the crisis in Michael's illness. The condition of his eyes, which had been proceeding at a slow pace, began to gallop off with him. When he was not hanging around the hospital, waiting to be admitted into Hans' sickroom, he spent the day lying on his bed, unshaven and unkempt, the curtains drawn close, his face turned to the wall. He would pile up magazines and books that I brought him, but he would not read them. "They are too dull," he would tell me. "Besides, reading makes me sleepy." But he did not sleep; he dozed during the day, and during the nights I heard him getting up every few hours and turning on the water in the bathroom. "What's the matter with you, Milky?" I would ask him, and he would answer: "I'm taking a hot shower. It's cold, isn't it?" Yet his forehead and hands were hot and dry, and when I finally persuaded him to take his temperature it was slightly up. We had a German thermometer, which showed 37.6 degrees Centigrade. It wasn't a fever and it wasn't normal either. It was the temperature Manfred Halban had had most of the time. There it is now, I thought. The little cloud, a veil of mist on Michael's horizon, had become black and heavy and covered the whole firmament, but it was still shapeless, unformed as clouds are. In the morning Michael's temperature was down again; he ate his breakfast and even got up and took a walk. He met Anneliese and he had a ten-minute visit with Hans from which he returned all pepped up. It's nothing, I am just overwrought, I told myself. In the evening the thermometer went up to 37.8 degrees, and I was lying awake all night, listening. No, he wasn't coughing. It's the excitement, I thought. It's this whole oppressive atmosphere and the waiting and the futile regret and the anxiety about young Streit. I myself felt chilly all the time, and in a shameful fit of cowardice I postponed from day to day taking the boy to a doctor.

I think it was Pimpernel's letter that reminded me first of Dr. Süsskind in Bergheim. The clerk at the desk handed it to me with a respectful bow because there was the Bergheim-Zuche coat of arms on the thick blue envelope.

"Dear Marion," the Grand Duchess wrote, "I don't know if you will still remember me. I heard through Clara Balbi that you are in Heidelberg, and I should have liked to have seen you again. Unfortunately I am an invalid in a wheelchair for the time being. You may have read in the papers about the plane crash in which I was hurt and my oldest son was killed.

It is very hard for us old people, but I have given up asking Why and trust that the Lord willed it thus.

"I am writing you on behalf of my younger son, who is a very fine engineer indeed and is looking for a job in the U.S.A. He holds a Ph.D. degree from California Institute of Technology and did some practical work at the Ford plant in Detroit. Would you put in a good word for him with your husband, who, I understand, is a very influential man? May my son send him his credentials and hope for his attention? If you are still in the vicinity when Dr. Süsskind permits me to see visitors I hope you will come and talk of old times with your friend,

"Eleonore Bergheim-Zuche (Pimpernel)

"P.S. The Grand Duke is well and sends you his best compliments."

A fine, sad, nostalgic scent rose from the crackling stationery with its useless coat of arms; the scent of a world gone and of youth past.

"Let's get out of here," I told Michael. "Let's make a trip to Bergheim, just for one day. It'll do us good and I want to see an old friend of mine."

I had written a note to Dr. Süsskind, for I had a feeling that a talk with the tough old battlehorse might do a lot in dispersing the black fogs that were brewing around us. We rented a car and drove a few hours on the new highway, of which they were so proud. There were the foothills with their familiar lines, with fields and orchards, barren now under the snow, and sleepy villages huddled around their old churches. We crossed the bridge across the Rhine, and I looked at the reflection of the Cathedral in the gray, wintry waters. Only one dried-up twist of twigs was lying at the feet of Saint Francis. Time after time I had been back in Bergheim in dreams, so that the dream town had become real to me and I did not recognize the real one. I cruised around searching for the high column with Hugo the Kind in his Roman toga and for the new Palace and never found it. The streets had new names, taken from the Nazi ranks, and where the new Palace had been there stood now a pseudo-Greek concrete building looking for all the world like a bank in Kansas City. I suppose it was the local seat of the government; it had a huge flag, and two sentries were posted outside, as motionless and darkly resolved as the figures on a war memorial.

Dr. Süsskind was expecting us. She, at least, had not changed much. She had been dry and hard as a pebble before, and pebbles don't change. "Good day, Marion," she said as if we had parted yesterday. "So this is the American product that worries you?" she said, shooting a sharp glance at Michael and slapping his shoulder. "What's the trouble, young fellow? You look as if you were living a bit too fast. Marion, would you like to see the new maternity ward in the general hospital? It's one of the sights of the town—electric incubators, babies behind glass, everything. And no more stigma on illegitimate offspring either! Too bad what's happened to the boy of the Grand Duchess, but better this way than dying piecemeal of a cirrhosis of the liver. That's what I told her, and she takes it quite sensibly."

"So now let's have a cup of coffee, but I mean real coffee, Marion. It might be unpatriotic to drink it as strong as I do, but it's the one thing an old woman like me needs to keep body and soul together. And then we'll have a look at this specimen of young manhood."

"So you trapped me into a medical examination," Michael whispered to me as we followed her into her living room. It was cold there. "With a blood pressure of over 200 one doesn't need much coal——" the old girl said, and it smelled of floor wax and disinfectant. The coffee was strong, but it too tasted of carbolic acid. With stern disapproval the Führer's picture with the swastika flag draped under it watched us wasting too many precious coffee beans.

Michael got on rather well with the old man hater. After five minutes they were deeply involved in some medical shop talk and I was left out entirely. "Groonemann is a great surgeon," I heard her say. "Young man, if you can get into Groonemann's classes you are lucky indeed." And then came Michael's report about what they had done to some Pfeiffer's and A Different Medium, and I looked out at the old trees in the park. If you see a young tree again after twenty years it makes all the difference in the world, but old trees don't change. "So now we'll give you the once over," Dr. Süsskind said, and gave me a nasty look when I sneaked into the surgery with them. But I felt tight around the chest and dreaded to be left alone; I had been waiting too much during those weeks.

Michael had gone through the same rigmarole ever since his childhood and began stripping before he was asked to. "Nicely built," Dr. Süsskind nodded to me approvingly, as if I had delivered a precise report about a welfare case. "A trifle under-weight maybe, but nice." The last weeks of hanging around in a stupor had not taken all the gold off Michael's skin; it was tanned into him by sun and snow and was rather durable. He breathed and held his breath, bent his head, crossed his hands, did this and that, almost mechanical and with an entirely dis-interested smile, while Dr. Süsskind's hard fingers and big-lobed ears and stethoscope wandered up and down his body.

"No, there's nothing the matter with him," she said at last. "He's a bit run down, that's all. His lungs are perfect as far as I can see. If you want to be absolutely sure, you can have some X-ray pictures made in Heidelberg. I don't like patients running a temperature without a reason though. There's usually a focal point hiding somewhere."

"There is a reason," I said. "That is, an emotional reason. Michael is having a bad time; his best friend tried to commit suicide."

"The slacker!" was all Dr. Süsskind had to say. "Why did he do it? Because of a girl?"

"A girl! Of course not," Michael said. "He had very serious reasons, very serious—and I feel responsible for it."

"In my time love was the most serious reason," Dr. Süsskind said, to my slight amazement. "But these youngsters have dif-ferent ideas. No, nothing the matter with his lungs. Any other trouble? How about venereal diseases? Want me to look at his southern parts, Marion? Never had a little attack of the clap, young man? No? Well, that's rare among students. How about a Wassermann?"

"The precondition for that sort of trouble is lacking, I'm sorry to confess," Michael said, obviously amused by the old girl's straight course. "I haven't lost my precious innocence in Heidelberg yet. The only thing that really troubles me are my eyes."

"Aha!" said Dr. Süsskind. "Rubbed some dirt into them? Some filthy little infection with Staphylococcus aureus? Well, I tell you, I am no eye specialist. You'd better see Professor Lamm about it, if you can afford his fee. He is the best man they have in Heidelberg. Professor Lamm on Neckar Street."

Michael seemed dissatisfied as he slowly slipped on his shirt again.

"Auf Wiedersehen, Marion," Dr. Süsskind said when we left. "No reason to worry about your filius. It's been nice seeing you again. Nice of you to remember the old dragon too." Suddenly she put her arms around my shoulders and kissed my cheek. Her lips were dry and hard. They felt like a newspaper that has been lying out in the rain and then put on the stove to dry.

"Yes, times have changed and things aren't what they were," she said. "Why don't you take this youngster of yours back to America? German suicides are contagious—like the German measles." It was the only indication that Dr. Süsskind was not a dyed-in-the-wool Nazi, but I had become sharp of hearing and perceived all the vibrating overtones in the air.

That was four days before Christmas, and the first station in our long pilgrimage from doctor to doctor. It left me slightly relieved, but Michael remained in a brooding and preoccupied state. "Why are you always harping on my lungs, Mony?" he asked me the following day. "It's a nasty little complex to have for an otherwise sensible mother."

"You were undernourished as a baby," I said. "And—and—there were some cases of T.B. in the family."

"Not on the Tillmann side," Michael said. My heart stopped for a second. Let's take the dive, I thought.

"No. Not on the Tillmann side," I answered. It was as close as I ever came to telling him the truth. I could not do it just then, he looked so sick and miserable. And he never has been with a girl yet, I thought; he has to know more about men and women and all their odd entanglements before I can tell him.

Professor Lamm was a pompous ass, choking with his own importance. He had heavy, sat-through, sagging leather chairs in his waiting room, and here too was the Führer's picture looking down on us, as sternly as if getting sick were a crime against the race and the fatherland. The professor found the eyes irritated and the retina inflamed. He too inquired about venereal diseases and insisted on doing a Wassermann test. It turned out negative; Michael was given some eyedrops and told not to read too much and to come for treatments twice a week.

"I couldn't read too much if I wanted to," he grumbled. "When I look into a book it's all a jumble; it makes me so tired it kills me." He looked strange with his big, dilated pupils, which the professor had treated with atropine. On Christmas eve we sat in my hotel room, and I tried to act cheerful and I had a little tree with candles as a surprise for Michael.

"That's lovely——" he said with a wan smile, and then he turned his head away. "The light hurts in these damned eyes," he said, embarrassed. "I'm sorry, Mony. Blow them out."

Two days later I found the book. It must have fallen under his bed while he was asleep. The grumpy chambermaid found it there and slammed it on my writing desk. It was a sober-looking schoolbook bound in gray linen. Lehrbuch der Augen-heilkunde. When I picked it up to carry it into Michael's room it fell open to where he had put a mark in it. There were some diagrams of sick eyes and also two photos of horrid-looking faces with distorted and destroyed eyes. I looked at them automatically and with a faintly sickish sensation. They were eaten up by pus and pus-filled bags dropped down in sunken cheeks. Then I began to read the marked page.

God, how happily ignorant I had been up to that day and how much I have learned about tuberculosis of the eye during those bitter years since. I had not even known that such a disease existed. Now I read about it, plowing through all the scientific expressions that I did not quite understand. What a fool I had been to lie awake at night and listen whether my boy was coughing. I looked at the photos and read and read again and then I felt sweat streaming down my flanks and my

back getting cold and clammy till my blouse stuck to my skin
as if I had been in the rain. So this is what the boy is thinking,
I thought. So this is what he is afraid of. Poor boy, poor, poor
Milky. I took the book and put it back into his room and
never talked to him about it. I went alone to Professor Lamm,
sat on his sagging waiting bench, and finally had a talk with him.

"You are making a mountain out of a molehill. Your boy has
a simple infection as we see it fifty times every day. We over
here just don't make a big fuss over nothing as your American
doctors do so they can work up a staggering bill," he said dis-
agreeably.

"Yes, but what sort of an infection, Professor?"

"You have to leave it to me what sort of an infection. I see
no sense in giving you explanations that you wouldn't understand anyway."

"Could it be T.B.?" I said, taking the jump.

"It could be but it isn't," the professor barked. "If you want
my frank opinion, your boy is pampered and uses his little
retinitis as an excuse for ditching his classes. Good day."

Dr. Flint was a dry, pedantic, thorough fellow who liked to
give long lectures, his hand with the probing instrument suspended in the air, while the patient sat in a fit of tense apprehension, staring desperately into the glaring mirror on the
doctor's forehead. He too made a Wassermann test and assured
us afterward in a long-winded speech that: "Whatever the
cause of this retinitis might be, it has not luetic origin."

Dr. Pastor, to whom we went from there, had the temperament of a terrier, the face of a bulldog, and the heavy, clumsy
hand of a champ's sparring partner. Dr. Manz was young and
nervous and overemotional. He had a fine skin, which blushed
easily, he made a tragedy over every patient, and he fell in
love with Michael. "I don't mind having my eyes burned out
by every chemical under the sun," Michael swore. "But I'll be
damned if I'll stand for being pawed by a goddamned pansy
specialist."

On a Friday during the first week of January we went to
Frankfort to interview Dr. Lanzhof, who had been recommended
to me as a great authority. He was an old-timer with a square

face that looked as if it had been molded after a discarded Hindenburg bust. He had good blue eyes and surprisingly small hands with soft, pink baby palms. He was a brisk and sharp-spoken old fellow with the manners of a former officer, and it rather surprised me that his receiving room looked like a library. There were bookshelves reaching up to the ceiling, and among the classics of the world literature I discovered many of the books that had been burned and banned a few years before. I knew that everybody avidly read those forbidden books, but only in deep secrecy. By displaying them so openly for anyone to see it was as if Dr. Lanzhof wanted to announce that he was a fearless man with enough pluck and power to do as he pleased and to hell with the Nazis.

"Let's have a little chat before I examine your ogles," he said to Michael. "Mama will keep quiet meanwhile and read a book, yes? What would you like to read?"

I took Thomas Mann's *The Magic Mountain* from the shelf and settled in a corner of the big, high-ceilinged room. I turned the pages, and over the rustling of them I heard scraps of the doctor's dialogue with Michael.

". . . yes, an iridocyclitis can be most unpleasant, as you must know as a student of medicine . . ."

". . . no pain at all, Professor, but it makes any organized work almost impossible . . ."

". . . occasionally a headache—affecting the trigenimus, no? . . ."

". . . I can tell you even now that you will have to have a lot of patience, Tillmann. Patience and rest and more patience . . ."

". . . but my second term begins next week, Herr Geheimrat. Don't you think I could at least attend lectures? . . ."

I had found the chapter I was looking for. ". . . Was nun Sie betrifft, so waren Sie ja wohl immer ziemlich bleichsuechtig, nicht? Aber muede wurden Sie gar nicht leicht bei koerperlicher Arbeit? Doch. . . . Wissen Sie, dass Sie schon frueher krank waren? Ich?" I read. I caught myself reading it over and over again without grasping the sense of it. "Wissen Sie, dass Sie schon frueher krank waren?" Ich? "Wissen Sie, dass Sie schon frueher krank waren?" Ich? Ich? Ich?

"Well, now let's have a look at that ugly retina of yours and I think we're going to do a little Pirquet. What do you think, Herr colleague," the professor said, getting up from his desk. I got up too, with the book still in my hands. "No, you better stay here. I don't like mamas in my torture chamber," he said genially, opening a padded door into the next room. "You can trust the studiosus to me; I am not going to hurt him—much." The door closed behind them, and the minutes dropped with a hollow sound from the clock on the console. In my fine grandparents' home there had been such a clock; very Victorian, with a muscular, bronze Father Time, brandishing his scythe while elegantly leaning against a wheel of black marble. After a while the clock cleared its throat and uttered a muffled chiming. The telephone on the doctor's desk rang a few times and stopped. The old nurse who had written out Michael's chart came tramping through the room and disappeared behind the padded door. Nothing happened for a long time. I picked up The Magic Mountain and tried to read, but my thoughts skidded off and went out of control. Then the door opened and the doctor came back. "Leave the pads on and relax for a few minutes," he called back to Michael, whom he had left inside, and then he closed the door and sat down at his desk. He picked up the chart and scanned it absent-mindedly before he turned his swivel chair toward me. "Do you want me to stall and lie or do you want to know the truth?" he asked.

"The truth. That's what we came for," I said, holding my breath.

"It looks bad, Frau Tillmann," he said. "Pretty bad."

"How bad?" I heard myself ask with a small voice.

"Very bad, if I am not mistaken. There are some patches at the back of the cornea that I don't like at all. The iris has gone down already. It takes those things a long, long time to develop. But when a case is gone as far as this one there's not much hope. Of course I might be wrong——"

"Is it T.B.?"

"So, you suspected it. Well, I don't know yet. Yes, if we take the special symptoms together with the general condition of the boy, T.B. would be the natural conclusion. We'll see how the test turns out. We have to wait seventy-two hours and then we'll know more, Frau Tillmann."

"And if it is tuberculosis—what will happen to him? Will he—is it dangerous—I mean—will I lose him?"

"No, that's not what I'm afraid of."

"But he won't get blind, Doctor, will he?"

The doctor picked up the chart and examined it as if the answer to my question were written on it.

"Let's hope he won't," he said. "Let's hope he won't, Frau Tillmann."

It's funny the things you see in such a moment. The cord of the telephone was coiled and twisted. The doctor had washed-out gray spots on his white coat. Silver nitrate, I thought. Volume eight and nine of Plato on the bookshelf were standing on their heads. I still had my finger between the pages of The Magic Mountain.

"Would you like a little brandy?" I heard the doctor ask.

"No, thanks. I'm all right."

That's what you always say when you feel the world revolve under your feet, as if it were shooting away with you into the blackness of the universe. There is a lot of fake bravado in that thing called self-control, but it helps at the moment. The doctor came over and patted my shoulder. "You've got to be a good little soldier," he said. "Excitement is bad for your son."

"Sure, Doctor. I know."

"He is no fool, our young studiosus. He knows damned well what this test means. Those next three days won't be much fun. Not for him and not for you. It would be a good idea to distract his mind if you can. You seem a sensible woman."

"I'll try my best."

"All right. I'm going back to our patient now. Let's hope things turn out to the best."

After a few minutes the doctor came back with Michael, who carried his coat over his arm. When he buttoned the sleeve of his shirt I noticed the two patches of adhesive tape side by side near the crock of his elbow. One for the tuberculin that had been injected and one for the control solution. It was the fourth time in Michael's life that this test had been made, and the three times before had been negative.

"Are you ready?" I said with a smile so stiff it crackled in the corners of my mouth.

"Ready, Ma'am," Michael said, also smiling. He put his dark glasses over his eyes. "You'll have to lead me," he said. "Atropine always makes me feel like a broken camera. You can't close the shutter."

"All right, Tillmann, take it easy. And come back, shall we say, Monday at the same time?"

The doctor seemed to have pushed a button, because the old nurse stuck her head into the door and he said: "Next, please." He handed her Michael's chart and remained standing behind his desk.

"Auf Wiedersehen," said Michael. "Auf Wiedersehen on Monday," I said. The doctor indicated a short, stiff bow. "My best respects, Tillmann. My best respects, Frau Tillmann," he said. It was an old-fashioned form of greeting, and I did not know whether he used it by habit or whether it was his way of acknowledging a real bad case among his patients.

"What would you like us to do now, Milky?" I asked when we stood on the street. "Hang around Frankfort until Monday or go back to Heidelberg? We can still make the five-fifteen train."

"I'll tell you what we're going to do if you are a good sport. We will take the five-fifteen and I will get my skis and wax them tonight, and first thing tomorrow morning we'll go into the mountains and have a roaring good time. I'll ask Anneliese to lend you her skis, you two are about the same height. Okay?"

"Wouldn't you rather take Anneliese along? I don't know how roaringly good a time you'll have with me."

"No. No. Anneliese can be fun, but I don't think she is the right company for a guy who has to wait seventy-two hours to see if his tuberculin test is going to itch or not. After all, a man's best friend is his mother."

When you read a collection of old letters written by mothers to their sons fifty or a hundred years ago they were full of beauti-

ful, big words and noble sentiments and benedictions and advice
and prayers. But my generation has learned to keep its mouth
shut, smoke a cigarette, and drink a brandy. I suppose it's only
a fashion. As Christopher says, everything comes in cycles and
our grandchildren will be back perhaps at being talkative and
dripping with demonstrative emotions. I have an idea that
people whose lives are tranquil have an urge to blow it up into
something high-sounding, like poetry and symphonic music and
grand opera and Sunday sermons. While we, living in a period
that is crowded with catastrophes, have to resort to a convention of understatements in order to stand it all. And so, knowing that my son might become blind and knowing that he knew
it too, the best I could do was not to speak about it.

Distress is a queer sort of drug; it affects you like a shot in
the arm. We were laughing when we arrived at the train, and
during the short ride we behaved like a couple of hopped-up
loons. We made silly puns and thought them screamingly funny.
We told old jokes and furnished new, absurd endings to them.
When the compartment became too crowded with people we
didn't like, Michael went into one of his improvisations. He
pretended that we were sideshow entertainers, that we had a
trained python in our suitcase; he spoke in the cosmopolitan
hodgepodge language of a circus clown and made me into
Princess Shuleima, the snake dancer. We had the whole compartment joining in the fun, and never in my life, never before
and never after, have I been so unhappy as during that train ride.

Back at the Neckarhof we had dinner in the dining room
where the band played and the sign JAZZ VERBOTEN hung undis-
turbed. Michael ordered a special bottle of wine, a sparkling,
rich Moselle, 1921, and we made wonderful plans for a motor
trip through France and knew all the time that we wouldn't
make it. Once in a while he touched his sleeve where the prick
of the tuberculin syringe was hidden under the adhesive tape,
and I pretended not to notice it. Afterward we went to a picture;
it wasn't the kind of picture to make you forget a toothache, but
it was the best we could find.

When we came out of the theater it was five minutes past
ten, and I was glad that six of the seventy-two hours were

killed and lived through. We went straight home, found our skis waxed and ready, set the alarm clock for six, and said good night. "Don't forget to take your temperature," I called to Michael when I heard him rummage in the bathroom.

"I'm taking it," he mumbled, hampered by the thermometer in his mouth.

"How much?" I asked after five minutes.

"I can't make it out. You read it yourself," he said, stepping through the doorway and holding the thermometer out to me. It showed 37.2 degrees.

"Well, what is Old Koch doing to me?" he asked.

"Almost normal," I said. "Let me sleep now or I won't be up in time."

"Good night, Mony."

"Good night, Milky."

"Good night. And don't worry."

"You know I'm not the worrying kind."

"Well—good night."

I listened for a while until all sounds in his room had subsided and he seemed asleep. After a while I turned my light off, and a little later I began praying.

There is something slightly schizophrenic about the prayers of people who do not believe in God and also something very pitiful. To the truly religious, prayer is elation and comfort, because he has faith and God is his friend. To the unthinking, undoubting people who are going to church because their parents did, it gives the righteous feeling of doing one's duty, like having clean teeth and a fresh shirt. To those who mumble their Om Manipadme hūm, turn their prayer wheels, or polish the beads of their rosaries, it is a powerful, peace-giving sedative, a pious way of counting sheep in endless repetition. To the dancing dervishes of every religion it brings the sacred frenzy, the trance, the boundless relief of letting yourself go, of breaking through the walls of reality. But to those who don't believe in God, prayer is like a fight in the dark with all the odds against them: like a fist that takes them at the scruff of the neck and forces them down onto their knees.

You can't do it, God, you can't let this happen, not to Michael,

not to my boy, please, God, please, listen to me, God, if you
exist. I know you are not there and if you are maybe you don't
care what happens, but there must be some order, there must
be some law. You, somebody, somewhere, listen to me! Don't
hurt my child, not him, he is young, he hasn't done any harm,
you can't hit him like this. Take me, hurt me, break me, let
me die, punish me, because it's all my fault and my guilt. God,
hear me, God, I don't know how to beg but hear me. Let me
talk to you, whoever you are. Don't let Michael get blind,
don't let him suffer, don't throw him into that awful darkness.
I offer myself to you, I give myself up, do with me what you
want, but save my child. I never asked you favors, God, and
I will never demand anything from you again if you will only
help me this time. If you exist at all, if you exist, God, Law,
Order, you can't be unjust. If you exist, you know where the
guilt is and you won't send the punishment the wrong way.
If it's revenge you want, take it on me, but let my child alone.
I have lived wrongly and sloppily, I have been slack and have
sinned and transgressed; if I have to pay for it, don't let me
pay with the eyesight of my child, God. Hear me, listen to
me, look down on me. Here I am crushed and humbled, crying
to you for mercy, if that is what you want. If you are God,
you must be just and kind, and you will help me. Strike me,
God, any day, any hour, any way you want, and I will not
complain. Thank you, God. Now I have delivered myself to
you and I am expecting your judgment. But save Michael, save
Michael, save Michael.

The night was translucent in front of my windows, filled
with cold, clear moonlight thrown back by the snow. Around
me the air was singing and roaring as in a storm, and the
walls of the room disappeared in a transparent cloudy emptiness.
My prayer was a cramp and a convulsion, painful as giving
birth. At last I was empty, and a deep exhaustion came over
me, and then a feeling of great relief, as if I had washed out
and cleansed myself from all my fears. For a while I cried
and then I remembered Putzi, my Common Little grandfather; all
the time he had been sitting on a fat cloud quite near to God
Father in a childish heaven. "When you're really unhappy you

will cry out: Help me, please, God help me!" he had told me once. "Yes, Putzi, you are right," I whispered into the strange diffused darkness. I felt so light and empty, as if I had no body any longer, and I thought: this is how it will feel to die. For a fleeting second I had got hold of an ultimate happiness, and then it was gone. I sobbed a few times; then the walls of my room returned, I came back into reality, the big German pillow beneath my cheeks felt wet, the white ruffles around it looked like faces, and there was the faintly singed smell of ironed linen. But the peace and deep contentment remained with me; I heard the church clock chime twice, and then I fell asleep.

IT HAD BEEN SNOWING during the night, and the black early-morning streets were wrapped in fresh white swaddling clothes when we left the hotel. All sounds were muffled, all trees stood motionless under their load, only once in a while a branch would move and stretch and spring back in place when a compact piece of frozen snow dropped off and released it. It was dark .yet, and the street cleaners had not begun to sweep the snow into heaps. The streets were empty, white and black, like a photographic negative. The air was still, with that peculiar stillness of an early snowed-in winter morning. As we stalked through the thick, soft whiteness that had leveled out all curbs, I remembered those mornings in Einsiedel when I had shoveled myself a trail from our house to the Gabel farm and how warm it had been in the stable when I came for the milk.

"Wouldn't it be nice in Einsiedel on a day like this?" Michael said, and I had to smile. Whenever we live close together for a while our thoughts begin to run on parallel tracks.

"Yes, that would be nice," I said. "Except that they have turned it into a prison camp."

"Who told you that?" Michael asked hotly.

"Someone who has been there. A refugee. An old friend of mine, in fact. Shani Kern. They busted his right ear which is too bad because he is a composer," I said and then there was silence.

"Let me carry your skis," Michael said after a while, as if to make up by personal kindness for the brutal wrongs the Nazis committed.

When it comes to summing up, the best thing to be said about us humans is that we have a limitless ability to be happy in the midst of unhappiness. This was our day and we made the best of it. This was not a black yesterday, nor a dreaded tomorrow. This was Now, and Now was good and we crammed it so full of greedy joy and fun and liveliness that it almost burst. It began with the foaming hot milk we drank in the small coffee shop opposite the station and it got better and better as the day went on. The local train was crowded with a gay, humming, buzzing freight of snow-hungry people. My old blue skiing outfit smelled of moth balls, for I hadn't used it since Michael had left America. I pushed my chin down into my collar and felt the roughness of the material like a clumsy caress and I was happy to go skiing with my boy again. Someone played on a mouth organ and a girl had a guitar and after a while the whole coach was singing. We were tightly packed onto the hard wooden benches and brimming with good fellowship. They sang the silly, nonsensical stuff skiers are singing all over the world, and you could forget for a while you were in a country with a nationalistic idée fixe.

At a small station we piled out of the train and into a waiting bus, which soon began a rattling up-hill climb. The road was cleared through the forest and the trees stood stiffly at both sides, packed with snow, leaning forward in an expectant and attentive attitude. As we reached the ridge of the first range the dawn had become liquid and a pink glow outlined the top of the higher mountains before us, which sat dark and massive—like heavy metal in the morning.

"You must take a look before we make the turn," Michael told me. "Doesn't the village seem from here like those toy villages at Eichheimer's?" I looked back into the valley, where the roofs leaned against the hillside; each one of the low farmhouses cut a neat rectangle around its farmyard; everything was covered with the fresh snow; only the dunghill formed a tiny dark spot in every farmyard, because the warmth of the dung melted the snow away. The air was so clear you could see some of the chimneys smoking their morning pipe, and the pink glow began creeping down from the heights and flirting with the weathervane on the spindly church spire.

While I still looked at the village, something arrived in my mind and fetched a faint resonance. "What did you say was the name of that village?" I asked Michael.

"Alpendorf," he said. "Why?"

"I don't know. It sounded familiar," I said.

"What's the matter? Did you see a ghost?" Michael asked at my side. You are getting too damned bright and sensitive, my little Milky, I thought. My heart felt tight as I recognized the road on which I had taken Walter Brandt to the station the day he went into the war.

The sun was out when we arrived, and the air had a sharp bite up there. We stamped our feet to get them warm while we waited for the bus driver to lug our skis from the bus top and sort them out. The snow had many colors under the sun, as if a careless painter had spilled his pails. Pink and gold and the hue of pale anemones and deep blues in the shade, where the trees stood bent over a frozen brook. But the old Paradise Inn had made space for a hotel.

The big hostelry was a rather pretentious piece of architecture, with the airs of a Bavarian castle about its front, but with tiny ratholes of rooms inside. Farther up the hill stood the Youth Hostel, complete with swastika flag and belligerent and re-solved looking troops of Hitler Youth marching in and out. From my window I had the view of the beginners' slope at the side of the hostelry, where screeching, awkward little figures were exercised by a stern, slim young skiing instructor. Farther up, a stretch of forest clung to the shoulder of the mountain and receded to leave a clearing free. From my window it seemed only a small patch of white on which three tiny dark insects were dancing; skiers doing their turns. But then it came with a pang of recognition to my mind that this might well be the meadow from which I had plucked a handful of grass during an unforgettable hour. No reason to get sentimental, my girl, I told myself. What has this long-ago to do with the now and today? You are Mrs. John Sprague, quite a different person from the one who was here in 1914. But don't you see how things repeat themselves? Like in a fixed pattern, like the tomatoes on my wallpaper, like the theme in a sonata. Once before you came here for three days to be happy and to forget the afterward. That doesn't prove a thing. There was a man you loved and there was a war and the man went away and never came back. That only proves that you can live through a lot of hardships and the crab apples bloom again and again. It just shows what a good hardened plant you are. Listen, Marion, my girl: Never be scared. Nothing can happen to you. That's the whole of it. If this here, this with Michael should go wrong, you'll stand it and it will pass. No, it won't and Michael is my child and if a child gets sick you feel it as if it were still inside of your womb and part of you. All right, that's enough now. Take your skis and don't spoil this day for the boy. Remember the little lady bug? Pommerland is on fire. Yes, it's on fire; the whole world has been on fire ever since that day in 1914. So now let's go and take a few spills.

There is no joy so sharp and clear-cut as being on skis. The pleasures of dancing and flying and fighting combined; being happy, drunk with speed, free of weight. There is the firm hold of my boots against my ankles and the first timid, gliding steps over the softly graded white space. The sway and delight of the turns, the hot labor of herring-boning up the steep shoulder of the mountain, the underbrush scratching against the roughness of my pants, sweat trickling down my face, the cold air brushing through my throat into my lungs, the blood dancing and singing in my veins. There is the wide view from the top and the impatient moment of rest up there and the sun warm on my hair, and the wind stinging cold against my eyelids and then, at last, the thrill of the downhill swoop. I can do it, I can do it, I shift my weight and gain confidence, the air rushes past my ears with the sound of tearing silk and my muscles are doing their work with precision; they are wonderful, my muscles, I did not know they still were so wonderful. A fir tree springs into my way and runs against me with unbelievable swiftness and is left behind. My long blue shadow races ahead of me over the snow and then another shadow joins mine and then Michael dashes past me with a shrill little yell, in an explosion of sunlit snow powder, like a bird passing another. I am leaning forward, feeling securely anchored in the hold of the cables and following Michael, faster, faster; we are racing each other, we overtake a group of skiers. Michael, still rushing on, waves his hand with the pole and slows down. I am still shooting downhill, then the ground pushes hard up against me, I feel a sharp jerk, I am catapulted into the air and land on my rear end, my legs a jumble and snow dropping from my twisted skis down into my surprised face. I lick it from my lips and brush it from my eyelashes. Carefully I sort out my limbs from the tangle and put myself back into a vertical position. Michael is standing farther down, where snow-laden pine trees form a crescent; he is signaling to me, shaking with laughter. I zoom toward him with my best Christy, though with the undignified feeling of having torn a big hole into the rear of my pants.

I tried to catch my breath. When I looked at the open level space ahead of us I recognized the little lake where I had been swimming as a young girl. For a dizzy second the past and the present blended into one full flash of delight. The most beautiful cloud I had ever seen pushed slowly up behind the pine trees, a gust of wind ran through the dry reed and the trees put their heads together and sighed. Michael's face was tense, almost greedy; I could not see his eyes behind the goggles but his mouth was open as though he wanted to swallow all the rich, lively world around us. I don't know why I felt so strong and sure at that moment. But it was the first time that I thought: Don't be afraid, Michael, I won't let it happen to you. You don't have to look at all the beautiful things as if you would never see them again; you don't have to store them away as a memory to take out and remember when you will be blind. It won't happen. I won't accept it, I'll fight and battle and not allow you to get hurt.

I wonder if birds ever get stiff muscles and sore shoulders from too much flying? I was stiff and sore that evening as if I had moved on wings all day long. My thighs and calves tingled with fatigue, the skin of my face was taut and hot, my lips began to crack, my ears were singing, and I was drunk with sun and snow and fresh air. A hot shower would have been wonderful, but as the hostelry had no such luxuries to offer, we crowded around the huge tiled stove in the lobby and heated our own furnace with hot, spiced Glühwein. For dinner we sat in a long row around a rough oak table and filled ourselves with thick split-pea soup, which is the best dish after a day in the snow. Just then the wistful little ghost of an old body chose to bob up behind my chair and whispered to me: "Gold and split-pea soup, don't forget. Gold and split-pea soup."

"Next time I'll know better," I murmured.

"What?" Michael asked surprised.

"Next time there'll be a war I'll have plenty of split-pea soup," I said.

I looked at Michael across the table. He had taken off his goggles and he gazed curiously at me. His eyelashes were much too long and his face shone with cold cream, it was gaunt and finely chiseled, like the saints Master Riemenschneider had carved for the churches of Würzburg and Nuremberg. I felt infinitely fond of him. I would have liked to stroke his hair or kiss his cheeks or take him on my lap like a baby. Well, such demonstrations of mother love were out of question between us. He took like a man what was coming to him, but, dear God, he was only a boy. I put down my fork and held out my hand to him.

"Hello, Milky——" I said.

"Hello, Ma'am," he answered. "Having fun?"

"Oodles of fun," I said, obediently falling into the vernacular.

"So am I," he said. "Oodles and oodles of fun. It's been the nicest day I've had in a long time."

Thank you, Milky, I thought. Thank you, my boy, thank you. That's all I wanted.

We sang, we banged our cups on the table, we joined hands with the crowd, we played silly games, we danced in our heavy boots to the music of the radio reinforced by intermittent offerings of the guitar and the mouth organ. Finally we crept upstairs into our tiny rooms and I took out the red leather case with the thermometer.

"If I have a little temperature it doesn't mean a thing," Michael muttered. "It's the altitude—and the work-out. And that's a scientific fact."

"Yes, Professor," I said. "Now keep it under your tongue and don't babble for a few minutes. And leave those adhesive pads alone."

"Yes, Ma'am, Mrs. Sprague," he said and pulled the sleeve of his pajama down over the two patches on his arm.

He showed 37 degrees. Normal. "Let's put it back for another minute," I said. It still was down to 37. Thank God. Thank you, God. It's all been a false alarm—but thank you all the same, from the bottom of my heart. If you want to take me at my word and have me break my neck tomorrow I won't kick and I won't complain, not ever again, God.

"Sleep well, Milky."

"I'm asleep already. Good night."

I undressed and went to bed. The door between our rooms stood open and wouldn't have stayed closed if we had wanted it. The bed was hard and the cover was a heavy, lumpy feather bed, the perfect design for creating nightmares and bad dreams. Tired. Stiff. Sore. Happy. Yes, happy. Confident. Confident in what? Just confident.

"Is your bed as bad as mine?" Michael asked sleepily when he heard me toss around on my creaking springs.

"I don't know how bad yours is. These Germans are geniuses in making life uncomfortable."

"So are the English. Even more so, aren't they?"

"I guess so."

"Yes, and that's as it should be. You've got to be tough and hardened and used to discomfort, so you can take it when you have to. You Americans are soft and pampered. Always worrying how to raise the high standard of living still a bit higher. It's your sacred cow."

"I don't like you saying 'You Americans.' You are an American yourself now, don't forget that."

"I'm a German. I'll always be a German. When I'm twenty-one I can choose my country and I will."

"I'm too sleepy to listen to your Weltanschauung now, Milky. Good night."

"Some day Germany and England will go together and then America will wake up and rub her eyes and find herself isolated and unfit and sissified. There will be trouble and America won't be prepared to stand it."

"Write it to your senator."

"If you don't use a muscle it atrophies. That's what happens over there. They are atrophied. Why they can't even walk three blocks without getting pooped. To me America seems like a rich man who's always complaining that he lost a thousand bucks at the races but doesn't care if his neighbor at the wrong side of the tracks is starving."

"Go climb a tree, Milky. I'm sleepy."

"No, Mony. I mean it. I know what I'm talking about (very serious). It's easy for a nation or for a person to be fair as long as the going is smooth. It's when things go wrong that you have to show your mettle. Nations, I mean, and persons too. It's better for you not to be pampered and not to feel sorry for yourself when things go wrong. Am I right?"

Poor boy, poor Milky, wrestling with his fate. He had been a cry baby and the tears had dropped on his knees and now he had to make himself hard and strong so he could take a blow standing up.

"Yes, I guess you are right there, Milky."

There was a long silence and I thought that he had fallen asleep. But then came a sharp squeak of his bed, as if he had sat up, and his voice in the dark.

"Mony? Are you asleep?"

"No, not quite."

"I've changed my mind, Mony. About Anneliese, I mean."

"Yes?"

"Yes, I'm—we were engaged, sort of—but I'm not going to marry her. I didn't tell you we were sort of engaged? Well, that's over. I suppose it was a little childish anyway. She did not quite live up to my ideas during the last weeks. I think she has a one-track mind. She is pretty, though. Do you think she is pretty, Mony?"

"Oh yes, very pretty."

"Yes, she is pretty. I suppose I would like to have a pretty wife even—even if my eyes should get worse and I couldn't see her so well. But Anneliese wouldn't be a good companion for a guy with bad eyes. You know, a person gets different ideas about what's pretty when a person has eye trouble. You get so damned subtle and sensitive about many things when your eyes let you down. Like about a voice, and what people talk and the way they enter a room. Anneliese has no music if you know what I mean. When we had that bad scene all I could see of her face was a blur but she made so much noise and she had no more conception of how I felt about the whole mess as if she were a piece of wood. By God, that's how she appeared to me. Like a squeaky door that drives you crazy."

"Your eyes won't let you down, Michael," I said. "You can trust me they won't. You'll take a few weeks' rest and a few treatments and they'll be as good as new."

There came no answer and after a while Michael picked up another thread.

"I must tell you something funny," he said. "It's about Hans Streit. We had a long talk the other day, that is, as long as they allow him to talk. He's still pretty low, but I think he'll soon be definitely out of danger. Well, he asked me if my father could get him to New York and maybe give him a job. He meant John, of course. Do you think John would do it? Hans is a decent kid and I owe him more of a compensation than I'll ever be able to pay. But isn't it funny? He said he wants to see how the world looks outside of Germany. Of course, he had a terrible shock and he went through quite a crisis and, no doubt, this Major Vitztum is a veritable hellhound and a skunk, but would you ever have thought that Hans would want to run out on his own country? Now that he can become an officer?"

What a tangled, twisted skein are the lives of all those bewildered, confused youngsters, I thought. Johnnie, the scion of an old American family in Madrid, fraternizing with the communists and braving the fascist air raids. Martin, my hundred-per-cent German eagerly turning himself into a true American. Hans, the German soldier fed up with it all and wanting to run away. And Michael, my brave fairhaired little half-Jew hanging on to Nazism by the skin of his teeth.

"However," he said in the dark. "Even if I won't marry Anneliese—I still think that Hitler is a genius."

Heaven have mercy on us if he is, I thought but I did not say it. I heard the creaking of the bed next door and then an amused chuckle as Michael lay back.

"Maybe we could go into business together, Hans and me," he said. "I could grind the organ and he could train a monkey. Or maybe we could sell gardenias at the corner of Fifty-second and Sixth. We'd make a nice pair, he with his lungs shot to pieces and I with my eyes gone. The halt and the blind. Is that what the Bible calls us?"

"So, and now it's really time to go to sleep and not to talk any nonsense," I said. I had recognized the Manfred Halban touch in Milky's last remark, the skeptic, bitter, self-destructive Jewish sort of humor.

"Good night, Mony," he mumbled. "Let's hope the weather will hold out tomorrow. It's been a wonderful day today."

In the morning his temperature had gone up a bit—37.3, well almost 37.4.

"That doesn't mean a thing," Michael said. "That's from my sunburn. My face itches so I can't even shave."

I had a sunburn too. I went into my room, closed the door by pushing the only chair against it, and in deep secrecy I took my own temperature. Yes, it was a bit above normal too: 37.2. I put the thermometer into its red leather case and began to sing.

The weather was holding out, at least until two o'clock in the afternoon. By that time the sun was gone, an endless herd of big, dirty cloud sheep were pushing across the ridge in a great hurry and spreading out over the blue sky pasture. The wind changed; it came in warm gusts from the south; some thin, watery snow began to dribble and to melt and to end up in a steady rain. The snow under our skis became spongy, and a nasty coat of sleet formed on top of it. When we came back to the hostelry the lounge was filled with loudly lamenting skiers, with the smell of wet clothes and greased shoes and with a general air of impatient boredom. Michael took off his goggles and stared desolately at a group who tried to coax something entertaining from the radio.

"I'm cold," he said. "The moment you stop moving around it gets chilly."

"Want some Glühwein?"

"The very idea! Glühwein at two o'clock. No, thanks."

"Hot chocolate? Hot milk?"

"No, thanks," he said listlessly. "The only thing I'd like is to get out of my things and go to bed and get warm."

"Why don't you do that? I'm feeling cold and tired myself."

Our rooms were cold, but the heavy feather beds looked promising. Michael closed the wooden shutters in front of his window and made himself an artificial night. My bed was warm though hard, and the rain played a steady sleepy cadenza on the window sill. I had fallen into a doze without knowing it when I heard Michael's voice.

"Mother——" he called. "Mother——"

I threw a quick glance upon my wrist watch. Not quite four o'clock. It was almost dark. I switched on the light.

"Mother——" Michael called me. It sounded urgent and queer. He never called me Mother, except in fun or in distress. I slipped my robe over my pajamas and went into his room. He too had his light burning; he was sitting up in his bed, staring at me with his sick eyes as if he could not see me.

"What is it, Michael?" I asked, frightened.

"Come here, Mother," he said. "Sit down here."

"Yes, Milky, what is it? Are you sick?"

"It didn't take seventy-two hours," he said. "We don't have to wait that long."

I searched his face. He nodded his head and he smiled. I think I smiled too. You see people smile at the craziest moments. He pushed back the sleeve of his pajama and held his arm before my eyes. It was a rather thin, boyish arm covered with white fluff. Traces of the sticky substance of the adhesive plaster were clinging to that fluff where he had taken off the two little pads. There was a little irritation, not bigger than a half-dollar, not much different from a mosquito bite.

"Is that all?" I said stupidly.

"Yes. That's all," he said. "That's the verdict. That's T.B."

"It doesn't mean anything," I said. "You'll be all right. You'll be all right, Milky. Doctors are so clever nowadays. We'll get you a good specialist. You'll be all right, we won't let you be ill, we'll fight it, you'll be all right."

"Sure. I'll be all right," he said. "I'm all right. Come, stay here. I'll be all right. Please turn off the light; it hurts me. Thanks."

In the dark he grabbed my hand and pressed it hard. His hand was hot and dry with fever, and I held it as firmly and tightly as I could. It was the old grip from the time when we had to change the bandages of our wounded men and were short of morphine. After a while he began to shake and the bed creaked softly under his convulsed shoulders.

"It's nothing. I'm having a bit of a chill," he whispered. I kept on holding his hand and put my other fist to his mouth. He bit into it as he had done as a child when he got an injection and when he had had a mastoid and the earache was unbearable. His teeth closed over the heel of my fist like a vise and he kept on shaking. Then it ebbed down into a trembling and I felt the boy relax. The rain beat against the wooden shutters, someone tramped down the corridor, there was the clatter of coffee cups and the plunking of a guitar downstairs.

"Damn it, damn it, damn it——" Michael whispered desperately.

"It's all over now. We'll fight it out together. You'll be all right."

"Funny. I'm seeing the most wonderful colors now——" he whispered. "Much better than the real ones."

He took a new grip on my hand and we became two links of a hard, stiff iron chain. The time went by; I heard my wrist watch ticking ahead in great haste. I tried to regulate my breath and breathe together with Michael. I compressed myself into those few inches where my hand touched his and tried a fakir trick. I tried to let every drop of strength and will and courage and faith and hope that was in me stream through our linked hands into him. It was almost like the time when he had been a newborn baby drinking from my breast. I don't know how long we remained welded together like that. But after an immeasurable time he began to loosen up and his breath brushed the air, quietly and gently, as if he had fallen asleep. I heard the bus start in front of the house amidst the jokes and shouts of the departing skiers and move off and fade away and then there was only rain again and my ticking watch. My arm was numb and my hand felt like dead cold lead. I moved it a little and Michael closed his fingers around it.

"Don't go away, Mother," he murmured. "I need you now."

In all the anxious black months to come this was the only time he asked for help. Not a complaint, not a cry, not a tear, not a trace of self-pity. Only strong, hard, young valor. Milky, my little boy, I am proud of you.

10

INTO the crevasse where Marion crouched, thinking, smoking, listening, remembering, fell a sheet of clarity and sudden enlightenment.

"Yes, God," she said. "I forgot that night when I prayed to you. I wanted to forget it. Actually I didn't think you would come some day and present the bill, correct and punctual as the tax assessor. But the right is on your side and I don't protest. I offered you my life if Michael would not get blind and I promised I wouldn't kick if you took it. All right. I'm keeping my word. I'm not kicking, God. I'm ready. I just think it is funny that you should be so accurate. I never thought of you as an adroit book-keeper like my father was. But if this is the price for Michael's eyesight, I must say I've made a bargain. In a way you are magnanimous, God, even if you are strict. You could have let me die of cancer or in some other horrible way. They say that freezing is the most pleasant way of dying. It's better than falling asleep and dreaming. There is music, they say, and a heavenly feeling of well-being. I thank you devotedly for making it so easy for me, God.

"So this is the ultimate soup I have cooked for myself and have to eat now. I think it's damned funny. I can't help it, God, I think it's the goddamnedest funniest thing I've ever heard of. I just hope that you'll treat the rest of this mortal mess and muddle just as judiciously as you did me and that you won't forget to let those who make the great mistakes pay for them just as you let me pay for my little mistake. I can feel myself sitting on the scale while you're reading the balance sheet. How do I make out in the final balance, God?

"And, listen, God, take good care of Michael after I'm gone. I never liked to let some unfinished business behind. I hated to put down a toy before it was carved and finished. Today I didn't take the time to finish Nero—and also, Michael is only a sketch yet. I can see the man who will grow from this sketch and I think it will be a good man and, perhaps, a happy one. I think the mixed strains in his blood will make him tolerant and understanding. I think his sickness and his struggle will have cleaned him of many impurities. I also think that there is enough of Europe in him and enough of America to make a happy synthesis of him. You know what a curious creature I've been all my life. I would like to watch Michael develop and grow and I would like to be at his wedding and carry my grandchildren in my arms. And like every human being since Adam and Eve, I hope that they will be better than we were and that they won't have to fight all over the fights we fought. I'm meeting my obligations, God. Now you go ahead and meet yours. Okay. I'm ready. Amen."

"So this is vienna," Michael said, peering out from behind his dark glasses. To look at things had become such a strain to him that his face wore a perpetual taut smile as a cover. He still could see, but already the apologetic expression of a blind man formed new lines around his mouth. I had bought him a cane with an ivory handle, and he attempted to use it with a certain swagger that was more pathetic to me than if he had openly searched his way in a world that became more blurred from day to day.

"Yes, this is Vienna——" I answered, rather bashfully, for there was not much to brag about in the sight before us.

"From what you told me I expected it to be something different," Michael said.

"I too," I had to admit. "But February is an unbecoming month anywhere."

"You said it would smell of violets. I think it smells of old dishwater," Michael said, sniffing into the air. His nose had become too damned sensitive since his eyesight began to let him down, but no doubt the odor of fried onions and stale grease emerged in little gusts from all those little basement restaurants where the little people of Vienna habitually ate their second breakfast. The streets were a bobbing trickle of wet black umbrellas, the rain was washing the dirty face of the pavement, softly gurgling rivulets rushed toward the clogged gullies, where they collected into stagnating black puddles; the policemen wore shining oilcloth coats with upturned collars and everything looked moody and down-at-the-heels; the houses, the people, their clothes, their shoes, their way of walking, their faces, their expressions. We had come from a visit at Dr. Konrad's and were standing at the corner of a dead, triste little street trying to catch a taxi. But the few that were rumbling by were all taken. Ever since the moment of our arrival I had had to struggle against the queer and slightly sickening sensation of knowing every stone, sound, smell of this town as I knew my own skin and yet of being a stranger and not knowing it at all. Maybe if I had returned to Vienna on a pleasure trip I would have been able to work up some glow of sentimental delight. But as it was, everything was blotted out by my one purpose and thought: Michael. Michael's eyes, Michael's future, Michael's very life.

"Look here, Frau Tillmann," Professor Lanzhof, in Frankfort, had told me, "I could wash my hands of this case and stick our studiosus into some T.B. sanatorium in the Odenwald and see what happens. Or I could tell you to take him to Arosa or to pack him up and ship him back to America and see what the fellows of the Mayo Clinic can do with him. But if you want my frank opinion, I'd advise you to go to Vienna first and see Kohn about it. He has devoted his whole life poking around tubercular eyes and nothing else. He is a fiend for hopeless cases, and, damn the little Jew, he has done quite a few miracles. Kohn in Vienna, Arthur Kohn. That is, he calls himself Dr. Konrad since he was chased from the university and out of Germany. Naturally I don't know his address, but I have followed his reports in some medical magazines; he seems to get astonishing results with his own special protein. Let me see—here I have it, Tubocolin 287 he calls it; it's something on the line of Old Koch but more— how shall I say—more dynamic. You understand, in a way it's still in the experimental stage. In some cases it not only doesn't work but aggravates the condition of the patient. But when it catches it does a lot of good and it's very well worth taking the risk. What I'm telling you here is high treason, Frau Tillmann. But I have an idea that if Hitler, Göring or Göbbels had some such serious trouble with their eyes they would go to Vienna and see Kohn about it. You go there too—and drop me a postcard once in a while and let me know how our studiosus is coming along. Bon voyage, Frau Tillmann, and my respects. My best respects."

There was some frantic cabling with John in New York, and he said yes, it was all right for me to try Konrad and stay in Europe for some while yet, and he also wired me all the money I might need for this expedition. I had never thought much about money—except when I had none at all—but now, for the first time, I was grateful it was there when it might buy me the eyesight of my child. Meanwhile I telephoned with Clara in Vienna; she located Dr. Konrad for us and, on an unfriendly evening late in February, we arrived in the town I had not visited for twenty-five years. I had forgotten how windy it always was there and how shabby the taxis looked and how urgent all hands were waiting for tips. We drove to a certain smart hotel on the Ring where, a few thousand years ago, I had spent an evening in the company of a silly pistol that had not gone off at the most important moment.

"In this hotel I wanted to commit suicide when I was a kid," I told Michael, who aimlessly wandered around in his room, furtively touching the edges of the furniture and the small objects on the desk to make himself acquainted with it. "Well did you?" he asked me in a flash of his own, brittle brand of humor.

"No. And it wouldn't have been worth it. Nothing is worth it, if you don't let it get you down," I said.

"You don't have to give me pep talks, Mony," he answered,

sharp of hearing as he had grown recently. "I'm not a deserter and I don't let it get me down. Okay?"

"Okay," I said. "The main thing is to keep your equilibrium."

"I'll keep mine if you'll keep yours," he said. It was a contract that we both have kept faithfully ever since, haven't we, Milky?

We both disliked Dr. Konrad at first sight, and I noticed that Michael flinched and tightened up every time the doctor came near him. "When he changed his name he should have had his nose fixed at the same time," he said bitterly. Dr. Konrad was a thin, slightly stooped man of indefinite age; he looked like a combination of all the Jewish caricatures on Nazi posters and in Nazi primers. His fingers were stained with nicotine—an unpleasantly filthy habit for a doctor; he was extremely nearsighted, and when he talked he came much too close to one, so that a whiff of mixed odors hit one square in the face. Tobacco and stale perspiration and yesterday's food and some antiseptic soap, embellished by a few drops of cheap eau de Cologne on his handkerchief. "He smells like they do in those unappetizing ads where even your best friend won't tell," Michael complained. "I don't mind him poking around in my eyes, but do I have to go through a gas attack every time he treats me? Maybe it's the Jewish sort of self-defense."

"If he is the one to get your eyes well you'll have to forget some of the Nazi teachings," I shouted at him, as angry as I could ever be at my unlucky child. But I had difficulties myself to find some contact with Dr. Konrad. He had a funny habit of hissing through his teeth and he had also a little speech defect that made every R come out as a W. Besides, he was utterly uncommunicative.

"Aha!" he would say, "Oho! Mhmm! Yes. No. Oh so. Well? Good." And that, without transcription into plain words, was his whole diagnosis. When he spoke at all he had a tantalizing way of leaving every sentence unfinished; it was like watching some sky-writing where the first letters dissolve into nothing before the last ones appear. "Who told you the boy would get? . . . Bunk! I have arrested worse cases of . . . Oho! You trust me? . . . Put him in my hands without . . . ' Good. I demand confidence and absolute obedience. Ab-so-lute! Yes? Mhmm! How

long? No question . . . No answer . . . Oh no! Six months,
two years, five . . . Damned dirty job, but . . . What? Oh so!
Well? Good."

However, after a few visits I began getting used to him and to
believe in him. Once, when he pushed his thick glasses up on his
forehead, I caught a brief glance of his eyes. They were dark
and big; limpid, beautiful eyes, tired, kind, and infinitely sad under his heavy wrinkled monkey eyelids. I guess those eyes made
me trust him.

Somehow the doctor's confidence in his own ability of per-
forming miracles braced Michael up, and by and by he dropped
some of his reluctance. I felt immensely relieved when he agreed
to let the doctor try his tricks for a while. He was put to bed,
fed according to order, taken out for a walk like a pet on a leash,
and put to bed again. Dr. Konrad wanted to keep him in Vienna
for the first two weeks of the treatment and then send him to
Alpenhof, his sanatorium in the mountains near the Semmering,
about two hours' distance from Vienna. The two weeks were
filled by examinations, tests, injections, reactions, and eye treatments. It was a strict routine that kept Michael busy, in the preoccupied way sick people are busy with their regimen until it
becomes an interesting substitute for the real substance of the
life they are missing. After a few days Michael was almost impatient for his visits to the doctor. Konrad had a queer sort of
humor, which Michael, being fifty per cent of a Jew himself
and a student of medicine besides, greatly appreciated. Konrad
never saw or discussed people. All he noticed were pathological
symptoms. He would call the most beautiful and adored actress
of Vienna "A slight case of Hutchinson's teeth." Professor Lanzhof was to him "a pretty well progressed Bright's disease," and
Florian Rieger, who usually drove us in his car, he referred to as
"a nice hyperthyroidism of the gastro-intestinal type." Michael
chuckled delightedly at such abstruse classifications, and everything went well.

Florian Rieger was what Clara called her husband, athough she
wasn't really married to him. He was a slim, elegant, quiet-spoken
gentleman who reminded me somewhat of my romantic Uncle
Theodor, the one with the captive eagle. His hair was not exactly

gray, but dusty-looking. Everything on him was narrow; his face, his shoulders, his hands and feet—even his mind, in certain respects. In his love for Austria he was slightly disgusting, like a man telling you too much about the more intimate charms of his wife. It made me impatient when he would stop his car and go into a trance of enchantment about some line, the sweep of a roof, the shape of a cornice, the noblesse of a baroque fountain or the beauty of the two Trajan columns in front of the Karlskirche, whose chiming had measured the hours of my childhood.

"Isn't it beautiful, Marion?" he would exclaim, his voice wavering with emotion, his eyes swimming in delight. "Look at it, just for one moment. Please do me the favor to look at it. Even if you got your taste spoiled by gazing at those horrid American skyscrapers, you must admit: This is beautiful!"

"It's beautiful, Flori," I would say, "but you haven't seen the Manhattan sky line at sunset yet. And also, may I point out, we're ten minutes late for our appointment."

Flori would sigh and reluctantly start his car again. "Quick, quick! Always in a hurry. No time to eat, no time to enjoy life. A real American!" he would complain. I would watch the clock on the dashboard and be glad to see his hands grip the steering wheel. But he would drop them once more, to guzzle another glance at the two columns, savor them, gulp them down, and smack his eyes.

"Too beautiful to let Herr Hitler throw bombs on them," he would murmur, and only then would we be on our way to Dr. Konrad.

Florian Rieger could not marry Clara for some very Austrian, very Catholic reason that had to do with the Pope, who would not agree to annulling Flori's first marriage and thus clear the way for a second. By and by I found out that Flori's wife had lost her mind and was vegetating in some institution, where he faithfully visited her every Wednesday to bring her candy and flowers. She would eat the candy and tear up the flowers without ever giving any sign of recognizing Flori. Meanwhile he and Clara lived together contentedly like husband and wife, and Clara had given up dancing and concentrated on bringing up Flori's daughter, Renate.

"Wouldn't you wish to be a devout Catholic like Flori?" Clara sighed occasionally. "Imagine what fun it must be to feel that it is sin and moral turpitude to keep house for him and get along on very little money and sew on his buttons and all the prosaic rest. I tell you something, baby; we are too goddamned broad-minded. It takes all the spice out of life."

"Well at least you haven't gone respectable as I have," I comforted her. "You should see me putting on the Mrs. John W. Sprague act at some social function. Jesus, how we kicked and rebelled against everything when we were young and look where it got us. You'll marry Flori the moment the Pope says the word, and I am a lawful wife with a trust fund."

"A trust fund? Sounds nasty," Clara said, puzzled. "What is it?"

"I don't know exactly. It's something John is very proud of. Every time we can't afford one thing or another it's because of the trust fund. I picture it more or less as a little pagan token that he worships in a secret nook in his office and that has to be appeased by sacrifices of money and gold from time to time."

Clara looked at me with eyes that were equally amused and troubled. "Yes, little monk, that's the end of it all. I got myself the goddamnedest out-and-out reactionary and you have married Big Money. We might as well have stayed home in the first place."

"Why did you give up dancing?" I asked her.

"Why did you give up fiddling? And why did you give up carving?"

"I have to see that Michael gets well. That's more important, isn't it?"

"Exactly. So is Flori. So is Renate."

Renate was a slim, lithe little creature of fifteen. She had big blue eyes under dark, serious eyebrows and blue-black shining hair—a rare combination, which made her very attractive. "Renate is like good music," Michael said of her, and also: "Renate is like ice cream with hot-chocolate sauce. Sweet and refreshing and when you find out how warm it all is underneath it gives you a bit of a shock." Renate on her part spent many hours with Michael, and I was more than grateful that she had entered our life just at the right moment, when he had to stay in bed most of the time and should be prevented from brooding. Renate—more often referred to by her droll nickname Bummerl—would read papers and magazines to him as well as the letters that John and Martin wrote him. Sometimes she brought her guitar and sang with the most innocent expression the ribald couplets she had snapped up from the cowherds on the mountain pastures. She sang with a fine, husky young voice and she had a lot of fun in her quiet, cunning way. She also taught Michael to plunk-plunk on the guitar, arranging his fingers on the chords as if they were made of wood. In return he gave her lessons in English and they lived in a happy little world full of whispered secrets, laughter, and perfect understanding. Renate would be a good teacher if Michael had to learn Braille, I caught myself thinking. It was a thought that burned, and I gave myself a strict command not to let any pessimism creep into my mind, because it was bad for Michael.

During the second week of our stay in Vienna, Florian Rieger became very nervous and fidgety and there were always new bumps in the fenders of his little old car. Clara spoke of her man with tender contempt. "He's such a fool, wearing himself ragged for a lost cause. But, you know, he has the rarest of all qualities in an Austrian: character. That's why I like him."

"Some of the finest characters I've met in the world are Austrians," I protested.

"Yes," Clara said, "once you transplant us to a tougher soil we do rather well. At home we choke ourselves with our own charm and our celebrated good food and with being sorry for ourselves. Flori isn't, though. Flori is all right. He isn't cut out to be a fighter, but he is fighting all the same. You can't ask more from a man, now can you?"

The thing Florian Rieger was fighting for in these hectic last February weeks was the decision that had been placed before the people of Austria after their Chancellor Schushnigg had returned from his ill-fated summons to Berchtesgaden. The town was a broiling cauldron; yet to the detached visitor it looked more as if the people were engaged in the preparations of a county fair than in the resolution whether Austria was to remain a sovereign and independent country or become an appendage of the Reich. After it had stopped raining, the streets seemed almost too colorful and there was a slight tinge of the old-fashioned Vienna operetta about this campaign. Many men strutted around in the old costumes of the mountains, wearing heavy knit white stockings, bare knees, and short, homespun trousers. This was a faintly ridiculous way of demonstrating one's allegiance to Hitler. There was hardly a lapel without a button, either the swastika or the red-and-white of the loyal Austrian; people had a funny way of looking at your lapel before looking into your face. There were parades marching down the Ring at all hours, competitions between partisans of the one side and the other. Being true Austrians, both parties had infinite faith in the exciting power of music, and so the brass instruments blared forth, the piccolo flutes squeaked, the drums rumbled their um-ta-ta, the men marched and grinned, and it was all very gay and pretty. To the innocent spectator it appeared like a nice show and also as if the Viennese enjoyed this free spectacle immensely.

Florian Rieger was busy day and night, writing newspaper articles, making speeches, kissing influential ladies' hands, and persuading men who were of his opinion anyway. He belonged to Schushnigg's Austria, body and soul. He had all the good and bad qualities of a through-and-through Austrian, brought up in the traditions of the old and settled hierarchy of officialdom. His grandfather and his father both had been officials of high rank, and his father had climbed, for a short while, to the lofty position of Minister of Transportation. Flori himself was something or the other in the Ministry of Justice, but he seemed to treat this as a side line and had branched out into writing. This too was an old Austrian tradition. The government was used to doling out modest clerk's wages to little geniuses who filled their office hours by writing manuscripts, sketching down plays, or constructing self-analytical sonnets on the official stationery.

Florian Rieger was convinced that at least eighty per cent of the votes would be for an independent Austria. Clara, on the other hand, was rather pessimistic about the outcome of the plebiscite. Her source was the janitor, this prototype and sample of the average Little Man. The janitor would vote for Schushnigg and sovereignty if everybody else would, that's what he said. He would vote for Hitler and the Anschluss if the majority would do so. "But, Jesus Maria, the majority of them are janitors," Clara shouted angrily. "Who is going to make up their minds for them?" In an attack of deep confidence the janitor had confessed to Clara that he really didn't care one way or the other. But he was no fool, the janitor. Although he preferred an independent Austria, with an emperor if possible, he had secretly become a member of the Nazi party—just in case. He also—and Clara laughed furiously when she told me about it—had never given up his membership in the Socialist party, which had run the country prior to 1934.

"What can you expect from such people?" Clara said with that new troubled expression that would frequently creep into her face and contradict her cheerful swearing. "Poor Flori, I wonder if he realizes how serious a game he is playing."

On a clear, cold Friday I borrowed Flori's car and drove Michael out of town and toward the mountains in the South to install him in Alpenhof. Renate had come along to make the trip more amusing for the boy and to keep me company on the way back. Dr. Konrad, in his erratic fashion, had ruled that I was not to hang around for more than an hour. "Oh no! Bad for his . . . Bored? Good for him to be . . . Best medicine. Improves fever curve and . . . Visit him every . . . If everything turns out . . ." he told me.

The air was sharp and clear, and while we drove through the sleepy villages, past small, modest old churches, along the vineyards of the southern slopes and later through forest and into the folds of steep mountain gorges, I felt for the first time that I was back in my homeland. There was a faint promise of spring in the air, and once we stopped and Renate plucked some snowdrops at the side of the road. They were a brave little vanguard, pointing the tiny lances of their leaves through the snow.

"Feel how cool they are, and how sturdy," Renate said, putting them into Michael's hand and closing his fingers around the white bells of the flower.

"Don't tickle me," Michael said with his good old grin. "Not even with snowdrops." He held them in his palms as though in a bowl and lifted them to his face. "Too bad they have no fragrance," Renate said.

"That's what you think," Michael told her. "A world of fragrance. They smell green and of snow and of earth and of a beginning." He leaned back and closed his eyes behind the dark glasses as he went on smiling at the flowers in his hand. I marveled how natural it was for Renate to say: "Feel the flowers" and not: "Look at the flowers." But then Renate was the product of generations that had bred tact and sensibility into their offspring. . . .

Dr. Konrad had arrived before us. He spent every week end in Alpenhof with his patients and stayed in Vienna from Tuesday to Friday. He pinched Renate's cheeks with his nicotine-stained fingers, and she accepted it with the smile of a martyr. "Good circulation. Well balanced glandular system," he muttered appreciatively. "Perhaps a tiny underfunction of the ovaries . . . But otherwise . . . Aha!" It was the most complete sentence I had heard from him so far, and I deduced that Renate's fine, uncommon beauty had made quite an impression on him. Michael's room was small but pleasant, with dark oak furniture and moss-green walls. It didn't look like a sick room at all, rather like the comfortable cell of a studious monk. The shade of the low overhanging roof softened the daylight into a flowing, diffused blue; the french door stood open and let the cool mountain air stream into the room. A near-by brook made a humming cradle of sound to rock you to sleep in its monotony. As I stepped out onto the balcony I could see the snow on the summit of the mountain, but the room was protected from the glare, and only the strong gray mountain flank was discernible through the door. The lamps had green shades, and I soon discovered that every detail in the house was efficiently and thoughtfully planned for the comfort of people with smarting eyes who feared the sun and yet needed it should they recover.

I went out onto the balcony to give the children time to say good-by. There was some whispering and suppressed laughter, and then the chiming of a small, whining church bell rose from the village in the valley and floated through the clear air up to us. Down there somebody played on a mouth organ, and for a second I was all wrapped in the feeling of being at home. Then the head nurse rumbled into the room to chase us out and pin a chart over Michael's bed. I promised to come and visit him the following week end, and then we got into the car and were on our way: Renate silent and thoughtful and I filled with a strange, unfounded, dawning, melting hope that everything would turn out well in the end.

"Did you ever try it, Aunt Marion?" Renate asked me after a long, long silence that had taken us through the gorge and out into the flat country.

"Try what?"

"Keeping your eyes closed and pretending to be blind and groping your way."

"No, child," I said. It was almost dark, but in the mirror of the car I saw dimly that she had her eyes closed even now.

"I do. I keep them closed for ten minutes or so every day. First I had to tie a handkerchief over them, but now I can keep them closed without cheating for five minutes in a row."

"Why do you do it, Renate?"

"Oh, just so. I want to know how it is to be . . . not being able to see, you know. Then I can imagine just what Michael might like or want or what is difficult for him. I mean—Aunt Marion, don't you think I could become a nurse and—and—take care of Michael if—if—he should need someone?"

"He is not going to be blind," I said stubbornly.

"You are right. I will never think that he might need a nurse. You can't send soldiers into a battle if they think they might lose. It's a battle, isn't it, and we must believe that he'll win. And when he's well again and goes back to America I can still become a nun and enter a convent. That's what I am going to do when Michael goes back to America. . . ."

I could hear how terribly sorry she was for herself in case Michael should get well, as sorry as you can be only when you are fifteen and lead the wonderful life of a tragic heroine and no one can guess the fathomless deep things that are going on inside of you because on the outside you are just a girl with two pigtails on which you chew when you forget yourself. . . .

When the next week end came around, Renate could not come

with me to visit Michael, because she had caught a bad cold, a condition that was taboo in Alpenhof. However, Clara offered to drive out with me. She was very fond of Michael and wanted to see him and also, I thought, she hoped to take her mind off the brewing trouble. It had been a hectic week, and she had hardly seen Flori at all. In these last days before the plebiscite Flori needed his car for himself, but he seemed to be rather glad to get Clara out of the way. She came for me with a car she had rented for the day.

The huge colored doorman who always paraded in front of the hotel helped me into the car and gave Clara a flashing smile.

"Comment allez vous, Ahmed?" she asked him.

"Merci bien, Madame, ça va. Les temps sont difficiles. . . ." he answered as he closed the door of the car. He wore wide pantaloons and a red fez like the funny little Sultan in Esquire; it was the Viennese idea of an appropriate costume for someone as exotic as a Negro.

"I wonder what they'll do to poor Ahmed if things should go wrong," Clara said, steering the car down the Ring, which was at the moment without any parades or processions. "He certainly is a polluter of racial purity."

"How come you know him?"

"Didn't I tell you? He is the father of Black Ignominy. Poor chap in his ludicrous get-up. Most decorative he is, but not a bit Aryan."

"How in the world did he ever get here, in front of the hotel?"

"He remained in Germany when his regiment went back to Africa, and he followed us to Berlin because he is a born family man and wanted to be with his woman and his child. He had a job in a night club there. Later, when I ran away, I took him along and Flori got him this job here. Ann, of course, stayed behind and married a Nazi."

"And Ignominy?"

"Oh, she is a torrent. She is the rage of Paris I understand. She's dancing at the Tabarin, and men cover her with synthetic rubies and cultured pearls. You know, Frenchmen are thrifty even when they are losing their heads, and synthetic rubies are inexpensive.

Yes, monky, our Black Ignominy has the makings of a whore in great style."

"Did you teach her dancing?"

"Well I don't think I taught her exactly what she is dancing now. It's called Ebony Eve, with nothing but a little fig leaf in front. She sent me a program with her photo on it. All I did was to limber her up a bit. It seems now she's so limbered up she is kicking Paris for a spin."

I tried in vain to picture the shy, dark baby I had carried in my arms as the rage of Paris. "I wonder if she would be a rage in Harlem——" I said condescendingly, and Clara gave a snorting little laugh. "What an American chauvinist you've turned out to be," she said, and then she had to concentrate on the rented car, which was of a moody and whimsical temperament.

"I wish we were a few days further ahead and would know what's going to happen to us," she said much later, when we had left the city behind. "This waiting gets you down."

"It's not like you to worry so much."

"It's easy not to worry as long as you are alone. Now there is Flori. And Renate. Once I had to run across a border for dear life. I wouldn't care very much for having to do it again, and with a man and a child."

"Why did you have to run the last time?"

"Oh, because of nothing. One of my dancers was a communist and I tried to hide her during those worst days in thirty-three."

"What became of her?"

Clara shrugged her shoulders. This shrug, this sigh, these puzzled frowns on her wide forehead, they all were new. She had one gray, almost white, skein of hair on her right temple, I traced it with my fingers as a hidden little caress. "You see, I am gray all over," she said. "I get a rinse to dye it blond, but I keep this strand white as an admission that I am really old and gray and have dyed hair."

"It's attractive and you know it."

"That's what Flori thinks, at least. He would make a good hair-dresser, don't you think so? Or a good headwaiter? Anything but a good politician. Well maybe he'll soon have to take up one of those polite professions. A week from now we shall know."

You know, we have all the odds against us. We are Austrians when it's wrong to be Austrian. Liberals when it's wrong to be liberal. Individualists when it's wrong to be individualists. It's a miracle people like us are still alive. It's tough to belong to the wrong generation. I am all for those cannibal tribes who eat their parents on their fortieth birthday. Saves a lot of trouble all around.

We found Michael well installed and quite content. It is so much easier for sick people to live with other patients than surrounded by coarse and ignorant health. To have sick eyes was normal in Alpenhof, and healthy visitors like ourselves soon felt a trifle wrong—freakish and abnormal. Imperceptibly I felt Michael gliding away from me into those twilight realms where nothing counted but the sickness and the cure. I found him calmer and less flickering than he had ever been. The strain of pretending that everything was well with him had been taken from him, and he seemed almost serene. Dr. Konrad was satisfied with him; he spoke about him as if he were a good if not very gifted disciple. "Good possibilities . . . reactions as anticipated . . . A pretty reliable patient if . . ." He even permitted us to take the boy for a little walk in the heady, brisk mountain air, along a narrow trail that cut across the lowest slope of the mountain. In the valley all the snow had melted, but up here there were still wide white patches of it and we had a modest little snowball fight and a timid imitation of a romp. Back in Alpenhof we drank the customary afternoon coffee with Michael, met some of the other patients at this occasion, watched the nurse taking his five o'clock temperature, and then I felt that the boy seemed almost impatient to see us go.

"Next time I am bringing Renate again," I said as we left him. Wrapped in his blankets he looked comfortable as he lay in his deckchair, without his dark glasses now that the evening descended, bathing his eyes in the healing, ice-cold air. The last bit of sun made a cone of raspberry ice cream of the summit, transparent and not quite real, and the narrow road on which we drove downhill caught a mauve mother-of-pearl twilight on its moist surface. But when we left the high altitude and reached the bottom of the valley the early evening had crept into every fold and wrinkle and filled it with a thick, padded darkness. My ears clicked, and then I could hear much clearer the steady fall of water from the stream way down in the steep gorge. The headlights of the car unwound the white thread of the road ahead of us. Once in a while a small animal scurried across and trees stepped into the light like curious strangers to look at us and turn away again.

At a small roadside inn we stopped for dinner, because the sharp air and the walk had made us hungry. The innkeeper was a shrill, thin woman who looked like the essence of determined and efficient widowhood. She fussed over us because ladies with a car did not belong to her usual class of customers. We were led through the taproom with its smell of stale beer and pipe smoke and passed the gaping, suddenly silenced crowd of beer-drinking men. The private saloon where the woman insisted on setting a table for us had the cold, murky atmosphere of a room seldom used. The old cuckoo clock was not wound up. The geraniums on the window sill were dry and dead. The stove was not heated. A photo, obviously taken at the widow's wedding, added to the general gloom; it showed a crowd in stiff Sunday clothes, surrounding the bridal couple and terrifiedly staring into the camera. However, the widow produced in no time an exceptionally well-cooked dinner, a strong hot bouillon, fried chicken Austrian style, and for dessert coffee and Apfelstrudel.

It was when the widow came from the taproom, carrying in the coffee, that Clara turned abruptly toward the door and listened. The men whose raucous laughter we had heard a few minutes ago had become breathlessly quiet, and all that could be heard was a voice coming from the radio in the corner. It was a poor contraption, full of static noises, but from the expression on Clara's face I knew that this quaking, wavering voice was of utmost importance.

"Don't close the door, please——" she whispered, rigid and motionless like a pointing bird dog as the widow was about to leave the room. "It's Schushnigg, isn't it?"

"If the ladies care to come and listen—I didn't think the ladies would be interested. Aren't the ladies foreigners?" the widow said, and Clara got up and followed her into the taproom. I went after her, but where she had treaded without a sound the loose old boards of the floor creaked under my steps and, not wanting to disturb the reception by more noises, I stopped and remained in a ridiculous, suspended pose, listening.

What we heard was the unexpected farewell of the chancellor to his country and his surrender to the crude new powers across the German border. When the painfully restrained impersonal voice had finished with a "Gott Schütze Oesterreich" there were a few moments of indecisive silence in the taproom. The men seemed to wait for more to come, for an explanation or an order what to do next. They were simple country folk with hard, gnarled features. I had carved many such peasant faces in bygone years. The lamp that hung over the zink counter shed a hard light upon them, and even the drifting heavy layers of blue smoke shone with a peculiar brightness of their own. Then the silence splintered as one of the men banged his glass down on the counter and ordered a round of beer for everybody. A murmur rose and grew, and at last a few arms flew up in the Nazi salute; someone in the back shouted: "Heil Hitler." What happened then was like in an oratorio when first the solo voices present the theme and then the chorus joins them and swells it to a triumphant hallelujah. Clara stood arrested in all the clamor, staring from one shouting, cheering man to the next. Then she turned abruptly, came back into the private room, and closed the door.

"Let's pay and get out of here——" she said in a dry whisper that sounded not at all like her. Only when I saw the tears streaming down her face in an angry rush did I realize that Austria was my country too and that it had just died. But all I felt was a detached regret and also a sudden strong desire to be with John—be back in America and forget the agonies of this troubled, confused, and terrified continent.

The widow came in, and when I paid her in a hurry she looked desperately at her Apfelstrudel, which we had not finished eating. "Didn't the ladies like the strudel?" she repeated unhappily. "Such a good Apfelstrudel, it's a shame to let it go to waste. Maybe the ladies would care to take it along, it's paid for anyway. No? Well, maybe the ladies don't know what's good. Good night," she concluded, hurt to the core in her soul of a proud cook. Clara walked off in a rage of anger and despair. "That's Austria for you," she said as we got into the car. "The Apfelstrudel! They carry their hearts in their stomachs. And that's just like me too. I would sit and eat Apfelstrudel instead of being with my man when it's a matter of life and death. Come on, monk, hurry."

"Shall I drive or will you?" I asked, discovering with surprise that my knees were weak and my hands trembling.

"You drive. You are the better driver. Go as fast as you can. No, let me," she added as an afterthought, pushing me from the wheel. "You aren't used to driving on the left side of the road." She put the car in gear and it shot away under us, tearing into the darkness beyond the small circle of light in front of the inn.

"Did you notice?" she asked me much later, when we entered one of the small towns along the highway.

"Yes, I did," I said. The lone policeman at the street crossing wore a badge with the swastika around his sleeve.

"He must have carried it in his pocket all the time, the swine," Clara grumbled. We turned into the main square, which swarmed with cheering, yelling, singing people. A frantic crowd filled the sidewalks and the whole square and our car crept slowly along, as through sticky molasses, with Clara furiously honking the horn and swearing under her breath. More people hung from the windows and fraternized with those down there. There was not a house without a swastika flag and not a person left with a white and red button. The faces that peered into the car were drunk with elation, their mouths gaping, their voices hoarse from yelling, their eyes blazing and yet numbed as though by a holy frenzy. Some boys jumped onto our running board, cheering wildly, waving little swastika flags into our faces.

From the corner beyond the church came the tramp-tramp of marching feet and a loud unison chorus. Then the windows caught a red and orange reflection as though from a blazing fire; an improvised torch parade gushed into the square, sweeping everybody along. Clara, bent over her wheel, looked as if she had to win an auto race. Her mouth was a firm, straight line, the white skein of hair had fallen over her forehead, and the tears kept streaming down her cheeks as she tried to steer the car against the current. Finally another policeman ordered us into a quieter side street; he too wore the swastika badge. At last, shaken and mangled, we reached the open road at the other end of the town, as if we had escaped from something as senseless, dangerous, and unpredictable as the eruption of a volcano that had been asleep for uncounted years.

All the little towns and villages along the highway were in the same uproar. Here and there shots tore holes in the night; they were fired by young boys out of sheer exuberance and to give vent to their emotions. We raced on and on in our rattling car— it was as if the speed would give Clara some relief—but we advanced only slowly. Several times we were stopped and questioned by stern-looking, tremendously important-mannered young busybodies, boys and girls who had conjured some party badges out of nowhere. They examined our Aryan features, demanded to see Clara's driver's license, yelled "Heil Hitler," and let us pass. Once we were held for a senseless half hour in a small police station. The entire spectacle that fermented out of the night had something fantastic, irrational, and incomprehensible. I had never seen a crowd so senselessly incensed, not during the War and not afterward, and this mass inflagration frightened me. "It's medieval," I said more to myself than to Clara. "It's unbelievable. And so utterly idiotic."

"Baby," Clara said, "you weren't there when the Reichstag burned. This is only the beginning of it. And Renate is alone at home. The child is alone at home. If anything should happen to her——"

The sentence remained unfinished and we went on racing toward an unknown, shapeless menace. What we saw on our way was only a small sample of the frenzy that had gripped Vienna. More people, more flags, more singing, marching, parading, more of this sudden flare of intoxication. "They are making a holiday of it," Clara said bitterly as we shuttled back and forth through side streets, trying to avoid the main thoroughfares with their unchained throngs.

It took us an endless time before we arrived at the old building where Clara lived. The janitor who opened the house door for us wore the swastika button on his sloppy old flannel housecoat. His suspenders were trailing down his backside. "Heil Hitler," he said, raising his right arm. "Good evening," Clara answered, pushing past him. He grinned at her, with a cunning twinkle which indicated that he didn't take any of it seriously. "Is my husband at home?" Clara asked him. "No, Herr Baron hasn't come home," the janitor said. "It's just as good maybe. There were two gentlemen asking for him, but I told them Herr Baron wasn't home."

"That's good of you," Clara said, dropping a tip into his expectant palm.

The street pounded with the steady roar of a surf against the thick walls of the house. We rushed upstairs round and round the old winding staircase, feeling at once safer and protected within the bounds of the old, old house that had seen wars and revolutions, victories and defeats.

Renate was sound asleep, looking very impish and innocent in her prim little nightgown of white batiste. She had put an orange on Clara's pillow and pinned a note to the bed:

Papa called up and said not to expect him home tonight and not to worry. He will let you know more as soon as possible. I waited for you until ten o'clock but am too sleepy. A good good night kiss from your

Bummerl

P.S. The orange is a present from me to you.

I would have liked to stay with you that night, Clara, my darling, but you were strict and stern and ordered me to go to my hotel at once. Maybe you thought that Flori might come and want to hide in my room there; but that happened only later, when they were after him. And so I spiraled down the winding stairs again and rang the bell for the janitor to open the house door for me and worked my way through the throng, back to my rented car, grinning all the time like a nitwit, because I was afraid of the crowd as you might be afraid of people senselessly drunk or insane. And I told myself furiously not to be sorry for the Austrian people, because whatever happened to them was what they had wanted and chosen.

It took me almost an hour to get back to my hotel, because the

Ring was a roaring Niagara Falls of enthusiasm, and also I was stopped four times by people who obviously had no business stopping me. When I finally arrived, Ahmed opened the car and helped me out of it.

He still wore his wide pantaloons and his fez and his face was black as the night. But he had added a badge with a swastika to his picturesque outfit.

I HAD OFTEN WONDERED what was meant when people said that something went underground, a movement or a person. It sounded jolly, like a gopher slipping into his burrow and only sticking his sly nose out of it as a periscope. It sounded as if going underground were fun. But when Flori Rieger went underground I discovered that it was no fun at all. It was part of the confusion and reshuffling that was going on all over town. Vienna had changed its face overnight; the crowds one saw on the streets were different from the crowds that had been there before; noisier, trumping, made of a cruder substance, shaped after a blunter mold, as if a new shift had taken over while the old shift went into hiding. There was the roaring of airplanes, diving low and not without menace, skimming the tops of the old plane trees along the Ring. Swastikas everywhere, on lapels, on badges and buttons, on uniforms, flags, on all the insignia of the trumping, tramping usurpers, which filled the streets of my childhood town with tanks and guns, as if there never had been chestnut trees and plumes of lilac and the soft, wistful cantilene of violins.

"You know who is speaking?" the telephone asked me somewhat dramatically two days after the tremendous show of the Führer's triumphant arrival in Vienna.

"Yes, of course," I cried, recognizing Florian Rieger's voice but deducing that he did not want me to mention his name. "Where are you? Clara is worrying her head off."

"I kiss your hand, Marion. Please, would you be so kind as to tell her not to worry. I prefer not to call her up in the apartment, for obvious reasons." (The Rieger flat had been searched twice, Flori's desk had been ransacked, and there was good cause to assume that the flat was kept under close observation.)

"Sure, I'll tell her at once. Anything else I can do for you?"

"If it isn't too much trouble for you I would be very grateful if you could ask Clara to give you my brown suit and some shirts and bring it to an address that you will receive in your mail today. But, please, keep Clara out of this. You will be so kind? Kiss your hand, I knew I could count on you. When you get there, please, ask for a black poodle. I'm sorry to trouble you. I kiss your hand."

When I put down the receiver I wondered if my telephone was tapped. It had been tapped in Moscow. Apparently it was impossible to free and redeem a people without secret police, prisons, and tapped telephones. I went downstairs at once to pick up my mail before it would pass through too many hands. One of the envelopes contained a printed advertisement with the address of a pet shop. "Buy your pet at Apfel's!" it said in neat green letters on yellow stationery. I assumed that this was it. With the address I hurried to Clara to bring her the good news that Flori hadn't been arrested yet like so many of his political friends. I was glad to find that she had got over her jitters and seemed more angry than anxious. "Now isn't this the absolute shit," she said; it made me feel good to hear her sound her old leitmotiv, the challenging bugle call that had accompanied all the battles of her life.

"Tell me word for word what he said," she asked me, and I told her word for word that Flori wanted her not to worry and to send him his brown suit and some shirts. "Is that all? Didn't he say anything else?" she asked again and again, and I assured her that this was all. "Isn't that just like Flori," she said with an angry laugh. "The brown suit. He loathes wearing the same suit two days in succession. He has only three, and he wears each one of them ten years, but never two days in a row."

She frowned and thought things over. We held a serious council, and then Clara decided not to send him that suit. "Look here, monk," she said. "You'll go away with that brown suit in a brown paper parcel, or in a suitcase, let's say. Now suppose they stop you and search that parcel. Or worse, they follow you and watch where you are taking this suspicious-looking parcel. It takes them straight to Flori, don't you see? Let him get along with his one suit. It's not worth taking chances, is it?"

"Maybe his suit is torn or got dirty or something. God knows, he might have had to climb over roofs; what do we know?"

Clara gave a deep sigh. "Yes, God knows," she said. "But let him buy a ready-made suit. Maybe—maybe, Mony, you could help him with some money. I suppose that's what he needs more than a brown suit at the moment. He'll have to pay Apfel plenty for shielding him."

"Do you know this pet shop?"

"Yes, Apfel is the man who married the former personal maid of Flori's mother. He was a horse trainer at the Tattersall stables, but he did a bad spill and broke a leg and had to give it up. I only hope he is reliable," Clara said. She wrote a letter for Florian, and Renate scribbled a row of little crosses at the bottom. "Each cross means a kiss and a prayer," she wrote on the margin. I received Clara's word of honor to stay put and not to make any nonsense and went on my way. The janitor, loitering in the doorway downstairs, greeted me with the party salute and with a wink that simultaneously made fun of it. Leaving the old house I peered up and down the street for anyone looking like an agent of the secret police. I felt pretty silly at that. If anyone should be following me I certainly was not intelligent enough to dodge him. I took a taxi and drove back to the hotel through streets that looked stranger and stranger to me from hour to hour. When I marched past Ahmed in his radiant regalia it seemed to me as if he were giving me some secret signal. This is like a visit in the fun house, I thought. You never know from where the next surprise will come. I went to the hotel bar and had a drink to steady my nerves, which had the consistency of jello. Then I took another taxi and drove to the pet shop.

Apfel's was a small store with two airedale pups asleep in a cage in the window and filled with the sharp odor of caged animals and wetted shavings and the shrill coloraturos of a gang of canaries. A moth-eaten little man came limping out from behind a curtain in back of the store and asked me about my wishes.

"I want to see about a black poodle——" I said, feeling foolish and absurd. He looked me over with a bland expression.

"A black poodle?" he echoed, clearing his throat.

"Yes, a black poodle. You sent me this advertisement, didn't you?" I said, producing the green and yellow slip.

"Are you the lady who lives at the Bristol Hotel?" he asked me.

"Yes, that's me," I said.

"Come inside if you please," he said, preceding me through a narrow chink in the curtain. We passed through an untidy kitchen, through a dark passage, through a glass door that was hung with a checkered gingham curtain, and arrived at last in a bedroom that was so cluttered up with furniture that I had to move sideways in order to squeeze past the big chiffoniere and the bed. Here too was the smell of animals. A sick-looking little rhesus monkey in too small a cage chattered and bared his teeth at me in a frightened or malicious grin. A little radio was going full blast, and two canaries tried to make more noise than the booming voice that came from it.

Florian Rieger got up from the bed where he had been sitting, bowed from the waist, and said in his most impeccable Austrian manner: "I kiss your hand, Marion. That's a charming little hat you're wearing." His eyes were red, as if he had not slept since I had seen him last, and he looked unshaven and unkempt. "How are you, Flori?" I asked him. "Still alive—that's something," he answered. I gave him Clara's letter and he read it eagerly. But he seemed disappointed when I explained to him about the brown suit. "I've worn this rag ever since Schushnigg gave up——" he said, looking down on himself and pinching his trousers where the crease had been rumpled. "I feel like a vagrant——"

Apfel stood beneath the monkey cage in a sloppily military posture. "Thank you, Apfel——" Flori said condescendingly, and the man limped off. "Clara wonders if he is reliable," I said after the glass door had clattered closed.

"Who is nowadays?" Flori said with all the defeatism of his kind.

"Have you stayed here since Friday?"

"Lord no. I don't dare stay in any one place longer than a few hours. The first two nights I just kept on wandering around where the crowd was the thickest. Last night I spent in a brothel, pretending to be drunk. That's a comparatively safe place, but expensive."

"I brought you some money," I said. Flori flinched when I stuffed it into his pocket after he had refused to take it. "It makes me feel like a pimp, taking money from a lady——" he said.

"I am no lady," I said. "And this is a good moment to forget your perfect manners anyway. What are your plans now? What am I to tell Clara? Can't you get out of the country?"

"I have no passport," he said. "And if I had one it wouldn't be much of a recommendation. You can be assured I would be arrested at the border. But I would feel much better if Clara and Bummerl would try and go to Prague at once. A stepsister of mine lives there. I am certain she would gladly take them in. I'm afraid they might arrest Clara as a hostage—or the child. The thought of it drives me crazy. It's the approved Nazi method of getting at people they want, isn't it?"

"I'll tell Clara," I said. "But I doubt that she would go away and leave you in the lurch."

"If I could only talk to her," he said, combing his fingers through his sandy hair. "If I could only see her for a few minutes. I could make her understand that it is the only sensible thing to do."

He did not seem very sensible himself. "What about you, Flori?" I said urgently. "You can't just keep running around on the streets and sleeping in brothels. You must make plans. You must have friends. What are the others doing? There must be a few millions in the same fix as you. The Gestapo can't follow every one of them every minute."

"If I could only get my brown suit," he said instead of an answer. "Fortunately I have a reversible raincoat, you know, an English one with camel hair on the inside. I look quite different when I turn it inside out. And I'm growing a mustache. You thought I was badly shaved; yes, I could see it on your face. No, no, Marion. It's just a little trick. How long do you think it'll take to grow it? Not more than a week, I'd say. And I'll wear eyeglasses too. They won't recognize me so easily, they won't."

He sounded as if he had pretty well gone to pieces. The radio sang the Horst Wessel song. The canaries trilled, and the little monkey chattered at them. It all seemed fantastic. "I'm afraid we are amateurs at this sort of thing," I said. "What else do you want me to tell Clara? And think hard what can be done to get you across the border. I understand they are tightening up their border control. You'd better try to get out quick."

"I'll get out," he said with a thin smile. "I'll get out eventually. After all, this is still Austria. We are sloppy people, as you know. There will always be a hole in the control to slip out somehow. There'll always be a way to fix up things. If I could only talk to Clara. Tell her that I love her. And if I could get my brown suit . . ."

This was the first of several secret meetings with Flori. I met him in shoddy coffee houses, on a park bench, in the Vienna woods while it was raining like mad, in the back of a stuffy, crowded little movie theater where the newsreels showed the frantic people of Austria welcoming the Führer. I got him his God-darned brown suit and I also arranged for him to meet Clara. Soon my nerves felt like a portion of scrambled eggs. Clara met him in my hotel room, where I had found Flori one evening, asleep on my couch, in complete exhaustion. It appeared that Ahmed, in spite of his Nazi badge, had smuggled him in via the basement. Of course Clara refused to leave the country while her man was in danger. Her mouth became a straight line and her forehead a map of wrinkles when the question was put before her, and I knew that no power on earth could shake her out of her resistance. We sent her home while Flori stayed in my room for two days and nights. I suppose the chambermaid knew that I was hiding a gentleman in my bathroom when she came in to fix the bed, but trained in smart discretion, she took it for a romantic escapade on my part. At least I hoped she did. Flori's presence was the reason why I didn't go up to Alpenhof to visit Michael that week end. I was afraid Flori would commit some sort of nonsense if I left him alone. He was as unfit as possible for the situation, a pathetic, bungling little gentleman of the old school trying to act as tough and brave as these new circumstances demanded. When I watched him bowing from the waist, kissing my hand, and making gallant jokes, it gave me a sensation as if someone took my heart and twisted it into a taut rope. I had a leisurely telephone conversation with Michael, who reported that everything with him was okay and hunky-dory, and on Friday I sent Renate to him as a welcome substitute. I also called up Dr. Konrad's office to learn from him how Michael was coming along; the nurse who answered the telephone told me that the doctor had not come to Vienna that week but had remained in Alpenhof. And then, during the following week, troubles began to pile up in such quick succession that I was thrashing around in a thick fog of dizzy confusion.

First Renate reported that two men in a car had followed her all the way to Alpenhof and back. "Maybe they thought you pretty and hoped for a bit of fun," Clara tried to make light of it. "No, they weren't that sort of men and they didn't make that sort of eyes at me," Renate said with the ample experience of a fifteen-year-old beauty growing up in a romantically inclined city. Next Florian Rieger disappeared for three days, so completely that we were almost sure he had been arrested and taken to secret-police headquarters. And what happened to people there everybody knew only too well. In spite of it Clara went valiantly to her hairdresser and had her gray roots done blond. "You know my motto," she said. "To dye but not surrender." The courage of women is made of a different substance than the courage of men, and to use facial cream in the midst of disaster is part of it. On Wednesday Clara went and took flowers and candy to Flori's wife in the insane asylum. "She won't miss him but she might miss the candy, and that might be bad for her," Clara said. I took Renate to a movie that afternoon to keep her from worrying about her father for a few hours. When I came to my hotel that evening I noticed Apfel limping up and down in front of it with a black poodle on a leash.

"What a cute dog——" I said, bending down and stroking the poodle. Apfel bent down too and whispered to me that he had news from Florian Rieger. He had left Vienna and was trying to get to his mother, who lived in a small town near the Czechoslovakian border. "He is trying to get smuggled across," Apfel whispered. "He'll need money. Please send it to his mother's address."

"Don't hang around here," I whispered back. "You want to get into trouble?" The poodle sat up and did his little tricks. I pretended to laugh about him, and when Apfel limped away and I met Ahmed's alert eyes I felt as if five hundred secret agents had watched our silly little act.

The following morning Clara was summoned to police head-quarters and kept there for six hours.

"What did they do to you?" I asked her when she finally came to my hotel room late that afternoon, looking as transparent and worn-out as she had done after dancing a strenuous new pro-gram to an unresponsive audience.

"Nothing. Give me a cigarette. They just asked me questions."

"A third degree?"

"What's that?"

"Did they hurt you? Did they put the squeeze on you?"

"If they did I didn't notice. No, I don't think so. The young man who put me through my paces seemed quite polite and con-siderate. He talked in a highfalutin way about the dance of the future. Seems he has seen me dance back in Munich. He appeared to think that I could be an asset to the Nazi movement. Kraft durch Freude and all that. Release unknown explosive powers of enthusiasm by reviving the old German folk dances, you know."

"Was it a bribe?"

"Possibly. I felt like cheering straight into his silly face. It's a clear sign that they haven't caught Flori yet, isn't it?"

"Certainly. They haven't got him and they aren't going to get him. What did you tell them?"

"The truth. That I'm nothing but Herr Rieger's housekeeper and that I have not the faintest idea where he's keeping himself at the moment. The young man told me to think it over and come back on Friday. He said he hoped I would know where Rieger is by then."

"Sounds bad, darling," I said, getting cold around my heart. Clara shrugged her shoulders. "Remember when Tosca was given in Vienna for the first time? People threatened to burn down the theater, they were so scandalized that the torture scene in the second act was shown publicly," she said, with the unexpected flash of a wistful smile in her gaunt face.

"They still don't torture publicly," I said. "What are you going to do now?"

"I don't know, really."

"Did they take away your passport?"

"No, not yet."

"Then I'll tell you what you have to do. You pack your things and catch the next plane for Prague. Get out while the going is good. I'll stay here and keep in contact with Flori and see that he gets across the border soon. It's so much easier for me, as an American citizen——"

"Don't tell me fairy tales, Mony. You know as well as I do that they won't let me through. You need a permit to leave for Czechoslovakia and I haven't got one. I'll just have to go through with this show. In a way I'm glad I really don't know where Flori is. Otherwise they might make me tell them on Friday. You never know how strong or weak you are until you've tried it out."

When she said this I was glad too that I hadn't had the opportunity of telling her that Flori was visiting his mother. Much better for her to worry and be kept uncertain than to know. I didn't even dare to ask for his mother's address, where I was supposed to send money. After Clara had gone home to give Renate her supper I spent most of the night pacing up and down in my room, smoking cigarettes and trying to find a clever way of whisking Clara out of the country before Friday. If she had not been watched before, I was sure she had some secret agent tailing her now. At four o'clock I took a sleeping powder because I figured that I might need a clear, rested mind the next morning. But I felt as if I had many thick woolen blankets wrapped around my head when my telephone woke me around eight.

"Yes——" I said drowsily, dusting my parchment lips with my flannel tongue.

"It's me, Milky——" the telephone said. "Did I wake you up?"

"Never mind," I said. "How are you, Milky?"

"Oh, I'm fine. How are you?"

"Fine too."

"That's good. I felt like saying good morning to you."

"It's a hell of an idea—but thanks all the same. Good morning."

"I missed you on Friday. I wondered if you could charter a car and come out today."

"I don't think so, Milky. I have a lot of very urgent things to attend to."

"What could be more urgent than visiting your ailing son?"

"Never mind. I'll tell you when I see you next time."

"Could you come tomorrow then?"

"For Christ's sake, don't sound like an impatient lover. What's the matter with you?"

"Oh—nothing with me directly. There has been a little trouble at Alpenholf, though."

"Have you been fresh with the doctor? Or did he hurt you?" I asked, making a quick calculation of the most probable troubles that might have occurred.

"Nothing of the kind. But I'm not in Alpenhof now. I spent the night in the Semmering Hotel. I hoped you could come and pick me up here."

I shook my head to get the dopey feeling out of it.

"Could you be a bit less cryptic, Milky?" I said softly. "I'm not quite up to solving puzzles before breakfast. I haven't slept out yesterday's Nembutal."

"I'm just trying to break it to you in a tactful fashion. Yesterday they came and took Dr. Konrad away. The nurses had left on Monday, but the old man and the one assistant who remained in the joint managed all right. But now he's gone for good."

"Who took him away? Where did they take him?" I yelled.

"Aren't you a bit hard of perception, my darling?" Michael said gently. "They took him away. They, you know. Just They. It makes not much sense to stay in a hospital without a doctor, does it? Besides, the people from the village came last evening and smashed everything in the laboratory. It was a magnificent display of furor teutonicus. Dr. Konrad's beautiful special Tubocolin 287 has gone the way of all proteins, I'm afraid. And later on we had a little fire in the house, that's why we trekked to the Semmering Hotel in the middle of the night. A funnier bunch of hitchhikers you've never seen. Blind as a bat, every one of us."

"Oh, Milky——" was all I could say to this grim report. "Oh Milky——"

"Yes, Mother. It's a tough break. Old man Konrad sure is the ugliest, smellingest skunk of a little Jew there ever was, but he sort of grows on you. I had an idea that he was the one guy to make me well again. Well that's over now. Are you coming with a car to get me?"

"Michael," I said pretty desperate, "I might have to stay in town today. Don't you think you could manage to hire a car there—or come back by train?"

"I'll try to if I have to," he said. "But I'm afraid of it. I've got so damned clumsy and dependent lately, I'm scared of bumping into something. Couldn't you send Bummerl for me?"

"No, that's just it. I can't send Bummerl," I shouted into the telephone to drown out the stab of pain that shot through me when Michael admitted that he did not dare to walk alone any more. "There is some trouble here too, don't you understand?"

"All right, all right, no use working yourself into a state," Michael said. "You take care of Bummerl—take good care of her, Mother, hear me—and I'll take care of myself."

Michael arrived around noon, pretending that everything was okay with him but looking as if he were made of thin white tissue paper. He was shuddering with chills, his temperature was up to 37.9 degrees. I put him to bed and had the hotel doctor send us an eye specialist. Obviously one could not break off the injections so abruptly without bad consequences. But as Michael had said, Dr. Konrad's Tubocolin didn't exist any longer and we had to get along as best we could. I wondered what the sudden change in the treatments would do to my boy. I had a bitter taste in my mouth, from the sleeping powder and from disgust. They haven't only smashed that laboratory, I thought, they've smashed my boy's eyes too.

"Do you mind staying alone for a while? I've to go and see Clara," I said, stopping at Michael's bedside. I had evolved a little plan of my own for getting Clara and Renate off, and I should have liked to discuss it with Michael. I felt bewildered and confused; by now I had so many problems to worry about that I felt like trying to get out of a swamp and being sucked in deeper and deeper.

"If it should be necessary to get them all out of the country by hook and crook, can I count on you?" I asked the boy.

"Of course you can," he said. "What a funny question, Mother dear."

"I never know exactly how much of a Nazi you still are. Or have your latest little experiences made a change in that?"

"I'm all for the Anschluss, if that's what you want to know. So are most Austrians. It wasn't very nice, what happened in Alpenhof, but you can be sure that if the Führer learned about such things he would be the first to punish the people who did it. You can't plant a field without digging the ground first."

"It's just too bad that they had to plow under a man like Konrad, isn't it, Milky?"

"I'm glad he was taken in protective custody before that horde from the village came. They would have killed him. They had an idea that he was using Aryans for guinea pigs," Michael said.

I gave a deep sigh over this my stubborn child; I felt like fighting it out with him right then and there, but after another glance at his drawn face with the cramped smile I gave up and went on my way to see Clara.

It was a nice, sunny day; the branches of the trees on the Ring were budding, the sparrows were chirping, and the crowd outside looked freshly starched and more cheerful than I could bear. When I passed Ahmed he did not greet me as usual but stared with a glassy expression straight ahead. Following the direction of his glance I discovered a car parked across the street with two harmless looking men in it. I had planned to take a taxi, but now I changed my mind and, forcing myself to walk slowly, I strolled down the Ring, turned into the Kaerntnerstrasse, stopped in front of a shop window, and saw in the glass that the car had followed me at a snail's pace. It gave me a chilly feeling at the nape of my neck; up to that moment I had only worried about my friends. Now the danger was gradually creeping up on me personally. Still, that people were dragged into cellars, beaten unconscious, tortured, imprisoned, killed seemed not like something that really could happen to me or to my friends but like something I had read in a cheap dime novel. I was very impatient to see Clara and discuss my plan with her. But now I changed my mind, circled the Opera House, and crossed the Ring. It didn't seem true at all that this had been my way to school when I was a child. Mechanically I turned into a side street; there was the jeweler where I had always caught a fleeting glance at the clock in the window when I was late. The shop was still there, but the clock was gone. There was the bakery with the same edifice of sweets and cakes and pastries built around a slightly soiled birthday cake that had seemed such a marvel when I was six. I looked around, the car had stopped at the corner, and one of the men got out of it. I walked on confusedly, and as I reached the next block I found myself facing the green square of the Schiller Platz. My heart was pounding with fear, and I sat down on a bench to calm it down. The crabapple tree that I had liked so much was still there, glowing with a faint blush but not in bloom yet. It surprised me that the trees and shrubs did not seem larger than they had been in my childhood; rather smaller and somewhat puny. Schiller looked sternly down from his black marble pedestal as if he were peeved at me. The man had stopped, pretending to light his cigarette. On that lawn Clara had danced for me with bare feet. Now they were going to take her and break her. The fear that any step I might make could be a disastrous mistake grew into a panic. But something had to be done, I could not just sit on a park bench and let my nerves run away with me. As soon as I get this business done I'll take the next boat and go back to U.S.A., I told myself. That was the thin little silver lining in the catastrophe that had befallen Dr. Konrad and his Alpenhof. There was nothing left now to keep me and Michael on this convulsed, diseased continent.

I pulled myself up from my bench, hailed a taxi, and drove straight to Clara's house. When I paid the driver and looked around I did not see any car or man following me. I pushed the bell of the Rieger apartment but did not hear it ring. However, Clara opened the door at once and pulled me inside. Her hands were shaking. More than anything else it frightened me that Clara's firm, steady hands whose grip I knew so well were shaking.

"I wrapped some cloth around the bell to muffle it," she whispered to me. "He's asleep. He's come back."

"Not Flori?"

She only nodded, tiptoeing ahead of me into the living room, where the portraits of former Riegers calmly twinkled down at us with their urbane old-fashioned dignity. "Yes, somehow he managed to sneak into the house without anyone watching him."

"But that's insane——" I said. "That's criminal, that's——"

"Give me a cigarette, I have run out of supply," Clara said, leaning against the grand piano. She looked at me with a strange, pale smile. "Yes, he has come back," she said. "He wants to give himself up. He is at the end of his rope I guess."

"You won't let him do it," I said.

"Of course not," Clara said. "Men are such frail creatures, aren't they?"

"Where is Renate?"

"She's out, having her piano lesson."

"Does she know?"

"No. It wouldn't do any good, would it?"

"Did he come back because he was afraid they would do things to you?" I asked, trying to penetrate the meaning of that strange, translucent smile in Clara's face.

"Yes, that's why he came. Isn't he a fool?" she said; the air of the room vibrated with the overtones of pride and tenderness and infinite affection in her words. "Isn't he a fool?"

"Telepathy?" I asked her. "Did he feel you were in danger?"

Clara shrugged her shoulders. "Who knows——" she said. "There are many funny things between two people who have lived as closely and happily as we——"

"Look here, Clara," I said briskly. "I've worked it all out. I've made two reservations on tomorrow's morning plane to Prague. You and Renate come to the airport as if to see us off, and never mind if you're watched or followed. We, Michael and I, will arrive at the last moment. You'll fall around my neck to kiss me good-by and Renate will hang onto Michael. You rush with us through the little gate. The man there tries to stop us; I pretend not to understand German, there is some confusion, a quarrel, I stall them—and meanwhile you and Renate get into the plane with our tickets. The plane is off before anyone realizes what has happened. Once you're off nobody can get you back. How is that for an idea?"

"It's the shit," Clara said. "And you are an idiot, little monk. Because the moment the plane is off they'll arrest you and we will be arrested at the first stop. Is that clear to you?"

"Yes, now that you say it——" I muttered, crestfallen. "Well—what else will we do then?"

"If I only knew, Marion, if I only knew," Clara said, linking her fingers tightly as she began pacing up and down the room. "Could I send Renate to you for tonight?" she asked. "It's better for the child not to know her father is here. And I have a lot to do. First I'll cook a good dinner for my man, a mushroom omelette, that's what he likes, and I'll put a bottle of champagne on ice. If we go down why not go down in grand style? And there is still a whole, long night ahead of us. Maybe we'll hit on some idea. If not, we'll have to—what does Michael call it? Face the music. After all, we have gone through worse things during the war, haven't we?"

"We certainly belong to a confounded generation, don't we? One thing after another crashing down on us. When will the world be normal again?"

"That's where you are wrong, little monk," Clara said. "The world is normal as it is now. It's just that sort of a world. There hasn't been a day without wars, revolutions, torture chambers somewhere as long as this world existed."

"Pessimism is a very unbecoming fashion for a girl like you," I said. "You go and cook your dinner now and put the champagne on ice, and I'm going home to wait for Renate. I'll keep the plane reservations, just in case."

"Thanks——" Clara whispered, leading me out. "And, Mony—if anything should go wrong—will you take care of Renate?"

"That's understood."

"As if she were your own child?"

"Yes. As if she were my own child."

"Servus," Clara said, with the smart old-fashioned greeting of our childhood, and opened the door.

"Servus, Clara," I said. When she gave me her hand it was warm and had stopped shaking.

I left the house, looking up and down the street, but there was neither car nor harmless-looking man to follow me. Maybe I'm just seeing ghosts, I thought. Seems a few months in Europe make you just as hysterical and scared as the rest of them. They certainly have a way of playing the xylophone on your nervous system that gets you down by and by. I had sounded pretty good when I talked to Clara, but I felt very downhearted and saw no way out. Marion, my girl, I told myself as I wound my way through the people who filled the narrow sidewalks, this turns out to be a thicker soup and more of it than you'll be able to eat. Michael's eyes. Dr. Konrad dragged into some camp from which he might never return. Flori at the end of his rope. Clara obviously resolved to go down with the ship. So what are you going to do about all this, Marion, my girl? I wish there were somebody to tell me what to do. God? You up there, you don't seem very interested in the muddle down here. Maybe you are inspecting some other planet just now and can't be bothered? Putzi? No, Putzi wouldn't understand the sort of trouble into which Austria had got herself. Max Wilde? Yes, the old reprobate knew danger and how to get out of it. You live through it or you die. Small consolation. It had begun to rain. Cold. Tired. Confused. Frightened. Yes, you little coward, frightened out of your wits. . . .

"There is a gentleman waiting for you," the clerk at the desk reported to me. The lobby of the hotel was a warm, bright, cozy refuge. People were laughing, chatting in many languages, sipping cocktails, drinking mocha, flirting, and the music in a corner played, full of sugar and spice.

"A gentleman?" I said. I felt my lips getting white and I had pain keeping my teeth from chattering. Here it is now, I thought. The man in the car. The Gestapo.

"Yes, Madame. He was very insistent. He wanted to go up to your room, but I managed to prevent him from doing so."

"Did he give his name?"

"No, he wanted to talk to your son, but as you had given

orders not to disturb the young gentleman I assumed that it would be correct to tell the gentleman to return later. However, the gentleman decided to wait for you. He told me to send for him the moment you came back. He is in the bar now."

The clerk lifted one nonchalant finger, and a page boy popped up at my side to take orders.

"Does Madame agree to see the gentleman presently?" the clerk asked me.

"Yes. Better get it over with——" I said feebly. The clerk gave the page boy a short explanation and the boy disappeared toward the bar. Why do page boys always have to wear such tight pants and caps, like monkeys, I thought; it can't be good for their self-respect. I'm an American citizen, I thought also. They can't simply arrest me or do things to me. I'm under the protection of the United States of America, I'll tell my Big Brother, I'll notify my Ambassador——

The page boy returned, pointing with his chin into my direction. I had put on my gloves and lighted a cigarette, but it seemed a tiny object to hold on to. I had my upper portion pretty well under control, but my knees were an undignified mass of jello. And then I saw who the insistent gentleman was who followed in the wake of the page boy, taller and wider of shoulders than anyone in the lobby and still wearing that funny old hat that I had wanted to throw away for the last three years. My heart was drumming fast and loud all over me, in my chest, my ears, my gums, my kidneys. This would be a nice moment for fainting, I told myself, and then John was standing in front of me and said: "Hello, kid."

"Hello, John," I said. "Hello there. Hello, John."

"You are much smaller than I remembered you," he said, coming down from his height, and there was the smell of whisky, and I had never smelled a lovelier perfume in all my life.

"I must have shrunk in the laundry," I said. I tore off my idiotic gloves to give him both my hands.

"Surprised to see me, kid?"

"Rather——" I said. "Why didn't you send me a cable?"

"Oh, just so. I wanted to see what sort of face you would make when I suddenly popped up in Vienna."

"Well what sort of a face do I make?"

"A silly one. Also one I'd like to kiss. And you have wet shoes again. I should have known it."

I looked guiltily at my feet. John linked his arm into mine. He was a huge human stove, giving out warmth.

"Do we have to hang around in this lousy lobby or can we go upstairs?"

"This is Mr. Sprague——" I said to the clerk. "We'll have to arrange for another room."

"Very well, Madame. May I have your passport, Mr. Sprague? And will you fill out this form, Mr. Sprague?"

"They're pretty strict with you here, eh?" John said good-naturedly. "What sort of a room is yours, Marion? Twin beds, double bed, or what?"

"A very chaste and very single bed," I said. "And Michael is sleeping in it just now. I guess he can keep my room and we'll take another one on the same floor. I might also need another single for a young lady who is coming to stay with us," I told the clerk. I clutched the sleeve of John's overcoat between my fingers, never to let him go away from me again. Warmth and safety emanated from him in thick, fat, happy rays.

"We want a two-room suite, with a sitting room or what have you, don't we, kid?" he said.

"Don't fuss now, John," I said. "I've got to go upstairs quick. I'll have to cry in a moment. I feel it coming."

"All right, all right, give us the best you have on that floor," John told the clerk, who importantly scanned the floor plan and jingled with keys. "And you, son, get my luggage from the porter. I left it with him. Here, that's for you."

The luggage consisted of a brown cardboard box tied with string. It traveled upstairs with us in the elevator and the hotel people tried to be tactful about it.

"Is that what Esquire prescribes now as the luggage of the smartly dressed American traveler?" I said, and then I pushed my face into the rough material of John's overcoat and began crying right there in the elevator as I hadn't cried since my third birthday. It must have been most embarrassing for the clerk, the porter, and the page boy who escorted us upstairs, but then, I guess, hotel employees are a hard-boiled lot.

"You see, I had no time to get my bag," I heard John say. "I made this hop rather suddenly, caught the boat directly from my office. I just bought me a tooth brush on board. . . . "

This made me cry still harder, and I kept on crying for quite a while after we were installed in 421–22, with John holding me on his lap as if I were a baby, patting my shoulder as if I were a horse, and muttering from time to time: "That's right. Have a good cry, kid. It'll do you good. Get it off your chest. My, that's a load of salt water you must have carried around. There, take my handkerchief."

Some men you love for their looks, some for their brain or their genius, some because they are good lovers, or good dancers, or good company on a fishing trip, in a bar, in bed. Some you love with your instinct, which senses that they will make good fathers for your children, and some with your mind, because you think alike. Some with your nerves because they are sensitive, some with your body because they have the same rhythm; some you just love for the way they cross their legs, smoke their cigarette, put their hands into their pockets, some because they need you, some because they resist you; and some you love for nothing but their shortcomings. I loved you best, John, when I felt ill, weak, scared, unhappy. I had fun with many of them, but you were the only one with whom I could be wonderfully unhappy and let myself go and cry. Thanks, John, for letting me blow my nose into your handkerchief. . . .

"Now tell me why you came all of a sudden like that, you with your cardboard box," I asked him when I had finished crying several gallons of tears and the rain barrel was empty.

"You don't seem to mind my being here, do you?"

"No, John. It could make me believe in God," I said, struggling with the hiccups, which had proceeded my crying jag. The chair on which John sat, holding me on his lap, was of a most uncomfortable Louis Seize design and creaked anxiously under its double load. There are always such counterpoints to burlesque the pathos in which we like to wallow.

"You'd better believe in him," John said. "But it wasn't God who sent me, if that's what you mean to say. It was simply Miss Crump. She told me so often I needed a vacation that I finally got annoyed and took one, see?"

"Is there anything the matter with your health, John?" I asked alarmed.

"Not at all. I'm in fine shape. But Miss Crump also shoved all sorts of clippings from the papers under my nose, just in case I should have overlooked the fact that Herr Hitler meanwhile has stuffed Austria into his pocket. Miss Crump seemed to think I'd better look after you in person. She didn't trust you would be intelligent enough to keep out of trouble all by yourself. And, damn it, Marion, do you realize you've been away from me for four months? Can't a guy get lonesome for his wife?"

"Yes, I know," I said, crestfallen. "I haven't been the sort of wife Miss Crump would have chosen for you. But John, you know that I had to see this through with Michael. I had no choice, had I?"

"How is the boy? Better?" John said, and his face was troubled as it hadn't been even in Dinky's worst times. I shook my head. "You'll see yourself," I said. "Of course he isn't always as low as you'll find him today. He takes little dips, you know——"

"Poor kids, you two have gone through a lot together, haven't you?" John said, pushing the knuckles of his fist under my chin as was his habit when he wanted to hide his emotions.

"Don't make me sorry for myself or I'll start crying all over," I said, hiccuping fiercely. John poured a glass of water for me and supervised my taking fourteen gulps as a remedy, and then I washed my face and we went over to 417 to spring the surprise on Michael.

That night we lay in our beds, with our hands linked across the Grand Canyon between them, and I told John all the twisted trouble in which I was involved. When I had finished he lit himself a cigarette, took a deep breath, and said: "Now let's get this straight." Then I saw the little glow of the cigarette wander to his mouth and away again and heard a faint jarring noise as he rubbed his chin, and I knew that he was thinking. It was an immeasurable relief to know that John was here to take over some of my load and get things straight.

"Now listen, kid," he said at last. "We have three different problems and we'll do best to treat them separately. There is first of all this Dr. Konrad. If you think and if Michael thinks that he can save his eyes, we must get the man out of here and to New York. I'll talk with our consul general tomorrow and see how it can be done. I'm sure they'll let him go if he has a quota visa for the U.S.A. I'll try my darnedest to get it for him as quickly as I can. Meanwhile I'll have the boys pull some strings to get him released from whatever hell they've put him in. Next we'll have to get this Clara woman away from here. They didn't take her passport. And they told her they would quiz her again on Friday, you say? That might have been a threat. On the other hand it might very well have been a friendly hint to get out pronto. I am inclined to think it was a hint—or why would they have left her the passport? I think the most sensible thing she can do is to take the train to Prague and cross the border quite legally and openly. If they shouldn't let her pass there, it's still time to make different plans.

"Now for the boy friend—he has no passport and if he had one they would pinch him at the border anyway. That means I'll have to borrow a passport for him from one of the boys and whisk him across the border illegally. That's how it's done all the time. Sure it's criminal, but so is that gang that wants him. I'll have to get a look at the fellow first thing tomorrow morning and a photo of his, so I can find a guy who resembles him to a certain degree and is willing to let me have his passport for a couple of days. D'you think he could pass for an American?"

"Flori? Certainly not. He is as Austrian as the double eagle."

"Hmm. That makes it a bit tougher. Couldn't he act like an American? Not to save his life?"

"No, not even to save his life. I doubt if he has ever seen an American except at the Salzburg Festival."

"Well—I'll get him across somehow. I'll talk it over with the boys. They know the ropes. Now will you be a good girl and not worry any more and get some sleep? You'll see, it's all quite simple."

"Yes, John," I said. "I didn't realize how simple it all is. I guess I'm just a stupid woman."

"You bet you are," he said, and I knew that he was grinning in the dark. Funny, I thought, now I'm almost forty-three and this is the first time, the very first time in all my life, that I feel protected. It's a wonderful feeling. Thank you for it, John, thank you. I don't want to be independent. I don't want to fight. I'm sick and tired of putting my head into the lion's mouth.

Of course there are still Michael's eyes, I thought then. They are my business and it's not simple, and no man can help me, not even John. When I thought that, I wanted to sigh, and when I tried to suppress the sigh, it came out as a loud lonely last hiccup.

"Suppose I moved over to you and took you in my arms—would that help?" John asked across the Grand Canyon.

"I guess it would," I said gratefully, making some space for him in my bed. I bedded my head into the warm, familiar hollow between his shoulder and his chest and closed my eyes. The radio in the room next door finished a speech and broke into their eternal Horst Wessel Lied. This was Vienna, the town I came from. And this was my husband, John W. Sprague III of the Hartford Spragues. You make lots of detours while you are alive. Soldiers marching down the Ring. Tramp tramp tramp tramp. The drums are out of rhythm, I thought, half asleep. It wasn't drums. It was John's heartbeat, close to my ear, and it was out of rhythm. Maybe because it's such a great heart, I thought, and then everything dissolved into the soft velvet of sleep and dream.

ONCE BEFORE I had left Vienna in rebellion and deep disgust. When the plane lifted itself into the air and the town began to revolve beneath us, with her churches and spires and steeples and domes, with the green squares of her parks, the slate-gray pattern of her old roofs; with the Danube a yellow snake coiling around her flanks and the hills rising softly curved, like the thighs and hips and breasts of a voluptuous woman, all I wanted and hoped for was never, never to see this beautiful corpse again. The plane climbed quickly, pierced through a mass of white cotton, and then we floated above a solid bank of clouds, left the pale morning sun on our right, and turned north toward the border. I saw that Renate had turned quite green around the gills and I smiled at her consolingly.

"You're not afraid of flying, child, are you?"

"Afraid? Jesus Maria, no. It's just because of my trauma. You know, when Hitler's airplanes came and dived so low and made such an unholy noise, it might have given me a little shock and now I'm having a trauma," she said nonchalantly.

"Where did you get that trauma stuff?"

"Oh, Michael told me all about it," she said eagerly. "You know, Clara told me all that dull bunk about sex and what the ovaries are and all that. But Michael doesn't treat me like a baby. He told me all about psychoanalysis and anal erotic and all that, he said it was time I transferred my father complex to him. It's as interesting as when you take an alarm clock apart. If I want to become a nurse I have to know all that, don't you see, and Michael——"

She gasped and clutched the golden cross she wore on a fine chain around her neck. The plane had taken a little bump, and Renate was flying for the first time. A little later she quietly took the little paper bag and, resignedly and well-mannered, began to spit into it.

John had organized the Rieger transport in three columns. My part in it was the easiest one. "You take Renate and shut up," I was told.

Clara had traveled by train with Michael the day before, supposedly as his nurse. He himself had worked out this idea and urgently pleaded with John to let him cover her exit that way. "That's at least one thing for which those wretched eyes of mine are useful," he said. John had smiled at him with raised eyebrows. "I thought you were all for the Nazis, son," he said. "How come you want to join in a conspiracy against them?"

"This is one case where the individual gets in conflict with the idea," Michael parried him in good humor. "I still believe in their philosophy but I couldn't let friends like Clara and—and—Renate down when they are in a jam, could I?"

"I guess you couldn't," John said, quite pleased. I was sorry for my boy who found himself in one emotional complication after another. Clara put herself into a Red Cross uniform with the pin and the medal she had received during the War, and Michael seemed as elated as an actor before an opening, like Manfred Halban when he had played a big part.

Clara's passport was a prize sample of correctness, full of stamps and transit visas, and she had her permit to leave, with a lovely visitor's visa for the U.S.A. as a climax. I was surprised to discover on this occasion that her real and legal name was nothing so colorful as Clara Balbi. In her passport she was simply and absurdly Fräulein Przestapinsky. Only the old Austria, with her medley of nationalities, could burden her subjects with names like this one; but it did marvelous service and got her safely across the border and into Prague. In my handbag I had Michael's wire with the message on which we had agreed: "Don't worry about my cold, it's much better today."

John had taken it upon himself to bring Florian Rieger into safety. For this purpose he had rigged up some sort of a stag party. Three of the boys were coming along to cover the transport, distract the attention of the border officials if necessary, and give the general impression that Flori was just one of a noisy, carefree, and slightly illuminated bunch of foreign businessmen. All this had been cooked up in a night session in our hotel room, where John had kept the radio going, the waiters buzzing in and out serving drinks and getting big tips, the bridge tables put up, and the boys singing Sweet Adeline at four in the morning. Everything exactly as loud and primitive as people imagined that foolish rich Americans would behave. Flori's skimpy new mustache had been shaved off again, his hair parted on the other side, and a pair of American-made horn-rimmed glasses administered to him. The only possible passport John had been able to produce was American after all; only Americans seemed to have enough pluck and sense of humor to take a chance and try cheating the authorities out of a victim. Michael had

spent hours in coaching poor Flori to say: "I don't understand
German" with a good Brooklyn accent—for Jake Conley, on
whose passport he was traveling, had the tough luck to hail
from Brooklyn. They were on the train, all five of them, but
they couldn't have reached the border yet. It took a very long
time for a minute to creep by, and my mind was with John and
Florian every minute. I could almost see them in their compartment, playing bridge on John's brown cardboard box, ordering
drinks, trying to make so much noise that no one would notice
how silent Jake Conley was. I wondered if Flori, our painstaking,
correct little gentleman of the old school, would manage to play
his part. "Don't answer if anybody talks German to you. Plug
your ears with Oropax so you don't hear them, that's the best and,
for Christ's sake, don't turn around if anybody shouts your
real name. Don't be fidgety. Don't wear gloves. Push your hat
back a bit more, that's it. Don't look at German newspapers.
Pretend to be asleep or drunk or something. You were in the
War, weren't you? You've been in tight spots before and pulled
out of it. Okay, this is war again. Just hold on to yourself,
boy."

Flori seemed to bog down under the load of good advice they
gave him. They had stuck him in a suit with a Brooks Brothers
label, had furnished him with a suitcase that bore the stickers
of the boats on which he was supposed to have crossed the
Atlantic, and filled it with American underwear for the perusal
of the customs men. They had given him an American wrist
watch and a batch of American newspapers to carry under his
arm. They had even remembered stuffing a few letters addressed
to Jake Conley into his breast pocket, together with Jake's
wallet containing the snapshots of Mrs. Jake Conley and the
two babies in Brooklyn. Still they were worried. "He's never
played football," they said. "He doesn't know what teamwork
is. If he fumbles, we'll all be sunk." I had an idea that John
would have liked to give Florian a powerful anesthetic for the
duration of the trip, or knock him out and drag him unconscious
through the border control. When I thought of everything that
might happen, I felt a bit sick myself. If I had had a golden
cross I would have clung to it too, and maybe said some silent

prayers as Renate did in the intermissions between spitting into her bag.

Our plane arrived at nine A. M., and the train with our men was supposed to be in at 4 P. M. but did not arrive until six. I remember those hours only in rags and patches as one remembers the hours after an operation, before the anesthetic wears off. It rained when we arrived, but Prague—like Paris—is a town to which silver gray veils are becoming. Michael was in bed with a temperature and a bit too cheerful. Clara had gone out, supposedly to look at the Hradčin. I assumed that she couldn't bear to sit still. Renate played nurse for a while, but when she heard the church bells call, she slipped off into the Tein Church, to pray.

Michael fell asleep, and Clara didn't come back. What now? I thought, looking across an endless ocean of waiting. God, who had worked several miracles for me recently, was helpful once more. On the writing desk I discovered a paperweight that was no more than a gnarled, bulging piece of wood. I picked it up and turned it in my fingers. It was much heavier than I had expected, and had a rough barky surface. I followed its shape and grain with my fingertips. It had a queer, cranky personality. I took my knife, the small one I always carried in my handbag, and began carving something that must have been on my mind without my knowing it. At first the wood was recalcitrant, but then it began to submit to the blade, and by and by it shaped itself into the figure of a prisoner. His hands were tied behind his back, he was kneeling, and his head was thrown back as though twisted by great pains. The old remedy worked once more. I forgot the time, Michael, John, and Florian Rieger. I did not hear it when the church bells chimed again because I had some trouble with the body of my little prisoner. It was still a very crude shape when Renate returned, her eyes as bright as if she had washed them with tears.

"Has Papa arrived?" she asked me.

"It's still almost two hours until the train arrives," I said.

She looked at my little man, who was still an embryo in the womb of the material, and began to laugh. "What is it going to be? A little monkey?"

"You're a little monkey yourself," I told her. "Go and wash your face and comb your hair. You want to look neat when Michael wakes up, don't you?"

She did not look into the mirror as she straightened her braids but touched her own head with her hand, stroking her hair back until it lay close and smooth to her skull. It was a strange little gesture, and then I understood that she was making herself attractive not to Michael's eyes but to the touch of his hand. It amazed me often enough in the months to come that she never for a minute forgot to consider how he, with his failing eyesight, would react. I myself forgot it frequently and hurt the boy by small slips and neglects, and then I was very angry with myself. I went over and put my cheek to hers to let her know how much I liked her. "I am terribly hungry," she said very seriously. "That's because I've turned my stomach inside out and puked myself empty."

That's one of the things I remember. I also remember very clearly the taste of the cake we ate after Clara had returned. I have the taste of it on my tongue even now. It was a yeast cake, filled with plum preserves and with a sprinkle of honeyed poppy-seeds on top. But I do not remember the nonsense we talked while we waited for the five-thirty train. We just tossed meaningless little bubbles of conversation into the air to fill the vacuum of time. At last the telephone rang, and there was John.

"Okay," he said. It sounded breathless, and I heard him panting.

"Okay? Everything?" I asked.

"Yes, everything okay. We are downstairs. I just called you before we're coming up—sort of a shock absorber, you know."

"Okay——" I said. I turned to Clara. "They are here. He says they are okay," I said, stupid with relief. Michael had his arm around Renate's thin shoulder. "Steady now, steady, Bummerl," I heard him whisper to her. Clara held my unfinished little prisoner in her hands. "Do you mind if I go to my room?" she said. "And will you send Flori to me? I don't care to make scenes in public——"

She walked stiffly toward the door, and for a moment I thought she would faint. It was a funny idea that Clara, my strong, bold archangel, should faint. But she got out in good countenance just when the elevator arrived with a click in the corridor outside. "Run along, Bummerl," Michael said, giving Renate a little pat and a shove. In the doorway she ran into John; she bent down, snatched his hand, kissed it, and was gone. John stood there, rubbing his hand with a baffled expression.

"Hello, saver of lives," I said. He seemed in no mood for jokes. He looked tired and strained. "Hello there——" he said tentatively. He went first of all to the telephone and picked it up. "Room service——" he said. "No, I can't speak Czech. You'd better understand English, see. I want you to send me a bottle of Scotch Whisky, yes, a whole bottle, and some mineral water and lots of ice."

"Was it hard, John?" I asked him late that night when we were lying in bed and he grabbed for my hand.

"No, it was fun," he said. "There were only two awful moments. One was at the border, in Bratislav. One of the men who inspected our passports knew Rieger. It seems he had been a waiter in one of those blasted coffeehouses where your Viennese spend their best years. Rieger pretty well went to pieces when he saw that man standing there in his uniform. 'It's all over,' he said. 'Je suis fini.' He babbled French in his excitement. We had a tough time pushing him out of the compartment and into the shed where they had their passport inspection. It meant taking a long chance, and, frankly, I didn't think myself that we would get him through. So then this man doesn't bat an eyelash. Not a trace of a sign of recognition. The boys and I thought Rieger was crazy. We thought he suffered from hallucinations when that man bowed and smiled and gave him the passport back and said in the lousiest English you've ever heard: 'Thanks, Mr. Conley.' And do you know what happened then? Just when we crawled back into the train this man pops up and, without looking at Rieger, he says: 'Happy voyage, Herr Baron Rieger, and much luck!' Funny people, your countrymen. I can tell you, my legs felt like cheese soufflé. . . . "

I watched John's cigarette wander to his mouth and listened to the deep breath he took. "And what else happened?" I asked him.

"What else? Oh yes, something that was still more awful. When we had passed the border we made sort of a beeline for the men's room, after all the excitement. And while we had to wait outside, this guy, Rieger, suddenly grabs my hand and kisses it. Just like that kid did before. It certainly is the goddamnedest sensation I ever had in my life. A man kissing my hand. Jesus Christ, it felt like five hundred rainworms crawling up my sleeve——"

"Well, you saved his life, don't forget, John, my darling," I said, laughing in the dark. "And Austrian sons are brought up by their mothers to kiss hands. Austrian daughters too—like that."

I felt John's hand squirm when I put my lips upon it, and I was so fond of him that for a while I even forgot Michael and his eyes.

The next morning, when we were all having breakfast in my room, a fat, smiling, sunny little gentleman came to see Florian Rieger. There was first a knock at the door, and instead of the waiter we had expected, that fat little man entered.

"I regret to disturb at this early hour," he said. "But I come on a rather urgent matter. Have I the pleasure to speak to Baron Florian Rieger?" he said, turning to Flori.

John did not understand him, because he spoke German. Clara kicked Flori under the table not to give himself away.

"This is my room and there seems to be a mistake," I said quickly, putting down my cup. "My husband, Mr. Sprague, and his friend, Mr. Conley, don't understand German. You'll have to talk with me and tell me what you want."

"I bring you a message from your mother, Herr Baron," the nice fat man continued, not paying any attention to my quavering protests but addressing Flori only. There was a moment's silence in which Renate dropped her spoon with a clank. She had been peeling a soft-boiled egg for Michael.

"Your mother, Frau Baronin Aloisia Rieger, lives in Villa Tannenruh in Thaya," the man said, producing an envelope from his breast pocket. "I have orders to bring you this letter from her. You don't want to read it? Well, I'll be glad to read it to you."

The little fat man brought out a pair of eyeglasses, adjusted them to the bridge of his nose, and took a letter from the envelope, which had not been sealed.

"My dear son," he read, entirely expressionless, "I have been arrested and will be held until your return to Vienna. Please come back at once and save the life of your unhappy mother."

He put the letter on the table, in front of Florian, between the butter and the jam. "You recognize your mother's handwriting?" he said softly. Flori read the letter, looked up, read it again, and then folded his napkin with an automatic gesture.

"Flori——" Clara said. Michael sat very stiffly, with Renate's little-girl's hand in his. She was chewing her pigtails frantically, but she neither screamed nor cried. John pushed back his chair and got up. "Say, what's all this?" he said.

"I give you ten minutes to make your decision, Herr Baron," the little man said amiably. "I have two men waiting outside to take you to the train if you decide to go back. You understand, we are not using any force. If you go back you do it entirely of your own free will. Do the ladies mind if I smoke?"

He lit himself a cigar and, with an abominable show of tact, went to the window and pretended to look out of it.

"Clara?" Flori said.

"Yes, dear——" she answered, looking straight at him, with an almost unbearable intensity.

"You know that I can't leave my mother in their hands?"

"Yes, Flori."

"You will forgive me if I go back?"

Clara nodded.

"You would not want me with you for such a price, would you?"

"Of course not, Flori."

"I knew it," he said. "Renate?"

"Yes, Papa."

"What would you do in my place?"

"The same, Papa."

"You'll take care of Clara, promise?"

"Yes, Papa. And I'll pray for you. You'll soon be free again."

"Certainly, child. Clara—she is your child from now on. You'll bring her up the way I would?"

"I want to go back with you," Clara said. "Marion will take care of Renate."

"Don't let's be sentimental," Flori said; poor Flori, who was the most sentimental person I had ever met in my life. "We must be rational about this. If you go back with me it would make everything a hundred times harder for me. As long as you are free you might be able to do something for me."

"Flori is right," I said. "We'll get him out, won't we, John? You have to stay with us. Maybe this is only a formality. They'll take him in protective confinement or something and we'll pull all the strings to get him out soon."

We all knew that this was nonsense, but at the moment we wanted to believe in it. When Flori took Clara in his arms to kiss her good-by I was afraid he would break, go to pieces, cry, make a horrible scene. But nothing of the sort happened. He had been embarrassingly voluble otherwise, but now he was taciturn and terse. Austrians are soft on the surface, but when it comes to a test, their underlining is as tough as corrugated iron. He kissed Clara and Renate, shook hands with John and Michael, and bowed to me.

"Thanks for everything, Marion," he said. "Auf Wiedersehen. Kiss your hand. Thanks, Mr. Sprague. I'm sorry I caused you so much trouble—with such unpleasant results. Grüss Gott. Au revoir."

He turned to the fat little man. "Do you mind if I take a second suit and some shirts along?" he asked. "I suppose you want to come with me when I go to my room and pack my underwear. Herr—what's your name?"

"It doesn't matter——" the little fat man muttered. He too bowed to all of us. "I regret having disturbed your breakfast," he said. He shoved Florian Rieger through the door. "After you, Herr Baron——" he said deferentially. Two other men were waiting outside. They wore no uniforms but they still had the shape and air of prison guards.

When I looked at Michael after they had taken Flori away I saw that he was holding my little carved prisoner in his hands;

he had broken the heavy wood in two and tears came rolling down from under his dark eyeglasses. John went over and patted his shoulder.

"Buck up, son," he said, "buck up, my boy. Now that you've had your fling it's time we all got out of this goddamned messy Europe and went home. Or do you still like it here?"

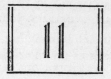

THERE CAME the great moment when Marion discovered the flask of enzian schnaps in her rucksack. It must have been left there, in the outer pocket, ever since her last ski trip with Christopher, and by a sheer miracle it had not broken when she fell into the crevasse. There is no better remedy against mountain sickness than a good hot gulp of this brandy that is distilled from the roots of the blue flaming gentian that grows in the Alps. After Marion had occupied herself for a few moments with this flask, all her resignation evaporated and all her optimism returned with a vengeance. New warmth spread through her body, and her lips which had been stiff began to thaw. Why this is absolutely luxurious, she thought. I'm dressed well, my leg doesn't hurt, and I have plenty of space for moving around and keeping myself warm. The sun is still shining, and Christopher must be on his way by now to search for me. I have cigarettes and chocolate, and now I have even this whole blessed flask full of buoyancy and self-assurance. My cigarette lighter is working, which is a small miracle in itself, and there, in my pocket, is that other piece of magic, my fountain pen. I can write letters to my friends to pass the time. I can drink half of my flask and still keep the other half for making a fire if I want to. Suppose I threw my rucksack into the flame if I felt cold; I could keep my fire burning for hours. Meanwhile it would be a good idea to look at the more pleasant sides of my little adventure. It's amazing that no chamber of commerce and no travel bureau has hit upon the idea of commercializing the crevasses on their glaciers. They could ask good money for taking people down here and just letting them look at all this beauty and glitter. Never in my life have I seen anything more thrilling than this depth of crystal into which I had the good luck to stumble. That's one thing we can't carve in wood, my girl. Maybe Walt Disney could make something of it. . . .

Tingling all over, Marion arranged herself in a comfortable position and began to get busy with her fountain pen.

"Dear Clara," she wrote, "don't be surprised if you receive a letter written on most sanitary but not very poetic toilet paper. I never go into the mountains without a small supply of this useful requisite, and it comes in handy just now. I have slipped down into a crevasse and am waiting for the rescue crew to haul me up. I'd like to send you a picture postcard from here, with all the blue and green fairy tale crystals down here, but all I have is toilet paper. Life is a succession of compromises, as you know, and we agreed long ago that there isn't such a thing as one hundred per cent. It's pretty and comfortable where I'm sitting, although a bit on the frigid side. I'm thinking of you and wondering what you are doing just now, Clara, my darling? Slapping some fat Park Avenue lady into shape? Or resting between work on your couch, which is as big as a full-size tent and as overcrowded as an old-time parlor?

"I just remembered the last time we were together. John was still alive but had gone to Albany, and we two were on our way home from some dull party. We had decided to take a little stroll along the park and have some fresh air before going home and to bed. The gardenias we had pinned to our shoulders had wilted; they were not brown yet but had reached the stage when they have the color of soft, warm butter. 'They're gone just about as much as we two,' I said, and you said, 'Yes, but that's when they smell best.' I don't remember how late it was, I suppose between five and six in the morning, for we had stopped on the way for a snack at Childs'. It was a chilly dawn, the streets were quiet and rather empty, and when we reached the park the top floors of the skyscrapers began to get pink and pearly. I had seen something in the middle of the street that interested me, and I left you on the sidewalk and went over to look at it. I hardly trusted my eyes, but it was true. There in the middle of the street was a little heap of horse apples, still warm, with a cloud of white steam hovering over it in the chilly air. I waved to you and you came after me to see what I had found. 'Pretty, isn't it?' I said. And you looked at it just as delighted as I was myself and you said: 'Miracle in Manhattan! How do you think it ever got here?'

" 'Maybe the horse of a milk cart has dropped it,' I suggested reluctantly. And you said: 'It's wonderful all the same, isn't it? The smell—doesn't it remind you of a hundred lovely things? And the color—like gold.'

" 'Yes, and a bit later the sparrows will come and pick out some grain and there will be a horse apple rush, sort of a sparrows' Alaska.'

" 'This makes the morning perfect,' you said. And I said: 'It's alive, that's what it is.' And then we went home and fixed ourselves some coffee and bacon and toast.

"You see, Clara, we both had our troubles and our fun, with men, with our professions, with our lives. But you are the only one to share with me the rapture over every little heap of horse manure we found on our way and the only one who knew everything about me without words.

"I wish you were here with me just now. You'd like it down here, and it would be twice as funny if we could laugh about it together. I don't have to tell you how I feel. It'll be too bad if you ever get this letter. But if you get it, my angry angel, you'll know everything I do not write down and you'll do all the things I would like you to do, without my asking for them."

Marion folded the letter away and thrust it into the rucksack, but she kept the fountain pen in her hand and played with it. Who said we are not progressing? she thought merrily. When Nefertiti in old Egypt wanted to send a love letter to her husband who was in some colonial war, she had to scratch it into bricks and some messenger had to tote a few tons of correspondence all across Egypt. Why even Moses had to chisel the ten commandments into blocks of stone. And Luther wrote his Bible with a huge quill, and when the devil came he threw his inkstand after him. But now look at this little wonder of perfection, a fountain pen. There were no fountain pens when I was a child; no typewriters, either; no phonographs, no movies, no radio, no airplanes, no automobiles, no Diesel motors. No rotogravure and no artificial silk, no air-raid shelters and no blackouts, no tanks either and no poison gas. No jazz bands and no atom smashing. No this and no that. Altogether those last forty years were pretty crowded, and no wonder people bump into one another once in a while. Forty years. My life. My generation. My period. Better—my periods; for it seems to me as if I had lived nine lives, like the proverbial cat. Lots of progress, lots of trouble. And where has it gotten us in the end? We're sitting in a crevasse and don't know how the hell we'll ever get out of it. But we have a fountain pen and an automatic cigarette lighter.

That sums it up nicely, doesn't it, Marion, my girl?

MARCH 1939. That first evening in Staufen, when I met Christopher. . . .

It was an evening as shut in and dark as if the whole village were locked inside of a nutshell. In Mexico they carve such naïve little landscapes into nutshells, with houses and trees and two Mexican fleas in their Sunday clothes going to church. I felt not bigger than a flea myself when I went out onto the veranda to cry. I had carried the tears with me for hours, feeling like an old rubber bag with a leak, afraid I might begin to dribble before Michael had gone to sleep.

We had arrived that noon with the bus that had picked us up at the station and taken us to the hotel, the only decent hotel in Staufen outside of a huge sanatorium for tuberculosis on the South Shore. In the afternoon we had walked to the small house where Dr. Konrad lived now, and he had made a thorough examination of Michael's eyes. Then I had taken Michael back along the shore to the hotel, had eaten dinner with him in the wood-paneled dining room, unobtrusively shoving plates and salt shakers and forks and spoons into his hands as had become my habit. The mountain air made him talkative, almost garrulous, and he embarked at once on some very funny efforts at imitating the Swiss Dutch of the waitresses. He talked so much and laughed so loud that people from other tables furtively turned their heads toward us and measured us newcomers with the cold disgust that older guests always display against new arrivals. I had a lot of trouble keeping my own voice steady and that heavy rubber bag full of tears from spilling. Michael had become terribly acute of hearing, and I had to be on guard all the time.

"Well, what had old smell-puss Konrad to say?"

"Oh, he seemed quite satisfied with you. You know how sure he is that he can cure your sort of trouble."

"Is he?"

"Definitely. He told me that he has improved his Tubocolin a lot."

"He has changed, Konrad, hasn't he?"

"How do you mean, changed?" I asked, wondering if Michael could still see enough to have noticed the damage they had done to Dr. Konrad's face. His jawbone had been smashed, his upper lip was pulled back, baring his new false teeth, which gave him an eager yet malicious expression. I had seen that expression before, on that little rhesus monkey in Apfel's bedroom.

"Well first of all he smells differently; dainty and practically fragrant. And then—didn't you notice? He loves to talk now. Remember how he used to shut up like a clam? Now you can hardly stop him from telling you stories."

"I suppose they weren't allowed to talk much in concentration camp. Now that he's free again he wants to make up for it."

"I hope he doesn't just talk. I hope he can do a bit more for me than they did in U.S.A."

"That's why we are here, Milky; isn't that it? You know what he demands. Confidence and ab-so-lute obedience."

"Okay, teacher, I confide and obey. But don't make me drink another glass of milk tonight or I'll bust."

I don't know why a man drinking his milk always seems so touching to women. It must have something to do with that utterly feminine machinery in our breasts. When Milky was propped up in his bed an hour later, I watched him empty the glass of warm milk I had coaxed into him; he clutched it between his two hands as he had done as a baby, and I had trouble keeping myself from getting too tender.

"Well, good night and dream something nice. You know the first dream in a new place always comes true," I said, tucking him in. I shouldn't have said it, because it gave a final little squeeze to my inside rubber bag, and Michael grabbed my hand and pulled me close to him.

"Why do you try so hard?" he said gently. "You don't have to lie to me, Mony. It's an insult, really. I'm not such a coward as all that. If I'm going to be blind it's much better for me to know it. I have to store away a lot of things as long as it's still time. Remember what that old guy Shakespeare said? Men must endure their going hence, even as their coming hither; ripeness is all! . . . "

As soon as Michael was asleep I slipped on the old raccoon coat, which I had brought along from New York, and stepped out onto the veranda that ran along the entire front of the inn. It was so dark out there that I had to grope my way to the railing. I could see neither the mountains across the lake nor the lake itself, except for a deeper black in the deep blackness of the night. There was no sky and no stars, only the low-hanging clouds that kept the village enclosed as in a velvet-lined box. All sounds were muffled and the lights in the windows of the village had gone. There was the clanking of a chain, the voice of a radio in a distant region of the hotel, the tiny moving light of a bicycle lantern, the small tinkle of its bell, and a girl's laughter somewhere. The clouds had sunk still lower; now all of Staufen was softly wrapped up in them. The wood of the railing felt moist under my fingers and a prickling cold dampness sprayed my hair and my cheeks. I felt small and utterly lonely and lost. I snuggled deeper into my coat, which was the only thing left of John, and then I began to cry.

All my life I have envied people who cried easily. It's like sending your heart to the laundry and getting it back, clean and freshly starched and every wrinkle ironed out. But I belong to that unfortunate race of hard criers who get a sore throat and cold, stiff hands and chills down the back and small but sharp knives everywhere—but no tears. The last time I had cried had been the day John had surprised me in Vienna. As I remembered that day, it made me cry still more.

I had not cried when Miss Crump called me up from the office to tell me in a climaxing outburst of grief and "I always told you so" that John had collapsed with a brain hemorrhage and been taken to the hospital in an ambulance. I hadn't cried in that damnably cheerful undertaker's parlor where a Presbyterian reverend with the face of an old vaudevillian worked his lungs overtime to make us cry; not when they invited me to take a last farewell from John in his coffin—they had him so nicely made up with grease paint and rouge that he looked like an oversized, smiling doll I had never seen before. I had not cried when the music played and the coffin under its mound of flowers slowly sank into the floor of the crematorium with that over-mechanized perfection that makes American funerals so inhuman. Not when John's will was read and the blessed trust fund came into action, and not when I cleaned his desk and found every one of the letters I had written him during the years before our marriage, together with the bill for the suite he had taken for me at the Savoy at that time and two menus, obviously of places where we had dined together. I had been a most decorous and unemotional bridegroom's mother in a purple dress at Martin's wedding; and when Johnnie went to China "to see what's going on in Chungking" I had given him and his friends a nice little farewell dinner and seen him off without losing my countenance. Only now, alone in this dark, muffled, alien night, wrapped in John's old raccoon coat, holding on to the wet railing of this unfamiliar veranda, I opened the dikes and cried.

I cried long and luxuriously, and the longer I cried the better I liked it. I heard myself sob and moan and it gave me a great relief to let go like that. I put my arms around one of the wet posts that supported the rail of the veranda, leaned my forehead against it, and cried. I felt the wood shake and vibrate as if it were alive and had pity with me, and this too helped me crying. At last I was only sobbing in a lovely, gentle, easy way, and I fumbled for my handkerchief and blew my nose.

And then I heard in the dripping stillness a small jarring sound, very close to me. Somebody struck a match; the tiny light flared up, prescribed a little arch, and alighted on a pipe. During that second I saw that part of the veranda was partitioned off by a rail from the rest. Beyond the rail stood a chair and on the chair a man was sitting. Then everything was dark again. I heard him draw on his pipe, there was the fleeting scent of smoke, and then a small glow. It lifted the sparse line of a chin and a cheek from the darkness and was gone.

I stopped sobbing at once. I was sure that the man on the chair had taken great pains to make his presence known by the most tactful maneuver he could perceive. It must be a hell of an embarrassing situation for a man sitting quietly on his veranda to be made the unwilling witness of the nervous breakdown of a woman he doesn't know. He could have been tactless and left the veranda with a masculine rumble of protest. But my invisible neighbor had been nice and sensitive with his pipe and match and I was infinitely grateful for it. Also, it helped me stop crying. I could hear him breathe evenly in the dripping black stillness.

"I'm very sorry——" I said, getting my voice under control. "I'm really not quite so hysterical as it may seem."

The darkness cleared its throat for an answer. "Not at all," it said softly. "This high altitude is rather upsetting for one's nervous system in the beginning. I remember I felt a great urge to smash plates the first week I was here."

"Yes, possibly it's the altitude," I said, grabbing for the life belt that was politely thrown to me.

"Quite. If you would count your pulse you'd find it much above normal. Imagine, it takes six minutes up here to boil a four-minute egg."

"Normally I do not cry in years," I said, faintly grateful.

"Please don't give it another thought or I should feel frightfully gauche."

"It's very dark tonight, isn't it?" I said, trying to make conversation.

"Yes, we'll possibly have rain tomorrow. Or even snow. Although I think it is too warm for snow."

"Warm? It seems like the North Pole to me."

"You'll soon get used to the mountain climate. Next week when the moon is waxing we'll have lovely weather. We had three lovely warm days last week. Only yesterday the weather changed."

I listened to the calm British voice. "How come English people always talk about the weather? It's so comforting."

"Yes, we're frightfully conventional and all that, aren't we?"

"Oxford?" I asked, seizing upon his accent.

"Not quite so bad as that; Cambridge——" the voice in the dark said. By that time I had got hold of myself. Having cried myself empty, I felt tired and relaxed. I grubbed in the pocket of my jacket for a cigarette.

"Have you a match for me?" I said into the darkness. There was the jarring sound again, the tiny flare, and then the flame came toward me, sheltered in the hollow of a hand that was made transparent by it. I could see the bones and the veins in it as it steadied the little flame while I lighted my cigarette. When I lifted my eyes I saw for a second his face, dimly suspended in the darkness all around us. He wore eyeglasses which caught a reflection, and the eyes behind them looked at me with the strong, concentrated glance peculiar to nearsighted people. "Thanks," I said and blew out the match. There was the darkness again, and we in it, very close, very unfamiliar, very isolated from the rest of the world. The smoke of his pipe and the smoke of my cigarette mixed their fragrance, and for a few minutes we were silent. Then I heard him get up from his chair.

"Well—good night——" he said. "I hope you'll feel better tomorrow."

"Don't go yet——" I said. "I mean—I would think I'd driven you away from your veranda if you go now. You wanted to smoke your pipe in peace and I spoiled it all with my silly crying jag."

"Well—if you'd like to chat a little longer——" he said tentatively. I felt more than I saw that he was now leaning against the rail that separated us. Some faint warmth of his body came across to me, the scent of wet tweed; sheep in the rain; he was much taller than I.

"Now I am getting used to the darkness. I'm beginning to see——" I said. I angled for my chair and sat down, and he sat down politely too.

"Have you been in this part of Switzerland before?" he asked with a renewed attempt at making conversation. "It is very lovely all year round. That is, if you like the mountains."

"Do you?"

"Beg your pardon? Yes, I do like them. They are the best friends I have."

"It must feel good to have such big strong friends."

"Do you care for skiing?"

"Yes, very much."

"Then you'll like it here. We have good skiing well into May. On the Kees over there we can ski almost the whole year." He pointed into the mist that hung like a thick, padded curtain around the house. "Too bad you cannot see the mountains to-night. They are beautiful. The Kees is the lower mountain across the lake; you have to go across the pass and traverse the glacier to get up on the Grauhorn, that's the high one behind it. There are seven glaciers in this region, but the Grauhorn glacier is the most beautiful one. He is shaped like a maple leaf, with five points running down the mountainside. You'll like him if you like the mountains."

"You talk of him as if he were a man."

"He seems a man to me. A big, hard, handsome, dangerous chap."

"Dangerous?"

"It's his dangerous time just now. Avalanche weather. Three years ago twelve people were buried by an avalanche, and only four survived."

"I've lived in the Bavarian Alps for several years. I'm not afraid of mountains," I said. "When you know them well enough they're not dangerous." There came no answer, and I realized that I must have sounded rather pompous, considering my moaning and sobbing a few minutes ago.

"I'm sorry I cried," I said in self-defense. "But you must believe me that I had a good reason for crying."

He took his pipe and knocked it against the railing. "I say—I am sorry——" he said after a brief embarrassed silence. Poor Christopher, we were not even formally introduced, and how you must have suffered in your reserved, well-mannered English soul when I began undressing my heart. But I came from America, where people tell about themselves and people are interested in one another's privatest private life and I had to talk or bust and the night was dark and close and secretive like the confessional of a Catholic priest and I let loose.

"I brought a patient to a doctor here and he gave me very little hope. That's why I cried," I said.

"I'm dreadfully sorry. But I understand they're doing amazing things with pulmonary surgery lately——" the voice in the dark said for a lame consolation. (My dear, first this woman cried like a loon, no self-control at all, and then she proceeded to tell me her entire life story. It was really the most frightfully embarrassing situation, and we were not even *introduced*, imagine——)

"It has nothing to do with his lungs. It's his eyes."

"Of course. How silly of me. I saw the young man with the dark glasses who was with you in the dining room. And I thought: what a merry young chap . . ."

"Yes, he carries it rather well——" I said. Suddenly the anonymity from which I had spoken into the dark was broken into pieces. There had been something romantic and mysterious about my invisible neighbor. A calm, soft voice, a long-boned hand sheltering a little flame in its transparent hollow. Now it all boiled down to one of a hundred banal young Englishmen who crowded the dining rooms of every Swiss hotel, staring arrogantly at the new guests.

"I am Mrs. Sprague," I said, by way of returning to flat correctness. "I came all the way from New York to see Dr. Konrad. But it seems I might as well have stayed over there."

"How do you do, Mrs. Sprague. My name is Christopher Lankersham."

"How do you do, Mr. Lankersham."

I squashed my cigarette on the wet railing which responded with a little hiss, and kept the stub in my fingers. The darkness had begun to lift and a car was heard laboriously taking in second gear a distant grade of the highway.

"A year ago Dr. Konrad was quite confident that he could cure or at least arrest the trouble. Today he gave me hardly any hope," I said. I knew that it was bad style to tell my troubles, but oh, so relaxing.

"Is Dr. Konrad the little hermit who lives in old Hammelin's house? They say that he is a great scientist who was held by the Nazis. He came here only recently, didn't he?"

"Yes, it took us almost a year to get him free. We hoped he would come to the United States, but he has not enough spunk to do it. He does not want to go through the necessary examinations and fight for a position. He is also afraid he couldn't learn the language. He seems like a man whose spine has been broken. All he wants is to hide and be left alone and follow up his research."

"That's understandable in his case, isn't it?"

"Yes, I suppose it is. Only—resignation is not my cup of tea. I came here to fight for Michael's eyesight. I counted on Dr. Konrad to help me win the fight, but he seems flaccid, like a balloon with all the air gone. It's dreadful what they are doing to people in those prison camps."

"If you like to fight you shouldn't have come to Staufen, Mrs. Sprague."

"Why not?"

"This is a place for escapists. Didn't you know that?"

"Are you an escapist?" I asked, and was sorry a moment later for being indiscreet.

"Well—yes. Yes, I'm afraid in a certain sense I'm an escapist too. I'm trying to escape from that vague disease known as island phobia. I simply couldn't bear living in England any longer. It's no wonder, is it? It had become so that the mere sight of an umbrella gave me the cramps."

"My country right or wrong——" I said, smiling toward the voice, which suddenly had come to life. It was two weeks after

Hitler had marched into Prague, and England's impotence had become disgracefully evident.

"Not only wrong but criminally stupid. I assure you, it is most unpleasant when you feel like apologizing to everybody: Excuse me, I'm really quite a decent chap in spite of being an Englishman. Perfectly disgusting!"

"Look!" I said. The clouds had torn apart and through the hole I could see a piece of the sky, a deep clear crystal blackness with a fine young moon etched into it and a sprinkle of stars, bigger and brighter than any stars I had ever seen. I watched the hole grow larger as the misty clouds receded. "An old friend of mine who knew the sky and the mountains used to say that it won't rain if you can see a clear piece of sky big enough to make a woman's shirt," I said.

"Yes, that's what the shepherds in Scotland believe too," Christopher said. He had filled and lighted his pipe once more, and now he got up and leaned over the railing to look up into the sky. I could see him quite clearly now. He was tall and lean and he had a mountaineer's face. Everything was big and strong in it, the nose, the mouth, and the deep eye sockets behind the glasses. He wore no overcoat, only a coarse turtle-necked sweater under his rough, loose tweed jacket, although the night seemed very cold to me.

"It's like looking through that hole straight into the universe, isn't it?" I said.

"There comes the Grauhorn now," he said, pointing with his chin into the distance. Slowly the misty clouds grew thin, luminous, transparent, and at last they had fallen away and the summit of the mountain rose out of the night, white and disembodied with that rare serene aloof beauty that makes you feel taut around the heart.

"Rather nice, isn't he?" Christopher said with the English genius for understatement. I thought that the mountain looked like those final things Beethoven was striving to express in the last movements of his symphonies without ever achieving it. But you could not say such a thing to a detached young Englishman whom you had hardly met.

"I will have to visit him soon," I said instead.

"Indeed, you should. If the weather holds out—I would be very glad to show you around a bit. I expect you brought your skis along?"

"Only one old pair. I trusted I could outfit myself up here."

"If not, you can always take the train to Arlingen; that's where you get everything. Thank heavens Staufen hasn't been discovered yet by the smart set."

Suddenly I noticed that I was dizzy with fatigue. My heart behaved funny and my ears sang and I was sure my pulse was beating at a crazy speed. "Now I am feeling the altitude," I said. "It has knocked me out all of a sudden. I think it's high time for me to go to bed."

I got up, still looking at the mountain. The clouds had formed into compact drifting layers that streaked across the range and covered the lake with a soft blanket. The night had grown still colder. It was so still and beautiful it almost hurt. Only then I realized that for the last fifteen minutes I had forgotten to be unhappy about Michael.

"Thanks for keeping me company——" I said.

"Thanks for letting me——" he said. I held my hand out across the rail, and he took it. My fingers were wet and cold and stiff and his were dry and warm. It was such a pleasant hand that I clung to it another moment. How come his hand is so warm? I thought. Because he has kept it in the pocket of his coat, I answered myself. Suddenly, unpredictably, I was overcome by the wish he might keep on holding my hand and let me snuggle it into his pocket, as young people do when they are in love and think that they have invented this precious caress. I wished it as urgently as if I were a wanderer lost in a blizzard and his pocket were a house at the wayside; light windows, a roof, a warm, snug shelter. I took my lonely cold hand and carried it into my bedroom, which was also cold.

That night I dreamed that I was a four-minute egg and I said: You must boil me much longer, I'm not even warm, and Dr. Konrad said: It is the altitude, and Michael said: Now I can see through a hole into the universe. And all through my dreams

I knew that something lovely had happened to me but I could not remember what.

June 14, 1940, I, Marion, am sitting in a mountain crevasse of the Walliser Alps, remembering my life. I remember the sound of the latchkey in my parents' home in Vienna, the feel of the banister under my hand in Paradise Inn, the smell of our flat in Hahnenstadt. I remember a million such insignificant things of long ago. But when I think of this last year I catch only shreds of conversations, the tremor of a voice, the form and flight of a cloud, the bewilderment of a world that is still bewildered. Those months between the rape of Czechoslovakia and the beginning of the war have a queer twilight quality, evasive and hard to grasp. I remember that people in the United States were hysterical and people in Europe seemed quiet and matter-of-fact. So what? they said. We've had wars before; we'll have another one. I remember that we had huge crates on board the French boat on which we sailed for Europe, and the crew said those were airplanes for France, and there was a rumor that we had German spies on board and a few weeks later I read in the papers that the boat had caught fire and been destroyed in its berth. I remember dancing with the first officer on the old-fashioned illuminated glass dance floor of that boat, and suddenly a man whose name I didn't know stopped us, pale in the face, and said in French: The Germans have marched into Prague. I remember the jokes everybody made about Hitler and the Nazis and how everybody on the boulevards of Paris and in the parks of London said that you've got to stop that fellow Hitler. The Maginot Line was still impregnable, the French army invincible. Holland could be flooded within a few hours, drowning any invading German army. In Hyde Park they had begun to dig trenches and to experiment with puny little shelters. Every man, woman, and child knew that the war was coming, but no one knew when and how and what face he would have this time. No one wanted this war and yet no one knew how to prevent it. We were just careening down a steep grade with all brakes out of order, staring fascinatedly at that last curve where the final smash-up would occur.

And while all this was happening to the world I began to fall in love with a boy fifteen years my junior. If there is anything more pathetic than a first love it's a last one. When you're falling in love for the first time you're defenseless; everything is singular and absolute and beyond comparison. There is no experience to warn us that love is a fragile article in any case. There is not a shade of distrust in a first love. Not against ourselves, not against our lover, and least of all against love. But falling in love for the last time is a bitter kind of delight. I knew too much, I knew the beginning, the climax, and the end, and I wanted to have none of it. Passion is a messy thing, always, and most unbecoming when you are past forty. I knew it, I told it to myself every morning, noon, and night. And yet there was that urge and yearning that whispered and sang: Just one more time, the last, the very last time to plunge into that hot, painful, blissful confusion. I never liked to go home before the fireworks were over and that last, lonely rocket had shot up into the midnight-blue sky and burst and died in a cascade of cheap radiant wonderful stars. I had been in love as long as I could remember, back to the time when I was four and sat on the oh, so masculine lap of the handsome guardsman August. And so, when I fell in love for the last time I was almost grateful, because it was in keeping with my style and it made me feel that I was still alive, and, besides, no one needed to know it. I've seen Cuban dancers go through all their wild movements with a filled glass of water balanced on their heads without shedding one single drop of it. That's how I felt while I carried my foolish love through those months, careful it should not spill over.

"Yesterday I made the acquaintance of your young brother," Christopher said to me when he met me near the mill where I had gone on a house-hunting campaign. "We pooled our phonograph records and had a very nice afternoon concert on our veranda."

"Yes, Michael told me. I wanted to thank you for keeping him company. He was very happy about it."

"He is an awfully nice chap, your brother."

I blushed, got angry at myself, and blushed still more. "He's not my brother, he's my son. My younger son," I said.

"Oh——" Christopher said. "I see. It didn't occur to me. You must have been very young when you got married."

"I can't exactly claim to have been raped at thirteen," I said. Christopher, thank heavens, was not shocked but began to chuckle. We looked at each other and laughed. It was the first time I had met him in full daylight. Suddenly the sun seemed terribly bright and I felt every wrinkle in my face like a deep canyon. I felt like a decaying little piece of something or other under a microscope. I wish he wouldn't wear glasses, I thought.

"Michael told me you were looking for a house. Did you find anything? I'm afraid the choice in Staufen is rather limited."

"I was just going to the top of the hill to look at the house where the two Italians moved away. They gave me the key at the mill."

"Mind if I toddle along?" Christopher said. Indeed, I didn't mind, and we walked up the hill together.

We always walked beautifully together, didn't we, Chris, my darling? We didn't talk much during that brief first walk, we just walked and walked and felt fine. After a while you looked down at me and you smiled, with the pipe clamped between your teeth, and you said: "Been doing some track work?"

"No, never," I said, surprised. "Why?"

"Usually my legs are a few yards too long when I walk with a lady; but not with you. You're walking like a man."

"Yes, I know. It made my mother quite unhappy when I was a little girl," I said.

"We must go up to the Arli Hütte together as soon as the weather is safe," you said. It was a promise and I carried it home with me and buried it as if it were a shining lump of gold and dug it up again to look at it and polished it and took it to bed with me the way Michael had taken his rabbit Nibble with the red eyes.

You looked at the house with me and helped me rent it. You went to the village carpenter with me and explained to him the sort of furniture I wanted him to make. You took me up to the mountains, you came to visit us every day, you made this lonesome corner of the world a home for us, and you became the first real friend Michael ever had.

Michael needed a friend just then. He had to resign himself to getting blind. To resign without resignation—which is the hardest task there is. It was during those months that he had to build up strong foundations from within; develop provinces of his soul and mind that had lain fallow up to then; sort out the shadow from the substance—(That's what you called it, Chris: sort out the shadow from the substance)—learn to be happy and useful In Spite.

"Wouldn't that be a good motto for your mother's coat of arms? In Spite——" I heard Chris say to Michael. "You're lucky to be her son. You simply can't help having inherited some of her genius for having fun in life. It's perfectly contagious." As on every afternoon, Michael was resting in his deckchair on the gallery and Chris kept him company. I did not hear what Michael answered because I went down to the kitchen to prepare some coffee for them and cut the cake I had baked. Fun in life, indeed! I thought. Just that day I had examined my body in front of the mirror and my body had flunked the examination. It was not a bad body, considering its age. It was strong and healthy; that was something, wasn't it? But it had stopped being a pleasure and a joy to me. There is a buoyant, purely physical joy in one's own body while one is young, and this joy had fizzled out. In fact, I was disgusted and bored with this body of mine; a coarsening here and a little sagging there; lines in the face and the bloom of the skin gone. Even my navel wasn't the same and had assumed a slack and bored expression. I couldn't be proud of myself if I were with a man. I would hide behind a lace gown and whisper: "Please, dear, turn off the light."

I remember what a witty old lady in Vienna had said: "Seventy is not old for a cathedral, but it's old for a woman." Well, forty-three wasn't old for a woman but too old for a lover. While I was cutting my cake downstairs I called myself an old, third-hand jallopy and swore once more that I would never, never allow myself to be carried away by some silly out-of-season emotions.

When I came upstairs with my cake they had changed the

subject. Apparently Christopher had been reading to Michael as he did every day to keep him in contact with the world. He held his index finger between the pages to discuss the point at which he had interrupted reading. I put my tray down on the table in Michael's room to listen without being noticed. I loved to look at the two heads out there, eagerly inclined toward each other. The distant mountains, to me, seemed the perfect background for Christopher's profile with the sharply jutting nose and chin.

". . . it is barely possible that all these convulsions, all these ugly and cruel demonstrations that accompany them, mean not more nor less than the search for a new religion. Mind you, it is a very long time that no new religion was founded. Religion, every religion, wants mystic martyrs and blood sacrifices. That's why I suspect that Nazism and communism are religious experiments in disguise. There is no doubt that the aims of Hitler, Mussolini, Stalin could be achieved in a much more rational and much less cruel and spectacular way. The lot of the workers could be bettered without a world revolution and Germany could get her Lebensraum by peaceful means, by the spreading of good will, by barter, even by purchase, as your United States got their expansion. But that could never be the start of a new religion. Religion wants crusades, inquisition, sacred wars. Not simply wars to get rubber or oil or gold, but a sacred war to turn the rest of humanity into Catholics, Protestants, Moslems or Nazis. Can't you see a hierarchy of saints and martyrs being created before our eyes with Horst Wessel as their pontifex maximus? You can watch the legends grow; the sacred sword is mowing down the unbelievers, and a hundred years from now there may well be churches for the worship of those new gods Hitler or Lenin. What they demand from their disciples is what all religions demand. Blind obedience, poverty, self-sacrifice. The faculty of independent thinking was never well liked by any church. And like the Catholic church they tolerate the sin of the flesh because it produces new cohorts of believers. Ever read the Bible? Remember the ranting of Jehovah against those who polluted the Jewish race by consorting with the children of Moab and Baal?

There's nothing new under the sun, my boy. Remind me to bring the Bible along tomorrow and you'll see what I mean."

Michael gave no answer, but I saw that it had set him to thinking. It was good to see how those long talks with Chris changed his immature picture of the world and made him see all sides instead of a flat one-dimensional primer for imbeciles.

I picked up my tray and served them coffee and cake on the gallery, and afterward we listened to the radio. We got a transcription from Paris, where Shani Kern was conducting Beethoven's eighth symphony, Debussy's Nuages, and his own new Concert Suite. It was funny to listen to my old friend from my hidden corner of the world; he was still fighting for vertical music while I was content that my cake had turned out well. . . .

It is true that I loved Christopher for the sparse line of his cheeks, for his lean, easy body, for his long-fingered sun-tanned hands, for all the silly physical reasons that cause women to fall in love with men. But I also loved him for his never-slackening effort to keep Michael interested, informed, alive, and hopeful. It happened all by itself that he took over Michael's mind while I began to train the boy's fingers to enjoy those things his eyes could not see any longer. I brought him flowers and fruit and the loveliest pebbles from the shore. Cats and dogs and babies and sometimes even old man Hammelin came to visit him and let him touch his tough, hairy, stringy arms. There was a wealth of things that were sweet to touch; there were all the textures, rough and smooth, shining and dull, wood and silk and glass and leaves. And again each leaf had a different texture; some were fuzzy and some slick as satin and some slightly sticky and some as fine and warm as the finest skin. I carved things for him too, simple shapes first, and then gradually more and more complicated ones to let his fingers guess what they were.

That's one of the things I would like to do if I ever get out of here: work out and carve a systematical succession of shapes for teaching blind people. . . .

Together we dabbled in plastiline and clay, which I had

ordered from Zürich, and at last we plunged into the art of Braille reading. Dr. Konrad furnished us with some primers for self-instruction in German and in English. First it was hard uphill work for both of us, but soon we got the knack of it. The day Michael could read his first piece in huge, childish letters—incidentally it was Lincoln's Gettysburg address—was the crowning climax of our labor.

Our afternoon concerts had become quite an institution. Often the children from the mill would come and listen in; they adored Michael because he clowned for them by the hour. He taught them songs and swapped his American slang for their Swiss Dutch. His talent for imitating everything within earshot was blooming as never before. By and by he had worked out a whole program. His rendering of Dr. Konrad's erratic oracles, his imitation of the radio, complete with static and with the babble of the German, Italian, and French that emanated from the different stations of Switzerland, were really funny. When he added a double-talk version of a Hitler speech I was not only amused, I knew that at last he had learned to laugh about the words and the spirit that has fascinated him for so long and I also knew that I had to thank Christopher for it. That evening when I said good night to Christopher I stretched out my hand and grabbed his. Usually I kept my hands linked behind my back while we had our last five-minute chat under the house door. The electric shock it gave me the moment my palm touched his was even stronger than I had feared. There is something like a little heart in the center of any palm, with a heartbeat and a sensitivity all of its own. Christopher kept my hand in his and looked at me with a queer kind of curiosity. I wondered if he had noticed any nonsense.

"Good night, Chris," I said; "If you hurry you'll get to the hotel before it starts to rain." The clouds had been hanging over the lake all afternoon, and there was a soft, warm, pregnant south wind. I pulled my hand back and he let go of it reluctantly as I stretched it out to see if the first drops were falling.

"And you, Marion," he said. "Don't stay up too long. Yesterday it was almost two before you went to bed."

"How do you know?" I asked, astonished. I had been restless,

as usual when we had a south wind, and when I could not
sleep I had decided to write letters.

"I can watch your light from my room," he said.

"That's not true. Your room looks out toward the lake, not
toward the foothills."

"Well then. I couldn't sleep and took a little stroll. I couldn't
help seeing that light."

"It's the south wind. It's almost a sirocco, isn't it? Well I hope
you'll sleep well tonight."

"Good night, Marion, darling."

"Good night, Chris."

Later it began to rain in heavy big drops which exploded on
the leaves of the tree behind the house. The millstream made
excited noises, as always when it rained. It sounded like a
grumbling old colonel with a chronic catarrh of the bronchia.
Otherwise the rain made the night still quieter; there was not
a breath of wind, not a stir of air, only that heavy, steady rain.
I remembered that I had left our Braille books on the gallery
and went out to get them before they became soaked. I had
brought my flashlight along because the night was a wet, steaming jungle of darkness; from the shingle roof hung a sheet of
water glimmering in the sharp, thin ray. And then I discovered
a figure in a mackintosh leaning against our fence and staring
up to the gallery.

"Christopher——" I said, startled. "What's the matter? What
are you doing here in the rain?"

"Waiting for the next street car, don't you see?" he said.

"No, really——"

"Taking my constitutional like every good Englishman."

"But seriously——"

"Seriously I've forgotten my tobacco pouch and I can't go
to sleep without my pipe. May I come in and get it?"

"Wait——" I said in wild confusion. "I'll—Michael's asleep—
I'll get it for you—just a second—I'll come downstairs——"

As usual the top of my pajamas was of a different breed than
the pants. Once you start the cycle wrong you'll never get
it straight. I should have been ravishingly dressed in a lovely
negligée of black chantilly lace over flesh-colored chiffon. But

here I was, with a crumpled blue pajama top, blue with red little stars, and a pair of also crumpled pants with blue stripes. My hair was an unbecoming tumble and my feet were bare and looked like something to be ashamed of. But I had never in my life possessed or worn any slippers. At least I have no cream on my face, I thought as I grabbed the tobacco pouch and carried it downstairs. Yes, my girl, and no make-up either, an ugly little voice whispered to me. Well, what's the matter? I thought. I don't want to seduce him, do I? It's just as well he sees how a middle-aged woman looks when she goes to bed. At least that'll cut off all nonsense for once and all. I handed him his confounded tobacco pouch through a chink of the door and crept into bed, disgusted with myself and the world. In the middle of the night I woke up and remembered that Christopher had received a big box of his special blended tobacco only three days ago. Why, he must have had enough for two months stored away in his room. Why then had he come tramping through the rain to stand under my window and watch my light? It was a question that stuck in me like a harpoon. The more I pulled to get away from it the deeper it drilled its barbed hooks into me.

Remember when we went to the Arli Hütte for the second time and I gave up in the upper chimney? You had me roped and I just felt that I wasn't strong enough to make it and you did all the work and practically dragged me up? I was mad at myself and I felt as old as Methuselah.

"I can understand Goethe's Faust perfectly," I said when we loafed on the bench outside of the hut and let the sun shine upon our closed eyelids.

"Can you, really?" you said lazily. "I can't. Not the second part anyway."

"If the devil would come to me and offer to make me sixteen again I would gladly go to hell for it. In fact there's nothing I'd wish better than that the devil would make me such an offer."

You didn't answer at once, and I thought you had not listened or that you had fallen asleep with that deep, good fatigue that comes after a hard climb.

"Mercy, how dull you would be, Marion, if you were sixteen, and how stupid. Besides, you would have a bad complexion and big, fat baby legs," you said at last.

The devil didn't come, but I felt better, much, much better when you said that. We were such good companions, Chris, weren't we? There was that rich, constant give and take between us, always. There's nothing but those fifteen years to keep us apart, I thought often. If I had been born later. If he had been born sooner. It isn't the number of years that makes you old, not the wrinkles and not the experience. It is that one belongs to the generation into which one is born and which puts its stamp upon one, indelibly. If I pictured myself making love to Christopher I felt as absurd as a Victorian sofa, complete with plush and antimacassars, in a streamlined glass and chromium ensemble.

So then Michael began hankering for a piano because he wanted to start studying music in earnest. "What has Templeton got that I haven't?" he said when we were rolling with laughter about one of his parodies. "Maybe I can make something of this little talent, as long as I can't become a doctor." It was rather lucky that during these months I could use whatever I had learned during a lifetime. Music, nursing, carving. A bit of patience and some optimism. The experience that nothing is so bad you couldn't get used to it. Why, if I remain stuck in this crevasse long enough I might begin to feel quite at home and even be sorry to be taken out of it. Like Captain Tillmann, who had been in the trenches so long he couldn't sleep in a bed any more. Maybe we all will get so used to living in shelters underground that when the last bomb has been dropped and the last town has been blasted we won't like to come back to the surface and sunlight again. . . .

"Let's go to Geneva together and rent a piano for Michael," Christopher suggested. He was quite at home in Geneva because he had been something or the other with the League of Nations. "I was no-gentleman's no-gentleman," he called it. I suppose he had been the secretary of some member of the English delegation in the unlucky session of 1936, and I also deduced that much of his bitterness and skepticism in regard to the world situation derived from that time.

"Couldn't you be an angel, Chris, and go to Geneva alone? I can't get away from Michael," I said nervously. Since that rainy night I had kept myself away from him as much as possible. I was not going to make a fool of myself, and yet it became harder and harder not to make a fool of myself.

"No, I won't be an angel. Michael is no baby, and Hammelin's daughter will gladly take care of him for two days. It'll do you good to get out of the rut, Marion," he said. "Besides, it's time for you to see a tailor in Geneva and have him make you a new skiing outfit. Your old one looks deplorable and God knows what will happen before next winter. Better be prepared."

Yes, and I can have something done to my hair, I thought, and that decided it. To have something done to her hair is one of the basic urges of any woman in love. Tresses down to my knees for Charles Dupont, who called them my cloak and dreamed of some sort of Lady Godiva act. Short ringlets for Walter Brandt. For Captain Tillmann a modest bun and the mousy texture that came from lack of vitamins. Bobbed and hennaed, permanent waved and bleached, blond and windblown for my flippant love affairs with strangers during my time as a career woman. For John I had returned to my own chestnut brown, and the tumble on my head had been kept strictly in check as was befitting for a Mrs. John W. Sprague. Now it was discolored by the mountain sun, stringy from washing it with hard spring water, and the first gray had put in an appearance. So far I had found only five gray hairs, but five gray hairs are enough to send you off in a panic, particularly if you are in love with a young boy.

We arrived in Geneva on the last evening in August, had dinner and a peaceful stroll through the town and along the lake. Chris had an appointment with some friends of his, and I went to bed early. In the morning I trotted to the beauty salon and turned my head over to a slender, effeminate wizard who decided on an oil treatment, a rinse to bring out the highlights, and an off-the-face and high-over-the-forehead hairdress. He went to it with the airs of a great surgeon while two breathless assistants handed him combs, scissors, and pins.

When I had come to the hairdresser there had still been

peace. When I left there was no doubt any longer that the war had started. In between lay Hitler's strangely restrained and almost sentimental speech, which the radio had drilled into my ears while one neat, oiled, shiny ringlet after the other was pinned around my forehead.

I remember that we took the little steamer that afternoon and went ashore at some small place whose name I have forgotten. We sat in front of a little tavern under a canopy of plane trees and we talked about everything but this new war. It was a soft, warm day with the first hazy blues of autumn in the air and the peace seemed unbelievably deep and lovely now that it was going to be taken away from us. We returned to town and rented the upright piano for Michael; I bought a piano instruction manual for beginners and some Clementi sonatinas and Chris loaded himself up with books. "It's about time I stopped gamboling about and really go to work on my Byzantine Empire," he said. "It's been a lovely day, Marion, hasn't it? In Spite, you know, In Spite."

What I remember most clearly just now is that little conversation we had on the train that night. I was standing in the corridor outside of my sleeping compartment to smoke a last cigarette before turning in. The train was swaying gently and I was swaying with it while I looked through the window into the night, which was like a cup of black glass. I felt content and calm in spite of this new war. This war wasn't anything like the old one. People seemed to be clear-eyed about it, very sensible, very sober, and completely without illusions. There was nothing glamorous or romantic about this new war. Somehow no one seemed to believe yet that this was going to be a real war. As if something must still turn back the clock and stop all the nonsense.

"War because of Danzig? Why, it's ridiculous," I had said to Chris. "It's the first time the Germans are right. Why would England start a war now when she didn't start one about Czechoslovakia?"

"They are shadow boxing," Chris said. "England has to declare war for reasons of prestige. It's only a gesture. Germany will take Danzig back, also for her prestige. It's also a gesture.

Then they'll make peace and go on appeasing until they're blue in the face."

"In six weeks we'll be in Paris and it'll all be over," Walter Brandt had said. How little even the least ignorant men knew . . .

I felt fine as I stood there in that corridor. I patted myself for having at last gotten out from under the spell that had held me so tightly in Staufen. Being cooped up with him in that small hamlet had made everything seem much too important. It had done me a lot of good to have come out for an airing. Also, if there was to be a war, it didn't really matter who was in love with whom and how old or young anybody was. I looked out into the gliding night and played bottom of the ocean. Strange creatures floated past, shrubs became corals in the glow of our passing, the lonesome lights way up on some invisible mountainside were luminous starfish. We shot down into a tangle of glassy seaweed and then an octopus swallowed us up in the dark stomach of a tunnel. I enjoyed myself immensely, standing there in the corridor all by myself, smoking, playing, thinking, and in peace. All my life I have needed great chunks of being alone, to replenish some tanks inside of me; it was as necessary to me as air and food and sleep. And yet, when Christopher stepped out of his compartment and posted himself at the next window I was once more overcome with that rich, full, senseless, vibrating delight of having him near.

"Oh—you're still about? How nice," he said. His hair was wet, as if he had brushed it back with water, and he smelled of toothpaste and leather and some lotion. He wore lounging pajamas and a dark green robe over them. "I couldn't sleep yet," he said. "A declaration of war isn't exactly a sedative, is it?"

He held his inevitable pipe and tobacco pouch in his hand when he came into the corridor. Obviously he had come there to smoke, but now he thrust both into the pocket of his robe and braced his arms against both sides of his window.

"What are your associations when you think of love?" I heard Christopher say. Coming from him, this was a most amazing question. Most of the time he observed the strict taboos that forbid people of his kind to talk about personal matters. "What do you mean?" I asked, slightly baffled.

"Oh, you know. Most people associate some definite picture with their idea of love. Some sort of an idée fixe or something. I expect the psychoanalysts have it all puzzled out. For instance, a friend of mine claims that love means the smell of a stiffly starched white apron. Most probably he had his first affair with the upstairs maid and he will be seeking for an upstairs maid in every girl he meets. I know a chap who told me that there is nothing so exciting as the creaking of a board in the floor when you are sneaking into the room of a married woman. You know, those week-end affairs in somebody's country place? I suppose that chap will have to sneak on stockinged feet into the bedroom of his lawful wedded wife. Well for me it is the smell and the movement and the atmosphere of a train. And for you?"

"As far as I can remember, when I was sixteen I dreamed of a man who would crush me in his strong arms and carry me across the threshold of an old marble palazzo," I said.

"How perfectly awful. I hope he didn't do it. And later, when you were grown up?"

"I don't know. An old raccoon coat, perhaps——" I said to my window.

"Would nothing else but an old raccoon coat do?" Chris asked his window.

"I knew a girl who liked the feel of a rough tweed coat against her cheek. And the sound of a man knocking his pipe against the mantelpiece," I said to my window, wondering if I had told too much. But Christopher seemed to have forgotten that I was there. I did not look at him but kept my eyes on the submarine landscape streaking past; but I could hear that he was smiling as he went on in his confessions.

"I assume it all has to do with a book I filched from my mother's bookshelf when I was ten. It gave a rather minute description of a seduction on a train. It excited me terribly. It still somehow does. You can keep your marble palazzo. I want to be on a train with the girl I love; I want to be alone with her in a tiny compartment with that blue night light and the printed warning of danger in three languages. The air is dry, it smells of luggage, leather, and spilled eau de Cologne; I turn the bolt and we're safe and on our way. The movement, you know, the wheels below, the tearing speed, the vibration—and later, when it is dark, I can see her face as some lights glide by. Did you ever watch the stripes of shade and light in a slat house? Well, something like it on the face of the girl I love. Look here—I do talk too much."

"Do all these lovely things occur with the girl from the book you filched? Or have you more definite ideas about her?" I asked. If he could be indiscreet so could I.

"Of course I have definite ideas. You'd be surprised how definite if I told you," he said to his window.

Immediately I stood in a blaze of jealousy. Up to that moment it had never occurred to me that Christopher had any other life than the one of which we had become such an integral part. Of course I knew that men didn't live like cauliflowers. But, like every woman in love, I had idiotically convinced myself that my man was the exception. I had accepted him as a recluse, a lonely escapist, and also a bit as my property. I should have known it, I thought bitterly; there is no such a thing as an unattached man. I conjured a picture of that girl out of the black window glass with the night behind it. She was blond and tall, with a peaches-and-cream complexion; she was arrogant without knowing it, and insupportably young.

"Is she English?" I asked, as tactless as I had ever been in my life. Christopher turned a surprised profile toward me and began to laugh.

"English? Lord, no! You know, there were too many centuries of inbreeding on our little island. There is no real tension between English men and women, I believe. We're all brothers and sisters, somehow. How could I get excited about another creature just as sand-colored, freckled, bony, and stiff as myself?"

What an idiot I was that night, Chris, my darling! All I could understand was that you were in love with another girl and that you had gone out of your way to let me know about it so that I should stop making a fool of myself. Just like that night when you had struck a match so I should stop crying. In headless retreat I muttered good night and dived into my compartment. And that was the only time we ever talked about anything as personal as love—until this morning, when you came into my room to say good-by. There was dew in your hair and you were chewing a grass-blade and I held on to my silly, petty, little dignity and if it killed me . . .

On my return to Staufen I found Michael in bed with a high fever. Not a simple temperature, but a real fever.

"I had a little palaver with old smell-puss Konrad," he reported, much too cheerful. "We decided to change the treatment. This is the first reaction."

"Not very much of a success, is it?" I asked him. "And just when I'm not here to take care of you."

"Oh, that's okay," Michael said. "You might have made difficulties. I didn't want you to wrestle with the decision. This is my own affair after all."

"What decision, Milky, for Christ's sake?"

"Konrad told me that we wouldn't get anywhere, proceeding with what he called a conservative treatment. He asked me if I were willing to take a chance, and I thought it over and said yes."

"What chance——" I asked feebly.

"Oh, the usual chance. The trouble that's localized now might get out of hand and spread and I might croak eventually. . . . You aren't mad at me, are you, Mony——" he said when I remained silent.

I knew that I was only a blurred dark shadow on his bedside and I shoved my hand into his, which was hot and shaky.

"Well—Milky——"

"To croak eventually is the thing a person has to do sooner or later, isn't it? Why make a fuss about it?"

"I don't make a fuss, do I?"

"Look here, Mony. If it were your eyes and your life that's at stake—you would take a chance too, now wouldn't you?"

"I suppose so——" I said.

"You bet you would. So there you are. If I croak I croak. If I don't croak I might win the jackpot yet and get my eyesight back. What's the importance anyway? Now that the war is on, millions and millions of boys like myself are going to croak— and under much less agreeable circumstances!"

The first week of the new treatment went by with Michael dozing in his bed, not wanting to talk, not wanting to eat, very tired and yet too restless to sleep. Dr. Konrad came every day, sometimes twice, to give him the new injections and watch the reactions. During the second week, when Michael was delirious, the doctor sometimes stayed late into the night in our house, absorbed by a most impersonal sort of fascination. He made notes and comparative charts, he did not trust my fever chart and my observations; he wanted to see everything with his own eyes and draw his own conclusions. He would hang around until two o'clock in the morning, would reluctantly transport himself off to old Hammelin's house where he lived, and would be back at half-past five to see what had happened during the few hours of his absence. To me it seemed that he looked upon Michael not as on a sick human being but as on a retort in which an experimental solution was boiling and brewing. He had only three patients all in all. Two more such desperate cases as Michael had followed him to Staufen to be treated by him. Sometimes, watching the gnomelike little man with his distorted face and his eyes of a fanatic, crouching at Michael's bedside, mumbling to himself, I wondered if that year in the concentration camp hadn't done something to his mind. But whatever his mental condition might have been, his scientific faculties were unimpaired and I had no other choice now than to trust him.

Michael wasted away during that second week of anxiety. Sometimes I was afraid the thin retort in which Dr. Konrad's great experiment was brewing might crack and burst. My child was so transparent, so burned out with fever that his long, gothic body showed every bone and sinew, like the body of a crucifixus on a primitive painting. Yet Michael had unexpected strength, and when he began to rave in his delirium I was not strong enough to hold him down in his bed. Christopher offered to move into our house and release me for hours at a time. I had stubbornly refused to have a nurse sent to us from Arlingen. To nurse Michael through was my business, of that I was sure; but I accepted Christopher's offer gladly, and he installed himself on the couch in Michael's room.

During the third week the fever began to subside, leaving

Michael as a gray little heap of embers and ashes in his bed. The piano we had rented in Geneva arrived and was placed in the downstairs room, but I wondered if Michael would ever play it. There came a letter from Renate, written in Braille, in the clumsy grade-one type that we—Michael and I—had just learned to master.

"Dear Michael," she wrote. "I am learning to write in Braille so that no one else has to read my letters to you. If your finger-tips are sensitive enough you will find a little kiss for you on every letter. Hope you will come to New York soon. I love it here but would love it a million times more if you were here too. Love from your friend,

"Renate Rieger."

This letter was a sweet bed companion for my sick boy, and I noticed that he kept it with him as he had done as a baby with his rabbit Nibble. Christopher moved out again, and I hardly noticed it. I pestered Dr. Konrad with questions, and he answered that everything developed according to his expectations—which was a rather vague answer. Toward the end of the third week Michael began to ask for food and to drink amazing amounts of milk and fruit juices.

And then, the second day of the fourth week, it was a Tuesday, something happened.

I had been on the gallery to water my geraniums. Michael was still in bed in his room, which had been kept dark for many weeks now. Our wooden shutters had a heart cut into the center, and sometimes a ray of sunlight would pierce through that heart and illuminate a miniature universe of dancing dust. I came from the gallery with my long-snouted little watering pot, leaving the door open to let the brisk autumn air into the room. Michael looked toward me as he always did when he heard me enter his room. Besides, he had never gone entirely blind; he could still perceive some moving shadows in his dim world.

"Come here, Mony," he called to me. I put down my watering pot and went over to his bed.

"No, bring that thing along, whatever it is——" Michael said.

Obediently I picked up the pot and carried it over. I did not think he had seen it. I thought he had heard the metallic clanking of its bottom against the floor when I put it down. I held it on my lap, and Michael stretched out his hands and touched it. Clunk, said the little pot. "Hm——" said Michael. He pushed the pot away, took my hands, and pulled me close. "Hm——" he said again. "Go back to the door and come in again——" he said after a moment. I got up, wondering what this meant, went to the brighter rectangle of the door, and back into the room.

"Do you wear a white apron?" Michael said.

"Of course——" I answered. "I'm antiseptic all over."

Only a moment afterward did I receive the full impact of his question. My knees grew weak and I plumped down on his bed. "Wait a moment——" he said, fingering the fabric of my dress the way thrifty old ladies do before they make a buy. "Wait, Mony. Would you say this dress is black?"

"Well—almost black. It's navy blue, but so dark that you could almost call it black——" I said. My tongue had suddenly grown thick, as if I were drunk.

Michael kept on fingering my skirt and staring at me. He moved his head to get a full view of me from every side. Then he traced with his fingers the outline of my white apron against the dark dress. "It's quite clear——" he said. "I can see it. It's lovely. It's white and dark. Now step back—I can still see it. Step back some more. Now it's gone. Come back here. I want to look at it some more. I think I can see your teeth too—that white flash up there—and your hair." He touched my teeth, and I was glad they were so big, and I held very still not to disturb the action that was of such shattering importance. "Well, Mony——" he said when he was through with it, "it looks as if we had hit the jackpot after all."

What else is there to remember? First came the winter and nothing happened and people grew slack again and made jokes about this war that was no war at all. The tramontana blew from the north, and Christopher withdrew into some shell and locked himself away from us with his Rise and Fall of the Byzantine Empire. The wind changed, it came from the south, and we had the first avalanches. A fat little general buzzed through Staufen to inspect the soldiers, and every man, woman, and child had a rifle and knew how to use it and they said they would rather die on the threshold of their houses than give up their ancient Swiss freedom. First there came the blackbirds, who fought bitterly for the nests of last year, and then Finland was lost. The swallows arrived punctually in the lower parts of the country and Norway was beaten. The violets and apple blossoms came and went and it was the turn of Holland and Belgium. And now that the first green cherries hang from our tree, France has fallen. I wonder if there will still be an England by the time the hazelnuts are changing from soft, green little buttons into hard golden kernels. . . .

This morning you came and brought me the first strawberries, Michael; you had found them with your own eyes, red in the green grass that grows along the trail. This morning you came to me, Christopher, your hair wet with dew, to bid me farewell. Remember that dark, foggy, muffled night when I cried on the veranda? It seems so long ago, almost prehistoric; because then there was still peace, but with this war a new age has begun. I've wandered a long way to meet you, Chris, my darling; forty-four years on the go; and now that I've found you it's only to let you go to fight in a war in which you don't believe. You have a vague idea against what you want to fight but not for what, and that's as bad as shooting with wet ammunition. And you, Martin, my good, straight, sober boy, I count on you and your cool mind and your good sense, because you are the salt of the earth. I love you just as much as I love Michael, even if you think I pampered him too much. It's up to you not to lose your head in these times but to go on drilling for water and building houses and machines and dams and airfields and planting corn and baking bread, all the simple, necessary, unglamorous things that you and millions like you are doing to keep the world on an even keel. I'm scribbling this little letter to you while I am stuck in a crevasse; I've remembered my whole life today in the hope of understanding where we are, how we got there, and whence we're going from here. But I'm just as bewildered and confused as before and pretty cold around the bottom. I'm not scared—No, I'm not scared. Never be scared. Nothing can happen to you. The main thing is to keep your equilibrium. I want to be a lion tamer. God have mercy on me. Good Lord, Marion, don't let's pretend now. You know that I love you. I love you too, Chris; I'm sorry I didn't tell you this morning. I love you with the tough, bitter, gnarled knowing love that lasts to the end. I'm a bit tired, Chris. I'd like to lie down and sleep and hibernate and not wake up until this war is over and the crabapple tree is blooming again. Do you mind, Chris, my dearest? . . .

12

HE SUN HAD CREPT further up, almost to the rim of the crevasse, and it had grown colder down there where Marion was crouching. Her fingers were so stiff that she could not hold the fountain pen any longer. However, the cigarette between her lips gave off as much heat as a stove. Never had any cigarette tasted so good as this one. The essence of anything good and warm and strong and fragrant and encouraging lived in that little glow. While Marion watched the tip of the cigarette it became for a second the glowing stove pipe in the warm room where she had made a present of herself to a sick stranger and had conceived Michael. The pipe kept on glowing and warming her for another moment, turned dark at last, and it was cold again. Marion dropped the extinguished cigarette to the bottom of the crevasse and listened for the inaudible sound of its arrival down in the black. Her body was numb with cold but her senses were sharpened to an unbelievable sensitivity. She could hear and feel and sense with some sixth sense that Christopher had arrived on the glacier by now and was searching every schrund and crevasse for her. Me and the world, she thought hazily; stuck in some place where we can't get out unless an Englishman comes to help us. The stripe of sun was not wider than one finger at the edge of the ice. Marion had still seven cigarettes and half a bottle of enzian schnaps. She called and yodeled, three times, but her voice did not carry. She kneeled on her sound leg and fumbled in her rucksack for the flask. I hope it is not frozen, she thought. Alcohol doesn't freeze so easily, you idiot. I must ask John at what temperature alcohol freezes. I mean Michael. Or Martin. She had trouble unscrewing the cap because her fingers were so numb and stiff, but she managed at last and drank two deep gulps. The miracle worked again. A minute afterward she felt strong and gay; in fact, she felt wonderful. She got up, bracing herself against the ice. She leaned over to bring her head out from under the overhanging roof of ice, which, it seemed to her, cut off her voice when she was calling. It was a precarious position, especially if you had one broken ankle. Hoop-la! The Queen of the air! Marion thought full of appreciation. Give her a hand, folks! That's it. Thank you, my friends! Balancing herself against a stalactite of ice she began calling, loud and systematically; not too often, in order to save her voice; not too seldom, so that no one would pass by her crevasse without noticing her. After a while it seemed to her as if she could perceive the very faintest answer to her call. She called and stopped and listened. She heard the glassy rustling in the ice that had become familiar to her and she called again.

She was very tired and sleepy and she felt fine. She had to take another gulp to keep herself awake and in good shape. She lifted the flask from her pocket, steadying herself with the other hand during the process. Her fingers were stiff and numb, as they say the fingers of lepers are. The flask dropped and fell; it made two leaps from the ledge of ice on which Marion balanced to the lower one, where it landed with a final bump and broke. Marion stared at her escaping and lost treasure, gaping. Then, suddenly, and as so often before in her life, something snapped in her and she began to laugh. This is funny! she thought. This is the goddamnedest funniest thing that ever happened to me! She bent over to look at the shatters of her bottle. It was lying in its little puddle of alcohol and looked guilty, like a baby after wetting its panties. God wants me to be sober when Christopher comes to find me, Marion thought. She kept on laughing, getting light and warm in her own laughter.

The sun had reached the rim of the crevasse and was gone.